SAMUEL JOHNSON

Rasselas, Poems, and Selected Prose

SAMUEL JOHNSON

Rasselas, Poems, and Selected Prose

**Third Edition Enlarged
with THE LIFE OF SAVAGE**

Edited with an
Introduction and Notes by

BERTRAND H. BRONSON

Holt, Rinehart and Winston, Inc.

NEW YORK • CHICAGO • SAN FRANCISCO • ATLANTA • DALLAS
MONTREAL • TORONTO • LONDON • SYDNEY

Holt Rinehart and Winston, Inc.
Introduction copyright 1952, © 1958, 1971 by Bertrand H. Bronson
ISBN: 0–03–082785–x
Printed in the United States of America
Library of Congress Catalog Card Number: 76–126576

56789 065 987654

CONTENTS

PRAYERS AND MEDITATIONS

CRITICISM

BIOGRAPHY

FICTION

INTRODUCTION

As September 18, 1768, drew to a close, Johnson wrote in his private notebook: "I have now begun the sixtieth year of my life. How the last year has past I am unwilling to terrify myself with thinking. This day has been past in great perturbation. . . ." Exactly one year later he wrote: "This day completes the sixtieth year of my age. What I have done and what I have left undone the unsettled state of my mind makes all endeavours to think improper. I hope to survey my life with more tranquillity, in some part of the time which God shall grant me."

These are the words of a man in violent spiritual tumult. They must not be discounted as overstatement for effect. They are a sober summary, written for no eye but his own, by one of the most vigorous intellects known to literary history, of his current state of mind—a state all too familiar to himself, if almost never acknowledged to anyone else. It is a condition so unusual, one suspects, in persons of comparable strength of character in our day that it is worth while to ask why Johnson was so perturbed and whether his alarm had human justification in his failures in performance.

The source of this brave man's terror was, of course, his religious conviction that, to an essential degree, eternal salvation waited upon the discharge of obligations inherent in the terms of earthly existence—in the personal endowments of body and mind, in environmental advantage or other conditions, in the length of life allotted and the liberty of choice. Johnson was a being gifted with very extraordinary powers of mind. There is little likelihood that he underestimated these, for he must have been reminded of them at every interchange of life. Nevertheless, he remained essentially and profoundly a humble man. Not that he could not display a sense of his own dignity if he thought he was being patronized. But in his relations with persons of mean abilities, like his friend and dependent, Dr. Levett, with servants, like Catherine Chambers, and with children, he never shows any trace of unconscious snobbery arising from his own sense of intellectual superiority. Nor does he do so in the long course of his moral teaching and writing, nor, indeed, except in the heat of controversy, with his companions in intellectual conversation. This radical humility he owed to his religion. For, by increasing his sense of mortal obligation, religion reduced him to the level of the humblest. Self-scrutiny in heaven's eye brought him too low for self-complacency. Thus, if his religion gave him little comfort and great disquiet, it yet contributed much to that wide sympathy and compassion for human weakness which in spite of strong moral principle is so indelible in his character. Of this truth, his charity toward the feckless Savage and the canting Dodd are shining instances.

In an age which has in great measure repudiated the only kind of fear that Johnson acknowledged, it takes a little effort to repossess the knowledge of certain positive consequences that follow from an outright acceptance of the point of view centering in religious humility. Of these, one of the foremost has to do with the communication of ideas: with the nature of the ideas and the way in which they are expressed. The assurance of a common commitment, common perils, and a common goal with all mankind at once justifies addressing one's fellow men on the perennial topics of mutual and ultimate concern. It is unnecessary to apologize for raising subjects universally acknowledged to be of profound importance. That these have been discussed before is insignificant in face of the fact that everything to come is still involved with them. Platitudes are not platitudes while they are being tested in the fire of personal experience. To an apprehension vital and unjaded a truism is a truth. And a conviction that our private welfare is implicated is a wonderful sharpener of attention. The enormous bulk of moral generalization and aphoristic statement in earlier English poetry as well as prose carries no suggestion that the appetite for this kind of food was then overestimated. Nor does its presence in large quantity imply a failure in intellectual (or physical) vigor. Indeed, intensely vital periods like the Elizabethan manifestly enjoyed a passion, a positive bulimy, for moral statement. The Elizabethans never tired of hearing that flesh is grass, and that "whatever fades but fading pleasure brings." To the unspoiled and vigorous intelligence no truths, perhaps, are too true.

> I know my body's of so frail a kind
>   As force without, fevers within, can kill;
> I know the heavenly nature of my mind,
>   But 'tis corrupted both in wit and will.
>
> I know my soul hath power to know all things,
>   Yet is she blind and ignorant in all;
> I know I am one of nature's little kings,
>   Yet to the least and vilest things am thrall.
>
> I know my life's a pain and but a span,
>   I know my sense is mocked with everything;
> And to conclude, I know myself a man,
>   Which is a proud, and yet a wretched thing.

So Sir John Davies, writing in the fifteen-nineties; and in the seventeen-fifties few Englishmen as yet rested content merely with hearing the parson's Sunday saw. In addition, they bought volumes of admired sermons and read them by the hundreds— both gentle and simple, clergy and laity, Sir Roger de Coverley and Thomas Turner, the country shopkeeper of East Hoathly. Not content with sermons, they also read moral essays; and like their forebears, welcomed moral generalization in their poetry, too. These things they did, not in the expectation of learning new truths, and certainly not because the senses failed to assert their vivid counterclaims; but because it was rational, they thought, for moral beings to give thought to morality, and because they added a dimension to their self-esteem by so doing.

When he commenced *The Rambler,* Johnson, in disclaiming the pursuit of novel truth, acutely remarked that "men more frequently require to be reminded than informed." The assumption that men are basically alike in all times and places, and that the sum total of scientific information already available or yet to be discovered is unlikely to make any radical alteration in human nature, obviously puts a premium upon the way in which the old truths are restated. This is not, it should be observed, to reduce the importance of the old truths, which are old because they are fundamental and therefore discovered early, and which, only because they are familiar, are likely to be rejected unless continually re-presented in fresh and agreeable forms.

Accepting their importance, and acknowledging the validity of this use of letters, the men of Johnson's day gave their highest praise, not to novelty, but to "what oft was thought but ne'er so well expressed." Since the content was of universal human concern, the ideal was to convey it in such a manner that it would immediately strike home to the widest possible audience with the pleasing shock of surprised recognition. It is no accident that Pope, who probably embodies this ideal more completely than any other author (always excepting Shakespeare) remains one of the most frequently quoted poets in our language.

It has been the business, partly deliberate, partly unconscious, of the next two centuries to undermine and then abolish this ideal. The enormous and accelerated accumulation of scientific information, and the concomitant ebbing of general religious belief and agreement as to the destiny of man, have robbed us of the assurance of general assent and the power of confident generalization, and induced a febrile self-consciousness, an insecure but absorbing egocentricity of which autobiography, direct or oblique, is the natural and inevitable mode of expression. Our focus of attention has shifted from the general to the particular, of which latter alone we feel relatively sure. Suspecting our personal insignificance, we strive to aggrandize our own importance as individuals by emphasizing our differences as claims to special consideration. We pursue and record novel excesses of experience and emotion, and invent semiarticulate verbal patterns in the vague hope of suggesting the incommunicable or unique. We are embarrassed by conventional truths, and prefer to be caught naked (if indeed we do not seek it) rather than to be caught in a cliché.

No doubt all this is the result of tides and currents beyond our power to control or even to analyze. But having been driven so far, there are signs lately appearing among us of an impulse to regain a common ground, to consolidate our position in a hostile universe around some basic core of elements in our common nature that may make for the reintegration of a society. After voyaging in strange seas of thought, alone, we long for the comfort of companionship and the strength of funded experience. One of the evidences of such a temper is the reawakening of curiosity, and even of respect, in and for the eighteenth-century figures, especially for Johnson himself, who spoke with impressive power and wrote with balanced and commanding eloquence out of convictions deeply rooted in our common humanity. For the possession of these qualities and for this kind of assurance, we find it natural to admire and envy him, and for his large humanity, to offer him our love.

It is not a sentimental nostalgia for a simpler and quieter time that motivates our present interest in Johnson's day. Not many of us would wish to recall it if we could, and certainly not for the sake of peace. For it was itself an age of profound and at times violent upheaval and change: an age of revolution, whether in the religious, the political, the social, economic, industrial, or the literary sphere. What interests us in Johnson is the spectacle of a man who, in a time (like our own) of rapidly shifting values, strove never to lose sight of fundamentals; who, without forgoing his humanity and becoming doctrinaire, fought strenuously throughout his life for just standards in thought and action, and cleared his own and others' minds of cant.

The perturbation from which Johnson was suffering in his sixtieth year made light of the product of thirty years and more of literary effort. By the time he was sixty he had already established himself as the foremost living English man of letters. Ten years earlier, Smollett, who was not given to idle compliment, was referring to him with casual irony as "that Great Cham of literature." He had won his way to the top in many different provinces: as a poet, as a biographer, as a moral essayist, as the nonpareil of lexicographers, as the author of a much admired work of fiction, and as the best of Shakespeare's editors to date. He had also done more miscellaneous anonymous writing than any one else knew, much of it as acts of friendship for people studious to conceal his assistance; had seen his play produced at Drury Lane (with sufficient success to net the author 300 pounds, and, if no theatrical triumph, certainly not the failure some have carelessly dubbed it); had been granted a royal pension for distinguished achievement in literature; and as head of the Literary Club, and elsewhere, had become widely known as one of the most brilliant talkers on record. In the fifteen years of life remaining to him, he would produce (besides four anonymous political tracts written at government request) his most attractive work, the prefaces known today as *The Lives of the Poets,* and his engaging travel book, *A Journey to the Western Islands.*

Aside from the more purely scholarly works—his Dictionary and the Shakespeare—most of his writing was performed with reluctance, in impulses of driving energy and determination to finish the task of the moment. His habitual condition during composition he described as one of being "unwilling to work and working with vigour and haste." He was no lover of his desk: he remembered composing sixty lines of his finest poem in his head of a morning, before writing anything down; he wrote forty-eight of the printed pages of his life of Savage at a sitting, working through the night; the *Rambler* papers were written in the same fashion, just before they were due at the press, sometimes without time allowed to read them over; his *Rasselas* was written in the evenings of one week; two of his major political tracts were written in the space of twenty-four hours apiece. If his writing gave him little pleasure in the doing, he spent little time in self-congratulation after it was done. He had no patience for the author-as-prima-donna, nothing but scorn for the ivory tower. "A man may write at any time," he once said, "if he will set himself doggedly to it." He doubtless got more satisfaction, in his private meditations, from his unrecorded acts of charity than from any of his written works.

Nevertheless, our own generation has come to recognize Johnson as one of the greatest masters of prose statement in the language. It is one of the grosser aberrations of nineteenth-century judgment that Taine found Johnson's prose monotonous and unvaried. For what calculated ends, and with what careful choice of words, Johnson shaped his periods in the fashion nicknamed Johnsonese has been recently shown in two penetrating studies by W. K. Wimsatt. He employed the "philosophic" vocabulary of seventeenth-century experimental science and empirical philosophy with a most just and subtle appreciation of its metaphorical possibilities, now with deep seriousness, now with delightful humor and self-mockery. "Johnson," writes Wimsatt finely,

> matches the physical scale of analogy, but especially the lower, mechanical, and elemental end of it, against the realm of mind. The two halves of experience, the mechanical outer, the vital, spiritual, and voluntary inner, with their partial resemblances (the mechanics of psychology) are his theme. And as he has the terms of either realm at his command, so he has the terms of the more transparent, algebraic realm where mechanics and psychology and all things else are subsumed. The thoughtful imagery of which Boswell spoke is an imagery of high shadows on the screen of categories, of lengthened metaphysical implications.

This is the special *Rambler* quality, as Wimsatt demonstrates; but in his letters he can be playful or solemn or simple, to suit his mood or his correspondent; in his *Lives* he can be free and various, ironic or tender or exact; and in his spoken prose he can be succinct and homely, or oracular, according to his need. "The Irish are a fair people;—they never speak well of one another." "Sir, it is not so much to be lamented that Old England is lost, as that the Scotch have found it." "No man is a hypocrite in his pleasures." "There is now less flogging in our great schools than formerly, but then less is learned there; so that what the boys get at one end they lose at the other." "Some people have a foolish way of not minding, or pretending to mind, what they eat. For my part, I mind my belly very studiously, and very carefully; for I look upon it, that he who does not mind his belly will hardly mind anything else." "Round numbers are always false." "All censure of a man's self is oblique praise." "Grief is a species of idleness." "It matters not how a man dies, but how he lives." "I have protracted my work till most of those whom I wished to please have sunk into the grave; and success and miscarriage are empty sounds."

Great writers do not remain static identities. Their stature is perpetually altering; they take on something of the color and appearance of every new age through which their works travel. Literary history has continually to be rewritten because it becomes less true with time. This reassessment of a great author by a new generation of readers is a mutually creative act. It is the duty of every age to strive to find its own truth; and, in the field of literature, to try to see, without falsifying the evidence, what was unnoticed by its predecessors because from their stretch of the road it was concealed. It is the fortune of a new age from time to time to get a clearer, though never a complete, view of an earlier genius; and it is a stroke of high good luck when the revolution of changing values brings us into positive relations with greatness, so that we chime, as it were, together. Happily, it is the privilege of our own time to see Johnson, not as the Tory die-hard he used to seem, but as a complex, vigorously dynamic figure whose life and art can enrich our own.

Bertrand H. Bronson

Berkeley, California
August, 1952

POSTSCRIPT

RASSELAS

Although there is not space for particular analysis, the inclusion of *Rasselas* in this fresh reprinting of Johnsonian selections offers occasion for a brief word on that masterpiece. The context of the book can be found where we commenced, in Johnson's diaries, so full, as we saw, of agonizing self-reproach in the periodic reviews of his spiritual state on private anniversaries and at intimate crises like the death of a near relation. His mother's imminent death, in the Lichfield house her son had not revisited in twenty years, touched the core of his emotional life and stirred into motion the whole train of early memories, which led to prolonged and somber meditation on the disparity between youth's hopes and plans, performance actual or possible in maturity, and the ultimate values accessible to man. To these reflections he decided to give the outward clothing of a currently popular literary *genre,* the Eastern Tale; but the autobiographical motivation is never long concealed.* If, as he later told Reynolds, he composed the work in

---

* A startling illustration of the contiguity of book and life is Imlac's anticipation of Johnson's actual homecoming—both the real and the imaginary occurring after an absence of twenty years. Imlac's words are, of course, Johnson's indirect discharge of feelings of guilt for never having gone home to visit during that period. Describing his return (*Rasselas,* Chapter XII), Imlac tells the Prince: "I now expected the caresses of my kinsmen, and the congratulations of my friends . . . But I was soon convinced that my thoughts were vain . . . of my companions the greater part was in the grave, of the rest some could with difficulty remember me, and some considered me as one corrupted by foreign manners." Three years *after* this was published, Johnson penned the following sardonic account of his subsequent return to Lichfield, in a letter to Joseph Baretti, of 20 July, 1762: "Last winter I went down to my native town, where I found the streets much narrower and shorter than I thought I had left them, inhabited by a new race of people, to whom I was very little known.

the evenings of that final week of his mother's life, in mid-January, 1759, he composed it as Mozart wrote down a symphony, with the whole work in mind, and with the pen travelling as fast as it could drive.. The maturity of the ideas and the precision of their expression are proof of an inward ripeness that required no further deliberation.

But the reader should be warned neither to expect a story nor to judge the book as such. Basically, *Rasselas* is a philosophical dialogue, of which the narrative outline advances the argument by providing the leads and transitional matter in the schematic conduct of the discourse. The voices in this enquiry are for the most part undifferentiated tonally, and bear labels chiefly in order to give a semblance of dramatic interchange to rational demonstration, and thus to lighten the proofs. One by one, in their appointed sequence as the work moves deliberately forward, the rush-lights of hypothetical earthly happiness gleam ahead of us but, when we come close to them, gutter out and leave us in the uncertain, but not unpeopled, dark. The surprising thing is that in its inexorably disillusioning course the book displays no bitterness nor cynicism, nor even impatience with youthful expectations or confident ignorance. The author's blend, condensed in the serene Imlac, of tested wisdom, sympathetic forbearance, and ironic compassion, leaves in our minds an abiding, pervasive impression of transcendent benevolence, under whose powerful spell we are half reconciled to the vanity of human wishes.

B. H. B.

February, 1958

My play-fellows were grown old, and forced me to suspect that I was no longer young . . . I wandered about for five days, and took the first convenient opportunity of returning to a place, where, if there is not much happiness, there is, at least, such a diversity of good and evil, that slight vexations do not fix upon the heart." Though London is not the Happy Valley, it is the best available surrogate.

A NOTE ON
THE LIFE OF SAVAGE

It is no common satisfaction to be able at length to include John-son's *Savage* in this anthology, for its absence hitherto has left unoccupied a space too conspicuous to be overlooked, in survey-ing the wide-ranging gallery of his works. In reading him, we continually get inklings of the abnormal reach of his sympathetic understanding of the human conditions; none the less, the life of Savage is our most unobstructed view of far horizons within the circumference of Johnson's humanity. As a manifestation of justice seasoned by mercy, it is godlike, irreplaceable.

This seems an extravagant claim, and may be countered by the charge that Johnson was blinded by credulous acceptance of un-verified statements, by partiality springing from shared experience. Johnson and Savage were veterans of a common battlefield, their grim fight against destitution. Poverty, Johnson was later to write, is not a simple condition, but a stratified one. There is *want of riches;* there is *want of competence;* there is *want of necessaries.* The two men had known together poverty's extreme degree. "The milder degrees of poverty are sometimes supported by hope, but the more severe often sink down in motionless despondence." "Life must be seen," he tells Jenyns and Pope, "before it can be known." Savage had seen it, losing neither hope nor cheerful-ness. Without the pennies for either food or lodging, he walked with Johnson round and round St. James's Square, hour after hour through the night, his talk running the gamut of his ob-servations from highest society to lowest, with nothing forgotten that might serve to enliven or hasten the new day: neither of them, Johnson assured Reynolds jauntily, looking back with com-placent amusement, "at all depressed, but in high spirits and brimful of patriotism"—a word Johnson chose to denigrate—"inveigh[ing] against the minister" [Sir Robert Walpole, the Whig who was trying to avoid foreign war] "and resolved they would *stand by their Country*." Unquestionably, such experience offered unequalled opportunities for exploring each other's mind and attitudes. Savage, like Dryden, had learned from life not books— had met everybody, had laid up his knowledge in a capacious memory, and was inexhaustibly communicative of illustrative anecdote and reflective comment. Of course Johnson, at least a decade younger, was grateful both for the entertainment and the instruction. "His conversation," Johnson testifies, "was so entertaining, and his address so pleasing, that few thought the pleasure which they received from him dearly purchased by paying for his wine." Then Johnson continues: "It was his peculiar happiness that he scarcely ever found a stranger whom he did not leave a friend; but it must likewise be added that he had not often a friend long, without obliging him to become a stranger." Unquestionably also, therefore, their intimacy left little likelihood that Johnson's perspicuity could be long or fundamentally deceived, had Savage deliberately set out to conceal an assumed identity of which he himself was not convinced. Johnson's belief in the basic truth of Savage's claim to be the son of the Countess of Macclesfield and Earl Rivers is the strongest evidence we shall find of the genuineness of Savage's own conviction that he was so. It will probably never be proved that he was not mistaken, and not in fact a changeling. Later research has disclosed many inaccuracies in the story as Johnson received and reported it. But these do not impugn the fundamental honesty of Savage's assumption of the name under which he passed through life.

"His character," writes Boswell, "was marked by profligacy, insolence, and ingratitude," and although Johnson does not dwell on the first of these faults of character, no reader will wish to qualify the other two accusations. One can but wonder, as Boswell says, that such a reprobate should have been for any length of time the intimate companion of Johnson, from whom at last, as Johnson recalls, he "parted with tears in his eyes." A shameless and ungrateful sponger, he was a man to run from if you saw him in time. His proud condescension and ticklish acceptance, or indignant rejection, of kindnesses were often unbearable. His conduct in the end alienated the friends who had tried hardest to help him. The virtue of his poetry has faded and lost most of its appeal over the years that have intervened. What is it that can interest posterity in this human derelict?

The answer, of course, is that Johnson found him interesting: so interesting that he wrote one of the most absorbing biographical narratives of all time about him. Reynolds told Boswell that when he ran across it, before he knew anything of Johnson, he "began to read it while he was standing with his arm leaning against a chimney-piece. It seized his attention so strongly, that, not being able to lay down the book till he had finished it, when he attempted to move, he found his arm totally benumbed." Reynolds, of course, as a portrait-painter and physiognomist, was a close student of the lineaments of character. But he was not alone among contemporaries in admiration. One of the book's first reviewers (quoted by Boswell) commended it above all works of its kind for its insight. It "opened," he said, "the recesses of the human heart." It was reprinted without change half a dozen times in the next thirty years. Noteworthy is the fact that when, toward the end of his life, Johnson reconsidered it for inclusion among the *Lives of the Poets,* he felt no need to make any significant alterations of judgment; only the longer quotations from Savage's poems were dropped, since these were now to be printed in their entirety. If his regard for the worth of the poetry had diminished meanwhile, he did not lessen or cancel his earlier praise; he must have been satisfied that the life as a whole did not misrepresent his mature opinions after nearly forty years.

When Johnson first wrote it, he was well aware of the sensational appeal of the story, and set out to capture the public attention reawakened by Savage's death in a Bristol jail, announcing his purpose in a letter to *The Gentleman's Magazine,* August, 1743, the very month when Savage died. Although his life did not appear until the following February, he wrote it in a white heat as soon as he had collected such materials as could be recovered in print or from correspondence, and finished before the middle of December, when Cave paid him fifteen guineas for it.

In a desultory conversation years later, at an inn at St. Andrews, the subject of rapid versus accurate composition arose, and Johnson, on hearing that Dr. Blair took a week to compose a sermon, casually remarked to his company that he had himself "composed about forty sermons. I have begun a sermon after dinner, and sent it off by the post that night. I wrote forty-eight of the printed octavo pages of the Life of Savage at a sitting; but then I sat up all night. . . I would say to a young divine, 'Here is your text; let me see how soon you can make a sermon.' Then I'd say, 'Let me see how much better you can make it.' "

At a first reading of the life, we are seized and at once horrified and fascinated by the melodramatic tale, by the unnatural cruelty of the mother, the pathetic plight of the abandoned son, the desperate episode of his killing a stranger, his being condemned to hang, his royal pardon, his elevation to the highest social levels, his subsequent destitution, and his dying in a debtors' prison. On a second reading, what most impresses is probably not the sensationalism but the incredible mismanagement by Savage, at every turn, of his own interests; his stupid arrogance and willful affronting of his friends, his slipshod disregard of all opportunities to better his fortunes, his imperious and ill-tempered demands that what could only be earned should be granted as his right and just due.

Our interest and concern for the man declines, the more we find him hopelessly irredeemable. But while this happens, our interest in his biographer grows. For we, like Savage's other friends, even the sorely tried Pope, (who supported him almost to the end,) have given him up. But Johnson has not. His clear-eyed acknowledgment ignores no facts in summing up the woeful shortcomings of his friend's character:

> "His temper was . . . uncertain and capricious . . . but he is accused of retaining his hatred more tenaciously than his benevolence. He was compassionate both by nature and principle . . . but when he was provoked (and very small offences were sufficient to provoke him), he would prosecute his revenge with the utmost acrimony till his passion had subsided.

"His friendship was therefore of little value; for though he was zealous in the support or vindication of those whom he loved, yet it was always dangerous to trust him, because he considered himself as discharged by the first quarrel from all ties of honour or gratitude, and would betray those secrets which, in the warmth of confidence, had been imparted to him . . . nor can it be denied that he was very ready to set himself free from the load of an obligation, for he could not bear to conceive himself in a state of dependence; his pride being equally powerful with his other passions, and appearing in the form of insolence at one time, and of vanity at another."

But then, after a short recapitulation of the strengths and weaknesses of Savage's verse, which he considers "the productions of a genius truly poetical" and original, with "very little to fear from the strictest moral and religious censure," he declares:

"For his life or for his writings none, who candidly consider his fortune, will think an apology either necessary or difficult. . . . The insolence and resentment of which he is accused were not easily to be avoided by a great mind, irritated by perpetual hardships, and constrained hourly to return the spurns of contempt and repress the insolence of prosperity; and vanity may surely readily be pardoned in him, to whom life afforded no other comforts than barren praises, and the consciousness of deserving them.

"Those are no proper judges of his conduct who have slumbered away their time on the down of plenty, nor will any wise man presume to say, 'Had I been in Savage's condition, I should have lived or written better than Savage.'"

In the presence of such compassionate forbearance, one can only bow with humility and awe.

Two or three points may be emphasized by way of conclusion. It is evident that what motivates Johnson in his account is not merely the spirit of Christian charity and forgiveness. He had a deep and ever-present consciousness of the insecurity of this mortal state. It was not only that none can foretell the events of tomorrow, but that we cannot be sure of the steadiness of our own purposes, nor be confident that today's resolve may not be subverted by tomorrow's emotional impulse. Nor, in fact, that what we know in the morning we shall know in the evening.

> In life's last scene what prodigies surprise,
> Fears of the brave, and follies of the wise?

In his discussion of Addison's Sir Roger, Johnson makes reference, in memorable phrases, to "the variable weather of the mind, the flying vapours of incipient madness, which from time to time cloud reason without eclipsing it."

With this persistent sense of the impermanence of weather conditions, Johnson set great store by the compass of moral principle, which establishes our direction, however the course may fluctuate; and he was ready to tolerate greater deviation, by reason of human weakness, than most of us can (in others), so long as no one tried to smash the compass or heave it overboard. He welcomed any sign, even the most trivial—like lifting one's hat when passing a church—that indicated good principles, however a man's conduct might vary.

Because of his radical distrust of human stability, Johnson had a tolerance which might be called a weakness for worldly-wise, intelligent, articulate companions with well-stocked minds but a streak of the profligate in them. He had many friends of this sort throughout his life. So long as he was sure they were well-principled, he tried to ignore their sensuality. Gilbert Walmsley, to whom Johnson pays tribute in the life of Edmund Smith, was one of these. Beauclerk was another, and we are not forgetting Boswell. Had the reckless Smith been of Johnson's generation instead of Addison's, it could easily have resulted that we should have had a companion piece for Savage, for Johnson would have known him at Oxford, and would not have been repelled by his madcap ways, since he was also a brilliant scholar and poet. He was rebellious against authority, and so, at Pembroke, was

Johnson. And though Smith (also a nobly sired bastard) got himself expelled, he was no more disreputable than Savage.

Among vices, Johnson had clear preferences—he wrote a memorable *Rambler* paper on the subject (No. 25). He had far greater tolerance for the positive faults than for the negative, for those that exceeded the middle point than those which fell short. For him it was better to be rash than cowardly, extravagant than avaricious, presumptuous than over-cautious. "Presumption," he wrote, "will be easily corrected. . . . It is the advantage of vehemence and activity, that they are always hastening to their own reformation. . . . But timidity is a disease of the mind more obstinate and fatal; for a man once persuaded that any impediment is insuperable. . . can scarcely strive with vigor and perseverance, when he has no hope of gaining the victory." And again, in *Idler* No. 57, in the character of Sophron the prudent, there is an unmistakable Johnsonian distaste and curling of the lip.

In addition to temperamental sympathy, Johnson was able to preserve for Savage respect: respect not only for the "courage never to submit or yield," but a respect based upon deeper, more philosophical grounds and a kindred moral outlook. The root of this attitude is in a passage that he quotes from Savage's most considerable poem, *The Wanderer*, a passage containing sentiments with which he is in profound agreement. Johnson characterizes the quoted lines as Savage's "first great position, 'that good is the consequence of evil,'" which the poem illustrates in various ways throughout, and to which Johnson himself gives impressive expression elsewhere. The idea is embodied in the couplet,

> That ev'n calamity, by thought refin'd,
> Inspirits and adorns the thinking mind.

And more distinctly in the following passage:

> By woe, the soul to daring action swells;
> By woe, in plaintless patience it excels;
> From patience, prudent clear experience springs,
> And traces knowledge thro' the course of things!

> Thence hope is form'd, thence fortitude, success,
> Renown. . . .

Johnson, giving it a more explicitly religious application, expresses the idea most powerfully in his *Idler* No. 89:

> But in a world like ours, where our senses assault us, and our hearts betray us, we should pass on from crime to crime, heedless and remorseless, if misery did not stand in our way, and our own pains admonish us of our folly . . . . If the senses were feasted with perpetual pleasure, they would always keep the mind in subjection. Reason has no authority over us, but by its power to warn us against evil.
>
> That misery does not make all virtuous experience too certainly informs us; but it is no less certain that of what virtue there is, misery produces far the greater part. Physical evil may be therefore endured with patience, since it is the cause of moral good; and patience itself is one virtue by which we are prepared for that state in which evil shall be no more.

Berkeley, California　　　　　　　　　　　　　　　　B. H. B.
January, 1970

CHRONOLOGY

Samuel Johnson born at Lichfield, September 18, 1709.

Attended Lichfield Grammar School under John Hunter, who "whipt me very well. Without that, Sir, I should have done nothing." 1719–1725.

At school, formed lifelong friendships with Edmund Hector and John (afterward Rev. Dr.) Taylor.

Attended Stourbridge Grammar School, Worcestershire, 1725–1726.

Entered Pembroke College, Oxford, October 31, 1728.

Left Oxford without a degree, Autumn, 1731.

His father, Michael Johnson, died, December, 1731.

Appointed usher (undermaster) in Market Bosworth School, Leicestershire, Spring, 1732; found it "complicated misery" and resigned post in July.

Having undertaken to translate Father Lobo's *Voyage to Abyssinia*, he kept the press waiting until persuaded to continue by his friend Hector. Thereupon, "he lay in bed with the book . . . before him, and dictated while Hector wrote." The translation was published in 1735.

Married Mrs. Elizabeth Porter, of Birmingham, at Derby, July 9, 1735.

Opened a private school at Edial, Staffordshire, early in 1736, with six to eight pupils, among them David Garrick.

Went up to London, March, 1737, with Garrick, taking turns riding on a single horse.

Worked at his unfinished tragedy, *Irene*, in Greenwich, during summer, 1737.

Brought his wife to London, late in 1737.

Worked for Edward Cave on *The Gentleman's Magazine*, from early 1738 onward, and became acquainted with Richard Savage.

Published *London, a Poem, in Imitation of the Third Satire of Juvenal*, May, 1738.

Wrote up the Parliamentary Debates for *The Gentleman's Magazine*, 1740–1743.

Published *An Account of the Life of Mr. Richard Savage*, February, 1744.

Published *Miscellaneous Observations on the Tragedy of Macbeth*, with proposals for a new edition of Shakespeare, April, 1745.

Wrote Prologue for Garrick's opening of Drury Lane Theatre, spoken September 15, 1747.

Published *Plan of a Dictionary of the English Language*, addressed to the Earl of Chesterfield, late 1747.

Published *The Vanity of Human Wishes. The Tenth Satire of Juvenal Imitated by Samuel Johnson*, January, 1749. His first signed work.

Irene: A Tragedy produced by Garrick, February 6, 1749, and eight succeeding nights, and published soon thereafter.

Wrote and published *The Rambler*, March 20, 1750, to March 14, 1752 (208 numbers, of which he wrote all but four and part of a fifth).

His wife died, March 28, 1752.

Contributed two dozen essays to *The Adventurer*, 1753–1754.

Published *A Dictionary of the English Language*, April, 1755.

Published *Proposals for Printing the Dramatick Works of William Shakespeare*, June, 1756.

Wrote and published *The Idler*, April 25, 1758, to April 5, 1760 (104 numbers, of which he wrote all but twelve).

His mother died, January, 1759.

Published *The Prince of Abissinia* (i.e., *Rasselas*), April, 1759.

Was granted a royal pension of 300 pounds a year, spring, 1762.

First met Boswell, who "came from Scotland," in Thomas Davies' back parlor, May 16, 1763.

With Reynolds, Burke, Goldsmith, Beauclerk, Langton, and three others, established the Literary Club, spring, 1764.

Became acquainted with Mr. and Mrs. Henry Thrale, 1764 or 1765.

Published *The Plays of William Shakespeare*, October, 1765.

Published *The False Alarm*, January, 1770.

Toured Scotland and the Hebrides with Boswell, August to November, 1773.

Published *The Patriot,* November, 1774.

Published *A Journey to the Western Islands of Scotland,* January, 1775.

Published *Taxation no Tyranny,* March, 1775.

Received from Oxford University the degree, Doctor in Civil Law, granted March 30, 1775.

Visited France with the Thrales, September to November, 1775.

Published *Prefaces, Biographical and Critical, to the Works of the English Poets,* afterward known as *The Lives of the Poets,* 1779–1781.

Died December 13, 1784.

BIBLIOGRAPHICAL NOTES

The texts included in this volume follow closely the most author-
itative editions of the separate works. The only intentional devia-
tions are either typographical or corrective of undeniable mis-
prints. The capitalization, spelling, and punctuation, although not
demonstrably Johnson's own, have been respected and preserved
because they are historically characteristic. For consistency's sake,
the new edition of the present collection has reverted from G. B.
Hill's text of Johnson's *Lives* of the Poets to the edition of 1783.
It is refreshing to observe the irregularities of spelling, the rhe-
torical pointing in defiance of our accustomed logical punctuation,
the casual capitalization and idiosyncratic printing practices flour-
ishing unabashed in the very citadel of the great Lawgiver.
Departing however in one case from our rule, the text of the
Letters included is the regulated, judicious text of R. W. Chap-
man in his selection for the *World's Classics*, 1925, but corrected
by the readings of his authoritative edition of the complete
Letters, 1952, wherever the recovery of holograph originals has
supplied a different wording, as in the letter to Mrs. Thrale of 6
October, 1777. The original spelling and punctuation are so
haphazard as to prove a serious distraction, and have been reg-
ularized in the conviction that Johnson himself, could he have
tolerated such an invasion of privacy, would have expected the
printer to perform this customary office.

The passages from the *Prayers and Meditations* follow the first
two editions, 1785, by the Rev. George Strahan, to whose care
Johnson committed the manuscripts. In the selections reprinted
here, the text does not differ materially from that of the recent

authoritative edition by E. L. McAdam, Jr. and Donald and Mary Hyde, the first volume of the Yale *Johnson*, 1958. The poetry is given from the Oxford text of 1941, edited by D. Nichol Smith and E. L. McAdam, Jr. This has been re-edited and revised by McAdam and George Milne for the Yale *Johnson*, vol. VI, 1964. The *Rambler* essays are printed from the fourth edition, 1756, the last one corrected by Johnson himself. (Cf. Curtis B. Bradford, *Samuel Johnson's Rambler*, Yale dissertation, 1937, unpublished.) A new edition with variant readings has lately appeared in the Yale *Johnson*, vols. III, IV, and V, edited by W. J. Bate and A. B. Strauss, published in 1969. The *Adventurer* papers are from the first edition. The *Idler* papers follow the third edition (2 vols., 1767. Cf. Boylston Green, *Samuel Johnson's Idler*, Yale dissertation, 1941, unpublished.) These can now be replaced by Vol. II of the Yale *Johnson*, edited by W. J. Bate, John M. Bullitt, and L. F. Powell, 1963. The review of Jenyns' *Enquiry* has been corrected from the earliest printing, in the May, June, and July, 1757, numbers of that scarce periodical, *The Literary Magazine: or, Universal Review*, through the kindness of Herman W. Liebert, Director of the Beinecke Library at Yale. The passage from *A Journey to the Western Islands of Scotland*, 1775, follows the edition of that and Boswell's *Tour* by R. W. Chapman (Oxford, 1924). The Preface to the *Dictionary* is printed from the fourth edition (2 volumes in folio, 1773), containing Johnson's latest corrections. The Preface to the edition of Shakespeare follows the text of the first edition, 1765. A variorum text is now available in the Yale *Johnson* (*Johnson on Shakespeare*, edited by Arthur Sherbo, vols. VII and VIII, 1968.) The notes to the plays are all (perhaps culpably) drawn for the present selection from Sir Walter A. Raleigh's admirable *Johnson on Shakespeare*, Oxford, 1908. The text of *Rasselas* follows that of the second edition of 1759 (reprinted and annotated by R. W. Chapman, Oxford, 1927). Grateful acknowledgments are due here to earlier editors and annotators, who have been robbed at need: especially George Birkbeck Hill, D. Nichol Smith, C. G. Osgood, and C. H. Conley.

Reading about Johnson naturally commences with Boswell's

*The Journal of a Tour to the Hebrides with Samuel Johnson,
LL. D.,* 1785 (best eds. by G. B. Hill, revised by L. F. Powell,
1950 and by R. W. Chapman, 1924), followed by Boswell's *Life
of Samuel Johnson, LL. D.,* 1791 (best ed. by G. B. Hill, revised
by L. F. Powell, 4 vols., Oxford, 1934, vols. v and vi, 1950). The
original manuscript of the *Tour* has been edited by F. A. Pottle
and C. H. Bennett, 1936, and again newly amplified and revised
by Pottle in 1961. For Johnson's letters, the student will find it
best to begin with R. W. Chapman's little *World's Classics* se-
lected Letters, 1925, or David Littlejohn's selection with connec-
tive biographical interpolations, *Dr. Johnson: His Life in Letters,*
1965. A very useful compendium of lesser biographical material
is the *Johnsonian Miscellanies* (2 vols., Oxford, 1897) edited by
G. B. Hill, containing among other valuable items Mrs. Thrale's
Anecdotes. Also valuable are C. B. Tinker, *Dr. Johnson and
Fanny Burney,* 1912, which contains the Johnsonian passages
from the latter's diaries; and Hugh Kingsmill's *Johnson without
Boswell: A Contemporary Portrait,* 1940.

After the large generalized characterizations of Carlyle and
Macaulay, Johnson began to be reinterpreted for our own century
most vigorously by Sir Walter A. Raleigh in *Six Essays on John-
son,* 1910 (among them essays of 1907 and 1908). Faithful work
on Johnson's family connections and early years was accomplished
by Aleyn Lyell Reade, in *Johnsonian Gleanings* (10 parts, 1909–
1946). This has been followed up by J. L. Clifford, *Young Sam
Johnson,* 1955, now available in paperback. There is a full-length
critical biography by Joseph Wood Krutch, *Samuel Johnson,*
1944. Stimulating if less scholarly portraits are Christopher Hollis,
Dr. Johnson, 1928, and Hugh Kingsmill, *Samuel Johnson,* 1933.
Other books of portraiture and interpretation are: John Bailey,
Dr. Johnson and His Circle, 1913; S. C. Roberts, *Dr. Johnson,*
1935; W. B. C. Watkins, *Perilous Balance,* 1939; B. H. Bronson,
Johnson Agonistes, 1946, revised 1965; W. J. Bate, *The Achieve-
ment of Samuel Johnson,* 1955; M. J. C. Hodgart, *Samuel John-
son and His Times,* 1962; Robert Voitle, *Samuel Johnson the
Moralist,* 1961; Paul K. Alkon, *Samuel Johnson and Moral Dis-
cipline,* 1967. More specialized are the following: W. K. Wim-

satt, Jr., *The Prose Style of Dr. Johnson*, 1942, and *Philosophic Words*, 1948; Jean H. Hagstrum, *Samuel Johnson's Literary Criticism*, 1952; Benjamin B. Hoover, *Johnson's Parliamentary Reporting*, 1953; James H. Sledd and Gwin J. Kolb, *Dr. Johnson's Dictionary*, 1955; Donald J. Greene, *The Politics of Samuel Johnson*, 1960; Chester F. Chapin, *The Religious Thought of Samuel Johnson*, 1968.

The Yale Edition of the Works, the first collected and independent edition since 1825 and the first and only one with conscientious textual collation, has now delivered eight volumes, all of which are mentioned above. Its completion may be expected in the coming decade. Indispensable tools for closer study are W. P. Courtney and D. Nichol Smith, *A Bibliography of Samuel Johnson*, 1915 and 1925, supplemented by R. W. Chapman and A. T. Hazen (Oxford Bibliographical Society, 1938); James L. Clifford, *Johnsonian Studies 1887–1950*; James L. Clifford and Donald J. Greene, *A Bibliography of Johnsonian Studies 1950–1960*.

LETTERS

TO WILLIAM STRAHAN

Nov. 1, 1751.

Dearest Sir

The message which you sent me by Mr. Stuart I do not consider
as at all your own, but if you were contented to be the deliverer of
it to me, you must favour me so far as to return my answer, which
I have written down to spare you the unpleasing office of doing
it in your own words. You advise me to write, I know with very
kind intentions, nor do I intend to treat your counsel with any
disregard when I declare that in the present state of the matter 'I
shall *not* write' otherwise than the words following:—

   'That my resolution has long been, and is *not* now altered,
and is now *less* likely to be altered, that I shall *not* see the Gen-
tlemen Partners till the first volume is in the press, which they
may forward or retard by dispensing or not dispensing with the
last message.'

   Be pleased to lay this my determination before them this morn-

3

ing, for I shall think of taking my measures accordingly to-morrow evening, only this that I mean no harm, but that my citadel shall not be taken by storm while I can defend it, and that if a blockade is intended, the country is under the command of my batteries, I shall think of laying it under contribution to-morrow Evening.*

I am Sir,
Your most obliged, most obedient,
and most humble servant,

SAM: JOHNSON.

TO THE RIGHT HONOURABLE THE EARL
OF CHESTERFIELD

FEBRUARY 7, 1755.

My Lord

I have been lately informed, by the proprietor of *The World,* that two papers,[1] in which my Dictionary is recommended to the publick, were written by your Lordship. To be so distinguished, is an honour, which, being very little accustomed to favours from the great, I know not well how to receive, or in what terms to acknowledge.

When, upon some slight encouragement, I first visited your Lordship, I was overpowered, like the rest of mankind, by the enchantment of your address; and could not forbear to wish that I might boast myself *Le vainqueur du vainqueur de la terre;* —that I might obtain that regard for which I saw the world contending; but I found my attendance so little encouraged, that neither pride nor modesty would suffer me to continue it. When I had once addressed your Lordship in publick, I had exhausted all the art of pleasing which a retired and uncourtly scholar can possess. I had done all that I could; and no man is well pleased to have his all neglected, be it ever so little.

Seven years, my Lord, have now past, since I waited in your

---

* Johnson is in effect threatening the publishers of the *Dictionary* to stop work on it unless they at once send him another remittance.

[1] Nos. 100, 101.

outward rooms, or was repulsed from your door; during which time I have been pushing on my work through difficulties, of which it is useless to complain, and have brought it, at last, to the verge of publication, without one act of assistance, one word of encouragement, or one smile of favour. Such treatment I did not expect, for I never had a Patron before.

The shepherd in Virgil grew at last acquainted with Love, and found him a native of the rocks.[2]

Is not a Patron, my Lord, one who looks with unconcern on a man struggling for life in the water, and, when he has reached ground, encumbers him with help? The notice which you have been pleased to take of my labours, had it been early, had been kind; but it has been delayed till I am indifferent, and cannot enjoy it; till I am solitary, and cannot impart it; till I am known, and do not want it. I hope it is no very cynical asperity not to confess obligations where no benefit has been received, or to be unwilling that the Publick should consider me as owing that to a Patron, which Providence has enabled me to do for myself.

Having carried on my work thus far with so little obligation to any favourer of learning, I shall not be disappointed though I should conclude it, if less be possible, with less; for I have been long wakened from that dream of hope, in which I once boasted myself with so much exultation, my Lord,

> your Lordship's most humble,
> most obedient servant,

SAM: JOHNSON.

TO MRS. MONTAGU

GRAY'S INN, DEC. 17, 1759.

Madam

Goodness so conspicuous as yours will be often solicited, and perhaps sometimes solicited by those who have little pretension to your favour. It is now my turn to introduce a petitioner, but such

---

[2] *Eclogue*, 8. 11. 43 ff. Johnson borrows his thrust from the pastoral, a form "easy, vulgar, and therefore disgusting."

as I have reason to believe you will think worthy of your notice.
Mrs. Ogle, who kept the music-room in Soho Square, a woman
who struggles with great industry for the support of eight children,
hopes by a benefit concert to set herself free from a few debts,
which she cannot otherwise discharge. She has, I know not why,
so high an opinion of me as to believe that you will pay less re-
gard to her application than to mine. You know, Madam, I am
sure you know, how hard it is to deny, and therefore would not
wonder at my compliance, though I were to suppress a motive
which you know not, the vanity of being supposed to be of any
importance to Mrs. Montagu. But though I may be willing to see
the world deceived for my advantage, I am not deceived myself,
for I know that Mrs. Ogle will owe whatever favours she shall
receive from the patronage which we humbly entreat on this oc-
casion, much more to your compassion for honesty in distress, than
to the request of,
      Madam,
      Your most obedient and most humble servant,
                                SAM: JOHNSON.

TO GEORGE STRAHAN

Dear George

To give pain ought always to be painful, and I am sorry that I
have been the occasion of any uneasiness to you, to whom I
hope never to do any thing but for your benefit or your pleasure.
Your uneasiness was without any reason on your part, as you
had written with sufficient frequency to me, and I had only
neglected to answer then, because as nothing new had been pro-
posed to your study, no new direction or incitement could be
offered you. But if it had happened that you had omitted what
you did not omit, and that I had for an hour, or a week, or a
much longer time, thought myself put out of your mind by some-
thing to which presence gave that prevalence, which presence will
sometimes give even where there is the most prudence and expe-
rience, you are not to imagine that my friendship is light enough

to be blown away by the first cross blast, or that my regard or kindness hangs by so slender a hair as to be broken off by the unfelt weight of a petty offence. I love you, and hope to love you long. You have hitherto done nothing to diminish my good will, and though you had done much more than you have supposed imputed to you, my good will would not have been diminished.

I write thus largely on this suspicion which you have suffered to enter your mind, because in youth we are apt to be too rigorous in our expectations, and to suppose that the duties of life are to be performed with unfailing exactness and regularity; but in our progress through life we are forced to abate much of our demands, and to take friends such as we can find them, not as we would make them.

These concessions every wise man is more ready to make to others, as he knows that he shall often want them for himself; and when he remembers how often he fails in the observance or cultivation of his best friends, is willing to suppose that his friends may in their turn neglect him, without any intention to offend him.

When therefore it shall happen, as happen it will, that you or I have disappointed the expectation of the other, you are not to suppose that you have lost me, or that I intended to lose you; nothing will remain but to repair the fault, and to go on as if it never had been committed.

> I am, Sir,
> Your affectionate servant,
>
> SAM: JOHNSON.

THURSDAY, JULY 14, 1763.

A MR. MR. BOSWELL, À LA COUR DE
L'EMPEREUR,[1] UTRECHT

Dear Sir

You are not to think yourself forgotten, or criminally neglected, that you have had yet no letter from me. I love to see my friends,

[1] The name of Boswell's inn.

to hear from them, to talk to them, and to talk of them; but it is not without a considerable effort of resolution that I prevail upon myself to write. I would not, however, gratify my own indolence by the omission of any important duty, or any office of real kindness.

To tell you that I am or am not well, that I have or have not been in the country, that I drank your health in the room in which we sat last together, and that your acquaintance continue to speak of you with their former kindness, topicks with which those letters are commonly filled which are written only for the sake of writing, I seldom shall think worth communicating; but if I can have it in my power to calm any harassing disquiet, to excite any virtuous desire, to rectify any important opinion or fortify any generous resolution, you need not doubt but I shall at least wish to prefer the pleasure of gratifying a friend much less esteemed than yourself, before the gloomy calm of idle vacancy. Whether I shall easily arrive at an exact punctuality of correspondence, I cannot tell. I shall, at present, expect that you will receive this in return for two which I have had from you. The first, indeed, gave me an account so hopeless of the state of your mind, that it hardly admitted or deserved an answer; by the second I was much better pleased: and the pleasure will still be increased by such a narrative of the progress of your studies, as may evince the continuance of an equal and rational application of your mind to some useful enquiry.

You will, perhaps, wish to ask, what study I would recommend. I shall not speak of theology, because it ought not to be considered as a question whether you shall endeavour to know the will of GOD.

I shall, therefore, consider only such studies as we are at liberty to pursue or to neglect; and of these I know not how you will make a better choice, than by studying the civil law, as your father advises, and the ancient languages, as you had determined for yourself; at least resolve, while you remain in any settled residence, to spend a certain number of hours every day amongst your books. The dissipation of thought, of which you complain, is nothing more than the vacillation of a mind suspended between different motives, and changing its direction as any motive gains or loses strength. If you can but kindle in your mind any strong desire, if you can but keep predominant any wish for some particular excellence or attainment, the gusts of imagination will break away, without any effect upon your conduct, and commonly without any traces left upon the memory.

There lurks, perhaps, in every human heart a desire of distinction, which inclines every man first to hope, and then to believe, that Nature has given him something peculiar to himself. This vanity makes one mind nurse aversions, and another actuate desires, till they rise by art much above their original state of power; and as affectation, in time, improves to habit, they at last tyrannise over him who at first encouraged them only for show. Every desire is a viper in the bosom, who, while he was chill, was harmless; but when warmth gave him strength, exerted it in poison. You know a gentleman,[2] who, when first he set his foot in the gay world, as he prepared himself to whirl in the vortex of pleasure, imagined a total indifference and universal negligence to be the most agreeable concomitants of youth, and the strongest indication of an airy temper and a quick apprehension. Vacant to every object, and sensible of every impulse, he thought that all appearance of diligence would deduct something from the reputation of genius; and hoped that he should appear to attain, amidst all the ease of carelessness, and all the tumult of diversion, that knowledge and those accomplishments which mortals of the common fabrick obtain only by mute abstraction and solitary drudgery. He tried this scheme of life awhile, was made weary of it by his sense and his virtue; he then wished to return to his studies; and finding long habits of idleness and pleasure harder to be cured than he expected, still willing to retain his claim to some extraordinary prerogatives, resolved the common consequences of irregularity into an unalterable decree of destiny, and concluded that Nature had originally formed him incapable of rational employment.

Let all such fancies, illusive and destructive, be banished hence-

[2] Presumably, Boswell himself.

forward from your thoughts for ever. Resolve, and keep your reso-
lution; choose, and pursue your choice. If you spend this day in
study, you will find yourself still more able to study to-morrow;
not that you are to expect that you shall at once obtain a com-
plete victory. Depravity is not very easily overcome. Resolution
will sometimes relax, and diligence will sometimes be interrupted;
but let no accidental surprize or deviation, whether short or long,
dispose you to despondency. Consider these failings as incident to
all mankind. Begin again where you left off, and endeavour to
avoid the seducements that prevailed over you before.

This, my dear Boswell, is advice which, perhaps, has been often
given you, and given you without effect. But this advice, if you
will not take from others, you must take from your own reflec-
tions, if you purpose to do the duties of the station to which the
bounty of Providence has called you.

Let me have a long letter from you as soon as you can. I hope
you continue your journal, and enrich it with many observations
upon the country in which you reside. It will be a favour if you
can get me any books in the Frisick language, and can enquire
how the poor are maintained in the Seven Provinces.

I am, dear Sir, your most affectionate servant,

SAM: JOHNSON.

LONDON, DEC. 8, 1763.

TO MRS. THRALE

OXFORD, APRIL 28, 1768.

Madam,

It is indeed a great alleviation of sickness to be nursed by a
mother, and it is a comfort in return to have the prospect of being
nursed by a daughter, even at that hour when all human atten-
tion must be vain. From that social desire of being valuable to
each other, which produces kindness and officiousness, it pro-
ceeds, and must proceed, that there is some pleasure in being able
to give pain. To roll the weak eye of helpless anguish, and see
nothing on any side but cold indifference, will, I hope, happen to

none whom I love or value; it may tend to withdraw the mind from life, but has no tendency to kindle those affections which fit us for a purer and a nobler state.

Yet when any man finds himself disposed to complain with how little care he is regarded, let him reflect how little he contributes to the happiness of others, and how little, for the most part, he suffers from their pains. It is perhaps not to be lamented, that those solicitudes are not long nor frequent, which must commonly be vain; nor can we wonder that, in a state in which all have so much to feel of their own evils, very few have leisure for those of another. However, it is so ordered, that few suffer from want of assistance; and that kindness which could not assist, however pleasing, may be spared.

These reflections do not grow out of any discontent at C—'s[1] behaviour: he has been neither negligent nor troublesome; nor do I love him less for having been ill in his house. This is no small degree of praise. I am better, having scarce eaten for seven days. I shall come home on Saturday.

> I am, &c.,

> SAM: JOHNSON.

TO JAMES BOSWELL

Dear Sir

Why do you charge me with unkindness? I have omitted nothing that could do you good, or give you pleasure, unless it be that I have forborne to tell you my opinion of your *Account of Corsica*. I believe my opinion, if you think well of my judgement, might have given you pleasure; but when it is considered how much vanity is excited by praise, I am not sure that it would have done you good. Your History is like other histories, but your Journal is in a very high degree curious and delightful. There is between the History and the Journal that difference which there will al-

---

[1] Robert, later Sir Robert, Chambers, principal of New Inn Hall, and Vinerian professor of law at Oxford. Johnson assisted him with his lectures.

ways be found between notions borrowed from without, and no-
tions generated within. Your History was copied from books; your
Journal rose out of your own experience and observation. You ex-
press images which operated strongly upon yourself, and you have
impressed them with great force upon your readers. I know
not whether I could name any narrative by which curiosity is
better excited, or better gratified.

I am glad that you are going to be married; and as I wish you
well in things of less importance, wish you well with proportionate
ardour in this crisis of your life. What I can contribute to your
happiness, I should be very unwilling to with-hold; for I have
always loved and valued you, and shall love you and value you
still more, as you become more regular and useful: effects which
a happy marriage will hardly fail to produce.

I do not find that I am likely to come back very soon from this
place. I shall, perhaps, stay a fortnight longer; and a fortnight is
a long time to a lover absent from his mistress. Would a fortnight
ever have an end?

> I am, dear Sir,
> your most affectionate humble servant,
>
> SAM: JOHNSON.

BRIGHTHELMSTONE, SEPT. 9, 1769.

TO MRS. THRALE

> ASHBOURNE, JULY 23, 1770.

Dearest Madam

There had not been so long an interval between my two last let-
ters, but that when I came hither I did not at first understand the
hours of the post.

I have seen the great bull; and very great he is. I have seen
likewise his heir apparent, who promises to inherit all the bulk
and all the virtues of his sire.[1] I have seen the man who offered
an hundred guineas for the young bull, while he was yet little
better than a calf. Matlock, I am afraid, I shall not see, but I

---

[1] Dr. John Taylor, whom Johnson was visiting, prided himself on his
purebred stock.

purpose to see Dovedale; and after all this seeing, I hope to see you.

I am Madam Your most obliged humble Servant

SAM: JOHNSON.

TO MRS. THRALE

ASHBOURNE, JULY 3, 1771.

Dear Madam

Last Saturday I came to Ashbourne; the dangers or the pleasures of the journey I have at present no disposition to recount; else might I paint the beauties of my native plains; might I tell of 'the smiles of nature, and the charms of art:' else might I relate how I crossed the Staffordshire canal, one of the great efforts of human labour, and human contrivance; which, from the bridge on which I viewed it, passed away on either side, and loses itself in distant regions, uniting waters that nature had divided, and dividing lands which nature had united. I might tell how these reflections fermented in my mind till the chaise stopped at Ashbourne, at Ashbourne in the Peak. Let not the barren name of the Peak terrify you; I have never wanted strawberries and cream. The great bull has no disease but age. I hope in time to be like the great bull; and hope you will be like him too a hundred years hence.

In the mean time, dearest Madam, you have many dangers to pass. I hope the danger of this year is now over, and you are safe in Bed with a pretty little Stranger in the cradle. I hope you do not think me indifferent about you, and therefore will take care to have me informed.

I am Madam Your most obedient
and most humble servant

SAM: JOHNSON.

TO MRS. THRALE

SKIE, SEPT. 21, 1773.

Dearest Madam

I am so vexed at the necessity of sending yesterday so short a letter, that I purpose to get a long letter beforehand by writing

something every day, which I may the more easily do, as a cold
makes me now too deaf to take the usual pleasure in conversation.
Lady Macleod is very kind to me, and the place at which we now
are is equal in strength of situation, in the wildness of the adjacent
country, and in the plenty and elegance of the domestick enter-
tainment, to a castle in Gothick romances. The sea with a little
island is before us; cascades play within view. Close to the house
is the formidable skeleton of an old castle probably Danish, and
the whole mass of building stands upon a protuberance of rock,
inaccessible till of late but by a pair of stairs on the sea side, and
secure in ancient times against any enemy that was likely to in-
vade the kingdom of Skie.

Macleod has offered me an island; if it were not too far off I
should hardly refuse it; my island would be pleasanter than
Brighthelmstone, if you and Master could come to it; but I cannot
think it pleasant to live quite alone.

Oblitusque meorum, obliviscendus et illis.[1]

That I should be elated by the dominion of an island to forget-
fulness of my friends at Streatham [I cannot believe], and I hope
never to deserve that they should be willing to forget me.

It has happened that I have been often recognized in my jour-
ney where I did not expect it. At Aberdeen I found one of my
acquaintance professor of physick; turning aside to dine with a
country gentleman, I was owned at table by one who had seen
me at a philosophical lecture; at Macdonald's I was claimed by a
naturalist, who wanders about the islands to pick up curiosities;
and I had once in London attracted the notice of Lady Macleod.
I will now go on with my account.

The Highland girl made tea, and looked and talked not inele-
gantly; her father was by no means an ignorant or a weak man;
there were books in the cottage, among which were some volumes
of Prideaux's Connexion.[2] This man's conversation we were glad

---

[1] Horace, *Epis.* I. xi. 9. My friends forgetting, and by them forgot.
[2] Humphrey Prideaux, *The Old and New Testament Connected*, 1716–
1718.

of while we staid. He had been *out,* as they call it, in forty five, and still retained his old opinions. He was going to America, because his rent was raised beyond what he thought himself able to pay.

At night our beds were made, but we had some difficulty in persuading ourselves to lie down in them, though we had put on our own sheets; at last we ventured, and I slept very soundly in the vale called Glenmorison amidst the rocks and mountains. Next morning our landlord liked us so well, that he walked some miles with us for our company, through a country so wild and barren that the proprietor does not, with all his pressure upon his tenants, raise more than four hundred [pounds] a year from near an hundred square miles, or sixty thousand acres. He let us know that he had forty head of black cattle, an hundred goats, and an hundred sheep, upon a farm which he remembred let at five pounds a year, but for which he now paid twenty. He told us some stories of their march into England. At last he left us, and we went forward, winding among mountains, sometimes green and sometimes naked, commonly so steep as not easily to be climbed by the greatest vigour and activity: our way was often crossed by little rivulets, and we were entertained with small streams trickling from the rocks, which after heavy rains must be tremendous torrents.

About noon we came to a small glen, so they call a valley, which compared with other places appeared rich and fertile; here our guides desired us to stop, that the horses might graze, for the journey was very laborious, and no more grass would be found. We made no difficulty of compliance, and I sat down to take notes on a green bank, with a small stream running at my feet, in the midst of savage solitude, with mountains before me, and on either hand, covered with heath. I looked round me, and wondered that I was not more affected, but the mind is not at all times equally ready to be put in motion; if my mistress and master and Queeney had been there we should have produced some reflections among us, either poetical or philosophical, for though *Solitude be the nurse of woe,*[3] conversation is often the parent of remarks and discoveries.

[3] T. Parnell, *A Hymn to Contentment.*

In about an hour we remounted, and persued our journey. The lake by which we had travelled for some time ended in a river, which we passed by a bridge, and came to another glen, with a collection of huts, called Auknashealds; the huts were generally built of clods of earth, held together by the intertexture of vegetable fibres, of which earth there are great levels in Scotland which they call mosses. Moss in Scotland is bog in Ireland, and moss-trooper is bog-trotter: there was, however, one hut built of loose stones, piled up with great thickness into a strong though not solid wall. From this house we obtained some great pails of milk, and having brought bread with us, were very liberally regaled. The inhabitants, a very coarse tribe, ignorant of any language but Earse, gathered so fast about us, that if we had not had Highlanders with us, they might have caused more alarm than pleasure; they are called the Clan of Macrae.

We had been told that nothing gratified the Highlanders so much as snuff and tobacco, and had accordingly stored ourselves with both at Fort Augustus. Boswell opened his treasure, and gave them each a piece of tobacco roll. We had more bread than we could eat for the present, and were more liberal than provident. Boswell cut it in slices and gave each of them an opportunity of tasting wheaten bread for the first time. I then got some halfpence for a shilling, and made up the deficiencies of Boswell's distribution, who had given some money among the children. We then directed that the mistress of the stone house should be asked what we must pay her: she, who perhaps had never sold any thing but cattle before, knew not, I believe, well what to ask, and referred herself to us. We obliged her to make some demand, and our Highlanders settled the account with her at a shilling. One of the men advised her, with the cunning that clowns never can be without, to ask more; but she said that a shilling was enough. We gave her half a crown, and she offered part of it again. The Macraes were so well pleased with our behaviour, that they declared it the best day they had seen since the time of the old Laird of Macleod, who, I suppose, like us, stopped in their valley, as he was travelling to Skie.

We were mentioning this view of the Highlander's life at Macdonald's, and mentioning the Macraes with some degree of pity, when a Highland lady informed us that we might spare our tenderness, for she doubted not but the woman who supplied us with milk was mistress of thirteen or fourteen milch cows.

I cannot forbear to interrupt my narrative. Boswell, with some of his troublesome kindness, has informed this family and reminded me that the 18th of September is my birth-day. The return of my birth-day, if I remember it, fills me with thoughts which it seems to be the general care of humanity to escape. I can now look back upon threescore and four years, in which little has been done, and little has been enjoyed; a life diversified by misery, spent part in the sluggishness of penury, and part under the violence of pain, in gloomy discontent or importunate distress. But perhaps I am better than I should have been if I had been less afflicted. With this I will try to be content.

In proportion as there is less pleasure in retrospective considerations, the mind is more disposed to wander forward into futurity; but at sixty-four what promises, however liberal of imaginary good, can futurity venture to make? yet something will be always promised, and some promises will always be credited. I am hoping and I am praying that I may live better in the time to come, whether long or short, than I have yet lived, and in the solace of that hope endeavour to repose. Dear Queeney's day is next, I hope she at sixty-four will have less to regret.

I will now complain no more, but tell my mistress of my travels. After we left the Macraes we travelled on through a country like that which we passed in the morning. The Highlands are very uniform, for there is little variety in universal barrenness; the rocks, however, are not all naked, some have grass on their sides, and birches and alders on their tops, and in the vallies are often broad and clear streams, which have little depth, and commonly run very quick: the channels are made by the violence of wintry floods, the quickness of the stream is in proportion to the declivity of the descent, and the breadth of the channel makes the water shallow in a dry season.

There are red deer and roebucks in the mountains, but we found only goats in the road, and had very little entertainment

as we travelled either for the eye or ear. There are, I fancy, no
singing birds in the Highlands.[4]

Towards night we came to a very formidable hill called Ratti-
ken, which we climbed with more difficulty than we had yet
experienced, and at last came to Glenelg, a place on the sea-side
opposite to Skie. We were by this time weary and disgusted, nor
was our humour much mended by an inn, which, though it was
built with lime and slate, the Highlander's description of a house
which he thinks magnificent, had neither wine, bread, eggs, nor
any thing that we could eat or drink. When we were taken up
stairs, a dirty fellow bounced out of the bed in which one of us was
to lie. Boswell blustered, but nothing could be got. At last a gentle-
man in the neighbourhood, who heard of our arrival, sent us rum
and white sugar. Boswell was now provided for in part, and the
landlord prepared some mutton chops, which we could not eat,
and killed two hens, of which Boswell made his servant broil a
limb, with what effect I know not. We had a lemon and a piece
of bread, which supplied me with my supper. When the repast
was ended, we began to deliberate upon bed; Mrs. Boswell had
warned us that we should *catch something,* and had given us
sheets for our *security,* for Sir Alexander and Lady Macdonald,
she said, came back from Skie, so scratching themselves. I thought
sheets a slender defence against the confederacy with which we
were threatened, and by this time our Highlanders had found a
place where they could get some hay: I ordered hay to be laid
thick upon the bed, and slept upon it in my great coat: Boswell
laid sheets upon his hay, and reposed in linen like a gentleman.
The horses were turned out to grass, with a man to watch them.
The hill Rattiken and the inn at Glenelg are the only things of
which we, or travellers yet more delicate, could find any preten-
sions to complain.

Sept. 2nd, I rose rustling from the hay, and went to tea, which
I forget whether we found or brought. We saw the isle of Skie
before us, darkening the horizon with its rocky coast. A boat was
procured, and we launched into one of the straits of the Atlantick
ocean. We had a passage of about twelve miles to the point where

[4] As Hill reminds us, it was then September.

Sir Alexander resided, having come from his seat in the midland part, to a small house on the shore, as we believe, that he might with less reproach entertain us meanly. If he aspired to meanness, his retrograde ambition was completely gratified, but he did not succeed equally in escaping reproach. He had no cook, nor I suppose much provision, nor had the Lady the common decencies of her tea-table: we picked up our sugar with our fingers. Boswell was very angry, and reproached him with his improper parsimony; I did not much reflect upon the conduct of a man with whom I was not likely to converse as long at any other time.

You will now expect that I should give you some account of the isle of Skie, of which, though I have been twelve days upon it, I have little to say. It is an island perhaps fifty miles long, so much indented by inlets of the sea that there is no part of it removed from the water more than six miles. No part that I have seen is plain; you are always climbing or descending, and every step is upon rock or mire. A walk upon ploughed ground in England is a dance upon carpets compared to the toilsome drudgery of wandering in Skie. There is neither town nor village in the island, nor have I seen any house but Macleod's, that is not much below your habitation at Brighthelmstone. In the mountains there are stags and roebucks, but no hares, and few rabbits; nor have I seen any thing that interested me, as Zoologist, except an otter, bigger than I thought an otter could have been.

You are perhaps imagining that I am withdrawn from the gay and the busy world into regions of peace and pastoral felicity, and am enjoying the reliques of the golden age; that I am surveying nature's magnificence from a mountain, or remarking her minuter beauties on the flowery bank of a winding rivulet; that I am invigorating myself in the sunshine, or delighting my imagination with being hidden from the invasion of human evils and human passions in the darkness of a thicket; that I am busy in gathering shells and pebbles on the shore, or contemplative on a rock, from which I look upon the water, and consider how many waves are rolling between me and Streatham.

The use of travelling is to regulate imagination by reality, and instead of thinking how things may be, to see them as they are.

Here are mountains which I should once have climbed, but to climb steeps is now very laborious, and to descend them dangerous; and I am now content with knowing, that by scrambling up a rock, I shall only see other rocks, and a wider circuit of barren desolation. Of streams, we have here a sufficient number, but they murmur not upon pebbles, but upon rocks. Of flowers, if Chloris herself were here, I could present her only with the bloom of heath. Of lawns and thickets, he must read that would know them, for here is little sun and no shade. On the sea I look from my window, but am not much tempted to the shore; for since I came to this island, almost every breath of air has been a storm, and what is worse, a storm with all its severity, but without its magnificence, for the sea is here so broken into channels that there is not a sufficient volume of water either for lofty surges or a loud roar.

On Sept. 6th, we left Macdonald, to visit Raarsa, the island which I have already mentioned. We were to cross part of Skie on horseback; a mode of travelling very uncomfortable, for the road is so narrow, where any road can be found, that only one can go, and so craggy that the attention can never be remitted; it allows, therefore, neither the gaiety of conversation, nor the laxity of solitude; nor has it in itself the amusement of much variety, as it affords only all the possible transpositions of bog, rock, and rivulet. Twelve miles, by computation, make a reasonable journey for a day.

At night we came to a tenant's house, of the first rank of tenants, where we were entertained better than at the landlord's. There were books both English and Latin. Company gathered about us, and we heard some talk of the second sight, and some talk of the events of forty-five; a year which will not soon be forgotten among the islanders. The next day we were confined by a storm. The company, I think, encreased, and our entertainment was not only hospitable but elegant. At night, a minister's sister, in very fine brocade, sung Earse songs; I wished to know the meaning, but the Highlanders are not much used to scholastick questions, and no translations could be obtained.

Next day, Sept. 8th, the weather allowed us to depart; a good

boat was provided us, and we went to Raarsa under the conduct
of Mr. Malcolm Macleod, a gentleman who conducted Prince
Charles through the mountains in his distresses. The Prince, he
says, was more active than himself; they were, at least, one night
without any shelter.

The wind blew enough to give the boat a kind of dancing agi-
tation, and in about three or four hours we arrived at Raarsa,
where we were met by the Laird and his friends upon the shore.
Raarsa, for such is his title, is master of two islands; upon the
smaller of which, called Rona, he has only flocks and herds. Rona
gives title to his eldest son. The money which he raises annually
by rent from all his dominions, which contain at least fifty thou-
sand acres, is not believed to exceed two hundred and fifty
pounds; but as he keeps a large farm in his own hands, he sells
every year great numbers of cattle which he adds to his revenue,
and his table is furnished from the farm and from the sea with
little expence, except for those things this country does not pro-
duce, and of those he is very liberal. The wine circulates vigor-
ously, and the tea and chocolate and coffee, however they are got,
are always at hand.

I am Madam Your most obedient servant

SAM: JOHNSON.

We are this morning trying to get out of Skie.

TO JAMES MACPHERSON

Mr. James Macpherson—
I received your foolish and impudent note. Whatever insult is
offered me I will do my best to repel, and what I cannot do for
myself, the law will do for me. I will not desist from detecting
what I think a cheat, from any fear of the menaces of a Ruffian.

You want me to retract. What shall I retract? I thought your
book an imposture from the beginning. I think it upon yet surer
reasons an imposture still. For this opinion I give the publick my
reasons which I here dare you to refute.

But however I may despise you, I reverence truth and if you can prove the genuineness of the work I will confess it. Your rage I defy, your abilities since your Homer are not so formidable, and what I have heard of your morals disposes me to pay regard not to what you shall say, but to what you can prove.

You may print this if you will.

SAM: JOHNSON.

[JAN. 20, 1775]

TO THE REVEREND DR. DODD

Dear Sir

That which is appointed to all men is now coming upon you. Outward circumstances, the eyes and the thoughts of men, are below the notice of an immortal being about to stand the trial for eternity, before the Supreme Judge of heaven and earth. Be comforted: your crime, morally or religiously considered, has no very deep dye of turpitude. It corrupted no man's principles; it attacked no man's life. It involved only a temporary and reparable injury. Of this, and of all other sins, you are earnestly to repent; and may GOD, who knoweth our frailty, and desireth not our death, accept your repentance, for the sake of his Son JESUS CHRIST our Lord.

In requital of those well-intended offices which you are pleased so emphatically to acknowledge, let me beg that you make in your devotions one petition for my eternal welfare.

I am, dear Sir, your affectionate servant,

SAM: JOHNSON.

JUNE 26, 1777.

TO MRS. BOSWELL

Madam

Though I am well enough pleased with the taste of sweetmeats, very little of the pleasure which I received at the arrival of your jar of marmalade arose from eating it. I received it as a token of friendship, as a proof of reconciliation, things much sweeter than sweetmeats, and upon this consideration I return you, dear Madam, my sincerest thanks. By having your kindness I think I have a double security for the continuance of Mr. Boswell's, which it is not to be expected that any man can long keep, when the influence of a lady so highly and so justly valued operates against him. Mr. Boswell will tell you that I was always faithful to your interest, and aways endeavoured to exalt you in his estimation. You must now do the same for me. We must all help one another, and you must now consider me, as

> Dear Madam, your most obliged,
> and most humble servant,

SAM: JOHNSON.

JULY 22, 1777.

TO MRS. THRALE

ASHBOURNE, OCTOBER 6, 1777.

Dear Madam

You are glad that I am absent; and I am glad that you are sick.[1] When you went away, what did you do with your aunt? I am glad she liked my Susy; I was always a Susy,[2] when nobody else was a Susy. How have you managed at your new place? Could you all get lodgings in one house, and meat at one table? Let me hear the whole series of misery; for, as Dr. Young says, *I love horrour*.[3]

Methinks you are now a great way off; and if I come, I have a great way to come to you; and then the sea is so cold, and the rooms are so dull; yet I do love to hear the sea roar and my mis-

---

[1] The Thrales were eager for a son.
[2] Possibly a jocular use of French à: in favor of, partisan to, for.
[3] Edward Young: *The Revenge*, 1721, Act I, Sc. 1, lines 3–5:
Zanga: But horrors now are not displeasing to me:
I like this rocking of the Battlements.
Rage on, ye Winds, burst Clouds, and Waters roar!

tress talk— For when she talks, ye gods! how she will talk.[4] I wish I were with you, but we are now near half the length of England asunder. It is frightful to think how much time must pass between writing this letter and receiving an answer, if any answer were necessary.

Taylor is now going to have a ram; and then, after Aries and Taurus, we shall have Gemini. His oats are now in the wet; here is a deal of rain. Mr. Langdon bought, at Nottingham fair, fifteen tun of cheese; which, at an ounce a-piece, will suffice after dinner for four hundred and eighty thousand men. This is all the news that the place affords. I purpose soon to be at Lichfield, but know not just when, having been defeated of my first design. When I come to town, I am to be very busy about my Lives.[5]—Could not you do some of them for me?

I am glad Master huspelled you,[6] and run you all on rucks,[7] and drove you about, and made you stir. Never be cross about it. Quiet and calmness you have enough of—a little hurry stirs life —and,

> Brushing o'er, adds motion to the pool.[8]

Now *pool* brings my master's excavations into my head. I wonder how I shall like them; I should like not to see them, till we all see them together. He will have no waterfall to roar like the Doctor's. I sat by it yesterday, and read Erasmus's *Militis Christiani Enchiridion*. Have you got that book?

Make my compliments to dear Queeney. I suppose she will dance at the Rooms, and your heart will go one knows not how.

I am, dearest, and dearest Lady,
Your most humble servant,

SAM: JOHNSON.

[4] Nathaniel Lee, *The Rival Queens*, Act I.
[5] I.e., of the Poets, published 1779–1781.
[6] Shook you about.
[7] Ridges or ruts.
[8] Dryden, *Cymon and Iphigenia*, l. 30.

TO MRS. THRALE

LICHFIELD, OCTOBER 27, 1777.

Dear Madam

You talk of writing and writing, as if you had all the writing to yourself. If our correspondence were printed, I am sure posterity, for posterity is always the authour's favourite, would say that I am a good writer too.—*Anch'io sono pittore*.[1] To sit down so often with nothing to say: to say something so often, almost without consciousness of saying, and without any remembrance of having said, is a power of which I will not violate my modesty by boasting, but I do not believe that every body has it.

Some, when they write to their friends, are all affection; some are wise and sententious; some strain their powers for efforts of gaiety: some write news, and some write secrets; but to make a letter without affection, without wisdom, without gaiety, without news, and without a secret, is, doubtless, the great epistolick art.

In a man's letters, you know, Madam, his soul lies naked, his letters are only the mirrour of his breast; whatever passes within him is shown undisguised in its natural process; nothing is inverted, nothing distorted; you see systems in their elements; you discover actions in their motives.

Of this great truth, sounded by the knowing to the ignorant, and so echoed by the ignorant to the knowing, what evidence have you now before you! Is not my soul laid open in these veracious pages? Do not you see me reduced to my first principles? This is the pleasure of corresponding with a friend, where doubt and distrust have no place, and every thing is said as it is thought. The original idea is laid down in its simple purity, and all the supervenient conceptions are spread over it *stratum super stratum*, as they happen to be formed. These are the letters by which souls are united, and by which minds naturally in unison move each other as they are moved themselves. I know, dearest Lady, that in the perusal of this, such is the consanguinity of our intellects, you will be touched as I am touched. I have indeed concealed nothing

[1] "I too am a painter": attributed to Correggio seeing the work of Rafael.

from you, nor do I expect ever to repent of having thus opened my heart.

> I am, Madam, Your most humble servant,

> SAM: JOHNSON.

TO MRS. GARRICK

Dr. Johnson sends most respectful condolence to Mrs. Garrick, and wishes that any endeavour of his could enable her [to] support a loss which the world cannot repair.[1]
FEB. 2. 1779.

TO JAMES BOSWELL

Dear Sir
I hoped you had got rid of all this hypocrisy of misery. What have you to do with Liberty and Necessity? Or what more than to hold your tongue about it? Do not doubt but I shall be most heartily glad to see you here again, for I love every part about you but your affectation of distress.

I have at last finished my *Lives*, and have laid up for you a load of copy, all out of order, so that it will amuse you a long time to set it right. Come to me, my dear Bozzy, and let us be as happy as we can. We will go again to the Mitre, and talk old times over.

> I am, dear Sir, yours affectionately,

> SAM: JOHNSON.

MARCH 14, 1781.

TO MRS. THRALE

> BOLT-COURT, FLEET-STREET,
> JUNE 19, 1783.

Dear Madam
I am sitting down in no cheerful solitude to write a narrative which would once have affected you with tenderness and sorrow,

[1] David Garrick died January 20 and was buried in Westminster Abbey on February 1.

but which you will perhaps pass over now with the careless glance of frigid indifference. For this diminution of regard however, I know not whether I ought to blame you, who may have reasons which I cannot know, and I do not blame myself, who have for a great part of human life done you what good I could, and have never done you evil.

I had been disordered in the usual way, and had been relieved by the usual methods, by opium and catharticks, but had rather lessened my dose of opium.

On Monday the 16th I sat for my picture, and walked a considerable way with little inconvenience. In the afternoon and evening I felt myself light and easy, and began to plan schemes of life. Thus I went to bed, and in a short time waked and sat up, as has been long my custom, when I felt a confusion and indistinctness in my head, which lasted I suppose about half a minute; I was alarmed, and prayed God, that however he might afflict my body, he would spare my understanding. This prayer, that I might try the integrity of my faculties, I made in Latin verse. The lines were not very good, but I knew them not to be very good: I made them easily, and concluded myself to be unimpaired in my faculties.

Soon after I perceived that I had suffered a paralytick stroke, and that my speech was taken from me. I had no pain, and so little dejection in this dreadful state, that I wondered at my own apathy, and considered that perhaps death itself when it should come would excite less horrour than seems now to attend it.

In order to rouse the vocal organs I took two drams. Wine has been celebrated for the production of eloquence. I put myself into violent motion, and I think repeated it; but all was vain. I then went to bed, and, strange as it may seem, I think, slept. When I saw light, it was time to contrive what I should do. Though God stopped my speech he left me my hand, I enjoyed a mercy which was not granted to my dear friend Lawrence, who now perhaps overlooks me as I am writing, and rejoices that I have what he wanted. My first note was necessarily to my servant, who came in talking, and could not immediately comprehend why he should read what I put into his hands.

I then wrote a card to Mr. Allen, that I might have a discreet friend at hand to act as occasion should require. In penning this note I had some difficulty, my hand, I knew not how nor why, made wrong letters. I then wrote to Dr. Taylor to come to me, and bring Dr. Heberden, and I sent to Dr. Brocklesby, who is my neighbour. My physicians are very friendly and very disinterested, and give me great hopes, but you may imagine my situation. I have so far recovered my vocal powers, as to repeat the Lord's Prayer with no very imperfect articulation. My memory, I hope, yet remains as it was; but such an attack produces solicitude for the safety of every faculty.

How this will be received by you I know not. I hope you will sympathise with me; but perhaps

> My mistress gracious, mild, and good,
> Cries! Is he dumb? 'Tis time he shou'd.[1]

But can this be possible? I hope it cannot. I hope that what, when I could speak, I spoke of you, and to you, will be in a sober and serious hour remembered by you; and surely it cannot be remembered but with some degree of kindness. I have loved you with virtuous affection; I have honoured you with sincere esteem. Let not all our endearment be forgotten, but let me have in this great distress your pity and your prayers. You see I yet turn to you with my complaints as a settled and unalienable friend; do not, do not drive me from you, for I have not deserved either neglect or hatred.

To the girls, who do not write often, for Susy has written only once, and Miss Thrale owes me a letter, I earnestly recommend, as their guardian and friend, that they remember their Creator in the days of their youth.

I suppose you may wish to know how my disease is treated by the physicians. They put a blister upon my back, and two from my ear to my throat, one on a side. The blister on the back has done little, and those on the throat have not risen. I bullied and bounced, (it sticks to our last sand)[2] and compelled the apothecary

---

[1] Adapted from Swift's *On the Death of Dr. Swift*.
[2] A quotation from Pope, *Moral Essays*, I. 225.

to make his salve according to the Edinburgh Dispensatory, that it might adhere better. I have two on now of my own prescription. They likewise give me salt of hartshorn, which I take with no great confidence, but am satisfied that what can be done is done for me.

O God! give me comfort and confidence in Thee: forgive my sins; and if it be Thy good pleasure, relieve my diseases for Jesus Christ's sake. Amen.

I am almost ashamed of this querulous letter, but now it is written, let it go.

I am, Madam Your most humble servant

SAM: JOHNSON.

TO MISS SUSANNA THRALE

(ABOUT JULY 5, 1783.)

Dearest Miss Susy

When you favoured me with your letter, you seemed to be in want of materials to fill it, having met with no great adventures either of peril or delight, nor done or suffered any thing out of the common course of life.

When you have lived longer, and considered more, you will find the common course of life very fertile of observation and reflection. Upon the common course of life must our thoughts and our conversation be generally employed. Our general course of life must denominate us wise or foolish; happy or miserable: if it is well regulated we pass on prosperously and smoothly; as it is neglected we live in embarrassment, perplexity, and uneasiness.

Your time, my love, passes, I suppose, in devotion, reading, work, and company. Of your devotions, in which I earnestly advise you to be very punctual, you may not perhaps think it proper to give me an account; and of work, unless I understood it better, it will be of no great use to say much; but books and company will always supply you with materials for your letters to me, as I shall be always pleased to know what you are reading, and with what you are pleased; and shall take great delight in knowing what impression new modes or new characters make upon you, and to

observe with what attention you distinguish the tempers, disposi-
tions, and abilities of your companions.

A letter may be always made out of the books of the morning or
talk of the evening; and any letters from you, my dearest, will be
welcome to

[Your, &c.,]

SAM: JOHNSON.

TO MRS. THRALE

LONDON, OCTOBER 9, 1783.

Madam . . .

. . . Two nights ago Mr. Burke sat with me a long time; he seems
much pleased with his journey. We had both seen Stonehenge
this summer for the first time. I told him that the view had
enabled me to confute two opinions which have been advanced
about it. One, that the materials are not natural stones, but an
artificial composition hardened by time. This notion is as old as
Camden's time; and has this strong argument to support it, that
stone of that species is no where to be found. The other opinion,
advanced by Dr. Charlton, is, that it was erected by the Danes.

Mr. Bowles made me observe, that the transverse stones were
fixed on the perpendicular supporters by a knob formed on the
top of the upright stone, which entered into a hollow cut in the
crossing stone. This is a proof that the enormous edifice was raised
by a people who had not yet the knowledge of mortar; which can-
not be supposed of the Danes who came hither in ships, and were
not ignorant certainly of the arts of life. This proves likewise the
stones not to be factitious; for they that could mould such durable
masses could do much more than make mortar, and could have
continued the transverse from the upright parts with the same
paste.

You have doubtless seen Stonehenge, and if you have not, I
should think it a hard task to make an adequate description.

It is, in my opinion, to be referred to the earliest habitation of
the Island, as a Druidical monument of at least two thousand
years; probably the most ancient work of man upon the Island.

Salisbury cathedral, and its neighbour Stonehenge, are two eminent monuments of art and rudeness, and may show the first essay, and the last perfection, in architecture.

I have not yet settled my thoughts about the generation of light air, which I indeed once saw produced, but I was at the height of my great complaint. I have made enquiry, and shall soon be able to tell you how to fill a ballon.

I am, Madam Your most humble servant

SAM: JOHNSON.

TO MRS. THRALE

Madam

If I interpret your letter right, you are ignominiously married; if it is yet undone, let us once talk together. If you have abandoned your children and your religion, God forgive your wickedness: if you have forfeited your fame and your country, may your folly do no further mischief.

If the last act is yet to do, I who have loved you, esteemed you, reverenced you, and served you, I who long thought you the first of humankind, entreat that, before your fate is irrevocable, I may once more see you. I was, I once was,

Madam, most truly yours,

SAM: JOHNSON.

JULY 2, 1784.
    I will come down, if you permit it.

TO MRS. THRALE

LONDON, JULY 8, 1784.

Dear Madam

What you have done, however I may lament it, I have no pretence to resent, as it has not been injurious to me: I therefore breathe out one sigh more of tenderness, perhaps useless, but at least sincere.

I wish that God may grant you every blessing, that you may be happy in this world for its short continuance, and eternally happy in a better state; and whatever I can contribute to your happiness I am very ready to repay, for that kindness which soothed twenty years of a life radically wretched.

Do not think slightly of the advice which I now presume to offer. Prevail upon Mr. Piozzi to settle in England: you may live here with more dignity than in Italy, and with more security: your rank will be higher, and your fortune more under your own eye. I desire not to detail all my reasons, but every argument of prudence and interest is for England, and only some phantoms of imagination seduce you to Italy.

I am afraid however that my counsel is vain, yet I have eased my heart by giving it.

When Queen Mary took the resolution of sheltering herself in England, the Archbishop of St. Andrew's, attempting to dissuade her, attended on her journey; and when they came to the irremeable stream that separated the two kingdoms, walked by her side into the water, in the middle of which he seized her bridle, and with earnestness proportioned to her danger and his own affection pressed her to return. The Queen went forward.——If the parallel reaches thus far, may it go no further.—The tears stand in my eyes.

I am going into Derbyshire, and hope to be followed by your good wishes, for I am, with great affection,

Your most humble servant,

SAM: JOHNSON.

Any letters that come for me hither will be sent me.

PRAYERS AND MEDITATIONS

April 25, 1752.

O Lord, our heavenly Father, almighty and most merciful God, in whose hands are life and death, who givest and takest away, castest down and raisest up, look with mercy on the affliction of thy unworthy servant, turn away thine anger from me, and speak peace to my troubled soul. Grant me the assistance and comfort of thy Holy Spirit, that I may remember with thankfulness the blessings so long enjoyed by me in the society of my departed wife;[1] make me so to think on her precepts and example, that I may imitate whatever was in her life acceptable in thy sight, and avoid all by which she offended Thee. Forgive me, O merciful Lord, all my sins, and enable me to begin and perfect that reformation which I promised her, and to persevere in that resolution, which she implored Thee to continue, in the purposes which I recorded in thy sight, when she lay dead before me, in obedience to thy laws, and faith in thy word. And now, O Lord, release me

[1] Elizabeth Johnson died March 28.

35

from my sorrow, fill me with just hopes, true faith, and holy consolations, and enable me to do my duty in that state of life to which Thou hast been pleased to call me, without disturbance from fruitless grief, or tumultuous imaginations; that in all my thoughts, words, and actions, I may glorify thy Holy Name, and finally obtain, what I hope Thou hast granted to thy departed servant, everlasting joy and felicity, through our Lord Jesus Christ. Amen.

EASTER EVE   (1757)

Almighty God, heavenly Father, who desirest not the death of a sinner, look down with mercy upon me, depraved with vain imaginations, and entangled in long habits of sin. Grant me that grace, without which I can neither will nor do what is acceptable to Thee. Pardon my sins; remove the impediments that hinder my obedience; enable me to shake off sloth, and to redeem the time mispent in idleness and sin, by a diligent application of the days yet remaining, to the duties which thy providence shall allot me. O God, grant me thy Holy Spirit, that I may repent and amend my life; grant me contrition, grant me resolution, for the sake of Jesus Christ, to whose covenant I now implore admission, of the benefits of whose death I implore participation. For his sake have mercy on me, O God; for his sake, O God, pardon and receive me. Amen.

EASTER EVE   1761.

Since the communion of last Easter, I have led a life so dissipated and useless, and my terrours and perplexities have so much encreased, that I am under great depression and discouragement; yet I purpose to present myself before God tomorrow, with humble hope that he will not break the bruised reed.

Come unto me all ye that travail.

I have resolved, I hope not presumptuously, till I am afraid to resolve again. Yet hoping in God, I stedfastly purpose to lead a new life. O God, enable me, for Jesus Christ's sake.

April 21, 1764, 3 in the morning.

My indolence, since my last reception of the Sacrament, has sunk into grosser sluggishness, and my dissipation spread into wilder negligence. My thoughts have been clouded with sensuality; and, except that from the beginning of this year I have in some measure forborn excess of strong drink, my appetites have predominated over my reason. A kind of strange oblivion has overspread me, so that I know not what has become of the last year; and perceive that incidents and intelligence pass over me without leaving any impression.

This is not the life to which heaven is promised. I purpose to approach the altar again to-morrow. Grant, O Lord, that I may receive the Sacrament with such resolutions of a better life as may by thy grace be effectual, for the sake of Jesus Christ. Amen.

April 21. I read the whole Gospel of St. John. Then sat up till the 22d.

My purpose is from this time, To reject or expel sensual images, and idle thoughts. To provide some useful amusement for leisure time. To avoid idleness. To rise early. To study a proper portion of every day. To worship God diligently. To read the Scriptures. To let no week pass without reading some part. To write down my observations. I will renew my resolutions made at Tetty's death.

I perceive an insensibility and heaviness upon me. I am less than commonly oppressed with the sense of sin, and less affected with the shame of idleness. Yet I will not despair. I will pray to God for resolution, and will endeavour to strengthen my faith in Christ, by commemorating his death. I prayed for Tett.

Sept. 18, 1764, about 6 evening.

This is my fifty-sixth birth-day, the day on which I have con-cluded fifty-five years.

I have outlived many friends. I have felt many sorrows. I have made few improvements. Since my resolution formed last Easter, I have made no advancement in knowledge or in goodness; nor do I recollect that I have endeavoured it. I am dejected, but not hope-less.

O God, for Jesus Christ's sake, have mercy upon me.

7 in the evening.

I went to church, prayed *to be loosed from the chain of my sins.*[1]

I have now spent fifty-five years in resolving; having from the earliest time almost that I can remember, been forming schemes of a better life. I have done nothing; the need of doing therefore is pressing, since the time of doing is short. O God, grant me to resolve aright, and to keep my resolution, for Jesus Christ's sake. Amen.

Sunday, Oct. 18, 1767.

Yesterday, Oct. 17, at about ten in the morning, I took my leave for ever of my dear old friend Catherine Chambers, who came to live with my mother about 1724, and has been but little parted from us since. She buried my father, my brother, and my mother. She is now fifty-eight years old.

I desired all to withdraw, then told her that we were to part for ever; that as Christians, we should part with prayer; and that I would, if she was willing, say a short prayer beside her. She expressed great desire to hear me; and held up her poor hands, as she lay in bed, with great fervour, while I prayed kneeling by her, nearly in the following words:

[1] Book of Common Prayer: "O God, whose nature and property."

Almighty and most merciful Father, whose loving-kindness is over all thy works, behold, visit, and relieve this thy servant, who is grieved with sickness. Grant that the sense of her weakness may add strength to her faith and seriousness to her repentance. And grant that by the help of thy Holy Spirit, after the pains and labours of this short life, we may all obtain everlasting happiness, through Jesus Christ our Lord; for whose sake hear our prayers. Amen. Our Father, &c.

I then kissed her. She told me, that to part was the greatest pain that she had ever felt, and that she hoped we should meet again in a better place. I expressed, with swelled eyes, and great emotion of tenderness, the same hopes. We kissed, and parted. I humbly hope to meet again, and to part no more.

Wednesday, March 28, 1770.

This is the day on which, in 1752, I was deprived of poor dear Tetty. Having left off the practice of thinking on her with some particular combinations, I have recalled her to my mind of late less frequently; but when I recollect the time in which we lived together, my grief for her departure is not abated; and I have less pleasure in any good that befalls me, because she does not partake it. On many occasions, I think what she would have said or done. When I saw the sea at Brighthelmstone, I wished for her to have seen it with me. But with respect to her, no rational wish is now left, but that we may meet at last where the mercy of God shall make us happy, and perhaps make us instrumental to the happiness of each other. It is now eighteen years.

June 1, 1770.

Every man naturally persuades himself that he can keep his resolutions, nor is he convinced of his imbecillity but by length of time and frequency of experiment. This opinion of our own constancy is so prevalent, that we always despise him who suffers his general and settled purpose to be overpowered by an occasional desire. They, therefore, whom frequent failures have made desperate, cease to form resolutions; and they who are become cunning, do not tell them. Those who do not make them are very few, but of their effect little is perceived; for scarcely any man persists in a course of life planned by choice, but as he is restrained from deviation by some external power. He who may live as he will, seldom lives long in the observation of his own rules.

Sept. 18, 1771, 9 at night.

I am now come to my sixty-third year. For the last year I have been slowly recovering both from the violence of my last illness and, I think, from the general disease of my life. My breath is less obstructed, and I am more capable of motion and exercise. My mind is less encumbered, and I am less interrupted in mental employment. Some advances I hope have been made towards regularity. I have missed church since Easter only two Sundays, both which I hope I have endeavoured to supply by attendance on divine worship in the following week. Since Easter, my evening devotions have been lengthened. But indolence and indifference has been neither conquered nor opposed. No plan of study has been pursued or formed, except that I have commonly read every week, if not on Sunday, a stated portion of the New Testament in Greek. But what is most to be considered, I have neither attempted nor formed any scheme of life by which I may do good, and please God.

One great hindrance is want of rest; my nocturnal complaints grow less troublesome towards morning; and I am tempted to repair the deficiencies of the night. I think, however, to try to rise every day by eight, and to combat indolence as I shall obtain strength. Perhaps Providence has yet some use for the remnant of my life.

Almighty and everlasting God, whose mercy is over all thy works, and who hast no pleasure in the death of a sinner, look with pity upon me, succour and preserve me; enable me to conquer evil habits, and surmount temptations. Give me grace so to use the degree of health which Thou hast restored to my mind and body, that I may perform the task Thou shalt yet appoint me. Look down, O gracious Lord, upon my remaining part of life; grant, if it please Thee, that the days few or many which Thou shalt yet allow me, may pass in reasonable confidence, and holy tranquillity. Withhold not thy Holy Spirit from me, but strengthen all good purposes, till they shall produce a life pleasing to Thee. And when Thou shalt call me to another state, forgive me my sins, and receive me to happiness, for the sake of Jesus Christ our Lord. Amen.

Safely brought us. &c.

EASTER DAY

April 16, 1775.

Almighty God, heavenly Father, whose mercy is over all thy works, look with pity on my miseries and sins. Suffer me to commemorate, in thy presence, my redemption by thy son Jesus Christ. Enable me so to repent of my mispent time, that I may pass the residue of my life in thy fear, and to thy glory. Relieve, O Lord, as seemeth best unto Thee, the infirmities of my body, and the perturbations of my mind. Fill my thoughts with awful love of thy goodness, with just fear of thine anger, and with humble confidence in thy mercy. Let me study thy laws, and labour in the duties which Thou shalt set before me. Take not from me thy Holy Spirit, but incite in me such good desires, as may produce diligent endeavours after thy glory and my own salvation; and when, after hopes and fears, and joys and sorrows, Thou shalt call me hence, receive me to eternal happiness, for the sake of Jesus Christ our Lord. Amen.

[March] 30, Easter Day, (1777), Imâ mane.[1]

The day is now come again, in which, by a custom which since the death of my wife I have by the divine assistance always observed, I am to renew the great covenant with my Maker and my

[1] One in the morning (i.e., *Prima [hora]*).

Judge. I humbly hope to perform it better. I hope for more efficacy of resolution, and more diligence of endeavour. When I survey my past life, I discover nothing but a barren waste of time, with some disorders of body, and disturbances of the mind very near to madness, which I hope He that made me, will suffer to extenuate many faults, and excuse many deficiencies. Yet much remains to be repented and reformed. I hope that I refer more to God than in former times, and consider more what submission is due to his dispensations. But I have very little reformed my practical life; and the time in which I can struggle with habits cannot be now expected to be long. Grant, O God, that I may no longer resolve in vain, or dream away the life which thy indulgence gives me, in vacancy and uselessness.

GOOD FRIDAY [1779]

11 P.M.

I am now to review the last year, and find little but dismal vacuity, neither business nor pleasure; much intended, and little done. My health is much broken; my nights afford me little rest. I have tried opium, but its help is counterbalanced with great disturbance; it prevents the spasms, but it hinders sleep. O God, have mercy on me.

Last week I published the Lives of the Poets, written, I hope, in such a manner as may tend to the promotion of piety.

In this last year I have made little acquisition; I have scarcely read any thing. I maintain Mrs. [Desmoulins] and her daughter. Other good of myself I know not where to find, except a little charity.

But I am now in my seventieth year; what can be done, ought not to be delayed.

[GOOD FRIDAY]

April 13, 1781.

I forgot my prayer and resolutions, till two days ago I found this paper.

Sometime in March I finished the Lives of the Poets, which I wrote in my usual way, dilatorily and hastily, unwilling to work, and working with vigour and haste.

On Wednesday 11, was buried my dear friend Thrale, who died on Wednesday 4; and with him were buried many of my hopes and pleasures.[1] About five, I think, on Wednesday morning he expired; I felt almost the last flutter of his pulse, and looked for the last time upon the face that for fifteen years had never been turned upon me but with respect or benignity. Farewel. May God, that delighteth in mercy, have had mercy on thee.

I had constantly prayed for him some time before his death.

The decease of him, from whose friendship I have obtained many opportunities of amusement, and to whom I turned my thoughts as to a refuge from misfortunes, has left me heavy. But my business is with myself.[2]

September 18 [1781]

My first knowledge of Thrale was in 1765. I enjoyed his favour for almost a fourth part of my life.

ON LEAVING MR. THRALE'S FAMILY

October 6, 1782.

Almighty God, Father of all mercy, help me, by thy grace, that I may with humble and sincere thankfulness remember the comforts and conveniences which I have enjoyed at this place, and that I may resign them with holy submission, equally trusting in thy protection when Thou givest and when Thou takest away. Have mercy upon me, O Lord, have mercy upon me.

To thy fatherly protection, O Lord, I commend this family. Bless, guide, and defend them, that they may so pass through this

[1] The Diary entry for April 14 begins at this point. For obvious reasons Strahan joined the two days.

[2] Refers to his self-examination before Easter.

world, as finally to enjoy in thy presence everlasting happiness, for Jesus Christ's sake. Amen.

O Lord, so far as, &c.—Thrale.

October 7 (1782)

I was called early. I packed up my bundles, and used the foregoing Prayer, with my morning devotions somewhat, I think, enlarged. Being earlier than the family, I read St. Paul's farewel in the Acts, and then read fortuitously in the Gospels, which was my parting use of the library.

AGAINST INQUISITIVE AND PERPLEXING
    THOUGHTS

August 12, 1784.

O Lord, my Maker and Protector, who hast graciously sent me into this world to work out my salvation, enable me to drive from me all such unquiet and perplexing thoughts as may mislead or hinder me in the practice of those duties which Thou hast required. When I behold the works of thy hands, and consider the course of thy providence, give me grace always to remember that thy thoughts are not my thoughts, nor thy ways my ways. And while it shall please Thee to continue me in this world, where much is to be done, and little is to be known, teach me, by thy Holy Spirit, to withdraw my mind from unprofitable and dangerous enquiries, from difficulties vainly curious, and doubts impossible to be solved. Let me rejoice in the light which Thou has imparted, let me serve Thee with active zeal and humble confidence, and wait with patient expectation for the time in which the soul which Thou receivest shall be satisfied with knowledge. Grant this, O Lord, for Jesus Christ's sake. Amen.

POETRY

To Mrs. Thrale

ON HER COMPLETING HER THIRTY-FIFTH YEAR

[AN IMPROMPTU] [1]

Oft in Danger yet alive
We are come to Thirty-five;
Long may better Years arrive,
Better Years than Thirty-five!
Could Philosophers contrive
Life to stop at Thirty-five,
Time his Hours should never drive
O'er the Bounds of Thirty-five:
High to soar and deep to dive
Nature gives at Thirty-five;
Ladies—stock and tend your Hive,
Trifle not at Thirty-five:

[1] "I went into his room the morning of my birth-day . . . and said to him, Nobody sends me any verses now, because I am five-and-thirty. . . . He burst out suddenly . . . without the least previous hesitation whatsoever. . . . 'And now (said he . . .), you may see what it is to come for poetry to a Dictionary-maker; you may observe that the rhymes run in alphabetical order.' "—Mrs. Thrale's *Anecdotes*. But she was already thirty-six, if not thirty-seven, as Boswell would have been pleased to observe.

47

For howe'er we boast and strive,
Life declines from Thirty-five;
He that ever hopes to thrive
Must begin by Thirty-five:
And those who wisely wish to wive,
Must look on Thrale at Thirty-five.

A Short Song of Congratulation

Long-expected one and twenty
   Ling'ring year at last is flown,
Pomp and Pleasure, Pride and Plenty
   Great Sir John,[1] are all your own.

Loosen'd from the Minor's tether,
   Free to mortgage or to sell,
Wild as wind, and light as feather
   Bid the slaves of thrift farewell.

Call the Bettys, Kates, and Jennys
   Ev'ry name that laughs at Care,   10
Lavish of your Grandsire's guineas,
   Show the Spirit of an heir.

All that prey on vice and folly
   Joy to see their quarry fly,

[1] Sir John Lade was the son of Henry Thrale's sister. On his asking Johnson whether or not to marry, the Doctor replied, "I would advise no man to marry, Sir, who is not likely to propagate understanding." The poem was sent to Mrs. Thrale, with injunctions not to show it. It was not published in Johnson's lifetime. Sir John is said to have followed the course prescribed for him in the poem.

Here the Gamester light and jolly
  There the Lender grave and sly.

Wealth, Sir John, was made to wander,
  Let it wander as it will;
See the Jocky, see the Pander,
  Bid them come, and take their fill.   20

When the bonny Blade carouses,
  Pockets full, and Spirits high,
What are acres? What are houses?
  Only dirt, or wet or dry.

If the Guardian or the Mother
  Tell the woes of wilful waste,
Scorn their counsel and their pother,
  You can hang or drown at last.

Prologue

SPOKEN BY MR. GARRICK, AT THE OPENING OF THE THEATRE
IN DRURY-LANE 1747

When Learning's Triumph o'er her barb'rous Foes
First rear'd the Stage, immortal SHAKESPEAR rose;
Each Change of many-colour'd Life he drew,
Exhausted Worlds, and then imagin'd new:
Existence saw him spurn her bounded Reign,
And panting Time toil'd after him in vain:
His pow'rful Strokes presiding Truth impress'd,
And unresisted Passion storm'd the Breast.
    Then JOHNSON[1] came, instructed from the School,

[1] Ben Jonson.

To please in Method, and invent by Rule;   10
His studious Patience, and laborious Art,
By regular Approach essay'd the Heart;
Cold Approbation gave the ling'ring Bays,   *laurels*
For those who durst not censure, scarce cou'd praise.
A Mortal born he met the general Doom,
But left, like *Egypt*'s Kings, a lasting Tomb.
  The Wits of *Charles* found easier Ways to Fame,
Nor wish'd for JOHNSON's Art, or SHAKESPEAR's Flame;
Themselves they studied, as they felt, they writ,
Intrigue was Plot, Obscenity was Wit.   20
Vice always found a sympathetick Friend;
They pleas'd their Age, and did not aim to mend.
Yet Bards like these aspir'd to lasting Praise,
And proudly hop'd to pimp in future Days.
Their Cause was gen'ral, their Supports were strong,
Their Slaves were willing, and their Reign was long;
Till Shame regain'd the Post that Sense betray'd,
And Virtue call'd Oblivion to her Aid.
  Then crush'd by Rules, and weaken'd as refin'd,
For Years the Pow'r of Tragedy declin'd;   30
From Bard, to Bard, the frigid Caution crept,
Till Declamation roar'd, while Passion slept.
Yet still did Virtue deign the Stage to tread.
Philosophy remain'd, though Nature fled.
But forc'd at length her antient Reign to quit,
She saw great *Faustus*[2] lay the Ghost of Wit:
Exulting Folly hail'd the joyful Day,
And Pantomime, and Song, confirm'd her Sway.
  But who the coming Changes can presage,
And mark the future Periods of the Stage?—   40
Perhaps if Skill could distant Times explore,
New *Behns*, new *Durfeys*, yet remain in Store.
Perhaps, where *Lear* has rav'd and *Hamlet* dy'd,
On flying Cars new Sorcerers may ride.

  [2] Doctor Faustus was a very popular subject of farces on the eighteenth-century stage.

Perhaps, for who can guess th' Effects of Chance?
Here *Hunt* may box, or *Mahomet* may dance.[3]
  Hard is his lot, that here by Fortune plac'd,
Must watch the wild Vicissitudes of Taste;
With ev'ry Meteor of Caprice must play,
And chase the new-blown Bubbles of the Day.   50
Ah! let not Censure term our Fate our Choice,
The Stage but echoes back the publick Voice.
The Drama's Laws the Drama's Patrons give,
For we that live to please, must please to live.
  Then prompt no more the Follies you decry,
As Tyrants doom their Tools of Guilt to die;
'Tis yours this Night to bid the Reign commence
Of rescu'd Nature, and reviving Sense;
To chase the Charms of Sound, the Pomp of Show,
For useful Mirth, and salutary Woe;   60
Bid scenic Virtue form the rising Age,
And Truth diffuse her Radiance from the Stage.

The Vanity of Human Wishes

THE TENTH SATIRE OF JUVENAL IMITATED

Let observation with extensive view,
Survey mankind, from China to Peru;
Remark each anxious toil, each eager strife,
And watch the busy scenes of crouded life;
Then say how hope and fear, desire and hate,
O'erspread with snares the clouded maze of fate,
Where wav'ring man, betray'd by vent'rous pride,

[3] A pugilist and a rope-dancer recently in public notice.

To tread the dreary paths without a guide,
As treach'rous phantoms in the mist delude,
Shuns fancied ills, or chases airy good;   10
How rarely reason guides the stubborn choice,
Rules the bold hand, or prompts the suppliant voice;
How nations sink, by darling schemes oppress'd,
When vengeance listens to the fool's request.[1]
Fate wings with ev'ry wish th' afflictive dart,
Each gift of nature, and each grace of art,
With fatal heat impetuous courage glows,
With fatal sweetness elocution flows,
Impeachment stops the speaker's pow'rful breath,
And restless fire precipitates on death.   20
    But scarce observ'd, the knowing and the bold
Fall in the gen'ral massacre of gold;
Wide-wasting pest! that rages unconfin'd,
And crouds with crimes the records of mankind;
For gold his sword the hireling ruffian draws,
For gold the hireling judge distorts the laws;
Wealth heap'd on wealth, nor truth nor safety buys,
The dangers gather as the treasures rise.
    Let hist'ry tell where rival kings command,
And dubious title shakes the madded land,   30
When statutes glean the refuse of the sword,
How much more safe the vassal than the lord;
Low skulks the hind beneath the rage of pow'r,
And leaves the wealthy traytor in the Tow'r,
Untouch'd his cottage, and his slumbers sound,
Tho' confiscation's vulturs hover round.
    The needy traveller, serene and gay,
Walks the wild heath, and sings his toil away.
Does envy seize thee? crush th' upbraiding joy,[2]

---

[1] Nations marked out for vengeance are destroyed by letting their foolish leaders have their way. The qualities, natural or acquired, that are our chief adornment are made the instruments of our subsequent affliction.

[2] If you are troubled by envy of the poor man's carefree lot, give him wealth and watch the results.

Increase his riches and his peace destroy;   40
Now fears in dire vicissitude invade,
The rustling brake alarms, and quiv'ring shade,
Nor light nor darkness bring his pain relief,
One shews the plunder, and one hides the thief.
   Yet still one gen'ral cry the skies assails,
And gain and grandeur load the tainted gales;
Few know the toiling statesman's fear or care,
Th' insidious rival and the gaping heir.
   Once more, Democritus, arise on earth,
With chearful wisdom and instructive mirth,   50
See motley life in modern trappings dress'd,
And feed with varied fools th' eternal jest:
Thou who couldst laugh where want enchain'd caprice,
Toil crush'd conceit, and man was of a piece;
Where wealth unlov'd without a mourner dy'd,
And scarce a sycophant was fed by pride;
Where ne'er was known the form of mock debate,
Or seen a new-made mayor's unwieldy state;
Where change of fav'rites made no change of laws,
And senates heard before they judg'd a cause;   60
How wouldst thou shake at Britain's modish tribe,
Dart the quick taunt, and edge the piercing gibe?
Attentive truth and nature to descry,
And pierce each scene with philosophic eye.
To thee were solemn toys or empty shew,
The robes of pleasure and the veils of woe:
All aid the farce, and all thy mirth maintain,
Whose joys are causeless, or whose griefs are vain.
   Such was the scorn that fill'd the sage's mind,
Renew'd at ev'ry glance on humankind;   70
How just that scorn ere yet thy voice declare,
Search every state, and canvass ev'ry pray'r.
   Unnumber'd suppliants croud Preferment's gate,
Athirst for wealth, and burning to be great;
Delusive Fortune hears th' incessant call,
They mount, they shine, evaporate, and fall.

On ev'ry stage the foes of peace attend,
Hate dogs their flight, and insult mocks their end.
Love ends with hope, the sinking statesman's door
Pours in the morning worshiper no more;   80
For growing names the weekly scribbler lies,
To growing wealth the dedicator flies,
From every room descends the painted face,
That hung the bright Palladium of the place,
And smok'd in kitchens, or in auctions sold,
To better features yields the frame of gold;
For now no more we trace in ev'ry line
Heroic worth, benevolence divine:
The form distorted justifies the fall,
And detestation rids th' indignant wall.   90
    But will not Britain hear the last appeal,
Sign her foes doom, or guard her fav'rites zeal?
Through Freedom's sons no more remonstrance rings,
Degrading nobles and controuling kings;
Our supple tribes repress their patriot throats,
And ask no questions but the price of votes;
With weekly libels and septennial ale,
Their wish is full to riot and to rail.
    In full-blown dignity, see Wolsey stand,
Law in his voice, and fortune in his hand: 100
To him the church, the realm, their pow'rs consign,
Thro' him the rays of regal bounty shine,
Turn'd by his nod the stream of honour flows,
His smile alone security bestows:
Still to new heights his restless wishes tow'r,
Claim leads to claim, and pow'r advances pow'r;
Till conquest unresisted ceas'd to please,
And rights submitted, left him none to seize.
At length his sov'reign frowns—the train of state
Mark the keen glance, and watch the sign to hate.   110
Where-e'er he turns he meets a stranger's eye,
His suppliants scorn him, and his followers fly;
At once is lost the pride of aweful state,

The golden canopy, the glitt'ring plate,
The regal palace, the luxurious board,
The liv'ried army, and the menial lord.
With age, with cares, with maladies oppress'd,
He seeks the refuge of monastic rest.
Grief aids disease, remember'd folly stings,
And his last sighs reproach the faith of kings.   120
    Speak thou, whose thoughts at humble peace repine,
Shall Wolsey's wealth, with Wolsey's end be thine?
Or liv'st thou now, with safer pride content,
The wisest justice on the banks of Trent?
For why did Wolsey near the steeps of fate,
On weak foundations raise th' enormous weight?
Why but to sink beneath misfortune's blow,
With louder ruin to the gulphs below?
    What gave great Villiers to th' assassin's knife,
And fixed disease on Harley's closing life?   130
What murder'd Wentworth, and what exil'd Hyde,
By kings protected, and to kings ally'd?
What but their wish indulg'd in courts to shine,
And pow'r too great to keep, or to resign?
    When first the college rolls receive his name,
The young enthusiast quits his ease for fame;
Through all his veins the fever of renown
Burns from the strong contagion of the gown;
O'er Bodley's dome[3] his future labours spread,
And Bacon's mansion trembles o'er his head.[4]   140
Are these thy views? proceed, illustrious youth,
And virtue guard thee to the throne of Truth!
Yet should thy soul indulge the gen'rous heat,
Till captive Science yields her last retreat;
Should Reason guide thee with her brightest ray,
And pour on misty Doubt resistless day;

[3] The Bodleian Library: *dome* in the sense of *domus*, house.
[4] *There is a tradition, that the study of friar Bacon, built on an arch
over the bridge, will fall, when a man greater than Bacon shall pass under
it.* [Johnson's note]

Should no false Kindness lure to loose delight,
Nor Praise relax, nor Difficulty fright;
Should tempting Novelty thy cell refrain,
And Sloth effuse her opiate fumes in vain;   150
Should Beauty blunt on fops her fatal dart,
Nor claim the triumph of a letter'd heart;
Should no Disease thy torpid veins invade,
Nor Melancholy's phantoms haunt thy shade;
Yet hope not life from grief or danger free,
Nor think the doom of man revers'd for thee:
Deign on the passing world to turn thine eyes,
And pause awhile from letters, to be wise;
There mark what ills the scholar's life assail,
Toil, envy, want, the patron, and the jail.   160
See nations slowly wise, and meanly just,
To buried merit raise the tardy bust.
If dreams yet flatter, once again attend,
Hear Lydiat's[5] life, and Galileo's end.
    Nor deem, when learning her last prize bestows,
The glitt'ring eminence exempt from foes;
See when the vulgar 'scape, despis'd or aw'd,
Rebellion's vengeful talons seize on Laud.
From meaner minds, tho' smaller fines content,
The plunder'd palace or sequester'd rent;   170
Mark'd out by dangerous parts he meets the shock,
And fatal Learning leads him to the block:
Around his tomb let Art and Genius weep,
But hear his death, ye blockheads, hear and sleep.[6]
    The festal blazes, the triumphal show,
The ravish'd standard, and the captive foe,
The senate's thanks, the gazette's pompous tale,
With force resistless o'er the brave prevail.
Such bribes the rapid Greek[7] o'er Asia whirl'd,

[5] A distinguished mathematician and Oxford don, Thomas Lydiat (1572–1646) lived and died a poor man.

[6] Archbishop Laud was executed by the Puritans in 1645. Blockheads are in no danger of such a death.

[7] Alexander.

For such the steady Romans shook the world;   180
For such in distant lands the Britons shine,
And stain with blood the Danube or the Rhine;
This pow'r has praise, that virtue scarce can warm,[8]
Till fame supplies the universal charm.
Yet Reason frowns on War's unequal game,
Where wasted nations raise a single name,
And mortgag'd states their grandsires wreaths regret,
From age to age in everlasting debt;
Wreaths which at last the dear-bought right convey
To rust on medals, or on stones decay.   190
   On what foundation stands the warrior's pride,
How just his hopes let Swedish Charles[9] decide;
A frame of adamant, a soul of fire,
No dangers fright him, and no labours tire;
O'er love, o'er fear, extends his wide domain,
Unconquer'd lord of pleasure and of pain;
No joys to him pacific scepters yield,
War sounds the trump, he rushes to the field;
Behold surrounding kings their pow'r combine,
And one capitulate, and one resign;   200
Peace courts his hand, but spreads her charms in vain;
'Think nothing gain'd,' he cries, 'till nought remain,
'On Moscow's walls till Gothic standards fly,
'And all be mine beneath the polar sky.'
The march begins in military state,
And nations on his eye suspended wait;
Stern Famine guards the solitary coast,
And Winter barricades the realms of Frost;
He comes, not want and cold his course delay;—
Hide, blushing Glory, hide Pultowa's day:[10]   210
The vanquish'd hero leaves his broken bands,
And shews his miseries in distant lands;

[8] The brave are tempted by the hope of glory, when the ideal of virtue by itself leaves them cold.
[9] Charles XII, king of Sweden, died 1718.
[10] A victory over Charles by Peter the Great, in 1709.

Condemn'd a needy supplicant to wait,
While ladies interpose, and slaves debate.
But did not Chance at length her error mend?
Did no subverted empire mark his end?
Did rival monarchs give the fatal wound?
Or hostile millions press him to the ground?
His fall was destin'd to a barren strand,
A petty fortress, and a dubious hand;   220
He left the name, at which the world grew pale,
To point a moral, or adorn a tale.
     All times their scenes of pompous woes afford,
From Persia's tyrant to Bavaria's lord.
In gay hostility, and barb'rous pride,
With half mankind embattled at his side,
Great Xerxes comes to seize the certain prey,
And starves exhausted regions in his way;
Attendant Flatt'ry counts his myriads o'er,
Till counted myriads sooth his pride no more;   230
Fresh praise is try'd till madness fires his mind,
The waves he lashes, and enchains the wind;
New pow'rs are claim'd, new pow'rs are still bestow'd,
Till rude resistance lops the spreading god;
The daring Greeks deride the martial show,
And heap their vallies with the gaudy foe;
Th' insulted sea with humbler thoughts he gains,
A single skiff to speed his flight remains;
Th' incumber'd oar scarce leaves the dreaded coast
Through purple billows and a floating host.   240
     The bold Bavarian,[11] in a luckless hour,
Tries the dread summits of Cesarean pow'r,
With unexpected legions bursts away,
And sees defenceless realms receive his sway;
Short sway! fair Austria[12] spreads her mournful charms,
The queen, the beauty, sets the world in arms;

[11] Charles Albert, elector of Bavaria, crowned emperor in 1742, died
ignominiously in 1745.
[12] Maria Theresa.

From hill to hill the beacons rousing blaze
Spreads wide the hope of plunder and of praise;
The fierce Croatian, and the wild Hussar,
And all the sons of ravage croud the war;   250
The baffled prince in honour's flatt'ring bloom
Of hasty greatness finds the fatal doom,
His foes derision, and his subjects blame,
And steals to death from anguish and from shame.
　　Enlarge my life with multitude of days,
In health, in sickness, thus the suppliant prays;
Hides from himself his state, and shuns to know,
That life protracted is protracted woe.
Time hovers o'er, impatient to destroy,
And shuts up all the passages of joy: 260
In vain their gifts the bounteous seasons pour,
The fruit autumnal, and the vernal flow'r,
With listless eyes the dotard views the store,
He views, and wonders that they please no more;
Now pall the tasteless meats, and joyless wines,
And Luxury with sighs her slave resigns.
Approach, ye minstrels, try the soothing strain,
Diffuse the tuneful lenitives of pain:
No sounds alas would touch th' impervious ear,
Though dancing mountains witness'd Orpheus near;   270
Nor lute nor lyre his feeble pow'rs attend,
Nor sweeter musick of a virtuous friend,
But everlasting dictates croud his tongue,
Perversely grave, or positively wrong.
The still returning tale, and ling'ring jest,
Perplex the fawning niece and pamper'd guest,
While growing hopes scarce awe the gath'ring sneer,
And scarce a legacy can bribe to hear;
The watchful guests still hint the last offence,
The daughter's petulance, the son's expence,   280
Improve his heady rage with treach'rous skill,
And mould his passions till they make his will.
　　Unnumber'd maladies his joints invade,

Lay siege to life and press the dire blockade;
But unextinguish'd Avarice still remains,
And dreaded losses aggravate his pains;
He turns, with anxious heart and crippled hands,
His bonds of debt, and mortgages of lands;
Or views his coffers with suspicious eyes,
Unlocks his gold, and counts it till he dies.   290
  But grant, the virtues of a temp'rate prime
Bless with an age exempt from scorn or crime;
An age that melts with unperceiv'd decay,
And glides in modest Innocence away;
Whose peaceful day Benevolence endears,
Whose night congratulating Conscience cheers;
The gen'ral fav'rite as the gen'ral friend:
Such age there is, and who shall wish its end?
  Yet ev'n on this her load Misfortune flings,
To press the weary minutes flagging wings: 300
New sorrow rises as the day returns,
A sister sickens, or a daughter mourns.
Now kindred Merit fills the sable bier,
Now lacerated Friendship claims a tear.
Year chases year, decay pursues decay,
Still drops some joy from with'ring life away;
New forms arise, and diff'rent views engage,
Superfluous lags the vet'ran on the stage,
Till pitying Nature signs the last release,
And bids afflicted worth retire to peace.   310
  But few there are whom hours like these await,
Who set unclouded in the gulphs of fate.
From Lydia's monarch[13] should the search descend,
By Solon caution'd to regard his end,
In life's last scene what prodigies surprise,
Fears of the brave, and follies of the wise?
From Marlb'rough's eyes the streams of dotage flow,
And Swift expires a driv'ler and a show.
  The teeming mother, anxious for her race,

  [13] Crœsus.

Begs for each birth the fortune of a face: 320
Yet Vane[14] could tell what ills from beauty spring;
And Sedley[15] curs'd the form that pleas'd a king.
Ye nymphs of rosy lips and radiant eyes,
Whom Pleasure keeps too busy to be wise,
Whom Joys with soft varieties invite,
By day the frolick, and the dance by night,
Who frown with vanity, who smile with art,
And ask the latest fashion of the heart,
What care, what rules your heedless charms shall save,
Each nymph your rival, and each youth your slave?   330
Against your fame with fondness hate combines,
The rival batters, and the lover mines.
With distant voice neglected Virtue calls,
Less heard and less, the faint remonstrance falls;
Tir'd with contempt, she quits the slipp'ry reign,
And Pride and Prudence take her seat in vain.
In croud at once, where none the pass defend,
The harmless Freedom, and the private Friend.
The guardians yield, by force superior ply'd;
By Int'rest, Prudence; and by Flatt'ry, Pride.   340
Now beauty falls betray'd, despis'd, distress'd,
And hissing Infamy proclaims the rest.
   Where then shall Hope and Fear their objects find?
Must dull Suspence corrupt the stagnant mind?
Must helpless man, in ignorance sedate,
Roll darkling down the torrent of his fate?
Must no dislike alarm, no wishes rise,
No cries attempt the mercies of the skies?
Enquirer, cease, petitions yet remain,
Which heav'n may hear, nor deem religion vain.   350
Still raise for good the supplicating voice,
But leave to heav'n the measure and the choice,

[14] Anne Vane, mistress of Frederick, Prince of Wales, died 1736, aged thirty-one.
[15] Catherine Sedley, mistress of James II, when Duke of York. He created her Countess of Dorchester in 1686.

Safe in his pow'r, whose eyes discern afar
The secret ambush of a specious pray'r.
Implore his aid, in his decisions rest,
Secure whate'er he gives, he gives the best.
Yet when the sense of sacred presence fires,
And strong devotion to the skies aspires,
Pour forth thy fervours for a healthful mind,
Obedient passions, and a will resign'd;   360
For love, which scarce collective man can fill;[16]
For patience sov'reign o'er transmuted ill;[17]
For faith, that panting for a happier seat,
Counts death kind Nature's signal of retreat:
These goods for man the laws of heav'n ordain,
These goods he grants, who grants the pow'r to gain;
With these celestial wisdom calms the mind,
And makes the happiness she does not find.

On the Death of Dr. Robert Levet [1]

Condemn'd to hope's delusive mine,
   As on we toil from day to day,

[16] The meaning of this line must challenge every reader. Query: love so all-embracing that mankind will hardly suffice it; Christian, unselfish love, an "obedient" passion. See I Corinthians, ch. 13. The thought is of universal benevolence. Compare Coleridge's *Ancient Mariner:*

He prayeth best who loveth best
   All things both great and small;
For the dear God who loveth us,
   He made and loveth all.

[17] Patience that presides over the ills which, by enduring, it has transmuted into benefits. Religious patience equates with St. Paul's *hope.*

[1] "One of the very few entirely sincere tributes paid by one whom the world calls a success to one whom the world calls a failure."—Christopher Hollis.

By sudden blasts, or slow decline,
    Our social comforts drop away.

Well tried through many a varying year,
    See LEVET to the grave descend;
Officious,[2] innocent, sincere,
    Of ev'ry friendless name the friend.

Yet still he fills affection's eye,
    Obscurely wise, and coarsely kind;   10
Nor, letter'd arrogance, deny
    Thy praise to merit unrefin'd.

When fainting nature call'd for aid,
    And hov'ring death prepar'd the blow,
His vig'rous remedy display'd
    The power of art without the show.

In misery's darkest cavern known,
    His useful care was ever nigh,
Where hopeless anguish pour'd his groan,
    And lonely want retir'd to die.   20

No summons mock'd by chill delay,
    No petty gain disdain'd by pride,
The modest wants of ev'ry day
    The toil of ev'ry day supplied.

His virtues walk'd their narrow round,
    Nor made a pause, nor left a void;
And sure th' Eternal Master found
    The single talent well employ'd.

The busy day, the peaceful night,
    Unfelt, uncounted, glided by;   30

[2] "Kind; doing good offices."—Johnson's *Dictionary*.

His frame was firm, his powers were bright,
   Tho' now his eightieth year was nigh.

Then with no throbbing fiery pain,
   No cold gradations of decay,
Death broke at once the vital chain,
   And free'd his soul the nearest way.

ESSAYS

FROM The Rambler

No. 4. SATURDAY, *March* 31, 1750.

Simul et jucunda et idonea dicere Vitæ.
And join both profit and delight in one.

HOR. [*Ars. Poet.* 334.]
CREECH.

The works of fiction, with which the present generation seems
more particularly delighted, are such as exhibit life in its true state,
diversified only by accidents that daily happen in the world, and
influenced by passions and qualities which are really to be found
in conversing with mankind.

This kind of writing may be termed not improperly the comedy
of romance, and is to be conducted nearly by the rules of comic
poetry. Its province is to bring about natural events by easy
means, and to keep up curiosity without the help of wonder: it
is therefore precluded from the machines and expedients of the
heroic romance, and can neither employ giants to snatch away a

67

lady from the nuptial rites, nor knights to bring her back from captivity; it can neither bewilder its personages in desarts, nor lodge them in imaginary castles.

I remember a remark made by Scaliger upon Pontanus,[1] that all his writings are filled with the same images; and that if you take from him his lillies and his roses, his satyrs and his dryads, he will have nothing left that can be called poetry. In like manner, almost all the fictions of the last age will vanish, if you deprive them of a hermit and a wood, a battle and a shipwreck.

Why this wild strain of imagination found reception so long, in polite and learned ages, it is not easy to conceive; but we cannot wonder that, while readers could be procured, the authors were willing to continue it: for when a man had by practice gained some fluency of language, he had no further care than to retire to his closet, let loose his invention, and heat his mind with incredibilities; a book was thus produced without fear of criticism, without the toil of study, without knowledge of nature, or acquaintance with life.

The task of our present writers is very different; it requires, together with that learning which is to be gained from books, that experience which can never be attained by solitary diligence, but must arise from general converse, and accurate observation of the living world. Their performances have, as Horace expresses it, *plus oneris quantum veniæ minus,*[2] little indulgence, and therefore more difficulty. They are engaged in portraits of which every one knows the original, and can detect any deviation from exactness of resemblance. Other writings are safe, except from the malice of learning, but these are in danger from every common reader; as the slipper ill executed was censured by a shoemaker who happened to stop in his way at the Venus of Apelles.

But the fear of not being approved as just copyers of human manners, is not the most important concern that an author of this sort ought to have before him. These books are written chiefly to the young, the ignorant, and the idle, to whom they serve as lectures of conduct, and introductions into life. They are the en-

[1] J. C. Scaliger, *Poetics,* V. iv.
[2] *Epistles,* II. i. 170.

tertainment of minds unfurnished with ideas, and therefore easily susceptible of impressions; not fixed by principles, and therefore easily following the current of fancy; not informed by experience, and consequently open to every false suggestion and partial account.

That the highest degree of reverence should be paid to youth, and that nothing indecent should be suffered to approach their eyes or ears; are precepts extorted by sense and virtue from an ancient writer,[3] by no means eminent for chastity of thought. The same kind, tho' not the same degree of caution, is required to every thing which is laid before them, to secure them from unjust prejudices, perverse opinions, and incongruous combinations of images.

In the romances formerly written, every transaction and sentiment was so remote from all that passes among men, that the reader was in very little danger of making any applications to himself; the virtues and crimes were equally beyond his sphere of activity; and he amused himself with heroes and with traitors, deliverers and persecutors, as with beings of another species, whose actions were regulated upon motives of their own, and who had neither faults nor excellencies in common with himself.

But when an adventurer is levelled with the rest of the world, and acts in such scenes of the universal drama, as may be the lot of any other man; young spectators fix their eyes upon him with closer attention, and hope by observing his behaviour and success to regulate their own practices, when they shall be engaged in the like part.

For this reason these familiar histories may perhaps be made of greater use than the solemnities of professed morality, and convey the knowledge of vice and virtue with more efficacy than axioms and definitions. But if the power of example is so great, as to take possession of the memory by a kind of violence, and produce effects almost without the intervention of the will, care ought to be taken that, when the choice is unrestrained, the best examples only should be exhibited; and that which is likely to operate so strongly, should not be mischievous or uncertain in its effects.

The chief advantage which these fictions have over real life

[3] Juvenal, in *Satires,* xiv.

is, that their authors are at liberty, tho' not to invent, yet to select objects, and to cull from the mass of mankind, those individuals upon which the attention ought most to be employ'd; as a diamond, though it cannot be made, may be polished by art, and placed in such a situation, as to display that lustre which before was buried among common stones.

It is justly considered as the greatest excellency of art, to imitate nature; but it is necessary to distinguish those parts of nature, which are most proper for imitation: greater care is still required in representing life, which is so often discoloured by passion, or deformed by wickedness. If the world be promiscuously described, I cannot see of what use it can be to read the account; or why it may not be as safe to turn the eye immediately upon mankind, as upon a mirror which shows all that presents itself without discrimination.

It is therefore not a sufficient vindication of a character, that it is drawn as it appears, for many characters ought never to be drawn; nor of a narrative, that the train of events is agreeable to observation and experience, for that observation which is called knowledge of the world, will be found much more frequently to make men cunning than good. The purpose of these writings is surely not only to show mankind, but to provide that they may be seen hereafter with less hazard; to teach the means of avoiding the snares which are laid by TREACHERY for INNOCENCE, without infusing any wish for that superiority with which the betrayer flatters his vanity; to give the power of counteracting fraud, without the temptation to practise it; to initiate youth by mock encounters in the art of necessary defence, and to increase prudence without impairing virtue.

Many writers, for the sake of following nature, so mingle good and bad qualities in their principal personages, that they are both equally conspicuous; and as we accompany them through their adventures with delight, and are led by degrees to interest ourselves in their favour, we lose the abhorrence of their faults, because they do not hinder our pleasure, or, perhaps, regard them with some kindness for being united with so much merit.

There have been men indeed splendidly wicked, whose en-

dowments threw a brightness on their crimes, and whom scarce
any villainy made perfectly detestable, because they never could
be wholly divested of their excellencies; but such have been in all
ages the great corrupters of the world, and their resemblance ought
no more to be preserved, than the art of murdering without pain.

Some have advanced, without due attention to the consequences
of this notion, that certain virtues have their correspondent faults,
and therefore that to exhibit either apart is to deviate from proba-
bility. Thus men are observed by Swift to be "grateful in the same
degree as they are resentful." This principle, with others of the
same kind, supposes man to act from a brute impulse, and persue
a certain degree of inclination, without any choice of the object;
for, otherwise, though it should be allowed that gratitude and
resentment arise from the same constitution of the passions, it
follows not that they will be equally indulged when reason is con-
sulted; yet unless that consequence be admitted, this sagacious
maxim becomes an empty sound, without any relation to practice
or to life.

Nor is it evident, that even the first motions to these effects
are always in the same proportion. For pride, which produces
quickness of resentment, will obstruct gratitude, by unwilling-
ness to admit that inferiority which obligation implies; and it is
very unlikely, that he who cannot think he receives a favour will
acknowledge or repay it.

It is of the utmost importance to mankind, that positions of this
tendency should be laid open and confuted; for while men con-
sider good and evil as springing from the same root, they will
spare the one for the sake of the other, and in judging, if not of
others at least of themselves, will be apt to estimate their virtues
by their vices. To this fatal error all those will contribute, who
confound the colours of right and wrong, and instead of helping
to settle their boundaries, mix them with so much art, that no
common mind is able to disunite them.

In narratives, where historical veracity has no place, I cannot dis-
cover why there should not be exhibited the most perfect idea of
virtue; of virtue not angelical, nor above probability, for what we
cannot credit we shall never imitate, but the highest and purest

that humanity can reach, which, exercised in such trials as the various revolutions of things shall bring upon it, may, by conquering some calamities, and enduring others, teach us what we may hope, and what we can perform. Vice, for vice is necessary to be shewn, should always disgust; nor should the graces of gaiety, or the dignity of courage, be so united with it, as to reconcile it to the mind. Wherever it appears, it should raise hatred by the malignity of its practices, and contempt by the meanness of its stratagems; for while it is supported by either parts or spirit, it will be seldom heartily abhorred. The Roman tyrant was content to be hated, if he was but feared; and there are thousands of the readers of romances willing to be thought wicked, if they may be allowed to be wits. It is therefore to be steadily inculcated, that virtue is the highest proof of understanding, and the only solid basis of greatness; and that vice is the natural consequence of narrow thoughts, that it begins in mistake, and ends in ignominy.

No. 5. TUESDAY, *April* 3, 1750.

Et nunc omnis ager, nunc omnis parturit arbos,
Nunc frondent silvae, nunc formosissimus annus.

VIRG. [*Ec.* III. v. 56.]

Now ev'ry field, now ev'ry tree is green;
Now genial nature's fairest face is seen.

ELPHINSTON.

Every man is sufficiently discontented with some circumstances of his present state, to suffer his imagination to range more or less in quest of future happiness, and to fix upon some point of time, in which, by the removal of the inconvenience which now perplexes him, or acquisition of the advantage which he at present wants, he shall find the condition of his life very much improved.

When this time, which is too often expected with great impatience, at last arrives, it generally comes without the blessing for which it was desired; but we solace ourselves with some new prospect, and press forward again with equal eagerness.

It is lucky for a man, in whom this temper prevails, when he turns his hopes upon things wholly out of his own power; since he forbears then to precipitate his affairs, for the sake of the great event that is to complete his felicity, and waits for the blissful hour, with less neglect of the measures necessary to be taken in the mean time.

I have long known a person of this temper, who indulged his dream of happiness with less hurt to himself than such chimerical wishes commonly produce, and adjusted his scheme with such address, that his hopes were in full bloom three parts of the year, and in the other part never wholly blasted. Many, perhaps, would be desirous of learning by what means he procured to himself such a cheap and lasting satisfaction. It was gained by a constant practice of referring the removal of all his uneasiness to the coming of the next spring; if his health was impaired, the spring would restore it; if what he wanted was at a high price, it would fall its value in the spring.

The spring, indeed, did often come without any of these effects, but he was always certain that the next would be more propitious; nor was ever convinced that the present spring would fail him before the middle of summer; for he always talked of the spring as coming 'till it was past, and when it was once past, every one agreed with him that it was coming.

By long converse with this man, I am, perhaps, brought to feel immoderate pleasure in the contemplation of this delightful season; but I have the satisfaction of finding many, whom it can be no shame to resemble, infected with the same enthusiasm; for there is, I believe, scarce any poet of eminence, who has not let some testimony of his fondness for the flowers, the zephyrs, and the warblers of the spring. Nor has the most luxuriant imagination been able to describe the serenity and happiness of the golden age, otherwise than by giving a perpetual spring, as the highest reward of uncorrupted innocence.

There is, indeed, something inexpressibly pleasing, in the an-

nual renovation of the world, and the new display of the treasures
of nature. The cold and darkness of winter, with the naked de-
formity of every object on which we turn our eyes, make us rejoice
at the succeeding season, as well for what we have escaped, as for
what we may enjoy; and every budding flower, which a warm
situation brings early to our view, is considered by us as a mes-
senger to notify the approach of more joyous days.

The Spring affords to a mind, so free from the disturbance of
cares or passions as to be vacant to calm amusements, almost every
thing that our present state makes us capable of enjoying. The
variegated verdure of the fields and woods, the succession of grate-
ful odours, the voice of pleasure pouring out its notes on every
side, with the gladness apparently conceived by every animal,
from the growth of his food, and the clemency of the weather,
throw over the whole earth an air of gaiety, significantly expressed
by the smile of nature.

Yet there are men to whom these scenes are able to give no
delight, and who hurry away from all the varieties of rural
beauty, to lose their hours, and divert their thoughts by cards,
or assemblies, a tavern dinner, or the prattle of the day.

It may be laid down as a position which will seldom deceive,
that when a man cannot bear his own company there is some-
thing wrong. He must fly from himself, either because he feels a
tediousness in life from the equipoise of an empty mind, which,
having no tendency to one motion more than another but as it is
impelled by some external power, must always have recourse to
foreign objects; or he must be afraid of the intrusion of some un-
pleasing ideas, and, perhaps, is struggling to escape from the
remembrance of a loss, the fear of a calamity, or some other
thought of greater horror.

Those whom sorrow incapacitates to enjoy the pleasures of
contemplation, may properly apply to such diversions, provided
they are innocent, as lay strong hold on the attention; and those,
whom fear of any future affliction chains down to misery, must
endeavour to obviate the danger.

My considerations shall, on this occasion, be turned on such
as are burthensome to themselves merely because they want sub-

jects for reflexion, and to whom the volume of nature is thrown open, without affording them pleasure or instruction, because they never learned to read the characters.

A French author has advanced this seeming paradox, that *very few men know how to take a walk*; and, indeed, it is true, that few know how to take a walk with a prospect of any other pleasure, than the same company would have afforded them at home.

There are animals that borrow their colour from the neighbouring body, and, consequently, vary their hue as they happen to change their place. In like manner it ought to be the endeavour of every man to derive his reflections from the objects about him; for it is to no purpose that he alters his position, if his attention continues fixed to the same point. The mind should be kept open to the access of every new idea, and so far disengaged from the predominance of particular thoughts, as easily to accommodate itself to occasional entertainment.

A Man that has formed this habit of turning every new object to his entertainment, finds in the productions of nature an inexhaustible stock of materials upon which he can employ himself, without any temptations to envy or malevolence; faults, perhaps, seldom totally avoided by those, whose judgment is much exercised upon the works of art. He has always a certain prospect of discovering new reasons for adoring the sovereign author of the universe, and probable hopes of making some discovery of benefit to others, or of profit to himself. There is no doubt but many vegetables and animals have qualities that might be of great use, to the knowledge of which there is not required much force of penetration, or fatigue of study, but only frequent experiments, and close attention. What is said by the chymists of their darling mercury, is, perhaps, true of every body through the whole creation, that if a thousand lives should be spent upon it, all its properties would not be found out.

Mankind must necessarily be diversified by various tastes, since life affords and requires such multiplicity of employments, and a nation of naturalists is neither to be hoped, or desired; but it is surely not improper to point out a fresh amusement to those who languish in health, and repine in plenty, for want of some source of diversion that may be less easily exhausted, and to inform the multitudes of both sexes, who are burthened with every new day, that there are many shows which they have not seen.

He that enlarges his curiosity after the works of nature, demonstrably multiplies the inlets to happiness; and, therefore, the younger part of my readers, to whom I dedicate this vernal speculation, must excuse me for calling upon them, to make use at once of the spring of the year, and the spring of life; to acquire, while their minds may be yet impressed with new images, a love of innocent pleasures, and an ardour for useful knowledge; and to remember, that a blighted spring makes a barren year, and that the vernal flowers, however beautiful and gay, are only intended by nature as preparatives to autumnal fruits.

No. 25. Tuesday, *June* 12, 1750.

Possunt quia posse videntur.

Virg. [*Æn.* V. 231.]

For they can conquer who believe they can.

Dryden.

There are some vices and errors, which, though often fatal to those in whom they are found, have yet, by the universal consent of mankind, been considered as entitled to some degree of respect, or have, at least, been exempted from contemptuous infamy, and condemned by the severest moralists with pity rather than detestation.

A constant and invariable example of this general partiality will be found in the different regard which has always been shown to rashness and cowardice, two vices, of which, though they may be conceived equally distant from the middle point, where true fortitude is placed, and may equally injure any publick or private

interest, yet the one is never mentioned without some kind of
veneration, and the other always considered as a topick of un-
limited and licentious censure, on which all the virulence of
reproach may be lawfully exerted.

The same distinction is made, by the common suffrage, between
profusion and avarice, and, perhaps, between many other opposite
vices: and, as I have found reason to pay great regard to the voice
of the people, in cases where knowledge has been forced upon
them by experience, without long deductions or deep researches,
I am inclined to believe that this distribution of respect, is not
without some agreement with the nature of things; and that in the
faults, which are thus invested with extraordinary privileges, there
are generally some latent principles of merit, some possibilities of
future virtue, which may, by degrees, break from obstruction, and
by time and opportunity be brought into act.

It may be laid down as an axiom, that it is more easy to take
away superfluities than to supply defects; and, therefore, he that
is culpable, because he has passed the middle point of virtue, is
always accounted a fairer object of hope, than he who fails by
falling short. The one has all that perfection requires, and more,
but the excess may be easily retrenched; the other wants the
qualities requisite to excellence, and who can tell how he shall
obtain them? We are certain that the horse may be taught to
keep pace with his fellows, whose fault is that he leaves them be-
hind. We know that a few strokes of the axe will lop a cedar; but
what arts of cultivation can elevate a shrub?

To walk with circumspection and steadiness in the right path,
at an equal distance between the extremes of error, ought to be
the constant endeavour of every reasonable being; nor can I think
those teachers of moral wisdom much to be honoured as bene-
factors to mankind, who are always enlarging upon the difficulty
of our duties, and providing rather excuses for vice than incentives
to virtue.

But, since to most it will happen often, and to all sometimes,
that there will be a deviation towards one side or the other, we
ought always to employ our vigilance, with most attention, on that

enemy from which there is greatest danger, and to stray, if we must stray, towards those parts from whence we may quickly and easily return.

Among other opposite qualities of the mind, which may become dangerous, though in different degrees, I have often had occasion to consider the contrary effects of presumption and despondency; of heady confidence, which promises victory without contest, and heartless pusillanimity, which shrinks back from the thought of great undertakings, confounds difficulty with impossibility, and considers all advancement towards any new attainment as irreversibly prohibited.

Presumption will be easily corrected. Every experiment will teach caution, and miscarriages will hourly shew, that attempts are not always rewarded with success. The most precipitate ardour will, in time, be taught the necessity of methodical gradation, and preparatory measures; and the most daring confidence be convinced that neither merit, nor abilities, can command events.

It is the advantage of vehemence and activity, that they are always hastening to their own reformation; because they incite us to try whether our expectations are well grounded, and therefore detect the deceits which they are apt to occasion. But timidity is a disease of the mind more obstinate and fatal; for a man once persuaded, that any impediment is insuperable, has given it, with respect to himself, that strength and weight which it had not before. He can scarcely strive with vigour and perseverance, when he has no hope of gaining the victory; and since he never will try his strength, can never discover the unreasonableness of his fears.

There is often to be found in men devoted to literature, a kind of intellectual cowardice, which whoever converses much among them, may observe frequently to depress the alacrity of enterprise, and, by consequence, to retard the improvement of science. They have annexed to every species of knowledge some chimerical character of terror and inhibition, which they transmit, without much reflexion, from one to another; they first fright themselves, and then propagate the panic to their scholars and acquaintance. One study is inconsistent with a lively imagination, another with a solid judgment; one is improper in the early parts of life, another requires so much time, that it is not to be attempted at an advanced age; one is dry and contracts the sentiments, another is diffuse and overburdens the memory; one is insufferable to taste and delicacy, and another wears out life in the study of words, and is useless to a wise man, who desires only the knowledge of things.

But of all the bugbears by which the *Infantes barbati*, boys both young and old, have been hitherto frighted from digressing into new tracts of learning, none has been more mischievously efficacious than an opinion that every kind of knowledge requires a peculiar genius, or mental constitution, framed for the reception of some ideas, and the exclusion of others; and that to him whose genius is not adapted to the study which he prosecutes, all labour shall be vain and fruitless, vain as an endeavour to mingle oil and water, or, in the language of chemistry, to amalgamate bodies of heterogeneous principles.

This opinion we may reasonably suspect to have been propagated, by vanity, beyond the truth. It is natural for those who have raised a reputation by any science, to exalt themselves as endowed by heaven with peculiar powers, or marked out by an extraordinary designation for their profession; and to fright competitors away by representing the difficulties with which they must contend, and the necessity of qualities which are supposed to be not generally conferred, and which no man can know, but by experience, whether he enjoys.

To this discouragement it may be possibly answered, that since a genius, whatever it be, is like fire in the flint, only to be produced by collision with a proper subject, it is the business of every man to try whether his faculties may not happily cooperate with his desires; and since they whose proficiency he admires, knew their own force only by the event, he needs but engage in the same undertaking, with equal spirit, and may reasonably hope for equal success.

There is another species of false intelligence, given by those who profess to shew the way to the summit of knowledge, of equal tendency to depress the mind with false distrust of itself, and weaken it by needless solicitude and dejection. When a scholar, whom they desire to animate, consults them at his entrance on some new study, it is common to make flattering representations of its pleasantness and facility. Thus they generally attain one of two ends almost equally desirable; they either incite his industry by elevating his hopes, or produce a high opinion of their own abilities, since they are supposed to relate only what they have found, and to have proceeded with no less ease than they promise to their followers.

The student, inflamed by this encouragement, sets forward in the new path, and proceeds a few steps with great alacrity, but he soon finds asperities and intricacies of which he has not been forewarned, and imagining that none ever were so entangled or fatigued before him, sinks suddenly into despair, and desists as from an expedition in which fate opposes him. Thus his terrors are multiplied by his hopes, and he is defeated without resistance, because he had no expectation of an enemy.

Of these treacherous instructors, the one destroys industry, by declaring that industry is vain, the other by representing it as needless; the one cuts away the root of hope, the other raises it only to be blasted. The one confines his pupil to the shore, by telling him that his wreck is certain, the other sends him to sea, without preparing him for tempests.

False hopes and false terrors are equally to be avoided. Every man, who proposes to grow eminent by learning, should carry in his mind, at once, the difficulty of excellence, and the force of industry; and remember that fame is not conferred but as the recompense of labour, and that labour, vigorously continued, has not often failed of its reward.

No. 32. SATURDAY, *July* 7, 1750.

Ὅσσά τε δαιμονίῃσι τύχαις βροτοὶ ἄλγε᾽ ἔχουσιν,
Ὧν ἂν μοῖραν ἔχῃς, πρᾴως φέρε, μηδ᾽ ἀγανάκτει·
Ἰᾶσθαι δὲ πρέπει κάθοσον δύνῃ.

PYTHAG.

> Of all the woes that load the mortal state,
> Whate'er thy portion, mildly meet thy fate;
> But ease it as thou can'st ←————

ELPHINSTON.

So large a part of human life passes in a state contrary to our natural desires, that one of the principal topics of moral instruction is the art of bearing calamities. And such is the certainty of evil, that it is the duty of every man to furnish his mind with those principles that may enable him to act under it with decency and propriety.

The sect of ancient philosophers, that boasted to have carried this necessary science to the highest perfection, were the stoics, or scholars of Zeno, whose wild enthusiastick virtue pretended to an exemption from the sensibilities of unenlightened mortals, and who proclaimed themselves exalted, by the doctrines of their sect, above the reach of those miseries, which embitter life to the rest of the world. They therefore removed pain, poverty, loss of friends, exile, and violent death, from the catalogue of evils; and passed, in their haughty stile, a kind of irreversible decree, by which they forbad them to be counted any longer among the objects of terror or anxiety, or to give any disturbance to the tranquillity of a wise man.

This edict was, I think, not universally observed, for though one of the more resolute, when he was tortured by a violent disease, cried out, that let pain harrass him to its utmost power, it should never force him to consider it as other than indifferent and neutral; yet all had not stubbornness to hold out against their senses: for a weaker pupil of Zeno is recorded to have confessed in the anguish of the gout, that *he now found pain to be an evil*.

It may however be questioned, whether these philosophers can be very properly numbered among the teachers of patience; for if pain be not an evil, there seems no instruction requisite how it may be borne; and therefore when they endeavour to arm their followers with arguments against it, they may be thought to have given up their first position. But such inconsistencies are to be expected from the greatest understandings, when they endeavour to grow eminent by singularity, and employ their strength in establishing opinions opposite to nature.

The controversy about the reality of external evils is now at an end. That life has many miseries, and that those miseries are, sometimes at least, equal to all the powers of fortitude, is now universally confessed; and therefore it is useful to consider not only how we may escape them, but by what means those which either the accidents of affairs, or the infirmities of nature must bring upon us, may be mitigated and lightened; and how we may make those hours less wretched, which the condition of our present existence will not allow to be very happy.

The cure for the greatest part of human miseries is not radical, but palliative. Infelicity is involved in corporeal nature, and interwoven with our being; all attempts therefore to decline it wholly are useless and vain: the armies of pain send their arrows against us on every side, the choice is only between those which are more or less sharp, or tinged with poison of greater or less malignity; and the strongest armour which reason can supply, will only blunt their points, but cannot repel them.

The great remedy which heaven has put in our hands is patience, by which, though we cannot lessen the torments of the body, we can in a great measure preserve the peace of the mind, and shall suffer only the natural and genuine force of an evil, without heightening its acrimony, or prolonging its effects.

There is indeed nothing more unsuitable to the nature of man in any calamity than rage and turbulence, which, without examining whether they are not sometimes impious, are at least always offensive, and incline others rather to hate and despise than to pity and assist us. If what we suffer has been brought upon us by ourselves, it is observed by an ancient poet, that patience is eminently our duty, since no one should be angry at feeling that which he has deserved.

> Leniter ex merito quicquid patiare ferendum est.[1]
> Let pain deserv'd without complaint be borne.

[1] Ovid, HEROIDES, v. 7.

And surely, if we are conscious that we have not contributed to our own sufferings, if punishment upon innocence, or disappointment happens to industry and prudence, patience, whether more necessary or not, is much easier, since our pain is then without aggravation, and we have not the bitterness of remorse to add to the asperity of misfortune.

In those evils which are allotted to us by providence, such as deformity, privation of any of the senses, or old age, it is always to be rememb[e]red, that impatience can have no present effect, but to deprive us of the consolations which our condition admits, by driving away from us those by whose conversation or advice we might be amused or helped; and that with regard to futurity it is yet less to be justified, since, without lessening the pain, it cuts off the hope of that reward, which he by whom it is inflicted will confer upon them that bear it well.

In all evils which admit a remedy, impatience is to be avoided, because it wastes that time and attention in complaints, that, if properly applied, might remove the cause. Turenne, among the acknowledgments which he used to pay in conversation to the memory of those by whom he had been instructed in the art of war, mentioned one with honour, who taught him not to spend his time in regretting any mistake which he had made, but to set himself immediately and vigorously to repair it.[2]

Patience and submission are very carefully to be distinguished from cowardice and indolence. We are not to repine, but we may lawfully struggle; for the calamities of life, like the necessities of nature, are calls to labour, and exercises of diligence. When we feel any pressure of distress, we are not to conclude that we can only obey the will of heaven by languishing under it, any more than when we perceive the pain of thirst we are to imagine that water is prohibited. Of misfortune it never can be certainly known whether, as proceeding from the hand of GOD, it is an act of favour, or of punishment: but since all the ordinary dispensations of providence are to be interpreted according to the

[2] Andrew Ramsay, *Histoire du Vicomte de Turenne* (1735), I. 85–86. The Duc de Weymar gave this salutary advice.

general analogy of things, we may conclude, that we have a right
to remove one inconvenience as well as another; that we are only
to take care lest we purchase ease with guilt; and that our Maker's
purpose, whether of reward or severity, will be answered by the
labours which he lays us under the necessity of performing.

This duty is not more difficult in any state, than in diseases
intensely painful, which may indeed suffer such exacerbations as
seem to strain the powers of life to their utmost stretch, and leave
very little of the attention vacant to precept or reproof. In this
state the nature of man requires some indulgence, and every ex-
travagance but impiety may be easily forgiven him. Yet, lest we
should think ourselves too soon entitled to the mournful privileges
of irresistible misery, it is proper to reflect that the utmost anguish
which human wit can contrive, or human malice can inflict, has
been borne with constancy; and that if the pains of disease be, as
I believe they are, sometimes greater than those of artificial torture,
they are therefore in their own nature shorter, the vital frame is
quickly broken, or the union between soul and body is for a time
suspended by insensibility, and we soon cease to feel our maladies
when they once become too violent to be born. I think there is
some reason for questioning whether the body and mind are not
so proportioned, that the one can bear all which can be inflicted
on the other, whether virtue cannot stand its ground as long as
life, and whether a soul well principled will not be separated
sooner than subdued.

In calamities which operate chiefly on our passions, such as
diminution of fortune, loss of friends, or declension of character,
the chief danger of impatience is upon the first attack, and many
expedients have been contrived, by which the blow may be
broken. Of these the most general precept is, not to take pleasure
in any thing, of which it is not in our power to secure the pos-
session to ourselves. This counsel, when we consider the enjoy-
ment of any terrestrial advantage, as opposite to a constant and
habitual solicitude for future felicity, is undoubtedly just, and
delivered by that authority which cannot be disputed; but in any
other sense, is it not like advice, not to walk lest we should stumble,
or not to see lest our eyes should light upon deformity? It seems

to me reasonable to enjoy blessings with confidence as well as to resign them with submission, and to hope for the continuance of good which we possess without insolence or voluptuousness, as for the restitution of that which we lose without despondency or murmurs.

The chief security against the fruitless anguish of impatience, must arise from frequent reflection on the wisdom and goodness of the GOD of nature, in whose hands are riches and poverty, honour and disgrace, pleasure and pain, and life and death. A settled conviction of the tendency of every thing to our good, and of the possibility of turning miseries into happiness, by receiving them rightly, will incline us to *bless the name of the* LORD, *whether he gives or takes away.*

"generation gap"

No. 50. SATURDAY, *September* 8, 1750.

Credebant hoc grande nefas, et morte piandum,
Si juvenis vetulo non assurrexerat, atque
Barbato cuicunque puer, licet ipse videret
Plura domi fraga, et majores glandis acervos.

JUV. [*Sat*. XIII. 54.]

And had not men the hoary head rever'd,
And boys paid rev'rence when a man appear'd,
Both must have died, tho' richer skins they wore,
And saw more heaps of acorns in their store.

CREECH.

I have always thought it the business of those who turn their speculations upon the living world, to commend the virtues, as well as to expose the faults of their contemporaries, and to confute a false as well as to support a just accusation; not only because it is peculiarly the business of a monitor to keep his own reputation untainted, lest those who can once charge him with partiality, should indulge themselves afterwards in disbelieving him at pleasure; but because he may find real crimes sufficient to give full employment to caution or repentance, without distracting the mind by needless scruples and vain solicitudes.

There are certain fixed and stated reproaches that one part of mankind has in all ages thrown upon another, which are regularly transmitted through continued successions, and which he that has once suffered them is certain to use with the same undistinguishing vehemence, when he has changed his station, and gained the prescriptive right of inflicting on others, what he had formerly endured himself.

To these hereditary imputations, of which no man sees the justice, till it becomes his interest to see it, very little regard is to be shewn; since it does not appear that they are produced by ratiocination or enquiry, but received implicitly, or caught by a kind of instantaneous contagion, and supported rather by willingness to credit, than ability to prove them.

It has been always the practice of those who are desirous to believe themselves made venerable by length of time, to censure the new comers into life, for want of respect to grey hairs and sage experience, for heady confidence in their own understandings, for hasty conclusions upon partial views, for disregard of counsels, which their fathers and grandsires are ready to afford them, and a rebellious impatience of that subordination to which youth is condemned by nature, as necessary to its security from evils into which it would be otherwise precipitated, by the rashness of passion, and the blindness of ignorance.

Every old man complains of the growing depravity of the world, of the petulance and insolence of the rising generation. He recounts the decency and regularity of former times, and celebrates the discipline and sobriety of the age in which his youth was passed; a happy age which is now no more to be expected, since confusion has broken in upon the world, and thrown down all the boundaries of civility and reverence.

It is not sufficiently considered how much he assumes, who dares to claim the privilege of complaining: for as every man has in his own opinion, a full share of the miseries of life, he is inclined to consider all clamorous uneasiness, as a proof of impatience rather than of affliction, and to ask, What merit has this man to show, by which he has acquired a right to repine at the distributions of nature? Or, why does he imagine that exemptions should be granted him from the general condition of man? We find ourselves excited rather to captiousness than pity, and instead of being in haste to sooth our complaints by sympathy and tenderness, we enquire, whether the pain be proportionate to the lamentation; and whether, supposing the affliction real, it is not the effect of vice and folly, rather than calamity.

The querulousness and indignation which is observed so often to disfigure the last scene of life, naturally leads us to enquiries like these. For surely it will be thought at the first view of things, that if age be thus contemned and ridiculed, insulted and neglected, the crime must at least be equal on either part. They who have had opportunities of establishing their authority over minds ductile and unresisting, they who have been the protectors of helplessness, and the instructors of ignorance, and who yet retain in their own hands the power of wealth, and the dignity of command, must defeat their influence by their own misconduct, and make use of all these advantages with very little skill, if they cannot secure to themselves an appearance of respect, and ward off open mockery, and declared contempt.

The general story of mankind will evince, that lawful and settled authority is very seldom resisted when it is well employed. Gross corruption, or evident imbecillity is necessary to the suppression of that reverence with which the majority of mankind look upon their governors, on those whom they see surrounded by splendour, and fortified by power. For tho' men are drawn by their passions into forgetfulness of invisible rewards and punishments, yet they are easily kept obedient to those who have temporal dominion in their hands, till their veneration is dissipated by such wickedness and folly as can neither be defended nor concealed.

It may, therefore, very reasonably be suspected that the old draw upon themselves the greatest part of those insults, which they so much lament, and that age is rarely despised but when it is contemptible. If men imagine that excess or debauchery can be made reverend by time, that knowledge is the consequence of

long life however idly and thoughtlessly employed, that priority
of birth will supply the want of steadiness or honesty, can it raise
much wonder that their hopes are disappointed, and that they see
their posterity rather willing to trust their own eyes in their
progress into life, than enlist themselves under guides who have
lost their way?

There are, indeed, many truths which time necessarily and
certainly teaches, and which might, by those who have learned
them from experience, be communicated to their successors at a
cheaper rate: but dictates, though liberally enough bestowed, are
generally without effect, the teacher gains few proselytes by in-
struction which his own behaviour contradicts; and young men
miss the benefit of counsel, because they are not very ready to
believe that those who fall below them in practice, can much
excel them in theory. Thus the progress of knowledge is retarded,
the world is kept long in the same state, and every new race is to
gain the prudence of their predecessors by committing and re-
dressing the same miscarriages.

To secure to the old that influence which they are willing to
claim, and which might so much contribute to the improvement of
the arts of life, it is absolutely necessary that they give them-
selves up to the duties of declining years; and contentedly resign
to youth its levity, its pleasures, its frolicks, and its fopperies. It is
a hopeless endeavour to unite the contrarieties of spring and
winter; it is unjust to claim the privileges of age, and retain the
play-things of childhood. The young always form magnificent
ideas of the wisdom and gravity of men, whom they consider as
placed at a distance from them in the ranks of existence, and
naturally look on those whom they find trifling with long beards,
with contempt and indignation, like that which women feel at
the effeminacy of men. If dotards will contend with boys in those
performances in which boys must always excel them; if they will
dress crippled limbs in embroidery, endeavour at gayety with
faltering voices; and darken assemblies of pleasure with the
ghastliness of disease, they may well expect those who find their
diversions obstructed will hoot them away; and that if they
descend to competition with youth, they must bear the insolence
of successful rivals.

Lusisti satis, edisti satis, atque bibisti:
Tempus abire tibi est.

[Hor. *Epist.* II. ii. 214.]

You've had your share of mirth, of meat and drink;
'Tis time to quit the scene—'tis time to think.
ELPHINSTON.

Another vice of age, by which the rising generation may be
alienated from it, is severity and censoriousness, that gives no
allowance to the failings of early life, that expects artfulness from
childhood, and constancy from youth, that is peremptory in every
command, and inexorable to every failure. There are many who
live merely to hinder happiness, and whose descendants can only
tell of long life, that it produces suspicion, malignity, peevish-
ness, and persecution: and yet even these tyrants can talk of the
ingratitude of the age, curse their heirs for impatience, and wonder
that young men cannot take pleasure in their fathers' company.

He that would pass the latter part of life with honour and
decency, must, when he is young, consider that he shall one day
be old; and remember, when he is old, that he has once been
young. In youth, he must lay up knowledge for his support, when
his powers of acting shall forsake him; and in age forbear to
animadvert with rigour on faults which experience only can
correct.

No. 59. TUESDAY, *October* 9, 1750.

Est aliquid fatale malum per verba levari,
    Hoc querulam Halcyonenque Proguen facit:
Hoc erat, in solo quare Pœantius antro
    Voce fatigaret Lemnia saxa sua.
Strangulat inclusus dolor atque exæstuat intus,
    Cogitur et vires multiplicare suas.

OVID. [*Trist.* V. 59.]

Complaining oft gives respite to our grief;
From hence the wretched *Progne* sought relief;
Hence the *Pœantian* chief his fate deplores,
And vents his sorrow to the *Lemnian* shores:
In vain by secresy we wou'd assuage
Our cares; conceal'd they gather tenfold rage.

F. Lewis.

It is common to distinguish men by the names of animals which they are supposed to resemble. Thus a hero is frequently termed a lion, and a statesman a fox, an extortioner gains the appellation of vultur, and a fop the title of monkey. There is also among the various anomalies of character, which a survey of the world exhibits, a species of beings in human form, which may be properly marked out as the screech-owls of mankind.

These screech-owls seem to be settled in an opinion that the great business of life is to complain, and that they were born for no other purpose than to disturb the happiness of others, to lessen the little comforts, and shorten the short pleasures of our condition, by painful remembrances of the past, or melancholy prognosticks of the future; their only care is to crush the rising hope, to damp the kindleing transport, and allay the golden hours of gaiety with the hateful dross of grief and suspicion.

To those, whose weakness of spirits, or timidity of temper, subjects them to impressions from others, and who are apt to suffer by fascination, and catch the contagion of misery, it is extremely unhappy to live within the compass of a screech-owl's voice; for it will often fill their ears in the hour of dejection, terrify them with apprehensions, which their own thoughts would never have produced, and sadden, by intruded sorrows, the day which might have been passed in amusements or in business; it will burthen the heart with unnecessary discontents, and weaken for a time that love of life, which is necessary to the vigorous prosecution of any undertaking.

Though I have, like the rest of mankind, many failings and weaknesses, I have not yet, by either friends or enemies, been charged with superstition; I never count the company which I enter, and I look at the new moon indifferently over either shoulder. I have, like most other philosophers, often heard the cuckoo without money in my pocket, and have been sometimes reproached as fool-hardy for not turning down my eyes when a raven flew over my head. I never go home abruptly because a snake crosses my way, nor have any particular dread of a climacterical year; yet I confess that, with all my scorn of old women, and their tales, I consider it as an unhappy day when I happen to be greeted, in the morning, by Suspirius the screech-owl.

I have now known Suspirius fifty-eight years and four months, and have never yet passed an hour with him in which he has not made some attack upon my quiet. When we were first acquainted, his great topick was the misery of youth without riches, and whenever we walked out together he solaced me with a long enumeration of pleasures, which, as they were beyond the reach of my fortune, were without the verge of my desires, and which I should never have considered as the objects of a wish, had not his unseasonable representations placed them in my sight.

Another of his topicks is the neglect of merit, with which he never fails to amuse every man whom he sees not eminently fortunate. If he meets with a young officer, he always informs him of gentlemen whose personal courage is unquestioned, and whose military skill qualifies them to command armies, that have, notwithstanding all their merit, grown old with subaltern commissions. For a genius in the church, he is always provided with a curacy for life. The lawyer he informs of many men of great parts and deep study, who have never had an opportunity to speak in the courts: And meeting Serenus the physician, "Ah, doctor, says he, what a-foot still, when so many blockheads are rattling their chariots? I told you seven years ago that you would never meet with encouragement, and I hope you will now take more notice, when I tell you, that your *Greek*, and your diligence, and your honesty, will never enable you to live like yonder apothecary, who prescribes to his own shop, and laughs at the physician."

Suspirius has, in his time, intercepted fifteen authors in their way to the stage; persuaded nine and thirty merchants to retire from a prosperous trade for fear of bankrup[t]cy, broke off an hundred and thirteen matches by prognostications of unhappiness, and enabled the small-pox to kill nineteen ladies, by perpetual alarms of the loss of beauty.

Whenever my evil stars bring us together, he never fails to represent to me the folly of my persuits, and informs me that we are much older than when we began our acquaintance, that the infirmities of decrepitude are coming fast upon me, that whatever I now get I shall enjoy but a little time, that fame is to a man tottering on the edge of the grave of very little importance, and that the time is at hand when I ought to look for no other pleasures than a good dinner and an easy chair.

Thus he goes on his unharmonious strain, displaying present miseries, and foreboding more, νυκτικόραξ ἄδει θανατηφόρον,[1] every syllable is loaded with misfortune, and death is always brought nearer to the view. Yet, what always raises my resentment and indignation, I do not perceive that his mournful meditations have much effect upon himself. He talks, and has long talked of calamities, without discovering, otherwise than by the tone of his voice, that he feels any of the evils which he bewails or threatens, but has the same habit of uttering lamentations, as others of telling stories, and falls into expressions of condolence for past, or apprehension of future mischiefs, as all men studious of their ease have recourse to those subjects upon which they can most fluently or copiously discourse.[2]

It is reported of the Sybarites, that they destroyed all their cocks, that they might dream out their morning dreams without disturbance. Though I would not so far promote effeminacy as to propose the Sybarites for an example, yet since there is no man so corrupt or foolish, but something useful may be learned from him, I could wish that, in imitation of a people not often to be copied, some regulations might be made to exclude screech-owls from all company, as the enemies of mankind, and confine them to some

[1] *Palatine Anthology,* XI. 186.

[2] Suspirius, the screechowl, is presumed by some to have suggested the character of Croaker to Goldsmith, in his comedy of the Good-natured Man. [1824 ed.]

proper receptacle, where they may mingle sighs at leisure, and thicken the gloom of one another.

Thou prophet of evil, says Homer's Agamemnon, *thou never foretellest me good, but the joy of thy heart is to predict misfortunes.*[3] Whoever is of the same temper might there find the means of indulging his thoughts, and improving his vein of denunciation, and the flock of screech-owls might hoot together without injury to the rest of the world.

Yet, though I have so little kindness for this dark generation, I am very far from intending to debar the soft and tender mind from the privilege of complaining, when the sigh rises from the desire not of giving pain, but of gaining ease. To hear complaints with patience, even when complaints are vain, is one of the duties of friendship; and though it must be allowed that he suffers most like a hero that hides his grief in silence,

> *Spem vultu simulat, premit altum corde dolorem.*[4]
> His outward smiles conceal'd his inward smart.
>
> DRYDEN.

yet, it cannot be denied that he who complains acts like a man, like a social being who looks for help from his fellow-creatures. Pity is to many of the unhappy a source of comfort in hopeless distresses, as it contributes to recommend them to themselves, by proving that they have not lost the regard of others; and heaven seems to indicate the duty even of barren compassion, by inclining us to weep for evils which we cannot remedy.

No. 60. SATURDAY, *October* 13, 1750.

—*Quid sit pulchrum, quid turpe, quid utile, quid non,*
Plenius et melius Chrysippo et Crantore dicit.

HOR. [*Epist.* I. ii. 3.]

[3] *Iliad,* I. 106.
[4] *Æneid,* I. 209.

Whose works the beautiful and base contain;
Of vice and virtue more instructive rules,
Than all the sober sages of the schools.

FRANCIS.

All joy or sorrow for the happiness or calamities of others is produced by an act of the imagination that realises the event however fictitious, or approximates it however remote, by placing us, for a time, in the condition of him whose fortune we contemplate; so that we feel, while the deception lasts, whatever motions would be excited by the same good or evil happening to ourselves.

Our passions are therefore more strongly moved, in proportion as we can more readily adopt the pains or pleasure proposed to our minds, by recognising them as once our own, or considering them as naturally incident to our state of life. It is not easy for the most artful writer to give us an interest in happiness or misery, which we think ourselves never likely to feel, and with which we have never yet been made acquainted. Histories of the downfal of kingdoms, and revolutions of empires, are read with great tranquillity; the imperial tragedy pleases common auditors only by its pomp of ornament, and grandeur of ideas; and the man whose faculties have been engrossed by business, and whose heart never fluttered but at the rise or fall of stocks, wonders how the attention can be seized, or the affection agitated by a tale of love.

Those parallel circumstances, and kindred images, to which we readily conform our minds, are, above all other writings, to be found in narratives of the lives of particular persons; and therefore no species of writing seems more worthy of cultivation than biography, since none can be more delightful or more useful, none can more certainly enchain the heart by irresistible interest, or more widely diffuse instruction to every diversity of condition.

The general and rapid narratives of history, which involve a thousand fortunes in the business of a day, and complicate innumerable incidents in one great transaction, afford few lessons applicable to private life, which derives its comforts and its wretchedness from the right or wrong management of things which nothing but their frequency makes considerable, *Parva, si non fiunt quotidie,* says Pliny,[1] and which can have no place in those relations which never descend below the consultation of senates, the motions of armies, and the schemes of conspirators.

I have often thought that there has rarely passed a life of which a judicious and faithful narrative would not be useful. For, not only every man has, in the mighty mass of the world, great numbers in the same condition with himself, to whom his mistakes and miscarriages, escapes and expedients, would be of immediate and apparent use; but there is such an uniformity in the state of man, considered apart from adventitious and separable decorations and disguises, that there is scarce any possibility of good or ill, but is common to human kind. A great part of the time of those who are placed at the greatest distance by fortune, or by temper, must unavoidably pass in the same manner; and though, when the claims of nature are satisfied, caprice, and vanity, and accident, begin to produce discriminations and peculiarities, yet the eye is not very heedful, or quick, which cannot discover the same causes still terminating their influence in the same effects, though sometimes accelerated, sometimes retarded, or perplexed by multiplied combinations. We are all prompted by the same motives, all deceived by the same fallacies, all animated by hope, obstructed by danger, entangled by desire, and seduced by pleasure.

It is frequently objected to relations of particular lives, that they are not distinguished by any striking or wonderful vicissitudes. The scholar who passed his life among his books, the merchant who conducted only his own affairs, the priest, whose sphere of action was not extended beyond that of his duty, are considered as no proper objects of publick regard, however they might have excelled in their several stations, whatever might have been their learning, integrity, and piety. But this notion arises from false measures of excellence and dignity, and must be eradicated by considering, that, in the esteem of uncorrupted reason, what is of most use is of most value.

[1] *Epistles,* III. i.

It is, indeed, not improper to take honest advantages of preju-
dice, and to gain attention by a celebrated name; but the business
of the biographer is often to pass slightly over those performances
and incidents, which produce vulgar greatness, to lead the thoughts
into domestick privacies, and display the minute details of daily
life, where exterior appendages are cast aside, and men excel
each other only by prudence and by virtue. The account of
Thuanus is, with great propriety, said by its author[2] to have been
written, that it might lay open to posterity the private and familiar
character of that man, *cujus ingenium et candorem ex ipsius
scriptis sunt olim semper miraturi,* whose candour and genius will
to the end of time be by his writings preserved in admiration.

There are many invisible circumstances which, whether we
read as inquirers[3] after natural or moral knowledge, whether we
intend to enlarge our science, or increase our virtue, are more im-
portant than publick occurrences. Thus Salust, the great master of
nature, has not forgot, in his account of Catiline,[4] to remark that
his walk was now quick, and again slow, as an indication of a
mind revolving something with violent commotion. Thus the story
of Melancthon affords a striking lecture on the value of time, by
informing us, that when he made an appointment, he expected
not only the hour, but the minute to be fixed, that the day might
not run out in the idleness of suspense;[5] and all the plans and
enterprizes of De Wit are now of less importance to the world,
than that part of his personal character which represents him as
careful of his health, and negligent of his life.[8]

But biography has often been allotted to writers who seem very
little acquainted with the nature of their task, or very negligent
about the performance. They rarely afford any other account than
might be collected from publick papers, but imagine themselves

[2] The phrase comes from Nic. Rigault's preface to de Thou's *Observa-
tions* (1733, p. 3, according to C. H. Conley).

[3] 1756: enquiries.

[4] *Conspiracy of Catiline,* XV. 5.

[5] Camerarius, *Vita Melancthonis* (1777, p. 62, according to C. G.
Osgood).

[6] Sir William Temple, *Works,* 1770, III, 244 (ref. W. Hale White.)

writing a life when they exhibit a chronological series of actions or preferments; and so little regard the manners or behaviour of their heroes, that more knowledge may be gained of a man's real character, by a short conversation with one of his servants, than from a formal and studied narrative, begun with his pedigree, and ended with his funeral.

If now and then they condescend to inform the world of particular facts, they are not always so happy as to select the most important. I know not well what advantage posterity can receive from the only circumstance by which Tickell has distinguished Addison from the rest of mankind, *the irregularity of his pulse:*[7] nor can I think myself overpaid for the time spent in reading the life of Malherb, by being enabled to relate, after the learned biographer,[8] that Malherb had two predominant opinions; one, that the looseness of a single woman might destroy all her boast of ancient descent; the other, that the French beggars made use very improperly and barbarously of the phrase *noble Gentleman,* because either word included the sense of both.

There are, indeed, some natural reasons why these narratives are often written by such as were not likely to give much instruction or delight, and why most accounts of particular persons are barren and useless. If a life be delayed till interest and envy are at an end, we may hope for impartiality, but must expect little intelligence; for the incidents which give excellence to biography are of a volatile and evanescent kind, such as soon escape the memory, and are rarely transmitted by tradition. We know how few can portray a living acquaintance, except by his most prominent and observable particularities, and the grosser features of his mind; and it may be easily imagined how much of this little knowledge may be lost in imparting it, and how soon a succession of copies will lose all resemblance of the original.

If the biographer writes from personal knowledge, and makes haste to gratify the publick curiosity, there is danger lest his interest, his fear, his gratitude, or his tenderness, overpower his fidelity,

[7] Preface to Addison's *Works,* 1721, I, xvi.
[8] H. de Racan, *Œuvres,* 1877, II, 258, 265.

and tempt him to conceal, if not to invent. There are many who think it an act of piety to hide the faults or failings of their friends, even when they can no longer suffer by their detection; we therefore see whole ranks of characters adorned with uniform panegyrick, and not to be known from one another, but by extrinsick and casual circumstances. "Let me remember, says Hale, when I find myself inclined to pity a criminal, that there is likewise a pity due to the country." [9] If we owe regard to the memory of the dead, there is yet more respect to be paid to knowledge, to virtue, and to truth.

No. 76. SATURDAY, *December* 8, 1750.

——*Silvis ubi passim*
Palantes error certo de tramite pellit,
Ille sinistrorsum, hic dextrorsum abit, unus utrique
Error, sed variis illudit partibus.

HOR.
[*Sat.* Bk. II, iii. 48]

While mazy error draws mankind astray
From truth's sure path, each takes his devious way:
One to the right, one to the left recedes,
Alike deluded, as each fancy leads.

ELIPHINSTON.

It is easy for every man, whatever be his character with others, to find reasons for esteeming himself, and therefore censure, contempt, or conviction of crimes, seldom deprive him of his own favour. Those, indeed, who can see only external facts, may look upon him with abhorrence, but when he calls himself to his own

---

[9] Gilbert Burnet, *Life and Death of Sir Matthew Hale*, 1805, p. 39.

tribunal, he finds every fault, if not absolutely effaced, yet so much palliated by the goodness of his intention, and the cogency of the motive, that very little guilt or turpitude remains; and when he takes a survey of the whole complication of his character, he discovers so many latent excellencies, so many virtues that want but an opportunity to exert themselves in act, and so many kind wishes for universal happiness, that he looks on himself as suffering unjustly under the infamy of single failings, while the general temper of his mind is unknown or unregarded.

It is natural to mean well, when only abstracted ideas of virtue are proposed to the mind, and no particular passion turns us aside from rectitude; and so willing is every man to flatter himself, that the difference between approving laws, and obeying them, is frequently forgotten; he that acknowledges the obligations of morality, and pleases his vanity with enforcing them to others, concludes himself zealous in the cause of virtue, though he has no longer any regard to her precepts, than they conform to his own desires; and counts himself among her warmest lovers, because he praises her beauty, though every rival steals away his heart.

There are, however, great numbers who have little recourse to the refinements of speculation, but who yet live at peace with themselves, by means which require less understanding, or less attention. When their hearts are burthened with the consciousness of a crime, instead of seeking for some remedy within themselves, they look round upon the rest of mankind, to find others tainted with the same guilt: they please themselves with observing, that they have numbers on their side; and that though they are hunted out from the society of good men, they are not likely to be condemned to solitude.

It may be observed, perhaps without exception, that none are so industrious to detect wickedness, or so ready to impute it, as they whose crimes are apparent and confessed. They envy an unblemished reputation, and what they envy they are busy to destroy: they are unwilling to suppose themselves meaner, and more corrupt than others, and therefore willingly pull down from their elevations those with whom they cannot rise to an equality. No man yet was ever wicked without secret discontent, and according to the different degrees of remaining virtue, or unextinguished reason, he either endeavours to reform himself, or corrupt others; either to regain the station which he has quitted, or prevail on others to imitate his defection.

It has been always considered as an alleviation of misery not to suffer alone, even when union and society can contribute nothing to resistance or escape; some comfort of the same kind seems to incite wickedness to seek associates, though indeed another reason may be given, for as guilt is propagated the power of reproach is diminished, and among numbers equally detestable every individual may be sheltered from shame, though not from conscience.

Another lenitive by which the throbs of the breast are assuaged, is, the contemplation, not of the same, but of different crimes. He that cannot justify himself by his resemblance to others, is ready to try some other expedient, and to enquire what will rise to his advantage from opposition and dissimilitude. He easily finds some faults in every human being, which he weighs against his own, and easily makes them preponderate while he keeps the balance in his own hand, and throws in or takes out at his pleasure circumstances that make them heavier or lighter. He then triumphs in his comparative purity, and sets himself at ease, not because he can refute the charges advanced against him, but because he can censure his accusers with equal justice, and no longer fears the arrows of reproach, when he has stored his magazine of malice with weapons equally sharp and equally envenomed.

This practice, though never just, is yet specious[1] and artful, when the censure is directed against deviations to the contrary extreme. The man who is branded with cowardice, may, with some appearance of propriety, turn all his force of argument against a stupid contempt of life, and rash precipitation into unnecessary danger. Every recession from temerity is an approach

[1] I.e., plausible.

towards cowardice, and though it be confessed that bravery like other virtues, stands between faults on either hand, yet the place of the middle point may always be disputed; he may therefore often impose upon careless understandings, by turning the attention wholly from himself, and keeping it fixed invariably on the opposite fault; and by shewing how many evils are avoided by his behaviour, he may conceal for a time those which are incurred.

But vice has not always opportunities or address for such artful subterfuges; men often extenuate their own guilt, only by vague and general charges upon others, or endeavour to gain rest to themselves, by pointing some other prey to the persuit of censure.

Every whisper of infamy is industriously circulated, every hint of suspicion eagerly improved, and every failure of conduct joyfully published, by those whose interest it is, that the eye and voice of the publick should be employed on any rather than on themselves.

All these artifices, and a thousand others equally vain and equally despicable, are incited by that conviction of the deformity of wickedness, from which none can set himself free, and by an absurd desire to separate the cause from the effects, and to enjoy the profit of crimes without suffering the shame. Men are willing to try all methods of reconciling guilt and quiet, and when their understandings are stubborn and uncomplying, raise their passions against them, and hope to over-power their own knowledge.

It is generally not so much the desire of men, sunk into depravity, to deceive the world as themselves, for when no particular circumstances make them dependant on others, infamy disturbs them little, but as it revives their remorse, and is echoed to them from their own hearts. The sentence most dreaded is that of reason and conscience, which they would engage on their side at any price but the labours of duty, and the sorrows of repentance. For this purpose every seducement and fallacy is sought, the hopes still rest upon some new experiment till life is at an end; and the last hour steals on unperceived, while the faculties are engaged in resisting reason, and repressing the sense of the divine disapprobation.

No. 117. TUESDAY, *April* 30, 1751.

"Οσσαν ἐπ' Οὐλύμπῳ μέμασαν θέμεν, αὐτὰρ ἐπ' "Οσσῃ
Πήλιον εἰνοσίφυλλον, ἵν' οὐρανὸς ἀμβατὸς εἴη.   Λ.
                                          [HOMER, *Od.* XI. 315.]

The gods they challenge, and affect the skies:
Heav'd on *Olympus* tott'ring *Ossa* stood;
On *Ossa, Pelion* nods with all his wood.

                                                  POPE.

TO THE RAMBLER

SIR,

Nothing has more retarded the advancement of learning than
the disposition of vulgar minds to ridicule and vilify what they
cannot comprehend. All industry must be excited by hope; and
as the student often proposes no other reward to himself than
praise, he is easily discouraged by contempt and insult. He who
brings with him into a clamorous multitude the timidity of recluse
speculation, and has never hardened his front in publick life, or
accustomed his passions to the vicissitudes and accidents, the
triumphs and defeats of mixed conversation, will blush at the
stare of petulant incredulity, and suffer himself to be driven, by a
burst of laughter, from the fortresses of demonstration. The
mechanist will be afraid to assert before hardy contradiction, the
possibility of tearing down bulwarks with a silk-worm's thread;
and the astronomer of relating the rapidity of light, the distance
of the fixed stars, and the height of the lunar mountains.

If I could by any efforts have shaken off this cowardice, I had
not sheltered myself under a borrowed name, nor applied to you
for the means of communicating to the public the theory of a
garret; a subject which, except some slight and transient strictures,
has been hitherto neglected by those who were best qualified to
adorn it, either for want of leisure to prosecute the various re-
searches in which a nice discussion must engage them, or because
it requires such diversity of knowledge, and such extent of curi-

osity, as is scarcely to be found in any single intellect: Or perhaps others foresaw the tumults which would be raised against them, and confined their knowledge to their own breasts, and abandoned prejudice and folly to the direction of chance.

That the professors of literature generally reside in the highest stories, has been immemorially observed. The wisdom of the ancients was well acquainted with the intellectual advantages of an elevated situation: why else were the *Muses* stationed on *Olympus* or *Parnassus* by those who could with equal right have raised them bowers in the vale of *Tempe,* or erected their altars among the flexures of *Meander?* Why was *Jove* himself nursed upon a mountain? or why did the goddesses, when the prize of beauty was contested, try the cause upon the top of *Ida?* Such were the fictions by which the great masters of the earlier ages endeavoured to inculcate to posterity the importance of a garret, which, though they had been long obscured by the negligence and ignorance of succeeding times, were well enforced by the celebrated symbol of *Pythagoras,* ἀνεμῶν πνεόντων, τὴν ἠχὼ προσκύνει;[1] "when the wind blows, worship its echo." This could not but be understood by his disciples as an inviolable injunction to live in a garret, which I have found frequently visited by the echo and the wind. Nor was the tradition wholly obliterated in the age of *Augustus,* for *Tibullus* evidently congratulates himself upon his garret, not without some allusion to the *Pythagorean* precept.

> *Quàm juvat immites ventos audire cubantem———*
> *Aut, gelidas hybernus aquas cum fuderit auster,*
> *Securum somnos, imbre juvante, sequi!*
>
> [*El.* I. i. 45]

> How sweet in sleep to pass the careless hours,
> Lull'd by the beating winds and dashing show'rs!

And it is impossible not to discover the fondness of *Lucretius,* an earlier writer, for a garret, in his description of the lofty towers

[1] Steele, in *The Tatler,* No. 214, explains this gnomic saying at some length, roughly to this effect: "Keep close during a storm."

of serene learning, and of the pleasure with which a wise man looks down upon the confused and erratic state of the world moving below him

> Sed nil dulcius est, bene quàm munita tenere
> Editâ doctrinâ sapientum templa serena;
> Despicere unde queas alios, passimque videre
> Errare, atque viam palanteis quærere vitæ

[Bk. II. 7.]

> ——'Tis sweet thy lab'ring steps to guide
> To virtue's heights, with wisdom well supply'd,
> And all the magazines of learning fortify'd:
> From thence to look below on human kind,
> Bewilder'd in the maze of life, and blind.

DRYDEN.

The institution has, indeed, continued to our own time; the garret is still the usual receptacle of the philosopher and poet; but this, like many ancient customs, is perpetuated only by an accidental imitation, without knowledge of the original reason for which it was established.

> Causa latet; res est notissima.

[VIRG. Æn. V. 5.]

> The cause is secret, but th' effect is known.

ADDISON.

Conjectures have, indeed, been advanced concerning these habitations of literature, but without much satisfaction to the judicious enquirer. Some have imagined, that the garret is generally chosen by the wits, as most easily rented; and concluded that no man rejoices in his aereal abode, but on the days of payment. Others suspect, that a garret is chiefly convenient, as it is remoter than any other part of the house from the outer door, which is often observed to be infested by visitants, who talk incessantly of beer, or linen, or a coat, and repeat the same sounds every morning, and sometimes again in the afternoon, without any variation, except that they grow daily more importunate and clamorous, and raise their voices in time from mournful murmurs to raging vociferations. This eternal monotony is always detestable to a man whose chief pleasure is to enlarge his knowledge, and vary his ideas. Others talk of freedom from noise, and abstraction from common business or amusements; and some, yet more visionary, tell us, that the faculties are inlarged by open prospects, and that the fancy is more at liberty, when the eye ranges without confinement.

These conveniencies may perhaps all be found in a well chosen garret; but surely they cannot be supposed sufficiently important to have operated unvariably upon different climates, distant ages, and separate nations. Of an universal practice, there must still be presumed an universal cause, which, however recondite and abstruse, may be perhaps reserved to make me illustrious by its discovery, and you by its promulgation.

It is universally known, that the faculties of the mind are invigorated or weakened by the state of the body, and that the body is in a great measure regulated by the various compressions of the ambient element. The effects of the air in the production or cure of corporal maladies have been acknowledged from the time of *Hippocrates*; but no man has yet sufficiently considered how far it may influence the operations of the genius, though every day affords instances of local understanding, of wits and reasoners, whose faculties are adapted to some single spot, and who, when they are removed to any other place, sink at once into silence and stupidity. I have discovered, by a long series of observations, that invention and elocution suffer great impediments from dense and impure vapours, and that the tenuity of a defecated air at a proper distance from the surface of the earth, accelerates the fancy, and sets at liberty those intellectual powers which were before shackled by too strong attraction, and unable to expand themselves under the pressure of a gross atmosphere. I have found dulness to quicken into sentiment in a thin ether, as water, though not very hot, boils in a receiver partly exhausted; and heads in appearance empty have teemed with notions upon rising ground, as the flaccid sides of a football would have swelled out into stiffness and extension.

For this reason I never think myself qualified to judge decisively of any man's faculties, whom I have only known in one degree of elevation; but take some opportunity of attending him from the cellar to the garret, and try upon him all the various degrees of rarefaction and condensation, tension and laxity. If he is neither vivacious aloft, nor serious below, I then consider him as hopeless; but as it seldom happens, that I do not find the temper to which the texture of his brain is fitted, I accommodate him in time with a tube of mercury, first marking the point most favourable to his intellects, according to rules which I have long studied, and which I may, perhaps, reveal to mankind in a complete treatise of barometrical pneumatology.

Another cause of the gaiety and sprightliness of the dwellers in garrets is probably the encrease of that vertiginous motion, with which we are carried round by the diurnal revolution of the earth. The power of agitation upon the spirits is well known; every man has felt his heart lightened in a rapid vehicle, or on a galloping horse; and nothing is plainer, than that he who towers to the fifth story, is whirled through more space by every circumrotation, than another that grovels upon the ground-floor. The nations between the tropicks are known to be fiery, inconstant, inventive and fanciful, because, living at the utmost length of the earth's diameter, they are carried about with more swiftness than those whom nature has placed nearer to the poles; and therefore, as it becomes a wise man to struggle with the inconveniencies of his country, whenever celerity and acuteness are requisite, we must actuate our languor by taking a few turns round the centre in a garret.

If you imagine that I ascribe to air and motion effects which they cannot produce, I desire you to consult your own memory, and consider whether you have never known a man acquire reputation in his garret, which, when fortune or a patron had placed him upon the first floor, he was unable to maintain and who never recovered his former vigour of understanding till he was restored to his original situation. That a garret will make every man a wit, I am very far from supposing; I know there are some who would continue blockheads even on the summit of the *Andes,* or on the peak of *Teneriffe.* But let not any man be considered as unimproveable till this potent remedy has been tried; for perhaps he was formed to be great only in a garret, as the joiner of *Aretæus* was rational in no other place but his own shop.

I think a frequent removal to various distances from the center so necessary to a just estimate of intellectual abilities, and consequently of so great use in education, that if I hoped that the public could be persuaded to so expensive an experiment, I would propose, that there should be a cavern dug, and a tower erected, like those which *Bacon* describes in *Solomon*'s house,[2] for the expansion and concentration of understanding, according to the exigence of different employments, or constitutions. Perhaps some that fume away in meditations upon time and space in the tower, might compose tables of interest at a certain depth; and he that upon level ground stagnates in silence, or creeps in narrative, might at the height of half a mile, ferment into merriment, sparkle with repartee, and froth with declamation.

Addison observes, that we may find the heat of *Virgil*'s climate, in some lines of his *Georgic*:[3] so, when I read a composition, I immediately determine the height of the author's habitation. As an elaborate performance is commonly said to smell of the lamp, my commendation of a noble thought, a sprightly sally, or a bold figure, is to pronounce it fresh from the garret; an expression which would break from me upon the perusal of most of your papers, did I not believe, that you sometimes quit the garret, and ascend into the cock-loft.

HYPERTATUS

No. 134. SATURDAY, *June* 29, 1751.

Quis scit, an adjiciant hodiernæ crastina summæ
Tempora Di superi!

HOR. [*Odes,* IV. vii. 17.]

[2] Sir Francis Bacon, in *The New Atlantis.* The Royal Society may have owed something to this imaginary community of scientists.

[3] Addison, *Works,* 1721, I, 256.

Who knows if Heav'n, with ever-bounteous pow'r,
Shall add to-morrow to the present hour.

FRANCIS.

I sat yesterday morning employed in deliberating on which, among the various subjects that occurred to my imagination, I should bestow the paper of to-day. After a short effort of meditation by which nothing was determined, I grew every moment more irresolute, my ideas wandered from the first intention, and I rather wished to think, than thought, upon any settled subject; till at last I was awakened from this dream of study by a summons from the press: the time was come for which I had been thus negligently purposing to provide, and, however dubious or sluggish, I was now necessitated to write.

Though to a writer whose design is so comprehensive and miscellaneous, that he may accommodate himself with a topick from every scene of life, or view of nature, it is no great aggravation of his task to be obliged to a sudden composition, yet I could not forbear to reproach myself for having so long neglected what was unavoidably to be done, and of which every moment's idleness increased the difficulty. There was however some pleasure in reflecting that I, who had only trifled till diligence was necessary, might still congratulate myself upon my superiority to multitudes, who have trifled till diligence is vain; who can by no degree of activity or resolution recover the opportunities which have slipped away; and who are condemned by their own carelessness to hopeless calamity and barren sorrow.

The folly of allowing ourselves to delay what we know cannot be finally escaped, is one of the general weaknesses, which, in spite of the instruction of moralists, and the remonstrances of reason, prevail to a greater or less degree in every mind; even they who most steadily withstand it, find it, if not the most violent, the most pertinacious of their passions, always renewing its attacks, and though often vanquished, never destroyed.

It is indeed natural to have particular regard to the time present, and to be most solicitous for that which is by its nearness enabled to make the strongest impressions. When therefore any sharp pain is to be suffered, or any formidable danger to be incurred, we can scarcely exempt ourselves wholly from the seducements of imagination; we readily believe that another day will bring some support or advantage which we now want; and are easily persuaded, that the moment of necessity which we desire never to arrive, is at a great distance from us.

Thus life is languished away in the gloom of anxiety, and consumed in collecting resolution which the next morning dissipates; in forming purposes which we scarcely hope to keep, and reconciling ourselves to our own cowardice by excuses, which, while we admit them, we know to be absurd. Our firmness is by the continual contemplation of misery hourly impaired; every submission to our fear enlarges its dominion; we not only waste that time in which the evil we dread might have been suffered and surmounted, but even where procrastination produces no absolute encrease of our difficulties, make them less superable to ourselves by habitual terrors. When evils cannot be avoided, it is wise to contract the interval of expectation; to meet the mischiefs which will overtake us if we fly; and suffer only their real malignity without the conflicts of doubt and anguish of anticipation.

To act is far easier than to suffer, yet we every day see the progress of life retarded by the *vis inertiæ,* the mere repugnance to motion, and find multitudes repining at the want of that which nothing but idleness hinders them from enjoying. The case of *Tantalus,* in the region of poetick punishment, was somewhat to be pitied, because the fruits that hung about him retired from his hand; but what tenderness can be claimed by those who though perhaps they suffer the pains of *Tantalus* will never lift their hands for their own relief?

There is nothing more common among this torpid generation than murmurs and complaints; murmurs at uneasiness which only vacancy and suspicion expose them to feel, and complaints of distresses which it is in their own power to remove. Laziness is commonly associated with timidity. Either fear originally prohibits endeavours by infusing despair of success; or the frequent failure of irresolute struggles, and the constant desire of avoiding labour, impress by degrees false terrors on the mind. But fear, whether natural or acquired, when once it has full possession of the fancy, never fails to employ it upon visions of calamity, such as if they are not dissipated by useful employment, will soon overcast it with horrors, and imbitter life not only with those miseries by which all earthly beings are really more or less tormented, but with those which do not yet exist, and which can only be discerned by the perspicacity of cowardice.

Among all who sacrifice future advantage to present inclination, scarcely any gain so little as those that suffer themselves to freeze in idleness. Others are corrupted by some enjoyment of more or less power to gratify the passions; but to neglect our duties, merely to avoid the labour of performing them, a labour which is always punctually rewarded, is surely to sink under weak temptations. Idleness never can secure tranquillity; the call of reason and of conscience will pierce the closest pavilion of the sluggard, and, though it may not have force to drive him from his down, will be loud enough to hinder him from sleep. Those moments which he cannot resolve to make useful by devoting them to the great business of his being, will still be usurped by powers that will not leave them to his disposal; remorse and vexation will seize upon them, and forbid him to enjoy what he is so desirous to appropriate.

There are other causes of inactivity incident to more active faculties and more acute discernment. He to whom many objects of persuit arise at the same time, will frequently hesitate between different desires, till a rival has precluded him, or change his course as new attractions prevail, and harrass himself without advancing. He who sees different ways to the same end, will, unless he watches carefully over his own conduct, lay out too much of his attention upon the comparison of probabilities, and the adjustment of expedients, and pause in the choice of his road, till some accident intercepts his journey. He whose penetration extends to remote consequences, and who, whenever he applies his attention to any design, discovers new prospects of advantage, and possibilities of improvement, will not easily be persuaded that his project is ripe for execution; but will superadd one contrivance to another, endeavour to unite various purposes in one operation, multiply complications, and refine niceties, till he is entangled in his own scheme, and bewildered in the perplexity of various intentions. He that resolves to unite all the beauties of situation in a new purchase, must waste his life in roving to no purpose from province to province. He that hopes in the same house to obtain every convenience, may draw plans and study *Palladio*, but will never lay a stone. He will attempt a treatise on some important subject, and amass materials, consult authors, and study all the dependent and collateral parts of learning, but never conclude himself qualified to write. He that has abilities to conceive perfection, will not easily be content without it; and since perfection cannot be reached, will lose the opportunity of doing well in the vain hope of unattainable excellence.

The certainty that life cannot be long, and the probability that it will be much shorter than nature allows, ought to awaken every man to the active prosecution of whatever he is desirous to perform. It is true that no diligence can ascertain success; death may intercept the swiftest career; but he who is cut off in the execution of an honest undertaking, has at least the honour of falling in his rank, and has fought the battle, though he missed the victory.

No. 144. Saturday, *August* 3, 1751.

————*Daphnidis arcum*
Fregisti et calamos: quæ tu, perverse Menalca,
Et cum vidisti puero donata, dolebas;
Et, si non aliqua nocuisses, mortuus esses.
Virg. [Ec. III. 12.]

The bow of *Daphnis* and the shafts you broke;
When the fair boy receiv'd the gift of right;
And but for mischief, you had dy'd for spite.
Dryden.

It is impossible to mingle in conversation without observing the difficulty with which a new name makes its way into the world. The first appearance of excellence unites multitudes against it; unexpected opposition rises up on every side; the celebrated and the obscure join in the confederacy; subtilty furnishes arms to impudence, and invention leads on credulity.

The strength and unanimity of this alliance is not easily conceived. It might be expected that no man should suffer his heart to be inflamed with malice, but by injuries; that none should busy himself in contesting the pretensions of another, but when some right of his own was involved in the question; that at least hostilities commenced without cause, should quickly cease; that the armies of malignity should soon disperse, when no common interest could be found to hold them together; and that the attack upon a rising character should be left to those who had something to hope or fear from the event.

The hazards of those that aspire to eminence would be much diminished if they had none but acknowledged rivals to encounter. Their enemies would then be few, and what is of yet greater importance, would be known. But what caution is sufficient to ward off the blows of invisible assailants, or what force can stand against unintermitted attacks, and a continual succession of enemies? Yet such is the state of the world, that no sooner can any man emerge from the crowd, and fix the eyes of the publick upon him, than he stands as a mark to the arrows of lurking calumny, and receives, in the tumult of hostility, from distant and from nameless hands, wounds not always easy to be cured.

It is probable that the onset against the candidates for renown, is originally incited by those who imagine themselves in danger of suffering by their success; but when war is once declared, volunteers flock to the standard, multitudes follow the camp only for want of employment, and flying squadrons are dispersed to every part, so pleased with an opportunity of mischief that they toil without prospect of praise, and pillage without hope of [1] profit.

When any man has endeavoured to deserve distinction, he will

[1] 1756: or.

be surprised to hear himself censured where he could not expect to have been named; he will find the utmost acrimony of malice among those whom he never could have offended.

As there are to be found in the service of envy men of every diversity of temper and degree of understanding, calumny is diffused by all arts and methods of propagation. Nothing is too gross or too refined, too cruel or too trifling to be practised; very little regard is had to the rules of honourable hostility, but every weapon is accounted lawful; and those that cannot make a thrust at life are content to keep themselves in play with petty malevolence, to teaze with feeble blows and impotent disturbance.

But as the industry of observation has divided the most miscellaneous and confused assemblages into proper classes, and ranged the insects of the summer, that torment us with their drones or stings, by their several tribes; the persecutors of merit, notwithstanding their numbers, may be likewise commodiously distinguished into Roarers, Whisperers, and Moderators.

The Roarer is an enemy rather terrible than dangerous. He has no other qualification for a champion of controversy than a hardened front and strong voice. Having seldom so much desire to confute as to silence, he depends rather upon vociferation than argument, and has very little care to adjust one part of his accusation to another, to preserve decency in his language, or probability in his narratives. He has always a store of reproachful epithets and contemptuous appellations, ready to be produced as occasion may require, which by constant use he pours out with resistless volubility. If the wealth of a trader is mentioned, he without hesitation devotes him to bankruptcy; if the beauty and elegance of a lady be commended, he wonders how the town can fall in love with rustick deformity; if a new performance of genius happens to be celebrated, he pronounces the writer a hopeless ideot, without knowledge of books or life, and without the understanding by which it must be acquired. His exaggerations are generally without effect upon those whom he compels to hear them; and though it will sometimes happen that the timorous are awed by his violence, and the credulous mistake his confidence for knowledge, yet the opinions which he endeavours to suppress soon recover their former strength, as the trees that bend to the tempest erect themselves again when its force is past.

The Whisperer is more dangerous. He easily gains attention by a soft address, and excites curiosity by an air of importance. As secrets are not to be made cheap by promiscuous publication, he calls a select audience about him, and gratifies their vanity with an appearance of trust by communicating his intelligence in a low voice. Of the trader he can tell that though he seems to manage an extensive commerce, and talks in high terms of the funds, yet his wealth is not equal to his reputation; he has lately suffered much by an expensive project, and had a greater share than is acknowledged in the rich ship that perished by the storm. Of the beauty he has little to say, but that they who see her in a morning do not discover all these graces which are admired in the park. Of the writer he affirms with great certainty, that though the excellence of the work be incontestable, he can claim but a small part of the reputation; that he owed most of the images and sentiments to a secret friend; and that the accuracy and equality of the stile was produced by the successive correction of the chief cricks of the age.

As every one is pleased with imagining that he knows something not yet commonly divulged, secret history easily gains credit; but it is for the most part believed only while it circulates in whispers, and when once it is openly told, is openly confuted.

The most pernicious enemy is the man of Moderation. Without interest in the question, or any motive but honest curiosity, this impartial and zealous enquirer after truth, is ready to hear either side, and always disposed to kind interpretations and favourable opinions. He has heard the trader's affairs reported with great variation, and after a diligent comparison of the evidence, concludes it probable that the splendid superstructure of business being originally built upon a narrow basis, has lately been found to totter; but between dilatory payment and bankruptcy there is a great distance; many merchants have supported themselves by expedients for a time, without any final injury to their creditors; and what is lost by one adventure may be recovered by another. He believes that a young lady pleased with admiration, and desirous to make perfect what is already excellent, may heighten her charms by artificial improvements, but surely most of her beauties must be genuine, and who can say that he is wholly what he endeavours to appear? The author he knows to be a man of diligence, who perhaps does not sparkle with the fire of *Homer,* but has the judgment to discover his own deficiencies, and to supply them by the help of others; and in his opinion modesty is a quality so amiable and rare, that it ought to find a patron wherever it appears, and may justly be preferred by the publick suffrage to petulant wit and ostentatious literature.

He who thus discovers failings with unwillingness, and extenuates the faults which cannot be denied, puts an end at once to doubt or vindication; his hearers repose upon his candour and veracity, and admit the charge without allowing the excuse.

Such are the arts by which the envious, the idle, the peevish, and the thoughtless, obstruct that worth which they cannot equal, and by artifices thus easy, sordid, and detestable, is industry defeated, beauty blasted, and genius depressed.

No. 148. SATURDAY, *August* 17, 1751.

Me pater sævis oneret catenis
Quod viro clemens misero peperci,
Me vel extremis Numidarum in oris
    Classe releget.

HOR. [Odes III. xi. 45.]

    Me let my father load with chains,
Or banish to *Numidia*'s farthest plains;
—My crime, that I a loyal wife,
In kind compassion sav'd [1] my husband's life.

FRANCIS.

Politicians remark that no oppression is so heavy or lasting as that which is inflicted by the perversion and exorbitance of legal au-

[1] 1756: spar'd.

thority. The robber may be seized, and the invader repelled when-
ever they are found; they who pretend no right but that of force,
may by force be punished or suppressed. But when plunder bears
the name of impost, and murder is perpetrated by a judicial sen-
tence, fortitude is intimidated and wisdom confounded; resistance
shrinks from an alliance with rebellion, and the villain remains
secure in the robes of the magistrate.

Equally dangerous and equally detestable are the cruelties often
exercised in private families, under the venerable sanction of
parental authority; the power which we are taught to honour from
the first moments of reason; which is guarded from insult and
violation by all that can impress awe upon the mind of man; and
which therefore may wanton in cruelty without controul, and
trample the bounds of right with innumerable transgressions, be-
fore duty and piety will dare to seek redress, or think themselves at
liberty to recur to any other means of deliverance than supplica-
tions by which insolence is elated, and tears by which cruelty is
gratified.

It was for a long time imagined by the *Romans,* that no son
could be the murderer of his father, and they had therefore no
punishment appropriated to parricide. They seem likewise to have
believed with equal confidence that no father could be cruel to his
child, and therefore they allowed every man the supreme judica-
ture in his own house, and put the lives of his offspring into his
hands. But experience informed them by degrees, that they had
determined too hastily in favour of human nature; they found that
instinct and habit were not able to contend with avarice or malice;
that the nearest relation might be violated; and that power, to
whomsoever entrusted, might be ill employed. They were there-
fore obliged to supply and to change their institutions; to deter the
parricide by a new law, and to transfer capital punishments from
the parent to the magistrate.

There are indeed many houses which it is impossible to enter
familiarly, without discovering that parents are by no means
exempt from the intoxications of dominion; and that he who is in
no danger of hearing remonstrances but from his own conscience,

will seldom be long without the art of controlling his convictions, and modifying justice by his own will.

If in any situation the heart were inaccessible to malignity, it might be supposed to be sufficiently secured by parental relation. To have voluntarily become to any being the occasion of its existence, produces an obligation to make that existence happy. To see helpless infancy stretching out her hands and pouring out her cries in testimony of dependance, without any powers to alarm jealousy, or any guilt to alienate affection, must surely awaken tenderness in every human mind; and tenderness once excited will be hourly encreased by the natural contagion of felicity, by the repercussion of communicated pleasure, and the consciousness of the dignity of benefaction. I believe no generous or benevolent man can see the vilest animal courting his regard, and shrinking at his anger, playing his gambols of delight before him, calling on him in distress, and flying to him in danger, without more kindness than he can persuade himself to feel for the wild and unsocial inhabitants of the air and water. We naturally endear to ourselves those to whom we impart any kind of pleasure, because we imagine their affection and esteem secured to us by the benefits which they receive.

There is indeed another method by which the pride of superiority may be likewise gratified. He that has extinguished all the sensations of humanity, and has no longer any satisfaction in the reflection that he is loved as the distributor of happiness, may please himself with exciting terror as the inflicter of pain; he may delight his solitude with contemplating the extent of his power and the force of his commands, in imagining the desires that flutter on the tongue which is forbidden to utter them, or the discontent which preys on the heart in which fear confines it; he may amuse himself with new contrivances of detection, multiplications of prohibition, and varieties of punishment; and swell with exultation when he considers how little of the homage that he receives he owes to choice.

That princes of this character have been known, the history of all absolute kingdoms will inform us; and since, as *Aristotle* observes, ἡ οἰκονομικὴ μοναρχία, *the government of a family is natu-*

rally monarchical,[2] it is like other monarchies too often arbitrarily administered. The regal and parental tyrant differ only in the extent of their dominions, and the number of their slaves. The same passions cause the same miseries; except that seldom any prince, however despotick, has so far shaken off all awe of the publick eye as to venture upon those freaks of injustice, which are sometimes indulged under the secrecy of a private dwelling. Capricious injunctions, partial decisions, unequal allotments, distributions of reward not by merit but by fancy, and punishments regulated not by the degree of the offence, but by the humour of the judge, are too frequent where no power is known but that of a father.

That he delights in the misery of others no man will confess, and yet what other motive can make a father cruel? The king may be instigated by one man to the destruction of another; he may sometimes think himself endangered by the virtues of a subject; he may dread the successful general or the popular orator; his avarice may point out golden confiscations; and his guilt may whisper that he can only be secure, by cutting off all power of revenge.

But what can a parent hope from the oppression of those who were born to his protection, of those who can disturb him with no competition, who can enrich him with no spoils? Why cowards are cruel may be easily discovered; but for what reason not more infamous than cowardice can that man delight in oppression who has nothing to fear?

The unjustifiable severity of a parent is loaded with this aggravation, that those whom he injures are always in his sight. The injustice of a prince is often exercised upon those of whom he never had any personal or particular knowledge; and the sentence which he pronounces, whether of banishment, imprisonment, or death, removes from his view the man whom he condemns. But the domestick oppressor dooms himself to gaze upon those faces which he clouds with terror and with sorrow; and beholds every moment the effects of his own barbarities. He that can bear to give continual pain to those who surround him, and can walk with satisfaction in the gloom of his own presence; he that can see sub-

[2] *Politics,* I. ii. 21.

missive misery without relenting, and meet without emotion the eye that implores mercy, or demands justice, will scarcely be amended by remonstrance or admonition; he has found means of stopping the avenues of tenderness, and arming his heart against the force of reason.

Even though no consideration should be paid to the great law of social beings, by which every individual is commanded to consult the happiness of others, yet the harsh parent is less to be vindicated than any other criminal, because he less provides for the happiness of himself. Every man, however little he loves others, would willingly be loved; every man hopes to live long, and therefore hopes for that time at which he shall sink back to imbecillity, and must depend for ease and chearfulness upon the officiousness of others. But how has he obviated the inconveniencies of old age, who alienates from him the assistance of his children, and whose bed must be surrounded in his last hours, in the hours of languor and dejection, of impatience and of pain, by strangers to whom his life is indifferent, or by enemies to whom his death is desirable?

Piety will indeed in good minds overcome provocation, and those who have been harrassed by brutality will forget the injuries which they have suffered so far as to perform the last duties with alacrity and zeal. But surely no resentment can be equally painful with kindness thus undeserved, nor can severer punishment be imprecated upon a man not wholly lost in meanness and stupidity, than through the tediousness of decrepitude, to be reproached by the kindness of his own children, to receive not the tribute but the alms of attendance, and to owe every relief of his miseries not to gratitude but to mercy.

No. 154. SATURDAY, *September* 7, 1751.

—*Tibi res antiquæ laudis & artis*
Aggredior, sanctos ausus recludere fontes.
VIRG. [*Georg.* II. 174.]

> For thee my tuneful accents will I raise,
> And treat of arts disclos'd in ancient days;
> Once more unlock for thee the sacred spring.
>
> DRYDEN.

The direction of *Aristotle* to those that study politicks, is, first to examine and understand what has been written by the ancients upon government, then to cast their eyes round upon the world, and consider by what causes the prosperity of communities is visibly influenced, and why some are worse, and others better administered.

The same method must be pursued by him who hopes to become eminent in any other part of knowledge. The first task is to search books, the next to contemplate nature. He must first possess himself of the intellectual treasures which the diligence of former ages has accumulated, and then endeavour to encrease them by his own collections.

The mental disease of the present generation, is impatience of study, contempt of the great masters of ancient wisdom, and a disposition to rely wholly upon unassisted genius and natural sagacity. The wits of these happy days have discovered a way to fame, which the dull caution of our laborious ancestors durst never attempt; they cut the knots of sophistry which it was formerly the business of years to untie, solve difficulties by sudden irradiations of intelligence, and comprehend long processes of argument by immediate intuition.

Men who have flattered themselves into this opinion of their own abilities, look down on all who waste their lives over books, as a race of inferior beings condemned by nature to perpetual pupillage, and fruitlessly endeavouring to remedy their barrenness by incessant cultivation, or succour their feebleness by subsidiary strength. They presume that none would be more industrious than they, if they were not more sensible of deficiencies, and readily conclude, that he who places no confidence in his own powers, owes his modesty only to his weakness.

It is however certain that no estimate is more in danger of erroneous calculations than those by which a man computes the force of his own genius. It generally happens at our entrance into the world, that by the natural attraction of similitude, we associate with men like ourselves young, sprightly, and ignorant, and rate our accomplishments by comparison with theirs; when we have once obtained an acknowledged superiority over our acquaintances, imagination and desire easily extend it over the rest of mankind, and if no accident forces us into new emulations, we grow old, and die in admiration of ourselves.

Vanity, thus confirmed in her dominion, readily listens to the voice of idleness, and sooths the slumber of life with continual dreams of excellence and greatness. A man elated by confidence in his natural vigour of fancy and sagacity of conjecture, soon concludes that he already possesses whatever toil and enquiry can confer. He then listens with eagerness to the wild objections which folly has raised against the common means of improvement; talks of the dark chaos of indigested knowledge; describes the mischievous effects of heterogeneous sciences fermenting in the mind; relates the blunders of lettered ignorance; expatiates on the heroick merit of those who deviate from prescription, or shake off authority; and gives vent to the inflations of his heart by declaring that he owes nothing to pedants and universities.

All these pretensions, however confident, are very often vain. The laurels which superficial acuteness gains in triumphs over ignorance unsupported by vivacity, are observed by *Locke*[1] to be lost whenever real learning and rational diligence appear against her; the sallies of gaiety are soon repressed by calm confidence, and the artifices of subtilty are readily detected by those who having carefully studied the question, are not easily confounded or surprised.

But though the contemner of books had neither been deceived by others nor himself, and was really born with a genius surpassing the ordinary abilities of mankind; yet surely such gifts of providence may be more properly urged as incitements to labour, than encouragements to negligence. He that neglects the culture of

[1] Perhaps in *Some Thoughts concerning Education,* §70.

ground, naturally fertile, is more shamefully culpable than he whose field would scarcely recompence his husbandry.

Cicero remarks, that not to know what has been transacted in former times is to continue always a child. If no use is made of the labours of past ages, the world must remain always in the infancy of knowledge. The discoveries of every man must terminate in his own advantage, and the studies of every age be employed on questions which the past generation had discussed and determined. We may with as little reproach borrow science as manufactures from our ancestors; and it is as rational to live in caves till our own hands have erected a palace, as to reject all knowledge of architecture, which our understandings will not supply.

To the strongest and quickest mind it is far easier to learn than to invent. The principles of arithmetick and geometry may be comprehended by a close attention in a few days; yet who can flatter himself that the study of a long life would have enabled him to discover them, when he sees them yet unknown to so many nations, whom he cannot suppose less liberally endowed with natural reason, than the *Grecians* or *Egyptians*?

Every science was thus far advanced towards perfection, by the emulous diligence of contemporary students, and the gradual discoveries of one age improving on another. Sometimes unexpected flashes of instruction were struck out by the fortuitous collision of happy incidents, or an involuntary concurrence of ideas, in which the philosopher to whom they happened had no other merit than that of knowing their value, and transmitting unclouded to posterity that light which had been kindled by causes out of his power. The happiness of these casual illuminations no man can promise to himself, because no endeavours can procure them; and therefore, whatever be our abilities or application, we must submit to learn from others what perhaps would have lain hid for ever from human penetration, had not some remote enquiry brought it to view; as treasures are thrown up by the ploughman and the digger in the rude exercise of their common occupations.

The man whose genius qualifies him for great undertakings,

must at least be content to learn from books the present state of human knowledge; that he may not ascribe to himself the invention of arts generally known; weary his attention with experiments of which the event has been long registered; and waste, in attempts which have already succeeded or miscarried, that time which might have been spent with usefulness and honour upon new undertakings.

But though the study of books is necessary, it is not sufficient to constitute literary eminence. He that wishes to be counted among the benefactors of posterity, must add by his own toil to the acquisitions of his ancestors, and secure his memory from neglect by some valuable improvement. This can only be effected by looking out upon the wastes of the intellectual world, and extending the power of learning over regions yet undisciplined and barbarous; or by surveying more exactly her antient dominions, and driving ignorance from the fortresses and retreats where she skulks undetected and undisturbed. Every science has its difficulties which yet call for solution before we attempt new systems of knowledge; as every country has its forests and marshes, which it would be wise to cultivate and drain, before distant colonies are projected as a necessary discharge of the exuberance of inhabitants.

No man ever yet became great by imitation. Whatever hopes for the veneration of mankind must have invention in the design or the execution; either the effect must itself be new, or the means by which it is produced. Either truths hitherto unknown must be discovered, or those which are already known enforced by stronger evidence, facilitated by clearer method, or ellucidated by brighter illustrations.

Fame cannot spread wide or endure long that is not rooted in nature, and manured by art. That which hopes to resist the blast of malignity, and stand firm against the attacks of time, must contain in itself some original principle of growth. The reputation which arises from the detail or transposition of borrowed sentiments, may spread for a while, like ivy on the rind of antiquity, but will be torn away by accident or contempt, and suffered to rot unheeded on the ground.

No. 155. TUESDAY, *September* 10, 1751.

————*Steriles transmisimus annos,*
Hæc ævi mihi prima dies, hæc limina vitæ.

STAT. [I. 362.]

————Our barren years are past;
Be this of life the first, of sloth the last.

ELPHINSTON.

No weakness of the human mind has more frequently incurred animadversion, than the negligence with which men overlook their own faults, however flagrant, and the easiness with which they pardon them, however frequently repeated.

It seems generally believed, that, as the eye cannot see itself, the mind has no faculties by which it can contemplate its own state, and that therefore we have not means of becoming acquainted with our real characters; an opinion which, like innumerable other postulates, an enquirer finds himself inclined to admit upon very little evidence, because it affords a ready solution of many difficulties. It will explain why the greatest abilities frequently fail to promote the happiness of those who possess them; why those who can distinguish with the utmost nicety the boundaries of vice and virtue, suffer them to be confounded in their own conduct; why the active and vigilant resign their affairs implicitly to the management of others; and why the cautious and fearful make hourly approaches towards ruin, without one sigh of solicitude or struggle for escape.

When a position teems thus with commodious consequences, who can without regret confess it to be false? Yet it is certain that declaimers have indulged a disposition to describe the dominion of the passions as extended beyond the limits that nature assigned. Self-love is often rather arrogant than blind; it does not hide our faults from ourselves, but persuades us that they escape the notice of others, and disposes us to resent censures lest we should confess them to be just. We are secretly conscious of defects and vices which we hope to conceal from the publick eye, and please ourselves with innumerable impostures, by which, in reality, no body is deceived.

In proof of the dimness of our internal sight, or the general inability of man to determine rightly concerning his own character, it is common to urge the success of the most absurd and incredible flattery, and the resentment always raised by advice, however soft, benevolent, and reasonable. But flattery, if its operation be nearly examined, will be found to owe its acceptance not to our ignorance but knowledge of our failures, and to delight us rather as it consoles our wants than displays our possessions. He that shall solicit the favour of his patron by praising him for qualities which he can find in himself, will be defeated by the more daring panegyrist who enriches him with adscititious excellence. Just praise is only a debt, but flattery is a present. The acknowledgement of those virtues on which conscience congratulates us, is a tribute that we can at any time exact with confidence, but the celebration of those which we only feign, or desire without any vigorous endeavours to attain them, is received as a confession of sovereignty over regions never conquered, as a favourable decision of disputable claims, and is more welcome as it is more gratuitous.

Advice is offensive, not because it lays us open to unexpected regret, or convicts us of any fault which had escaped our notice, but because it shows us that we are known to others as well as to ourselves; and the officious monitor is persecuted with hatred, not because his accusation is false, but because he assumes that superiority which we are not willing to grant him, and has dared to detect what we desired to conceal.

For this reason advice is commonly ineffectual. If those who follow the call of their desires, without enquiry whither they are going, had deviated ignorantly from the paths of wisdom, and were rushing upon dangers unforeseen, they would readily listen to information that recals them from their errors, and catch the first alarm by which destruction or infamy is denounced. Few that wander in the wrong way mistake it for the right; they only find it more smooth and flowery, and indulge their own choice rather than approve it: therefore few are persuaded to quit it by admonition or reproof, since it impresses no new conviction, nor confers any powers of action or resistance. He that is gravely informed how soon profusion will annihilate his fortune, hears with little advantage what he knew before, and catches at the next occasion of expence, because advice has no force to suppress his vanity. He that is told how certainly intemperance will hurry him to the grave, runs with his usual speed to a new course of luxury, because his reason is not invigorated, nor his appetite weakened.

The mischief of flattery is, not that it persuades any man that he is what he is not, but that it suppresses the influence of honest ambition, by raising an opinion that honour may be gained without the toil of merit; and the benefit of advice arises commonly, not from any new light imparted to the mind, but from the discovery which it affords of the publick suffrages. He that could withstand conscience, is frighted at infamy, and shame prevails when reason was defeated.

As we all know our own faults, and know them commonly with many aggravations which human perspicacity cannot discover, there is, perhaps, no man, however hardened by impudence or dissipated by levity, sheltered by hypocrisy, or blasted by disgrace, who does not intend some time to review his conduct, and to regulate the remainder of his life by the laws of virtue. New temptations indeed attack him, new invitations are offered by pleasure and interest, and the hour of reformation is always delayed; every delay gives vice another opportunity of fortifying itself by habit; and the change of manners, though sincerely intended and rationally planned, is referred to the time when some craving passion shall be fully gratified, or some powerful allurement cease its importunity.

Thus procrastination is accumulated on procrastination, and one impediment succeeds another, till age shatters our resolution, or death intercepts the project of amendment. Such is often the end of salutary purposes, after they have long delighted the imagination, and appeased that disquiet which every mind feels from known misconduct, when the attention is not diverted by business or by pleasure.

Nothing surely can be more unworthy of a reasonable nature, than to continue in a state so opposite to real happiness, as that all the peace of solitude and felicity of meditation, must arise from resolutions of forsaking it. Yet the world will often afford examples of men, who pass months and years in a continual war with their own convictions, and are daily dragged by habit or betrayed by passion into practices, which they closed and opened their eyes with purposes to avoid; purposes which, though settled on conviction, the first impulse of momentary desire totally overthrows.

The influence of custom is indeed such that to conquer it will require the utmost efforts of fortitude and virtue, nor can I think any man more worthy of veneration and renown, than those who have burst the shackles of habitual vice. This victory however has different degrees of glory as of difficulty; it is more heroic as the objects of guilty gratification are more familiar, and the recurrence of solicitation more frequent. He that from experience of the folly of ambition resigns his offices, may set himself free at once from temptation to squander his life in courts, because he cannot regain his former station. He who is inslaved by an amorous passion, may quit his tyrant in disgust, and absence will without the help of reason overcome by degrees the desire of returning. But those appetites to which every place affords their proper object, and which require no preparatory measures or gradual advances, are more tenaciously adhesive; the wish is so near the enjoyment, that compliance often precedes consideration, and before the powers of reason can be summoned, the time for employing them is past.

Indolence is therefore one of the vices from which those whom it once infects are seldom reformed. Every other species of luxury operates upon some appetite that is quickly satiated, and requires some concurrence of art or accident which every place will not supply; but the desire of ease acts equally at all hours, and the longer it is indulged is the more encreased. To do nothing is in every man's power; we can never want an opportunity of omitting duties. The lapse to indolence is soft and imperceptible, because it is only a mere cessation of activity; but the return to diligence is difficult, because it implies a change from rest to motion, from privation to reality.

————*Facilis descensus Averni:*
Noctes atque dies patet atri janua Ditis:
Sed revocare gradum, superasque evadere ad auras,
Hoc opus, hic labor est.————

[VIR. *Æn.* VI. 126.]

The gates of *Hell* are open night and day;
Smooth the descent, and easy is the way:
But, to return, and view the chearful skies;
In this, the task and mighty labour lies.

DRYDEN.

Of this vice, as of all others, every man who indulges it is conscious; we all know our own state, if we could be induced to consider it; and it might perhaps be useful to the conquest of all these ensnarers of the mind, if at certain stated days life was reviewed. Many things necessary are omitted, because we vainly imagine that they may be always performed, and what cannot be done without pain will for ever be delayed if the time of doing it be left unsettled. No corruption is great but by long negligence, which can scarcely prevail in a mind regularly and frequently awakened by periodical remorse. He that thus breaks his life into parts, will find in himself a desire to distinguish every stage of his existence by some improvement, and delight himself with the approach of the day of recollection, as of the time which is to begin a new series of virtue and felicity.

No. 160. SATURDAY, *September* 28, 1751.

————*Inter se convenit ursis.*

JUV. [*Sat.* XV. 164.]

Beasts of each kind their fellows spare;
Bear lives in amity with bear.

"The world," says *Locke,* "has people of all sorts." As in the general hurry produced by the superfluities of some, and necessities of others, no man needs to stand still for want of employment, so in the innumerable gradations of ability, and endless varieties of study and inclination, no employment can be vacant for want of a man qualified to discharge it.

Such is probably the natural state of the universe, but it is so much deformed by interest and passion, that the benefit of this adaptation of men to things is not always perceived. The folly or indigence of those who set their services to sale, inclines them to boast of qualifications which they do not possess, and attempt business which they do not understand; and they who have the power of assigning to others the task of life, are seldom honest or seldom happy in their nominations. Patrons are corrupted by avarice, cheated by credulity, or overpowered by resistless solicitation. They are sometimes too strongly influenced by honest prejudices of friendship, or the prevalence of virtuous compassion. For, whatever cool reason may direct, it is not easy for a man of tender and scrupulous goodness to overlook the immediate effect of his own actions, by turning his eyes upon remoter consequences, and to do that which must give present pain, for the sake of obviating evil yet unfelt, or securing advantage in time to come. What is distant is in itself obscure, and, when we have no wish to see it, easily escapes our notice, or takes such a form as desire or imagination bestows upon it.

Every man might for the same reason in the multitudes that swarm about him, find some kindred mind with which he could unite in confidence and friendship; yet we see many straggling single about the world, unhappy for want of an associate, and pining with the necessity of confining their sentiments to their own bosoms.

This inconvenience arises in like manner from struggles of the will against the understanding. It is not often difficult to find a suitable companion, if every man would be content with such as he is qualified to please. But if vanity tempts him to forsake his rank, and post himself among those with whom no common interest or mutual pleasure can ever unite him, he must always live in a state of unsocial separation, without tenderness and without trust.

There are many natures which can never approach within a certain distance, and which when any irregular motive impels them towards contact, seem to start back from each other by some invincible repulsion. There are others which immediately cohere whenever they come into the reach of mutual attraction, and with very little formality of preparation mingle intimately as soon as they meet. Every man whom either business or curiosity has thrown at large into the world, will recollect many instances of fondness and dislike, which have forced themselves upon him without the intervention of his judgment; of dispositions, to court some and avoid others, when he could assign no reason for the preference, or none adequate to the violence of his passions; of influence that acted instantaneously upon his mind, and which no arguments or persuasions could ever overcome.

Among those with whom time and intercourse have made us familiar, we feel our affections divided in different proportions without much regard to moral or intellectual merit. Every man knows some whom he cannot induce himself to trust, though he has no reason to suspect that they would betray him; those to whom he cannot complain, though he never observed them to want compassion; those in whose presence he never can be gay, though excited by invitations to mirth and freedom; and those from whom he cannot be content to receive instruction, though they never insulted his ignorance by contempt or ostentation.

That much regard is to be had to those instincts of kindness and dislike, or that reason should blindly follow them, I am far from intending to inculcate: it is very certain that by indulgence we may give them strength which they have not from nature, and almost every example of ingratitude and treachery proves that by obeying them we may commit our happiness to those who are very unworthy of so great a trust. But it may deserve to be remarked, that since few contend much with their inclinations, it is generally vain to solicit the good will of those whom we perceive thus involuntarily alienated from us; neither knowledge nor virtue will reconcile antipathy, and though officiousness may for a time be admitted, and diligence applauded, they will at last be dismissed with coldness, or discouraged by neglect.

Some have indeed an occult power of stealing upon the affections, of exciting universal benevolence, and disposing every heart to fondness and friendship. But this is a felicity granted only to the favourites of nature. The greater part of mankind find a different reception from different dispositions; they sometimes obtain unexpected caresses from those whom they never flattered with uncommon regard, and sometimes exhaust all their arts of pleasing without effect. To these it is necessary to look round and attempt every breast in which they find virtue sufficient for the foundation of friendship; to enter into the crowd, and try whom chance will offer to their notice, till they fix on some temper congeneal to their own, as the magnet rolled in the dust collects the fragments of its kindred metal from a thousand particles of other substances.

Every man must have remarked the facility with which the kindness of others is sometimes gained by those to whom he never could have imparted his own. We are by our occupations, education and habits of life divided almost into different species, which regard one another for the most part with scorn and malignity. Each of these classes of the human race has desires, fears, and conversation, vexations and merriment peculiar to itself; cares which another cannot feel; pleasures which he cannot partake; and modes of expressing every sensation which he cannot understand. That frolick which shakes one man with laughter will convulse another with indignation; the strain of jocularity which in one place obtains treats and patronage, would in another be heard with indifference, and in a third with abhorrence.

To raise esteem we must benefit others, to procure love we must please them. *Aristotle* observes, that old men do not readily form friendships, because they are not easily susceptible of pleasure. He that can contribute to the hilarity of the vacant hour, or partake with equal gust the favourite amusement, he whose mind is employed on the same objects, and who therefore never harrasses the understanding with unaccustomed ideas, will be welcomed with ardour, and left with regret, unless he destroys those recommendations by faults with which peace and security cannot consist.

It were happy if, in forming friendships, virtue could concur with pleasure; but the greatest part of human gratifications ap-

proach so nearly to vice, that few who make the delight of others
their rule of conduct, can avoid disingenuous compliances; yet
certainly he that suffers himself to be driven or allured from
virtue, mistakes his own interest, since he gains succour by means,
for which his friend, if ever he becomes wise, must scorn him, and
for which at last he must scorn himself.

No. 161. TUESDAY, *October* 1, 1751.

Οἴη περ φύλλων γενεή, τοίη δὲ καὶ ἀνδρῶν.
HOMER [*Il*. VI. 146.]

Frail as the leaves that quiver on the sprays,
Like them man flourishes, like them decays.

MR. RAMBLER

SIR,
You have formerly observed that curiosity often terminates in bar-
ren knowledge, and that the mind is prompted to study and en-
quiry rather by the uneasiness of ignorance, than the hope of
profit. Nothing can be of less importance to any present interest
than the fortune of those who have been long lost in the grave,
and from whom nothing now can be hoped or feared. Yet to rouse
the zeal of a true antiquary little more is necessary than to men-
tion a name which mankind have conspired to forget; he will
make his way to remote scenes of action thro' obscurity and con-
tradiction, as *Tully* sought amidst brushes and brambles the tomb
of *Archimedes*.[1]

It is not easy to discover how it concerns him that gathers the
produce or receives the rent of an estate, to know through what
families the land has passed, who is registered in the conqueror's
survey as its possessor, how often it has been forfeited by treason,

[1] Cicero, *Tusculan Disputations*, V. 23.

or how often sold by prodigality. The power or wealth of the present inhabitants of a country cannot be much encreased by an enquiry after the names of those barbarians, who destroyed one another twenty centuries ago, in contests for the shelter of woods or convenience of pasturage. Yet we see that no man can be at rest in the enjoyment of a new purchase till he has learned the history of his grounds from the antient inhabitants of the parish, and that no nation omits to record the actions of their ancestors, however bloody, savage, and rapacious.

The same disposition, as different opportunities call it forth, discovers itself in great or little things. I have always thought it unworthy of a wise man to slumber in total inactivity only because he happens to have no employment equal to his ambition or genius; it is therefore my custom to apply my attention to the objects before me, and as I cannot think any place wholly unworthy of notice that affords a habitation to a man of letters, I have collected the history and antiquities of the several garrets in which I have resided:

> *Quantulacunque estis, vos ego magna voco.*[2]
> How small to others, but how great to me!

Many of these narratives my industry has been able to extend to a considerable length; but the woman with whom I now lodge has lived only eighteen months in the house, and can give no account of its ancient revolutions; the plaisterer, having, at her entrance, obliterated by his white-wash, all the smoky memorials which former tenants had left upon the cieling, and perhaps drawn the veil of oblivion over politicians, philosophers, and poet.

When I first cheapened my lodgings, the landlady told me, that she hoped I was not an author, for the lodgers on the first floor had stipulated that the upper rooms should not be occupied by a noisy trade. I very readily promised to give no disturbance to her family, and soon dispatched a bargain on the usual terms.

I had not slept many nights in my new apartment before I began to enquire after my predecessors, and found my landlady, whose

[2] Ovid, *Amores,* III. xv. 14.

imagination is filled chiefly with her own affairs, very ready to give me information.

Curiosity, like all other desires, produces pain as well as pleasure. Before she began her narrative, I had heated my head with expectations of adventures and discoveries, of elegance in disguise, and learning in distress; and was somewhat mortified when I heard, that the first tenant was a taylor, of whom nothing was remembered but that he complained of his room for want of light; and, after having lodged in it a month, and paid only a week's rent, pawned a piece of cloth which he was trusted to cut out, and was forced to make a precipitate retreat from this quarter of the town.

The next was a young woman newly arrived from the country, who lived for five weeks with great regularity, and became by frequent treats very much the favourite of the family, but at last received visits so frequently from a cousin in *Cheapside*, that she brought the reputation of the house into danger, and was therefore dismissed with good advice.

The room then stood empty for a fortnight; my landlady began to think that she had judged hardly, and often wished for such another lodger. At last an elderly man of a grave aspect, read the bill, and bargained for the room, at the very first price that was asked. He lived in close retirement, seldom went out till evening, and then returned early sometimes chearful, and at other times dejected. It was remarkable, that whatever he purchased, he never had small money in his pocket, and tho' cool and temperate on other occasions, was always vehement and stormy till he received his change. He paid his rent with great exactness, and seldom failed once a week to requite my landlady's civility with a supper. At last, such is the fate of human felicity, the house was alarm'd at midnight by the constable, who demanded to search the garrets. My landlady assuring him that he had mistaken the door, conducted him up stairs, where he found the tools of a coiner; but the tenant had crawled along the roof to an empty house, and escaped; much to the joy of my landlady, who declares him a very honest man, and wonders why any body should be hanged for making money when such numbers are in want of it. She however confesses that she shall for the future always question the character of those who take her garret without beating down the price.

The bill was then placed again in the window, and the poor woman was teazed for seven weeks by innumerable passengers, who obliged her to climb with them every hour up five stories, and then disliked the prospect, hated the noise of a publick street, thought the stairs narrow, objected to a low cieling, required the walls to be hung with fresher paper, asked questions about the neighbourhood, could not think of living so far from their acquaintance, wished the window had looked to the south rather than the west, told how the door and chimney might have been better disposed, bid her half the price that she asked, or promised to give her earnest the next day, and came no more.

At last, a short meagre man, in a tarnish'd waistcoat, desired to see the garret, and when he had stipulated for two long shelves and a larger table, hired it at a low rate. When the affair was completed, he looked round him with great satisfaction, and repeated some words which the woman did not understand. In two days he brought a great box of books, took possession of his room, and lived very inoffensively, except that he frequently disturbed the inhabitants of the next floor by unseasonable noises. He was generally in bed at noon, but from evening to midnight he sometimes talked aloud with great vehemence, sometimes stamped as in rage, sometimes threw down his poker, then clattered his chairs, then sat down in deep thought, and again burst out into loud vociferations; sometimes he would sigh as oppressed with misery, and sometimes shake with convulsive laughter. When he encountered any of the family he gave way or bowed, but rarely spoke, except that as he went up stairs he often repeated,

—Ὃς ὑπέρτατα δώματα ναίει.[3]
This habitant th' aerial regions boast.

hard words, to which his neighbors listened so often, that they learned them without understanding them. What was his employment she did not venture to ask him, but at last heard a printer's boy enquire for the author.

[3] Hesiod, *Works and Days,* I. 8.

My landlady was very often advised to beware of this strange man, who, tho' he was quiet for the present, might perhaps become outrageous in the hot months; but as she was punctually paid, she could not find any sufficient reason for dismissing him, till one night he convinced her by setting fire to his curtains, that it was not safe to have an author for her inmate.

She had then for six weeks a succession of tenants, who left the house on Saturday, and instead of paying their rent, stormed at their landlady. At last she took in two sisters, one of whom had spent her little fortune in procuring remedies for a lingering disease, and was now supported and attended by the other: she climbed with difficulty to the apartment, where she languished eight weeks, without impatience or lamentation, except for the expence and fatigue which her sister suffered, and then calmly and contentedly expired. The sister followed her to the grave, paid the few debts which they had contracted, wiped away the tears of useless sorrow, and returning to the business of common life, resigned to me the vacant habitation.

Such, Mr. *Rambler,* are the changes which have happened in the narrow space where my present fortune has fixed my residence. So true is it that amusement and instruction are always at hand for those who have skill and willingness to find them; and so just is the observation of *Juvenal,*[4] that a single house will shew whatever is done or suffered in the world.

I am, Sir, &c.

No. 183. TUESDAY, *December* 17, 1751.

Nulla fides regni sociis, omnisque potestas
Impatiens consortis erit.

LUCAN [*Phar.* I. 92.]

No faith of partnership dominion owns;
Still discord hovers o'er divided thrones.

[4] *Satires,* XIII. 159–160.

The hostility perpetually exercised between one man and another, is caused by the desire of many for that which only few can possess. Every man would be rich, powerful, and famous; yet fame, power, and riches, are only the names of relative conditions, which imply the obscurity, dependence, and poverty of greater numbers.

This universal and incessant competition, produces injury and malice by two motives, interest, and envy; the prospect of adding to our possessions what we can take from others, and the hope of alleviating the sense of our disparity by lessening others, though we gain nothing to ourselves.

Of these two malignant and destructive powers, it seems probable at the first view, that interest has the strongest and most extensive influence. It is easy to conceive that opportunities to seize what has been long wanted, may excite desires almost irresistible; but surely, the same eagerness cannot be kindled by an accidental power of destroying that which gives happiness to another. It must be more natural to rob for gain, than to ravage only for mischief.

Yet I am inclined to believe, that the great law of mutual benevolence is oftener violated by envy than by interest, and that most of the misery which the defamation of blameless actions, or the obstruction of honest endeavours brings upon the world, is inflicted by men that propose no advantage to themselves but the satisfaction of poisoning the banquet which they cannot taste, and blasting the harvest which they have no right to reap.

Interest can diffuse itself but to a narrow compass. The number is never large of those who can hope to fill the posts of degraded power, catch the fragments of shattered fortune, or succeed to the honours of depreciated beauty. But the empire of envy has no limits, as it requires to its influence very little help from external circumstances. Envy may always be produced by idleness and pride, and in what place will not they be found?

Interest requires some qualities not universally bestowed. The ruin of another will produce no profit to him, who has not discernment to mark his advantage, courage to seize, and activity to pursue it; but the cold malignity of envy may be exerted in a torpid and quiescent state, amidst the gloom of stupidity, in the coverts of cowardice. He that falls by the attacks of interest, is torn by hungry tigers; he may discover and resist his enemies. He that perishes in the ambushes of envy, is destroyed by unknown and invisible assailants, and dies like a man suffocated by a poisonous vapour, without knowledge of his danger, or possibility of contest.

Interest is seldom pursued but at some hazard. He that hopes to gain much, has commonly something to lose, and when he ventures to attack superiority, if he fails to conquer, is irrecoverably crushed. But envy may act without expence, or danger. To spread suspicion, to invent calumnies, to propagate scandal, requires neither labour nor courage. It is easy for the author of a lye, however malignant, to escape detection, and infamy needs very little industry to assist its circulation.

Envy is almost the only vice which is praticable at all times, and in every place; the only passion which can never lie quiet for want of irritation: its effects therefore are every where discoverable, and its attempts always to be dreaded.

It is impossible to mention a name which any advantageous distinction has made eminent, but some latent animosity will burst out. The wealthy trader, however he may abstract himself from publick affairs, will never want those who hint, with *Shylock,* that ships are but boards. The beauty, adorned only with the unambitious graces of innocence and modesty, provokes, whenever she appears, a thousand murmurs of detraction. The genius, even when he endeavours only to entertain or instruct, yet suffers persecution from innumerable criticks, whose acrimony is excited merely by the pain of seeing others pleased, and of hearing applauses which another enjoys.

The frequency of envy makes it so familiar, that it escapes our notice; nor do we often reflect upon its turpitude or malignity, till we happen to feel its influence. When he that has given no provocation to malice, but by attempting to excel, finds himself pursued by multitudes whom he never saw with all the implacability of personal resentment; when he perceives clamour and malice let loose upon him as a publick enemy, and incited by every stratagem of defamation; when he hears the misfortunes of his family, or the follies of his youth exposed to the world; and every failure of conduct, or defect of nature aggravated and ridiculed; he then learns to abhor those artifices at which he only laughed before, and discovers how much the happiness of life would be advanced by the eradication of envy from the human heart.

Envy is, indeed, a stubborn weed of the mind, and seldom yields to the culture of philosophy. There are, however, considerations, which if carefully implanted and diligently propagated, might in time overpower and repress it, since no one can nurse it for the sake of pleasure, as its effects are only shame, anguish, and perturbation.

It is above all other vices inconsistent with the character of a social being, because it sacrifices truth and kindness to very weak temptations. He that plunders a wealthy neighbour, gains as much as he takes away, and may improve his own condition in the same proportion as he impairs another's; but he that blasts a flourishing reputation, must be content with a small dividend of additional fame, so small as can afford very little consolation to balance the guilt by which it is obtained.

I have hitherto avoided that dangerous and empirical morality, which cures one vice by means of another. But envy is so base and detestable, so vile in its original, and so pernicious in its effects, that the predominance of almost any other quality is to be preferred. It is one of those lawless enemies of society, against which poisoned arrows may honestly be used. Let it, therefore, be constantly remembered, that whoever envies another, confesses his superiority, and let those be reformed by their pride who have lost their virtue.

It is no slight aggravation of the injuries which envy incites, that they are committed against those who have given no intentional provocation; and that the sufferer is often marked out for ruin, not because he has failed in any duty, but because he has dared to do more than was required.

Almost every other crime is practised by the help of some quality which might have produced esteem or love, if it had been well employed; but envy is mere unmixed and genuine evil; it pursues a hateful end by despicable means, and desires not so much its own happiness as another's misery. To avoid depravity like this, it is not necessary that any one should aspire to heroism or sanctity, but only, that he should resolve not to quit the rank which nature assigns him, and wish to maintain the dignity of a human being.

No. 184. SATURDAY, *December 21, 1751.*

Permittes ipsis expendere numinibus, quid
Conveniat nobis, rebusque sit utile nostris.

Juv. [*Sat.* X. 347.]

Intrust thy fortune to the pow'rs above:
Leave them to manage for thee, and to grant
What their unerring wisdom sees thee want.

DRYDEN.

As every scheme of life, so every form of writing has its advantages and inconveniencies, though not mingled in the same proportions. The writer of essays, escapes many embarrassments to which a large work would have exposed him; he seldom harrasses his reason with long trains of consequence, dims his eyes with the perusal of antiquated volumes, or burthens his memory with great accumulations of preparatory knowledge. A careless glance upon a favourite author, or transient survey of the varieties of life, is sufficient to supply the first hint or seminal idea, which enlarged by the gradual accretion of matter stored in the mind, is by the warmth of fancy easily expanded into flowers, and sometimes ripened into fruit.

The most frequent difficulty, by which the authors of these petty compositions are distressed, arises from the perpetual demand of novelty and change. The compiler of a system of science lays his invention at rest, and employs only his judgment, the faculty exerted with least fatigue. Even the relator of feigned adventures, when once the principal characters are established, and the great events regularly connected, finds incidents and episodes crouding upon his mind; every change opens new views, and the latter part of the story grows without labour out of the former. But he that attempts to entertain his reader with unconnected pieces, finds the irksomeness of his task rather encreased than lessened by every production. The day calls afresh upon him for a new topick, and he is again obliged to choose, without any principle to regulate his choice.

It is indeed true, that there is seldom any necessity of looking far, or enquiring long for a proper subject. Every diversity of art or nature, every public blessing or calamity, every domestick pain or gratification, every sally of caprice, blunder of absurdity, or stratagem of affectation may supply matter to him whose only rule is to avoid uniformity. But it often happens, that the judgment is distracted with boundless multiplicity, the imagination ranges from one design to another, and the hours pass imperceptibly away till the composition can be no longer delayed, and necessity enforces the use of those thoughts which then happen to be at hand. The mind rejoicing at deliverance on any terms from perplexity and suspense, applies herself vigorously to the work before her, collects embellishments and illustrations, and sometimes finishes with great elegance and happiness what in a state of ease and leisure she never had begun.

It is not commonly observed, how much, even of actions considered as particularly subject to choice, is to be attributed to accident, or some cause out of our own power, by whatever name it be distinguished. To close tedious deliberations with hasty resolves, and after long consultations with reason to refer the question to caprice, is by no means peculiar to the essayist. Let him that peruses this paper, review the series of his life, and enquire how he was placed in his present condition. He will find that of the good or ill which he has experienced, a great part came unexpected, without any visible gradations of approach; that every

event has been influenced by causes acting without his interven-
tion; and that whenever he pretended to the prerogative of fore-
sight, he was mortified with new conviction of the shortness of his
views.

The busy, the ambitious, the inconstant, and the adventurous,
may be said to throw themselves by design into the arms of for-
tune, and voluntarily to quit the power of governing themselves;
they engage in a course of life in which little can be ascertained
by previous measures; nor is it any wonder that their time is past
between elation and despondency, hope and disappointment.

Some there are who appear to walk the road of life with more
circumspection, and make no step till they think themselves secure
from the hazard of a precipice; when neither pleasure nor profit
can tempt them from the beaten path; who refuse to climb lest
they should fall, or to run lest they should stumble, and move
slowly forward without any compliance with those passions by
which the heady and vehement are seduced and betrayed.

Yet even the timorous prudence of this judicious class is far
from exempting them from the dominion of chance, a subtle and
insidious power, who will intrude upon privacy and embarrass
caution. No course of life is so prescribed and limited, but that
many actions must result from arbitrary election. Every one must
form the general plan of his conduct by his own reflections; he
must resolve whether he will endeavour at riches or at content;
whether he will exercise private or publick virtues; whether he
will labour for the general benefit of mankind, or contract his
beneficence to his family and dependants.

This question has long exercised the schools of philosophy, but
remains yet undecided; and what hope is there that a young man,
unacquainted with the arguments on either side, should determine
his own destiny otherwise than by chance?

When chance has given him a partner of his bed, whom he
prefers to all other women, without any proof of superior desert,
chance must again direct him in the education of his children;
for, who was ever able to convince himself by arguments, that
he had chosen for his son that mode of instruction to which his

understanding was best adapted, or by which he would most easily be made wise or virtuous?

Whoever shall enquire by what motives he was determined on these important occasions, will find them such, as his pride will scarcely suffer him to confess; some sudden ardour of desire, some uncertain glimpse of advantage, some petty competition, some inaccurate conclusion, or some example implicitly reverenced. Such are often the first causes of our resolves; for it is necessary to act, but impossible to know the consequences of action, or to discuss all the reasons which offer themselves on every part to inquisitiveness and solicitude.

Since life itself is uncertain, nothing which has life for its basis, can boast much stability. Yet this is but a small part of our perplexity. We set out on a tempestuous sea, in quest of some port, where we expect to find rest, but where we are not sure of admission; we are not only in danger of sinking in the way, but of being misled by meteors mistaken for stars, of being driven from our course by the changes of the wind, and of losing it by unskilful steerage; yet it sometimes happens, that cross winds blow us to a safer coast, that meteors draw us aside from whirlpools, and that negligence or error contributes to our escape from mischiefs to which a direct course would have exposed us. Of those that by precipitate conclusions, involve themselves in calamities without guilt, very few, however they may reproach themselves, can be certain that other measures would have been more successful.

In this state of universal uncertainty, where a thousand dangers hover about us, and none can tell whether the good that he persues is not evil in disguise, or whether the next step will lead him to safety or destruction, nothing can afford any rational tranquillity, but the conviction that, however we amuse ourselves with unideal sounds, nothing in reality is governed by chance, but that the universe is under the perpetual superintendence of him who created it; that our being is in the hands of omnipotent goodness, by whom what appears casual to us is directed for ends ultimately kind and merciful; and that nothing can finally hurt him who debars not himself from the divine favour.

No. 185. Tuesday, *December* 24, 1751.

At vindicta bonum vita jucundius ipsa,
Nempe hoc indocti. ————————
Chrysippus *non dicet idem, nec mite* Thaletis
Ingenium, dulcique senex vicinus Hymetto,
Qui partem acceptæ sæva inter vincla Cicutæ
Accusatori nollet dare.————*Quippe minuti*
Semper, et infirmi est Animi, exiguique Voluptas
Ultio.

Juv. [Sat. XIII. 180–191.]

But O! revenge is sweet.
Thus think the crowd; who, eager to engage,
Take quickly fire, and kindle into rage.
Not so mild *Thales*, nor *Chrysippus* thought,
Nor that good man, who drank the pois'nous draught
With mind serene; and could not wish to see
His vile accuser drink as deep as he:
Exalted *Socrates!* divinely brave!
Injur'd he fell, and dying he forgave,
Too noble for revenge; which still we find
The weakest frailty of a feeble mind.

Dryden.

No vitious dispositions of the mind more obstinately resist both the counsels of philosophy and the injunctions of religion, than those which are complicated with an opinion of dignity; and which we cannot dismiss without leaving in the hands of opposition some advantage iniquitously obtained, or suffering from our own prejudices some imputation of pusillanimity.

For this reason scarcely any law of our Redeemer is more openly transgressed, or more industriously evaded, than that by which he commands his followers to forgive injuries, and prohibits, under the sanction of eternal misery, the gratification of the desire which every man feels to return pain upon him that inflicts it. Many who could have conquered their anger, are unable to combat pride, and pursue offences to extremity of vengeance, lest they should be insulted by the triumph of an enemy.

But certainly no precept could better become him, at whose birth *peace* was proclaimed *to the earth*. For, what would so soon destroy all the order of society, and deform life with violence and ravage, as a permission to every one to judge his own cause, and to apportion his own recompence for imagined injuries?

It is difficult for a man of the strictest justice not to favour himself too much, in the calmest moments of solitary meditation. Every one wishes for the distinctions for which thousands are wishing at the same time, in their own opinion, with better claims. He that, when his reason operates in its full force, can thus, by the mere prevalence of self-love, prefer himself to his fellow-beings, is very unlikely to judge equitably when his passions are agitated by a sense of wrong, and his attention wholly engrossed by pain, interest, or danger. Whoever arrogates to himself the right of vengeance, shows how little he is qualified to decide his own claims, since he certainly demands what he would think unfit to be granted to another.

Nothing is more apparent than that, however injured, or however provoked, some must at last be contented to forgive. For it can never be hoped, that he who first commits an injury, will contentedly acquiesce in the penalty required: the same haughtiness of contempt, or vehemence of desire, that prompt the act of injustice, will more strongly incite its justification; and resentment can never so exactly balance the punishment with the fault, but there will remain an overplus of vengeance which even he who condemns his first action will think himself entitled to retaliate. What then can ensue but a continual exacerbation of hatred, an unextinguishable feud, an incessant reciprocation of mischief, a mutual vigilance to entrap, and eagerness to destroy?

Since then the imaginary right of vengeance must be at last remitted, because it is impossible to live in perpetual hostility, and equally impossible that of two enemies, either should first think himself obliged by justice to submission, it is surely eligible to forgive early. Every passion is more easily subdued before it has been long accustomed to possession of the heart; every idea is obliterated with less difficulty, as it has been more slightly impressed, and less frequently renewed. He who has often brooded over his wrongs, pleased himself with schemes of malignity, and glutted his pride with the fancied supplications of humbled enmity, will not easily open his bosom to amity and reconciliation, or indulge the gentle sentiments of benevolence and peace.

It is easiest to forgive, while there is yet little to be forgiven. A single injury may be soon dismissed from the memory; but a long succession of ill offices by degrees associates itself with every idea, a long contest involves so many circumstances, that every place and action will recal it to the mind, and fresh remembrance of vexation must still enkindle rage, and irritate revenge.

A wise man will make haste to forgive, because he knows the true value of time, and will not suffer it to pass away in unnecessary pain. He that willingly suffers the corrosions of inveterate hatred, and gives up his days and nights to the gloom of malice, and perturbations of stratagem, cannot surely be said to consult his ease. Resentment is an union of sorrow with malignity, a combination of a passion which all endeavour to avoid, with a passion which all concur to detest. The man who retires to meditate mischief, and to exasperate his own rage; whose thoughts are employed only on means of distress and contrivances of ruin; whose mind never pauses from the remembrance of his own sufferings, but to indulge some hope of enjoying the calamities of another, may justly be numbered among the most miserable of human beings, among those who are guilty without reward, who have neither the gladness of prosperity, nor the calm of innocence.

Whoever considers the weakness both of himself and others, will not long want persuasives to forgiveness. We know not to what degree of malignity any injury is to be imputed; or how much its guilt, if we were to inspect the mind of him that committed it, would be extenuated by mistake, precipitance, or negligence; we cannot be certain how much more we feel than was intended to be inflicted, or how much we encrease the mischief to ourselves by voluntary aggravations. We may charge to design the effects of accident; we may think the blow violent only because we have made ourselves delicate and tender; we are on every side in danger of error and of guilt, which we are certain to avoid only by speedy forgiveness.

From this pacifick and harmless temper, thus propitious to others and ourselves, to domestick tranquility and to social happiness, no man is with-held but by pride, by the fear of being insulted by his adversary or despised by the world.

It may be laid down as an unfailing and universal axiom, that, "all pride is abject and mean." It is always an ignorant, lazy, or cowardly acquiescence in a false appearance of excellence, and proceeds not from consciousness of our attainments, but insensibility of our wants.

Nothing can be great which is not right. Nothing which reason condemns can be suitable to the dignity of the human mind. To be driven by external motives from the path which our own heart approves, to give way to any thing but conviction, to suffer the opinion of others to rule our choice, or overpower our resolves, is to submit tamely to the lowest and most ignominious slavery, and to resign the right of directing our own lives.

The utmost excellence at which humanity can arrive, is a constant and determinate pursuit of virtue, without regard to present dangers or advantage; a continual reference of every action to the divine will; an habitual appeal to everlasting justice; and an unvaried elevation of the intellectual eye to the reward which perseverance only can obtain. But that pride which many who presume to boast of generous sentiments, allow to regulate their measures, has nothing nobler in view than the approbation of men, of beings whose superiority we are under no obligation to acknowledge, and who, when we have courted them with the utmost assiduity, can confer no valuable or permanent reward; of beings who ignorantly judge of what they do not understand, or partially determine what they never have examined; and whose sentence is therefore of no weight till it has received the ratification of our own conscience.

He that can descend to bribe suffrages like these, at the price of his innocence; he that can suffer the delight of such acclamations to with-hold his attention from the commands of the universal sovereign, has little reason to congratulate himself upon the greatness of his mind; whenever he awakes to seriousness and reflection, he must become despicable in his own eyes, and shrink with shame from the remembrance of his cowardice and folly.

Of him that hopes to be forgiven it is indispensibly required, that he forgive. It is therefore superfluous to urge any other motive. On this great duty eternity is suspended, and to him that refuses to practise it, the throne of mercy is inaccessible, and the SAVIOUR of the world has been born in vain.

No. 200. SATURDAY, *February* 15, 1752.

Nemo petit modicis quæ mittebantur amicis
A Seneca, quæ Piso bonus, quæ Cotta solebat
Largiri, nempe et titulis et fascibus olim
Major habebatur donandi gloria; solum
Poscimus ut cœnes civiliter; hoc face, et esto
Esto, ut nunc multi, dives tibi, pauper amicis.

JUV. [*Sat.* V. 108.]

No man expects (for who so much a sot,
Who has the times he lives in so forgot?)
What *Seneca*, what *Piso* us'd to send,
To raise, or to support a sinking friend.
Those godlike men, to wanting virtue kind,
Bounty well-plac'd, preferr'd, and well design'd,
To all their titles, all that height of pow'r,
Which turns the brains of fools, and fools alone adore.
When your poor client is condemn'd t' attend,
'Tis all we ask, receive him as a friend:
Descend to this, and then we ask no more;
Rich to yourself, to all beside be poor.

BOWLES.

To the RAMBLER

Mr. RAMBLER,
Such is the tenderness or infirmity of many minds, that when any affliction oppresses them, they have immediate recourse to lamentation and complaint, which, though it can only be allowed reasonable when evils admit of remedy, and then only when addressed to those from whom the remedy is expected, yet seems even in hopeless and incurable distresses to be natural, since those by

whom it is not indulged, imagine that they give a proof of extraordinary fortitude by suppressing it.

I am one of those who, with the *Sancho* of *Cervantes*, leave to higher characters the merit of suffering in silence, and give vent without scruple to any sorrow that swells in my heart. It is therefore to me a severe aggravation of a calamity, when it is such as in the common opinion will not justify the acerbity of exclamation, or support the solemnity of vocal grief. Yet many pains are incident to a man of delicacy, which the unfeeling world cannot be persuaded to pity, and which, when they are separated from their peculiar and personal circumstances, will never be considered as important enough to claim attention, or deserve redress.

Of this kind will appear to gross and vulgar apprehensions, the miseries which I endured in a morning visit to *Prospero*, a man lately raised to wealth by a lucky project, and too much intoxicated by sudden elevation, or too little polished by thought and conversation, to enjoy his present fortune with elegance and decency.

We set out in the world together; and for a long time mutually assisted each other in our exigencies, as either happened to have money or influence beyond his immediate necessities. You know that nothing generally endears men so much as participation of dangers and misfortunes; I therefore always considered *Prospero* as united with me in the strongest league of kindness, and imagined that our friendship was only to be broken by the hand of death. I felt at his sudden shoot of success an honest and disinterested joy; but as I want no part of his superfluities, am not willing to descend from that equality in which we hitherto have lived.

Our intimacy was regarded by me as a dispensation from ceremonial visits; and it was so long before I saw him at his new house, that he gently complained of my neglect, and obliged me to come on a day appointed. I kept my promise, but found that the impatience of my friend arose not from any desire to communicate his happiness, but to enjoy his superiority.

When I told my name at the door, the footman went to see if his master was at home, and, by the tardiness of his return, gave me reason to suspect that time was taken to deliberate. He then informed me, that *Prospero* desired my company, and showed the staircase carefully secured by mats from the pollution of my feet. The best apartments were ostentatiously set open, that I might have a distant view of the magnificence which I was not permitted to approach; and my old friend receiving me with all the insolence of condescension at the stop of the stairs, conducted me to a back room, where he told me he always breakfasted when he had not great company.

On the floor where we sat, lay a carpet covered with a cloth, of which *Prospero* ordered his servant to lift up a corner, that I might contemplate the brightness of the colours, and the elegance of the texture, and asked me whether I had ever seen any thing so fine before? I did not gratify his folly with any outcries of admiration, but coldly bade[1] the footman let down the cloth.

We then sat down, and I began to hope that pride was glutted with persecution, when *Prospero* desired that I would give the servant leave to adjust the cover of my chair, which was slipt a little aside to show the damask; he informed me that he had bespoke ordinary chairs for common use, but had been disappointed by his tradesman. I put the chair aside with my foot, and drew another so hastily, that I was entreated not to rumple the carpet.

Breakfast was at last set, and as I was not willing to indulge the peevishness that began to seize me, I commended the tea; *Prospero* then told me, that another time I should taste his finest sor[t], but that he had only a very small quantity rema[i]ning, and reserved it for those whom he thought himself obliged to treat with particular respect.

While we were conversing upon such subjects as imagination happened to suggest, he frequently digressed into directions to the servant that waited, or made a slight enquiry after the jeweller or silversmith; and once as I was pursuing an argument with some degree of earnestness, he started from his posture of attention, and ordered, that if lord *Lofty* called on him that morning, he should be shewn into the best parlour.

[1] 1756: bad.

My patience was not yet wholly subdued. I was willing to promote his satisfaction, and therefore observed, that the figures on the china were eminently pretty. *Prospero* had now an opportunity of calling for his *Dresden* china, which, says he, I always associate with my chased tea-kettle. The cups were brought; I once resolved not to have looked upon them, but my curiosity prevailed. When I had examined them a little, *Prospero* desired me to set them down, for they who were accustomed only to common dishes, seldom handled china with much care. You will, I hope, commend my philosophy, when I tell you that I did not dash his baubles to the ground.

He was now so much elevated with his own greatness, that he thought some humility necessary to avert the glance of envy, and therefore told me with an air of soft composure, that I was not to estimate life by external appearance, that all these shineing acquisitions had added little to his happiness, that he still remembered with pleasure the days in which he and I were upon the level, and had often, in the moment of reflection, been doubtful, whether he should lose much by changing his condition for mine.

I began now to be afraid lest his pride should, by silence and submission, be emboldened to insults that could not easily be borne, and, therefore, cooly considered, how I should repress it without such bitterness of reproof as I was yet unwilling to use. But he interrupted my meditation, by asking leave to be dressed, and told me, that he had promised to attend some ladies in the park, and, if I was going the same way, would take me in his chariot. I had no inclination to any other favours, and, therefore, left him without any intention of seeing him again, unless some misfortune should restore his understanding.

I *am,* &c.

ASPER.

Though I am not wholly insensible of the provocations which my correspondent has received, I cannot altogether commend the keenness of his resentment, nor encourage him to persist in his resolution of breaking off all commerce with his old acquaintance. One of the golden precepts of *Pythagoras* directs that *a friend should not be hated for little faults*,[2] and surely, he, upon whom nothing worse can be charged, than that he mats his stairs, and covers his carpet, and sets out his finery to show before those whom he does not admit to use it, has yet committed nothing that should exclude him from common degrees of kindness. Such improprieties often proceed rather from stupidity than malice. Those who thus shine only to dazzle, are influenced merely by custom and example, and neither examine, nor are qualified to examine, the motives of their own practice, or to state the nice limits between elegance and ostentation. They are often innocent of the pain which their vanity produces, and insult others when they have no worse purpose than to please themselves.

He that too much refines his delicacy will always endanger his quiet. Of those with whom nature and virtue oblige us to converse, some are ignorant of the arts of pleasing, and offend when they design to caress; some are negligent, and gratify themselves without regard to the quiet of another; some, perhaps, are malicious, and feel no greater satisfaction in prosperity, than that of raising envy and trampling inferiority. But whatever be the motive of insult, it is always best to overlook it, for folly scarcely can deserve resentment, and malice is punished by neglect.[3]

No. 204. SATURDAY, *February* 29, 1752.

Nemo tam divos habuit faventes,
Crastinum ut possit sibi polliceri.
SENECA. [*Thyestes*, Act III, Chorus.]

[2] *Fragmenta Philosophorum Graecorum*, ed. Mullach, 1860–1881, I, 428.

[3] Garrick's little vanities are recognized by all in the character of Prospero. Mr. Boswell informs us, that he never forgave its pointed satire. On the same authority we are assured, that though Johnson so dearly loved to ridicule his pupil, yet he so habitually considered him as his own property, that he would permit no one beside to hold up his weaknesses to derision. [1824 ed.]

Of heav'n's protection who can be
So confident to utter this?—
To-morrow I will spend in bliss.

F. Lewis.

Seged, lord of *Ethiopia,* to the inhabitants of the world: To the
sons of *presumption,* humility, and fear; and to the daughters of
sorrow, content and acquiescence.

Thus, in the twenty-seventh year of his reign, spoke *Seged,*
the monarch of forty nations, the distributer of the waters of the
Nile. "At length, *Seged,* thy toils are at an end, thou hast recon-
ciled disaffection, thou hast suppressed rebellion, thou hast pacified
the jealousies of thy courtiers, thou hast[1] chased war from thy
confines, and erected fortresses in the lands of thy enemies. All
who have offended thee, tremble in thy presence, and wherever
thy voice is heard, it is obeyed. Thy throne is surrounded by
armies, numerous as the locusts of the summer, and resistless as
the blasts of pestilence. Thy magazines are stored with ammuni-
tion, thy treasuries overflow with the tribute of conquered king-
doms. Plenty waves upon thy fields, and opulence glitters in thy
cities. Thy nod is as the earthquake that shakes the mountains, and
thy smile as the dawn of the vernal day. In thy hand is the strength
of thousands, and thy health is the health of millions. Thy palace
is gladdened by the song of praise, and thy path perfumed by
the breath of benediction. Thy subjects gaze upon thy greatness,
and think of danger or misery no more. Why, *Seged,* wilt not thou
partake the blessings thou bestowest? Why shouldst thou only
forbear to rejoice in this general felicity? Why should thy face
be clouded with anxiety, when the meanest of those who call thee
sovereign, gives the day to festivity, and the night to peace. At
length, *Seged,* reflect and be wise. What is the gift of conquest but
safety, why are riches collected but to purchase happiness?"

Seged then ordered the house of pleasure, built in an island of
the lake *Dambea,* to be prepared for his reception. "I will retire,
says he, for ten days from tumult and care, from counsels and
decrees. Long quiet is not the lot of the governors of nations, but a

[1] 1756: had.

cessation of ten days cannot be denied me. This short interval of happiness may surely be secured from the interruption of fear or perplexity, sorrow or disappointment. I will exclude all trouble from my abode, and remove from my thoughts whatever may confuse the harmony of the concert, or abate the sweetness of the banquet. I will fill the whole capacity of my soul with enjoyment, and try what it is to live without a wish unsatisfied."

In a few days the orders were performed, and *Seged* hasted to the palace of *Dambea,* which stood in an island cultivated only for pleasure, planted with every flower that spreads its colours to the sun, and every shrub that sheds fragrance in the air. In one part of this extensive garden, were open walks for excursions in the morning; in another, thick groves, and silent arbours, and bubbling fountains for repose at noon. All that could solace the sense, or flatter the fancy, all that industry could extort from nature, or wealth furnish to art, all that conquest could seize, or beneficence attract, was collected together, and every perception of delight was excited and gratified.

Into this delicious region *Seged* summoned all the persons of his court, who seemed eminently qualified to receive, or communicate pleasure. His call was readily obeyed; the young, the fair, the vivacious, and the witty, were all in haste to be sated with felicity. They sailed jocund over the lake, which seemed to smooth its surface before them: Their passage was cheered with musick, and their hearts dilated with expectation.

Seged, landing here with his band of pleasure, determined from that hour to break off all acquaintance with discontent, to give his heart for ten days to ease and jollity, and then fall back to the common state of man, and suffer his life to be diversified, as before, with joy and sorrow.

He immediately entered his chamber, to consider where he should begin his circle of happiness. He had all the artists of delight before him, but knew not whom to call, since he could not enjoy one, but by delaying the performance of another. He chose and rejected, he resolved and changed his resolution, till his faculties were harrassed, and his thoughts confused; then returned to the apartment where his presence was expected, with languid eyes and clouded countenance, and spread the infection of uneasiness over the whole assembly. He observed their depression, and was offended, for he found his vexation encreased by those whom he expected to dissipate and relieve it. He retired again to his private chamber, and sought for consolation in his own mind; one thought flowed in upon another; a long succession of images seized his attention; the moments crept imperceptibly away through the gloom of pensiveness, till having recovered his tranquillity, he lifted his head, and saw the lake brightened by the setting sun. "Such," said *Seged*, sighing, "is the longest day of human existence: Before we have learned to use it, we find it at an end."

The regret which he felt for the loss of so great a part of his first day, took from him all disposition to enjoy the evening; and, after having endeavoured, for the sake of his attendants, to force an air of gaiety, and excite that mirth which he could not share, he resolved to refer his hopes to the next morning, and lay down to partake with the slaves of labour and poverty the blessing of sleep.

He rose early the second morning, and resolved now to be happy. He therefore fixed upon the gate of the palace an edict, importing, that whoever, during nine days, should appear in the presence of the king with dejected countenance, or utter any expression of discontent or sorrow, should be driven for ever from the palace of *Dambea*.

This edict was immediately made known in every chamber of the court, and bower of the gardens. Mirth was frighted away, and they who were before dancing in the lawns, or singing in the shades, were at once engaged in the care of regulating their looks, that *Seged* might find his will punctually obeyed, and see none among them liable to banishment.

Seged now met every face settled in a smile; but a smile that betrayed solicitude, timidity, and constraint. He accosted his favourites with familiarity and softness; but they durst not speak without premeditation, lest they should be convicted of discontent or sorrow. He proposed diversions, to which no objection was made, because objection would have implied uneasiness; but they were regarded with indifference by the courtiers, who had no other desire than to signalize themselves by clamorous exultation. He offered various topics of conversation, but obtained only forced jests, and laborious laughter, and after many attempts to animate his train to confidence and alacrity, was obliged to confess to himself the impotence of command, and resign another day to grief and disappointment.

He at last relieved his companions from their terrors, and shut himself up in his chamber to ascertain, by different measures, the felicity of the succeeding days. At length, he threw himself on the bed and closed his eyes, but imagined, in his sleep, that his palace and gardens were overwhelmed by an inundation, and waked with all the terrors of a man struggling in the water. He composed himself again to rest, but was affrighted by an imaginary irruption into his kingdom, and striving, as is usual in dreams, without ability to move, fancied himself betrayed to his enemies, and again started up with horror and indignation.

It was now day, and fear was so strongly impressed on his mind, that he could sleep no more. He rose, but his thoughts were filled with the deluge and invasion, nor was he able to disengage his attention, or mingle with vacancy and ease in any amusement. At length his perturbation gave way to reason, and he resolved no longer to be harrassed by visionary miseries; but before this resolution could be completed half the day had elapsed: He felt a new conviction of the uncertainty of human schemes, and could not forbear to bewail the weakness of that being, whose quiet was to be interrupted by vapours of the fancy. Having been first disturbed by a dream, he afterwards grieved that a dream could disturb him. He at last discovered, that his terrors and grief were equally vain, and, that to lose the present in lamenting the past, was voluntarily to protract a melancholy vision. The third day was now declining, and *Seged* again resolved to be happy on the morrow.

No. 205. Tuesday, *March* 3, 1752.

> *Volat ambiguis*
> *Mobilis alis hora. nec ulli*
> *Præstat velox Fortuna fidem.*
>
>   Seneca [*Hippol.* 1141.]

On fickle wings the minutes haste,
And fortune's favours never last.

                                           F. Lewis.

On the fourth morning *Seged* rose early, refreshed with sleep, vigorous with health, and eager with expectation. He entered the garden, attended by the princes and ladies of his court, and seeing nothing about him but airy cheerfulness, began to say to his heart, "This day shall be a day of pleasure." The sun played upon the water, the birds warbled in the groves, and the gales quivered among the branches. He roved from walk to walk as chance directed him, and sometimes listened to the songs, sometimes mingled with the dancers, sometimes let loose his imagination in flights of merriment; and sometimes uttered grave reflections, and sententious maxims, and feasted on the admiration with which they were received.

Thus the day rolled on, without any accident of vexation, or intrusion of melancholy thoughts. All that beheld him caught gladness from his looks, and the sight of happiness conferred by himself filled his heart with satisfaction: But having passed three hours in this harmless luxury, he was alarmed on a sudden by an universal scream among the women, and turning back, saw the whole assembly flying in confusion. A young crocodile had risen out of the lake, and was ranging the garden in wantonness or hunger. *Seged* beheld him with indignation, as a disturber of his felicity, and chased him back into the lake, but could not persuade his retinue to stay, or free their hearts from the terror which had seized upon them. The princesses inclosed themselves in the palace, and could yet scarcely believe themselves in safety. Every attention was fixed upon the late danger and escape, and no mind was any longer at leisure for gay sallies or careless prattle.

Seged had now no other employment than to contemplate the innumerable casualties which lie in ambush on every side to intercept the happiness of man, and break in upon the hour of delight and tranquillity. He had, however, the consolation of thinking, that he had not been now disappointed by his own fault, and that the accident which had blasted the hopes of the day, might easily be prevented by future caution.

That he might provide for the pleasure of the next morning, he resolved to repeal his penal edict, since he had already found that discontent and melancholy were not to be frighted away by the threats of authority, and that pleasure would only reside where she was exempted from controul. He therefore invited all the companions of his retreat to unbounded pleasantry, by proposing prizes for those who should, on the following day, distinguish themselves by any festive performances; the tables of the antechamber were covered with gold and pearls, and robes and garlands, decreed the rewards of those who could refine elegance or heighten pleasure.

At this display of riches every eye immediately sparkled, and every tongue was busied in celebrating the bounty and magnificence of the emperor. But when *Seged* entered in hopes of uncommon entertainment from universal emulation, he found that any passion too strongly agitated, puts an end to that tranquillity which is necessary to mirth, and that the mind, that is to be moved by the gentle ventilations of gaiety, must be first smoothed by a total calm. Whatever we ardently wish to gain, we must in the same degree be afraid to lose, and fear and pleasure cannot dwell together.

All was now care and solicitude. Nothing was done or spoken, but with so visible an endeavour at perfection, as always failed to delight, though it sometimes forced admiration: And *Seged* could not but observe with sorrow, that his prizes had more influence than himself. As the evening approached, the contest grew more earnest, and those who were forced to allow themselves excelled, began to discover the malignity of defeat, first by angry glances, and at last by contemptuous murmurs. *Seged* likewise shared the anxiety of the day, for considering himself as obliged to distribute with exact justice the prizes which had been so zealously sought, he durst never remit his attention, but passed his time upon the rack of doubt in balancing different kinds of merit, and adjusting the claims of all the competitors.

At last knowing, that no exactness could satisfy those whose hopes he should disappoint, and thinking that on a day set apart for happiness, it would be cruel to oppress any heart with sorrow, he declared that all had pleased him alike, and dismissed all with presents of equal value.

Seged soon saw that his caution had not been able to avoid offence. They who had believed themselves secure of the highest prizes, were not pleased to be levelled with the crowd; and though by the liberality of the king, they received more than his promise had intitled them to expect, they departed unsatisfied, because they were honoured with no distinction, and wanted an opportunity to triumph in the mortification of their opponents. "Behold here," said *Seged*, "the condition of him who places his happiness in the happiness of others." He then retired to meditate, and, while the courtiers were repining at his distributions, saw the fifth sun go down in discontent.

The next dawn renewed his resolution to be happy. But having learned how little he could effect by settled schemes or preparatory measures, he thought it best to give up one day entirely to chance, and left every one to please and be pleased his own way.

This relaxation of regularity diffused a general complacence through the whole court, and the emperor imagined, that he had at last found the secret of obtaining an interval of felicity. But as he was roving in this careless assembly with equal carelessness, he overheard one of his courtiers in a close arbour murmuring alone: "What merit has *Seged* above us, that we should thus fear and obey him, a man, whom, whatever he may have formerly performed, his luxury now shews to have the same weakness with ourselves." This charge affected him the more, as it was uttered by one whom he had always observed among the most abject of his flatterers. At first his indignation prompted him to severity; but reflecting, that what was spoken, without intention to be heard, was to be considered as only thought, and was perhaps but the sudden burst of casual and temporary vexation, he invented some decent pretence to send him away, that his retreat might not be tainted with the breath of envy, and after the struggle of deliberation was past, and all desire of revenge utterly suppressed, passed the evening not only with tranquillity, but triumph, though none but himself was conscious of the victory.

The remembrance of this clemency cheered the beginning of the

seventh day, and nothing happened to disturb the pleasure of
Seged, till looking on the tree that shaded him, he recollected,
that under a tree of the same kind he had passed the night after
his defeat in the kingdom of *Goiama*. The reflection on his loss,
his dishonour, and the miseries which his subjects suffered from
the invader, filled him with sadness. At last he shook off the weight
of sorrow, and began to solace himself with his usual pleasures,
when his tranquillity was again disturbed by jealousies which the
late contest for the prizes had produced, and which, having in vain
tried to pacify them by persuasion, he was forced to silence by
command.

On the eighth morning *Seged* was awakened early by an un-
usual hurry in the apartments, and enquiring the cause, was told,
that the princess *Balkis* was seized with sickness. He rose, and call-
ing the physicians, found that they had little hope of her recovery.
Here was an end of jollity: All his thoughts were now upon his
daughter, whose eyes he closed on the tenth day.

Such were the days which *Seged* of *Ethiopia* had appropriated
to a short respiration from the fatigues of war and the cares of
government. This narrative he has bequeathed to future genera-
tions, that no man hereafter may presume to say, "This day shall be
a day of happiness."

No. 207. TUESDAY, *March* 10, 1752.

Solve senescentem mature sanus equum, ne
Peccet ad extremum ridendus.

HOR.
[*Epistles*, Bk. I, i. 8]

The voice of reason cries with winning force,
  Loose from the rapid car your aged horse,
Lest, in the race derided, left behind,
  He drag his jaded limbs and burst his wind.

FRANCIS.

Such is the emptiness of human enjoyment, that we are always impatient of the present. Attainment is followed by neglect, and possession by disgust; and the malicious remark of the *Greek* epigrammatist on marriage may be applied to every other course of life, that its two days of happiness are the first and the last.[1]

Few moments are more pleasing than those in which the mind is concerting measures for a new undertaking. From the first hint that wakens the fancy, till the hour of actual execution, all is improvement and progress, triumph and felicity. Every hour brings additions to the original scheme, suggests some new expedient to secure success, or discovers consequential advantages not hitherto foreseen. While preparations are made, and materials accumulated, day glides after day through elysian prospects, and the heart dances to the song of hope.

Such is the pleasure of projecting, that many content themselves with a succession of visionary schemes, and wear out their allotted time in the calm amusement of contriving what they never attempt or hope to execute.

Others, not able to feast their imagination with pure ideas, advance somewhat nearer to the grossness of action, with great diligence collect whatever is requisite to their design, and, after a thousand researches and consultations, are snatched away by death, as they stand *in procinctu* waiting for a proper opportunity to begin.

If there were no other end of life, than to find some adequate solace for every day, I know not whether any condition could be preferred to that of the man who involves himself in his own thoughts, and never suffers experience to shew him the vanity of speculation; for no sooner are notions reduced to practice, than tranquillity and confidence forsake the breast; every day brings its task, and often without bringing abilities to perform it: Difficulties embarrass, uncertainty perplexes, opposition retards, censure exasperates, or neglect depresses. We proceed, because we have begun; we complete our design, that the labour already spent may not be vain: but as expectation gradually dies away, the gay smile of alacrity disappears, we are compelled to implore severer powers, and trust the event to patience and constancy.

[1] Palladus, *Greek Anthology*, xi. 381.

When once our labour has begun, the comfort that enables us
to endure it is the prospect of its end; for though in every long
work there are some joyous intervals of self-applause, when the
attention is recreated by unexpected facility, and the imagination
soothed by incidental excellencies; yet the toil with which perform-
ance struggles after idea, is so irksome and disgusting, and so fre-
quent is the necessity of resting below that perfection which we
imagined within our reach, that seldom any man obtains more
from his endeavours than a painful conviction of his defects, and
a continual resuscitation of desires which he feels himself unable
to gratify.

So certainly is weariness the concomitant of our undertakings,
that every man, in whatever he is engaged, consoles himself with
the hope of change; if he has made his way by assiduity to publick
employment, he talks among his friends of the delight of retreat;
if by the necessity of solitary application he is secluded from the
world, he listens with a beating heart to distant noises, longs to
mingle with living beings, and resolves to take hereafter his fill of
diversions, or display his abilities on the universal theatre, and
enjoy the pleasure of distinction and applause.

Every desire, however innocent, grows dangerous, as by long in-
dulgence it becomes ascendent in the mind. When we have been
much accustomed to consider any thing as capable of giving happi-
ness, it is not easy to restrain our ardour, or to forbear some pre-
cipitation in our advances, and irregularity in our persuits. He
that has cultivated the tree, watched the swelling bud and opening
blossom, and pleased himself with computing how much every
sun and shower add to its growth, scarcely stays till the fruit has
obtained its maturity, but defeats his own cares by eagerness to
reward them. When we have diligently laboured for any purpose,
we are willing to believe that we have attained it, and because
we have already done much, too suddenly conclude that no more
is to be done.

All attraction is encreased by the approach of the attracting
body. We never find ourselves so desirous to finish, as in the latter
part of our work, or so impatient of delay, as when we know that
delay cannot be long. This unseasonable importunity of discon-
tent may be partly imputed to languor and weariness, which must

always oppress those more whose toil has been longer continued; but the greater part usually proceeds from frequent contemplation of that ease which is now considered as within reach, and which, when it has once flattered our hopes, we cannot suffer to be withheld.

In some of the noblest compositions of wit, the conclusion falls below the vigour and spirit of the first books; and as a genius is not to be degraded by the imputation of human failings, the cause of this declension is commonly sought in the structure of the work, and plausible reasons are given why in the defective part less ornament was necessary, or less could be admitted. But, perhaps, the author would have confessed, that his fancy was tired, and his perseverance broken; that he knew his design to be unfinished, but that, when he saw the end so near, he could no longer refuse to be at rest.

Against the instillations of this frigid opiate, the heart should be secured by all the considerations which once concurred to kindle the ardour of enterprize. Whatever motive first incited action, has still greater force to stimulate perseverance; since he that might have lain still at first in blameless obscurity, cannot afterwards desist but with infamy and reproach. He, whom a doubtful promise of distant good, could encourage to set difficulties at defiance, ought not to remit his vigour, when he has almost obtained his recompence. To faint or loiter, when only the last efforts are required, is to steer the ship through tempests, and abandon it to the winds in sight of land; it is to break the ground and scatter the seed, and at last to neglect the harvest.

The masters of rhetorick direct, that the most forcible arguments be produced in the latter part of an oration, lest they should be effaced or perplexed by supervenient images. This precept may be justly extended to the series of life: Nothing is ended with honour, which does not conclude better than it begun. It is not sufficient to maintain the first vigour; for excellence loses its effect upon the mind by custom, as light after a time ceases to dazzle. Admiration must be continued by that novelty which first produced it, and how much soever is given, there must always be reason to imagine that more remains.

We not only are most sensible of the last impressions, but such is the unwillingness of mankind to admit transcendent merit, that, though it be difficult to obliterate the reproach of miscarriages by any subsequent atchievement, however illustrious, yet the reputation raised by a long train of success, may be finally ruined by a single failure, for weakness or error will be always remembered by that malice and envy which it gratifies.

For the prevention of that disgrace, which lassitude and negligence may bring as last upon the greatest performances, it is necessary to proportion carefully our labour to our strength. If the design comprises many parts, equally essential, and therefore not to be separated, the only time for caution is before we engage; the powers of the mind must be then impartially estimated, and it must be remembered, that not to complete the plan, is not to have begun it; and that nothing is done, while any thing is omitted.

But, if the task consists in the repetition of single acts, no one of which derives its efficacy from the rest, it may be attempted with less scruple, because there is always opportunity to retreat with honour. The danger is only lest we expect from the world the indulgence with which most are disposed to treat themselves; and in the hour of listlessness imagine, that the diligence of one day will atone for the idleness of another, and that applause begun by approbation will be continued by habit.

He that is himself weary will soon weary the public. Let him therefore lay down his employment, whatever it be, who can no longer exert his former activity or attention; let him not endeavour to struggle with censure, or obstinately infest the stage till a general hiss commands him to depart.

No. 208. SATURDAY, *March* 14, 1752.

Ἡράκλειτος ἐγώ· τί με ὦ κάτω ἕλκετ᾽ ἄμουσι;
Οὐχ᾽ ὑμῖν ἐπόνουν, τοῖς δὲ μ᾽ ἐπισταμένοις·
Εἷς ἐμοὶ ἄνθρωπος τρισμύριοι· οἱ δ᾽ ἀνάριθμοι
Οὐδείς· ταῦτ᾽ αὐδῶ καὶ παρὰ Περσεφόνῃ·

DIOG. LAERT.

Begone, ye blockheads, *Heraclitus* cries,
And leave my labours to the learn'd and wise,
By wit, by knowledge, studious to be read,
I scorn the multitude, alive and dead.

Time, which puts an end to all human pleasures and sorrows, has likewise concluded the labours of the RAMBLER. Having supported, for two years, the anxious employment of a periodical writer, and multiplied my essays to four volumes, I have now determined to desist.

The reasons of this resolution it is of little importance to declare, since justification is unnecessary when no objection is made. I am far from supposing, that the cessation of my performances will raise any inquiry, for I have never been much a favourite of the publick, nor can boast that, in the progress of my undertaking, I have been animated by the rewards of the liberal, the caresses of the great, or the praises of the eminent.

But I have no design to gratify pride by submission, or malice by lamentation; nor think it reasonable to complain of neglect from those whose regard I never solicited. If I have not been distinguished by the distributers of literary honours, I have seldom descended to the arts by which favour is obtained. I have seen the meteors of fashion rise and fall, without any attempt to add a moment to their duration. I have never complied with temporary curiosity, nor enabled my readers to discuss the topick of the day; I have rarely exempl[if]ied my assertions by living characters; in my papers, no man could look for censures of his enemies, or praises of himself; and they only were expected to peruse them, whose passions left them leisure for abstracted truth, and whom virtue could please by its naked dignity.

To some, however, I am indebted for encouragement, and to others for assistance. The number of my friends was never great, but they have been such as would not suffer me to think that I was writing in vain, and I did not feel much dejection from the want of popularity.

My obligations having not been frequent, my acknowledgements may be soon dispatched. I can restore to all my correspondents their productions, with little diminution of the bulk of my volumes, though not without the loss of some pieces to which particular honours have been paid.

The parts from which I claim no other praise than that of having given them an opportunity of appearing, are the four billets in the tenth paper, the second letter in the fifteenth, the thirtieth, the forty-fourth, the ninety-seventh, and the hundredth papers, and the second letter in the hundred and seventh.

Having thus deprived myself of many excuses which candor might have admitted for the inequality of my compositions, being no longer able to alledge the necessity of gratifying correspondents, the importunity with which publication was solicited, or obstinacy with which correction was rejected, I must remain accountable for all my faults, and submit, without subterfuge, to the censures of criticism, which, however, I shall not endeavour to soften by a formal deprecation, or to overbear by the influence of a patron. The supplications of an author never yet reprieved him a moment from oblivion; and, though greatness has sometimes sheltered guilt, it can afford no protection to ignorance or dulness. Having hitherto attempted only the propagation of truth, I will not at last violate it by the confession of terrors which I do not feel: Having laboured to maintain the dignity of virtue, I will not now degrade it by the meanness of dedication.

The seeming vanity with which I have sometimes spoken of myself, would perhaps require an apology, were it not extenuated by the example of those who have published essays before me, and by the privilege which every nameless writer has been hitherto allowed. "A mask," says *Castiglione,* "confers a right of acting and speaking with less restraint, even when the wearer happens to be known." He that is discovered without his own consent, may claim some indulgence, and cannot be rigorously called to justify those sallies or frolicks which his disguise must prove him desirous to conceal.

But I have been cautious lest this offence should be frequently or grossly committed; for, as one of the philosophers directs us to live with a friend, as with one that is some time to become an enemy, I have always thought it the duty of an anonymous author to write, as if he expected to be hereafter known.

I am willing to flatter myself with hopes, that, by collecting these papers, I am not preparing for my future life, either shame or repentance. That all are happily imagined, or accurately polished, that the same sentiments have not sometimes recurred, or the same expressions been too frequently repeated, I have not confidence in my abilities sufficient to warrant. He that condemns himself to compose on a stated day, will often bring to his task an attention dissipated, a memory embarrassed, an imagination overwhelmed, a mind distracted with anxieties, a body languishing with disease. He will labour on a barren topick, till it is too late to change it; or in the ardour of invention, diffuse his thoughts into wild exuberance, which the pressing hour of publication cannot suffer judgment to examine or reduce.

Whatever shall be the final sentence of mankind, I have at least endeavoured to deserve their kindness. I have laboured to refine our language to grammatical purity, and to clear it from colloquial barbarisms, licentious idioms, and irregular combinations. Something, perhaps, I have added to the elegance of its construction, and something to the harmony of its cadence. When common words were less pleasing to the ear, or less distinct in their signification, I have familiarized the terms of philosophy by applying them to popular ideas, but have rarely admitted any word not authorized by former writers; for I believe that whoever knows the *English* tongue in its present extent, will be able to express his thoughts without further help from other nations.

As it has been my principal design to inculcate wisdom or piety, I have allotted few papers to the idle sports of imagination. Some, perhaps, may be found, of which the highest excellence is harmless merriment, but scarcely any man is so steadily serious, as not to complain, that the severity of dictatorial instruction has been too seldom relieved, and that he is driven by the sternness of the Rambler's philosophy to more chearful and airy companions.

Next to the excursions of fancy are the disquisitions of criticism, which, in my opinion, is only to be ranked among the subordinate and instrumental arts. Arbitrary decision and general exclamation I have carefully avoided, by asserting nothing without a reason, and establishing all my principles of judgment on unalterable and evident truth.

In the pictures of life I have never been so studious of novelty or surprize, as to depart wholly from all resemblance; a fault which writers deservedly celebrated frequently commit, that they may raise, as the occasion requires, either mirth or abhorrence. Some enlargement may be allowed to declamation, and some exaggeration to burlesque; but as they deviate farther from reality, they become less useful, because their lessons will fail of application. The mind of the reader is carried away from the contemplation of his own manners; he finds in himself no likeness to the phantom before him; and though he laughs or rages, is not reformed.

The essays professedly serious, if I have been able to execute my own intentions, will be found exactly conformable to the precepts of Christianity, without any accommodation to the licentiousness and levity of the present age. I therefore look back on this part of my work with pleasure, which no blame or praise of man shall diminish or augment. I shall never envy the honours which wit and learning obtain in any other cause, if I can be numbered among the writers who have given ardour to virtue, and confidence to truth.

Αὐτῶν ἐκ μακάρων ἀντάξιος εἴη ἀμοιβή.

Celestial pow'rs! that piety regard,
From you my labours wait their last reward.

FROM The Adventurer

No. 67. TUESDAY, *June* 26, 1753.

Inventas——vitam excoluere per artes.
VIRG. [*Æn*. VI. 663.]

They polish life by useful arts.

That familiarity produces neglect, has been long observed. The effect of all external objects, however great or splendid, ceases with their novelty: the courtier stands without emotion in the royal presence; the rustic tramples under his foot the beauties of the spring, with little attention to their colours or their fragrance; and the inhabitant of the coast darts his eye upon the immense diffusion of waters, without awe, wonder, or terror.

Those who have past much of their lives in this great city, look upon its opulence and its multitudes, its extent and variety, with cold indifference; but an inhabitant of the remoter parts of the kingdom is immediately distinguished by a kind of dissipated curiosity, a busy endeavour to divide his attention amongst a thousand objects, and a wild confusion of astonishment and alarm.

The attention of a new-comer is generally first struck by the multiplicity of cries that stun him in the streets, and the variety of merchandise and manufactures which the shopkeepers expose on every hand; and he is apt, by unwary bursts of admiration, to excite the merriment and contempt of those, who mistake the use of their eyes for effects of their understanding, and confound accidental knowledge with just reasoning.

But, surely, these are subjects on which any man may without reproach employ his meditations: the innumerable occupations, among which the thousands that swarm in the streets of London are distributed, may furnish employment to minds of every cast, and capacities of every degree. He that contemplates the extent of this wonderful city, finds it difficult to conceive, by what method plenty is maintained in our markets, and how the inhabitants are regularly supplied with the necessaries of life; but when he examines the shops and warehouses, sees the immense stores of every kind of merchandise piled up for sale, and runs over all the manufactures of art and products of nature, which are every where attracting his eye and soliciting his purse, he will be inclined to conclude, that such quantities cannot easily be exhausted, and that part of mankind must soon stand still for want of employment, till the wares already provided shall be worn out and destroyed.

As Socrates was passing through the fair at Athens, and casting his eyes over the shops and customers, "how many things are here," says he, "that I do not want!" [1] The same sentiment is every moment rising in the mind of him that walks the streets of London, however inferior in philosophy to Socrates: he beholds a thousand shops crouded with goods, of which he can scarcely tell the use, and which, therefore, he is apt to consider as of no value; and, indeed, many of the arts by which families are supported, and wealth is heaped together, are of that minute and superfluous kind, which nothing but experience could evince possible to be prosecuted with advantage, and which, as the world might easily want, it could scarcely be expected to encourage.

But so it is, that custom, curiosity, or wantonness, supplies every art with patrons, and finds purchasers for every manufacture; the

[1] Diogenes Laertius, *Socrates,* II. 25.

world is so adjusted, that not only bread, but riches may be obtained without great abilities, or arduous performances: the most unskilful hand and unenlightened mind have sufficient incitements to industry; for he that is resolutely busy, can scarcely be in want: there is, indeed, no employment, however despicable, from which a man may not promise himself more than competence, when he sees thousands and myriads raised to dignity, by no other merit than that of contributing to supply their neighbours with the means of sucking smoke through a tube of clay; and others raising contributions upon those, whose elegance disdains the grossness of smoky luxury, by grinding the same materials into a powder, that may at once gratify and impair the smell.

Not only by these popular and modish trifles, but by a thousand unheeded and evanescent kinds of business, are the multitudes of this city preserved from idleness, and consequently from want: in the endless variety of tastes and circumstances that diversify mankind, nothing is so superfluous, but that some one desires it; or so common, but that some one is compelled to buy it. As nothing is useless but because it is in improper hands, what is thrown away by one is gathered up by another; and the refuse of part of mankind furnishes a subordinate class with the materials necessary to their support.

When I look round upon those who are thus variously exerting their qualifications, I cannot but admire the secret concatenation of society, that links together the great and the mean, the illustrious and the obscure; and consider with benevolent satisfaction, that no man, unless his body or mind be totally disabled, has need to suffer the mortification of seeing himself useless or burdensome to the community: he that will diligently labour, in whatever occupation, will deserve the sustenance which he obtains, and the protection which he enjoys; and may lie down every night with the pleasing consciousness, of having contributed something to the happiness of life.

Contempt and admiration are equally incident to narrow minds: he whose comprehension can take in the whole subordination of mankind, and whose perspicacity can pierce to the real state of things through the thin veils of fortune or of fashion, will discover meanness in the highest stations, and dignity in the meanest; and find that no man can become venerable but by virtue, or contemptible but by wickedness.

In the midst of this universal hurry, no man ought to be so little influenced by example, or so void of honest emulation, as to stand a lazy spectator of incessant labour; or please himself with the mean happiness of a drone, while the active swarms are buzzing about him: no man is without some quality, by the due application of which he might deserve well of the world; and whoever he be that has but little in his power, should be in haste to do that little, lest he be confounded with him that can do nothing.

By this general concurrence of endeavours, arts of every kind have been so long cultivated, that all the wants of man may be immediately supplied; idleness can scarcely form a wish which she may not gratify by the toil of others, or curiosity dream of a toy which the shops are not ready to afford her.

Happiness is enjoyed only in proportion as it is known; and such is the state or folly of man, that it is known only by experience of its contrary: we who have long lived amidst the conveniencies of a town immensely populous, have scarce an idea of a place where desire cannot be gratified by money. In order to have a just sense of this artificial plenty, it is necessary to have passed some time in a distant colony, or those parts of our island which are thinly inhabited: he that has once known how many trades every man in such situations is compelled to exercise, with how much labour the products of nature must be accommodated to human use, how long the loss or defect of any common utensil must be endured, or by what aukward expedients it must be supplied, how far men may wander with money in their hands before any can sell them what they wish to buy, will know how to rate at its proper value the plenty and ease of a great city.

But that the happiness of man may still remain imperfect, as wants in this place are easily supplied, new wants likewise are easily created: every man, in surveying the shops of London, sees numberless instruments and conveniences, of which, while he did not know them, he never felt the need; and yet, when use has

---

made them familiar, wonders how life could be supported without them. Thus it comes to pass, that our desires always increase with our possessions; the knowledge that something remains yet unenjoyed, impairs our enjoyment of the good before us.

They who have been accustomed to the refinements of science, and multiplications of contrivance, soon lose their confidence in the unassisted powers of nature, forget the paucity of our real necessities, and overlook the easy methods by which they may be supplied. It were a speculation worthy of a philosophical mind, to examine how much is taken away from our native abilities, as well as added to them by artificial expedients. We are so accustomed to give and receive assistance, that each of us singly can do little for himself; and there is scarce any one among us, however contracted may be his form of life, who does not enjoy the labour of a thousand artists.

But a survey of the various nations that inhabit the earth will inform us, that life may be supported with less assistance, and that the dexterity, which practice enforced by necessity produces, is able to effect much by very scanty means. The nations of Mexico and Peru erected cities and temples without the use of iron; and at this day the rude Indian supplies himself with all the necessaries of life: sent like the rest of mankind naked into the world, as soon as his parents have nursed him up to strength, he is to provide by his own labour for his own support. His first care is to find a sharp flint among the rocks; with this he undertakes to fell the trees of the forest, he shapes his bow, heads his arrows, builds his cottage, and hollows his canoe, and from that time lives in a state of plenty and prosperity; he is sheltered from the storms, he is fortified against beasts of prey, he is enabled to persue the fish of the sea, and the deer of the mountains; and as he does not know, does not envy the happiness of polished nations, where gold can supply the want of fortitude and skill, and he whose laborious ancestors have made him rich, may lie stretched upon a couch, and see all the treasures of all the elements poured down before him.

This picture of a savage life, if it shews how much individuals may perform, shews likewise how much society is to be desired:

though the perseverance and address of the Indian excite our admiration, they nevertheless cannot procure him the conveniences which are enjoyed by the vagrant beggar of a civilized country: he hunts like a wild beast to satisfy his hunger; and when he lies down to rest after a successful chace, cannot pronounce himself secure against the danger of perishing in a few days; he is, perhaps, content with his condition, because he knows not that a better is attainable by man; as he that is born blind does not long for the perception of light, because he cannot conceive the advantages which light would afford him: but hunger wounds and weariness are real evils, though he believes them equally incident to all his fellow creatures; and when a tempest compels him to lie starving in his hut, he cannot justly be concluded equally happy with those whom art has exempted from the power of chance, and who make the foregoing year provide for the following.

To receive and to communicate assistance, constitutes the happiness of human life: man may indeed preserve his existence in solitude, but can enjoy it only in society; the greatest understanding of an individual, doomed to procure food and cloathing for himself, will barely supply him with expedients to keep off death from day to day; but as one of a large community performing only his share of the common business, he gains leisure for intellectual pleasures, and enjoys the happiness of reason and reflection.

No. 84. SATURDAY, *August 25*, 1753.

——————————— *Tolle periclum,*
Jam vaga prosiliet frænis natura remotis.

HOR. [*Sat.* II. vii. 73.]

But take the danger and the shame away,
And vagrant nature bounds upon her prey.

FRANCIS.

To the ADVENTURER

SIR,

It has been observed, I think, by Sir WILLIAM TEMPLE,[1] and after him by almost every other writer, that England affords a greater variety of characters, than the rest of the world. This is ascribed to the liberty prevailing amongst us, which gives every man the privilege of being wise or foolish his own way, and preserves him from the necessity of hypocrisy, or the servility of imitation.

That the position itself is true, I am not completely satisfied. To be nearly acquainted with the people of different countries can happen to very few; and in life, as in every thing else beheld at a distance, there appears an even uniformity; the petty discriminations which diversify the natural character, are not discoverable but by a close inspection; we therefore find them most at home, because there we have most opportunities of remarking them. Much less am I convinced, that this peculiar diversification, if it be real, is the consequence of peculiar liberty: for where is the government to be found, that superintends individuals with so much vigilance, as not to leave their private conduct without restraint? Can it enter into a reasonable mind to imagine, that men of every other nation are not equally masters of their own time or houses with ourselves, and equally at liberty to be parsimonious or profuse, frolic or sullen, abstinent or luxurious? Liberty is certainly necessary to the full play of predominant humours; but such liberty is to be found alike under the government of the many or the few; in monarchies or in commonwealths.

How readily the predominant passion snatches an interval of liberty, and how fast it expands itself when the weight of restraint is taken away, I had lately opportunity to discover, as I took a short journey into the country in a stage coach; which, as every journey is a kind of adventure, may be very properly related to you, though I can display no such extraordinary assembly as CERVANTES had collected at DON QUIXOTE's inn.

[1] *Of Poetry. Works,* 1720, I, 248.

In a stage coach the passengers are for the most part wholly un-known to one another, and without expectation of ever meeting again when their journey is at an end; one should therefore imag-ine, that it was of little importance to any of them, what conjec-tures the rest should form concerning him. Yet so it is, that as all think themselves secure from detection, all assume that character of which they are most desirous, and on no occasion is the general ambition of superiority more apparently indulged.

On the day of our departure, in the twilight of the morning, I ascended the vehicle, with three men and two women my fellow travellers. It was easy to observe the affected elevation of mien with which every one entered, and the supercilious civility with which they paid their compliments to each other. When the first cere-mony was dispatched, we sat silent for a long time, all employed in collecting importance into our faces, and endeavouring to strike reverence and submission into our companions.

It is always observable that silence propagates itself, and that the longer talk has been suspended, the more difficult it is to find any thing to say. We began now to wish for conversation; but no one seemed inclined to descend from his dignity, or first to propose a topic of discourse. At last a corpulent gentleman, who had equipped himself for this expedition with a scarlet surtout, and a large hat with a broad lace, drew out his watch, looked on it in silence, and then held it dangling at his finger. This was, I sup-pose, understood by all the company as an invitation to ask the time of the day; but no body appeared to heed his overture: and his desire to be talking so far overcame his resentment, that he let us know of his own accord it was past five, and that in two hours we should be at breakfast.

His condescension was thrown away, we continued all obdurate: the ladies held up their heads: I amused myself with watching their behaviour; and of the other two, one seemed to employ him-self in counting the trees as we drove by them, the other drew his hat over his eyes, and counterfeited a slumber. The man of benevo-lence, to shew that he was not depressed by our neglect, hummed a tune and beat time upon his snuff-box.

Thus universally displeased with one another, and not much de-

lighted with ourselves, we came at last to the little inn appointed
for our repast, and all began at once to recompense themselves for
the constraint of silence by innumerable questions and orders to
the people that attended us. At last, what every one had called for
was got, or declared impossible to be got at that time, and we were
persuaded to sit round the same table; when the gentleman in the
red surtout looked again upon his watch, told us that we had half
an hour to spare, but he was sorry to see so little merriment among
us; that all fellow travellers were for the time upon the level, and
that it was always his way to make himself one of the company.
I remember, says he, it was on just such a morning as this that I
and my lord Mumble and the duke of Tenterden were out upon a
ramble; we called at a little house as it might be this; and my land-
lady, I warrant you, not suspecting to whom she was talking, was
so jocular and facetious, and made so many merry answers to our
questions, that we were all ready to burst with laughter. At last the
good woman happened to overhear me whispering to the duke and
calling him by his title, was so surprised and confounded that we
could scarcely get a word from her: and the duke never met me
from that day to this, but he talks of the little house, and quarrels
with me for terrifying the woman.

He had scarcely had time to congratulate himself on the venera-
tion which this narrative must have procured him from the com-
pany, when one of the ladies having reached out for a plate on a
distant part of the table, began to remark the inconveniences of
travelling, and the difficulty which they who never sat at home
without a great number of attendants found in performing for
themselves such offices as the road required; but that people of
quality often travelled in disguise, and might be generally known
from the vulgar by their condescension to poor inn-keepers, and
the allowance which they made for any defect in their entertain-
ment: that for her part, while people were civil and meant well, it
was never her custom to find fault; for one was not to expect upon
a journey all that one enjoyed at one's own house.

A general emulation seemed now to be excited. One of the men,
who had hitherto said nothing, called for the last newspaper; and
having perused it a while with deep pensiveness, It is impossible,

says he, for any man to guess how to act with regard to the stocks; last week it was the general opinion that they would fall; and I sold out twenty thousand pound in order to a purchase: they have now risen unexpectedly; and I make no doubt but at my return to London I shall risk thirty thousand pound amongst them again.

A young man, who had hitherto distinguished himself only by the vivacity of his look, and a frequent diversion of his eyes from one object to another, upon this closed his snuff-box, and told us that he had a hundred times talked with the chancellor and the judges on the subject of the stocks; that for his part he did not pretend to be well acquainted with the principles on which they were established, but had always heard them reckoned pernicious to trade, uncertain in their produce, and unsolid in their foundation; and that he had been advised by three judges, his most intimate friends, never to venture his money in the funds, but to put it out upon land security, till he could light upon an estate in his own country.

It might be expected that, upon these glimpses of latent dignity, we should all have begun to look round us with veneration, and have behaved like the princes of romance, when the enchantment that disguises them is dissolved, and they discover the dignity of each other; yet it happened, that none of these hints made much impression on the company; every one was apparently suspected of endeavouring to impose false appearances upon the rest; all continued their haughtiness, in hopes to enforce their claims; and all grew every hour more sullen, because they found their representations of themselves without effect.

Thus we travelled on four days with malevolence perpetually increasing, and without any endeavour but to outvie each other in superciliousness and neglect; and when any two of us could separate ourselves for a moment, we vented our indignation at the sauciness of the rest.

At length the journey was at an end, and time and chance, that strip off all disguises, have discovered that the intimate of lords and dukes is a nobleman's butler, who has furnished a shop with the money he has saved; the man who deals so largely in the funds, is the clerk of a broker in Change-alley; the lady who so carefully concealed her quality, keeps a cookshop behind the Exchange; and the young man who is so happy in the friendship of the judges, engrosses and transcribes for bread in a garret of the Temple. Of one of the women only I could make no disadvantageous detection, because she had assumed no character, but accommodated herself to the scene before her, without any struggle for distinction or superiority.

I could not forbear to reflect on the folly of practising a fraud, which as the event shewed, had been already practised too often to succeed, and by the success of which no advantage could have been obtained; of assuming a character, which was to end with the day; and of claiming upon false pretences honours which must perish with the breath that paid them.

But MR. ADVENTURER, let not those who laugh at me and my companions, think this folly confined to a stage coach. Every man in the journey of life takes the same advantage of the ignorance of his fellow travellers, disguises himself in counterfeited merit, and hears those praises with complacency which his conscience reproaches him for accepting. Every man deceives himself while he thinks he is deceiving others; and forgets that the time is at hand when every illusion shall cease; when fictitious excellence shall be torn away; and ALL must be shown to ALL in their real state.

I am, SIR,
Your humble Servant,

VIATOR.

No. 111. *Tuesday, 17 November 1753.*

———*Quae non fecimus ipsi,*
Vix ea nostra voco.

OVID, *Metamorphoses,* XIII. 140–41.

The deeds of long descended ancestors
Are but by grace of imputation ours.

DRYDEN.

The evils inseparably annexed to the present condition of man, are so numerous and afflictive, that it has been, from age to age, the task of some to bewail, and of others to solace them: and he, therefore, will be in danger of seeming a common enemy, who shall attempt to depreciate the few pleasures and felicities which nature has allowed us.

Yet I will confess, that I have sometimes employed my thoughts in examining the pretensions that are made to happiness, by the splendid and envied conditions of life; and have not thought the hour unprofitably spent, when I have detected the imposture of counterfeit advantages, and found disquiet lurking under false appearances of gayety and greatness.

It is asserted by a tragic poet, that "est miser nemo nisi comparatus," [1] "no man is miserable, but as he is compared with others happier than himself:" this position is not strictly and philosophically true. He might have said, with rigorous propriety, that no man is happy, but as he is compared with the miserable; for such is the state of this world, that we find in it absolute misery but happiness only comparative; we may incur as much pain as we can possibly endure, though we can never obtain as much happiness as we might possibly enjoy.

Yet it is certain likewise, that many of our miseries are merely comparative: we are often made unhappy, not by the presence of any real evil, but by the absence of some fictitious good; of something which is not required by any real want of nature, which has not in itself any power of gratification, and which neither reason nor fancy would have prompted us to wish, did we not see it in the possession of others.

For a mind diseased with vain longings after unattainable advantages, no medicine can be prescribed, but an impartial enquiry into the real worth of that which is so ardently desired. It is well known, how much the mind, as well as the eye, is deceived by distance; and, perhaps, it will be found, that of many imagined blessings it may be doubted, whether he that wants or possesses them has more reason to be satisfied with his lot.

---

[1] Seneca, *Troades*, Act IV, chorus.

The dignity of high birth and long extraction, no man, to whom nature has denied it, can confer upon himself; and, therefore, it deserves to be considered, whether the want of that which can never be gained, may not easily be endured. It is true, that if we consider the triumph and delight, with which most of those recount their ancestors who have ancestors to recount, and the artifices by which some who have risen to unexpected fortune endeavour to insert themselves into an honourable stem, we shall be inclined to fancy, that wisdom or virtue may be had by inheritance, or that all the excellencies of a line of progenitors are accumulated on their descendant. Reason, indeed, will soon inform us, that our estimation of birth is arbitrary and capricious, and that dead ancestors can have no influence but upon imagination: let it then be examined, whether one dream may not operate in the place of another; whether he that owes nothing to forefathers, may not receive equal pleasure from the consciousness of owing all to himself; whether he may not, with a little meditation, find it more honourable to found than to continue a family, and to gain dignity than transmit it; whether, if he receives no dignity from the virtues of his family, he does not likewise escape the danger of being disgraced by their crimes; and whether he that brings a new name into the world, has not the convenience of playing the game of life without a stake, an opportunity of winning much though he has nothing to lose.

There is another opinion concerning happiness, which approaches much more nearly to universality, but which may, perhaps, with equal reason, be disputed. The pretensions to ancestral honours many of the sons of earth easily see to be ill grounded; but all agree to celebrate the advantage of hereditary riches, and to consider those as the minions of fortune, who are wealthy from their cradles; whose estate is "res non parta labore sed relicta," [2] "the acquisition of another, not of themselves;" and whom a father's industry has dispensed from a laborious attention to arts or commerce, and left at liberty to dispose of life as fancy shall direct them.

[2] Martial, x. 47. 3.

If every man were wise and virtuous, capable to discern the best use of time, and resolute to practise it; it might be granted, I think, without hesitation, that total liberty would be a blessing; and that it would be desirable to be left at large to the exercise of religious and social duties, without the interruption of importunate avocations.

But since felicity is relative, and that which is the means of happiness to one man may be to another the cause of misery, we are to consider, what state is best adapted to human nature in its present degeneracy and frailty. And, surely, to far the greater number it is highly expedient, that they should by some settled scheme of duties be rescued from the tyranny of caprice, that they should be driven on by necessity through the paths of life, with their attention confined to a stated task, that they may be less at leisure to deviate into mischief at the call of folly.

When we observe the lives of those whom an ample inheritance has let loose to their own direction, what do we discover that can excite our envy? Their time seems not to pass with much applause from others, or satisfaction to themselves; many squander their exuberance of fortune in luxury and debauchery, and have no other use of money than to inflame their passions, and riot in a wider range of licentiousness; others, less criminal indeed, but, surely, not much to be praised, lie down to sleep and rise up to trifle, are employed every morning in finding expedients to rid themselves of the day, chase pleasure through all the places of public resort, fly from London to Bath and from Bath to London, without any other reason for changing place, but that they go in quest of company as idle and as vagrant as themselves, always endeavouring to raise some new desire that they may have something to persue, to rekindle some hope which they know will be disappointed, changing one amusement for another which a few months will make equally insipid, or sinking into languor and disease, for want of something to actuate their bodies or exhilarate their minds.

Whoever has frequented those places, where idlers assemble to escape from solitude, knows that this is generally the state of the wealthy; and from this state it is no great hardship to be debarred.

No man can be happy in total idleness: he that should be condemned to lie torpid and motionless, "would fly for recreation," says South, "to the mines and the gallies;"[3] and it is well, when nature or fortune find employment for those, who would not have known how to procure it for themselves.

He, whose mind is engaged by the acquisition or improvement of a fortune, not only escapes the insipidity of indifference, and the tediousness of inactivity; but gains enjoyments wholly unknown to those, who live lazily on the toil of others; for life affords no higher pleasure, than that of surmounting difficulties, passing from one step of success to another, forming new wishes and seeing them gratified. He that labours in any great or laudable undertaking, has his fatigues first supported by hope, and afterwards rewarded by joy; he is always moving to a certain end, and when he has attained it, an end more distant invites him to a new persuit.

It does not, indeed, always happen, that diligence is fortunate; the wisest schemes are broken by unexpected accidents; the most constant perseverance sometimes toils through life without a recompence; but labour, though unsuccessful, is more eligible than idleness: he that prosecutes a lawful purpose by lawful means, acts always with the approbation of his own reason; he is animated through the course of his endeavours by an expectation which though not certain, he knows to be just; and is at last comforted in his disappointment, by the consciousness that he has not failed by his own fault.

That kind of life is most happy which affords us most opportunities of gaining our own esteem; and what can any man infer in his own favour from a condition to which, however prosperous, he contributed nothing, and which the vilest and weakest of the species would have obtained by the same right, had he happened to be the son of the same father?

To strive with difficulties, and to conquer them, is the highest human felicity; the next, is to strive, and deserve to conquer: but he whose life has passed without a contest, and who can

[3] Robert South, *Sermons*, 1823, I, 20 [ref. Powell and Bate].

boast neither success nor merit, can survey himself only as a useless filler of existence; and if he is content with his own character, must owe his satisfaction to insensibility.

Thus it appears that the satyrist advised rightly, when he directed us to resign ourselves to the hands of Heaven, and to leave to superior powers the determination of our lot:

> *Permittes ipsis expendere Numinibus, quid*
> *Conveniat nobis, rebusque sit utile nostris,*
> *Carior est illis homo quam sibi.*
>
> JUVENAL, *Satires*, x. 347–48, 350.

> Intrust thy fortune to the pow'rs above:
> Leave them to manage for thee, and to grant
> What their unerring wisdom sees thee want.
> In goodness as in greatness they excell,
> Ah! that we lov'd ourselves but half so well.
>
> DRYDEN.

What state of life admits most happiness is uncertain; but that uncertainty ought to repress the petulance of comparison, and silence the murmurs of discontent.

✓ No. 16. SATURDAY, *July* 29, 1758.

carpet

I paid a visit yesterday to my old friend *Ned Drugget*, at his country-lodgings. *Ned* began trade with a very small fortune; he took a small house in an obscure street, and for some years dealt only in remnants. Knowing that *light gains make a heavy purse*, he was content with moderate profit; having observed or heard the effects of civility, he bowed down to the counter edge at the entrance and departure of every customer, listened, without impatience, to the objections of the ignorant, and refused, without resentment, the offers of the penurious. His only Recreation was to stand at his own door and look into the street. His dinner was sent him from a neighbouring Alehouse, and he opened and shut the shop at a certain hour with his own hands.

His reputation soon extended from one end of the street to the other, and Mr. *Drugget's* exemplary conduct was recommended by every master to his apprentice, and by every father to his son. *Ned* was not only considered as a thriving trader, but as a man of Elegance and Politeness, for he was remarkably neat in his dress, and would wear his coat threadbare without spotting it; his hat was always brushed, his shoes glossy, his wig nicely curled, and his stockings without a wrinkle. With such qualifications it was not very difficult for him to gain the heart of Miss *Comfit,* the only daughter of Mr. *Comfit* the confectioner.

Ned is one of those whose happiness marriage has encreased. His wife had the same disposition with himself, and his method of life was very little changed, except that he dismissed the lodgers from the first floor, and took the whole house into his own hands.

He had already, by his parsimony, accumulated a considerable sum, to which the fortune of his wife was now added. From this time he began to grasp at greater acquisitions, and was always ready, with money in his hand, to pick up the refuse of a Sale, or to buy the Stock of a Trader who retired from business. He soon added his parlour to his shop, and was obliged, a few months afterwards, to hire a warehouse.

He had now a Shop splendidly and copiously furnished with every thing that time had injured, or fashion had degraded, with fragments of tissues, odd yards of brocade, vast bales of faded silk, and innumerable boxes of antiquated ribbons. His shop was soon celebrated through all quarters of the town, and frequented by every form of ostentatious Poverty. Every maid, whose misfortune it was to be taller than her Lady, matched her gown at Mr. *Drugget*'s; and many a maiden who had passed a winter with her aunt in *London,* dazzled the Rustics, at her return, with cheap finery which *Drugget* had supplied. His shop was often visited in a morning by Ladies, who left their coaches in the next street, and crept through the Alley in linnen gowns. *Drugget* knows the rank of his customers by their bashfulness, and when he finds them unwilling to be seen, invites them up stairs, or retires with them to the back window.

I rejoiced at the encreasing prosperity of my friend, and imagined that as he grew rich, he was growing happy. His mind has partaken the enlargement of his fortune. When I stepped in for the first five years, I was welcomed only with a shake of the hand; in the next period of his life, he beckoned across the way for a pot of beer; but, for six years past, he invites me to dinner; and, if he bespeaks me the day before, never fails to regale me with a fillet of veal.

His riches neither made him uncivil nor negligent. He rose at the same hour, attended with the same assiduity, and bowed with the same gentleness. But for some years he has been much inclined to talk of the fatigues of business, and the confinement of a shop, and to wish that he had been so happy as to have renewed his uncle's lease of a farm, that he might have lived without noise and hurry, in a pure air, in the artless society of honest Villagers, and the contemplation of the works of nature.

I soon discovered the cause of my friend's Philosophy. He thought himself grown rich enough to have a lodging in the country, like the mercers on *Ludgate-hill*, and was resolved to enjoy himself in the decline of life. This was a revolution not to be made suddenly. He talked three years of the pleasures of the country, but passed every night over his own shop. But at last he resolved to be happy, and hired a lodging in the Country, that he may steal some hours in the week from business; for, says he, *when a man advances in life he loves to entertain himself sometimes with his own thoughts.*

I was invited to this seat of quiet and contemplation among those whom Mr. *Drugget* considers as his most reputable friends, and desires to make the first witnesses of his elevation to the highest dignities of a Shopkeeper. I found him at *Islington*, in a room which overlooked the high road, amusing himself with looking through the window, which the clouds of dust would not suffer him to open. He embraced me, told me I was welcome into the Country, and asked me, If I did not feel myself refreshed. He then desired that dinner might be hastened, for fresh air always sharpened his appetite, and ordered me a toast and a glass of wine after my walk. He told me much of the pleasures he found in retirement, and wondered what had kept him so long out of the Country. After dinner company came in, and Mr. *Drugget* again repeated the praises of the Country, recommended the pleasures of Meditation, and told them, that he had been all the morning at the window, counting the carriages as they passed before him.

√ No. 18. SATURDAY, *August* 12, 1758.

To the IDLER

Sir,

It commonly happens to him who endeavours to obtain distinction by ridicule, or censure, that he teaches others to practise his own arts against himself; and that, after a short enjoyment of the applause paid to his sagacity, or of the mirth excited by his wit, he is doomed to suffer the same severities of scrutiny, to hear inquiry detecting his faults, and exaggeration sporting with his failings.

The natural discontent of inferiority will seldom fail to operate in some degree of malice against him, who professes to superintend the conduct of others, especially if he seats himself uncalled in the chair of Judicature, and exercises Authority by his own commission.

You cannot, therefore, wonder that your observations on human folly, if they produce laughter at one time, awaken criticism at another; and that among the numbers whom you have taught to scoff at the retirement of *Drugget,* there is one who offers his apology.

The mistake of your old friend is by no means peculiar. The public pleasures of far the greater part of mankind are counterfeit. Very few carry their philosophy to places of diversion, or are very careful to analyse their enjoyments. The general condition of life is so full of misery, that we are glad to catch delight without enquiring whence it comes, or by what power it is bestowed.

The mind is seldom quickened to very vigorous operations but by pain, or the dread of pain. We do not disturb ourselves with the detection of fallacies which do us no harm, nor willingly decline a pleasing effect to investigate its cause. He that is happy, by whatever means, desires nothing but the continuance of happiness, and is no more sollicitous to distribute his sensations into their proper species, than the common gazer on the beauties of the spring to separate light into its original rays.

Pleasure is therefore seldom such as it appears to others, nor often such as we represent it to ourselves. Of the Ladies that sparkle at a musical performance, a very small number has any quick sensibility of harmonious sounds. But every one that goes has her pleasure. She has the pleasure of wearing fine cloaths, and of shewing them, of outshining those whom she suspects to envy her; she has the pleasure of appearing among other Ladies in a place whither the race of meaner mortals seldom intrudes, and of reflecting that, in the conversations of the next morning, her name will be mentioned among those that sat in the first row; she has the pleasure of returning courtesies, or refusing to return them, of receiving compliments with civility, or rejecting them with disdain. She has the pleasure of meeting some of her acquaintance, of guessing why the rest are absent, and of telling them that she saw the opera, on pretence of inquiring why they would miss it. She has the pleasure of being supposed to be pleased with a refined amusement, and of hoping to be numbered among the votresses of harmony. She has the pleasure of escaping for two hours the superiority of a sister, or the controul of a husband; and from all these pleasures she concludes that heavenly music is the balm of life.

All assemblies of gaiety are brought together by motives of the same kind. The Theatre is not filled with those that know or regard the skill of the Actor, nor the Ball-room by those who dance, or attend to the Dancers. To all places of general resort, where the standard of pleasure is erected, we run with equal eagerness, or appearance of eagerness, for very different reasons. One goes that he may say he has been there, another because he never misses. This man goes to try what he can find, and that to discover what others find. Whatever diversion is costly will be frequented by those who desire to be thought rich; and whatever has, by an accident, become fashionable, easily continues its reputation, because every one is ashamed of not partaking it.

To every place of entertainment we go with expectation, and desire of being pleased; we meet others who are brought by the same motives; no one will be the first to own the disappointment; one face reflects the smile of another, till each believes the rest delighted, and endeavours to catch and transmit the circulating rapture. In time, all are deceived by the cheat to which all contribute. The fiction of happiness is propagated by every tongue, and confirmed by every look, till at last all profess the joy which they do not feel, consent to yield to the general delusion; and when the voluntary dream is at an end, lament that bliss is of so short a duration.

If *Drugget* pretended to pleasures, of which he had no perception, or boasted of one amusement where he was indulging another, what did he which is not done by all those who read his story? of whom some pretend delight in conversation, only because they dare not be alone; some praise the quiet of solitude, because they are envious of sense and impatient of folly; and some gratify their pride, by writing characters which expose the vanity of life.

    I am, Sir,
    Your humble Servant.

No. 31. Saturday, *November* 18, 1758.

Many moralists have remarked, that Pride has of all human vices the widest dominion, appears in the greatest multiplicity of forms, and lies hid under the greatest variety of disguises; of disguises, which, like the moon's *veil of brightness,* are both *its lustre and its shade,* and betray it to others, tho' they hide it from ourselves.

It is not my intention to degrade Pride from this pre-eminence of mischief, yet I know not whether Idleness may not maintain a very doubtful and obstinate competition.

There are some that profess Idleness in its full dignity, who call themselves the *Idle,* as *Busiris* in the play *calls himself the Proud;*[1] who boast that they do nothing, and thank their stars that they have nothing to do; who sleep every night till they can sleep no

[1] Edward Young, *Busiris,* 1719, I. i. 13.

longer, and rise only that exercise may enable them to sleep again; who prolong the reign of darkness by double curtains, and never see the sun but to *tell him how they hate his beams;*[2] whose whole labour is to vary the postures of indulgence, and whose day differs from their night but as a couch or chair differs from a bed.

These are the true and open votaries of Idleness, for whom she weaves the garlands of poppies, and into whose cup she pours the waters of oblivion; who exist in a state of unruffled stupidity, forgetting and forgotten; who have long ceased to live, and at whose death the survivors can only say, that they have ceased to breathe.

But Idleness predominates in many lives where it is not suspected; for being a vice which terminates in itself, it may be enjoyed without injury to others; and is therefore not watched like Fraud, which endangers property, or like Pride, which naturally seeks its gratifications in another's inferiority. Idleness is a silent and peaceful quality, that neither raises envy by ostentation, nor hatred by opposition; and therefore no body is busy to censure or detect it.

As Pride sometimes is hid under humility, Idleness is often covered by turbulence and hurry. He that neglects his known duty and real employment, naturally endeavours to croud his mind with something that may bar out the remembrance of his own folly, and does any thing but what he ought to do with eager diligence, that he may keep himself in his own favour.

Some are always in a state of preparation, occupied in previous measures, forming plans, accumulating materials, and providing for the main affair. These are certainly under the secret power of Idleness. Nothing is to be expected from the workman whose tools are for ever to be sought. I was once told by a great master, that no man ever excelled in painting, who was eminently curious about pencils and colours.

There are others to whom Idleness dictates another expedient, by which life may be passed unprofitably away without the tediousness of many vacant hours. The art is, to fill the day with

[2] *Paradise Lost,* IV. 37.

petty business, to have always something in hand which may raise curiosity, but not solicitude, and keep the mind in a state of action, but not of labour.

This art has for many years been practised by my old friend *Sober*, with wonderful success. *Sober* is a man of strong desires and quick imagination, so exactly ballanced by the love of ease, that they can seldom stimulate him to any difficult undertaking; they have, however, so much power, that they will not suffer him to lie quite at rest, and though they do not make him sufficiently useful to others, they make him at least weary of himself.

Mr. *Sober*'s chief pleasure is conversation; there is no end of his talk or his attention; to speak or to hear is equally pleasing; for he still fancies that he is teaching or learning something, and is free for the time from his own reproaches.

But there is one time at night when he must go home, that his friends may sleep; and another time in the morning, when all the world agrees to shut out interruption. These are the moments of which poor *Sober* trembles at the thought. But the misery of these tiresome intervals, he has many means of alleviating. He has persuaded himself that the manual arts are undeservedly overlooked; he has observed in many trades the effects of close thought, and just ratiocination. From speculation he proceeded to practice, and supplied himself with the tools of a carpenter, with which he mended his coal-box very successfully, and which he still continues to employ, as he finds occasion.

He has attempted at other times the crafts of the Shoemaker, Tinman, Plumber, and Potter; in all these arts he has failed, and resolves to qualify himself for them by better information. But his daily amusement is Chemistry. He has a small furnace, which he employs in distillation, and which has long been the solace of his life. He draws oils and waters, and essences and spirits, which he knows to be of no use; sits and counts the drops as they come from his retort, and forgets that, whilst a drop is falling, a moment flies away.

Poor *Sober!* I have often teazed him with reproof, and he has often promised reformation; for no man is so much open to conviction as the *Idler*, but there is none on whom it operates so little. What will be the effect of this paper I know not; perhaps he will read it and laugh, and light the fire in his furnace; but my hope is that he will quit his trifles, and betake himself to rational and useful diligence.[3]

No. 32. SATURDAY, *November* 25, 1758.

Among the innumerable mortifications that way-lay human arrogance on every side may well be reckoned our ignorance of the most common objects and effects, a defect of which we become more sensible by every attempt to supply it. Vulgar and inactive minds confound familiarity with knowledge, and conceive themselves informed of the whole nature of things when they are shewn their form or told their use; but the Speculatist, who is not content with superficial views, harrasses himself with fruitless curiosity, and still as he enquires more perceives only that he knows less.

Sleep is a state in which a great part of every life is passed. No animal has been yet discovered, whose existence is not varied with intervals of insensibility; and some late Philosophers have extended the empire of Sleep over the vegetable world.

Yet of this change so frequent, so great, so general, and so necessary, no searcher has yet found either the efficient or final cause; or can tell by what power the mind and body are thus chained down in irresistible stupefaction; or what benefits the animal receives from this alternate suspension of its active powers.

Whatever may be the multiplicity or contrariety of opinions upon this subject, Nature has taken sufficient care that Theory shall have little influence on Practice. The most diligent enquirer is not able long to keep his eyes open; the most eager disputant will begin about midnight to desert his argument; and once in

[3] In Mr. Sober, we may recognize traits of Dr. Johnson's own character. No. 67 of the Idler is another portrait of him. [1824 ed.]

four and twenty hours, the gay and the gloomy, the witty and the dull, the clamorous and the silent, the busy and the idle, are all overpowered by the gentle tyrant, and all lie down in the equality of Sleep.

Philosophy has often attempted to repress insolence, by asserting that all conditions are levelled by Death; a position which, however it may deject the happy, will seldom afford much comfort to the wretched. It is far more pleasing to consider that Sleep is equally a leveller with Death; that the time is never at a great distance, when the balm of rest shall be effused alike upon every head, when the diversities of life shall stop their operation, and the high and the low shall lie down together.

It is somewhere recorded of *Alexander*, that in the pride of conquests, and intoxication of flattery, he declared that he only perceived himself to be a man by the necessity of Sleep. Whether he considered Sleep as necessary to his mind or body, it was indeed a sufficient evidence of human infirmity; the body which required such frequency of renovation gave but faint promises of immortality; and the mind which, from time to time, sunk gladly into insensibility, had made no very near approaches to the felicity of the supreme and selfsufficient Nature.

I know not what can tend more to repress all the passions that disturb the peace of the world, than the consideration that there is no height of happiness or honour, from which man does not eagerly descend to a state of unconscious repose, that the best condition of life is such, that we contentedly quit its good to be disentangled from its evils; that in a few hours splendor fades before the eye, and praise itself deadens in the ear; the senses withdraw from their objects, and reason favours the retreat.

What then are the hopes and prospects of covetousness, ambition, and rapacity? Let him that desires most have all his desires gratified, he never shall attain a state, which he can, for a day and a night, contemplate with satisfaction, or from which, if he had the power of perpetual vigilance, he would not long for periodical separations.

All envy would be extinguished if it were universally known that there are none to be envied, and surely none can be much envied who are not pleased with themselves. There is reason to suspect that the distinctions of mankind have more shew than value, when it is found that all agree to be weary alike of pleasures and of cares; that the powerful and the weak, the celebrated and obscure, join in one common wish, and implore from Nature's hand the nectar of oblivion.

Such is our desire of abstraction from ourselves, that very few are satisfied with the quantity of stupefaction which the needs of the body force upon the mind. *Alexander* himself added intemperance to sleep, and solaced with the fumes of wine the sovereignty of the world; and almost every man has some art, by which he steals his thoughts away from his present state.

It is not much of life that is spent in close attention to any important duty. Many hours of every day are suffered to fly away without any traces left upon the intellects. We suffer phantoms to rise up before us, and amuse ourselves with the dance of airy images, which after a time we dismiss for ever, and know not how we have been busied.

Many have no happier moments than those that they pass in solitude, abandoned to their own imagination, which sometimes puts sceptres in their hands or mitres on their heads, shifts the scene of pleasure with endless variety, bids all the forms of beauty sparkle before them, and gluts them with every change of visionary luxury.

It is easy in these semi-slumbers to collect all the possibilities of happiness, to alter the course of the Sun, to bring back the past, and anticipate the future, to unite all the beauties of all seasons, and all the blessings of all climates, to receive and bestow felicity, and forget that misery is the lot of man. All this is a voluntary dream, a temporary recession from the realities of life to airy fictions; and habitual subjection of reason to fancy.[1]

Others are afraid to be alone, and amuse themselves by a perpetual succession of companions: but the difference is not great; in solitude we have our dreams to ourselves, and in com-

[1] Johnson's reflections here forecast the Astronomer in *Rasselas*, chs. 40 ff.

pany we agree to dream in concert. The end sought in both is forgetfulness of ourselves.

No. 41. SATURDAY, *January 27, 1759.*

The following Letter relates to an affliction[1] perhaps not necessary to be imparted to the Public, but I could not persuade myself to suppress it, because I think I know the sentiments to be sincere, and I feel no disposition to provide for this day any other entertainment.

> *At tu quisquis eris, miseri qui cruda poetæ*
>   *Credideris fletu funera digna tuo,*
> *Hæc postrema tibi sit flendi causa, fluatque*
>   *Lenis inoffenso vitaque morsque gradu.*[2]
>
> OVID.

Mr. Idler,

Notwithstanding the warnings of Philosophers, and the daily examples of losses and misfortunes which life forces upon our observation, such is the absorption of our thoughts in the business of the present day, such the resignation of our reason to empty hopes of future felicity, or such our unwillingness to foresee what we dread, that every calamity comes suddenly upon us, and not only presses us as a burthen, but crushes as a blow.

There are evils which happen out of the common course of nature, against which it is no reproach not to be provided. A flash of lightning intercepts the traveller in his way. The concussion of an earthquake heaps the ruins of cities upon their

---

[1] This paper was occasioned by the death of Johnson's mother.

[2] "But thou, whoever thou shalt be, that shalt deem worthy thy tears the untimely fate of the poet, mayst thou have no further cause to mourn, and may life and death flow easily with gentle pace." The passage has not been found in Ovid.

inhabitants. But other miseries time brings, though silently yet visibly forward by its even lapse, which yet approach us unseen because we turn our eyes away, and seize us unresisted because we could not arm ourselves against them, but by setting them before us.

That it is vain to shrink from what cannot be avoided, and to hide that from ourselves which must some time be found, is a truth which we all know, but which all neglect, and perhaps none more than the speculative reasoner, whose thoughts are always from home, whose eye wanders over life, whose fancy dances after meteors of happiness kindled by itself, and who examines every thing rather than his own state.

Nothing is more evident than that the decays of age must terminate in death; yet there is no man, says *Tully*,[3] who does not believe that he may yet live another year; and there is none who does not, upon the same principle, hope another year for his parent or his friend; but the fallacy will be in time detected; the last year, the last day must come. It has come and is past. The life which made my own life pleasant is at an end, and the gates of death are shut upon my prospects.

The loss of a friend upon whom the heart was fixed, to whom every wish and endeavour tended, is a state of dreary desolation in which the mind looks abroad impatient of itself, and finds nothing but emptiness and horror. The blameless life, the artless tenderness, the pious simplicity, the modest resignation, the patient sickness, and the quiet death, are remembered only to add value to the loss, to aggravate regret for what cannot be amended, to deepen sorrow for what cannot be recalled.

These are the calamities by which Providence gradually disengages us from the love of life. Other evils fortitude may repel, or hope may mitigate; but irreparable privation leaves nothing to exercise resolution or flatter expectation. The dead cannot return, and nothing is left us here but languishment and grief.

Yet such is the course of nature, that whoever lives long must outlive those whom he loves and honours. Such is the condition

[3] Cicero, *De Senectute*, 24.

of our present existence, that life must one time lose its associa-
tions, and every inhabitant of the earth must walk downward to
the grave alone and unregarded, without any partner of his joy
or grief, without any interested witness of his misfortunes or
success.

Misfortune, indeed, he may yet feel, for where is the bottom
of the misery of man? But what is success to him that has none
to enjoy it. Happiness is not found in self-contemplation; it is
perceived only when it is reflected from another.

We know little of the state of departed souls, because such
knowledge is not necessary to a good life. Reason deserts us at
the brink of the grave, and can give no further intelligence.
Revelation is not wholly silent. *There is joy in the Angels of
Heaven over one Sinner that repenteth*,[4] and surely this joy is
not incommunicable to souls disentangled from the body, and
made like Angels.

Let Hope therefore dictate, what Revelation does not confute,
that the union of souls may still remain; and that we who are
struggling with sin, sorrow, and infirmities, may have our part
in the attention and kindness of those who have finished their
course, and are now receiving their reward.

These are the great occasions which force the mind to take
refuge in Religion: When we have no help in ourselves, what
can remain but that we look up to a higher and a greater Power;
and to what hope may we not raise our eyes and hearts, when we
consider that the Greatest POWER is the BEST?

Surely there is no man who, thus afflicted, does not seek succour
in the *Gospel*, which has brought *Life and Immortality to light*.[5]
The Precepts of *Epicurus,* who teaches us to endure what the
Laws of the Universe make necessary, may silence but not content
us. The dictates of *Zeno,* who commands us to look with indif-
ference on external things, may dispose us to conceal our sorrow,
but cannot assuage it. Real alleviation of the loss of friends, and
rational tranquility in the prospect of our own dissolution, can be

[4] Luke 15: 10.
[5] II Tim. 1: 10.

received only from the promises of him in whose hands are life and death, and from the assurance of another and better state, in which all tears will be wiped from the eyes, and the whole soul shall be filled with joy. Philosophy may infuse stubbornness, but Religion only can give Patience.

I am, &c.

No. 57. Saturday, *May* 19, 1759.

Prudence is of more frequent use than any other intellectual quality; it is exerted on slight occasions, and called into act by the cursory business of common life.

Whatever is universally necessary, has been granted to mankind on easy terms. Prudence, as it is always wanted, is without great difficulty obtained. It requires neither extensive view nor profound search, but forces itself, by spontaneous impulse, upon a mind neither great nor busy, neither ingrossed by vast designs nor distracted by multiplicity of attention.

Prudence operates on life in the same manner as rules on composition; it produces vigilance rather than elevation, rather prevents loss than procures advantage; and often escapes miscarriages, but seldom reaches either power or honour. It quenches that ardour of enterprize, by which every thing is done that can claim praise or admiration; and represses that generous temerity which often fails and often succeeds. Rules may obviate faults, but can never confer beauties; and Prudence keeps life safe, but does not often make it happy. The world is not amazed with prodigies of excellence, but when Wit tramples upon Rules, and Magnanimity breaks the chains of Prudence.

One of the most prudent of all that have fallen within my observation, is my old companion *Sophron,* who has passed through the world in quiet, by perpetual adherence to a few plain maxims, and wonders how contention and distress can so often happen.

The first principle of *Sophron* is to *run no hazards.* Tho' he loves money, he is of opinion, that frugality is a more certain source of riches than industry. It is to no purpose that any prospect of large profit is set before him; he believes little about futurity, and does not love to trust his money out of his sight, for nobody knows what may happen. He has a small estate which he lets at the old rent, because *it is better to have a little than nothing;* but he rigorously demands payment on the stated day, for *he that cannot pay one quarter cannot pay two.* If he is told of any improvements in Agriculture, he likes the old way, has observed that changes very seldom answer expectation, is of opinion that our forefathers knew how to till the ground as well as we, and concludes with an argument that nothing can overpower, that the expence of planting and fencing is immediate, and the advantage distant, and that *he is no wise man who will quit a certainty for an uncertainty.*

Another of *Sophron*'s rules is, *to mind no business but his own.* In the State he is of no party; but hears and speaks of publick affairs with the same coldness as of the administration of some ancient republick. If any flagrant act of Fraud or Oppression is mentioned, he hopes that *all is not true that is told:* If Misconduct or Corruption puts the nation in a flame, he hopes that *every man means well.* At Elections he leaves his dependents to their own choice, and declines to vote himself, for every Candidate is a good man, whom he is unwilling to oppose or offend.

If disputes happen among his neighbours, he observes an invariable and cold neutrality. His punctuality has gained him the reputation of honesty, and his caution that of wisdom, and few would refuse to refer their claims to his award. He might have prevented many expensive law-suits, and quenched many a feud in its first smoke, but always refuses the office of Arbitration, because he must decide against one or the other.

With the affairs of other families he is always unacquainted. He sees estates bought and sold, squandered and increased, without praising the economist or censuring the spendthrift. He never courts the rising lest they should fall, nor insults the fallen lest they should rise again. His caution has the appearance of virtue, and all who do not want his help praise his benevolence; but if any man solicits his assistance, he has just sent away all his money; and when the petitioner is gone, declares to his family that he is sorry for his misfortunes, has always looked upon him with particular kindness, and therefore could not lend him money, lest he should destroy their friendship by the necessity of enforcing payment.

Of domestic misfortunes he has never heard. When he is told the hundredth time of a Gentleman's daughter who has married the coachman, he lifts up his hands with astonishment, for he always thought her a very sober girl. When nuptial quarrels, after having filled the country with talk and laughter, at last end in separation, he never can conceive how it happened, for he looked upon them as a happy couple.

If his advice is asked, he never gives any particular direction, because events are uncertain, and he will bring no blame upon himself; but he takes the consulter tenderly by the hand, tells him he makes his case his own, and advises him not to act rashly, but to weigh the reasons on both sides; observes that a man may be as easily too hasty as too slow, and that as many fail by doing too much as too little; that *a wise man has two ears and one tongue*; and *that little said is soon amended*; that he could tell him this and that, but that after all every man is the best judge of his own affairs.

With this some are satisfied, and go home with great reverence of *Sophron*'s wisdom, and none are offended, because every one is left in full possession of his own opinion.

Sophron gives no characters. It is equally vain to tell him of Vice and Virtue, for he has remarked that no man likes to be censured, and that very few are delighted with the praises of another. He has a few terms which he uses to all alike. With respect to fortune, he believes every family to be in good circumstances; he never exalts any understanding by lavish praise, yet he meets with none but very sensible people. Every man is honest and hearty, and every woman is a good creature.

Thus *Sophron* creeps along, neither loved nor hated, neither favoured nor opposed; he has never attempted to grow rich for fear of growing poor, and has raised no friends for fear of making enemies.

Criticism

No. 60. SATURDAY, *June* 9, 1759.

Criticism is a study by which men grow important and formidable at a very small expence. The power of invention has been conferred by Nature upon few, and the labour of learning those sciences which may, by mere labour, be obtained, is too great to be willingly endured; but every man can exert such judgment as he has upon the works of others; and he whom Nature has made weak, and Idleness keeps ignorant, may yet support his vanity by the name of a Critick.

I hope it will give comfort to great numbers who are passing thro' the world in obscurity, when I inform them how easily distinction may be obtained. All the other powers of literature are coy and haughty, they must be long courted, and at last are not always gained; but Criticism is a goddess easy of access and forward of advance, who will meet the slow and encourage the timorous; the want of meaning she supplies with words, and the want of spirit she recompenses with malignity.

This profession has one recommendation peculiar to itself, that it gives vent to malignity without real mischief. No genius was ever blasted by the breath of Criticks. The poison which if confined, would have burst the heart, fumes away in empty hisses, and malice is set at ease with very little danger to merit. The Critick is the only man whose triumph is without another's pain, and whose greatness does not rise upon another's ruin.

To a study at once so easy and so reputable, so malicious and so harmless, it cannot be necessary to invite my readers by a long or laboured exhortation; it is sufficient, since all would be Critics if they could, to shew by one eminent example that all can be Criticks if they will.

Dick Minim, after the common course of puerile studies,

not a good student

in which he was no great proficient, was put apprentice to a Brewer, with whom he had lived two years, when his uncle died in the city, and left him a large fortune in the stocks. *Dick* had for six months before used the company of the lower players, of whom he had learned to scorn a trade, and being now at liberty to follow his genius, he resolved to be a man of wit and humour. That he might be properly initiated in his new character, he frequented the coffee-houses near the theatres, where he listened very diligently, day after day, to those who talked of language and sentiments, and unities and catastrophes, till by slow degrees he began to think that he understood something of the Stage, and hoped in time to talk himself.

But he did not trust so much to natural sagacity, as wholly to neglect the help of books. When the Theatres were shut, he retired to *Richmond* with a few select writers, whose opinions he impressed upon his memory by unwearied diligence; and when he returned with other wits to the town, was able to tell, in very proper phrases, that the chief business of art is to copy nature; that a perfect writer is not to be expected, because genius decays as judgment increases; that the great art is the art of blotting; and that according to the rule of *Horace*, every piece should be kept nine years.[1]

Of the great Authors he now began to display the Characters, laying down as an universal position, that all had beauties and defects. His opinion was, that *Shakespear*, committing himself wholly to the impulse of Nature, wanted that correctness which learning would have given him; and that *Jonson*, trusting to learning, did not sufficiently cast his eye on Nature. He blamed the *Stanza* of *Spenser*, and could not bear the *Hexameters* of *Sidney*. *Denham* and *Waller* he held the first reformers of *English* Numbers, and thought that if *Waller* could have obtained the strength of *Denham*, or *Denham* the sweetness of *Waller*, there had been nothing wanting to complete a Poet.[2] He often expressed his commiseration of *Dryden*'s poverty, and his indig-

---

[1] *Ars Poetica*, 388.
[2] Cf. Pope, *An Essay on Criticism*, 361.

play by Dryden

nation at the age which suffered him to write for bread; he repeated with rapture the first lines of *All for Love,* but wondered at the corruption of taste which could bear any thing so unnatural as rhyming tragedies. In *Otway* he found uncommon powers of moving the passions, but was disgusted by his general negligence, and blamed him for making a Conspirator his Hero; and never concluded his disquisition, without remarking how happily the sound of the clock is made to alarm the audience. *Southern* would have been his favourite, but that he mixes comick with tragick scenes, intercepts the natural course of the passions, and fills the mind with a wild confusion of mirth and melancholy. The versification of *Rowe* he thought too melodious for the stage, and too little varied in different passions. He made it the great fault of *Congreve,* that all his persons were wits, and that he always wrote with more art than nature. He considered *Cato* rather as a poem than a play, and allowed *Addison* to be the complete master of Allegory and grave humour, but paid no great deference to him as a Critick. He thought the chief merit of *Prior* was in his easy tales and lighter poems, tho' he allowed that his *Solomon* had many noble sentiments elegantly expressed. in *Swift* he discovered an inimitable vein of irony, and an easiness which all would hope and few would attain. *Pope* he was inclined to degrade from a Poet to a Versifier, and thought his numbers rather luscious than sweet. He often lamented the neglect of *Phædra and Hippolytus,*[3] and wished to see the stage under better regulations.

These assertions passed commonly uncontradicted;[4] and if now and then an opponent started up, he was quickly repressed by the suffrages of the company, and *Minim* went away from every dispute with elation of heart and increase of confidence.

He now grew conscious of his abilities, and began to talk of the present state of dramatick Poetry; wondered what was become of the comick genius which supplied our ancestors with wit and

[3] By Edmund Smith, 1707. So also, as Osgood notes, thought Addison in *The Spectator,* No. 18.
[4] The point, of course, is that the foregoing are all critical clichés of the age.

pleasantry, and why no writer could be found that durst now venture beyond a Farce. He saw no reason for thinking that the vein of humour was exhausted, since we live in a country where liberty suffers every character to spread itself to its utmost bulk, and which therefore produces more originals than all the rest of the world together.[5] Of Tragedy he concluded business to be the soul, and yet often hinted that love predominates too much upon the modern stage.

He was now an acknowledged Critick, and had his own seat in a coffee-house, and headed a party in the pit. *Minim* has more vanity than ill-nature, and seldom desires to do much mischief; he will perhaps murmur a little in the ear of him that sits next him, but endeavours to influence the audience to favour, by clapping when an actor exclaims *ye Gods,* or laments the misery of his country.

By degrees he was admitted to Rehearsals, and many of his friends are of opinion, that our present Poets are indebted to him for their happiest thoughts; by his contrivance the bell was rung twice in *Barbarossa,*[6] and by his persuasion the author of *Cleone*[7] concluded his Play without a couplet; for what can be more absurd, said *Minim,* than that part of a play should be rhymed, and part written in blank verse? and by what acquisition of faculties is the Speaker who never could find rhymes before, enabled to rhyme at the conclusion of an Act?

He is the great investigator of hidden beauties, and is particularly delighted when he finds *the Sound an Echo to the Sense.*[8] He has read all our Poets with particular attention to this delicacy of Versification, and wonders at the supineness with which their Works have been hitherto perused, so that no man has found the sound of a Drum in this distich,

> When Pulpit, Drum ecclesiastic,
> Was beat with fist instead of a stick,[9]

[5] Cf. *ante, The Adventurer,* No. 84.
[6] By Dr. John Brown, 1754.
[7] By Robert Dodsley, 1758.
[8] Pope, *An Essay on Criticism,* l. 365.
[9] Samuel Butler, *Hudibras,* I. i. 11–12.

and that the wonderful lines upon Honour and a Bubble have
hitherto passed without notice,

> Honour is like the glassy Bubble,
> Which costs Philosophers such trouble;
> Where one part crack'd, the whole does fly,
> And Wits are crack'd to find out why.[10]

In these Verses, says *Minim*, we have two striking accommoda-
tions of the Sound to the Sense. It is impossible to utter the [first]
two lines emphatically without an act like that which they
describe; *Bubble* and *Trouble* causing a momentary inflation of
the Cheeks by the retention of the breath, which is afterwards
forcibly emitted, as in the practice of *blowing bubbles*. But the
greatest excellence is in the third line, which is *crack'd* in the
middle to express a crack, and then shivers into monosyllables.
Yet has this diamond lain neglected with common stones, and
among the innumerable admirers of *Hudibras* the observation of
this superlative passage has been reserved for the sagacity of
Minim.

No. 61. Saturday, *June* 16, 1759.

Mr. Minim had now advanced himself to the zenith of critical
reputation; when he was in the Pit, every eye in the Boxes was
fixed upon him; when he entered his Coffee-house, he was sur-
rounded by circles of candidates, who passed their noviciate of
literature under his tuition; his opinion was asked by all who had
no opinion of their own, and yet loved to debate and decide; and
no composition was supposed to pass in safety to posterity, till it
had been secured by *Minim*'s approbation.

Minim professes great admiration of the wisdom and munifi-
cence by which the Academies of the continent were raised, and

[10] *Ibid.,* II. ii. 385–388.

often wishes for some standard of taste, for some tribunal, to which merit may appeal from caprice, prejudice, and malignity. He has formed a plan for an Academy of Criticism, where every work of Imagination may be read before it is printed, and which shall authoritatively direct the Theatres what pieces to receive or reject, to exclude or to revive.

Such an institution would, in *Dick's* opinion, spread the fame of *English* Literature over *Europe,* and make *London* the metropolis of elegance and politeness, the place to which the learned and ingenious of all countries would repair for instruction and improvement, and where nothing would any longer be applauded or endured that was not conformed to the nicest rules, and finished with the highest elegance.

Till some happy conjunction of the planets shall dispose our Princes or Ministers to make themselves immortal by such an Academy, *Minim* contents himself to preside four nights in a week in a Critical Society selected by himself, where he is heard without contradiction, and whence his judgment is disseminated through the great vulgar and the small.

When he is placed in the chair of Criticism, he declares loudly for the noble simplicity of our ancestors, in opposition to the petty refinements, and ornamental luxuriance. Some-times he is sunk in despair, and perceives false delicacy daily gaining ground, and sometimes brightens his countenance with a gleam of hope, and predicts the revival of the true sublime. He then fulminates his loudest censures against the monkish barbarity of rhyme; wonders how beings that pretend to reason can be pleased with one line always ending like another; tells how unjustly and unnaturally sense is sacrificed to sound; how often the best thoughts are mangled by the necessity of confining or extending them to the dimensions of a couplet; and rejoices that genius has, in our days, shaken off the shackles which had encumbered it so long. Yet he allows that rhyme may sometimes be borne, if the lines be often broken, and the pauses judiciously diversified.

From Blank Verse he makes an easy transition to *Milton,* whom he produces as an example of the slow advance of lasting reputation. *Milton* is the only writer whose books *Minim* can read for ever without weariness. What cause it is that exempts this pleasure from satiety he has long and diligently enquired, and believes it to consist in the perpetual variation of the numbers, by which the ear is gratified and the attention awakened. The lines that are commonly thought rugged and unmusical, he conceives to have been written to temper the melodious luxury of the rest, or to express things by a proper cadence: for he scarcely finds a verse that has not this favourite beauty; he declares that he could shiver in a hot-house when he reads that

> the ground
> Burns frore, and cold performs th' effect of fire;[1]

and that when *Milton* bewails his blindness, the verse

> So thick a drop serene has quench'd these orbs,[2]

has, he knows not how, something that strikes him with an obscure sensation like that which he fancies would be felt from the sound of Darkness.

Minim is not so confident of his rules of Judgment as not very eagerly to catch new light from the name of the author. He is commonly so prudent as to spare those whom he cannot resist, unless, as will sometimes happen, he finds the publick combined against them. But a fresh pretender to fame he is strongly inclined to censure, 'till his own honour requires that he commend him. 'Till he knows the success of a composition, he intrenches himself in general terms; there are some new thoughts and beautiful passages, but there is likewise much which he would have advised the author to expunge. He has several favourite epithets, of which he has never settled the meaning, but which are very commodiously applied to books which he has not read, or cannot understand. One is *manly,* another is *dry,* another *stiff,* and another *flimzy;* sometimes he discovers delicacy of style, and sometimes meets with *strange expressions.*

He is never so great, or so happy, as when a youth of promis-

[1] *Paradise Lost,* II. 595.
[2] *Ibid.,* III. 25.

ing parts is brought to receive his directions for the prosecution of his studies. He then puts on a very serious air; he advises the pupil to read none but the best Authors, and, when he finds one congenial to his own mind, to study his beauties, but avoid his faults, and, when he sits down to write, to consider how his favourite Author would think at the present time on the present occasion. He exhorts him to catch those moments when he finds his thoughts expanded and his genius exalted, but to take care lest imagination hurry him beyond the bounds of Nature. He holds Diligence the mother of Success, yet enjoins him, with great earnestness, not to read more than he can digest, and not to confuse his mind by pursuing studies of contrary tendencies. He tells him, that every man has his genius, and that *Cicero* could never be a Poet. The boy retires illuminated, resolves to follow his genius, and to think how *Milton* would have thought; and *Minim* feasts upon his own beneficence till another day brings another Pupil.

a joke

No. 72. SATURDAY, *September* 1, 1759.

Men complain of nothing more frequently than of deficient Memory; and indeed, every one finds that many of the ideas which he desired to retain have slipped irretrievably away; that the acquisitions of the mind are sometimes equally fugitive with the gifts of fortune; and that a short intermission of attention more certainly lessens knowledge than impairs an estate.

To assist this weakness of our nature many methods have been proposed, all of which may be justly suspected of being ineffectual; for no art of memory, however its effects have been boasted or admired, has been ever adopted into general use, nor have those who possessed it, appeared to excel others in readiness of recollection or multiplicity of attainments.

There is another art of which all have felt the want, tho' *Themistocles* only confessed it. We suffer equal pain from the

pertinacious adhesion of unwelcome images, as from the eva-
nescence of those which are pleasing and useful; and it may be
doubted whether we should be more benefited by the art of
Memory or the art of Forgetfulness.

Forgetfulness is necessary to Remembrance. Ideas are retained
by renovation of that impression which time is always wearing
away, and which new images are striving to obliterate. If useless
thoughts could be expelled from the mind, all the valuable parts
of our knowledge would more frequently recur, and every re-
currence would reinstate them in their former place.

It is impossible to consider, without some regret, how much
might have been learned, or how much might have been invented
by a rational and vigorous application of time, uselessly or pain-
fully passed in the revocation of events, which have left neither
good nor evil behind them, in grief for misfortunes either repaired
or irreparable, in resentment of injuries known only to ourselves,
of which death has put the authors beyond our power.

Philosophy has accumulated precept upon precept, to warn
us against the anticipation of future calamities. All useless misery
is certainly folly, and he that feels evils before they come may be
deservedly censured; yet surely to dread the future is more
reasonable than to lament the past. The business of life is to go
forwards; he who sees evil in prospect meets it in his way, but
he who catches it by retrospection turns back to find it. That
which is feared may sometimes be avoided, but that which is
regretted to-day may be regretted again to-morrow.

Regret is indeed useful and virtuous, and not only allowable
but necessary, when it tends to the amendment of life, or to
admonition of error which we may be again in danger of com-
mitting. But a very small part of the moments spent in medita-
tion on the past, produce any reasonable caution or salutary
sorrow. Most of the mortifications that we have suffered, arose
from the concurrence of local and temporary circumstances,
which can never meet again; and most of our disappointments
have succeeded those expectations, which life allows not to be
formed a second time.

It would add much to human happiness, if an art could be

taught of forgetting all of which the remembrance is at once useless and afflictive, if that pain which never can end in pleasure could be driven totally away, that the mind might perform its functions without incumbrance, and the past might no longer encroach upon the present.

Little can be done well to which the whole mind is not applied; the business of every day calls for the day to which it is assigned; and he will have no leisure to regret yesterday's vexations who resolves not to have a new subject of regret tomorrow.

But to forget or to remember at pleasure, are equally beyond the power of man. Yet as memory may be assisted by method, and the decays of knowledge repaired by stated times of recollection, so the power of forgetting is capable of improvement. Reason will, by a resolute contest, prevail over imagination, and the power may be obtained of transferring the attention as judgment shall direct.

The incursions of troublesome thoughts are often violent and importunate; and it is not easy to a mind accustomed to their inroads to expel them immediately by putting better images into motion; but this enemy of quiet is above all others weakened by every defeat; the reflection which has been once overpowered and ejected, seldom returns with any formidable vehemence.

Employment is the great instrument of intellectual dominion. The mind cannot retire from its enemy into total vacancy, or turn aside from one object but by passing to another. The gloomy and the resentful are always found among those who have nothing to do, or who do nothing. We must be busy about good or evil, and he to whom the present offers nothing will often be looking backward on the past.

No. 88. SATURDAY, *December* 22, 1759.

When the Philosophers of the last Age were first congregated into the Royal Society, great expectations were raised of the

sudden progress of useful Arts; the time was supposed to be near
when Engines should turn by a perpetual motion, and Health
be secured by the universal Medicine; when Learning should be
facilitated by a real Character, and Commerce extended by ships
which could reach their Ports in defiance of the Tempest.

But Improvement is naturally slow. The Society met and
parted without any visible diminution of the miseries of life. The
Gout and Stone were still painful, the Ground that was not
plowed brought no Harvest, and neither Oranges nor Grapes
would grow upon the Hawthorn. At last, those who were dis-
appointed began to be angry; those likewise who hated innova-
tion were glad to gain an opportunity of ridiculing men who had
depreciated, perhaps with too much arrogance, the Knowledge of
Antiquity. And it appears from some of their earliest Apologies,
that the Philosophers felt with great sensibility the unwelcome
importunities of those who were daily asking, "What have ye
done?"

The truth is, that little had been done compared with what
Fame had been suffered to promise; and the question could only
be answered by general apologies and by new hopes, which, when
they were frustrated, gave a new occasion to the same vexatious
enquiry.

This fatal question has disturbed the quiet of many other minds.
He that in the latter part of his life too strictly enquires what he
has done, can very seldom receive from his own heart such an
account as will give him satisfaction.

We do not indeed so often disappoint others as ourselves. We
not only think more highly than others of our own abilities, but
allow ourselves to form hopes which we never communicate, and
please our thoughts with employments which none ever will
allot us, and with elevations to which we are never expected to
rise; and when our days and years have passed away in common
business or common amusements, and we find at last that we have
suffered our purposes to sleep till the time of action is past, we are
reproached only by our own reflections; neither our friends nor
our enemies wonder that we live and die like the rest of mankind;

that we live without notice and die without memorial; they know not what task we had proposed, and therefore cannot discern whether it is finished.

He that compares what he has done with what he has left undone, will feel the effect which must always follow the comparison of imagination with reality; he will look with contempt on his own unimportance, and wonder to what purpose he came into the world; he will repine that he shall leave behind him no evidence of his having been, that he has added nothing to the system of life, but has glided from Youth to Age among the crowd, without any effort for distinction.

Man is seldom willing to let fall the opinion of his own dignity, or to believe that he does little only because every individual is a very little being. He is better content to want Diligence than Power, and sooner confesses the Depravity of his Will than the Imbecillity of his Nature.

From this mistaken notion of human Greatness it proceeds, that many who pretend to have made great Advances in Wisdom so loudly declare that they despise themselves. If I had ever found any of the Self-contemners much irritated or pained by the consciousness of their meanness, I should have given them consolation by observing, that a little more than nothing is as much as can be expected from a being who with respect to the multitudes about him is himself little more than nothing. Every man is obliged by the supreme Master of the Universe to improve all the opportunities of Good which are afforded him, and to keep in continual activity such Abilities as are bestowed upon him. But he has no reason to repine, though his Abilities are small and his Opportunities few. He that has improved the Virtue or advanced the Happiness of one Fellow-creature, he that has ascertained a single moral Proposition, or added one useful Experiment to natural Knowledge, may be contented with his own Performance, and, with respect to mortals like himself, may demand, like *Augustus*,[1] to be dismissed at his departure with Applause.

[1] Suetonius, *Octavius*, 99.

Easter

No. 103. SATURDAY, *April* 5, 1760.

Respicere ad longæ jussit spatia ultima vitæ.

Juv. [*Sat.* X. 275.]

"bade him regard the last period of a long life."

Much of the Pain and Pleasure of mankind arises from the con-
jectures which every one makes of the thoughts of others; we all
enjoy praise which we do not hear, and resent contempt which
we do not see. The *Idler* may therefore be forgiven, if he suffers
his Imagination to represent to him what his readers will say or
think when they are informed that they have now his last paper
in their hands.

Value is more frequently raised by scarcity than by use. That
which lay neglected when it was common, rises in estimation as
its quantity becomes less. We seldom learn the true want of what
we have till it is discovered that we can have no more.

This essay will, perhaps, be read with care even by those who
have not yet attended to any other; and he that finds this late
attention recompensed, will not forbear to wish that he had
bestowed it sooner.

Though the *Idler* and his readers have contracted no close
friendship, they are perhaps both unwilling to part. There are
few things not purely evil, of which we can say, without some
emotion of uneasiness, *this is the last*. Those who never could
agree together, shed tears when mutual discontent has deter-
mined them to final separation; of a place which has been fre-
quently visited, tho' without pleasure, the last look is taken with
heaviness of heart; and the *Idler*, with all his chilness of tran-
quility, is not wholly unaffected by the thought that his last
essay is now before him.

This secret horrour of the last is inseparable from a thinking
being whose life is limited, and to whom death is dreadful. We
always make a secret comparison between a part and the whole;
the termination of any period of life reminds us that life itself

has likewise its termination; when we have done any thing for the last time, we involuntarily reflect that a part of the days allotted us is past, and that as more is past there is less remaining.

It is very happily and kindly provided, that in every life there are certain pauses and interruptions, which force consideration upon the careless, and seriousness upon the light; points of time where one course of action ends and another begins: and by vicissitude of fortune, or alteration of employment, by change of place, or loss of friendship, we are forced to say of something, *this is the last*.

An even and unvaried tenour of life always hides from our apprehension the approach of its end. Succession is not perceived but by variation; he that lives to-day as he lived yesterday, and expects that, as the present day is such will be the morrow, easily conceives time as running in a circle and returning to itself. The uncertainty of our duration is impressed commonly by dissimilitude of condition; it is only by finding life changeable that we are reminded of its shortness.

This conviction, however forcible at every new impression, is every moment fading from the mind; and partly by the inevitable incursion of new images, and partly by voluntary exclusion of unwelcome thoughts, we are again exposed to the universal fallacy; and we must do another thing for the last time, before we consider that the time is nigh when we shall do no more.

As the last *Idler* is published in that solemn week which the Christian world has always set apart for the examination of the conscience, the review of life, the extinction of earthly desires and the renovation of holy purposes, I hope that my readers are already disposed to view every incident with seriousness, and improve it by meditation; and that when they see this series of trifles brought to a conclusion, they will consider that by outliving the *Idler,* they have passed weeks, months, and years which are now no longer in their power; that an end must in time be put to every thing great as to every thing little; that to life must come its last hour, and to this system of being its last day, the hour at which probation ceases, and repentance will be vain; the day in which every work of the hand, and imagination of the heart shall be brought to judgment, and an everlasting futurity shall be determined by the past.

CRITICISM

FROM a review of Soame Jenyns' A Free Inquiry into the Nature and Origin of Evil

This doctrine of the regular subordination of beings, the scale of existence, and the chain of nature, I have often considered, but always left the Inquiry in doubt and uncertainty.

That every being not infinite, compared with infinity, must be imperfect, is evident to intuition; that whatever is imperfect must have a certain line which it cannot pass, is equally certain. But the reason which determined this limit, and for which such being was suffered to advance thus far and no further, we shall never be able to discern. Our discoverers tell us, the Creator has made beings of all orders, and that therefore one of them must be such as man. But this system seems to be established on a concession which if it be refused cannot be extorted.

Every reason which can be brought to prove, that there are beings of every possible sort, will prove that there is the greatest number possible of every sort of beings; but this with respect to man we know, if we know any thing, not to be true.

It does not appear even to the imagination, that of three orders of being, the first and the third receive any advantage from the

imperfection of the second, or that indeed they may not equally
exist, though the second had never been, or should cease to be,
and why should that be concluded necessary, which cannot be
proved even to be useful?

The scale of existence from infinity to nothing, cannot possibly
have being. The highest being not infinite must be, as has been
often observed, at an infinite distance below infinity. *Cheyne,*[1]
who, with the desire inherent in mathematicians to reduce every
thing to mathematical images, considers all existence as a *cone,*
allows that the basis is at an infinite distance from the body. And
in this distance between finite and infinite, there will be room for
ever for an infinite series of indefinable existence.

Between the lowest positive existence and nothing, wherever we
suppose positive existence to cease, is another chasm infinitely
deep; where there is room again for endless orders of sub-
ordinate nature, continued for ever and for ever and yet infinitely
superior to non-existence.

To these meditations humanity is unequal. But yet we may
ask, not of our maker, but of each other, since on the one side
creation, wherever it stops, must stop infinitely below infinity,
and on the other infinitely above nothing, what necessity there
is that it should proceed so far either way, that beings so high
or so low should ever have existed. We may ask; but I believe no
created wisdom can give an adequate answer.

Nor is this all. In the scale, wherever it begins or ends, are
infinite vacuities. At whatever distance we suppose the next order
of beings to be above man, there is room for an intermediate order
of beings between them; and if for one order then for infinite
orders; since every thing that admits of more or less, and con-
sequently all the parts of that which admits them, may be in-
finitely divided. So that, as far as we can judge, there may be
room in the vacuity between any two steps of the scale, or be-
tween any two points of the cone of being for infinite exertion
of infinite power.

[1] George Cheyne, *Philosophical Principles of Natural Religion,* 1705–
1715.

Thus it appears how little reason those who repose their reason upon the scale of being have to triumph over them who recur to any other expedient of solution, and what difficulties arise on every side to repress the rebellions of presumptuous decision. *Qui pauca considerat, facile pronunciat.*[2] In our passage through the boundless ocean of disquisition we often take fogs for land, and after having long toiled to approach them, find instead of repose and harbours, new storms of objection and fluctuations of uncertainty.

We are next entertained with *Pope's* alleviations of those evils which we are doomed to suffer.

"Poverty, or the want of riches, is generally compensated by having more hopes and fewer fears, by a greater share of health, and a more exquisite relish of the smallest enjoyments, than those who possess them are usually bless'd with. The want of taste and genius, with all the pleasures that arise from them, are commonly recompenced by a more useful kind of common sense, together with a wonderful delight, as well as success, in the busy pursuits of a scrambling world. The sufferings of the sick are greatly relieved by many trifling gratifications imperceptible to others, and sometimes almost repaid by the inconceivable transports occasioned by the return of health and vigour. Folly cannot be very grievous, because imperceptible; and I doubt not but there is some truth in that rant of a mad poet, that there is a pleasure in being mad, which none but madmen know. Ignorance, or the want of knowledge and literature, the appointed lot of all born to poverty, and the drudgeries of life, is the only opiate capable of infusing that insensibility which can enable them to endure the miseries of the one, and the fatigues of the other. It is a cordial administered by the gracious hand of providence; of which they ought never to be deprived by an ill-judged and improper education. It is the basis of all subordination, the support of society, and the privilege of individuals: and I have ever thought it a most remarkable instance of the divine wisdom, that whereas in all animals, whose individuals rise little above the rest of their species,

---

[2] "Answers are easy for the unthinking."

knowledge is instinctive; in man, whose individuals are so widely
different, it is acquired by education; by which means the prince
and the labourer, the philosopher and the peasant, are in some
measure fitted for their respective situations."

Much of these positions is perhaps true, and the whole para-
graph might well pass without censure, were not objections
necessary to the establishment of knowledge. *Poverty* is very
gently paraphrased by *want of riches*. In that sense almost every
man may in his own opinion be poor. But there is another poverty
which is *want of competence,* of all that can soften the miseries
of life, of all that can diversify attention, or delight imagina-
tion. There is yet another poverty which is *want of necessaries,*
a species of poverty which no care of the publick, no charity of
particulars, can preserve many from feeling openly, and many
secretly.

That hope and fear are inseparably or very frequently con-
nected with poverty, and riches, my surveys of life have not in-
formed me. The milder degrees of poverty are sometimes sup-
ported by hope, but the more severe often sink down in motionless
despondence. Life must be seen before it can be known. This
author and *Pope* perhaps never saw the miseries which they im-
agine thus easy to be born. The poor indeed are insensible of
many little vexations which sometimes imbitter the possessions
and pollute the enjoyment, of the rich. They are not pained by
casual incivility, or mortified by the mutilation of a compliment;
but this happiness is like that of a malefactor who ceases to feel
the cords that bind him when the pincers are tearing his flesh.

That want of taste for one enjoyment is supplied by the
pleasures of some other, may be fairly allowed. But the com-
pensations of sickness I have never found near to equivalence,
and the transports of recovery only prove the intenseness of the
pain.

With folly no man is willing to confess himself very intimately
acquainted, and therefore its pains and pleasures are kept secret.
But what the author says of its happiness seems applicable only
to fatuity, or gross dulness, for that inferiority of understanding
which makes one man without any other reason the slave, or tool,

or property of another, which makes him sometimes useless, and sometimes ridiculous, is often felt with very quick sensibility. On the happiness of madmen, as the case is not very frequent, it is not necessary to raise a disquisition, but I cannot forbear to observe, that I never yet knew disorders of mind encrease felicity: every madman is either arrogant and irascible, or gloomy and suspicious, or possessed by some passion or notion destructive to his quiet. He has always discontent in his look, and malignity in his bosom. And, if we had the power of choice, he would soon repent who should resign his reason to secure his peace.

Concerning the portion of ignorance necessary to make the condition of the lower classes of mankind safe to the public and tolerable to themselves, both morals and policy exact a nicer enquiry than will be very soon or very easily made. There is undoubtedly a degree of knowledge which will direct a man to refer all to providence, and to acquiesce in the condition which omniscient goodness has determined to allot him; to consider this world as a phantom that must soon glide from before his eyes, and the distresses and vexations that encompass him, as dust scattered in his path, as a blast that chills him for a moment, and passes off for ever.

Such wisdom, arising from the comparison of part with the whole of our existence, those that want it most cannot possibly obtain from philosophy, nor unless the method of education and the general tenour of life are changed, will very easily receive it from religion. The bulk of mankind is not likely to be very wise or very good: and I know not whether there are not many states of life, in which all knowledge less than the highest wisdom, will produce discontent and danger. I believe it may be sometimes found, that a *little learning* is to a poor man a *dangerous thing*.[3] But such is the condition of humanity, that we easily see, or quickly feel the wrong, but cannot always distinguish the right. Whatever knowledge is superfluous, in irremediable poverty, is hurtful, but the difficulty is to determine when poverty is irremediable, and at what point superfluity begins. Gross ignorance every man has found equally dangerous with perverted knowledge. Men

[3] Pope, *An Essay on Criticism*, 1. 215.

left wholly to their appetites and their instincts, with little sense of moral or religious obligation, and with very faint distinctions of right and wrong, can never be safely employed or confidently trusted: they can be honest only by obstinacy, and diligent only by compulsion or caprice. Some instruction, therefore, is necessary, and much perhaps may be dangerous.

Though it should be granted that those who are *born to poverty and drudgery* should not be *deprived* by an *improper education* of the *opiate* of *ignorance*; even this concession will not be of much use to direct our practice, unless it be determined who are those that are *born to poverty*. To entail irreversible poverty upon generation after generation only because the ancestor happened to be poor, is in itself cruel, if not unjust, and is wholly contrary to the maxims of a commercial nation, which always suppose and promote a rotation of property, and offer every individual a chance of mending his condition by his diligence. Those who communicate literature to the son of a poor man, consider him as one not born to poverty, but to the necessity of deriving a better fortune from himself. In this attempt, as in others, many fail and many succeed. Those that fail will feel their misery more acutely; but since poverty is now confessed to be such a calamity as cannot be born without the opiate of insensibility, I hope the happiness of those whom education enables to escape from it, may turn the ballance against that exacerbation which the others suffer.

I am always afraid of determining on the side of envy or cruelty. The privileges of education may sometimes be improperly bestowed, but I shall always fear to with-hold them, lest I should be yielding to the suggestions of pride, while I persuade myself that I am following the maxims of policy; and under the appearance of salutary restraints, should be indulging the lust of dominion, and that malevolence which delights in seeing others depressed.

Pope's doctrine is at last exhibited in a comparison, which, like other proofs of the same kind, is better adapted to delight the fancy than convince the reason.

"Thus the universe resembles a large and well-regulated family, in which all the officers and servants, and even the domestic animals, are subservient to each other in a proper subordination: each enjoys the privileges and perquisites peculiar to his place, and at the same time contributes by that just subordination to the magnificence and happiness of the whole."

The magnificence of a house is of use or pleasure always to the master, and sometimes to the domestics. But the magnificence of the universe adds nothing to the supreme Being; for any part of its inhabitants with which human knowledge is acquainted, an universe much less spacious or splendid would have been sufficient; and of happiness it does not appear that any is communicated from the Beings of a lower world to those of a higher. . . .

When this author presumes to speak of the universe, I would advise him a little to distrust his own faculties, however large and comprehensive. Many words easily understood on common occasion, become uncertain and figurative when applied to the works of Omnipotence. Subordination in human affairs is well understood, but when it is attributed to the universal system, its meaning grows less certain, like the petty distinctions of locality, which are of good use upon our own globe, but have no meaning with regard to infinite space, in which nothing is *high* or *low*. . . .

Having thus dispatched the consideration of particular evils, he comes at last to a general reason for which *evil* may be said to be *our good*. He is of opinion that there is some inconceivable benefit in pain abstractedly considered; that pain however inflicted, or wherever felt, communicates some good to the general system of being, and that every animal is some way or other the better for the pain of every other animal. This opinion he carries so far as to suppose that there passes some principle of union through all animal life, as attraction is communicated to all corporeal nature, and that the evils suffered on this globe, may by some inconceivable means contribute to the felicity of the inhabitants of the remotest planet.

How the origin of evil is brought nearer to human conception by any *inconceivable* means, I am not able to discover. We believed that the present system of creation was right, though we could not explain the adaptation of one part to the other, or for the whole succession of causes and consequences. Where has this enquirer added to the little knowledge that we had before? He has told us of the benefits of evil, which no man feels, and relations between distant parts of [the] universe, which he cannot himself conceive. There was enough in this question inconceivable before, and we have little advantage from a new inconceivable solution.

I do not mean to reproach this author for not knowing what is equally hidden from learning and from ignorance. The shame is to impose words for ideas upon ourselves or others. To imagine that we are going forward when we are only turning round. To think that there is any difference between him that gives no reason, and him that gives a reason, which by his own confession cannot be conceived.

But that he may not be thought to conceive nothing but things inconceivable, he has at last thought on a way by which human sufferings may produce good effects. He imagines that as we have not only animals for food, but choose some for our diversion, the same privilege may be allowed to some beings above us, *who may deceive, torment, or destroy us for the ends only of their own pleasure or utility.* This he again finds impossible to be conceived, *but that impossibility lessens not the probability of the conjecture, which by analogy is so strongly confirmed.*

I cannot resist the temptation of contemplating this analogy, which I think he might have carried further very much to the advantage of his argument. He might have shewn that these *hunters whose game is man* have many sports analogous to our own. As we drown whelps and kittens, they amuse themselves now and then with sinking a ship, and stand round the fields of *Blenheim* or the walls of *Prague,* as we encircle a cock-pit. As we shoot a bird flying, they take a man in the midst of his business or pleasure, and knock him down with an apoplexy. Some of them, perhaps, are virtuosi, and delight in the operations of an asthma, as a human philosopher in the effects of the air pump. To swell a man with a tympany is as good sport as to blow a frog. Many a merry bout have these frolic beings at the vicissitudes of an ague, and good sport it is to see a man tumble with an epilepsy, and revive and tumble again, and all this he knows not why. As they are wiser and more powerful than we, they have

more exquisite diversions, for we have no way of procuring any
sport so brisk and so lasting as the paroxysms of the gout and stone
which undoubtedly must make high mirth, especially if the play
be a little diversified with the blunders and puzzles of the blind
and deaf. We know not how far their sphere of observation may
extend. Perhaps now and then a merry being may place himself
in such a situation as to enjoy at once all the varieties of an epi-
demical disease, or amuse his leisure with the tossings and con-
tortions of every possible pain exhibited together.

One sport the merry malice of these beings has found means
of enjoying to which we have nothing equal or similar. They now
and then catch a mortal proud of his parts, and flattered either by
the submission of those who court his kindness, or the notice of
those who suffer him to court theirs. A head thus prepared for the
reception of false opinions, and the projection of vain designs,
they easily fill with idle notions, till in time they make their
plaything an author: their first diversion commonly begins with
an Ode or an epistle, then rises perhaps to a political irony, and
is at last brought to its height, by a treatise of philosophy. Then
begins the poor animal to entangle himself in sophisms, and
flounder in absurdity, to talk confidently of the scale of being,
and to give solutions which himself confesses impossible to be
understood. Sometimes, however, it happens that their pleasure
is without much mischief. The author feels no pain, but while
they are wondering at the extravagance of his opinion, and
pointing him out to one another as a new example of human folly,
he is enjoying his own applause, and that of his companions, and
perhaps is elevated with the hope of standing at the head of a new
sect.

Many of the books which now croud the world, may be justly
suspected to be written for the sake of some invisible order of
beings, for surely they are of no use to any of the corporeal inhab-
itants of the world. Of the productions of the last bounteous year,
how many can be said to serve any purpose of use or pleasure. The
only end of writing is to enable the readers better to enjoy life,
or better to endure it: and how will either of those be put more
in our power by him who tells us, that we are puppets, of which

some creature not much wiser than ourselves manages the wires. That a set of beings unseen and unheard, are hovering about us, trying experiments upon our sensibility, putting us in agonies to see our limbs quiver, torturing us to madness, that they may laugh at our vagaries, sometimes obstructing the bile, that they may see how a man looks when he is yellow; sometimes breaking a traveller's bones to try how he will get home; sometimes wasting a man to a skeleton, and sometimes killing him fat for the greater elegance of his hide.

This is an account of natural evil which though, like the rest, not quite new is very entertaining, though I know not how much it may contribute to patience. The only reason why we should contemplate evil is, that we may bear it better, and I am afraid nothing is much more placidly endured, for the sake of making others sport. . . .

FROM a Journey to the Western Islands of Scotland

Of the Earse language, as I understand nothing, I cannot say more than I have been told. It is the rude speech of a barbarous people, who had few thoughts to express, and were content, as they conceived grossly, to be grossly understood. After what has been lately talked of Highland Bards, and Highland genius, many will startle when they are told, that the *Earse* never was a written language; that there is not in the world an Earse manuscript a hundred years old; and that the sounds of the Highlanders were never expressed by letters, till some little books of piety were translated, and a metrical version of the Psalms was made by the synod of *Argyle*. Whoever therefore now writes in this language, spells according to his own perception of the sound, and his own idea of the power of the letters. The *Welsh* and the *Irish* are cultivated tongues. The Welsh, two hundred years ago, insulted their *English* neighbours for the instability of their Orthography; while the *Earse* merely floated in the breath of the people, and could therefore receive little improvement.

When a language begins to teem with books, it is tending to refinement; as those who undertake to teach others must have undergone some labour in improving themselves, they set a proportionate value on their own thoughts, and wish to enforce them by efficacious expressions; speech becomes embodied and permanent; different modes and phrases are compared, and the best obtains an establishment. By degrees one age improves upon another. Exactness is first obtained, and afterwards elegance. But diction, merely vocal, is always in its childhood. As no man leaves his eloquence behind him, the new generations have all to learn. There may possibly be books without a polished language, but there can be no polished language without books.

That the Bards could not read more than the rest of their countrymen, it is reasonable to suppose; because, if they had read, they could probably have written; and how high their compositions may reasonably be rated, an inquirer may best judge by considering what stores of imagery, what principles of ratiocination, what comprehension of knowledge, and what delicacy of elocution he has known any man attain who cannot read. The state of the Bards was yet more hopeless. He that cannot read, may now converse with those that can; but the Bard was a barbarian among barbarians, who, knowing nothing himself, lived with others that knew no more.

There has lately been in the Islands one of these illiterate poets, who hearing the Bible read at church, is said to have turned the sacred history into verse. I heard part of a dialogue, composed by him, translated by a young lady in *Mull,* and thought it had more meaning than I expected from a man totally uneducated; but he had some opportunities of knowledge; he lived among a learned people. After all that has been done for the instruction of the Highlanders, the antipathy between their language and literature still continues; and no man that has learned only *Earse* is, at this time, able to read.

The *Earse* has many dialects, and the words used in some Islands are not always known in others. In literate nations, though the pronunciation, and sometimes the words of common speech may differ, as now in *England,* compared with the South of *Scotland,* yet there is a written diction, which pervades all dialects, and is understood in every province. But where the whole language is colloquial, he that has only one part, never gets the rest, as he cannot get it but by change of residence.

In an unwritten speech, nothing that is not very short is transmitted from one generation to another. Few have opportunities of hearing a long composition often enough to learn it, or have inclination to repeat it so often as is necessary to retain it; and what is once forgotten is lost for ever. I believe there cannot be recovered, in the whole *Earse* language, five hundred lines of which there is any evidence to prove them a hundred years old. Yet I hear that the father of Ossian boasts of two chests more of ancient poetry, which he suppresses, because they are too good for the *English*.

He that goes into the Highlands with a mind naturally acquiescent, and a credulity eager for wonders, may come back with an opinion very different from mine; for the inhabitants knowing the ignorance of all strangers in their language and antiquities, perhaps are not very scrupulous adherents to truth; yet I do not say that they deliberately speak studied falsehood, or have a settled purpose to deceive. They have inquired and considered little, and do not always feel their own ignorance. They are not much accustomed to be interrogated by others; and seem never to have thought upon interrogating themselves; so that if they do not know what they tell to be true, they likewise do not distinctly perceive it to be false.

Mr. Boswell was very diligent in his inquiries; and the result of his investigations was, that the answer to the second question was commonly such as nullified the answer to the first.

We were a while told, that they had an old translation of the scriptures; and told it till it would appear obstinacy to inquire again. Yet by continued accumulation of questions we found, that the translation meant, if any meaning there were, was nothing else than the *Irish* Bible.

We heard of manuscripts that were, or that had been in the hands of somebody's father, or grandfather; but at last we had no reason to believe they were other than Irish. Martin mentions Irish, but never any Earse manuscripts, to be found in the Islands in his time.

I suppose my opinion of the poems of Ossian is already discovered: I believe they never existed in any other form than that which we have seen. The editor, or author, never could shew the original; nor can it be shewn by any other; to revenge reasonable incredulity, by refusing evidence, is a degree of insolence, with which the world is not yet acquainted, and stubborn audacity is the last refuge of guilt. It would be easy to shew it if he had it; but whence could it be had? It is too long to be remembered, and the language formerly had nothing written. He has doubtless inserted names that circulate in popular stories, and may have translated some wandering ballads, if any can be found; and the names, and some of the images being recollected, make an inaccurate auditor imagine, by the help of Caledonian bigotry, that he has formerly heard the whole.

I asked a very learned Minister in Sky, who had used all arts to make me believe the genuineness of the book, whether at last he believed it himself? but he would not answer. He wished me to be deceived, for the honour of his country; but would not directly and formally deceive me. Yet has this man's testimony been publickly produced, as of one that held Fingal to be the work of Ossian.

It is said, that some men of integrity profess to have heard parts of it, but they all heard them when they were boys; and it was never said that any of them could recite six lines. They remember names, and, perhaps, some proverbial sentiments; and, having no distinct ideas, coin a resemblance without an original. The persuasion of the Scots, however, is far from universal; and in a question so capable of proof, why should doubt be suffered to continue? The editor has been heard to say, that part of the poem was received by him, in the Saxon character. He has then found, by some peculiar fortune, an unwritten language, written in a character which the natives probably never beheld.

I have yet supposed no imposture but in the publisher, yet I am far from certainty, that some translations have not been lately made, that may now be obtruded as parts of the original work. Credulity on one part is a strong temptation to deceit on the other, especially to deceit of which no personal injury is the consequence, and which flatters the author with his own ingenuity. The Scots have something to plead for their easy reception of an improbable fiction: they are seduced by their fondness for their supposed ancestors. A Scotchman must be a very sturdy moralist, who does not love *Scotland* better than truth: he will always love it better than inquiry; and if falsehood flatters his vanity, will not be very diligent to detect it. Neither ought the *English* to be much influenced by *Scotch* authority; for of the past and present state of the whole *Earse* nation, the Lowlanders are at least as ignorant as ourselves. To be ignorant is painful; but it is dangerous to quiet our uneasiness by the delusive opiate of hasty persuasion.

But this is the age in which those who could not read, have been supposed to write; in which the giants of antiquated romance have been exhibited as realities. If we know little of the ancient Highlanders, let us not fill the vacuity with *Ossian*. If we have not searched the *Magellanick* regions, let us however forbear to people them with *Patagons*.

Preface to A Dictionary
of the English
Language

It is the fate of those who toil at the lower employments of life, to be rather driven by the fear of evil, than attracted by the prospect of good; to be exposed to censure, without hope of praise; to be disgraced by miscarriage, or punished for neglect, where success would have been without applause, and diligence without reward.

Among these unhappy mortals is the writer of dictionaries; whom mankind have considered, not as the pupil, but the slave of science, the pionier of literature, doomed only to remove rubbish and clear obstructions from the paths through which Learning and Genius press forward to conquest and glory, without bestowing a smile on the humble drudge that facilitates their progress. Every other authour may aspire to praise; the lexicographer can only hope to escape reproach, and even this negative recompense has been yet granted to very few.

I have, notwithstanding this discouragement, attempted a dictionary of the *English language,* which, while it was employed in the cultivation of every species of literature, has itself been hitherto neglected; suffered to spread, under the direction of chance, into wild exuberance; resigned to the tyranny of time and fashion; and exposed to the corruptions of ignorance, and caprices of innovation.

When I took the first survey of my undertaking, I found our speech copious without order, and energetick without rules: wherever I turned my view, there was perplexity to be disentangled, and confusion to be regulated; choice was to be made out of boundless variety, without any established principle of selection; adulterations were to be detected, without a settled test of purity; and modes of expression to be rejected or received, without the suffrages of any writers of classical reputation or acknowledged authority.

Having therefore no assistance but from general grammar, I applied myself to the perusal of our writers; and noting whatever might be of use to ascertain or illustrate any word or phrase, accumulated in time the materials of a dictionary, which, by degrees, I reduced to method, establishing to myself, in the progress of the work, such rules as experience and analogy suggested to me; experience, which practice and observation were continually increasing; and analogy, which, though in some words obscure, was evident in others.

In adjusting the ORTHOGRAPHY, which has been to this time unsettled and fortuitous, I found it necessary to distinguish those irregularities that are inherent in our tongue, and perhaps coeval with it, from others which the ignorance or negligence of later writers has produced. Every language has its anomalies, which, though inconvenient, and in themselves once unnecessary, must be tolerated among the imperfections of human things, and which require only to be registered, that they may not be increased, and ascertained, that they may not be confounded: but every language has likewise its improprieties and absurdities, which it is the duty of the lexicographer to correct or proscribe.

As language was at its beginning merely oral, all words of necessary or common use were spoken before they were written; and while they were unfixed by any visible signs, must have been spoken with great diversity, as we now observe those who cannot read catch sounds imperfectly, and utter them negligently. When this wild and barbarous jargon was first reduced to an alphabet, every penman endeavoured to express, as he could, the sounds which he was accustomed to pronounce or to receive, and vitiated in writing such words as were already vitiated in speech. The powers of the letters, when they were applied to a new language, must have been vague and unsettled, and therefore different hands would exhibit the same sound by different combinations.

From this uncertain pronunciation arise in a great part the various dialects of the same country, which will always be observed to grow fewer, and less different, as books are multiplied; and from this arbitrary representation of sounds by letters, proceeds that diversity of spelling observable in the *Saxon* remains, and I suppose in the first books of every nation, which perplexes or destroys analogy, and produces anomalous formations, that, being once incorporated, can never be afterward dismissed or reformed.

Of this kind are the derivatives *length* from *long*, *strength* from *strong*, *darling* from *dear*, *breadth* from *broad*, from *dry*, *drought*, and from *high*, *height*, which *Milton*, in zeal for analogy, writes *highth*; *Quid te exempta juvat spinis de pluribus una* (Horace, *Epistles*, II. ii. 212); to change all would be too much, and to change one is nothing.

This uncertainty is most frequent in the vowels, which are so capriciously pronounced, and so differently modified, by accident or affectation, not only in every province, but in every mouth, that to them, as is well known to etymologists, little regard is to be shewn in the deduction of one language from another.

Such defects are not errours in orthography, but spots of barbarity impressed so deep in the *English* language, that criticism can never wash them away: these, therefore, must be permitted to remain untouched; but many words have likewise been altered by accident, or depraved by ignorance, as the pronunciation of the vulgar has been weakly followed; and some still continue to be variously written, as authours differ in their care or skill: of these it was proper to enquire the true orthography, which I have always considered as depending on their derivation, and have therefore referred them to their original languages: thus I write *enchant, enchantment, enchanter*, after the *French*, and *incantation* after the *Latin*; thus *entire* is chosen rather than *intire*, because it passed to us not from the *Latin integer,* but from the *French entier.*

Of many words it is difficult to say whether they were immediately received from the *Latin* or the *French,* since at the time when we had dominions in *France,* we had *Latin* service in our churches. It is, however, my opinion, that the *French* generally supplied us; for we have few *Latin* words, among the terms of domestick use, which are not *French;* but many *French,* which are very remote from *Latin.*

Even in words of which the derivation is apparent, I have been often obliged to sacrifice uniformity to custom; thus I write, in compliance with a numberless majority, *convey* and *inveigh, deceit* and *receipt, fancy* and *phantom;* sometimes the derivative varies from the primitive, as *explain* and *explanation, repeat* and *repetition.*

Some combinations of letters having the same power are used indifferently without any discoverable reason of choice, as in *choak, choke; soap, sope; fewel, fuel,* and many others; which I have sometimes inserted twice, that those who search for them under either form, may not search in vain.

In examining the orthography of any doubtful word, the mode of spelling by which it is inserted in the series of the dictionary, is to be considered as that to which I give, perhaps not often rashly, the preference. I have left, in the examples, to every authour his own practice unmolested, that the reader may balance suffrages, and judge between us: but this question is not always to be determined by reputed or by real learning; some men, intent upon greater things, have thought little on sounds and derivations; some, knowing in the ancient tongues, have neglected those in which our words are commonly to be sought. Thus *Hammond* writes *fecibleness* for *feasibleness,* because I suppose he imagined it derived immediately from the *Latin;* and some words, such as *dependant, dependent; dependance, dependence,* vary their final syllable, as one or another language is present to the writer.

In this part of the work, where caprice has long wantoned without controul, and vanity sought praise by petty reformation,

I have endeavoured to proceed with a scholar's reverence for
antiquity, and a grammarian's regard to the genius of our tongue.
I have attempted few alterations, and among those few, perhaps
the greater part is from the modern to the ancient practice; and
I hope I may be allowed to recommend to those, whose thoughts
have been perhaps employed too anxiously on verbal singularities,
not to disturb, upon narrow views, or for minute propriety, the
orthography of their fathers. It has been asserted, that for the law
to be *known,* is of more importance than to be *right.* Change, says
Hooker, is not made without inconvenience, even from worse to
better.[1] There is in constancy and stability a general and lasting
advantage, which will always overbalance the slow improvements
of gradual correction. Much less ought our written language to
comply with the corruptions of oral utterance, or copy that which
every variation of time or place makes different from itself, and
imitate those changes, which will again be changed, while imita-
tion is employed in observing them.

This recommendation of steadiness and uniformity does not
proceed from an opinion, that particular combinations of letters
have much influence on human happiness; or that truth may not
be successfully taught by modes of spelling fanciful and erroneous:
I am not yet so lost in lexicography, as to forget that *words are
the daughters of earth, and that things are the sons of heaven.*
Language is only the instrument of science, and words are but
the signs of ideas: I wish, however, that the instrument might be
less apt to decay, and that signs might be permanent, like the
things which they denote.

In settling the orthography, I have not wholly neglected the
pronunciation, which I have directed, by printing an accent upon
the acute or elevated syllable. It will sometimes be found, that
the accent is placed by the authour quoted, on a different syllable
from that marked in the alphabetical series; it is then to be under-
stood, that custom has varied, or that the authour has, in my
opinion, pronounced wrong. Short directions are sometimes given
where the sound of letters is irregular; and if they are sometimes

[1] *Ecclesiastical Polity,* IV. xiv.

omitted, defect in such minute observations will be more easily excused, than superfluity.

In the investigation both of the orthography and signification of words, their ETYMOLOGY was necessarily to be considered, and they were therefore to be divided into primitives and derivatives. A primitive word, is that which can be traced no further to any *English* root; thus *circumspect, circumvent, circumstance, delude, concave,* and *complicate,* though compounds in the *Latin,* are to us primitives. Derivatives are all those that can be referred to any word in *English* of greater simplicity.

The derivatives I have referred to their primitives, with an accuracy sometimes needless; for who does not see that *remoteness* comes from *remote, lovely* from *love, concavity* from *concave,* and *demonstrative* from *demonstrate?* but this grammatical exuberance the scheme of my work did not allow me to repress. It is of great importance in examining the general fabrick of a language, to trace one word from another, by noting the usual modes of derivation and inflection; and uniformity must be preserved in systematical works, though sometimes at the expence of particular propriety.

Among other derivatives I have been careful to insert and elucidate the anomalous plurals of nouns and preterites of verbs, which in the *Teutonick* dialects are very frequent, and though familiar to those who have always used them, interrupt and embarrass the learners of our language.

The two languages from which our primitives have been derived are the *Roman* and *Teutonick*: under the *Roman* I comprehend the *French* and provincial tongues; and under the *Teutonick* range the *Saxon, German,* and all their kindred dialects. Most of our polysyllables are *Roman,* and our words of one syllable are very often *Teutonick.*

In assigning the *Roman* original, it has perhaps sometimes happened that I have mentioned only the *Latin,* when the word was borrowed from the *French;* and considering myself as employed only in the illustration of my own language, I have not been very careful to observe whether the *Latin* word be pure or barbarous, or the *French* elegant or obsolete.

For the Teutonick etymologies, I am commonly indebted to
Junius and *Skinner,* the only names which I have forborn to
quote when I copied their books; not that I might appropriate
their labours or usurp their honours, but that I might spare a
perpetual repetition by one general acknowledgment. Of these,
whom I ought not to mention but with the reverence due to in-
structors and benefactors, *Junius* appears to have excelled in
extent of learning, and *Skinner* in rectitude of understanding.
Junius was accurately skilled in all the northern languages, *Skin-
ner* probably examined the ancient and remoter dialects only by
occasional inspection into dictionaries; but the learning of *Junius*
is often of no other use than to show him a track by which he may
deviate from his purpose, to which *Skinner* always presses forward
by the shortest way. *Skinner* is often ignorant, but never ridic-
ulous: *Junius* is always full of knowledge; but his variety distracts
his judgment, and his learning is very frequently disgraced by
his absurdities.

The votaries of the northern muses will not perhaps easily
restrain their indignation, when they find the name of *Junius*
thus degraded by a disadvantageous comparison; but whatever
reverence is due to his diligence, or his attainments, it can be
no criminal degree of censoriousness to charge that etymologist
with want of judgment, who can seriously derive *dream* from
drama, because *life is a drama, and a drama is a dream,* and who
declares with a tone of defiance, that no man can fail to derive
moan from μόνος, *monos, single* or *solitary,* who considers that
grief naturally loves to be *alone.*[2]

Our knowledge of the northern literature is so scanty, that of

[2] That I may not appear to have spoken too irreverently of *Junius,* I
have here subjoined a few Specimens of his etymological extravagance.

BANISH, *religare, ex banno vel territorio exigere, in exilium agere.* G.
bannir. It. *bandire, bandeggiare.* H. *bandir.* B. *bannen.* Ævi medii scrip-
tores bannire dicebant. V. Spelm. in Bannum & in Banleuga. Quoniam verò
regionum urbiumq; limites arduis plerumq; montibus, altis fluminibus,
longis deniq; flexuosisq; angustissimarum viarum anfractibus includebantur,
fieri potest id genus limites *ban* dici ab eo quod Βαννάται & Βαννάτροι
Tarentinis olim, sicuti tradit Hesychius, vocabantur αἱ λοξοὶ καὶ μὴ
ἰθυτενεῖς ὁδοί, "obliquæ ac minimè in rectum tendentes viæ." Ac fortasse

words undoubtedly *Teutonick* the original is not always to be found in any ancient language; and I have therefore inserted *Dutch* or *German* substitutes, which I consider not as radical but parallel, not as the parents, but sisters of the *English*.

The words which are represented as thus related by descent or cognation, do not always agree in sense; for it is incident to words, as to their authours, to degenerate from their ancestors, and to change their manners when they change their country. It is sufficient, in etymological enquiries, if the senses of kindred words be found such as may easily pass into each other, or such as may both be referred to one general idea.

The etymology, so far as it is yet known, was easily found in the volumes where it is particularly and professedly delivered; and, by proper attention to the rules of derivation, the orthography was soon adjusted. But to COLLECT the WORDS of our language was a task of greater difficulty: the deficiency of dictionaries was immediately apparent; and when they were exhausted, what was yet wanting must be sought by fortuitous and unguided excursions into books, and gleaned as industry should find, or chance should offer it, in the boundless chaos of a living speech. My search, how-

---

quoque huc facit quod Βανοὺς, eodem Hesychio teste, dicebant ὄρη στραγγύλη, montes arduos.

EMPTY, emtie, *vacuus, inanis.* A. S. Æmtiჳ. Nescio an sint ab ἐμέω vel ἐμετάω. Vomo, evomo, vomitu evacuo. Videtur iterim etymologiam hanc non obscurè firmare codex Rush. Mat. xii. 22. ubi antiquè scriptum invenimus ჳemoeteδ hit emetiჳ. "Invenit eam vacantem."

HILL, *mons, collis.* A. S. hyll. Quod videri potest abscissum ex κολώνη vel κολωνός. Collis, tumulus, locus in plano editior. Hom. Il. b. v. 811, ἔστι δέ τις προπάροιθε πόλεως αἰπεῖα κολώνη. Ubi authori brevium scholiorum κολώνη exp. τόπος εἰς ὕψος ἀνήκων, γεώλοφος ἐξοχή.

NAP, *to take a nap. Dormire, condormiscere.* Cym. heppian. A. S. hnæppan. Quod postremum videri potest desumptum ex κνέφας, obscuritas, tenebræ: nihil enim æque solet conciliare somnum, quam caliginosa profundæ noctis obscuritas.

STAMMERER, Balbus, blæsus. Goth. STAMMS. A. S. stamer, stamur. D. *stam.* B. *stameler.* Su. *stamma.* Isl. *stamr.* Sunt a στωμυλεῖν vel στωμύλλειν, nimia loquacitate alios offendere; quod impeditè loquentes libentissimè garrire soleant; vel quod aliis nimii semper videantur, etiam parcissimè loquentes. [Johnson's note]

ever, has been either skilful or lucky; for I have much augmented the vocabulary.

As my design was a dictionary, common or appellative, I have omitted all words which have relation to proper names; such as *Arian, Socinian, Calvinist, Benedictine, Mahomentan;* but have retained those of a more general nature, as *Heathen, Pagan.*

Of the terms of art I have received such as could be found either in books of science or technical dictionaries; and have often inserted, from philosophical writers, words which are supported perhaps only by a single authority, and which being not admitted into general use, stand yet as candidates or probationers, and must depend for their adoption on the suffrage of futurity.

The words which our authours have introduced by their knowledge of foreign languages, or ignorance of their own, by vanity or wantonness, by compliance with fashion or lust of innovation, I have registred as they occurred, though commonly only to censure them, and warn others against the folly of naturalizing useless foreigners to the injury of the natives.

I have not rejected any by design, merely because they were unnecessary or exuberant; but have received those which by different writers have been differently formed, as *viscid,* and *viscidity, viscous,* and *viscosity.*

Compounded or double words I have seldom noted, except when they obtain a signification different from that which the components have in their simple state. Thus *highwayman, woodman,* and *horsecourser,* require an explanation; but of *thieflike* or *coachdriver* no notice was needed, because the primitives contain the meaning of the compounds.

Words arbitrarily formed by a constant and settled analogy, like diminutive adjectives in *ish,* as *greenish, bluish,* adverbs in *ly,* as *dully, openly,* substantives in *ness,* as *vileness, faultiness,* were less diligently sought, and sometimes have been omitted, when I had no authority that invited me to insert them; not that they are not genuine and regular offsprings of *English* roots, but because their relation to the primitive being always the same, their signification cannot be mistaken.

The verbal nouns in *ing,* such as the *keeping* of the *castle,* the *leading* of the *army,* are always neglected, or placed only to illustrate the sense of the verb, except when they signify things as well as actions, and have therefore a plural number, as *dwelling, living;* or have an absolute and abstract signification, as *colouring, painting, learning.*

The participles are likewise omitted, unless, by signifying rather habit or quality than action, they take the nature of adjectives; as a *thinking* man, a man of prudence; a *pacing* horse, a horse that can pace: these I have ventured to call *participial adjectives.* But neither are these always inserted, because they are commonly to be understood, without any danger of mistake, by consulting the verb.

Obsolete words are admitted, when they are found in authours not obsolete, or when they have any force or beauty that may deserve revival.

As composition is one of the chief characteristicks of a language, I have endeavoured to make some reparation for the universal negligence of my predecessors, by inserting great numbers of compounded words, as may be found under *after, fore, new, night, fair,* and many more. These, numerous as they are, might be multiplied, but that use and curiosity are here satisfied, and the frame of our language and modes of our combination amply discovered.

Of some forms of composition, such as that by which *re* is prefixed to note *repetition,* and *un* to signify *contrariety* or *privation,* all the examples cannot be accumulated, because the use of these particles, if not wholly arbitrary, is so little limited, that they are hourly affixed to new words as occasion requires, or is imagined to require them.

There is another kind of composition more frequent in our language than perhaps in any other, from which arises to foreigners the greatest difficulty. We modify the signification of many verbs by a particle subjoined; as to *come off,* to escape by a fetch; to *fall on,* to attack; to *fall off,* to apostatize; to *break off,* to stop abruptly; to *bear out,* to justify; to *fall in,* to comply; to *give over,* to cease; to *set off,* to embellish; to *set in,* to begin a continual tenour; to *set out,* to begin a course or journey; to *take off,* to copy; with innumerable expressions of the same kind, of which some appear wildly irregular, being so far distant from the sense of the simple words, that no sagacity will be able to trace the steps by which they arrived at the present use. These I have noted with great care; and though I cannot flatter myself that the collection is complete, I believe I have so far assisted the students of our language, that this kind of phraseology will be no longer insuperable; and the combinations of verbs and particles, by chance omitted, will be easily explained by comparison with those that may be found.

Many words yet stand supported only by the name of *Bailey, Ainsworth, Philips,* or the contracted *Dict.* for *Dictionaries* subjoined; of these I am not always certain that they are read in any book but the works of lexicographers. Of such I have omitted many, because I had never read them; and many I have inserted, because they may perhaps exist, though they have escaped my notice: they are, however, to be yet considered as resting only upon the credit of former dictionaries. Others, which I considered as useful, or know to be proper, though I could not at present support them by authorities, I have suffered to stand upon my own attestation, claiming the same privilege with my predecessors of being sometimes credited without proof.

The words, thus selected and disposed, are grammatically considered; they are referred to the different parts of speech; traced, when they are irregularly inflected, through their various terminations; and illustrated by observations, not indeed of great or striking importance, separately considered, but necessary to the elucidation of our language, and hitherto neglected or forgotten by *English* grammarians.

That part of my work on which I expect malignity most frequently to fasten, is the *Explanation;* in which I cannot hope to satisfy those, who are perhaps not inclined to be pleased, since I have not always been able to satisfy myself. To interpret a language by itself is very difficult; many words cannot be explained by synonimes, because the idea signified by them has not more than one appellation; nor by paraphrase, because simple ideas cannot be described. When the nature of things is unknown, or the notion unsettled and indefinite, and various in various minds, the words by which such notions are conveyed, or such things denoted, will be ambiguous and perplexed. And such is the fate of hapless lexicography, that not only darkness, but light, impedes and distresses it; things may be not only too little, but too much known, to be happily illustrated. To explain, requires the use of terms less abstruse than that which is to be explained, and such terms cannot always be found; for as nothing can be proved but by supposing something intuitively known, and evident without proof, so nothing can be defined but by the use of words too plain to admit a definition.

Other words there are, of which the sense is too subtle and evanescent to be fixed in a paraphrase; such are all those which are by the grammarians termed *expletives,* and, in dead languages, are suffered to pass for empty sounds, of no other use than to fill a verse, or to modulate a period, but which are easily perceived in living tongues to have power and emphasis, though it be sometimes such as no other form of expression can convey.

My labour has likewise been much increased by a class of verbs too frequent in the *English* language, of which the signification is so loose and general, the use so vague and indeterminate, and the senses detorted so widely from the first idea, that it is hard to trace them through the maze of variation, to catch them on the brink of utter inanity, to circumscribe them by any limitations, or interpret them by any words of distinct and settled meaning; such are *bear, break, come, cast, full, get, give, do, put, set, go, run, make, take, turn, throw.* If of these the whole power is not accurately delivered, it must be remembered, that while our language is yet living, and variable by the caprice of every one that speaks it, these words are hourly shifting their relations, and can no more be ascertained in a dictionary, than a grove, in the agitation of a storm, can be accurately delineated from its picture in the water.

The particles are among all nations applied with so great latitude, that they are not easily reducible under any regular scheme of explication: this difficulty is not less, nor perhaps greater, in *English,* than in other languages. I have laboured them with diligence, I hope with success; such at least as can be expected in a task, which no man, however learned or sagacious, has yet been able to perform.

Some words there are which I cannot explain, because I do not understand them; these might have been omitted very often with little inconvenience, but I would not so far indulge my vanity as to decline this confession: for when *Tully* owns himself ignorant whether *lessus,* in the twelve tables, means a *funeral song,* or *mourning garment,*[3] and *Aristotle* doubts whether οὐρεὺς in the Iliad, signifies a *mule,* or *muleteer,* I may surely, without shame, leave some obscurities to happier industry, or future information.

The rigour of interpretative lexicography requires that *the explanation, and the word explained, should be always reciprocal;* this I have always endeavoured, but could not always attain. Words are seldom exactly synonimous; a new term was not introduced, but because the former was thought inadequate: names, therefore, have often many ideas, but few ideas have many names. It was then necessary to use the proximate word, for the deficiency of single terms can very seldom be supplied by circumlocution; nor is the inconvenience great of such mutilated interpretations, because the sense may easily be collected entire from the examples.

In every word of extensive use, it was requisite to mark the progress of its meaning, and show by what gradations of intermediate sense it has passed from its primitive to its remote and accidental signification; so that every foregoing explanation should tend to that which follows, and the series be regularly concatenated from the first notion to the last.

This is specious, but not always practicable; kindred senses may be so interwoven, that the perplexity cannot be disentangled, nor any reason be assigned why one should be ranged before the other. When the radical idea branches out into parallel ramifications, how can a consecutive series be formed of senses in their nature collateral? The shades of meaning sometimes pass imperceptibly into each other; so that though on one side they ap-

---

[3] Cicero, *Laws,* II. xxiii. 59.

parently differ, yet it is impossible to mark the point of contact. Ideas of the same race, though not exactly alike, are sometimes so little different, that no words can express the dissimilitude, though the mind easily perceives it, when they are exhibited together; and sometimes there is such a confusion of acceptations, that discernment is wearied, and distinction puzzled, and persever-ance herself hurries to an end, by crouding together what she can-not separate.

These complaints of difficulty will, by those that have never considered words beyond their popular use, be thought only the jargon of a man willing to magnify his labours, and procure ven-eration to his studies by involution and obscurity. But every art is obscure to those that have not learned it: this uncertainty of terms, and commixture of ideas, is well known to those who have joined philosophy with grammar; and if I have not expressed them very clearly, it must be remembered that I am speaking of that which words are insufficient to explain.

The original sense of words is often driven out of use by their metaphorical acceptations, yet must be inserted for the sake of a regular origination. Thus I know not whether *ardour* is used for *material heat,* or whether *flagrant,* in *English,* ever signifies the same with *burning;* yet such are the primitive ideas of these words, which are therefore set first, though without examples, that the figurative senses may be commodiously deduced.

Such is the exuberance of signification which many words have obtained, that it was scarcely possible to collect all their senses; sometimes the meaning of derivatives must be sought in the mother term, and sometimes deficient explanations of the primitive may be supplied in the train of derivation. In any case of doubt or difficulty, it will be always proper to examine all the words of the same race; for some words are slightly passed over to avoid repeti-tion, some admitted easier and clearer explanation than others, and all will be better understood, as they are considered in greater variety of structures and relations.

All the interpretations of words are not written with the same skill, or the same happiness: things equally easy in themselves, are not all equally easy to any single mind. Every writer of a long work commits errours, where there appears neither ambiguity to mislead, nor obscurity to confound him; and in a search like this, many felicities of expression will be casually overlooked, many convenient parallels will be forgotten, and many particulars will admit improvement from a mind utterly unequal to the whole performance.

But many seeming faults are to be imputed rather to the nature of the undertaking, than the negligence of the performer. Thus some explanations are unavoidably reciprocal or circular, as *hind, the female of the stag; stag, the male of the hind:* sometimes easier words are changed into harder, as *burial* into *sepulture* or *interment, drier* into *desiccative, dryness* into *siccity* or *aridity, fit* into *paroxysm;* for the easiest word, whatever it be, can never be translated into one more easy. But easiness and difficulty are merely relative, and if the present prevalence of our language should invite foreigners to this dictionary, many will be assisted by those words which now seem only to increase or produce obscurity. For this reason I have endeavoured frequently to join a *Teutonick* and *Roman* interpretation, as to CHEER, to *gladden,* or *exhilarate,* that every learner of *English* may be assisted by his own tongue.

The solution of all difficulties, and the supply of all defects, must be sought in the examples, subjoined to the various senses of each word, and ranged according to the time of their authours.

When first I collected these authorities, I was desirous that every quotation should be useful to some other end than the illustration of a word; I therefore extracted from philosophers principles of science; from historians remarkable facts; from chymists complete processes; from divines striking exhortations; and from poets beautiful descriptions. Such is design, while it is yet at a distance from execution. When the time called upon me to range this accumulation of elegance and wisdom into an alphabetical series, I soon discovered that the bulk of my volumes would fright away the student, and was forced to depart from my scheme of including all that was pleasing or useful in *English* literature, and reduce my transcripts very often to clusters of words, in which scarcely any meaning is retained; thus to the weariness of copying, I was condemned to add the vexation of expunging. Some passages I have yet spared, which may relieve the labour of verbal searches, and intersperse with verdure and flowers the dusty desarts of barren philology.

The examples, thus mutilated, are no longer to be considered as conveying the sentiments or doctrine of their authours; the word for the sake of which they are inserted, with all its appendant clauses, has been carefully preserved; but it may sometimes happen, by hasty detruncation, that the general tendency of the sentence may be changed: the divine may desert his tenets, or the philosopher his system.

Some of the examples have been taken from writers who were never mentioned as masters of elegance or models of stile; but words must be sought where they are used; and in what pages, eminent for purity, can terms of manufacture or agriculture be found? Many quotations serve no other purpose, than that of proving the bare existence of words, and are therefore selected with less scrupulousness than those which are to teach their structures and relations.

My purpose was to admit no testimony of living authours, that I might not be misled by partiality, and that none of my cotemporaries might have reason to complain; nor have I departed from this resolution, but when some performance of uncommon excellence excited my veneration, when my memory supplied me, from late books, with an example that was wanting, or when my heart, in the tenderness of friendship, solicited admission for a favourite name.

So far have I been from any care to grace my pages with modern decorations, that I have studiously endeavoured to collect examples and authorities from the writers before the restoration, whose works I regard as *the wells of English undefiled,* as the pure sources of genuine diction. Our language, for almost a century, has, by the concurrence of many causes, been gradually departing from its original *Teutonick* character, and deviating towards a *Gallick* structure and phraseology, from which it ought to be our endeavour to recal it, by making our ancient volumes the ground-work of stile, admitting among the additions of later times, only such as may supply real deficiencies, such as are readily adopted by the genius of our tongue, and incorporate easily with our native idioms.

But as every language has a time of rudeness antecedent to perfection, as well as of false refinement and declension, I have been cautious lest my zeal for antiquity might drive me into times too remote, and croud my book with words now no longer understood. I have fixed *Sidney*'s work for the boundary, beyond which I make few excursions. From the authours which rose in the time of *Elizabeth,* a speech might be formed adequate to all the purposes of use and elegance. If the language of theology were extracted from *Hooker* and the translation of the Bible; the terms of natural knowledge from *Bacon;* the phrases of policy, war, and navigation from *Raleigh;* the dialect of poetry and fiction from *Spenser* and *Sidney;* and the diction of common life from *Shakespeare,* few ideas would be lost to mankind, for want of *English* words, in which they might be expressed.

It is not sufficient that a word is found, unless it be so combined as that its meaning is apparently determined by the tract and tenour of the sentence; such passages I have therefore chosen, and when it happened that any authour gave a definition of a term, or such an explanation as is equivalent to a definition, I have placed his authority as a supplement to my own, without regard to the chronological order, that is otherwise observed.

Some words, indeed, stand unsupported by any authority, but they are commonly derivative nouns or adverbs, formed from their primitives by regular and constant analogy, or names of things seldom occurring in books, or words of which I have reason to doubt the existence.

There is more danger of censure from the multiplicity than paucity of examples; authorities will sometimes seem to have been accumulated without necessity or use, and perhaps some will be found, which might, without loss, have been omitted. But a work of this kind is not hastily to be charged with superfluities: those quotations, which to careless or unskilful perusers appear only to repeat the same sense, will often exhibit, to a more accurate examiner, diversities of signification, or, at least, afford different shades of the same meaning: one will shew the word applied to persons, another to things; one will express an ill, another a good, and a third a neutral sense; one will prove the expression genuine from an ancient authour; another will shew it elegant from a modern: a doubtful authority is corroborated by another of more credit; an ambiguous sentence is ascertained by a passage clear and determinate; the word, how often soever repeated, appears with new associates and in different combinations, and every quotation contributes something to the stability or enlargement of the language.

When words are used equivocally, I receive them in either sense; when they are metaphorical, I adopt them in their primitive acceptation.

I have sometimes, though rarely, yielded to the temptation of exhibiting a genealogy of sentiments, by shewing how one authour copied the thoughts and diction of another: such quotations are indeed little more than repetitions, which might justly be censured, did they not gratify the mind, by affording a kind of intellectual history.

The various syntactical structures occurring in the examples have been carefully noted; the licence or negligence with which many words have been hitherto used, has made our stile capricious and indeterminate; when the different combinations of the same word are exhibited together, the preference is readily given to propriety, and I have often endeavoured to direct the choice.

Thus have I laboured by settling the orthography, displaying the analogy, regulating the structures, and ascertaining the signification of *English* words, to perform all the parts of a faithful lexicographer: but I have not always executed my own scheme, or satisfied my own expectations. The work, whatever proofs of diligence and attention it may exhibit, is yet capable of many improvements: the orthography which I recommend is still controvertible, the etymology which I adopt is uncertain, and perhaps frequently erroneous; the explanations are sometimes too much contracted, and sometimes too much diffused, the significations are distinguished rather with subtilty than skill, and the attention is harrassed with unnecessary minuteness.

The examples are too often injudiciously truncated, and perhaps sometimes, I hope very rarely, alleged in a mistaken sense; for in making this collection I trusted more to memory, than, in a state of disquiet and embarrassment, memory can contain, and purposed to supply at the review what was left incomplete in the first transcription.

Many terms appropriated to particular occupations, though necessary and significant, are undoubtedly omitted; and of the words most studiously considered and exemplified, many senses have escaped observation.

Yet these failures, however frequent, may admit extenuation and apology. To have attempted much is always laudable, even when the enterprize is above the strength that undertakes it: To rest below his own aim is incident to every one whose fancy is active, and whose views are comprehensive; nor is any man satisfied with himself because he has done much, but because he can conceive little. When first I engaged in this work, I resolved to leave neither words nor things unexamined, and pleased myself with a prospect of the hours which I should revel away in feasts of literature, with the obscure recesses of northern learning, which I should enter and ransack; the treasures with which I expected every search into those neglected mines to reward my labour, and the triumph with which I should display my acquisitions to mankind. When I had thus enquired into the original of words, I resolved to show likewise my attention to things; to pierce deep into every science, to enquire the nature of every substance of which I inserted the name, to limit every idea by a definition strictly logical, and exhibit every production of art or nature in an accurate description, that my book might be in place of all other dictionaries whether appellative or technical. But these were the dreams of a poet doomed at last to wake a lexicographer. I soon found that it is too late to look for instruments, when the work calls for execution, and that whatever abilities I had brought to my task, with those I must finally perform it. To deliberate whenever I doubted, to enquire whenever I was ignorant, would have protracted the undertaking without end, and, perhaps, without much improvement; for I did not find by my first experiments, that what I had not of my own was easily to be obtained: I saw that one enquiry only gave occasion to another, that book referred to book, that to search was not always to find, and to find was not always to be informed; and that thus to persue perfection, was, like the first inhabitants of Arcadia, to chace the sun, which, when they had reached the hill where he seemed to rest, was still beheld at the same distance from them.

I then contracted my design, determining to confide in myself, and no longer to solicit auxiliaries, which produced more incumbrance than assistance: by this I obtained at least one advantage, that I set limits to my work, which would in time be ended, though not completed.

Despondency has never so far prevailed as to depress me to negligence; some faults will at last appear to be the effects of anxious diligence and persevering activity. The nice and subtle ramifications of meaning were not easily avoided by a mind intent upon accuracy, and convinced of the necessity of disentangling combinations, and separating similitudes. Many of the distinctions which to common readers appear useless and idle, will be found real and important by men versed in the school philosophy, without which no dictionary shall ever be accurately compiled, or skilfully examined.

Some senses however there are, which, though not the same, are yet so nearly allied, that they are often confounded. Most men think indistinctly, and therefore cannot speak with exactness; and consequently some examples might be indifferently put to either signification: this uncertainty is not to be imputed to me, who do not form, but register the language; who do not teach men how they should think, but relate how they have hitherto expressed their thoughts.

The imperfect sense of some examples I lamented, but could not remedy, and hope they will be compensated by innumerable passages selected with propriety, and preserved with exactness; some shining with sparks of imagination, and some replete with treasures of wisdom.

The orthography and etymology, though imperfect, are not imperfect for want of care, but because care will not always be successful, and recollection or information come too late for use.

That many terms of art and manufacture are omitted, must be frankly acknowledged; but for this defect I may boldly allege that it was unavoidable: I could not visit caverns to learn the miner's language, nor take a voyage to perfect my skill in the dialect of navigation, nor visit the warehouses of merchants, and shops of artificers, to gain the names of wares, tools and operations, of which no mention is found in books; what favourable accident, or easy enquiry brought within my reach, has not been neglected; but it had been a hopeless labour to glean up words, by courting living information, and contesting with the sullenness of one, and the roughness of another.

To furnish the academicians *della Crusca* with words of this kind, a series of comedies called *la Fiera,* or *the Fair,* was professedly written by *Buonaroti;* but I had no such assistant, and therefore was content to want what they must have wanted likewise, had they not luckily been so supplied.

Nor are all words which are not found in the vocabulary, to be lamented as omissions. Of the laborious and mercantile part of the people, the diction is in a great measure casual and mutable; many of their terms are formed for some temporary or local convenience, and though current at certain times and places, are in others utterly unknown. This fugitive cant, which is always in a state of increase or decay, cannot be regarded as any part of the durable materials of a language, and therefore must be suffered to perish with other things unworthy of preservation.

Care will sometimes betray to the appearance of negligence. He that is catching opportunities which seldom occur, will suffer those to pass by unregarded, which he expects hourly to return; he that is searching for rare and remote things, will neglect those that are obvious and familiar: thus many of the most common and cursory words have been inserted with little illustration, because in gathering the authorities, I forbore to copy those which I thought likely to occur whenever they were wanted. It is remarkable that, in reviewing my collection, I found the word SEA unexemplified.

Thus it happens, that in things difficult there is danger from ignorance, and in things easy from confidence; the mind, afraid of greatness, and disdainful of littleness, hastily withdraws herself from painful searches, and passes with scornful rapidity over tasks not adequate to her powers, sometimes too secure for caution, and again too anxious for vigorous effort; sometimes idle in a plain path, and sometimes distracted in labyrinths, and dissipated by different intentions.

A large work is difficult because it is large, even though all its parts might singly be performed with facility; where there are many things to be done, each must be allowed its share of time and labour, in the proportion only which it bears to the whole; nor can it be expected, that the stones which form the dome of a temple, should be squared and polished like the diamond of a ring.

Of the event of this work, for which, having laboured it with so much application, I cannot but have some degree of parental fondness, it is natural to form conjectures. Those who have been persuaded to think well of my design, will require that it should fix our language, and put a stop to those alterations which time and chance have hitherto been suffered to make in it without opposition. With this consequence I will confess that I flattered myself for a while; but now begin to fear that I have indulged expectation which neither reason nor experience can justify. When we see men grow old and die at a certain time one after another, from century to century, we laugh at the elixir that promises to prolong life to a thousand years; and with equal justice may the lexicographer be derided, who being able to produce no example of a nation that has preserved their words and phrases from mutability, shall imagine that his dictionary can embalm his language, and secure it from corruption and decay, that it is in his power to change sublunary nature, and clear the world at once from folly, vanity, and affectation.

With this hope, however, academies have been instituted, to guard the avenues of their languages, to retain fugitives, and repulse intruders; but their vigilance and activity have hitherto been vain; sounds are too volatile and subtile for legal restraints; to enchain syllables, and to lash the wind, are equally the undertakings of pride, unwilling to measure its desires by its strength.

The *French* language has visibly changed under the inspection of the academy; the stile of *Amelot*'s translation of Father *Paul*[4] is observed by *Le Courayer* to be *un peu passé;* and no *Italian* will maintain that the diction of any modern writer is not perceptibly different from that of *Boccace, Machiavel,* or *Caro.*

Total and sudden transformations of a language seldom happen; conquests and migrations are now very rare: but there are other causes of change, which, though slow in their operation, and invisible in their progress, are perhaps as much superiour to human resistance, as the revolutions of the sky, or intumescence of the tide. Commerce, however necessary, however lucrative, as it depraves the manners, corrupts the language; they that have frequent intercourse with strangers, to whom they endeavour to accommodate themselves, must in time learn a mingled dialect, like the jargon which serves the traffickers on the *Mediterranean* and *Indian* coasts. This will not always be confined to the exchange, the warehouse, or the port, but will be communicated by degrees to other ranks of the people, and be at last incorporated with the current speech.

There are likewise internal causes equally forcible. The language most likely to continue long without alteration, would be that of a nation raised a little, and but a little above barbarity, secluded from strangers, and totally employed in procuring the conveniencies of life; either without books, or, like some of the *Mahometan* countries, with very few: men thus busied and unlearned, having only such words as common use requires, would perhaps long continue to express the same notions by the same signs. But no such constancy can be expected in a people polished by arts, and classed by subordination, where one part of the community is sustained and accommodated by the labour of the other. Those who have much leisure to think, will always be enlarging the stock of ideas, and every increase of knowledge, whether real or fancied, will produce new words, or combinations of words. When the mind is unchained from necessity, it will range after convenience; when it is left at large in the fields of speculation,

[4] Paolo Sarpi, *History of the Council of Trent,* 1619; ed. Amelot, 1683; ed. Courayer, 1736.

it will shift opinions; as any custom is disused, the words that expressed it must perish with it; as any opinion grows popular, it will innovate speech in the same proportion as it alters practice.

As by the cultivation of various sciences, a language is amplified, it will be more furnished with words deflected from original sense; the geometrician will talk of a courtier's zenith, or the excentrick virtue of a wild hero, and the physician of sanguine expectations and phlegmatick delays. Copiousness of speech will give opportunities to capricious choice, by which some words will be preferred, and others degraded; vicissitudes of fashion will enforce the use of new, or extend the signification of known terms. The tropes of poetry will make hourly encroachments, and the metaphorical will become the current sense: pronunciation will be varied by levity or ignorance, and the pen must at length comply with the tongue; illiterate writers will at one time or other, by publick infatuation, rise into renown, who, not knowing the original import of words, will use them with colloquial licentiousness, confound distinction, and forget propriety. As politeness increases, some expressions will be considered as too gross and vulgar for the delicate, others as too formal and ceremonious for the gay and airy; new phrases are therefore adopted, which must, for the same reasons, be in time dismissed. *Swift,* in his petty treatise on the *English* language,[5] allows that new words must sometimes be introduced, but proposes that none should be suffered to become obsolete. But what makes a word obsolete, more than general agreement to forbear it? and how shall it be continued, when it conveys an offensive idea, or recalled again into the mouths of mankind, when it has once become unfamiliar by disuse, and unpleasing by unfamiliarity?

There is another cause of alteration more prevalent than any other, which yet in the present state of the world cannot be obviated. A mixture of two languages will produce a third distinct from both, and they will always be mixed, where the chief part of education, and the most conspicuous accomplishment, is skill in ancient or in foreign tongues. He that has long cultivated an-

[5] *A Proposal for Correcting, Improving and Ascertaining the English Tongue,* 1712.

other language, will find its words and combinations croud upon
his memory; and haste and negligence, refinement and affectation,
will obtrude borrowed terms and exotick expressions.

The great pest of speech is frequency of translation. No book
was ever turned from one language into another, without impart-
ing something of its native idiom; this is the most mischievous and
comprehensive innovation; single words may enter by thousands,
and the fabrick of the tongue continue the same, but new phrase-
ology changes much at once; it alters not the single stones of the
building, but the order of the columns. If an academy should be
established for the cultivation of our stile, which I, who can never
wish to see dependance multiplied, hope the Spirit of *English*
liberty will hinder or destroy, let them, instead of compiling
grammars and dictionaries, endeavour, with all their influence, to
stop the licence of translatours, whose idleness and ignorance, if
it be suffered to proceed, will reduce us to babble a dialect of
France.

If the changes that we fear be thus irresistible, what remains
but to acquiesce with silence, as in the other insurmountable dis-
tresses of humanity? It remains that we retard what we cannot
repel, that we palliate what we cannot cure. Life may be length-
ened by care, though death cannot be ultimately defeated:
tongues, like governments, have a natural tendency to degenera-
tion; we have long preserved our constitution, let us make some
struggles for our language.

In hope of giving longevity to that which its own nature for-
bids to be immortal, I have devoted this book, the labour of years,
to the honour of my country, that we may no longer yield the
palm of philology, without a contest, to the nations of the con-
tinent. The chief glory of every people arises from its authours:
whether I shall add any thing by my own writings to the reputa-
tion of *English* literature, must be left to time: much of my life
has been lost under the pressures of disease; much has been trifled
away; and much has always been spent in provision for the day
that was passing over me; but I shall not think my employment
useless or ignoble, if by my assistance foreign nations, and distant
ages, gain access to the propagators of knowledge, and understand

the teachers of truth; if my labours afford light to the repositories of science, and add celebrity to *Bacon*, to *Hooker*, to *Milton*, and to *Boyle*.

When I am animated by this wish, I look with pleasure on my book, however defective, and deliver it to the world with the spirit of a man that has endeavoured well. That it will immediately become popular I have not promised to myself: a few wild blunders, and risible absurdities, from which no work of such multiplicity was ever free, may for a time furnish folly with laughter, and harden ignorance in contempt; but useful diligence will at last prevail, and there never can be wanting some who distinguish desert; who will consider that no dictionary of a living tongue ever can be perfect, since while it is hastening to publication, some words are budding, and some falling away; that a whole life cannot be spent upon syntax and etymology, and that even a whole life would not be sufficient; that he, whose design includes whatever language can express, must often speak of what he does not understand; that a writer will sometimes be hurried by eagerness to the end, and sometimes faint with weariness under a task, which *Scaliger* compares[6] to the labours of the anvil and the mine; that what is obvious is not always known, and what is known is not always present; that sudden fits of inadvertency will surprize vigilance, slight avocations will seduce attention, and casual eclipses of the mind will darken learning; and that the writer shall often in vain trace his memory at the moment of need, for that which yesterday he knew with intuitive readiness, and which will come uncalled into his thoughts tomorrow.

In this work, when it shall be found that much is omitted, let it not be forgotten that much likewise is performed; and though no book was ever spared out of tenderness to the authour, and the world is little solicitous to know whence proceeded the faults of that which it condemns; yet it may gratify curiosity to inform it, that the *English Dictionary* was written with little assistance of the learned, and without any patronage of the great; not in the soft obscurities of retirement, or under the shelter of academick

[6] *In Lexicorum Compilatores. Poemata Omnia*, Berlin, 1868, p. 38. [C. H. Conley]

bowers, but amidst inconvenience and distraction, in sickness and in sorrow. It may repress the triumph of malignant criticism to observe, that if our language is not here fully displayed, I have only failed in an attempt which no human powers have hitherto completed. If the lexicons of ancient tongues, now immutably fixed, and comprised in a few volumes, be yet, after the toil of successive ages, inadequate and delusive; if the aggregated knowledge, and co-operating diligence of the *Italian* academicians, did not secure them from the censure of *Beni;* if the embodied criticks of *France,* when fifty years had been spent upon their work, were obliged to change its oeconomy, and give their second edition another form, I may surely be contented without the praise of perfection, which, if I could obtain, in this gloom of solitude, what would it avail me? I have protracted my work till most of those whom I wished to please have sunk into the grave, and success and miscarriage are empty sounds: I therefore dismiss it with frigid tranquillity, having little to fear or hope from censure or from praise.

Preface to
Shakespeare

That praises are without reason lavished on the dead, and that the honours due only to excellence are paid to antiquity, is a complaint likely to be always continued by those, who, being able to add nothing to truth, hope for eminence from the heresies of paradox; or those, who, being forced by disappointment upon consolatory expedients, are willing to hope from posterity what the present age refuses, and flatter themselves that the regard which is yet denied by envy, will be at last bestowed by time.

Antiquity, like every other quality that attracts the notice of mankind, has undoubtedly votaries that reverence it, not from reason, but from prejudice. Some seem to admire indiscriminately whatever has been long preserved, without considering that time has sometimes co-operated with chance; all perhaps are more willing to honour past than present excellence; and the mind contemplates genius through the shades of age, as the eye surveys the sun through artificial opacity. The great contention of criticism is to find the faults of the moderns, and the beauties of the ancients. While an authour is yet living we estimate his powers by his worst performance, and when he is dead we rate them by his best.

To works, however, of which the excellence is not absolute and definite, but gradual and comparative; to works not raised upon principles demonstrative and scientifick, but appealing wholly to observation and experience, no other test can be applied than length of duration and continuance of esteem. What mankind have long possessed they have often examined and compared, and if they persist to value the possession, it is because frequent comparisons have confirmed opinion in its favour. As among the works of nature no man can properly call a river deep or a mountain high, without the knowledge of many mountains and many rivers; so in the productions of genius, nothing can be stiled excellent till it has been compared with other works of the same kind. Demonstration immediately displays its power, and has nothing to hope or fear from the flux of years; but works tentative and experimental must be estimated by their proportion to the general and collective ability of man, as it is discovered in a long succession of endeavours. Of the first building that was raised, it might be with certainty determined that it was round or square, but whether it was spacious or lofty must have been referred to time. The Pythagorean scale of numbers was at once discovered to be perfect;[1] but the poems of *Homer* we yet know not to transcend the common limits of human intelligence, but by remarking, that nation after nation, and century after century, has been able to do little more than transpose his incidents, new name his characters, and paraphrase his sentiments.

The reverence due to writings that have long subsisted arises therefore not from any credulous confidence in the superior wisdom of past ages, or gloomy persuasion of the degeneracy of mankind, but is the consequence of acknowledged and indubitable positions, that what has been longest known has been most considered, and what is most considered is best understood.

The Poet, of whose works I have undertaken the revision, may now begin to assume the dignity of an ancient, and claim the privilege of established fame and prescriptive veneration. He has long outlived his century, the term commonly fixed as the test of literary merit. Whatever advantages he might once derive from personal allusions, local customs, or temporary opinions, have for

---

[1] Cf. Aristotle, *Metaphysics.* I. v.

many years been lost; and every topick of merriment or motive of sorrow, which the modes of artificial life afforded him, now only obscure the scenes which they once illuminated. The effects of favour and competition are at an end; the tradition of his friendships and his enmities has perished; his works support no opinion with arguments, nor supply any faction with invectives; they can neither indulge vanity nor gratify malignity, but are read without any other reason than the desire of pleasure, and are therefore praised only as pleasure is obtained; yet, thus unassisted by interest or passion, they have past through variations of taste and changes of manners, and, as they devolved from one generation to another, have received new honours at every transmission.

But because human judgment, though it be gradually gaining upon certainty, never becomes infallible; and approbation, though long continued, may yet be only the approbation of prejudice or fashion; it is proper to inquire, by what peculiarities of excellence *Shakespeare* has gained and kept the favour of his countrymen.

Nothing can please many, and please long, but just representations of general nature. Particular manners can be known to few, and therefore few only can judge how nearly they are copied. The irregular combinations of fanciful invention may delight a-while, by that novelty of which the common satiety of life sends us all in quest; but the pleasures of sudden wonder are soon exhausted, and the mind can only repose on the stability of truth.

Shakespeare is above all writers, at least above all modern writers, the poet of nature; the poet that holds up to his readers a faithful mirrour of manners and of life. His characters are not modified by the customs of particular places, unpractised by the rest of the world; by the peculiarities of studies or professions, which can operate but upon small numbers; or by the accidents of transient fashions or temporary opinions: they are the genuine progeny of common humanity, such as the world will always supply, and observation will always find. His persons act and speak by the influence of those general passions and principles by which all minds are agitated, and the whole system of life is continued in motion. In the writings of other poets a character is too often an individual; in those of *Shakespeare* it is commonly a species.

It is from this wide extension of design that so much instruction is derived. It is this which fills the plays of *Shakespeare* with practical axioms and domestick wisdom. It was said of *Euripides,* that every verse was a precept;[2] and it may be said of *Shakespeare,* that from his works may be collected a system of civil and œconomical prudence. Yet his real power is not shown in the splendour of particular passages, but by the progress of his fable, and the tenour of his dialogue; and he that tries to recommend him by select quotations, will succeed like the pedant in *Hierocles,*[3] who, when he offered his house to sale, carried a brick in his pocket as a specimen.

It will not easily be imagined how much *Shakespeare* excells in accommodating his sentiments to real life, but by comparing him with other authours. It was observed of the ancient schools of declamation, that the more diligently they were frequented, the more was the student disqualified for the world, because he found nothing there which he should ever meet in any other place. The same remark may be applied to every stage but that of *Shakespeare.* The theatre, when it is under any other direction, is peopled by such characters as were never seen, conversing in a language which was never heard, upon topicks which will never arise in the commerce of mankind. But the dialogue of this authour is often so evidently determined by the incident which produces it, and is pursued with so much ease and simplicity, that it seems scarcely to claim the merit of fiction, but to have been gleaned by diligent selection out of common conversation, and common occurrences.

Upon every other stage the universal agent is love, by whose power all good and evil is distributed, and every action quickened or retarded. To bring a lover, a lady and a rival into the fable; to entangle them in contradictory obligations, perplex them with oppositions of interest, and harrass them with violence of desires inconsistent with each other; to make them meet in rapture and part in agony; to fill their mouths with hyperbolical joy and out-

[2] Cicero, *Epistolae ad Familiares,* XVI. 8.

[3] *Hieroclis Commentarius in Aurea Carmina,* ed. Needham, 1709, p. 462. [D. Nichol Smith]

rageous sorrow; to distress them as nothing human ever was distressed; to deliver them as nothing human ever was delivered, is the business of a modern dramatist. For this probability is violated, life is misrepresented, and language is depraved. But love is only one of many passions, and as it has no great influence upon the sum of life, it has little operation in the dramas of a poet, who caught his ideas from the living world, and exhibited only what he saw before him. He knew, that any other passion, as it was regular or exorbitant, was a cause of happiness or calamity.

Characters thus ample and general were not easily discriminated and preserved, yet perhaps no poet ever kept his personages more distinct from each other. I will not say with *Pope,* that every speech may be assigned to the proper speaker,[4] because many speeches there are which have nothing characteristical; but, perhaps, though some may be equally adapted to every person, it will be difficult to find, any that can be properly transferred from the present possessor to another claimant. The choice is right, when there is reason for choice.

Other dramatists can only gain attention by hyperbolical or aggravated characters, by fabulous and unexampled excellence or depravity, as the writers of barbarous romances invigorated the reader by a giant and a dwarf; and he that should form his expectations of human affairs from the play, or from the tale, would be equally deceived. *Shakespeare* has no heroes; his scenes are occupied only by men, who act and speak as the reader thinks that he should himself have spoken or acted on the same occasion: Even where the agency is supernatural the dialogue is level with life. Other writers disguise the most natural passions and most frequent incidents; so that he who contemplates them in the book will not know them in the world: *Shakespeare* approximates the remote, and familiarizes the wonderful; the event which he represents will not happen, but if it were possible, its effects would be probably such as he has assigned; and it may be said, that he has not only shewn human nature as it acts in real exigences, but as it would be found in trials, to which it cannot be exposed.

[4] Pope's Preface, ¶4.

This therefore is the praise of *Shakespeare*, that his drama is the mirrour of life; that he who has mazed his imagination, in following the phantoms which other writers raise up before him, may here be cured of his delirious extasies, by reading human sentiments in human language; by scenes from which a hermit may estimate the transactions of the world, and a confessor predict the progress of the passions.

His adherence to general nature has exposed him to the censure of criticks, who form their judgments upon narrower principles. *Dennis* and *Rhymer* think his *Romans* not sufficiently Roman; and *Voltaire* censures his kings as not completely royal. *Dennis* is offended, that *Menenius,* a senator of *Rome,* should play the buffoon;[5] and *Voltaire* perhaps thinks decency violated when the *Danish* Usurper is represented as a drunkard. But *Shakespeare* always makes nature predominate over accident; and if he preserves the essential character, is not very careful of distinctions superinduced and adventitious. His story requires Romans or kings, but he thinks only on men. He knew that *Rome,* like every other city, had men of all dispositions; and wanting a buffoon, he went into the senate-house for that which the senate-house would certainly have afforded him. He was inclined to shew an usurper and a murderer not only odious but despicable, he therefore added drunkenness to his other qualities, knowing that kings love wine like other men, and that wine exerts its natural power upon kings. These are the petty cavils of petty minds; a poet overlooks the casual distinction of country and condition, as a painter, satisfied with the figure, neglects the drapery.

The censure which he has incurred by mixing comick and tragick scenes, as it extends to all his works, deserves more consideration. Let the fact be first stated, and then examined.

Shakespeare's plays are not in the rigorous and critical sense either tragedies or comedies, but compositions of a distinct kind; exhibiting the real state of sublunary nature, which partakes of good and evil, joy and sorrow, mingled with endless variety of proportion and innumerable modes of combination; and express-

---

[5] *An Essay on the Genius and Writings of Shakespear,* 1712 (ed. Hooker, 1943, II, 5).

ing the course of the world, in which the loss of one is the gain of another; in which, at the same time, the reveller is hasting to his wine, and the mourner burying his friend; in which the malignity of one is sometimes defeated by the frolick of another; and many mischiefs and many benefits are done and hindered without design.

Out of this chaos of mingled purposes and casualties the ancient poets, according to the laws which custom had prescribed, selected some the crimes of men, and some their absurdities; some the momentous vicissitudes of life, and some the lighter occurrences; some the terrours of distress, and some the gayeties of prosperity. Thus rose the two modes of imitation, known by the names of *tragedy* and *comedy,* compositions intended to promote different ends by contrary means, and considered as so little allied, that I do not recollect among the *Greeks* or *Romans* a single writer who attempted both.

Shakespeare has united the powers of exciting laughter and sorrow not only in one mind, but in one composition. Almost all his plays are divided between serious and ludicrous characters, and, in the successive evolutions of the design, sometimes produce seriousness and sorrow, and sometimes levity and laughter.

That this is a practice contrary to the rules of criticism will be readily allowed; but there is always an appeal open from criticism to nature. The end of writing is to instruct; the end of poetry is to instruct by pleasing. That the mingled drama may convey all the instruction of tragedy or comedy cannot be denied, because it includes both in its alter[n]ations of exhibition, and approaches nearer than either to the appearance of life, by shewing how great machinations and slender designs may promote or obviate one another, and the high and the low co-operate in the general system by unavoidable concatenation.

It is objected, that by this change of scenes the passions are interrupted in their progression, and that the principal event, being not advanced by a due gradation of preparatory incidents, wants at last the power to move, which constitutes the perfection of dramatick poetry. This reasoning is so specious, that it is received as true even by those who in daily experience feel it to be

false. The interchanges of mingled scenes seldom fail to produce
the intended vicissitudes of passion. Fiction cannot move so much,
but that the attention may be easily transferred; and though it
must be allowed that pleasing melancholy be sometimes inter-
rupted by unwelcome levity, yet let it be considered likewise, that
melancholy is often not pleasing, and that the disturbance of one
man may be the relief of another; that different auditors have dif-
ferent habitudes; and that, upon the whole, all pleasure consists
in variety.

The players, who in their edition[6] divided our authour's works
into comedies, histories, and tragedies, seem not to have distin-
guished the three kinds, by any very exact or definite ideas.

An action which ended happily to the principal persons, how-
ever serious or distressful through its intermediate incidents, in
their opinion constituted a comedy. This idea of a comedy con-
tinued long amongst us, and plays were written, which, by chang-
ing the catastrophe, were tragedies to-day and comedies to-morrow.

Tragedy was not in those times a poem of more general dignity
or elevation than comedy; it required only a calamitous conclu-
sion, with which the common criticism of that age was satisfied,
whatever lighter pleasure it afforded in its progress.

History was a series of actions, with no other than chrono-
logical succession, independent of [7] each other, and without any
tendency to introduce or regulate the conclusion. It is not always
very nicely distinguished from tragedy. There is not much nearer
approach to unity of action in the tragedy of *Antony and Cleo-
patra,* than in the history of *Richard the Second.* But a history
might be continued through many plays; as it had no plan, it
had no limits.

Through all these denominations of the drama, *Shakespeare's*
mode of composition is the same; an interchange of seriousness
and merriment, by which the mind is softened at one time, and
exhilarated at another. But whatever be his purpose, whether to
gladden or depress, or to conduct the story, without vehemence

---

[6] The first folio (1623) is meant: John Heming and Henry Condell,
members of Shakespeare's theatrical company, were responsible for it.

[7] 1778: on.

or emotion, through tracts of easy and familiar dialogue, he never fails to attain his purpose; as he commands us, we laugh or mourn, or sit silent with quiet expectation, in tranquillity without indifference.

When *Shakespeare*'s plan is understood, most of the criticisms of *Rhymer* and *Voltaire* vanish away. The play of *Hamlet* is opened, without impropriety, by two sentinels; *Iago* bellows at *Brabantio*'s window, without injury to the scheme of the play, though in terms which a modern audience would not easily endure; the character of *Polonius* is seasonable and useful; and the Grave-diggers themselves may be heard with applause.

Shakespeare engaged in dramatick poetry with the world open before him; the rules of the ancients were yet known to few; the publick judgment was unformed; he had no example of such fame as might force him upon imitation, nor criticks of such authority as might restrain his extravagance: He therefore indulged his natural disposition, and his disposition, as *Rhymer* has remarked, led him to comedy. In tragedy he often writes with great appearance of toil and study, what is written at last with little felicity; but in his comick scenes, he seems to produce without labour, what no labour can improve. In tragedy he is always struggling after some occasion to be comick, but in comedy he seems to repose, or to luxuriate, as in a mode of thinking congenial to his nature. In his tragick scenes there is always something wanting, but his comedy often surpasses expectation or desire. His comedy pleases by the thoughts and the language, and his tragedy for the greater part by incident and action. His tragedy seems to be skill, his comedy to be instinct.

The force of his comick scenes has suffered little diminution from the changes made by a century and a half, in manners or in words. As his personages act upon principles arising from genuine passion, very little modified by particular forms, their pleasures and vexations are communicable to all times and to all places; they are natural, and therefore durable; the adventitious peculiarities of personal habits, are only superficial dies, bright and pleasing for a little while, yet soon fading to a dim tinct, without any remains of former lustre; but the discriminations of true passion are the colours of nature; they pervade the whole mass, and can only perish with the body that exhibits them. The accidental compositions of heterogeneous modes are dissolved by the chance which combined them; but the uniform simplicity of primitive qualities neither admits increase, nor suffers decay. The sand heaped by one flood is scattered by another, but the rock always continues in its place. The stream of time, which is continually washing the dissoluble fabricks of other poets, passes without injury by the adamant of *Shakespeare*.

If there be, what I believe there is, in every nation, a stile which never becomes obsolete, a certain mode of phraseology so consonant and congenial to the analogy and principles of its respective language as to remain settled and unaltered; this stile is probably to be sought in the common intercourse of life, among those who speak only to be understood, without ambition of elegance. The polite are always catching modish innovations, and the learned depart from established forms of speech, in hope of finding or making better; those who wish for distinction forsake the vulgar, when the vulgar is right; but there is a conversation above grossness and below refinement, where propriety resides, and where this poet seems to have gathered his comick dialogue. He is therefore more agreeable to the ears of the present age than any other authour equally remote, and among his other excellencies deserves to be studied as one of the original masters of our language.

These observations are to be considered not as unexceptionably constant, but as containing general and predominant truth. *Shakespeare*'s familiar dialogue is affirmed to be smooth and clear, yet not wholly without ruggedness or difficulty; as a country may be eminently fruitful, though it has spots unfit for cultivation: His characters are praised as natural, though their sentiments are sometimes forced, and their actions improbable; as the earth upon the whole is spherical, though its surface is varied with protuberances and cavities.

Shakespeare with his excellencies has likewise faults, and faults sufficient to obscure and overwhelm any other merit. I shall shew them in the proportion in which they appear to me, without envious malignity or superstitious veneration. No question can be more innocently discussed than a dead poet's pretensions to renown; and little regard is due to that bigotry which sets candour higher than truth.

His first defect is that to which may be imputed most of the evil in books or in men. He sacrifices virtue to convenience, and is so much more careful to please than to instruct, that he seems to write without any moral purpose. From his writings indeed a system of social duty may be selected, for he that thinks reasonably must think morally; but his precepts and axioms drop casually from him; he makes no just distribution of good or evil, nor is always careful to shew in the virtuous a disapprobation of the wicked; he carries his persons indifferently through right and wrong, and at the close dismisses them without further care, and leaves their examples to operate by chance. This fault the barbarity of his age cannot extenuate; for it is always a writer's duty to make the world better, and justice is a virtue independant on time or place.

The plots are often so loosely formed, that a very slight consideration may improve them, and so carelessly pursued, that he seems not always fully to comprehend his own design. He omits opportunities of instructing or delighting which the train of his story seems to force upon him, and apparently rejects those exhibitions which would be more affecting, for the sake of those which are more easy.

It may be observed, that in many of his plays the latter part is evidently neglected. When he found himself near the end of his work, and, in view of his reward, he shortened the labour, to snatch the profit. He therefore remits his efforts where he should most vigorously exert them, and his catastrophe is improbably produced or imperfectly represented.

He had no regard to distinction of time or place, but gives to one age or nation, without scruple, the customs, institutions, and opinions of another, at the expence not only of likelihood, but of possibility. These faults *Pope* has endeavoured, with more zeal than judgment, to transfer to his imagined interpolators. We need not wonder to find *Hector* quoting *Aristotle,* when we see the

loves of *Theseus* and *Hippolyta* combined with the *Gothick* my-
thology of fairies. *Shakespeare*, indeed, was not the only violator
of chronology, for in the same age *Sidney*, who wanted not the
advantages of learning, has, in his *Arcadia,* confounded the pas-
toral with the feudal times, the days of innocence, quiet and secu-
rity, with those of turbulence, violence and adventure.

In his comick scenes he is seldom very successful, when he
engages his characters in reciprocations of smartness and contest
of sarcasm; their jests are commonly gross, and their pleasantry
licentious; neither his gentlemen nor his ladies have much deli-
cacy, nor are sufficiently distinguished from his clowns by any
appearance of refined manners. Whether he represented the real
conversation of his time is not easy to determine; the reign of
Elizabeth is commonly supposed to have been a time of state-
liness, formality and reserve, yet perhaps the relaxations of that
severity were not very elegant. There must, however, have been
always some modes of gayety preferable to others, and a writer
ought to chuse the best.

In tragedy his performance seems constantly to be worse, as his
labour is more. The effusions of passion which exigence forces
out are for the most part striking and energetick; but whenever
he solicits his invention, or strains his faculties, the offspring of
his throes is tumour, meanness, tediousness, and obscurity.

In narration he affects a disproportionate pomp of diction and
a wearisome train of circumlocution, and tells the incident im-
perfectly in many words, which might have been more plainly
delivered in few. Narration in dramatick poetry is naturally tedi-
ous, as it is unanimated and inactive, and obstructs the progress
of the action; it should therefore always be rapid, and enlivened
by frequent interruption. *Shakespeare* found it an encumbrance,
and instead of lightening it by brevity, endeavoured to recommend
it by dignity and splendour.

His declamations or set speeches are commonly cold and weak,
for his power was the power of nature; when he endeavoured, like
other tragick writers, to catch opportunities of amplification, and
instead of inquiring what the occasion demanded, to show how

much his stores of knowledge could supply, he seldom escapes without the pity or resentment of his reader.

It is incident to him to be now and then entangled with an unwieldy sentiment, which he cannot well express, and will not reject; he struggles with it a while, and if it continues stubborn, comprises it in words such as occur, and leaves it to be disentangled and evolved by those who have more leisure to bestow upon it.

Not that always where the language is intricate the thought is subtle, or the image always great where the line is bulky; the equality of words to things is very often neglected, and trivial sentiments and vulgar ideas disappoint the attention, to which they are recommended by sonorous epithets and swelling figures.

But the admirers of this great poet [8] have never less reason to indulge their hopes of supreme excellence, than when he seems fully resolved to sink them in dejection, and mollify them with tender emotions by the fall of greatness, the danger of innocence, or the crosses of love. He is not long soft and pathetick without some idle conceit, or contemptible equivocation. He no sooner begins to move, than he counteracts himself; and terrour and pity, as they are rising in the mind, are checked and blasted by sudden frigidity.

A quibble is to *Shakespeare*, what luminous vapours are to the traveller; he follows it at all adventures, it is sure to lead him out of his way, and sure to engulf him in the mire. It has some malignant power over his mind, and its fascinations are irresistible. Whatever be the dignity or profundity of his disquisition, whether he be enlarging knowledge or exalting affection, whether he be amusing attention with incidents, or enchaining it in suspense, let but a quibble spring up before him, and he leaves his work unfinished. A quibble is the golden apple for which he will always turn aside from his career, or stoop from his elevation. A quibble poor and barren as it is, gave him such delight, that he was con-

[8] 1778 reads: "have most reason to complain when he approaches nearest to his highest excellence, and seems fully resolved . . . crosses of love. What he does best, he soon ceases to do. He is . . . ."

tent to purchase it, by the sacrifice of reason, propriety and truth. A quibble was to him the fatal *Cleopatra* for which he lost the world, and was content to lose it.

It will be thought strange, that, in enumerating the defects of this writer, I have not yet mentioned his neglect of the unities; his violation of those laws which have been instituted and established by the joint authority of poets and of criticks.

For his other deviations from the art of writing, I resign him to critical justice, without making any other demand in his favour, than that which must be indulged to all human excellence; that his virtues be rated with his failings: But, from the censure which this irregularity may bring upon him, I shall, with due reverence to that learning which I must oppose, adventure to try how I can defend him.

His histories, being neither tragedies nor comedies, are not subject to any of their laws; nothing more is necessary to all the praise which they expect, than that the changes of action be so prepared as to be understood, that the incidents be various and affecting, and the characters consistent, natural and distinct. No other unity is intended, and therefore none is to be sought.

In his other works he has well enough preserved the unity of action. He has not, indeed, an intrigue regularly perplexed and regularly unravelled; he does not endeavour to hide his design only to discover it, for this is seldom the order of real events, and *Shakespeare* is the poet of nature: But his plan has commonly what *Aristotle* requires, a beginning, a middle, and an end; one event is concatenated with another, and the conclusion follows by easy consequence. There are perhaps some incidents that might be spared, as in other poets there is much talk that only fills up time upon the stage; but the general system makes gradual advances, and the end of the play is the end of expectation.

To the unities of time and place he has shewn no regard, and perhaps a nearer view of the principles on which they stand will diminish their value, and withdraw from them the veneration which, from the time of *Corneille*, they have very generally received by discovering that they have given more trouble to the poet, than pleasure to the auditor.

The necessity of observing the unities of time and place arises from the supposed necessity of making the drama credible. The criticks hold it impossible, that an action of months or years can be possibly believed to pass in three hours; or that the spectator can suppose himself to sit in the theatre, while ambassadors go and return between distant kings, while armies are levied and towns besieged, while an exile wanders and returns, or till he whom they saw courting his mistress, shall lament the untimely fall of his son. The mind revolts from evident falsehood, and fiction loses its force when it departs from the resemblance of reality.

From the narrow limitation of time necessarily arises the contraction of place. The spectator, who knows that he saw the first act at *Alexandria*, cannot suppose that he sees the next at *Rome*, at a distance to which not the dragons of *Medea* could, in so short a time, have transported him; he knows with certainty that he has not changed his place; and he knows that place cannot change itself; that what was a house cannot become a plain; that what was *Thebes* can never be *Persepolis*.

Such is the triumphant language with which a critick exults over the misery of an irregular poet, and exults commonly without resistance or reply. It is time therefore to tell him, by the authority of *Shakespeare*, that he assumes, as an unquestionable principle, a position, which, while his breath is forming it into words, his understanding pronounces to be false. It is false, that any representation is mistaken for reality; that any dramatick fable in its materiality was ever credible, or, for a single moment, was ever credited.

The objection arising from the impossibility of passing the first hour at *Alexandria*, and the next at *Rome*, supposes, that when the play opens the spectator really imagines himself at *Alexandria*, and believes that his walk to the theatre has been a voyage to *Egypt*, and that he lives in the days of *Antony* and *Cleopatra*. Surely he that imagines this, may imagine more. He that can take the stage at one time for the palace of the *Ptolemies*, may take it in half an hour for the promontory of *Actium*. Delusion, if delusion be admitted, has no certain limitation; if the spectator can be once persuaded, that his old acquaintance are *Alexander* and *Cæsar,* that a room illuminated with candles is the plain of *Pharsalia,* or the bank of *Granicus,* he is in a state of elevation above the reach of reason, or of truth, and from the heights of empyrean poetry, may despise the circumscriptions of terrestrial nature. There is no reason why a mind thus wandering in extasy should count the clock, or why an hour should not be a century in that calenture of the brains that can make the stage a field.

The truth is, that the spectators are always in their senses, and know, from the first act to the last, that the stage is only a stage, and that the players are only players. They come to hear a certain number of lines recited with just gesture and elegant modulation. The lines relate to some action, and an action must be in some place; but the different actions that compleat a story may be in places very remote from each other; and where is the absurdity of allowing that space to represent first *Athens,* and then *Sicily,* which was always known to be neither *Sicily* nor *Athens,* but a modern theatre?

By supposition, as place is introduced, time may be extended; the time required by the fable elapses for the most part between the acts; for, of so much of the action as is represented, the real and poetical duration is the same. If, in the first act, preparations for war against *Mithridates* are represented to be made in *Rome,* the event of the war may, without absurdity, be represented, in the catastrophe, as happening in *Pontus;* we know that there is neither war, nor preparation for war; we know that we are neither in *Rome* nor *Pontus;* that neither *Mithridates* nor *Lucullus* are before us. The drama exhibits successive imitations of successive actions, and why may not the second imitation represent an action that happened years after the first; if it be so connected with it, that nothing but time can be supposed to intervene? Time is, of all modes of existence, most obsequious to the imagination; a lapse of years is as easily conceived as a passage of hours. In contemplation we easily contract the time of real actions, and therefore willingly permit it to be contracted when we only see their imitation.

It will be asked, how the drama moves, if it is not credited.

It is credited with all the credit due to a drama. It is credited, whenever it moves, as a just picture of a real original; as representing to the auditor what he would himself feel, if he were to do or suffer what is there feigned to be suffered or to be done. The reflection that strikes the heart is not, that the evils before us are real evils, but that they are evils to which we ourselves may be exposed. If there be any fallacy, it is not that we fancy the players, but that we fancy ourselves unhappy for a moment; but we rather lament the possibility than suppose the presence of misery, as a mother weeps over her babe, when she remembers that death may take it from her. The delight of tragedy proceeds from our consciousness of fiction; if we thought murders and treasons real, they would please no more.

Imitations produce pain or pleasure, not because they are mistaken for realities, but because they bring realities to mind. When the imagination is recreated by a painted landscape, the trees are not supposed capable to give us shade, or the fountains coolness; but we consider, how we should be pleased with such fountains playing beside us, and such woods waving over us. We are agitated in reading the history of *Henry* the Fifth, yet no man takes his book for the field of *Agencourt*. A dramatick exhibition is a book recited with concomitants that encrease or diminish its effect. Familiar comedy is often more powerful on the theatre, than in the page; imperial tragedy is always less. The humour of *Petruchio* may be heightened by grimace; but what voice or what gesture can hope to add dignity or force to the soliloquy of *Cato*.[9]

A play read, affects the mind like a play acted. It is therefore evident, that the action is not supposed to be real, and it follows that between the acts a longer or shorter time may be allowed to pass, and that no more account of space or duration is to be taken by the auditor of a drama, than by the reader of a narrative, before whom may pass in an hour the life of a hero, or the revolutions of an empire.

Whether *Shakespeare* knew the unities, and rejected them by design, or deviated from them by happy ignorance, it is, I think,

[9] Addison, *Cato.* V. i.

impossible to decide, and useless to inquire.[10] We may reasonably
suppose, that, when he rose to notice, he did not want[11] the
counsels and admonitions of scholars and criticks, and that he at
last deliberately persisted in a practice, which he might have
begun by chance. As nothing is essential to the fable, but unity
of action, and as the unities of time and place arise evidently from
false assumptions, and, by circumscribing the extent of the drama,
lessen its variety, I cannot think it much to be lamented, that they
were not known by him, or not observed: Nor, if such another
poet could arise, should I very vehemently reproach him, that his
first act passed at *Venice*, and his next in *Cyprus*. Such violations
of rules merely positive, become the comprehensive genius of
Shakespeare, and such censures are suitable to the minute and
slender criticism of *Voltaire*:

> *Non usque adeo permiscuit imis*
> *Longus summa dies, ut non, si voce Metelli*
> *Serventur leges, maline a Cæsare tolli.*[12]

Yet when I speak thus slightly of dramatick rules, I cannot but
recollect how much wit and learning may be produced against
me; before such authorities I am afraid to stand, not that I think
the present question one of those that are to be decided by mere
authority, but because it is to be suspected, that these precepts
have not been so easily received but for better reasons than I
have yet been able to find. The result of my enquiries, in which
it would be ludicrous to boast of impartiality, is, that the unities
of time and place are not essential to a just drama, that though
they may sometimes conduce to pleasure, they are always to be
sacrificed to the nobler beauties of variety and instruction; and
that a play, written with nice observation of critical rules, is to be
contemplated as an elaborate curiosity, as the product of super-

---

[10] 1778: enquire.

[11] i.e., lack.

[12] Lucan, *Pharsalia*, III. 138–140. "The course of time has not wrought
such confusion that the laws would not rather be trampled on by Caesar
than saved by Metellus." [tr. J. D. Duff]

fluous and ostentatious art, by which is shewn, rather what is possible, than what is necessary.

He that, without diminution of any other excellence, shall preserve all the unities unbroken, deserves the like applause with the architect, who shall display all the orders of architecture in a citadel, without any deduction from its strength; but the principal beauty of a citadel is to exclude the enemy; and the greatest graces of a play, are to copy nature and instruct life.

Perhaps, what I have here not dogmatically but deliberately[13] written, may recal the principles of the drama to a new examination. I am almost frighted at my own temerity; and when I estimate the fame and the strength of those that maintain the contrary opinion, am ready to sink down in reverential silence; as *Æneas* withdrew from the defence of *Troy*, when he saw *Neptune* shaking the wall, and *Juno* heading the besiegers.[14]

Those whom my arguments cannot persuade to give their approbation to the judgment of *Shakespeare*, will easily, if they consider the condition of his life, make some allowance for his ignorance.

Every man's performances, to be rightly estimated, must be compared with the state of the age in which he lived, and with his own particular opportunities; and though to the reader a book be not worse or better for the circumstances of the authour, yet as there is always a silent reference of human works to human abilities, and as the enquiry, how far man may extend his designs, or how high he may rate his native force, is of far greater dignity than in what rank we shall place any particular performance, curiosity is always busy to discover the instruments, as well as to survey the workmanship, to know how much is to be ascribed to original powers, and how much to casual and adventitious help. The palaces of *Peru* or *Mexico* were certainly mean and incommodious habitations, if compared to the houses of *European* monarchs; yet who could forbear to view them with astonishment, who remembered that they were built without the use of iron?

[13] Unpaged preface of First (1765) Edition: "deliberatively."
[14] *Æneid,* II. 610.

The *English* nation, in the time of *Shakespeare,* was yet strug-
gling to emerge from barbarity. The philology of *Italy* had been
transplanted hither in the reign of *Henry* the Eighth; and the
learned languages had been successfully cultivated by *Lilly,*[15]
Linacer,[16] and *More;* by *Pole, Cheke,* and *Gardiner;*[17] and after-
wards by *Smith, Clerk, Haddon,*[18] and *Ascham.* Greek was now
taught to boys in the principal schools; and those who united
elegance with learning, read, with great diligence, the *Italian*
and *Spanish* poets. But literature was yet confined to professed
scholars, or to men and women of high rank. The publick was
gross and dark; and to be able to read and write, was an ac-
complishment still valued for its rarity.

Nations, like individuals, have their infancy. A people newly
awakened to literary curiosity, being yet unacquainted with the
true state of things, knows not how to judge of that which is
proposed as its resemblance. Whatever is remote from common
appearances is always welcome to vulgar, as to childish credulity;
and of a country unenlightened by learning, the whole people
is the vulgar. The study of those who then aspired to plebeian
learning was laid out upon adventures, giants, dragons, and en-
chantments. *The Death of Arthur* was the favourite volume.

The mind, which has feasted on the luxurious wonders of
fiction, has no taste of the insipidity of truth. A play which im-
itated only the common occurrences of the world, would, upon
the admirers of *Palmerin* and *Guy* of *Warwick,* have made little
impression; he that wrote for such an audience was under the
necessity of looking round for strange events and fabulous trans-
actions, and that incredibility, by which maturer knowledge is

[15] William Lily, author of a famous Latin grammer, used by Shakes-
peare.

[16] Thomas Linacre, physician and humanist, taught Greek at Oxford.

[17] Stephen Gardiner and Reginald Pole, scholar-statesmen and church-
men, both became chancellor of Cambridge; Sir John Cheke was regius
professor of Greek there.

[18] Sir Thomas Smith was vice-chancellor of Cambridge, as was also
Walter Haddon; both were regius professors of civil law, and the latter be-
came president of Magdalen College, Oxford. John Clerk was Wolsey's
chaplain and bishop of Bath and Wells.

offended, was the chief recommendation of writings, to unskilful curiosity.

Our authour's plots are generally borrowed from novels, and it is reasonable to suppose, that he chose the most popular, such as were read by many, and related by more; for his audience could not have followed him through the intricacies of the drama, had they not held the thread of the story in their hands.

The stories, which we now find only in remoter authours, were in his time accessible and familliar. The fable of *As you like it,* which is supposed to be copied from *Chaucer's* Gamelyn, was a little pamphlet of those times;[19] and old Mr. *Cibber*[20] remembered the tale of *Hamlet* in plain *English* prose, which the cricks have now to seek in *Saxo Grammaticus.*

His *English* histories he took from *English* chronicles and *English* ballads; and as the ancient writers were made known to his countrymen by versions, they supplied him with new subjects; he dilated some of *Plutarch's* lives into plays, when they had been translated by *North.*[21]

His plots, whether historical or fabulous, are always crouded with incidents, by which the attention of a rude people was more easily caught than by sentiment or argumentation; and such is the power of the marvellous even over those who despise it, that every man finds his mind more strongly seized by the tragedies of *Shakespeare* than of any other writer; others please us by particular speeches, but he always makes us anxious for the event, and has perhaps excelled all but *Homer* in securing the first purpose of a writer, by exciting restless and unquenchable curiosity, and compelling him that reads his work to read it through.

The shows and bustle with which his plays abound have the same original. As knowledge advances, pleasure passes from the eye to the ear, but returns, as it declines, from the ear to the eye. Those to whom our authour's labours were exhibited had more

[19] The tale of *Gamelyn,* no longer regarded as Chaucer's work, was the ancestor of Thomas Lodge's *Rosalynde* (1590), which in turn supplied Shakespeare with a plot.

[20] Colley Cibber.

[21] 1579, 1595, augmented 1603.

skill in pomps or processions than in poetical language, and
perhaps wanted some visible and discriminated events, as com-
ments on the dialogue. He knew how he should most please;
and whether his practice is more agreeable to nature, or whether
his example has prejudiced the nation, we still find that on our
stage something must be done as well as said, and inactive decla-
mation is very coldly heard, however musical or elegant, passionate
or sublime.

Voltaire expresses his wonder,[22] that our authour's extrava-
gancies are endured by a nation, which has seen the tragedy of
Cato. Let him be answered, that *Addison* speaks the language of
poets, and *Shakespeare,* of men. We find in *Cato* innumerable
beauties which enamour us of its authour, but we see nothing
that acquaints us with human sentiments or human actions; we
place it with the fairest and the noblest progeny which judgment
propagates by conjunction with learning, but *Othello* is the
vigorous and vivacious offspring of observation impregnated by
genius. *Cato* affords a splendid exhibition of artificial and fictitious
manners, and delivers just and noble sentiments, in diction easy,
elevated and harmonious, but its hopes and fears communicate
no vibration to the heart; the composition refers us only to the
writer; we pronounce the name of *Cato,* but we think on *Addison.*

The work of a correct and regular writer is a garden accurately
formed and diligently planted, varied with shades, and scented
with flowers; the composition of *Shakespeare* is a forest, in which
oaks extend their branches, and pines tower in the air, interspersed
sometimes with weeds and brambles, and sometimes giving shelter
to myrtles and to roses; filling the eye with awful pomp, and
gratifying the mind with endless diversity. Other poets display
cabinets of precious rarities, minutely finished, wrought into shape,
and polished unto brightness. *Shakespeare* opens a mine which
contains gold and diamonds in unexhaustible plenty, though
clouded by incrustations, debased by impurities, and mingled
with a mass of meaner minerals.

It has been much disputed, whether *Shakespeare* owed his

[22] *Œuvres,* 1785, XLVII, 303.

excellence to his own native force, or whether he had the common helps of scholastick education, the precepts of critical science, and the examples of ancient authours.

There has always prevailed a tradition, that *Shakespeare* wanted learning, that he had no regular education, nor much skill in the dead languages. *Johnson*,[23] his friend, affirms, that *he had small Latin, and no Greek;* who, besides that he had no imaginable temptation to falsehood, wrote at a time when the character and acquisitions of *Shakespeare* were known to multitudes. His evidence ought therefore to decide the controversy, unless some testimony of equal force could be opposed.

Some have imagined, that they have discovered deep learning in many imitations of old writers; but the examples which I have known urged, were drawn from books translated in his time; or were such easy coincidencies of thought, as will happen to all who consider the same subjects; or such remarks on life or axioms of morality as float in conversation, and are transmitted through the world in proverbial sentences.

I have found it remarked, that, in this important sentence, *Go before, I'll follow,* we read a translation of, *I prae, sequar.*[24] I have been told, that when *Caliban,* after a pleasing dream, says, *I cry'd to sleep again,* the authour imitates *Anacreon,* who had, like every other man, the same wish on the same occasion.

There are a few passages which may pass for imitations, but so few, that the exception only confirms the rule; he obtained them from accidental quotations, or by oral communication, and as he used what he had, would have used more if he had obtained it.

The *Comedy of Errors* is confessedly taken from the *Menæchmi* of *Plautus;* from the only play of *Plautus* which was then in *English.* What can be more probable, than that he who copied that, would have copied more; but that those which were not translated were inaccessible?

[23] Ben Jonson, in his verses to the memory of Shakespeare, prefixed to the first folio and later editions. He said "less Greek."

[24] Zachary Grey, *Critical, historical, and explanatory Notes on Shakespeare,* 1754, II, 53. (*Richard III,* I. i. 143; Terence, *Andria,* 1. 171.)

Whether he knew the modern languages is uncertain. That his plays have some *French* scenes proves but little; he might easily procure them to be written, and probably, even though he had known the language in the common degree, he could not have written it without assistance. In the story of *Romeo* and *Juliet* he is observed to have followed the *English* translation, where it deviates from the *Italian;* but this on the other part proves nothing against his knowledge of the original. He was to copy, not what he knew himself, but what was known to his audience.

It is most likely that he had learned *Latin* sufficiently to make him acquainted with construction, but that he never advanced to an easy perusal of the *Roman* authours. Concerning his skill in modern languages, I can find no sufficient ground of determination; but as no imitations of *French* or *Italian* authours have been discovered, though the *Italian* poetry was then high in esteem, I am inclined to believe, that he read little more than *English,* and chose for his fables only such tales as he found translated.

That much knowledge is scattered over his works is very justly observed by *Pope,* but it is often such knowledge as books did not supply. He that will understand *Shakespeare,* must not be content to study him in the closet, he must look for his meaning sometimes among the sports of the field, and sometimes among the manufactures of the shop.

There is however proof enough that he was a very diligent reader, nor was our language then so indigent of books, but that he might very liberally indulge his curiosity without excursion into foreign literature. Many of the *Roman* authours were translated, and some of the *Greek*;[25] the reformation had filled the kingdom with theological learning; most of the topicks of human disquisition had found *English* writers; and poetry had been cultivated, not only with diligence, but success. This was a stock of knowledge sufficient for a mind so capable of appropriating and improving it.

But the greater part of his excellence was the product of his

[25] See the list of "Ancient Translations from Classic Authors" drawn up by Steevens (and Malone), printed in the Variorum ed., 1821, I, 371–391.

own genius. He found the *English* stage in a state of the utmost rudeness; no essays either in tragedy or comedy had appeared, from which it could be discovered to what degree of delight either one or other might be carried. Neither character nor dialogue were yet understood. *Shakespeare* may be truly said to have introduced them both amongst us, and in some of his happier scenes to have carried them both to the utmost height.

By what gradations of improvement he proceeded, is not easily known; for the chronology of his works is yet unsettled. *Rowe* is of opinion, that *perhaps we are not to look for his beginning, like those of other writers, in his least perfect works; art had so little, and nature so large a share in what he did, that for ought I know,* says he, *the performances of his youth, as they were the most vigorous, were the best.*[26] But the power of nature is only the power of using to any certain purpose the materials which diligence procures, or opportunity supplies. Nature gives no man knowledge, and when images are collected by study and experience, can only assist in combining or applying them. *Shakespeare,* however favoured by nature, could impart only what he had learned; and as he must increase his ideas, like other mortals, by gradual acquisition, he, like them, grew wiser as he grew older, could display life better, as he knew it more, and instruct with more efficacy, as he was himself more amply instructed.

There is a vigilance of observation and accuracy of distinction which books and precepts cannot confer; from this almost all original and native excellence proceeds. *Shakespeare* must have looked upon mankind with perspicacity, in the highest degree curious and attentive. Other writers borrow their characters from preceding writers, and diversify them only by the accidental appendages of present manners; the dress is a little varied, but the body is the same. Our authour had both matter and form to provide; for except the characters of *Chaucer,* to whom I think he is not much indebted, there were no writers in *English,* and perhaps not many in other modern languages, which shewed life in its native colours.

The contest about the original benevolence or malignity of man

[26] Rowe's "Life of Shakespeare," prefixed to his edition, 1709, ¶4.

had not yet commenced. Speculation had not yet attempted to analyse the mind, to trace the passions to their sources, to unfold the seminal principles of vice and virtue, or sound the depths of the heart for the motives of action. All those enquiries, which from that time that human nature became the fashionable study, have been made sometimes with nice discernment, but often with idle subtilty, were yet unattempted. The tales, with which the infancy of learning was satisfied, exhibited only the superficial appearances of action, related the events but omitted the causes, and were formed for such as delighted in wonders rather than in truth. Mankind was not then to be studied in the closet; he that would know the world, was under the necessity of gleaning his own remarks, by mingling as he could in its business and amusements.

Boyle congratulated himself upon his high birth, because it favoured his curiosity, by facilitating his access.[27] *Shakespeare* had no such advantage; he came to *London* a needy adventurer, and lived for a time by very mean employments. Many works of genius and learning have been performed in states of life, that appear very little favourable to thought or to enquiry; so many, that he who considers them is inclined to think that he sees enterprise and perseverance predominating over all external agency, and bidding help and hindrance vanish before them. The genius of *Shakespeare* was not to be depressed by the weight of poverty, nor limited by the narrow conversation to which men in want are inevitably condemned; the incumbrances of his fortune were shaken from his mind, *as dewdrops from a lion's mane.*[28]

Though he had so many difficulties to encounter, and so little assistance to surmount them, he has been able to obtain an exact knowledge of many modes of life, and many casts of native dispositions; to vary them with great multiplicity; to mark them by nice distinctions; and to shew them in full view by proper combinations. In this part of his performances he had none to imitate,

[27] D. Nichol Smith refers to Birch, *Life of Robert Boyle,* 1744, pp. 18–19.
   [28] *Troilus and Cressida,* III. iii. 225.

but has himself been imitated by all succeeding writers; and it may be doubted, whether from all his successors more maxims of theoretical knowledge, or more rules of practical prudence, can be collected, than he alone has given to his country.

Nor was his attention confined to the actions of men; he was an exact surveyor of the inanimate world; his descriptions have always some peculiarities, gathered by contemplating things as they really exist. It may be observed, that the oldest poets of many nations preserve their reputation, and that the following genera- tions of wit, after a short celebrity, sink into oblivion. The first, whoever they be, must take their sentiments and descriptions im- mediately from knowledge; the resemblance is therefore just, their descriptions are verified by every eye, and their sentiments acknowl- edged by every breast. Those whom their fame invites to the same studies, copy partly them, and partly nature, till the books of one age gain such authority, as to stand in the place of nature to another, and imitation, always deviating a little, becomes at last capricious and casual. *Shakespeare,* whether life or nature be his subject, shews plainly, that he has seen with his own eyes; he gives the image which he receives, not weakened or distorted by the intervention of any other mind; the ignorant feel his repre- sentations to be just, and the learned see that they are compleat.

Perhaps it would not be easy to find any authour, except *Homer,* who invented so much as *Shakespeare,* who so much advanced the studies which he cultivated, or effused so much novelty upon his age or country. The form, the characters, the language, and the shows of the *English* drama are his. *He seems,* says *Dennis, to have been the very original of our* English *tragical harmony, that is, the harmony of blank verse, diversified often by dissyllable and trissyllable terminations. For the diversity distinguishes it from heroick harmony, and by bringing it nearer to common use makes it more proper to gain attention, and more fit for action and dialogue. Such verse we make when we are writing prose; we make such verse in common conversation.*[29]

I know not whether this praise is rigorously just. The dissyllable termination, which the critick rightly appropriates to the drama,

[29] *An Essay on the Genius and Writings of Shakespear,* 1712, ¶2.

is to be found, though, I think, not in *Gorboduc* which is con-
fessedly before our author; yet in *Hieronnymo*,[30] of which the
date is not certain, but which there is reason to believe at least
as old as his earliest plays. This however is certain, that he is the
first who taught either tragedy or comedy to please, there being no
theatrical piece of any older writer, of which the name is known,
except to antiquaries and collectors of books, which are sought
because they are scarce, and would not have been scarce, had they
been much esteemed.

To him we must ascribe the praise, unless *Spenser* may divide
it with him, of having first discovered to how much smoothness
and harmony the *English* language could be softened. He has
speeches, perhaps sometimes scenes, which have all the delicacy
of *Rowe*, without his effeminacy. He endeavours indeed com-
monly to strike by the force and vigour of his dialogue, but he
never executes his purpose better, than when he tries to sooth
by softness.

Yet it must be at last confessed, that as we owe every thing
to him, he owes something to us; that, if much of his praise is
paid by perception and judgement, much is likewise given by
custom and veneration. We fix our eyes upon his graces, and
turn them from his deformities, and endure in him what we
should in another loath or despise. If we endured without prais-
ing, respect for the father of our drama might excuse us; but I
have seen, in the book of some modern critick,[31] a collection of
anomalies which shew that he has corrupted language by every
mode of depravation, but which his admirer has accumulated as
a monument of honour.

He has scenes of undoubted and perpetual excellence, but
perhaps not one play, which, if it were now exhibited as the
work of a contemporary writer, would be heard to the conclusion.
I am indeed far from thinking, that his works were wrought to
his own ideas of perfection; when they were such as would

[30] Printed 1605, anonymous, and though a forepiece to Kyd's *Spanish
Tragedy*, probably later. But possibly the reference is to *The Spanish
Tragedy* itself.
    [31] John Upton, *Critical Observations on Shakespeare*, 1746, 1748.

satisfy the audience, they satisfied the writer. It is seldom that authours, though more studious of fame than *Shakespeare,* rise much above the standard of their own age; to add a little of what is best will always be sufficient for present praise, and those who find themselves exalted into fame, are willing to credit their encomiasts, and to spare the labour of contending with themselves.

It does not appear, that *Shakespeare* thought his works worthy of posterity, that he levied any ideal tribute upon future times, or had any further prospect, than of present popularity and present profit. When his plays had been acted, his hope was at an end; he solicited no addition of honour from the reader. He therefore made no scruple to repeat the same jests in many dialogues, or to entangle different plots by the same knot of perplexity, which may be at least forgiven him, by those who recollect, that of *Congreve*'s four comedies, two are concluded by a marriage in a mask, by a deception, which perhaps never happened, and which, whether likely or not, he did not invent.

So careless was this great poet of future fame, that, though he retired to ease and plenty, while he was yet little *declined into the vale of years,*[32] before he could be disgusted with fatigue, or disabled by infirmity, he made no collection of his works, nor desired to rescue those that had been already published from the depravations that obscured them, or secure to the rest a better destiny, by giving them to the world in their genuine state.

Of the plays which bear the name of *Shakespeare* in the late editions, the greater part were not published till about seven years after his death, and the few which appeared in his life are apparently thrust into the world without the care of the authour, and therefore probably without his knowledge.

Of all the publishers, clandestine or professed, their negligence and unskilfulness has by the late revisers been sufficiently shown. The faults of all are indeed numerous and gross, and have not only corrupted many passages perhaps beyond recovery, but have brought others into suspicion, which are only obscured by obsolete phraseology, or by the writer's unskilfulness and affectation. To

[32] *Othello,* III. iii. 265.

alter is more easy than to explain, and temerity is a more common quality than diligence. Those who saw that they must employ conjecture to a certain degree, were willing to indulge it a little further. Had the authour published his own works, we should have sat quietly down to disentangle his intricacies, and clear his obscurities; but now we tear what we cannot loose, and eject what we happen not to understand.

The faults are more than could have happened without the concurrence of many causes. The stile of *Shakespeare* was in itself ungrammatical, perplexed and obscure; his works were transcribed for the players by those who may be supposed to have seldom understood them; they were transmitted by copiers equally unskilful, who still multiplied errours; they were perhaps sometimes mutilated by the actors, for the sake of shortening the speeches; and were at last printed without correction of the press.

In this state they remained, not as Dr. *Warburton* supposes, because they were unregarded,[33] but because the editor's art was not yet applied to modern languages, and our ancestors were accustomed to so much negligence of *English* printers, that they could very patiently endure it. At last an edition was undertaken by *Rowe*; not because a poet was to be published by a poet, for *Rowe* seems to have thought very little on correction or explanation, but that our authour's works might appear like those of his fraternity, with the appendages of a life and recommendatory preface. *Rowe* has been clamorously blamed for not performing what he did not undertake, and it is time that justice be done him, by confessing, that though he seems to have had no thought of corruption beyond the printer's errours, yet he has made many emendations, if they were not made before, which his successors have received without acknowledgment, and which, if they had produced them, would have filled pages and pages with censures of the stupidity by which the faults were committed, with displays of the absurdities which they involved, with ostentatious expositions of the new reading, and self congratulations on the happiness of discovering it.

Of *Rowe*, as of all the editors, I have preserved the preface,

[33] Warburton's Preface, 1747, ¶2.

and have likewise retained the authour's life, though not written with much elegance or spirit; it relates however what is now to be known, and therefore deserves to pass through all succeeding publications.

The nation had been for many years content enough with Mr. *Rowe*'s performance, when Mr. *Pope* made them acquainted with the true state of *Shakespear[e]*'s text, shewed that it was extremely corrupt, and gave reason to hope that there were means of reforming it. He collated the old copies, which none had thought to examine before, and restored many lines to their integrity; but, by a very compendious criticism, he rejected whatever he disliked, and thought more of amputation than of cure.

I know not why he is commended by Dr. *Warburton* for distinguishing the genuine from the spurious plays. In this choice he exerted no judgement of his own; the plays which he received, were given by *Hemings* and *Condel,* the first editors; and those which he rejected, though, according to the licentiousness of the press in those times, they were printed during *Shakespear[e]*'s life, with his name, had been omitted by his friends, and were never added to his works before the edition of 1664, from which they were copied by the later printers.

This was a work which *Pope* seems to have thought unworthy of his abilities, being not able to suppress his contempt of *the dull duty of an editor*.[34] He understood but half his undertaking. The duty of a collator is indeed dull, yet, like other tedious tasks, is very necessary; but an emendatory critick would ill discharge his duty, without qualities very different from dulness. In perusing a corrupted piece, he must have before him all possibilities of meaning, with all possibilities of expression. Such must be his comprehension of thought, and such his copiousness of language. Out of many readings possible, he must be able to select that which best suits with the state, opinions, and modes of language prevailing in every age, and with his authour's particular cast of thought, and turn of expression. Such must be his knowledge, and such his taste. Conjectural criticism demands more than humanity possesses, and he that exercises it with most praise has

[34] Pope's Preface, 1725, penultimate paragraph.

very frequent need of indulgence. Let us now be told no more of the dull duty of an editor.

Confidence is the common consequence of success. They whose excellence of any kind has been loudly celebrated, are ready to conclude, that their powers are universal. *Pope*'s edition fell below his own expectations, and he was so much offended, when he was found to have left any thing for others to do, that he past the latter part of his life in a state of hostility with verbal criticism.

I have retained all his notes, that no fragment of so great a writer may be lost; his preface, valuable alike for elegance of composition and justness of remark, and containing a general criticism on his authour, so extensive that little can be added, and so exact, that little can be disputed, every editor has an interest to suppress, but that every reader would demand its insertion.

Pope was succeeded by *Theobald,* a man of narrow comprehension and small acquisitions, with no native and intrinsick splendour of genius, with little of the artificial light of learning, but zealous for minute accuracy, and not negligent in pursuing it. He collated the ancient copies, and rectified many errors. A man so anxiously scrupulous might have been expected to do more, but what little he did was commonly right.

In his report of copies and editions he is not to be trusted, without examination. He speaks sometimes indefinitely of copies, when he has only one. In his enumeration of editions, he mentions the two first folios as of high, and the third folio as of middle authority; but the truth is, that the first is equivalent to all others, and that the rest only deviate from it by the printer's negligence. Whoever has any of the folios has all, excepting those diversities which mere reiteration of editions will produce. I collated them all at the beginning, but afterwards used only the first.

Of his notes I have generally retained those which he retained himself in his second edition, except when they were confuted by subsequent annotators, or were too minute to merit preservation. I have sometimes adopted his restoration of a comma, without inserting the panegyrick in which he celebrated himself for his achievement. The exuberant excrescence of [his] diction I have often lopped, his triumphant exultations over *Pope* and *Rowe* I have sometimes suppressed, and his contemptible ostentation I have frequently concealed; but I have in some places shewn him, as he would have shewn himself, for the reader's diversion, that the inflated emptiness of some notes may justify or excuse the contraction of the rest.

Theobald, thus weak and ignorant, thus mean and faithless, thus petulant and ostentatious, by the good luck of having *Pope* for his enemy, has escaped, and escaped alone, with reputation, from this undertaking. So willingly does the world support those who solicite favour, against those who command reverence; and so easily is he praised, whom no man can envy.

Our authour fell then into the hands of Sir *Thomas Hanmer,* the *Oxford* editor, a man, in my opinion, eminently qualified by nature for such studies. He had, what is the first requisite to emendatory criticism, that intuition by which the poet's intention is immediately discovered, and that dexterity of intellect which dispatches its work by the easiest means. He had undoubtedly read much; his acquaintance with customs, opinions, and traditions, seems to have been large; and he is often learned without shew. He seldom passes what he does not understand, without an attempt to find or to make a meaning, and sometimes hastily makes what a little more attention would have found. He is solicitous to reduce to grammar, what he could not be sure that his authour intended to be grammatical. *Shakespeare* regarded more the series of ideas, than of words; and his language, not being designed for the reader's desk, was all that he desired it to be, if it conveyed his meaning to the audience.

Hanmer's care of the metre has been too violently censured. He found the measures reformed in so many passages, by the silent labours of some editors, with the silent acquiescence of the rest, that he thought himself allowed to extend a little further the license, which had already been carried so far without reprehension; and of his corrections in general, it must be confessed, that they are often just, and made commonly with the least possible violation of the text.

But, by inserting his emendations, whether invented or borrowed, into the page, without any notice of varying copies, he has appropriated the labour of his predecessors, and made his own edition of little authority. His confidence indeed, both in himself and others, was too great; he supposes all to be right that was done by *Pope* and *Theobald*; he seems not to suspect a critick of fallibility, and it was but reasonable that he should claim what he so liberally granted.

As he never writes without careful enquiry and diligent consideration, I have received all his notes, and believe that every reader will wish for more.

Of the last editor[35] it is more difficult to speak. Respect is due to high place, tenderness to living reputation, and veneration to genius and learning; but he cannot be justly offended at that liberty of which he has himself so frequently given an example, nor very solicitous what is thought of notes, which he ought never to have considered as part of his serious employments, and which, I suppose, since the ardour of composition is remitted, he no longer numbers among his happy effusions.

The original and predominant errour of his commentary, is acquiescence in his first thoughts; that precipitation which is produced by consciousness of quick discernment; and that confidence which presumes to do, by surveying the surface, what labour only can perform, by penetrating the bottom. His notes exhibit sometimes perverse interpretations, and sometimes improbable conjectures; he at one time gives the authour more profundity of meaning than the sentence admits, and at another discovers absurdities, where the sense is plain to every other reader. But his emendations are likewise often happy and just; and his interpretation of obscure passages learned and sagacious.

Of his notes, I have commonly rejected those, against which the general voice of the publick has exclaimed, or which their own incongruity immediately condemns, and which, I suppose, the authour himself would desire to be forgotten. Of the rest, to part I have given the highest approbation, by inserting the offered reading in the text; part I have left to the judgment of the reader, as doubtful, though specious; and part I have censured without

---

[35] Warburton.

reserve, but I am sure without bitterness of malice, and, I hope, without wantonness of insult.

It is no pleasure to me, in revising my volumes, to observe how much paper is wasted in confutation. Whoever considers the revolutions of learning, and the various questions of greater or less importance, upon which wit and reason have exercised their powers, must lament the unsuccessfulness of enquiry, and the slow advances of truth, when he reflects, that great part of the labour of every writer is only the destruction of those that went before him. The first care of the builder of a new system, is to demolish the fabricks which are standing. The chief desire of him that comments an authour, is to shew how much other commentators have corrupted and obscured him. The opinions prevalent in one age, as truths above the reach of controversy, are confuted and rejected in another, and rise again to reception in remoter times. Thus the human mind is kept in motion without progress. Thus sometimes truth and errour, and sometimes contrarieties of errour, take each other's place by reciprocal invasion. The tide of seeming knowledge which is poured over one generation, retires and leaves another naked and barren; the sudden meteors of intelligence which for a while appear to shoot their beams into the regions of obscurity, on a sudden withdraw their lustre, and leave mortals again to grope their way.

These elevations and depressions of renown, and the contradictions to which all improvers of knowledge must for ever be exposed, since they are not escaped by the highest and brightest of mankind, may surely be endured with patience by criticks and annotators, who can rank themselves but as the satellites of their authours. How canst thou beg for life, says *Achilles* to his captive, when thou knowest that thou art now to suffer only what must another day be suffered by *Achilles?* [36]

Dr. *Warburton* had a name sufficient to confer celebrity on those who could exalt themselves into antagonists, and his notes have raised a clamour too loud to be distinct. His chief assailants are the authours of *the Canons of criticism*[37] and of the *Review*

[36] *Iliad.* XXI. 99 ff.
[37] By Thomas Edwards, 1748.

of Shakespeare's *text*,[38] of whom one ridicules his errours with
airy petulance, suitable enough to the levity of the controversy;
the other attacks them with gloomy malignity, as if he were
dragging to justice an assassin or incendiary. The one stings like
a fly, sucks a little blood, takes a gay flutter, and returns for
more; the other bites like a viper, and would be glad to leave
inflammations and gangrene behind him. When I think on one,
with his confederates, I remember the danger of *Coriolanus,* who
was afraid that *girls with spits, and boys with stones, should slay
him in puny battle;* when the other crosses my imagination, I
remember the prodigy in *Macbeth,*

> *An eagle tow'ring in his pride of place,*
> *Was by a mousing owl hawk'd at and kill'd.*

Let me however do them justice. One is a wit, and one a scholar.
They have both shewn acuteness sufficient in the discovery of
faults, and have both advanced some probable interpretations of
obscure passages; but when they aspire to conjecture and emenda-
tion, it appears how falsely we all estimate our own abilities, and
the little which they have been able to perform might have taught
them more candour to the endeavours of others.

Before Dr. *Warburton*'s edition, *Critical observations on* Shake-
speare had been published by Mr. *Upton,*[39] a man skilled in
languages, and acquainted with books, but who seems to have
had no great vigour of genius or nicety of taste. Many of his
explanations are curious and useful, but he likewise, though he
professed to oppose the licentious confidence of editors, and adhere
to the old copies, is unable to restrain the rage of emendation,
though his ardour is ill seconded by his skill. Every cold empirick,
when his heart is expanded by a successful experiment, swells
into a theorist, and the laborious collator at some unlucky moment
frolicks in conjecture.

Critical, historical and explanatory notes have been likewise

[38] By Benjamin Heath, 1765. The proper title is *Revisal,* not *Review.*
[39] 1746.

published upon *Shakespeare* by Dr. *Grey*,[40] whose diligent perusal of the old *English* writers has enabled him to make some useful observations. What he undertook he has[41] well enough performed, but as he neither attempts judicial nor emendatory criticism, he employs rather his memory than his sagacity. It were to be wished that all would endeavour to imitate his modesty who have not been able to surpass his knowledge.

I can say with great sincerity of all my predecessors, what I hope will hereafter be said of me, that not one has left *Shakespeare* without improvement, nor is there one to whom I have not been indebted for assistance and information. Whatever I have taken from them it was my intention to refer to its original authour, and it is certain, that what I have not given to another, I believed when I wrote it to be my own. In some perhaps I have been anticipated; but if I am ever found to encroach upon the remarks of any other commentator, I am willing that the honour, be it more or less, should be transferred to the first claimant, for his right, and his alone, stands above dispute; the second can prove his pretensions only to himself, nor can himself always distinguish invention, with sufficient certainty, from recollection.

They have all been treated by me with candour, which they have not been careful of observing to one another. It is not easy to discover from what cause the acrimony of a scholiast can naturally proceed. The subjects to be discussed by him are of very small importance; they involve neither property nor liberty; nor favour the interest of sect or party. The various readings of copies, and different interpretations of a passage, seem to be questions that might exercise the wit, without engaging the passions. But, whether it be, that *small things make mean men proud*,[42] and vanity catches small occasions; or that all contrariety of opinion, even in those that can defend it no longer, makes proud men angry; there is often found in commentaries a spontaneous strain of invective and contempt, more eager and venomous than is

[40] Zachary Grey, 2 vols., 1754.
[41] 1768: undertook was.
[42] 2 *Henry VI*, IV. i. 106.

vented by the most furious controvertist in politicks against those
whom he is hired to defame.

Perhaps the lightness of the matter may conduce to the vehe-
mence of the agency; when the truth to be investigated is so near
to inexistence, as to escape attention, its bulk is to be enlarged by
rage and exclamation: That to which all would be indifferent in
its original state, may attract notice when the fate of a name is
appended to it. A commentator has indeed great temptations to
supply by turbulence what he wants of dignity, to beat his little
gold to a spacious surface, to work that to foam which no art or
diligence can exalt to spirit.

The notes which I have borrowed or written are either illus-
trative, by which difficulties are explained; or judicial, by which
faults and beauties are remarked; or emendatory, by which dep-
ravations are corrected.

The explanations transcribed from others, if I do not subjoin
any other interpretation, I suppose commonly to be right, at least
I intend by acquiescence to confess, that I have nothing better
to propose.

After the labours of all the editors, I found many passages which
appeared to me likely to obstruct the greater number of readers,
and thought it my duty to facilitate their passage. It is impossible
for an expositor not to write too little for some, and too much for
others. He can only judge what is necessary by his own experience;
and how long soever he may deliberate, will at last explain many
lines which the learned will think impossible to be mistaken, and
omit many for which the ignorant will want his help. These are
censures merely relative, and must be quietly endured. I have
endeavoured to be neither superfluously copious, nor scrupulously
reserved, and hope that I have made my authour's meaning acces-
sible to many who before were frighted from perusing him, and
contributed something to the publick, by diffusing innocent and
rational pleasure.

The compleat explanation of an authour not systematick and
consequential, but desultory and vagrant, abounding in casual
allusions and light hints, is not to be expected from any single
scholiast. All personal reflections, when names are suppressed,

must be in a few years irrecoverably obliterated; and customs, too minute to attract the notice of law, such as modes of dress, formalities of conversation, rules of visits, disposition of furniture, and practices of ceremony, which naturally find places in familiar dialogue, are so fugitive and unsubstantial, that they are not easily retained or recovered. What can be known, will be collected by chance, from the recesses of obscure and obsolete papers, perused commonly with some other view. Of this knowledge every man has some, and none has much; but when an authour has engaged the publick attention, those who can add any thing to his illustration, communicate their discoveries, and time produces what had eluded diligence.

To time I have been obliged to resign many passages, which, though I did not understand them, will perhaps hereafter be explained, having, I hope, illustrated some, which others have neglected or mistaken, sometimes by short remarks, or marginal directions, such as every editor has added at his will, and often by comments more laborious than the matter will seem to deserve; but that which is most difficult is not always most important, and to an editor nothing is a trifle by which his authour is obscured.

The poetical beauties or defects I have not been very diligent to observe. Some plays have more, and some fewer judicial observations, not in proportion to their difference of merit, but because I gave this part of my design to chance and to caprice. The reader, I believe, is seldom pleased to find his opinion anticipated; it is natural to delight more in what we find or make, than in what we receive. Judgement, like other faculties, is improved by practice, and its advancement is hindered by submission to dictatorial decisions, as the memory grows torpid by the use of a table book. Some initiation is however necessary; of all skill, part is infused by precept, and part is obtained by habit; I have therefore shewn so much as may enable the candidate of criticism to discover the rest.

To the end of most plays, I have added short strictures, containing a general censure of faults, or praise of excellence; in which I know not how much I have concurred with the current opinion; but I have not, by any affectation of singularity, deviated from it. Nothing is minutely and particularly examined, and therefore it is to be supposed, that in the plays which are condemned there is much to be praised, and in these which are praised much to be condemned.

The part of criticism in which the whole succession of editors has laboured with the greatest diligence, which has occasioned the most arrogant ostentation, and excited the keenest acrimony, is the emendation of corrupted passages, to which the publick attention having been first drawn by the violence of contention between *Pope* and *Theobald,* has been continued by the persecution, which, with a kind of conspiracy, has been since raised against all the publishers of *Shakespeare.*

That many passages have passed in a state of depravation through all the editions is indubitably certain; of these the restoration is only to be attempted by collation of copies or sagacity of conjecture. The collator's province is safe and easy, the conjecturer's perilous and difficult. Yet as the greater part of the plays are extant only in one copy, the peril must not be avoided, nor the difficulty refused.

Of the readings which this emulation of amendment has hitherto produced, some from the labours of every publisher I have advanced into the text; those are to be considered as in my opinion sufficiently supported; some I have rejected without mention, as evidently erroneous; some I have left in the notes without censure or approbation, as resting in equipoise between objection and defence; and some, which seemed specious but not right, I have inserted with a subsequent animadversion.

Having classed the observations of others, I was at last to try what I could substitute for their mistakes, and how I could supply their omissions. I collated such copies as I could procure, and wished for more, but have not found the collectors of these rarities very communicative. Of the editions which chance or kindness put into my hands I have given an enumeration, that I may not be blamed for neglecting what I had not the power to do.

By examining the old copies, I soon found that the later publishers, with all their boasts of diligence, suffered many passages to stand unauthorised, and contented themselves with *Rowe's* regulation of the text, even where they knew it to be arbitrary, and with a little consideration might have found it to be wrong. Some of these alterations are only the ejection of a word for one that appeared to him more elegant or more intelligible. These corruptions I have often silently rectified; for the history of our language, and the true force of our words, can only be preserved, by keeping the text of authours free from adulteration. Others, and those very frequent, smoothed the cadence, or regulated the measure; on these I have not exercised the same rigour; if only a word was transposed, or a particle inserted or omitted, I have sometimes suffered the line to stand; for the inconstancy of the copies is such, as that some liberties may be easily permitted. But this practice I have not suffered to proceed far, having restored the primitive diction wherever it could for any reason be preferred.

The emendations, which comparison of copies supplied, I have inserted in the text; sometimes where the improvement was slight, without notice, and sometimes with an account of the reasons of the change.

Conjecture, though it be sometimes unavoidable, I have not wantonly nor licentiously indulged. It has been my settled principle, that the reading of the ancient books is probably true, and therefore is not to be disturbed for the sake of elegance, perspicuity, or mere improvement of the sense. For though much credit is not due to the fidelity, nor any to the judgement of the first publishers, yet they who had the copy before their eyes were more likely to read it right, than we who only read it by imagination. But it is evident that they have often made strange mistakes by ignorance or negligence, and that therefore something may be properly attempted by criticism, keeping the middle way between presumption and timidity.

Such criticism I have attempted to practise, and where any passage appeared inextricably perplexed, have endeavoured to discover how it may be recalled to sense, with least violence. But my first labour is, always to turn the old text on every side, and try if there be any interstice, through which light can find its way; nor would *Huetius*[43] himself condemn me, as refusing the

[43] Pierre Huet, *De Interpretatione libri duo*, 1661.

trouble of research, for the ambition of alteration. In this modest industry I have not been unsuccessful. I have rescued many lines from the violations of temerity, and secured many scenes from the inroads of correction. I have adopted the *Roman* sentiment, that it is more honourable to save a citizen, than to kill an enemy, and have been more careful to protect than to attack.

I have preserved the common distribution of the plays into acts, though I believe it to be in almost all the plays void of authority. Some of those which are divided in the later editions have no division in the first folio, and some that are divided in the folio have no division in the preceding copies. The settled mode of the theatre requires four intervals in the play, but few, if any, of our authour's compositions can be properly distributed in that manner. An act is so much of the drama as passes without intervention of time or change of place. A pause makes a new act. In every real, and therefore in every imitative action, the intervals may be more or fewer, the restriction of five acts being accidental and arbitrary. This *Shakespeare* knew, and this he practised; his plays were written, and at first printed in one unbroken continuity, and ought now to be exhibited with short pauses, interposed as often as the scene is changed, or any considerable time is required to pass. This method would at once quell a thousand absurdities.

In restoring the authour's works to their integrity, I have considered the punctuation as wholly in my power; for what could be their care of colons and commas, who corrupted words and sentences. Whatever could be done by adjusting points is therefore silently performed, in some plays with much diligence, in others with less; it is hard to keep a busy eye steadily fixed upon evanescent atoms, or a discursive mind upon evanescent truth.

The same liberty has been taken with a few particles, or other words of slight effect. I have sometimes inserted or omitted them without notice. I have done that sometimes, which the other editors have done always, and which indeed the state of the text may sufficiently justify.

The greater part of readers, instead of blaming us for passing trifles, will wonder that on mere trifles so much labour is expended, with such importance of debate, and such solemnity of diction. To these I answer with confidence, that they are judging of an art which they do not understand; yet cannot much reproach them with their ignorance, nor promise that they would become in general, by learning criticism, more useful, happier or wiser.

As I practised conjecture more, I learned to trust it less; and after I had printed a few plays, resolved to insert none of my own readings in the text. Upon this caution I now congratulate myself, for every day encreases my doubt of my emendations.

Since I have confined my imagination to the margin, it must not be considered as very reprehensible, if I have suffered it to play some freaks in its own dominion. There is no danger in conjecture, if it be proposed as conjecture; and while the text remains un-injured, those changes may be safely offered, which are not con-sidered even by him that offers them as necessary or safe.

If my readings are of little value, they have not been ostenta-tiously displayed or importunately obtruded. I could have written longer notes, for the art of writing notes is not of difficult attain-ment. The work is performed, first by railing at the stupidity, negligence, ignorance, and asinine tastelessness of the former editors, and shewing, from all that goes before and all that follows, the inelegance and absurdity of the old reading; then by pro-posing something, which to superficial readers would seem specious, but which the editor rejects with indignation; then by producing the true reading, with a long paraphrase, and con-cluding with loud acclamations on the discovery, and a sober wish for the advancement and prosperity of genuine criticism.

All this may be done, and perhaps done sometimes without im-propriety. But I have always suspected that the reading is right, which requires many words to prove it wrong; and the emenda-tion wrong, that cannot without so much labour appear to be right. The justness of a happy restoration strikes at once, and the moral precept may be well applied to criticism, *quod dubitas ne feceris*.[44]

To dread the shore which he sees spread with wrecks, is natural to the sailor. I had before my eye, so many critical adventures

[44] "When in doubt, refrain."

ended in miscarriage, that caution was forced upon me. I encountered in every page Wit struggling with its own sophistry, and Learning confused by the multiplicity of its views. I was forced to censure those whom I admired, and could not but reflect, while I was dispossessing their emendations, how soon the same fate might happen to my own, and how many of the readings which I have corrected may be by some other editor defended and established.

> Criticks, I saw, that other's names efface,
> And fix their own, with labour, in the place;
> Their own, like others, soon their place resign'd,
> Or disappear'd, and left the first behind.[45]
>
> POPE.

That a conjectural critick should often be mistaken, cannot be wonderful, either to others or himself, if it be considered, that in his art there is no system, no principal and axiomatical truth that regulates subordinate positions. His chance of errour is renewed at every attempt; an oblique view of the passage, a slight misapprehension of a phrase, a casual inattention to the parts connected, is sufficient to make him not only fail, but fail ridiculously; and when he succeeds best, he produces perhaps but one reading of many probable, and he that suggests another will always be able to dispute his claims.

It is an unhappy state, in which danger is hid under pleasure. The allurements of emendation are scarcely resistible. Conjecture has all the joy and all the pride of invention, and he that has once started a happy change, is too much delighted to consider what objections may rise against it.

Yet conjectural criticism has been of great use in the learned world; nor is it my intention to depreciate a study, that has exercised so many mighty minds, from the revival of learning to our own age, from the Bishop of *Aleria*[46] to English *Bentley*. The

---

[45] *Temple of Fame*, ll. 37–40 (inaccurately quoted).

[46] Joannes Andreas (1417–c. 1480), Pope Sixtus IV's librarian, and a great classical editor.

cricks on ancient authours have, in the exercise of their sagacity, many assistances, which the editor of *Shakespeare* is condemned to want. They are employed upon grammatical and settled languages, whose construction contributes so much to perspicuity, that *Homer* has fewer passages unintelligible than *Chaucer*. The words have not only a known regimen, but invariable quantities, which direct and confine the choice. There are commonly more manuscripts than one; and they do not often conspire in the same mistakes. Yet *Scaliger* could confess to *Salmasius* how little satisfaction his emendations gave him. *Illudunt nobis conjecturæ nostræ, quarum nos pudet, posteaquam in meliores codices incidimus.*[47] And *Lipsius* could complain, that cricks were making faults, by trying to remove them, *Ut olim vitiis, ita nunc remediis laboratur.*[48] And indeed, where mere conjecture is to be used, the emendations of *Scaliger* and *Lipsius,* notwithstanding their wonderful sagacity and erudition, are often vague and disputable, like mine or *Theobald*'s.

Perhaps I may not be more censured for doing wrong, than for doing little; for raising in the publick expectations, which at last I have not answered. The expectation of ignorance is indefinite, and that of knowledge is often tyrannical. It is hard to satisfy those who know not what to demand, or those who demand by design what they think impossible to be done. I have indeed disappointed no opinion more than my own; yet I have endeavoured to perform my task with no slight solicitude. Not a single passage in the whole work has appeared to me corrupt, which I have not attempted to restore; or obscure, which I have not endeavoured to illustrate. In many I have failed like others; and from many, after all my efforts, I have retreated, and confessed the repulse. I have not passed over, with affected superiority, what is equally difficult to the reader and to myself, but where I could not instruct him, have owned my ignorance. I might easily have accumulated a mass of seeming learning upon easy scenes;

[47] "Our conjectures make fools of us, putting us to shame, when later we hit upon better MSS."

[48] "As formerly we toiled over corruptions, so now we struggle with corrections."

but it ought not to be imputed to negligence, that, where nothing was necessary, nothing has been done, or that, where others have said enough, I have said no more.

Notes are often necessary, but they are necessary evils. Let him, that is yet unacquainted with the powers of *Shakespeare,* and who desires to feel the highest pleasure that the drama can give, read every play from the first scene to the last, with utter negligence of all his commentators. When his fancy is once on the wing, let it not stoop at correction or explanation. When his attention is strongly engaged, let it disdain alike to turn aside to the name of *Theobald* and [of] *Pope.* Let him read on through brightness and obscurity, through integrity and corruption; let him preserve his comprehension of the dialogue and his interest in the fable. And when the pleasures of novelty have ceased, let him attempt exactness; and read the commentators.

Particular passages are cleared by notes, but the general effect of the work is weakened. The mind is refrigerated by interruption; the thoughts are diverted from the principal subject; the reader is weary, he suspects not why; and at last throws away the book, which he has too diligently studied.

Parts are not to be examined till the whole has been surveyed; there is a kind of intellectual remoteness necessary for the comprehension of any great work in its full design and its true proportions; a close approach shews the smaller niceties, but the beauty of the whole is discerned no longer.

It is not very grateful to consider how little the succession of editors has added to this authour's power of pleasing. He was read, admired, studied, and imitated, while he was yet deformed with all the improprieties which ignorance and neglect could accumulate upon him; while the reading was yet not rectified, nor his allusions understood; yet then did *Dryden* pronounce "that *Shakespeare* was the man, who, of all modern and perhaps ancient poets, had the largest and most comprehensive soul. All the images of nature were still present to him, and he drew them not laboriously, but luckily: When he describes any thing, you more than see it, you feel it too. Those who accuse him to have wanted learning, give him the greater commendation: he was naturally learned: he needed not the spectacles of books to read nature; he looked inwards, and found her there. I cannot say he is every where alike; were he so, I should do him injury to compare him with the greatest of mankind. He is many times flat and insipid; his comick wit degenerating into clenches, his serious swelling into bombast. But he is always great, when some great occasion is presented to him: No man can say, he ever had a fit subject for his wit, and did not then raise himself as high above the rest of poets,

Quantum lenta solent inter viburna cupressi." [49]

It is to be lamented, that such a writer should want a commentary; that his language should become obsolete, or his sentiments obscure. But it is vain to carry wishes beyond the condition of human things; that which must happen to all, has happened to *Shakespeare,* by accident and time; and more than has been suffered by any other writer since the use of types, has been suffered by him through his own negligence of fame, or perhaps by that superiority of mind, which despised its own performances, when it compared them with its powers, and judged those works unworthy to be preserved, which the criticks of following ages were to contend for the fame of restoring and explaining.

Among these candidates of inferiour fame, I am now to stand the judgment of the publick; and wish that I could confidently produce my commentary as equal to the encouragement which I have had the honour of receiving. Every work of this kind is by its nature deficient, and I should feel little solicitude about the sentence, were it to be pronounced only by the skilful and the learned.

[49] Dryden, *An Essay of Dramatic Poesy,* 1668 (*Essays,* ed. W. P. Ker, 1926, I, 78–80). The Latin is Virgil, *Eclogue,* I. 25: "as among the bending osiers is the habit of cypresses."

Notes on the Plays

There is perhaps not one of *Shakespear*'s plays more darkened than this by the peculiarities of its Authour, and the unskilfulness of its Editors, by distortions of phrase, or negligence of transscription.

ACT I. SCENE i. (I . i. 7–9.)

> *Then no more remains:*
> *But that to your sufficiency, as your worth is able,*
> *And let them work.*

This is a passage which has exercised the sagacity of the Editors, and is now to employ mine.

Sir *Tho. Hanmer* having caught from Mr. *Theobald* a hint that a line was lost, endeavours to supply it thus.

> ——*Then no more remains,*
> *But that to your sufficiency* you join
> A will to serve us, *as your worth is able.*

308

He has by this bold conjecture undoubtedly obtained a meaning, but, perhaps not, even in his own opinion, the meaning of *Shakespear*.

That the passage is more or less corrupt, I believe every reader will agree with the Editors. I am not convinced that a line is lost, as Mr. *Theobald* conjectures, nor that the change of *but* to *put*, which Dr. *Warburton* has admitted after some other Editor, will amend the fault. There was probably some original obscurity in the expression, which gave occasion to mistake in repetition or transcription. I therefore suspect that the Authour wrote thus,

> *Then no more remains,*
> *But that to your* sufficiencies *your worth is* abled,
> *And let them work.*

Then nothing remains more than to tell you that your Virtue is now invested with power equal to your knowledge and wisdom. Let therefore your knowledge and your virtue now work together. It may easily be conceived how *sufficiencies* was, by an inarticulate speaker, or inattentive hearer, confounded with *sufficiency as,* and how *abled,* a word very unusual, was changed into *able.* For *abled,* however, an authority is not wanting. *Lear* uses it in the same sense, or nearly the same, with the Duke. As for *sufficiencies, D. Hamilton,* in his dying speech, prays that *Charles* II. *may exceed both the* virtues *and* sufficiencies *of his father.*

ACT I. SCENE ii. (I. i. 51.)

> *We have with a* leaven'd *and prepared choice.*

> *Leaven'd* has no sense in this place: we should read
> LEVEL'D *choice.* The allusion is to archery, when a man
> has fixed upon his object, after taking good aim.
>   —WARBURTON.

No emendation is necessary. *Leaven'd choice* is one of *Shakespear*'s harsh metaphors. His train of ideas seems to be this. *I have proceeded to you with choice* mature, concocted, fermented, *leaven'd.* When Bread is *leaven'd,* it is left to ferment: a *leaven'd* choice is therefore a choice not hasty, but considerate, not declared as soon as it fell into the imagination, but suffered to work long in the mind. Thus explained, it suits better with *prepared* than *levelled.*

ACT II. SCENE ix. (II. iii. 11–12.)

> *Who falling in the* flaws *of her own youth,*
> *Hath* blister'd *her report.*

Who doth not see that the integrity of the metaphor requires we should read FLAMES *of her own youth.*
—WARBURTON.

Who does not see that upon such principles there is no end of correction.

ACT III. SCENE i. (III. i. 13–15.)

> *Thou art not noble:*
> *For all th' accommodations, that thou bear'st,*
> *Are nurs'd by baseness.*

Dr. *Warburton* is undoubtedly mistaken in supposing that by *baseness* is meant *self-love* here assigned as the motive of all human actions. *Shakespear* meant only to observe, that a minute analysis of life at once destroys that splendour which dazzles the imagination. Whatever grandeur can display, or luxury enjoy, is procured by *baseness,* by offices of which the mind shrinks from the contemplation. All the delicacies of the table may be traced back to the shambles and the dunghill, all magnificence of building was hewn from the quarry, and all the pomp of ornaments, dug from among the damps and darkness of the mine.

ACT III. SCENE i. (III. i. 16–17.)

> The soft and tender fork
> Of a poor worm.

Worm is put for any creeping thing or *serpent*. *Shakespear* supposes falsely, but according to the vulgar notion, that a serpent wounds with his tongue, and that his tongue is *forked*. He confounds reality and fiction, a serpent's tongue is *soft* but not *forked* nor hurtful. If it could hurt, it could not be soft. In *Midsummer-Night's Dream* he has the same notion.

> —————With doubler *tongue*
> *Than thine, O serpent, never adder* stung.

ACT III. SCENE i. (III. i. 32–4.)

> Thou hast nor youth, nor age:
> But as it were an after dinner's sleep,
> Dreaming on both.

This is exquisitely imagined. When we are young we busy ourselves in forming schemes for succeeding time, and miss the gratifications that are before us; when we are old we amuse the languour of age with the recollection of youthful pleasures or performances; so that our life, of which no part is filled with the business of the present time, resembles our dreams after dinner, when the events of the morning are mingled with the designs of the evening.

ACT III. SCENE i. (III. i. 36–8.)

> When thou'rt old and rich,
> Thou hast neither heat, affection, limb, nor beauty
> To make thy riches pleasant.

But how does beauty make *riches pleasant*? We should
read BOUNTY, which compleats the sense, and is this; Thou
hast neither the pleasure of enjoying riches thy self, for
thou wantest vigour: nor of seeing it enjoyed by others,
for thou wantest *bounty*. Where the making the want of
bounty as inseparable from old age as the want of *health*,
is extremely satyrical tho' not altogether just.

—WARBURTON.

I am inclined to believe that neither man nor woman will have
much difficulty to tell how *beauty makes riches pleasant*. Surely
this emendation, though it is elegant and ingenious, is not such
as that an opportunity of inserting it should be purchased by de-
claring ignorance of what every one knows, by confessing insensi-
bility of what every one feels.

ACT III. SCENE ii. (III. i. 137–8.)

> *Is't not a kind of incest, to take life*
> *From thine own sister's shame?*

In *Isabella*'s declamation there is something harsh, and some-
thing forced and far-fetched. But her indignation cannot be
thought violent when we consider her not only as a virgin but as
a nun.

ACT IV. SCENE viii. (IV. iii. 4–5.)

> *First here's young Mr.* Rash, *&c.*

This enumeration of the inhabitants of the prison affords a
very striking view of the practices predominant in *Shakespear*'s
age. Besides those whose follies are common to all times, we have
four fighting men and a traveller. It is not unlikely that the origi-
nals of these pictures were then known.

ACT IV. SCENE xiii. (IV. V. I.)

> DUKE. *These letters at fit time deliver me.*

Peter never delivers the letters, but tells his story without any credentials. The poet forgot the plot which he had formed.

ACT V. SCENE vii. (V. i. 448.)

> *'Till he did look on me.*

The *Duke* has justly observed that *Isabel* is *importuned against all sense* to solicit for *Angelo*, yet here *against all sense* she solicits for him. Her argument is extraordinary.

> *A due sincerity govern'd his deeds,*
> *'Till he did look on me; since it is so,*
> *Let him not die.*

That *Angelo* had committed all the crimes charged against him, as far as he could commit them, is evident. The only *intent* which *his act did not overtake,* was the defilement of *Isabel.* Of this *Angelo* was only intentionally guilty.

Angelo's crimes were such, as must sufficiently justify punishment, whether its end be to secure the innocent from wrong, or to deter guilt by example; and I believe every reader feels some indignation when he finds him spared. From what extenuation of his crime can *Isabel,* who yet supposes her brother dead, form any plea in his favour. *Since he was good 'till he looked on me, let him not die.* I am afraid our Varlet Poet intended to inculcate, that women think ill of nothing that raises the credit of their beauty, and are ready, however virtuous, to pardon any act which they think incited by their own charms.

ACT V. SCENE viii. (V. i. 479 ff.)

It is somewhat strange, that *Isabel* is not made to express either gratitude, wonder or joy at the sight of her brother.

After the pardon of two murderers *Lucio* might be treated by the good *Duke* with less harshness; but perhaps the Poet intended to show, what is too often seen, *that men easily forgive wrongs which are not committed against themselves.*

The novel of *Cynthio Giraldi,* from which *Shakespear* is supposed to have borrowed this fable, may be read in *Shakespear illustrated,*[1] elegantly translated, with remarks which will assist the enquirer to discover how much absurdity *Shakespear* has admitted or avoided.

I cannot but suspect that some other had new modelled the novel of *Cynthio,* or written a story which in some particulars resembled it, and that *Cinthio* was not the authour whom *Shakespear* immediately followed. The Emperour in *Cinthio* is named *Maximine,* the Duke, in *Shakespear's* enumeration of the persons of the drama, is called *Vincentio.* This appears a very slight remark; but since the Duke has no name in the play, nor is ever mentioned but by his title, why should he be called *Vincentio* among the *Persons,* but because the name was copied from the story, and placed superfluously at the head of the list by the mere habit of transcription? It is therefore likely that there was then a story of *Vincentio* Duke of *Vienna,* different from that of *Maximine* Emperour of the *Romans.*

Of this play the light or comick part is very natural and pleasing, but the grave scenes, if a few passages be excepted, have more labour than elegance. The plot is rather intricate than artful. The time of the action is indefinite; some time, we know not how much, must have elapsed between the recess of the *Duke* and the imprisonment of *Claudio;* for he must have learned the story of *Mariana* in his disguise, or he delegated his power to a man already known to be corrupted. The unities of action and place are sufficiently preserved.

[1] By Charlotte Lennox, 1753–1754.

HENRY IV

None of *Shakespeare's* plays are more read than the first and second parts of *Henry* the fourth. Perhaps no authour has ever in two plays afforded so much delight. The great events are interesting, for the fate of kingdoms depends upon them; the slighter occurrences are diverting, and, except one or two, sufficiently probable; the incidents are multiplied with wonderful fertility of invention, and the characters diversified with the utmost nicety of discernment, and the profoundest skill in the nature of man.

The prince, who is the hero both of the comick and tragick part, is a young man of great abilities and violent passions, whose sentiments are right, though his actions are wrong; whose virtues are obscured by negligence, and whose understanding is dissipated by levity. In his idle hours he is rather loose than wicked, and when the occasion forces out his latent qualities, he is great without effort, and brave without tumult. The trifler is roused into a hero, and the hero again reposes in the trifler. This character is great, original, and just.

Piercy is a rugged soldier, cholerick, and quarrelsome, and has only the soldier's virtues, generosity and courage.

But *Falstaff* unimitated, unimitable *Falstaff*, how shall I describe thee? Thou compound of sense and vice; of sense which may be admired but not esteemed, of vice which may be despised, but hardly detested. *Falstaff* is a character loaded with faults, and with those faults which naturally produce contempt. He is a thief, and a glutton, a coward, and a boaster, always ready to cheat the weak, and prey upon the poor; to terrify the timorous and insult the defenceless. At once obsequious and malignant, he satirises in their absence those whom he lives by flattering. He is familiar with the prince only as an agent of vice, but of this familiarity he is so proud as not only to be supercilious and haughty with common men, but to think his interest of importance to the duke of *Lancaster*. Yet the man thus corrupt, thus despicable, makes himself necessary to the prince that despises him, by the most pleasing of all qualities, perpetual gaiety, by an unfailing power of exciting laughter, which is the more freely indulged, as his wit is not of the splendid or ambitious kind, but consists in easy escapes and sallies of levity, which make sport but raise no envy. It must be observed that he is stained with no enormous or sanguinary crimes, so that his licentiousness is not so offensive but that it may be borne for his mirth.

The moral to be drawn from this representation is, that no man is more dangerous than he that with a will to corrupt, hath the power to please; and that neither wit nor honesty ought to think themselves safe with such a companion when they see *Henry* seduced by *Falstaff*.

HENRY V

ACT II. SCENE iv. (II. iii. 27–8.)

Cold as any stone.

Such is the end of *Falstaff*, from whom *Shakespeare* had promised us in his epilogue to *Henry* IV. that we should receive more entertainment. It happened to *Shakespeare* as to other writers, to have his imagination crowded with a tumultuary confusion of images, which, while they were yet unsorted and unexamined, seemed sufficient to furnish a long train of incidents, and a new variety of merriment, but which, when he was to produce them to view, shrunk suddenly from him, or could not be accommodated to his general design. That he once designed to have brought *Falstaff* on the scene again, we know from himself; but whether he could contrive no train of adventures suitable to his character, or could match him with no companions likely to quicken his humour, or could open no new vein of pleasantry, and was afraid to continue the same strain lest it should not find the same reception, he has here for ever discarded him, and made haste to dispatch him, perhaps for the same reason for which *Addison* killed Sir *Roger,* that no other hand might attempt to exhibit him.

Let meaner authours learn from this example, that it is dangerous to sell the bear which is yet not hunted, to promise to the publick what they have not written.

KING LEAR

The Tragedy of *Lear* is deservedly celebrated among the dramas of *Shakespeare*. There is perhaps no play which keeps the attention so strongly fixed; which so much agitates our passions and interests our curiosity. The artful involutions of distinct interests, the striking opposition of contrary characters, the sudden changes of fortune, and the quick succession of events, fill the mind with a perpetual tumult of indignation, pity, and hope. There is no scene which does not contribute to the aggravation of the distress or conduct of the action, and scarce a line which does not conduce to the progress of the scene. So powerful is the current of the poet's imagination, that the mind, which once ventures within it, is hurried irresistibly along.

On the seeming improbability of *Lear's* conduct it may be observed, that he is represented according to histories at that time vulgarly received as true. And perhaps if we turn our thoughts upon the barbarity and ignorance of the age to which this story is referred, it will appear not so unlikely as while we estimate *Lear's* manners by our own. Such preference of one daughter to another, or resignation of dominion on such conditions, would be yet credible, if told of a petty prince of *Guinea* or *Madagascar*. *Shakespeare,* indeed, by the mention of his Earls and Dukes, has given us the idea of times more civilised, and of life regulated by softer manners; and the truth is, that though he so nicely discriminates, and so minutely describes the characters of men, he commonly neglects and confounds the characters of ages, by mingling customs ancient and modern, *English* and foreign.

My learned friend Mr. *Warton,* who has in the *Adventurer*[2]

[2] Nos. 113, 116, 122, by Joseph Warton. The strictures are at the end of the third paper.

very minutely criticised this play, remarks, that the instances of
cruelty are too savage and shocking, and that the intervention of
Edmund destroys the simplicity of the story. These objections
may, I think, be answered, by repeating, that the cruelty of the
daughters is an historical fact, to which the poet has added little,
having only drawn it into a series by dialogue and action. But I
am not able to apologise with equal plausibility for the extrusion
of *Gloucester*'s eyes, which seems an act too horrid to be endured
in dramatick exhibition, and such as must always compel the mind
to relieve its distress by incredulity. Yet let it be remembered that
our authour well knew what would please the audience for which
he wrote.

The injury done by *Edmund* to the simplicity of the action is
abundantly recompensed by the addition of variety, by the art
with which he is made to co-operate with the chief design, and
the opportunity which he gives the poet of combining perfidy with
perfidy, and connecting the wicked son with the wicked daughters,
to impress this important moral, that villany is never at a stop,
that crimes lead to crimes, and at last terminate in ruin.

But though this moral be incidentally enforced, *Shakespeare*
has suffered the virtue of *Cordelia* to perish in a just cause, con-
trary to the natural ideas of justice, to the hope of the reader, and,
what is yet more strange, to the faith of chronicles. Yet this con-
duct is justified by the Spectator, who blames *Tate* for giving
Cordelia success and happiness in his alteration, and declares, that,
in his opinion, *the tragedy has lost half its beauty*.[3] *Dennis* has
remarked, whether justly or not, that, to secure the favourable
reception of *Cato, the town was poisoned with much false and
abominable criticism*,[4] and that endeavours had been used to
discredit and decry poetical justice. A play in which the wicked
prosper, and the virtuous miscarry, may doubtless be good, because
it is a just representation of the common events of human life:
but since all reasonable beings naturally love justice, I cannot
easily be persuaded, that the observation of justice makes a play

[3] *The Spectator*, No. 40, by Addison.
[4] *Remarks upon Cato, a Tragedy*, 1713. (*Critical Works of John
Dennis*, ed. Hooker, 1943, II, 43.)

worse; or, that if other excellencies are equal, the audience will not always rise better pleased from the final triumph of persecuted virtue.

In the present case the publick has decided. *Cordelia,* from the time of *Tate,* has always retired with victory and felicity. And, if my sensations could add any thing to the general suffrage, I might relate, that I was many years ago so shocked by *Cordelia*'s death, that I know not whether I ever endured to read again the last scenes of the play till I undertook to revise them as an editor.

ROMEO AND JULIET

ACT I. SCENE ii. (1. i. 181 ff.)

> *Why then, O brawling love! O loving hate! &c.*

Of these lines neither the sense nor occasion is very evident. He is not yet in love with an enemy, and to love one and hate another is no such uncommon state, as can deserve all this toil of antithesis.

ACT I. SCENE iii. (1. ii. 25.)

> *Earth-treading stars that make dark* HEAVEN's *light.*

This nonsense should be reformed thus,

> *Earth-treading stars that make dark* EVEN *light.*

> WARBURTON.

But why nonsense? Is anything more commonly said, than that beauties eclipse the sun? Has not *Pope* the thought and the word?

> *Sol through white curtains shot a tim'rous ray,*
> *And ope'd those eyes that must eclipse the day.*[5]

[5] *The Rape of the Lock,* I. 13–14.

320 CRITICISM

Both the old and the new reading are philosophical nonsense, but they are both, and both equally poetical sense.

ACT I. SCENE iii. (I. ii. 26–8.)

> Such comfort as do lusty young men feel,
> When well-apparel'd April on the heel
> Of limping Winter treads.

To say, and to say in pompous words, that a *young man shall feel* as much in an assembly of beauties, *as young men feel in the month of April,* is surely to waste sound upon a very poor sentiment. I read,

> Such comfort as do lusty yeomen feel.

You shall feel from the sight and conversation of these ladies, such hopes of happiness and such pleasure, as the farmer receives from the spring, when the plenty of the year begins, and the prospect of the harvest fills him with delight.

ACT I. SCENE iv. (I. iii. 92.)

> That in gold clasps locks in the golden Story.

The *golden story* is perhaps the *golden legend,* a book in the darker ages of popery much read, and doubtless often exquisitely embellished, but of which *Canus,* one of the popish doctors, proclaims the author to have been *homo ferrei oris, plumbei cordis.*[6]

ACT I. SCENE vi. (I. v. 34.)

> Good cousin Capulet.

This cousin *Capulet* is *unkle* in the paper of invitation, but as *Capulet* is described as old, *cousin* is probably the right word in both places. I know not how *Capulet* and his lady might agree,

[6] A being with iron tongue and heart of lead.

their ages were very disproportionate; he has been past masking for thirty years, and her age, as she tells Juliet, is but eight and twenty.

ACT I. CHORUS. (II. PROLOGUE.)

The use of this chorus is not easily discovered, it conduces nothing to the progress of the play, but relates what is already known, or what the next scenes will shew; and relates it without adding the improvement of any moral sentiment.

ACT II. SCENE vi. (II. vi. 15.)

> *Too swift arrives as tardy as too slow.*

He that travels too fast is as long before he comes to the end of his journey, as he that travels slow. Precipitation produces mishap.

ACT III. SCENE i. (III. i. 2.)

> *The day is hot.*

It is observed that in *Italy* almost all assassinations are committed during the heat of summer.

ACT III. SCENE iii. (III. i. 183.)

> *Affection makes him false.*

The charge of falshood on *Bentivolio*, though produced at hazard, is very just. The authour, who seems to intend the character of *Bentivolio* as good, meant perhaps to shew, how the best minds, in a state of faction and discord, are detorted to criminal partiality.

ACT III. SCENE viii. (III. v. 84.)

> *And, yet, no Man like he doth grieve my heart.*

Juliet's equivocations are rather too artful for a mind disturbed by the loss of a new lover.

ACT IV. SCENE iii. (IV. iii. 2–3.)

> Leave me to myself to-night;
> For I have need of many orisons.

Juliet plays most of her pranks under the appearance of religion: perhaps *Shakespeare* meant to punish her hypocrisy.

ACT V. SCENE i. (V. i. 3.)

> *My bosom's Lord sits lightly on this throne,* &c.

These three lines are very gay and pleasing. But why does *Shakespeare* give *Romeo* this involuntary cheerfulness just before the extremity of unhappiness? Perhaps to shew the vanity of trusting to those uncertain and casual exaltations or depressions, which many consider as certain foretokens of good and evil.

ACT V. SCENE v. (V. iii. 229.)

> FRIAR. *I will be brief.*

It is much to be lamented that the Poet did not conclude the dialogue with the action, and avoid a narrative of events which the audience already knew.

This play is one of the most pleasing of our Author's performances. The scenes are busy and various, the incidents numerous and important, the catastrophe irresistably affecting, and the process of the action carried on with such probability, at least with such congruity to popular opinions, as tragedy requires.
Here is one of the few attempts of *Shakespeare* to exhibit the conversation of gentlemen, to represent the airy sprightliness of juvenile elegance. Mr. *Dryden* mentions a tradition, which might easily reach his time, of a declaration made by *Shakespeare,* that *he was obliged to kill* Mercutio *in the third act, lest he should have been killed by him.* Yet he thinks him *no such formidable*

person, but that he might have lived through the play, and died in his bed, without danger to a poet.[7] *Dryden* well knew, had he been in quest of truth, that, in a pointed sentence, more regard is commonly had to the words than the thought, and that it is very seldom to be rigorously understood. *Mercutio's* wit, gaiety and courage, will always procure him friends that wish him a longer life; but his death is not precipitated, he has lived out the time allotted him in the construction of the play; nor do I doubt the ability of *Shakespeare* to have continued his existence, though some of his sallies are perhaps out of the reach of *Dryden;* whose genius was not very fertile of merriment, nor ductile to humour, but acute, argumentative, comprehensive, and sublime.

The Nurse is one of the characters in which the Authour delighted: he has, with great subtility of distinction, drawn her at once loquacious and secret, obsequious and insolent, trusty and dishonest.

His comick scenes are happily wrought, but his pathetick strains are always polluted with some unexpected depravations. His persons, however distressed, *have a conceit left them in their misery, a miserable conceit.*

HAMLET

ACT II. SCENE ii. (II. i. 114–17.)

> It is as proper to our age
> To cast beyond ourselves in our opinions,
> As it is common for the younger sort
> To lack discretion.

This is not the remark of a weak man. The vice of age is too much suspicion. Men long accustomed to the wiles of life *cast* commonly *beyond themselves,* let their cunning go further than

[7] *Defence of the Epilogue,* 1672. *Essays,* ed. Ker, I, 174.

reason can attend it. This is always the fault of a little mind, made artful by long commerce with the world.

ACT II. SCENE iv. (II. ii.)

Polonius is a man bred in courts, exercised in business, stored with observation, confident of his knowledge, proud of his eloquence, and declining into dotage. His mode of oratory is truly represented as designed to ridicule the practice of those times, of prefaces that made no introduction, and of method that embarrassed rather than explained. This part of his character is accidental, the rest is natural. Such a man is positive and confident, because he knows that his mind was once strong, and knows not that it is become weak. Such a man excels in general principles, but fails in the particular application. He is knowing in retrospect, and ignorant in foresight. While he depends upon his memory, and can draw from his repositories of knowledge, he utters weighty sentences, and gives useful counsel; but as the mind in its enfeebled state cannot be kept long busy and intent, the old man is subject to sudden dereliction of his faculties, he loses the order of his ideas, and entangles himself in his own thoughts, till he recovers the leading principle, and falls again into his former train. This idea of dotage encroaching upon wisdom, will solve all the phænomena of the character of *Polonius*.

If the dramas of *Shakespeare* were to be characterised, each by the particular excellence which distinguishes it from the rest, we must allow to the tragedy of *Hamlet* the praise of variety. The incidents are so numerous, that the argument of the play would make a long tale. The scenes are interchangeably diversified with merriment and solemnity; with merriment that includes judicious and instructive observations, and solemnity, not strained by poetical violence above the natural sentiments of man. New characters appear from time to time in continual succession, exhibiting various forms of life and particular modes of conversation. The pretended madness of *Hamlet* causes much mirth, the mournful distraction of *Ophelia* fills the heart with tenderness, and every personage produces the effect intended, from the apparition that in the first act chills the blood with horror, to the fop in the last, that exposes affectation to just contempt.

The conduct is perhaps not wholly secure against objections. The action is indeed for the most part in continual progression, but there are some scenes which neither forward nor retard it. Of the feigned madness of *Hamlet* there appears no adequate cause, for he does nothing which he might not have done with the reputation of sanity. He plays the madman most, when he treats *Ophelia* with so much rudeness, which seems to be useless and wanton cruelty.

Hamlet is, through the whole play, rather an instrument than an agent. After he has, by the stratagem of the play, convicted the King, he makes not attempt to punish him, and his death is at last effected by an incident which *Hamlet* has no part in producing.

The catastrophe is not very happily produced; the exchange of weapons is rather an expedient of necessity, than a stroke of art. A scheme might easily have been formed, to kill *Hamlet* with the dagger, and *Laertes* with the bowl.

The poet is accused of having shewn little regard to poetical justice, and may be charged with equal neglect of poetical probability. The apparition left the regions of the dead to little purpose; the revenge which he demands is not obtained but by the death of him that was required to take it; and the gratification which would arise from the destruction of an usurper and a murderer, is abated by the untimely death of *Ophelia*, the young, the beautiful, the harmless, and the pious.

OTHELLO

ACT V. SCENE vi. (v. ii. 63–5.)

> *Oh perjur'd woman! thou dost stone my heart,*
> *And mak'st me call, what I intend to do,*
> *A murder, which I thought a sacrifice.*

This line is difficult. *Thou hast harden'd my heart, and makest me* kill thee with the rage of a *murderer,* when *I thought to have sacrificed* thee to justice with the calmness of a priest striking a victim.

It must not be omitted, that one of the elder quarto's reads, *thou dost stone* thy *heart;* which I suspect to be genuine. The meaning then will be, *thou forcest me* to dismiss thee from the world in the state of the *murdered* without preparation for death, *when I intended* that thy punishment should have been *a sacrifice* atoning for thy crime.

I am glad that I have ended my revisal of this dreadful scene. It is not to be endured.

The beauties of this play impress themselves so strongly upon the attention of the reader, that they can draw no aid from critical illustration. The fiery openness of *Othello,* magnanimous, artless, and credulous, boundless in his confidence, ardent in his affection, inflexible in his resolution, and obdurate in his revenge; the cool malignity of *Iago,* silent in his resentment, subtle in his designs, and studious at once of his interest and his vengeance; the soft simplicity of *Desdemona,* confident of merit, and conscious of innocence, her artless perseverance in her suit, and her slowness to suspect that she can be suspected, are such proofs of *Shakespeare's* skill in human nature, as, I suppose, it is vain to seek in any modern writer. The gradual progress which *Iago* makes in the Moor's conviction, and the circumstances which he employs to inflame him, are so artfully natural, that, though it will perhaps not be said of him as he says of himself, that he is *a man not easily jealous,* yet we cannot but pity him when at last we find him *perplexed in the extreme.*

There is always danger lest wickedness conjoined with abilities should steal upon esteem, though it misses of approbation; but the character of *Iago* is so conducted, that he is from the first scene to the last hated and despised.

Even the inferiour characters of this play would be very conspicuous in any other piece, not only for their justness but their strength. *Cassio* is brave, benevolent, and honest, ruined only by his want of stubbornness to resist an insidious invitation. *Rod-*

erigo's suspicious credulity, and impatient submission to the cheats which he sees practised upon him, and which by persuasion he suffers to be repeated, exhibit a strong picture of a weak mind betrayed by unlawful desires, to a false friend; and the virtue of *Æmilia* is such as we often find, worn loosely, but not cast off, easy to commit small crimes, but quickened and alarmed at atrocious villanies.

The Scenes from the beginning to the end are busy, varied by happy interchanges, and regularly promoting the progression of the story; and the narrative in the end, though it tells but what is known already, yet is necessary to produce the death of *Othello*.

Had the scene opened in *Cyprus,* and the preceding incidents been occasionally related, there had been little wanting to a drama of the most exact and scrupulous regularity.

BIOGRAPHY

FROM **Milton**

Milton has the reputation of having been in his youth eminently beautiful, so as to have been called the Lady of his college. His hair, which was of a light brown, parted at the foretop, and hung down upon his shoulders, according to the picture which he has given of Adam. He was, however, not of the heroick stature, but rather below the middle size, according to Mr. Richardson, who mentions him as having narrowly escaped from being *short and thick.*[1] He was vigorous and active, and delighted in the exercise of the sword, in which he is related to have been eminently skilful. His weapon was, I believe, not the rapier, but the backsword, of which he recommends the use in his book on Education.

His eyes are said never to have been bright; but, if he was a dexterous fencer, they must have been once quick.

His domestick habits, so far as they are known, were those of a severe student. He drank little strong drink of any kind, and fed without excess in quantity, and in his earlier years without delicacy of choice. In his youth he studied late at night; but afterwards

[1] Jonathan Richardson, *Explanatory Notes and Remarks on Paradise Lost,* 1734, p. 2.

changed his hours, and rested in bed from nine to four in the summer, and five in winter. The course of his day was best known after he was blind. When he first rose, he heard a chapter in the Hebrew Bible, and then studied till twelve; then took some exercise for an hour; then dined; then played on the organ, and sung, or heard another sing; then studied to six; then entertained his visitors till eight; then supped, and, after a pipe of tobacco and a glass of water, went to bed.

So is his life described; but this even tenour appears attainable only in Colleges. He that lives in the world will sometimes have the succession of his practice broken and confused. Visiters, of whom Milton is represented to have had great numbers, will come and stay unseasonably; business, of which every man has some, must be done when others will do it.

When he did not care to rise early, he had something read to him by his bedside; perhaps at this time his daughters were employed. He composed much in the morning, and dictated in the day, sitting obliquely in an elbow-chair, with his leg thrown over the arm.

Fortune appears not to have had much of his care. In the civil wars he lent his personal estate to the parliament; but when, after the contest was decided, he solicited repayment, he met not only with neglect, but *sharp rebuke*; and, having tired both himself and his friends, was given up to poverty and hopeless indignation, till he shewed how able he was to do greater service. He was then made Latin secretary, with two hundred pounds a year; and had a thousand pounds for his *Defence of the People*. His widow, who, after his death, retired to Namptwich in Cheshire, and died about 1729, is said to have reported that he lost two thousand pounds by entrusting it to a scrivener; and that, in the general depredation upon the Church, he had grasped an estate of about sixty pounds a year belonging to Westminster-Abbey, which, like other sharers of the plunder of rebellion, he was afterwards obliged to return. Two thousand pounds, which he had placed in the Excise-office, were also lost. There is yet no reason to believe that he was ever reduced to indigence. His wants, being few were competently supplied. He sold his library before his death, and left his family fifteen hundred pounds, on which his widow laid hold, and only gave one hundred to each of his daughters.

His literature was unquestionably great. He read all the languages which are considered either as learned or polite: Hebrew, with its two dialects, Greek, Latin, Italian, French, and Spanish. In Latin his skill was such as places him in the first rank of writers and criticks; and he appears to have cultivated Italian with uncommon diligence. The books in which his daughter, who used to read to him, represented him as most delighting, after Homer, which he could almost repeat, were Ovid's Metamorphoses and Euripides. His Euripides is, by Mr. Cradock's kindness, now in my hands: the margin is sometimes noted; but I have found nothing remarkable.

Of the English poets he set most value upon Spenser, Shakspeare, and Cowley. Spenser was apparently his favourite: Shakspeare he may easily be supposed to like, with every other skilful reader; but I should not have expected that Cowley, whose ideas of excellence were different from his own, would have had much of his approbation. His character of Dryden, who sometimes visited him, was, that he was a good rhymist, but no poet.

His theological opinions are said to have been first Calvinistical; and afterwards, perhaps when he began to hate the Presbyterians, to have tended towards Arminianism. In the mixed questions of theology and government, he never thinks that he can recede far enough from popery, or prelacy; but what Baudius says of Erasmus seems applicable to him, *magis habuit quod fugeret, quam quod sequeretur.* He had determined rather what to condemn, than what to approve. He has not associated himself with any denomination of Protestants: we know rather what he was not, than what he was. He was not of the church of Rome; he was not of the church of England.

To be of no church, is dangerous. Religion, of which the rewards are distant, and which is animated only by Faith and Hope, will glide by degrees out of the mind, unless it be invigorated and reimpressed by external ordinances, by stated calls to worship, and the salutary influence of example. Milton, who appears to have had full conviction of the truth of Christianity, and to have re-

garded the Holy Scriptures with the profoundest veneration, to
have been untainted by an heretical peculiarity of opinion, and
to have lived in a confirmed belief of the immediate and occasional
agency of Providence, yet grew old without any visible worship.
In the distribution of his hours, there was no hour of prayer, either
solitary, or with his household; omitting publick prayers, he
omitted all.

Of this omission the reason has been sought, upon a supposition
which ought never to be made, that men live with their own
approbation, and justify their conduct to themselves. Prayer cer-
tainly was not thought superfluous by him, who represents our first
parents as praying acceptably in the state of innocence, and
efficaciously after their fall. That he lived without prayer can
hardly be affirmed; his studies and meditations were an habitual
prayer. The neglect of it in his family was probably a fault for
which he condemned himself, and which he intended to correct,
but that death, as too often happens, intercepted his reformation.

His political notions were those of an acrimonious and surly
republican, for which it is not known that he gave any better
reason than that *a popular government was the most frugal; for
the trappings of a monarchy would set up an ordinary common-
wealth*.[2] It is surely very shallow policy, that supposes money to
be the chief good; and even this, without considering that the
support and expence of a Court is, for the most part, only a particu-
lar kind of traffick, by which money is circulated, without any
national impoverishment.

Milton's republicanism was, I am afraid, founded in an envious
hatred of greatness, and a sullen desire of independence; in petu-
lance impatient of controul, and pride disdainful of superiority.
He hated monarchs in the state, and prelates in the church; for he
hated all whom he was required to obey. It is to be suspected, that
his predominant desire was to destroy rather than establish, and
that he felt not so much the love of liberty as repugnance to au-
thority.

It has been observed, that they who most loudly clamour for
liberty do not most liberally grant it. What we know of Milton's

[2] John Toland, *Life of Milton*, p. 139.

character, in domestick relations, is, that he was severe and arbi-
trary. His family consisted of women; and there appears in his
books something like a Turkish contempt of females, as subordi-
nate and inferior beings. That his own daughters might not break
the ranks, he suffered them to be depressed by a mean and penuri-
ous education. He thought woman made only for obedience, and
man only for rebellion. . . .

* * *

One of the poems on which much praise has been bestowed is
Lycidas; of which the diction is harsh, the rhymes uncertain, and
the numbers unpleasing. What beauty there is, we must therefore
seek in the sentiments and images. It is not to be considered as the
effusion of real passion; for passion runs not after remote allusions
and obscure opinions. Passion plucks no berries from the myrtle
and ivy, nor calls upon Arethuse and Mincius, nor tells of rough
satyrs and *fauns with cloven heel.* Where there is leisure for fiction
there is little grief.

In this poem there is no nature, for there is no truth; there is
no art, for there is nothing new. Its form is that of a pastoral, easy,
vulgar, and therefore disgusting: whatever images it can supply,
are long ago exhausted; and its inherent improbability always
forces dissatisfaction on the mind. When Cowley tells of Hervey
that they studied together, it is easy to suppose how much he
must miss the companion of his labours, and the partner of his
discoveries; but what image of tenderness can be excited by these
lines!

> We drove a field, and both together heard
> What time the grey fly winds her sultry horn,
> Battening our flocks with the fresh dews of night.

We know that they never drove a field, and that they had no
flocks to batten; and though it be allowed that the representation
may be allegorical, the true meaning is so uncertain and remote,
that it is never sought because it cannot be known when it is
found.

Among the flocks, and copses, and flowers, appear the heathen deities; Jove and Phœbus, Neptune and Æolus, with a long train of mythological imagery, such as a College easily supplies. Nothing can less display knowledge, or less exercise invention, than to tell how a shepherd has lost his companion, and must now feed his flocks alone, without any judge of his skill in piping; and how one god asks another god what is become of Lycidas, and how neither god can tell. He who thus grieves will excite no sympathy; he who thus praises will confer no honour.

This poem has yet a grosser fault. With these trifling fictions are mingled the most awful and sacred truths, such as ought never to be polluted with such irreverend combinations. The shepherd likewise is now a feeder of sheep, and afterwards an ecclesiastical pastor, a superintendent of a Christian flock. Such equivocations are always unskilful; but here they are indecent, and at least approach to impiety, of which, however, I believe the writer not to have been conscious.

Such is the power of reputation justly acquired that its blaze drives away the eye from nice examination. Surely no man could have fancied that he read *Lycidas* with pleasure, had he not known its author.

Of the two pieces, *L'Allegro* and *Il Penseroso,* I believe opinion is uniform; every man that reads them, reads them with pleasure. The author's design is not, what Theobald has remarked, merely to shew how objects derive their colours from the mind, by representing the operation of the same things upon the gay and the melancholy temper, or upon the same man as he is differently disposed; but rather how, among the successive variety of appearances, every disposition of mind takes hold on those by which it may be gratified.

The *chearful* man hears the lark in the morning; the *pensive* man hears the nightingale in the evening. The *chearful* man sees the cock strut, and hears the horn and hounds echo in the wood; then walks *not unseen* to observe the glory of the rising sun, or listen to the singing milk-maid, and view the labours of the plowman and the mower; then casts his eyes about him over scenes of smiling plenty, and looks up to the distant tower, the residence of some fair inhabitant; thus he pursues rural gaiety through a day of labour or of play, and delights himself at night with the fanciful narratives of superstitious ignorance.

The *pensive* man, at one time, walks *unseen* to muse at midnight, and at another hears the sullen curfew. If the weather drives him home, he sits in a room lighted only by *glowing embers;* or by a lonely lamp outwatches the North Star, to discover the habitation of separate souls, and varies the shades of meditation, by contemplating the magnificent or pathetick scenes of tragick and epick poetry. When the morning comes, a morning gloomy with rain and wind, he walks into the dark trackless woods, falls asleep by some murmuring water, and with melancholy enthusiasm expects some dream of prognostication, or some musick played by aerial performers.

Both Mirth and Melancholy are solitary, silent inhabitants of the breast that neither receive nor transmit communication; no mention is therefore made of a philosophical friend, or a pleasant companion. The seriousness does not arise from any participation of calamity, nor the gaiety from the pleasures of the bottle.

The man of *chearfulness*, having exhausted the country, tries what *towered cities* will afford, and mingles with scenes of splendor, gay assemblies, and nuptial festivities; but he mingles a mere spectator, as, when the learned comedies of Jonson, or the wild dramas of Shakspeare, are exhibited, he attends the theatre.

The *pensive* man never loses himself in crowds, but walks the cloister, or frequents the cathedral. Milton probably had not yet forsaken the Church.

Both his characters delight in musick; but he seems to think that chearful notes would have obtained from Pluto a compleat dismission of Eurydice, of whom solemn sounds only procured a conditional release.

For the old age of Chearfulness he makes no provision; but Melancholy he conducts with great dignity to the close of life. His Chearfulness is without levity, and his Pensiveness without asperity.

Through these two poems the images are properly selected, and nicely distinguished; but the colours of the diction seem not suffi-

ciently discriminated. I know not whether the characters are kept
sufficiently apart. No mirth can, indeed, be found in his melan-
choly; but I am afraid that I always meet some melancholy in his
mirth. They are two noble efforts of imagination. . . .

[*Comus* is examined, and the Sonnets are dismissed.]

Those little pieces may be dispatched without much anxiety; a
greater work calls for greater care. I am now to examine *Paradise
Lost*; a poem, which, considered with respect to design, may claim
the first place, and with respect to performance the second, among
the productions of the human mind.

By the general consent of criticks, the first praise of genius is
due to the writer of an epick poem, as it requires an assemblage
of all the powers which are singly sufficient for other compositions.
Poetry is the art of uniting pleasure with truth, by calling imagi-
nation to the help of reason. Epick poetry undertakes to teach the
most important truths by the most pleasing precepts, and there-
fore relates some great event in the most affecting manner. History
must supply the writer with the rudiments of narration, which he
must improve and exalt by a nobler art, must animate by dramatick
energy, and diversify by retrospection and anticipation; morality
must teach him the exact bounds, and different shades, of vice and
virtue; from policy, and the practice of life, he has to learn the
discriminations of character, and the tendency of the passions,
either single or combined; and physiology must supply him with
illustrations and images. To put these materials to poetical use, is
required an imagination capable of painting nature, and realizing
fiction. Nor is he yet a poet till he has attained the whole extension
of his language, distinguished all the delicacies of phrase, and
all the colours of words, and learned to adjust their different
sounds to all the varieties of metrical modulation.

Bossu is of opinion that the poet's first work is to find a *moral*,
which his fable is afterwards to illustrate and establish.[3] This
seems to have been the process only of Milton; the moral of other
poems is incidental and consequent; in Milton's only it is essential

[3] *Traité du Poëme Épique*, Bk. I, ch. 7.

and intrinsick. His purpose was the most useful and the most arduous; *to vindicate the ways of God to man;* to shew the reasonableness of religion, and the necessity of obedience to the Divine Law.

To convey this moral, there must be a *fable,* a narration artfully constructed, so as to excite curiosity, and surprise expectation. In this part of his work, Milton must be confessed to have equalled every other poet. He has involved in his account of the Fall of Man the events which preceded, and those that were to follow it: he has interwoven the whole system of theology with such propriety, that every part appears to be necessary; and scarcely any recital is wished shorter for the sake of quickening the progress of the main action.

The subject of an epick poem is naturally an event of great importance. That of Milton is not the destruction of a city, the conduct of a colony, or the foundation of an empire. His subject is the fate of worlds, the revolutions of heaven and of earth; rebellion against the Supreme King, raised by the highest order of created beings; the overthrow of their host, and the punishment of their crime; the creation of a new race of reasonable creatures; their original happiness and innocence, their forfeiture of immortality, and their restoration to hope and peace.

Great events can be hastened or retarded only by persons of elevated dignity. Before the greatness displayed in Milton's poem, all other greatness shrinks away. The weakest of his agents are the highest and noblest of human beings, the original parents of mankind; with whose actions the elements consented; on whose rectitude, or deviation of will, depended the state of terrestrial nature, and the condition of all the future inhabitants of the globe.

Of the other agents in the poem, the chief are such as it is irreverence to name on slight occasions. The rest were lower powers;

> —of which the least could wield
> Those elements, and arm him with the force
> Of all their regions;[4]

[4] *Paradise Lost,* VI. 221.

powers, which only the controul of Omnipotence restrains from laying creation waste, and filling the vast expanse of space with ruin and confusion. To display the motives and actions of beings thus superiour, so far as human reason can examine them, or human imagination represent them, is the task which this mighty poet has undertaken and performed.

In the examination of epick poems much speculation is commonly employed upon the *characters*. The characters in the *Paradise Lost* which admit of examination, are those of angels and of man; of angels good and evil; of man in his innocent and sinful state.

Among the angels, the virtue of Raphael is mild and placid, of easy condescension and free communication; that of Michael is regal and lofty, and, as may seem, attentive to the dignity of his own nature. Abdiel and Gabriel appear occasionally, and act as every incident requires; the solitary fidelity of Abdiel is very amiably painted.[5]

Of the evil angels the characters are more diversified. To Satan, as Addison observes, such sentiments are given as suit *the most exalted and most depraved. being.*[6] Milton has been censured, by Clarke, for the impiety which sometimes breaks from Satan's mouth. For there are thoughts, as he justly remarks, which no observation of character can justify, because no good man would willingly permit them to pass, however transiently, through his own mind.[7] To make Satan speak as a rebel, without any such expressions as might taint the reader's imagination, was indeed one of the great difficulties in Milton's undertaking, and I cannot but think that he has extricated himself with great happiness. There is in Satan's speeches little that can give pain to a pious ear. The language of rebellion cannot be the same with that of obedience. The malignity of Satan foams in haughtiness and obstinacy; but his expressions are commonly general, and no otherwise offensive than as they are wicked.

The other chiefs of the celestial rebellion are very judiciously

[5] *Ibid.*, V. 803 ff.
[6] *Spectator*, No. 303.
[7] John Clarke, *Essay upon Study*, 1731, p. 204.

discriminated in the first and second books; and the ferocious character of Moloch appears, both in the battle and the council, with exact consistency.

To Adam and to Eve are given, during their innocence, such sentiments as innocence can generate and utter. Their love is pure benevolence and mutual veneration; their repasts are without luxury, and their diligence without toil. Their addresses to their Maker have little more than the voice of admiration and gratitude. Fruition left them nothing to ask, and Innocence left them nothing to fear.

But with guilt enter distrust and discord, mutual accusation, and stubborn self-defence; they regard each other with alienated minds, and dread their Creator as the avenger of their transgression. At last they seek shelter in his mercy, soften to repentance, and melt in supplication. Both before and after the Fall, the superiority of Adam is diligently sustained.

Of the *probable* and the *marvellous,* two parts of a vulgar epick poem which immerge the critick in deep consideration, the *Paradise Lost* requires little to be said. It contains the history of a miracle, of Creation and Redemption; it displays the power and the mercy of the Supreme Being; the probable therefore is marvellous, and the marvellous is probable. The substance of the narrative is truth; and as truth allows no choice, it is, like necessity, superior to rule. To the accidental or adventitious parts, as to every thing human, some slight exceptions may be made. But the main fabrick is immovably supported.

It is justly remarked by Addison[8] that this poem has, by the nature of its subject, the advantage above all others, that it is universally and perpetually interesting. All mankind will, through all ages, bear the same relation to Adam and to Eve, and must partake of that good and evil which extend to themselves.

Of the *machinery,* so called from ϑεὸς ἀπὸ μηχανῆς,[9] by which is meant the occasional interposition of supernatural power, another fertile topic of critical remarks, here is no room to speak, because every thing is done under the immediate and visible direc-

[8] *Spectator,* No. 273.
[9] Aristotle. *Poetics,* XV. 10. "Deus ex machina."

tion of Heaven; but the rule is so far observed, that no part of the action could have been accomplished by any other means.

Of *episodes,* I think there are only two, contained in Raphael's relation of the war in heaven, and Michael's prophetick account of the changes to happen in this world.[10] Both are closely connected with the great action; one was necessary to Adam as a warning, the other as a consolation.

To the compleatness or *integrity* of the design nothing can be objected; it has distinctly and clearly what Aristotle requires, a beginning, a middle, and an end. There is perhaps no poem, of the same length, from which so little can be taken without apparent mutilation. Here are no funeral games, nor is there any long description of a shield. The short digressions at the beginning of the third, seventh, and ninth books, might doubtless be spared; but superfluities so beautiful, who would take away? or who does not wish that the author of the *Iliad* had gratified succeeding ages with a little knowledge of himself? Perhaps no passages are more frequently or more attentively read than those extrinsick paragraphs; and, since the end of poetry is pleasure, that cannot be unpoetical with which all are pleased.

The questions, whether the action of the poem be strictly *one,* whether the poem can be properly termed *heroick,* and who is the hero, are raised by such readers as draw their principles of judgement rather from books than from reason. Milton, though he intituled *Paradise Lost* only a *poem,* yet calls it himself *heroick song.*[11] Dryden, petulantly and indecently, denies the heroism of Adam, because he was overcome; but there is no reason why the hero should not be unfortunate, except established practice, since success and virtue do not go necessarily together. Cato is the hero of Lucan, but Lucan's authority will not be suffered by Quintilian to decide. However, if success be necessary, Adam's deceiver was at last crushed; Adam was restored to his Maker's favour, and therefore may securely resume his human rank.

After the scheme and fabrick of the poem, must be considered its component parts, the sentiments and the diction.

[10] *Paradise Lost,* V. 577 ff.; XI. 334 ff.
[11] *Ibid.,* IX. 25.

The *sentiments,* as expressive of manners, or appropriated to characters, are, for the greater part, unexceptionably just.

Splendid passages, containing lessons of morality, or precepts of prudence, occur seldom. Such is the original formation of this poem, that as it admits no human manners till the Fall, it can give little assistance to human conduct. Its end is to raise the thoughts above sublunary cares or pleasures. Yet the praise of that fortitude, with which Abdiel maintained his singularity of virtue against the scorn of multitudes, may be accommodated to all times; and Raphael's reproof of Adam's curiosity after the planetary motions, with the answer returned by Adam, may be confidently opposed to any rule of life which any poet has delivered.[12]

The thoughts which are occasionally called forth in the progress, are such as could only be produced by an imagination in the highest degree fervid and active, to which materials were supplied by incessant study and unlimited curiosity. The heat of Milton's mind might be said to sublimate his learning, to throw off into his work the spirit of science, unmingled with its grosser parts.[13]

He had considered creation in its whole extent, and his descriptions are therefore learned. He had accustomed his imagination to unrestrained indulgence, and his conceptions therefore were extensive. The characteristick quality of his poem is sublimity. He sometimes descends to the elegant, but his element is the great. He can occasionally invest himself with grace; but his natural port is gigantick loftiness. He can please when pleasure is required; but it is his peculiar power to astonish.

He seems to have been well acquainted with his own genius, and to know what it was that Nature had bestowed upon him more bountifully than upon others; the power of displaying the vast, illuminating the splendid, enforcing the awful, darkening the gloomy, and aggravating the dreadful: he therefore chose a subject on which too much could not be said, on which he might tire his fancy without the censure of extravagance.

The appearances of nature, and the occurrences of life, did not

[12] *Ibid.,* VIII. 66 ff.
[13] Cf. Wordsworth, Preface to *Lyrical Ballads:* "Poetry . . . is the impassioned expression which is in the countenance of all Science."

satiate his appetite of greatness. To paint things as they are, requires a minute attention, and employs the memory rather than the fancy. Milton's delight was to sport in the wide regions of possibility; reality was a scene too narrow for his mind. He sent his faculties out upon discovery, into worlds where only imagination can travel, and delighted to form new modes of existence, and furnish sentiment and action to superior beings, to trace the counsels of hell, or accompany the choirs of heaven.

But he could not be always in other worlds: he must sometimes revisit earth, and tell of things visible and known. When he cannot raise wonder by the sublimity of his mind, he gives delight by its fertility.

Whatever be his subject, he never fails to fill the imagination. But his images and descriptions of the scenes or operations of Nature do not seem to be always copied from original form, nor to have the freshness, raciness, and energy of immediate observation. He saw Nature, as Dryden expresses it, *through the spectacles of books;*[14] and on most occasions calls learning to his assistance. The garden of Eden brings to his mind the vale of *Enna,* where Proserpine was gathering flowers. Satan makes his way through fighting elements, like *Argo* between the *Cyanean* rocks, or *Ulysses* between the two *Sicilian* whirlpools, when he shunned *Charybdis* on the *larboard.* The mythological allusions have been justly censured,[15] as not being always used with notice of their vanity; but they contribute variety to the narration, and produce an alternate exercise of the memory and the fancy.

His similies are less numerous, and more various, than those of his predecessors. But he does not confine himself within the limits of rigorous comparison: his great excellence is amplitude, and he expands the adventitious image beyond the dimensions which the occasion required. Thus, comparing the shield of Satan to the orb of the Moon, he crouds the imagination with the discovery of the telescope, and all the wonders which the telescope discovers.

Of his moral sentiments it is hardly praise to affirm that they excel those of all other poets; for this superiority he was indebted

[14] *Essays,* ed. Ker, I, 80.
[15] *Spectator,* No. 297.

to his acquaintance with the sacred writings. The ancient epick poets, wanting the light of Revelation, were very unskilful teachers of virtue: their principal characters may be great, but they are not amiable. The reader may rise from their works with a greater degree of active or passive fortitude, and sometimes of prudence; but he will be able to carry away few precepts of justice, and none of mercy.

From the Italian writers it appears, that the advantages of even Christian knowledge may be possessed [16] in vain. Ariosto's pravity is generally known; and though the *Deliverance of Jerusalem* may be considered as a sacred subject, the poet[17] has been very sparing of moral instruction.

In Milton every line breathes sanctity of thought, and purity of manners, except when the train of the narration requires the introduction of the rebellious spirits; and even they are compelled to acknowledge their subjection to God, in such a manner as excites reverence, and confirms piety.

Of human beings there are but two; but those two are the parents of mankind, venerable before their fall for dignity and innocence, and amiable after it for repentance and submission. In their first state their affection is tender without weakness, and their piety sublime without presumption. When they have sinned, they shew how discord begins in mutual frailty, and how it ought to cease in mutual forbearance; how confidence of the divine favour is forfeited by sin, and how hope of pardon may be obtained by penitence and prayer. A state of innocence we can only conceive, if indeed, in our present misery, it be possible to conceive it; but the sentiments and worship proper to a fallen and offending being, we have all to learn, as we have all to practise.

The poet, whatever be done, is always great. Our progenitors, in their first state, conversed with angels; even when folly and sin had degraded them, they had not in their humiliation *the port of mean suitors;*[18] and they rise again to reverential regard, when we find that their prayers were heard.

---

[16] 1783: supposed.
[17] Torquato Tasso.
[18] *Paradise Lost*, XI. 8.

As human passions did not enter the world before the Fall, there is in the *Paradise Lost* little opportunity for the pathetick; but what little there is has not been lost. That passion which is peculiar to rational nature, the anguish arising from the consciousness of transgression, and the horrours attending the sense of the Divine Displeasure, are very justly described and forcibly impressed. But the passions are moved only on one occasion; sublimity is the general and prevailing quality in this poem; sublimity variously modified, sometimes descriptive, sometimes argumentative.

The defects and faults of *Paradise Lost,* for faults and defects every work of man must have, it is the business of impartial criticism to discover. As, in displaying the excellence of Milton, I have not made long quotations, because of selecting beauties there had been no end, I shall in the same general manner mention that which seems to deserve censure; for what Englishman can take delight in transcribing passages, which, if they lessen the reputation of Milton, diminish in some degree the honour of our country?

The generality of my scheme does not admit the frequent notice of verbal inaccuracies; which Bentley,[19] perhaps better skilled in grammar than in poetry, has often found, though he sometimes made them, and which he imputed to the obtrusions of a reviser whom the author's blindness obliged him to employ. A supposition rash and groundless, if he thought it true; and vile and pernicious, if, as is said, he in private allowed it to be false.

The plan of *Paradise Lost* has this inconvenience, that it comprises neither human actions nor human manners. The man and woman who act and suffer, are in a state which no other man or woman can ever know. The reader finds no transaction in which he can be engaged; beholds no condition in which he can by any effort of imagination place himself; he has, therefore, little natural curiosity or sympathy.

We all, indeed, feel the effects of Adam's disobedience; we all sin like Adam, and like him must all bewail our offences; we have restless and insidious enemies in the fallen angels, and in the blessed spirits we have guardians and friends; in the Redemption

[19] Preface to his edition of *Paradise Lost,* 1732.

of mankind we hope to be included: in the description of heaven and hell we are surely interested, as we are all to reside hereafter either in the regions of horrour or of bliss.

But these truths are too important to be new: they have been taught to our infancy; they have mingled with our solitary thoughts and familiar conversation, and are habitually interwoven with the whole texture of life. Being therefore not new, they raise no unaccustomed emotion in the mind; what we knew before, we cannot learn; what is not unexpected, cannot surprise.

Of the ideas suggested by these awful scenes, from some we recede with reverence, except when stated hours require their association; and from others we shrink with horrour, or admit them only as salutary inflictions, as counterpoises to our interests and passions. Such images rather obstruct the career of fancy than incite it.

Pleasure and terrour are indeed the genuine sources of poetry; but poetical pleasure must be such as human imagination can at least conceive, and poetical terrour such as human strength and fortitude may combat. The good and evil of Eternity are too ponderous for the wings of wit; the mind sinks under them in passive helplessness, content with calm belief and humble adoration.

Known truths, however, may take a different appearance, and be conveyed to the mind by a new train of intermediate images. This Milton has undertaken, and performed with pregnancy and vigour of mind peculiar to himself. Whoever considers the few radical positions which the Scriptures afforded him will wonder by what energetick operation he expanded them to such extent, and ramified them to so much variety, restrained as he was by religious reverence from licentiousness of fiction.

Here is a full display of the united force of study and genius; of a great accumulation of materials, with judgement to digest, and fancy to combine them: Milton was able to select from nature, or from story, from ancient fable, or from modern science, whatever could illustrate or adorn his thoughts. An accumulation of knowledge impregnated his mind, fermented by study, and exalted by imagination.

It has been therefore said, without an indecent hyperbole, by one of his encomiasts, that in reading *Paradise Lost* we read a book of universal knowledge.

But original deficience cannot be supplied. The want of human interest is always felt. *Paradise Lost* is one of the books which the reader admires and lays down, and forgets to take up again. None ever wished it longer than it is. Its perusal is a duty rather than a pleasure. We read Milton for instruction, retire harassed and over-burdened, and look elsewhere for recreation; we desert our master, and seek for companions.

Another inconvenience of Milton's design is, that it requires the description of what cannot be described, the agency of spirits. He saw that immateriality supplied no images, and that he could not show angels acting but by instruments of action; he therefore invested them with form and matter. This, being necessary, was therefore defensible; and he should have secured the consistency of his system, by keeping immateriality out of sight, and enticing his reader to drop it from his thoughts. But he has unhappily perplexed his poetry with his philosophy. His infernal and celestial powers are sometimes pure spirit, and sometimes animated body. When Satan walks with his lance upon the *burning marle*, he has a body; when in his passage between hell and the new world, he is in danger of sinking in the vacuity, and is supported by a gust of rising vapours, he has a body; when he animates the toad, he seems to be mere spirit, that can penetrate matter at pleasure; when he *starts up in his own shape*, he has at least a determined form; and when he is brought before Gabriel, he has *a spear and a shield*, which he had the power of hiding in the toad, though the arms of the contending angels are evidently material.[20]

The vulgar inhabitants of Pandæmonium, being *incorporeal spirits,* are *at large, though without number,* in a limited space; yet in the battle, when they were overwhelmed by mountains, their armour hurt them, *crushed in upon their substance, now grown gross by sinning.* This likewise happened to the uncorrupted angels, who were overthrown *the sooner for their arms, for unarmed they*

[20] For the above allusions, cf. Paradise Lost, I. 296; II. 931; IV. 800, 819, 990.

might easily as spirits have evaded by contraction or remove. Even
as spirits they are hardly spiritual; for *contraction* and *remove* are
images of matter; but if they could have escaped without their
armour, they might have escaped from it, and left only the empty
cover to be battered. Uriel, when he rides on a sunbeam, is mate-
rial; Satan is material when he is afraid of the prowess of Adam.[21]

The confusion of spirit and matter which pervades the whole
narration of the war of heaven fills it with incongruity; and the
book, in which it is related, is, I believe, the favourite of children,
and gradually neglected as knowledge is increased.

After the operation of immaterial agents, which cannot be
explained, may be considered that of allegorical persons, which
have no real existence. To exalt causes into agents, to invest
abstract ideas with form, and animate them with activity, has
always been the right of poetry. But such airy beings are, for the
most part, suffered only to do their natural office, and retire. Thus
Fame tells a tale, and Victory hovers over a general, or perches on
a standard; but Fame and Victory can do no more. To give them
any real employment, or ascribe to them any material agency, is to
make them allegorical no longer, but to shock the mind by ascrib-
ing effects to non-entity. In the *Prometheus* of Æschylus, we see
Violence and *Strength*, and in the *Alcestis* of Euripides, we see
Death, brought upon the stage, all as active persons of the drama;
but no precedents can justify absurdity.

Milton's allegory of Sin and Death is undoubtedly faulty. Sin
is indeed the mother of Death, and may be allowed to be the
portress of hell; but when they stop the journey of Satan, a journey
described as real, and when Death offers him battle, the allegory is
broken. That Sin and Death should have shewn the way to hell,
might have been allowed; but they cannot facilitate the passage by
building a bridge, because the difficulty of Satan's passage is de-
scribed as real and sensible, and the bridge ought to be only
figurative. The hell assigned to the rebellious spirits is described
as not less local than the residence of man. It is placed in some
distant part of space, separated from the regions of harmony and
order by a chaotick waste and an unoccupied vacuity; but *Sin* and

[21] *Ibid.*, I. 789; VI. 651, 595; IV. 555, 590; IX. 480.

Death worked up a *mole* of *aggregated* [22] *soil,* cemented with *asphaltus;* a work too bulky for ideal architects. [23]

This unskilful allegory appears to me one of the greatest faults of the poem; and to this there was no temptation, but the author's opinion of its beauty.

To the conduct of the narrative some objections may be made. Satan is with great expectation brought before Gabriel in Paradise, and is suffered to go away unmolested. The creation of man is represented as the consequence of the vacuity left in heaven by the expulsion of the rebels; yet Satan mentions it as a report *rife in heaven* before his departure. [24]

To find sentiments for the state of innocence, was very difficult; and something of anticipation perhaps is now and then discovered. Adam's discourse of dreams seems not to be the speculation of a new-created being. I know not whether his answer to the angel's reproof for curiosity does not want something of propriety: it is the speech of a man acquainted with many other men. Some philosophical notions, especially when the philosophy is false, might have been better omitted. The angel, in a comparison, speaks of *timorous deer,* before deer were yet timorous, and before Adam could understand the comparison. [25]

Dryden remarks, that Milton has some flats among his elevations. [26] This is only to say, that all the parts are not equal. In every work, one part must be for the sake of others; a palace must have passages; a poem must have transitions. It is no more to be required that wit should always be blazing, than that the sun should always stand at noon. In a great work there is a vicissitude of luminous and opaque parts, as there is in the world a succession of day and night. Milton, when he has expatiated in the sky, may be allowed sometimes to revisit earth; for what other author ever soared so high, or sustained his flight so long?

Milton, being well versed in the Italian poets, appears to have

[22] 1783: aggravated.
[23] Cf. *Paradise Lost,* II. 648 ff.; X. 293 ff.
[24] *Ibid.,* IV. 874; VII. 150; I. 650.
[25] *Ibid.,* V. 100; VIII. 179; VI. 857.
[26] Preface to *Sylvae. Essays,* ed. Ker, I, 268.

borrowed often from them; and, as every man catches something from his companions, his desire of imitating Ariosto's levity has disgraced his work with the *Paradise of Fools;* a fiction not in itself ill-imagined, but too ludicrous for its place.[27]

His play on words, in which he delights too often; his equivocations, which Bentley endeavours to defend by the example of the ancients; his unnecessary and ungraceful use of terms of art; it is not necessary to mention, because they are easily remarked, and generally censured, and at last bear so little proportion to the whole, that they scarcely deserve the attention of a critick.

Such are the faults of that wonderful performance *Paradise Lost;* which he who can put in balance with its beauties must be considered not as nice but as dull, as less to be censured for want of candour, than pitied for want of sensibility. . . .

Rhyme, he says, and says truly, *is no necessary adunct of true poetry.*[28] But perhaps, of poetry as a mental operation, metre or musick is no necessary adjunct: it is however by the musick of metre that poetry has been discriminated in all languages; and in languages melodiously constructed with a due proportion of long and short syllables, metre is sufficient. But one language cannot communicate its rules to another: where metre is scanty and imperfect, some help is necessary. The musick of the English heroick line strikes the ear so faintly that it is easily lost, unless all the syllables of every line co-operate together: this co-operation can be only obtained by the preservation of every verse unmingled with another, as a distinct system of sounds; and this distinctness is obtained and preserved by the artifice of rhyme. The variety of pauses, so much boasted by the lovers of blank verse, changes the measures of an English poet to the periods of a declaimer; and there are only a few skilful and happy readers of Milton, who enable their audience to perceive where the lines end or begin. *Blank verse,* said an ingenious critick, *seems to be verse only to the eye.*[29]

Poetry may subsist without rhyme, but English poetry will not

[27] *Ibid.,* III. 444 ff.
[28] Preface to *Paradise Lost.*
[29] William Locke. Cf. Boswell's *Johnson,* ed. Hill, IV, 43.

often please; nor can rhyme ever be safely spared but where the subject is able to support itself. Blank verse makes some approach to that which is called the *lapidary style;* has neither the easiness of prose, nor the melody of numbers, and therefore tires by long continuance. Of the Italian writers without rhyme, whom Milton alleges as precedents, not one is popular; what reason could urge in its defence, has been confuted by the ear.

But, whatever be the advantage of rhyme, I cannot prevail on myself to wish that Milton had been a rhymer; for I cannot wish his work to be other than it is; yet, like other heroes, he is to be admired rather than imitated. He that thinks himself capable of astonishing, may write blank verse; but those that hope only to please, must condescend to rhyme.

The highest praise of genius is original invention. Milton cannot be said to have contrived the structure of an epick poem, and therefore owes reverence to that vigour and amplitude of mind to which all generations must be indebted for the art of poetical narration, for the texture of the fable, the variation of incidents, the interposition of dialogue, and all the stratagems that surprise and enchain attention. But, of all the borrowers from Homer, Milton is perhaps the least indebted. He was naturally a thinker for himself, confident of his own abilities, and disdainful of help or hindrance: he did not refuse admission to the thoughts or images of his predecessors, but he did not seek them. From his contemporaries he neither courted nor received support; there is in his writings nothing by which the pride of other authors might be gratified, or favour gained; no exchange of praise, nor solicitation of support. His great works were performed under discountenance, and in blindness, but difficulties vanished at his touch; he was born for whatever is arduous; and his work is not the greatest of heroick poems, only because it is not the first.

FROM Cowley

The Life of Cowley, notwithstanding the penury of English biography, has been written by Dr. Sprat,[1] an author whose pregnancy of imagination and elegance of language have deservedly set him high in the ranks of literature; but his zeal of friendship, or ambition of eloquence, has produced a funeral oration rather than a history: he has given the character, not the life of Cowley; for he writes with so little detail, that scarcely anything is distinctly known, but all is shewn confused and enlarged through the mist of panegyrick.

Abraham Cowley was born in the year one thousand six hundred and eighteen. His father was a grocer, whose condition Dr. Sprat conceals under the general appellation of a citizen; and, what would probably not have been less carefully suppressed, the omission of his name in the register of St. Dunstan's parish gives reason to suspect that his father was a sectary. Whoever he was, he died before the birth of his son, and consequently left him to the care of his mother; whom Wood represents as struggling earnestly

[1] Thomas Sprat, distinguished churchman and man of Letters, published his account of Cowley in 1668.

to procure him a literary education, and who, as she lived to the age of eighty, had her solicitude rewarded by seeing her son eminent, and, I hope, by seeing him fortunate, and partaking his prosperity. We know at least, from Sprat's account, that he always acknowledged her care, and justly paid the dues of filial gratitude.

In the window of his mother's apartment lay Spenser's Fairy Queen; in which he very early took delight to read, till, by feeling the charms of verse, he became, as he relates, irrecoverably a poet. Such are the accidents, which, sometimes remembered, and perhaps sometimes forgotten, produce that particular designation of mind, and propensity for some certain science or employment, which is commonly called Genius. The true Genius is a mind of large general powers, accidentally determined to some particular direction. Sir Joshua Reynolds, the great Painter of the present age, had the first fondness for his art excited by the perusal of Richardson's treatise.

By his mother's solicitation he was admitted into Westminster school, where he was soon distinguished. He was wont, says Sprat, to relate, "that he had this defect in his memory at that time, that his teachers never could bring it to retain the ordinary rules of grammar."

This is an instance of the natural desire of man to propagate a wonder. It is surely very difficult to tell any thing as it was heard, when Sprat could not refrain from amplifying a commodious incident, though the book to which he prefixed his narrative contained its confutation. A memory admitting some things, and rejecting others, an intellectual digestion that concocted the pulp of learning, but refused the husks, had the appearance of an instinctive elegance, of a particular provision made by Nature for literary politeness. But in the author's own honest relation, the marvel vanishes: he was, he says, such "an enemy to all constraint, that his master never could prevail on him to learn the rules without book." He does not tell that he could not learn the rules, but that, being able to perform his exercises without them, and being an "enemy to constraint," he spared himself the labour.

Among the English poets, Cowley, Milton, and Pope, might be said "to lisp in numbers;" and have given such early proofs, not

only of powers of language, but of comprehension of things, as to
more tardy minds seems scarcely credible. But of the learned
puerilities of Cowley there is no doubt, since a volume of his
poems was not only written but printed in his thirteenth year;
containing, with other poetical compositions, "The tragical His-
tory of Pyramus and Thisbe," written when he was ten years old;
and "Constantia and Philetus," written two years after.

*   *   *

In the year 1647, his "Mistress" was published; for he imagined,
as he declared in his preface to a subsequent edition, that "poets
are scarce thought freemen of their company without paying some
duties, or obliging themselves to be true to Love."

This obligation to amorous ditties owes, I believe, its original to
the fame of Petrarch, who, in an age rude and uncultivated, by
his tuneful homage to his Laura, refined the manners of the let-
tered world, and filled Europe with love and poetry. But the basis
of all excellence is truth: he that professes love ought to feel its
power. Petrarch was a real lover, and Laura doubtless deserved
his tenderness. Of Cowley, we are told by Barnes,[2] who had means
enough of information, that, whatever he may talk of his own
inflammability, and the variety of characters by which his heart
was divided, he in reality was in love but once, and then never had
resolution to tell his passion.

This consideration cannot but abate, in some measure, the
reader's esteem for the work and the author. To love excellence,
is natural; it is natural likewise for the lover to solicit reciprocal
regard by an elaborate display of his own qualifications. The
desire of pleasing has in different men produced actions of hero-
ism, and effusions of wit; but it seems as reasonable to appear the
champion as the poet of an "airy nothing," and to quarrel as to
write for what Cowley might have learned from his master Pindar
to call the "dream of a shadow."

It is surely not difficult, in the solitude of a college, or in the

[2] Joshua Barnes, Professor of Greek, Cambridge University, in the
preface to *Anacreon*, 1705, p. 32. See the quoted passage in G. B. Hill's
edition of Johnson's *Lives*, 1905, I, 6–7n.

bustle of the world, to find useful studies and serious employment. No man needs to be so burthened with life as to squander it in voluntary dreams of fictitious occurrences. The man that sits down to suppose himelf charged with treason or peculation, and heats his mind to an elaborate purgation of his character from crimes which he was never within the possibility of committing, differs only by the infrequency of his folly from him who praises beauty which he never saw, complains of jealousy which he never felt; supposes himself sometimes invited, and sometimes forsaken; fatigues his fancy, and ransacks his memory, for images which may exhibit the gaiety of hope, or the gloominess of despair, and dresses his imaginary Chloris or Phyllis sometimes in flowers fading as her beauty, and sometimes in gems lasting as her virtues.

*   *   *

A doctor of physic however he was made at Oxford, in December 1657; and in the commencement of the Royal Society, of which an account has been published by Dr. Birch,[3] he appears busy among the experimental philosophers with the title of Doctor Cowley.

There is no reason for supposing that he ever attempted practice; but his preparatory studies have contributed something to the honor of his country. Considering Botany as necessary to a physician, he retired into Kent to gather plants; and as the predominance of a favourite study affects all subordinate operations of the intellect, Botany in the mind of Cowley turned into poetry. He composed in Latin several books on Plants, of which the first and second display the qualities of Herbs, in elegiac verse; the third and fourth the beauties of Flowers in various measures; and in the fifth and sixth, the uses of Trees in heroick numbers.

At the same time were produced from the same university, the two great Poets, Cowley and Milton, of dissimilar genius, of opposite principles; but concurring in the cultivation of Latin poetry,

___

[3] Thomas Birch (1705–1766), divine, and secretary of the Royal Society, 1752–65. Johnson reviewed his History in the year of its publication (1756).

in which the English, till their works and May's poem[4] appeared, seemed unable to contest the palm with any other of the lettered nations.

If the Latin performances of Cowley and Milton be compared, for May I hold to be superior to both, the advantage seems to lie on the side of Cowley. Milton is generally content to express the thoughts of the ancients in their language; Cowley, without much loss of purity or elegance, accommodates the diction of Rome to his own conceptions.

*   *   *

Wit, like all other things subject by their nature to the choice of man, has its changes and fashions, and at different times takes different forms. About the beginning of the seventeenth century appeared a race of writers that may be termed the metaphysical poets; of whom, in a criticism on the works of Cowley, it is not improper to give some account.

The metaphysical poets were men of learning, and to shew their learning was their whole endeavour; but, unluckily resolving to shew it in rhyme, instead of writing poetry, they only wrote verses, and very often such verses as stood the trial of the finger better than of the ear; for the modulation was so imperfect, that they were only found to be verses by counting the syllables.

If the father of criticism has rightly denominated poetry $\tau\acute{\epsilon}\chi\nu\eta$ $\mu\iota\mu\eta\tau\iota\kappa\acute{\eta}$, *an imitative art,* these writers will, without great wrong, lose their right to the name of poets; for they cannot be said to have imitated any thing; they neither copied nature nor life; neither painted the forms of matter, nor represented the operations of intellect.

Those however who deny them to be poets, allow them to be wits. Dryden confesses of himself and his contemporaries, that they fall below Donne in wit, but maintains that they surpass him in poetry.[5]

If Wit be well described by Pope, as being, "that which has

---

[4] *Supplementum Lucani,* 1640, by Thomas May (1599–1650).
[5] *Essays, ed.* Ker, II, 102.

been often thought, but was never before so well expressed,"[6] they certainly never attained, nor ever sought it, for they endeavoured to be singular in their thoughts, and were careless of their diction. But Pope's account of wit is undoubtedly erroneous: he depresses it below its natural dignity, and reduces it from strength of thought to happiness of language.

If by a more noble and more adequate conception that be considered as Wit, which is at once natural and new, that which, though not obvious, is, upon its first production, acknowledged to be just; if it be that, which he that never found it, wonders how he missed; to wit of this kind the metaphysical poets have seldom risen. Their thoughts are often new, but seldom natural; they are not obvious, but neither are they just; and the reader, far from wondering that he missed them, wonders more frequently by what perverseness of industry they were ever found.

But Wit, abstracted from its effects upon the hearer, may be more rigorously and philosophically considered as a kind of *discordia concors*; a combination of dissimilar images, or discovery of occult resemblances in things apparently unlike. Of wit, thus defined, they have more than enough. The most heterogeneous ideas are yoked by violence together; nature and art are ransacked for illustrations, comparisons, and allusions; their learning instructs, and their subtilty surprises; but the reader commonly thinks his improvement dearly bought, and, though he sometimes admires, is seldom pleased.

From this account of their compositions it will be readily inferred, that they were not successful in representing or moving the affections. As they were wholly employed on something unexpected and surprising, they had no regard to that uniformity of sentiment which enables us to conceive and to excite the pains and the pleasure of other minds: they never enquired what, on any occasion, they should have said or done; but wrote rather as beholders than partakers of human nature; as Beings looking upon good and evil, impassive and at leisure; as Epicurean deities making remarks on the actions of men, and the vicissitudes of life, without interest and without emotion. Their courtship was void of

[6] *Essay on Criticism,* ll. 297–298.

fondness, and their lamentation of sorrow. Their wish was only to say what they hoped had been never said before.

Nor was the sublime more within their reach than the pathetick; for they never attempted that comprehension and expanse of thought which at once fills the whole mind, and of which the first effect is sudden astonishment, and the second rational admiration. Sublimity is produced by aggregation, and littleness by dispersion. Great thoughts are always general, and consist in positions not limited by exceptions, and in descriptions not descending to minuteness. It is with great propriety that Subtlety, which in its original import means exility of particles, is taken in its metaphorical meaning for nicety of distinction. Those writers who lay on the watch for novelty could have little hope of greatness; for great things cannot have escaped former observation. Their attempts were always analytick; they broke every image into fragments: and could no more represent, by their slender conceits and laboured particularities, the prospects of nature, or the scenes of life, than he, who dissects a sun-beam with a prism, can exhibit the wide effulgence of a summer noon.

What they wanted however of the sublime, they endeavoured to supply by hyperbole; their amplification had no limits; they left not only reason but fancy behind them; and produced combinations of confused magnificence, that not only could not be credited, but could not be imagined.

Yet great labour, directed by great abilities, is never wholly lost: if they frequently threw away their wit upon false conceits, they likewise sometimes struck out unexpected truth: if their conceits were far-fetched, they were often worth the carriage. To write on their plan, it was at least necessary to read and think. No man could be born a metaphysical poet, nor assume the dignity of a writer, by descriptions copied from descriptions, by imitations borrowed from imitations, by traditional imagery, and hereditary similies, by readiness of rhyme, and volubility of syllables.

In perusing the works of this race of authors, the mind is exercised either by recollection or inquiry; either something already learned is to be retrieved, or something new is to be examined. If their greatness seldom elevates, their acuteness often surprises; if

the imagination is not always gratified, at least the powers of re-
flection and comparison are employed; and in the mass of mate-
rials which ingenious absurdity has thrown together, genuine wit
and useful knowledge may be sometimes found, buried perhaps in
grossness of expression, but useful to those who know their value;
and such as, when they are expanded to perspicuity, and polished
to elegance, may give lustre to works which have more propriety
though less copiousness of sentiment.

*   *   *

Having thus endeavoured to exhibit a general representation of
the style and sentiments of the metaphysical poets, it is now proper
to examine particularly the works of Cowley, who was almost the
last of that race, and undoubtedly the best.

His Miscellanies contain a collection of short compositions, writ-
ten some as they were dictated by a mind at leisure, and some as
they were called forth by different occasions; with great variety of
style and sentiment, from burlesque levity to awful grandeur.
Such an assemblage of diversified excellence no other poet has
hitherto afforded. To choose the best, among many good, is one of
the most hazardous attempts of criticism. I know not whether
Scaliger himself has persuaded many readers to join with him in
his preference of the two favourite odes, which he estimates in his
raptures at the value of a kingdom.[7] I will however venture to
recommend Cowley's first piece, which ought to be inscribed *To
my muse,* for want of which the second couplet is without refer-
ence. When the title is added, there will still remain a defect; for
every piece ought to contain in itself whatever is necessary to make
it intelligible. Pope has some epitaphs without names; which are
therefore epitaphs to be let, occupied indeed for the present, but
hardly appropriated.

The ode on Wit is almost without a rival. It was about the time
of Cowley that *Wit,* which had been till then used for *Intellection,*

---

[7] Hill, in his edition of this *Life,* quotes (I, p. 35n) a passage from
the elder Scaliger, in which two of Horace's odes (IV.3 and III.9) are
judged sweeter than nectar and ambrosia, and which he would rather have
composed than be king of Tarracona.

in contradistinction to *Will,* took the meaning, whatever it be, which it now bears.

Of all the passages in which poets have exemplified their own precepts, none will easily be found of greater excellence than that in which Cowley condemns exuberance of Wit:

> Yet 'tis not to adorn and gild each part,
>   That shews more cost than art.
> Jewels at nose and lips but ill appear;
>   Rather than all things wit, let none be there.
>   Several lights will not be seen,
>   If there be nothing else between.
> Men doubt, because they stand so thick i' th' sky,
> If those be stars which paint the galaxy. . . .

*   *   *

The *Chronicle* is a composition unrivalled and alone: such gaiety of fancy, such facility of expression, such varied similitude, such a succession of images, and such a dance of words, it is vain to expect except from Cowley. His strength always appears in his agility; his volatility is not the flutter of a light, but the bound of an elastick mind. His levity never leaves his learning behind it; the moralist, the politician, and the critick, mingle their influence even in this airy frolick of genius. To such a performance Suckling could have brought the gaiety, but not the knowledge; Dryden could have supplied the knowledge, but not the gaiety.

The verses to Davenant, which are vigorously begun, and happily concluded, contain some hints of criticism very justly conceived and happily expressed. Cowley's critical abilities have not been sufficiently observed: the few decisions and remarks which his prefaces and his notes on the Davideis supply, were at that time accessions to English literature, and shew such skill as raises our wish for more examples.

The lines from Jersey are a very curious and pleasing specimen of the familiar descending to the burlesque.

His two metrical disquisitions *for* and *against* Reason, are no mean specimens of metaphysical poetry. The stanzas against knowl-

edge produce little conviction. In those which are intended to exalt
the human faculties, Reason has its proper task assigned it; that
of judging, not of things revealed, but of the reality of revela-
tion. . . .

Cowley seems to have had, what Milton is believed to have
wanted, the skill to rate his own performances by their just value,
and has therefore closed his Miscellanies with the verses upon
Crashaw, which apparently excel all that have gone before them,
and in which there are beauties which common authors may
justly think not only above their attainment, but above their am-
bition.

To the Miscellanies succeed the *Anacreontiques,* or paraphrasti-
cal translations of some little poems, which pass, however justly,
under the name of Anacreon. Of those songs dedicated to festivity
and gaiety, in which even the morality is voluptuous, and which
teach nothing but the enjoyment of the present day, he has given
rather a pleasing than a faithful representation, having retained
their spriteliness, but lost their simplicity. The Anacreon of Cow-
ley, like the Homer of Pope, has admitted the decoration of some
modern graces, by which he is undoubtedly made more amiable to
common readers, and perhaps, if they would honestly declare their
own perceptions, to far the greater part of those whom courtesy
and ignorance are content to style the Learned.

These little pieces will be found more finished in their kind
than any other of Cowley's works. The diction shews nothing of
the mould of time, and the sentiments are at no great distance
from our present habitudes of thought. Real mirth must be always
natural, and nature is uniform. Men have been wise in very dif-
ferent modes; but they have always laughed the same way.

Levity of thought naturally produced familiarity of language,
and the familiar part of language continues long the same: the
dialogue of comedy, when it is transcribed from popular manners
and real life, is read from age to age with equal pleasure. The
artifice of inversion, by which the established order of words is
changed, or of innovation, by which new words or new meanings
of words are introduced, is practised, not by those who talk to be
understood, but by those who write to be admired.

The Anacreontiques therefore of Cowley give now all the pleasure which they ever gave. If he was formed by nature for one kind of writing more than for another, his power seems to have been greatest in the familiar and the festive.

*   *   *

In the general review of Cowley's poetry it will be found, that he wrote with abundant fertility, but negligent or unskilful selection; with much thought; but with little imagery; that he is never pathetick, and rarely sublime, but always either ingenious or learned, either acute or profound.

It is said by Denham in his elegy,

> To him no author was unknown;
> Yet what he writ was all his own.

This wide position requires less limitation, when it is affirmed of Cowley, than perhaps of any other poet—He read much, and yet borrowed little.

His character of writing was indeed not his own: he unhappily adopted that which was predominant. He saw a certain way to present praise, and not sufficiently enquiring by what means the ancients have continued to delight through all the changes of human manners, he contented himself with a deciduous laurel, of which the verdure in its spring was bright and gay, but which time has been continually stealing from his brows.

He was in his own time considered as of unrivalled excellence. Clarendon represents him as having taken flight beyond all that went before him[8]; and Milton is said to have declared, that the three greatest English poets were Spenser, Shakspeare, and Cowley.

His manner he had in common with others: but his sentiments were his own. Upon every subject he thought for himself; and such was his copiousness of knowledge, that something at once

[8] Henry Hyde, first Earl of Clarendon (1609–74), in his autobiography, first published 1759. For the relevant quotation, see Hill's edition of Johnson's *Lives*, I, 56n and 58n.

remote and applicable rushed into his mind; yet it is not likely that
he always rejected a commodious idea merely because another had
used it: his known wealth was so great, that he might have bor-
rowed without loss of credit. . . .

*   *   *

It is related by Clarendon, that Cowley always acknowledged
his obligation to the learning and industry of Jonson; but I have
found no traces of Jonson in his works: to emulate Donne, appears
to have been his purpose; and from Donne he may have learned
that familiarity with religious images, and that light allusion to
sacred things, by which readers far short of sanctity are frequently
offended; and which would not be born in the present age, when
devotion, perhaps not more fervent, is more delicate. . . .

His diction was in his own time censured as negligent. He seems
not to have known, or not to have considered, that words being
arbitrary must owe their power to association, and have the influ-
ence, and that only, which custom has given them. Language is
the dress of thought; and as the noblest mien, or most graceful
action, would be degraded and obscured by a garb appropriated to
the gross employments of rusticks or mechanicks, so the most he-
roick sentiments will lose their efficacy, and the most splendid
ideas drop their magnificence, if they are conveyed by words used
commonly upon low and trivial occasions, debased by vulgar
mouths, and contaminated by inelegant applications.

Truth indeed is always truth, and reason is always reason; they
have an intrinsick and unalterable value, and constitute that intel-
lectual gold which defies destruction: but gold may be so con-
cealed in baser matter, that only a chymist can recover it; sense
may be so hidden in unrefined and plebeian words, that none but
philosophers can distinguish it; and both may be so buried in im-
purities, as not to pay the cost of their extraction.

*   *   *

After so much criticism on his Poems, the Essays which accom-
pany them must not be forgotten. What is said by Sprat of his
conversation, that no man could draw from it any suspicion of his

excellence in poetry, may be applied to these compositions. No author ever kept his verse and his prose at a greater distance from each other. His thoughts are natural, and his style has a smooth and placid equability, which has never yet obtained its due commendation. Nothing is far-sought, or hard-laboured; but all is easy without feebleness, and familiar without grossness.

It has been observed by Felton, in his Essay on the Classicks, that Cowley was beloved by every Muse that he courted; and that he has rivalled the Ancients in every kind of poetry but tragedy.[9]

It may be affirmed, without any encomiastick fervour, that he brought to his poetick labours a mind replete with learning, and that his pages are embellished with all the ornaments which books could supply; that he was the first who imparted to English numbers the enthusiasm of the greater ode, and the gaiety of the less; that he was equally qualified for spritely sallies, and for lofty flights; that he was among those who freed translation from servility, and, instead of following his author at a distance, walked by his side; and that if he left versification yet improvable, he left likewise from time to time such specimens of excellence as enabled succeeding poets to improve it.

[9] Henry Felton, *A Dissertation on Reading the Classics*, ed. of 1730, p. 27 [Hill].

FROM **Dryden**

Dryden may be properly considered as the father of English criticism, as the writer who first taught us to determine upon principles the merit of composition. Of our former poets, the greatest dramatist wrote without rules, conducted through life and nature by a genius that rarely misled, and rarely deserted him. Of the rest, those who knew the laws of propriety had neglected to teach them.

Two *Arts of English Poetry* were written in the days of Elizabeth by Webb and Puttenham,[1] from which something might be learned, and a few hints had been given by Jonson and Cowley; but Dryden's *Essay on Dramatick Poetry*[2] was the first regular and valuable treatise on the art of writing.

He who, having formed his opinions in the present age of English literature, turns back to peruse this dialogue, will not perhaps find much increase of knowledge, or much novelty of instruction; but he is to remember that critical principles were then in the hands of a few, who had gathered them partly from the Ancients,

[1] William Webbe, *A Discourse of English Poetrie*, 1586; George Puttenham, *The Arte of English Poesie*, 1589.
[2] *Of Dramatick Poesie, an Essay* (1668).

and partly from the Italians and French. The structure of dramatick poems was not then generally understood. Audiences applauded by instinct, and poets perhaps often pleased by chance.

A writer who obtains his full purpose loses himself in his own lustre. Of an opinion which is no longer doubted, the evidence ceases to be examined. Of an art universally practised, the first teacher is forgotten. Learning once made popular is no longer learning; it has the appearance of something which we have bestowed upon ourselves, as the dew appears to rise from the field which it refreshes.

To judge rightly of an author, we must transport ourselves to his time, and examine what were the wants of his contemporaries, and what were his means of supplying them. That which is easy at one time was difficult at another. Dryden at least imported his science, and gave his country what it wanted before; or rather, he imported only the materials, and manufactured them by his own skill.

The dialogue on the Drama was one of his first essays of criticism, written when he was yet a timorous candidate for reputation, and therefore laboured with that diligence which he might allow himself somewhat to remit, when his name gave sanction to his positions, and his awe of the public was abated, partly by custom, and partly by success. It will not be easy to find, in all the opulence of our language, a treatise so artfully variegated with successive representations of opposite probabilities, so enlivened with imagery, so brightned with illustrations. His portraits of the English dramatists are wrought with great spirit and diligence. The account of Shakspeare may stand as a perpetual model of encomiastick criticism;[3] exact without minuteness, and lofty without exaggeration. The praise lavished by Longinus, on the attestation of the heroes of Marathon, by Demosthenes, fades away before it.[4] In a few lines is exhibited a character, so extensive in its comprehension, and so curious in its limitations, that nothing can be

[3] Johnson quotes it in his own Preface to Shakespeare; cf. *ante*. p. 306–307.

[4] Longinus, *On the Sublime,* XVI; Demosthenes, *On the Crown,* 263. 11.

added, diminished, or reformed; nor can the editors and admirers of Shakspeare, in all their emulation of reverence, boast of much more than of having diffused and paraphrased this epitome of excellence, of having changed Dryden's gold for baser metal, of lower value though of greater bulk.

In this, and in all his other essays on the same subject, the criticism of Dryden is the criticism of a poet; not a dull collection of theorems, nor a rude detection of faults, which perhaps the censor was not able to have committed; but a gay and vigorous dissertation, where delight is mingled with instruction, and where the author proves his right of judgement, by his power of performance.

The different manner and effect with which critical knowledge may be conveyed, was perhaps never more clearly exemplified than in the performances of Rymer and Dryden. It was said of a dispute[5] between two mathematicians, "malim cum Scaligero errare, quam cum Clavio recte sapere;" that *it was more eligible to go wrong with one than right with the other*. A tendency of the same kind every mind must feel at the perusal of Dryden's prefaces and Rymer's discourses. With Dryden we are wandering in quest of Truth; whom we find, if we find her at all, drest in the graces of elegance; and if we miss her, the labour of the pursuit rewards itself; we are led only through fragrance and flowers: Rymer, without taking a nearer, takes a rougher way; every step is to be made through thorns and brambles; and Truth, if we meet her, appears repulsive by her mien, and ungraceful by her habit. Dryden's criticism has the majesty of a queen; Rymer's has the ferocity of a tyrant.

As he had studied with great diligence the art of poetry, and enlarged or rectified his notions, by experience perpetually increasing, he had his mind stored with principles and observations; he poured out his knowledge with little labour; for of labour, notwithstanding the multiplicity of his productions, there is sufficient

---

[5] About the correction of the Calendar, ordered by Gregory XIII. Christopher Clavius (1537–1612), strictly speaking, was the only mathematician. Joseph Scaliger (1540–1609) was a great classical scholar and an authority on Greek and Latin writing on chronological matters (*De Emendatione Temporum*, 1583; *Thesaurus Temporum*, 1606).

reason to suspect that he was not a lover. To write *con amore*, with
fondness for the employment, with perpetual touches and re-
touches, with unwillingness to take leave of his own idea, and an
unwearied pursuit of unattainable perfection, was, I think, no part
of his character.

His Criticism may be considered as general or occasional. In his
general precepts, which depend upon the nature of things, and
the structure of the human mind, he may doubtless be safely rec-
ommended to the confidence of the reader; but his occasional and
particular positions were sometimes interested, sometimes negli-
gent, and sometimes capricious. It is not without reason that
Trapp, speaking[6] of the praises which he bestows on Palamon and
Arcite, says,

> Novimus judicium Drydeni de poemate quodam *Chau-*
> *ceri*, pulchro sane illo, et admodum laudando, nimirum
> quod non modo vere epicum sit, sed *Iliada* etiam atque
> *Æneida* æquet, imo superet. Sed novimus eodem tempore
> viri illius maximi non semper accuratissimas esse censuras,
> nec ad severissimam critices normam exactas: illo judice id
> plerumque optimum est, quod nunc præ manibus habet,
> et in quo nunc occupatur.[7]

He is therefore by no means constant to himself. His defence
and desertion of dramatick rhyme is generally known. *Spence*,[8]
in his remarks on Pope's Odyssey, produces what he thinks an
unconquerable quotation from Dryden's preface to the Æneid, in
favour of translating an epick poem into blank verse; but he forgets

[6] In *Praelectiones Poeticae*, 1722, p. 386.
[7] Translated by Trapp, *Lectures on Poetry*, 1742, p. 348, as follows:
"We know our countryman Mr. Dryden's judgment about a poem of
Chaucer's, truly beautiful indeed and worthy of praise; namely that it was
not only equal, but even superior to the *Iliad* and *Aeneid*. But we know
likewise that his opinion was not always the most accurate, nor formed
upon the severest rules of criticism. What was in hand was generally most
in esteem; if it was uppermost in his thoughts it was so in his judgment
too."
[8] *Essay*, 1737, p. 121.

that when his author attempted the Iliad, some years afterwards, he departed from his own decision, and translated into rhyme.

When he has any objection to obviate, or any license to defend, he is not very scrupulous about what he asserts, nor very cautious, if the present purpose be served, not to entangle himself in his own sophistries. But when all arts are exhausted, like other hunted animals, he sometimes stands at bay; when he cannot disown the grossness of one of his plays, he declares that he knows not any law that prescribes morality to a comick poet.

His remarks on ancient or modern writers are not always to be trusted. His parallel of the versification of Ovid with that of Claudian has been very justly censured by Sewel.[9] His comparison of the first line of Virgil with the first of Statius is not happier.[10] Virgil, he says, is soft and gentle, and would have thought Statius mad if he had heard him thundering out

Quae superimposito moles geminata colosso[11]

Statius perhaps heats himself, as he proceeds, to exaggerations somewhat hyperbolical; but undoubtedly Virgil would have been too hasty, if he had condemned him to straw for one sounding line. Dryden wanted an instance, and the first that occurred was imprest into the service.

What he wishes to say, he says at hazard; he cited Gorbuduc, [sic] which he had never seen; gives a false account of Chapman's versification; and discovers in the preface to his Fables that he translated the first book of the Iliad, without knowing what was in the second.[12]

It will be difficult to prove that Dryden ever made any great advances in literature. As having distinguished himself at Westminster under the tuition of Busby, who advanced his scholars to a height of knowledge very rarely attained in grammar-schools, he

---

[9] Preface to Ovid's *Metamorphoses*. [Johnson's note]

[10] *A Parallel of Poetry and Painting. Essays*, ed. Ker, II, 149.

[11] Statius, *Sylvae*, I. i. 1. "What huge mass, doubled by the colossus set upon it."

[12] *Essays*, ed. Ker, I, 5, 12; II, 254.

resided afterwards at Cambridge, it is not to be supposed, that his skill in the ancient languages was deficient, compared with that of common students; but his scholastick acquisitions seem not proportionate to his opportunities and abilities. He could not, like Milton or Cowley, have made his name illustrious merely by his learning. He mentions but few books, and those such as lie in the beaten track of regular study; from which if ever he departs, he is in danger of losing himself in unknown regions.

In his Dialogue on the Drama, he pronounces with great confidence that the Latin tragedy of Medea is not Ovid's, because it is not sufficiently interesting and pathetick. He might have determined the question upon surer evidence; for it is quoted by Quintilian as the work of Seneca; and the only line which remains of Ovid's play, for one line is left us, is not there to be found. There was therefore no need of the gravity of conjecture, or the discussion of plot or sentiment, to find what was already known upon higher authority than such discussions can ever reach.

His literature, though not always free from ostentation, will be commonly found either obvious, and made his own by the art of dressing it; or superficial, which, by what he gives, shews what he wanted; or erroneous, hastily collected, and negligently scattered.

Yet it cannot be said that his genius is ever unprovided of matter, or that his fancy languishes in penury of ideas. His works abound with knowledge, and sparkle with illustrations. There is scarcely any science or faculty that does not supply him with occasional images and lucky similitudes; every page discovers a mind very widely acquainted both with art and nature, and in full possession of great stores of intellectual wealth. Of him that knows much, it is natural to suppose that he has read with diligence; yet I rather believe that the knowledge of Dryden was gleaned from accidental intelligence and various conversation, by a quick apprehension, a judicious selection, and a happy memory, a keen appetite of knowledge, and a powerful digestion; by vigilance that permitted nothing to pass without notice, and a habit of reflection that suffered nothing useful to be lost. A mind like Dryden's, always curious, always active, to which every understanding was proud to be associated, and of which every one solicited the regard, by an

ambitious display of himself, had a more pleasant, perhaps a nearer
way, to knowledge than by the silent progress of solitary reading.
I do not suppose that he despised books, or intentionally neglected
them; but that he was carried out, by the impetuosity of his
genius, to more vivid and speedy instructors; and that his studies
were rather desultory and fortuitous than constant and systemati-
cal.

It must be confessed that he scarcely ever appears to want book-
learning but when he mentions books; and to him may be trans-
ferred the praise which he gives his master Charles:

> His conversation, wit, and parts,
> His knowledge in the noblest useful arts,
>   Were such, dead authors could not give,
>   But habitudes of those that live;
> Who, lighting him, did greater lights receive:
>   He drain'd from all, and all they knew,
> His apprehension quick, his judgement true:
>   That the most learn'd with shame confess
> His knowledge more, his reading only less.[13]

Of all this, however, if the proof be demanded, I will not un-
dertake to give it; the atoms of probability, of which my opinion
has been formed, lie scattered over all his works; and by him who
thinks the question worth his notice, his works must be perused
with very close attention.

Criticism, either didactick or defensive, occupies almost all his
prose, except those pages which he has devoted to his patrons; but
none of his prefaces were ever thought tedious. They have not the
formality of a settled style, in which the first half of the sentence
betrays the other. The clauses are never balanced, nor the periods
modelled; every word seems to drop by chance, though it falls into
its proper place. Nothing is cold or languid; the whole is airy,
animated, and vigorous; what is little, is gay; what is great, is
splendid. He may be thought to mention himself too frequently;
but while he forces himself upon our esteem, we cannot refuse

[13] *Threnodia Augustalis*, ll. 337 ff.

him to stand high in his own. Every thing is excused by the play of images and the spriteliness of expression. Though all is easy, nothing is feeble; though all seems careless, there is nothing harsh; and though, since his earlier works, more than a century has passed, they have nothing yet uncouth or obsolete.

He who writes much, will not easily escape a manner, such a recurrence of particular modes as may be easily noted. Dryden is always *another and the same*,[14] he does not exhibit a second time the same elegances in the same form, nor appears to have any art other than that of expressing with clearness what he thinks with vigour. His style could not easily be imitated, either seriously or ludicrously; for, being always equable and always varied, it has no prominent or discriminative characters. The beauty who is totally free from disproportion of parts and features, cannot be ridiculed by an overcharged resemblance.

From his prose, however, Dryden derives only his accidental and secondary praise; the veneration with which his name is pronounced by every cultivator of English literature, is paid to him as he refined the language, improved the sentiments, and tuned the numbers of English Poetry.

After about half a century of forced thoughts, and rugged metre, some advances toward nature and harmony had been already made by Waller and Denham; they had shewn that long discourses in rhyme grew more pleasing when they were broken into couplets, and that verse consisted not only in the number but the arrangement of syllables.

But though they did much, who can deny that they left much to do? Their works were not many, nor were their minds of very ample comprehension. More examples of more modes of composition were necessary for the establishment of regularity, and the introduction of propriety in word and thought.

Every language of a learned nation necessarily divides itself into diction scholastick and popular, grave and familiar, elegant and gross; and from a nice distinction of these different parts, arises a great part of the beauty of style. But if we except a few minds, the favourites of nature, to whom their own original rectitude was

[14] A phrase from Pope's *Dunciad*, Bk. III, 32 (*Poems*, ed. Butt, 1963).

in the place of rules, this delicacy of selection was little known to our authors; our speech lay before them in a heap of confusion, and every man took for every purpose what chance might offer him.

There was therefore before the time of Dryden no poetical diction, no system of words at once refined from the grossness of domestick use, and free from the harshness of terms appropriated to particular arts. Words too familiar, or too remote, defeat the purpose of a poet. From those sounds which we hear on small or on coarse occasions, we do not easily receive strong impressions, or delightful images; and words to which we are nearly strangers, whenever they occur, draw that attention on themselves which they should transmit to things.

Those happy combinations of words which distinguish poetry from prose, had been rarely attempted; we had few elegances or flowers of speech, the roses had not yet been plucked from the bramble, or different colours had not been joined to enliven one another.

It may be doubted whether Waller and Denham could have over-born the prejudices which had long prevailed, and which even then were sheltered by the protection of Cowley. The new versification, as it was called, may be considered as owing its establishment to Dryden; from whose time it is apparent that English poetry has had no tendency to relapse to its former savageness.

The affluence and comprehension of our language is very illustriously displayed in our poetical translations of Ancient Writers; a work which the French seem to relinquish in despair, and which we were long unable to perform with dexterity. Ben Jonson thought it necessary to copy Horace almost word by word; Feltham, his contemporary and adversary, considers it as indispensably requisite in a translation to give line for line. It is said that Sandys, whom Dryden calls the best versifier of the last age, has struggled hard to comprise every book of his English Metamorphoses in the same number of verses with the original. Holyday had nothing in view but to shew that he understood his author, with so little regard to the grandeur of his diction, or the volubility of his numbers, that his metres can hardly be called verses; they cannot be read without reluctance, nor will the labour always be rewarded by understanding them. Cowley saw that such *copyers* were a *servile race*;[15] he asserted his liberty, and spread his wings so boldly that he left his authors. It was reserved for Dryden to fix the limits of poetical liberty, and give us just rules and examples of translation.

When languages are formed upon different principles, it is impossible that the same modes of expression should always be elegant in both. While they run on together, the closest translation may be considered as the best; but when they divaricate, each must take its natural course. Where correspondence cannot be obtained, it is necessary to be content with something equivalent. *Translation therefore,* says Dryden, *is not so loose as paraphrase, nor so close as metaphrase.*[16]

All polished languages have different styles; the concise, the diffuse, the lofty, and the humble. In the proper choice of style consists the resemblance which Dryden principally exacts from the translator. He is to exhibit his author's thoughts in such a dress of diction as the author would have given them, had his language been English: rugged magnificence is not to be softened: hyperbolical ostentation is not to be repressed, nor sententious affectation to have its points blunted. A translator is to be like his author: it is not his business to excel him.

The reasonableness of these rules seems sufficient for their vindication; and the effects produced by observing them were so happy, that I know not whether they were ever opposed but by Sir Edward Sherburne, a man whose learning was greater than his powers of poetry; and who, being better qualified to give the meaning than the spirit of Seneca, has introduced his version of three tragedies by a defence of close translation. The authority of Horace,[17] which the new translators cited in defence of their practice, he has, by a judicious explanation, taken fairly from them; but reason wants not Horace to support it.

[15] Preface to *Pindaric Odes.*
[16] Dedication of the *Æneis.* In *Essays,* ed. W. P. Ker, II, 227.
[17] Horace, *Ars Poetica,* l. 133: "nor make it your prime care to render word for word."

It seldom happens that all the necessary causes concur to any great effect: will is wanting to power, or power to will, or both are impeded by external obstructions. The exigences in which Dryden was condemned to pass his life, are reasonably supposed to have blasted his genius, to have driven out his works in a state of immaturity, and to have intercepted the full-blown elegance which longer growth would have supplied.

Poverty, like other rigid powers, is sometimes too hastily accused. If the excellence of Dryden's works was lessened by his indigence, their number was increased; and I know not how it will be proved, that if he had written less he would have written better; or that indeed he would have undergone the toil of an author, if he had not been solicited by something more pressing than the love of praise.

*   *   *

In a general survey of Dryden's labours, he appears to have had a mind very comprehensive by nature, and much enriched with acquired knowledge. His compositions are the effects of a vigorous genius operating upon large materials.

The power that predominated in his intellectual operations, was rather strong reason than quick sensibility. Upon all occasions that were presented, he studied rather than felt, and produced sentiments not such as Nature enforces, but meditation supplies. With the simple and elemental passions, as they spring separate in the mind, he seems not much acquainted; and seldom describes them but as they are complicated by the various relations of society, and confused in the tumults and agitations of life.

What he says of love may contribute to the explanation of his character:

> Love various minds does variously inspire;
> It stirs in gentle bosoms gentle fire,
> Like that of incense on the altar laid;
> But raging flames tempestuous souls invade,
> A fire which every windy passion blows;
> With pride it mounts, or with revenge it glows.[18]

[18] *Tyrannic Love*, II. iii.

Dryden's was not one of the *gentle bosoms*: Love, as it subsists
in itself, with no tendency but to the person loved, and wishing
only for correspondent kindness; such love as shuts out all other
interest; the Love of the Golden Age, was too soft and subtle to
put his faculties in motion. He hardly conceived it but in its tur-
bulent effervescence with some other desires; when it was in-
flamed by rivalry, or obstructed by difficulties: when it invigorated
ambition, or exasperated revenge.

He is therefore, with all his variety of excellence, not often
pathetick; and had so little sensibility of the power of effusions
purely natural, that he did not esteem them in others. Simplicity
gave him no pleasure; and for the first part of his life he looked on
Otway with contempt, though at last, indeed very late, he con-
fessed that in his play *there was Nature, which is the chief
beauty.*[19]

We do not always know our own motives. I am not certain
whether it was not rather the difficulty which he found in exhibit-
ing the genuine operations of the heart, than a servile submission
to an injudicious audience, that filled his plays with false magnifi-
cence. It was necessary to fix attention; and the mind can be cap-
tivated only by recollection, or by curiosity; by reviving natural
sentiments, or impressing new appearances of things: sentences
were readier at his call than images; he could more easily fill the
ear with some splendid novelty, than awaken those ideas that
slumber in the heart.

The favourite exercise of his mind was ratiocination; and, that
argument might not be too soon at an end, he delighted to talk of
liberty and necessity, destiny and contingence; these he discusses
in the language of the school with so much profundity, that the
terms which he uses are not always understood. It is indeed learn-
ing, but learning out of place.

When once he had engaged himself in disputation, thoughts
flowed in on either side: he was now no longer at a loss; he had
always objections and solutions at command; *verbaque provisam*

[19] *A Parallel,* etc., *Essays,* ed. Ker, II, 145.

rem[20]—give him matter for his verse, and he finds without difficulty verse for his matter.

In Comedy, for which he professes himself not naturally qualified, the mirth which he excites will perhaps not be found so much to arise from any original humour, or peculiarity of character nicely distinguished and diligently pursued, as from incidents and circumstances, artifices and surprizes; from jests of action rather than of sentiment. What he had of humorous or passionate, he seems to have had not from nature, but from other poets; if not always as a plagiary, at least as an imitator.

Next to argument, his delight was in wild and daring sallies of sentiment, in the irregular and excentrick violence of wit. He delighted to tread upon the brink of meaning, where light and darkness begin to mingle; to approach the precipice of absurdity, and hover over the abyss of unideal vacancy. This inclination sometimes produced nonsense, which he knew, as,

> Move swiftly, sun, and fly a lover's pace,
> Leave weeks and months behind thee in thy race.[21]

> Amariel flies . . .
> To guard thee from the demons of the air;
> My flaming sword above them to display,
> All keen, and ground upon the edge of day.[22]

And sometimes it issued in absurdities, of which perhaps he was not conscious:

> Then we upon our orb's last verge shall go,
>   And see the ocean leaning on the sky;
> From thence our rolling neighbours we shall know,
>   And on the lunar world securely pry.[23]

[20] Horace, *Ars Poetica*, l. 311.
[21] *Conquest of Granada*, Pt. 2, V. ii.
[22] *Tyrannic Love*, IV. i.
[23] *Annus Mirabilis*, st. 164.

These lines have no meaning; but may we not say, in imitation of Cowley on another book,

> 'Tis so like *sense* 'twil serve the turn as well? [24]

This endeavour after the grand and the new, produced many sentiments either great or bulky, and many images either just or splendid:

> I am as free as Nature first made man,
> Ere the base laws of servitude began,
> When wild in woods the noble savage ran.[25]

> 'Tis but because the Living death ne'er knew,
> They fear to prove it as a thing that's new:
> Let me th' experiment before you try,
> I'll show you first how easy 'tis to die.[26]

> There with a forest of their darts he strove,
> And stood like *Capaneus* defying Jove;
> With his broad sword the boldest beating down,
> While Fate grew pale lest he should win the town,
> And turn'd the iron leaves of his dark book
> To make new dooms, or mend what it mistook.[27]

> I beg no pity for this mouldering clay;
> For if you give it burial, there it takes
> Possession of your earth;
> If burnt, and scatter'd in the air, the winds
> That strew my dust diffuse my royalty,
> And spread me o'er your clime; for where one atom
> Of mine shall light, know there Sebastian reigns.[28]

Of these quotations the two first may be allowed to be great, the two later only tumid.

[24] *Ode to Mr. Hobbes.*
[25] *Conquest of Granada,* Pt. 1, I. i.
[26] *Tyrannic Love,* V. i.
[27] *Ibid.,* I. i.
[28] *Don Sebastian,* I. i.

Of such selection there is no end. I will add only a few more passages; of which the first, though it may perhaps not be quite clear in prose, is not too obscure for poetry, as the meaning that it has is noble:

> No, there is a necessity in Fate,
> Why still the brave bold man is fortunate;
> He keeps his object ever full in sight,
> And that assurance holds him firm and right;
> True, 'tis a narrow way that leads to bliss,
> But right before there is no precipice;
> Fear makes men look aside, and so their footing miss.[29]

Of the images which the two following citations afford, the first is elegant, the second magnificent; whether either be just, let the reader judge:

> What precious drops are these,
> Which silently each other's track pursue,
> Bright as young diamonds in their infant dew? [30]

> "Resign your castle."
> "Enter, brave Sir; for when you speak the word,
> The gates shall open of their own accord;
> The genius of the place its Lord shall meet,
> And bow its towery forehead at your feet." [31]

These bursts of extravagance, Dryden calls the *Dalilahs* of the Theatre; and owns that many noisy lines of Maximin and Alamanzor call out for vengeance upon him; but *I knew,* says he, *that they were bad enough to please, even when I wrote them.*[32] There is surely reason to suspect that he pleased himself as well as his audience; and that these, like the harlots of other men, had his love, though not his approbation.

[29] *Conquest of Granada,* Pt. 1, IV. ii.
[30] *Ibid.,* Pt. 2, III. i.
[31] *Ibid.,* Pt. 2, III. iii.
[32] Dedication of *The Spanish Friar. Works,* 1883, VI, 406.

He had sometimes faults of a less generous and splendid kind. He makes, like almost all other poets, very frequent use of mythology, and sometimes connects religion and fable too closely without distinction.

He descends to display his knowledge with pedantick ostentation; as when, in translating Virgil, he says, *tack to the larboard*— and *veer starboard;*[33] and talks, in another work, of *virtue spooming before the wind.*[34] His vanity now and then betrays his ignorance:

> They Nature's king through Nature's opticks view'd;
> Revers'd they view'd him lessen'd to their eyes.[35]

He had heard of reversing a telescope, and unluckily reverses the object.

He is sometimes unexpectedly mean. When he describes the Supreme Being as moved by prayer to stop the Fire of London, what is his expression?

> A hollow crystal pyramid he takes,
>   In firmamental waters dipp'd above,
> Of this a broad *extinguisher* he makes,
>   And *hoods* the flames that to their quarry strove.[36]

When he describes the Last Day, and the decisive tribunal, he intermingles this image:

> When rattling bones together fly,
> From the four quarters of the sky.[37]

It was indeed never in his power to resist the temptation of a jest. In his Elegy on Cromwell:

[33] *Æneid*, III. 525.
[34] *The Hind and the Panther*, III, 96.
[35] *Ibid.*, I, 57.
[36] *Annus Mirabilis*, st. 281.
[37] *Ode to Mrs. Killigrew*, l. 184.

No sooner was the Frenchman's cause embrac'd,
Than the *light Monsieur* the *grave Don* outweigh'd;
His fortune turn'd the scale.[38]

He had a vanity, unworthy of his abilities, to shew, as may be suspected, the rank of the company with whom he lived, by the use of French words, which had then crept into conversation; such as *fraicheur* for *coolness, fougue* for *turbulence,*[39] and a few more, none of which the language has incorporated or retained. They continue only where they stood first, perpetual warnings to future innovators.

These are his faults of affectation; his faults of negligence are beyond recital. Such is the unevenness of his compositions, that ten lines are seldom found together without something of which the reader is ashamed. Dryden was no rigid judge of his own pages; he seldom struggled after supreme excellence, but snatched in haste what was within his reach; and when he could content others, was himself contented. He did not keep present to his mind, an idea of pure perfection; nor compare his works, such as they were, with what they might be made. He knew to whom he should be opposed. He had more musick than Waller, more vigour than Denham, and more nature than Cowley; and from his contemporaries he was in no danger. Standing therefore in the highest place, he had no care to rise by contending with himself; but while there was no name above his own, was willing to enjoy fame on the easiest terms.

He was no lover of labour. What he thought sufficient, he did not stop to make better; and allowed himself to leave many parts unfinished, in confidence that the good lines would overbalance the bad. What he had once written, he dismissed from his thoughts; and, I believe, there is no example to be found of any correction or improvement made by him after publication. The hastiness of his productions might be the effect of necessity; but his subsequent neglect could hardly have any other cause than impatience of study. . . .

[38] *On the Death of Cromwell*, st. 23.
[39] *On the Coronation*, l. 101; *Astraea Redux*, l. 203.

Of Dryden's works it was said by Pope,[40] that *he could select from them better specimens of every mode of poetry than any other English writer could supply*. Perhaps no nation ever produced a writer that enriched his language with such variety of models. To him we owe the improvement, perhaps the completion of our metre, the refinement of our language, and much of the correctness of our sentiments. By him we were taught *sapere et fari*, to think naturally and express forcibly. Though Davies has reasoned in rhyme before him, it may be perhaps maintained that he was the first who joined argument with poetry. He shewed us the true bounds of a translator's liberty. What was said of Rome, adorned by Augustus, may be applied by an easy metaphor to English poetry embellished by Dryden, *lateritiam invenit, marmoream reliquit*,[41] he found it brick, and he left it marble.

[40] Perhaps to Spence: not located.
[41] Suetonius, *Augustus*, XXIX.

FROM Smith

Edmund Smith is one of those lucky writers who have, without much labour, attained high reputation, and who are mentioned with reverence rather for the possession than the exertion of uncommon abilities.

Of his life little is known; and that little claims no praise but what can be given to intellectual excellence, seldom employed to any virtuous purpose. His character, as given by Mr. Oldisworth,[1] with all the partiality of friendship, . . . is said by Dr. Burton to show *what fine things one man of parts can say of another;* . . . I shall subjoin such little memorials as accident has enabled me to collect.

[Johnson here transcribes Oldisworth's eulogistic sketch at length, and then proceeds with "a plainer tale," as follows]

*   *   *

Edmund Neal, known by the name of Smith, was born at Handley, the seat of the Lechmeres, in Worcestershire. The year of his birth is uncertain.

[1] William Oldisworth (1680–1734), author, translator, and editor of the Tory *Examiner.*

He was educated at Westminster. It is known to have been the practice of Dr. Busby to detain those youths long at school, of whom he had formed the highest expectations. Smith took his Master's degree on the 8th of July 1696: he therefore was probably admitted into the university in 1689, when we may suppose him twenty years old.

His reputation for literature in his college was such as has been told; but the indecency and licentiousness of his behaviour drew upon him, Dec. 24, 1694, while he was yet only Batchelor, a publick admonition, entered upon record, in order to his expulsion. Of this reproof the effect is not known. He was probably less notorious. At Oxford, as we all know, much will be forgiven to literary merit; and of that he had exhibited sufficient evidence by his excellent ode on the death of the great Orientalist, Dr. Pocock, who died in 1691, and whose praise must have been written by Smith when he had been yet but two years in the university.

This ode, which closed the second volume of the *Musæ Anglicanæ*, though perhaps some objections may be made to its Latinity, is by far the best Lyrick composition in that collection; nor do I know where to find it equalled among the modern writers. It expresses, with great felicity, images not classical in classical diction: its digressions and returns have been deservedly recommended by Trapp as models for imitation.[2]

*   *   *

He proceeded to take his degree of Master of Arts July 8, 1696. Of the exercises which he performed on that occasion, I have not heard any thing memorable.

As his years advanced, he advanced in reputation: for he continued to cultivate his mind, though he did not amend his irregularities, by which he gave so much offence, that, April 24, 1700, the Dean and Chapter declared "the place of Mr. Smith void, he having been convicted of riotous misbehaviour in the house of Mr. Cole an apothecary; but it was referred to the Dean

[2] Joseph Trapp (1679–1747), in *Praelectiones Poeticae,* 1711 and later, his lectures as Oxford Professor of Poetry.

when and upon what occasion the sentence should be put in execution."

Thus tenderly was he treated: the governors of his college could hardly keep him, and yet wished that he would not force them to drive him away.

Some time afterwards he assumed an appearance of decency; in his own phrase, he *whitened* himself, having a desire to obtain the censorship, an office of honour and some profit in the college; but when the election came, the preference was given to Mr. *Foulkes,* his junior; the same, I suppose, that joined with *Freind* in an edition of part of Demosthenes; the censor is a tutor, and it was not thought proper to trust the superintendance of others to a man who took so little care of himself.

From this time Smith employed his malice and his wit against the Dean, Dr. Aldrich,[3] whom he considered as the opponent of his claim. Of his lampoon upon him, I once heard a single line too gross to be repeated.

But he was still a genius and a scholar, and Oxford was unwilling to lose him; he was endured, with all his pranks and his vices, two years longer; but on Dec. 20, 1705, at the instance of all the canons, the sentence declared five years before was put in execution.

The execution was, I believe, silent and tender; for one of his friends, from whom I learned much of his life, appeared not to know it.

He was now driven to London, where he associated himself with the Whigs, whether because they were in power, or because the Tories had expelled him, or because he was a Whig by principle, may perhaps be doubted. He was however caressed by men of great abilities, whatever were their party, and was supported by the liberality of those who delighted in his conversation.

There was once a design hinted at by Oldisworth, to have made him useful. One evening, as he was sitting with a friend at a tavern, he was called down by the waiter; and, having staid some

[3] Henry Aldrich (1647–1710), Dean of Christ Church, Oxford, and an excellent musician.

time below, came up thoughtful. After a pause, said he to his friend, "He that wanted me below was Addison, whose business was to tell me that a History of the Revolution was intended, and to propose that I should undertake it. I said, what shall I do with the character of Lord Sunderland?[4] and Addison immediately returned, When, Rag, were you drunk last? and went away."

Captain *Rag* was a name which he got at Oxford by his negligence of dress.

This story I heard from the late Mr. Clark of Lincoln's Inn, to whom it was told by the friend of Smith.

Such scruples might debar him from some profitable employments; but as they could not deprive him of any real esteem, they left him many friends; and no man was ever better introduced to the theatre than he, who, in that violent conflict of parties, had a Prologue and Epilogue from the first wits on either side.

But learning and nature will now and then take different courses. His play[5] pleased the criticks, and the criticks only. It was, as Addison has recorded, hardly heard the third night. Smith had indeed trusted entirely to his merit; had ensured no band of applauders, nor used any artifice to force success, and found that naked excellence was not sufficient for its own support.

The play, however, was bought by Lintot, who advanced the price from fifty guineas, the current rate, to sixty; and Halifax, the general patron, accepted the dedication. Smith's indolence kept him from writing the dedication, till Lintot, after fruitless importunity, gave notice that he would publish the play without it. Now therefore it was written; and Halifax expected the author with his book, and had prepared to reward him with a place of three hundred pounds a year. Smith, by pride, or caprice, or indolence, or bashfulness, neglected to attend him, though doubtless warned and pressed by his friends, and at last missed his reward by not going to solicit it.

Addison has, in the *Spectator*, mentioned the neglect of Smith's

---

[4] Probably Robert Spencer, second Earl (1640–1702), a notoriously crafty and unscrupulous politician and intriguer.

[5] *Phaedra and Hippolitus*, 1707–08. The Prologue was written by Addison, the Epilogue by Prior.

tragedy as disgraceful to the nation, and imputes it to the fondness for operas then prevailing.[6] The authority of Addison is great; yet the voice of the people, when to please the people is the purpose, deserves regard. In this question, I cannot but think the people in the right. The fable is mythological, a story which we are accustomed to reject as false, and the manners are so distant from our own, that we know them not from sympathy, but by study: the ignorant do not understand the action, the learned regard it as a school-boy's tale; *incredulus odi*. What I cannot for a moment believe, I cannot for a moment behold with interest or anxiety. The sentiments thus remote from life, are removed yet further by the diction, which is too luxuriant and splendid for dialogue, and envelopes the thoughts rather than displays them. It is a scholar's play, such as may please the reader rather than the spectator; the work of a vigorous and elegant mind, accustomed to please itself with its own conceptions, but of little acquaintance with the course of life. . . .

In 1709, a year after the exhibition of *Phaedra*, died John Philips, the friend and fellow-collegian of Smith, who, on that occasion, wrote a poem, which justice must place among the best elegies which our language can shew, an elegant mixture of fondness and admiration, of dignity and softness. There are some passages too ludicrous; but every human performance has its faults.

This elegy it was the mode among his friends to purchase for a guinea; and, as his acquaintance was numerous, it was a very profitable poem.

Of his *Pindar,* mentioned by Oldisworth, I have never otherwise heard. His *Longinus* he intended to accompany with some illustrations, and had selected his instances of the false *Sublime* from the works of Blackmore.

He resolved to try again the fortune of the Stage, with the story of Lady Jane Grey. It is not unlikely that his experience of the inefficacy and incredibility of a mythological tale, might determine him to choose an action from English History, at no great distance from our own times, which was to end in a real event, produced by the operation of known characters.

⁶ *Spectator,* no. 18 (March 21, 1711).

A subject will not easily occur that can give more opportunities of informing the understanding, for which Smith was unquestionably qualified, or for moving the passions, in which I suspect him to have had less power.

Having formed his plan, and collected materials, he declared that a few months would complete his design; and, that he might pursue his work with less frequent avocations, he was, in June 1710, invited by Mr. George Ducket to his house at Gartham in Wiltshire. Here he found such opportunities of indulgence as did not much forward his studies, and particularly some strong ale, too delicious to be resisted. He ate and drank till he found himself plethorick: and then, resolving to ease himself by evacuation, he wrote to an apothecary in the neighbourhood a prescription of a purge so forcible, that the apothecary thought it his duty to delay it till he had given notice of its danger. Smith, not pleased with the contradiction of a shopman, and boastful of his own knowledge, treated the notice with rude contempt, and swallowed his own medicine, which, in July 1710, brought him to the grave. He was buried at Gartham.

*   *   *

Of Smith I can yet say a little more. He was a man of such estimation among his companions, that the casual censures or praises which he dropped in conversation were considered, like those of Scaliger, as worthy of preservation.

He had great readiness and exactness of criticism, and by a cursory glance over a new composition would exactly tell all its faults and beauties.

He was remarkable for the power of reading with great rapidity, and of retaining with great fidelity what he so easily collected.

He therefore always knew what the present question required; and when his friends expressed their wonder at his acquisitions, made in a state of apparent negligence and drunkenness, he never discovered his hours of reading or method of study, but involved himself in affected silence, and fed his own vanity with their admiration and conjectures.

One practice he had, which was easily observed: if any thought or image was presented to his mind, that he could use or improve, he did not suffer it to be lost; but, amidst the jollity of a tavern, or in the warmth of conversation, very diligently committed it to paper.

Thus it was that he had gathered two quires of hints for his new tragedy; of which Rowe, when they were put into his hands, could make, as he says, very little use, but which the collector considered as a valuable stock of materials.

When he came to London, his way of life connected him with the licentious and dissolute; and he affected the airs and gaiety of a man of pleasure; but his dress was always deficient: scholastick cloudiness still hung about him; and his merriment was sure to produce the scorn of his companions.

With all his carelessness, and all his vices, he was one of the murmurers at Fortune; and wondered why he was suffered to be poor, when Addison was caressed and preferred: nor would a very little have contented him; for he estimated his wants at six hundred pounds a year.

In his course of reading it was particular, that he had diligently perused, and accurately remembered, the old romances of knight-errantry.

He had a high opinion of his own merit, and something contemptuous in his treatment of those whom he considered as not qualified to oppose or contradict him. He had many frailties; yet it cannot but be supposed that he had great merit, who could obtain to the same play a prologue from Addison, and an epilogue from Prior; and who could have at once the patronage of Halifax, and the praise of Oldisworth.

For the power of communicating these minute memorials, I am indebted to my conversation with Gilbert Walmsley, late registrar of the ecclesiastical court of Lichfield, who was acquainted both with Smith and Ducket. . . .

Of Gilbert Walmsley,[7] thus presented to my mind, let me indulge myself in the remembrance. I knew him very early; he

[7] Walmsley, or Walmisley (1680–1751), born in Lichfield, is now chiefly remembered as Johnson's early friend. It is odd that no correspondence survives from this friendship.

was one of the first friends that literature procured me, and I hope that at least my gratitude made me worthy of his notice.

He was of an advanced age, and I was only not a boy; yet he never received my notions with contempt. He was a Whig, with all the virulence and malevolence of his party; yet difference of opinion did not keep us apart. I honoured him, and he endured me.

He had mingled with the gay world, without exemption from its vices or its follies, but had never neglected the cultivation of his mind; his belief of Revelation was unshaken; his learning preserved his principles; he grew first regular, and then pious.

His studies had been so various, that I am not able to name a man of equal knowledge. His acquaintance with books was great; and what he did not immediately know, he could at least tell where to find. Such was his amplitude of learning, and such his copiousness of communication, that it may be doubted whether a day now passes in which I have not some advantage from his friendship.

At this man's table I enjoyed many chearful and instructive hours, with companions such as are not often found; with one who has lengthened, and one who has gladdened life; with Dr. James, whose skill in physick will be long remembered;[8] and with David Garrick, whom I hoped to have gratified with this character of our common friend: but what are the hopes of man! I am disappointed by that stroke of death,[9] which has eclipsed the gaiety of nations, and impoverished the publick stock of harmless pleasure.

[8] Dr. Robert James (1705–1776), author of a Medical Dictionary (1743) and a *Dissertation on Fevers* (1748); remembered for his famous fever-powder and pill, feared to have hastened Oliver Goldsmith's death, but generally in favor with his contemporaries.

[9] Jan. 20, 1779. See *ante*, p. 26, letter to Mrs. Garrick.

FROM Addison

Before the Tatler and Spectator, if the writers for the theatre are excepted, England had no masters of common life. No writers had yet undertaken to reform either the savageness of neglect, or the impertinence of civility; to shew when to speak, or to be silent; how to refuse, or how to comply. We had many books to teach us our more important duties, and to settle opinions in philosophy or politicks; but an *Arbiter elegantiarum*, a judge of propriety, was yet wanting, who should survey the track of daily conversation, and free it from thorns and prickles, which teaze the passer, though they do not wound him.

For this purpose nothing is so proper as the frequent publication of short papers, which we read not as study but amusement. If the subject be slight, the treatise likewise is short. The busy may find time, and the idle may find patience. . . .

It has been suggested that the Royal Society was instituted soon after the Restoration, to divert the attention of the people from publick discontent. The Tatler and Spectator had the same tendency: they were published at a time when two parties, loud, restless, and violent, each with plausible declarations, and each perhaps without any distinct termination of its views, were agitating the nation; to minds heated with political contest, they supplied cooler and more inoffensive reflections; and it is said by Addison, in a subsequent work, that they had a perceptible influence upon the conversation of that time, and taught the frolick and the gay to unite merriment with decency; an effect which they can never wholly lose, while they continue to be among the first books by which both sexes are initiated in the elegances of knowledge.

The Tatler and Spectator adjusted, like Casa,[1] the unsettled practice of daily intercourse by propriety and politeness; and, like La Bruyère, exhibited the *Characters and Manners of the Age.* The personages introduced in these papers were not merely ideal; they were then known, and conspicuous in various stations. Of the Tatler this is told by Steele in his last paper, and of The Spectator by Budgell in the Preface to Theophrastus[2]; a book which Addison has recommended, and which he was suspected to have revised, if he did not write it. Of those portraits, which may be supposed to be sometimes embellished, and sometimes aggravated, the originals are now partly known, and partly forgotten.

But to say that they united the plans of two or three eminent writers, is to give them but a small part of their due praise; they superadded literature and criticism, and sometimes towered far above their predecessors; and taught, with great justness of argument and dignity of language, the most important duties and sublime truths.

All these topicks were happily varied with elegant fictions and refined allegories, and illuminated with different changes of style and felicities of invention.

It is recorded by Budgell, that of the characters feigned or exhibited in the Spectator, the favourite of Addison was Sir Roger de Coverley, of whom he had formed a very delicate and discriminated idea, which he would not suffer to be violated; and

---

[1] Giovanni della Casa, *Il Galateo,* 1558.
[2] Eustace Budgell, *The Moral Characters of Theophrastus,* 1714, p. 7.

therefore when Steele had shewn him innocently picking up a girl in the Temple, and taking her to a tavern, he drew upon himself so much of his friend's indignation, that he was forced to appease him by a promise of forbearing Sir Roger for the time to come.

The reason which induced Cervantes to bring his hero to the grave, *para mi sola nacio Don Quixote, y yo para el,* made Addison declare, with an undue vehemence of expression, that he would kill Sir Roger; being of opinion that they were born for one another, and that any other hand would do him wrong.

It may be doubted whether Addison ever filled up his original delineation. He describes his Knight as having his imagination somewhat warped; but of this perversion he has made very little use. The irregularities in Sir Roger's conduct, seem not so much the effects of a mind deviating from the beaten track of life, by the perpetual pressure of some overwhelming idea, as of habitual rusticity, and that negligence which solitary grandeur naturally generates.

The variable weather of the mind, the flying vapours of incipient madness, which from time to time cloud reason, without eclipsing it, it requires so much nicety to exhibit, that Addison seems to have been deterred from prosecuting his own design.

To Sir Roger, who, as a country gentleman, appears to be a Tory, or, as it is gently expressed, an adherent to the landed interest, is opposed Sir Andrew Freeport, a new man, a wealthy merchant, zealous for the moneyed interest, and a Whig. Of this contrariety of opinions, it is probable more consequences were at first intended, than could be produced when the resolution was taken to exclude party from the paper. Sir Andrew does but little, and that little seems not to have pleased Addison, who, when he dismissed him from the club, changed his opinions. Steele had made him, in the true spirit of unfeeling commerce, declare that he *would not build an hospital for idle people;* but at last he buys land, settles in the country, and builds not a manufactory, but an hospital for twelve old husbandmen, for men with whom a merchant has little acquaintance, and whom he commonly considers with little kindness.

Of essays thus elegant, thus instructive, and thus commodiously distributed, it is natural to suppose the approbation general and the sale numerous. I once heard it observed, that the sale may be calculated by the product of the tax, related in the last number to produce more than twenty pounds a week, and therefore stated at one and twenty pounds, or three pounds ten shillings a day: this, at a half-penny a paper, will give sixteen hundred and eighty for the daily number.

*   *   *

The tragedy of *Cato,* which, contrary to the rule observed in selecting the works of other poets, has by the weight of its character forced its way into the late collection, is unquestionably the noblest production of Addison's genius. Of a work so much read, it is difficult to say any thing new. About things on which the public thinks long, it commonly attains to think right; and of *Cato* it has been not unjustly determined that it is rather a poem in dialogue than a drama, rather a succession of just sentiments in elegant language than a representation of natural affections, or of any state probable or possible in human life. Nothing here *excites or asswages emotion;* here is *no magical power of raising phantastick terror or wild anxiety.* The events are expected without solicitude, and are remembered without joy or sorrow. Of the agents we have no care: we consider not what they are doing, or what they are suffering; we wish only to know what they have to say. Cato is a being above our solicitude; a man of whom the gods take care, and whom we leave to their care with heedless confidence. To the rest, neither gods nor men can have much attention; for there is not one amongst them that strongly attracts either affection or esteem. But they are made the vehicles of such sentiments and such expression, that there is scarcely a scene in the play which the reader does not wish to impress upon his memory.

*   *   *

Addison is now to be considered as a critick; a name which the present generation is scarcely willing to allow him. His criticism is condemned as tentative or experimental, rather than scientifick, and he is considered as deciding by taste rather than by principles.

It is not uncommon for those who have grown wise by the labour of others, to add a little of their own, and overlook their masters. Addison is now despised by some who perhaps would never have seen his defects, but by the lights which he afforded them. That he always wrote as he would think it necessary to write now, cannot be affirmed; his instructions were such as the character of his readers made proper. That general knowledge which now circulates in common talk, was in his time rarely to be found. Men not professing learning were not ashamed of ignorance; and in the female world, any acquaintance with books was distinguished only to be censured. His purpose was to infuse literary curiosity, by gentle and unsuspected conveyance, into the gay, the idle, and the wealthy; he therefore presented knowledge in the most alluring form, not lofty and austere, but accessible and familiar. When he shewed them their defects, he shewed them likewise that they might be easily supplied. His attempt succeeded; enquiry was awakened, and comprehension expanded. An emulation of intellectual elegance was excited, and from his time to our own, life has been gradually exalted, and conversation purified and enlarged.

Dryden had, not many years before, scattered criticism over his Prefaces with very little parcimony; but, though he sometimes condescended to be somewhat familiar, his manner was in general too scholastick for those who had yet their rudiments to learn, and found it not easy to understand their master. His observations were framed rather for those that were learning to write, than for those that read only to talk.

An instructor like Addison was now wanting, whose remarks being superficial, might be easily understood, and being just, might prepare the mind for more attainments. Had he presented *Paradise Lost* to the publick with all the pomp of system and severity of science, the criticism would perhaps have been admired, and the poem still have been neglected; but by the blandishments of gentleness and facility, he has made Milton an universal favourite, with whom readers of every class think it necessary to be pleased.

He descended now and then to lower disquisitions; and by a serious display of the beauties of *Chevy Chase*,[3] exposed himself to the ridicule of Wagstaff, who bestowed a like pompous character on *Tom Thumb*; and to the contempt of Dennis, who, considering the fundamental position of his criticism, that *Chevy Chase* pleases, and ought to please, because it is natural, observes "that there is a way of deviating from nature, by bombast or tumour, which soars above nature, and enlarges images beyond their real bulk; by affectation, which forsakes nature in quest of something unsuitable; and by imbecillity, which degrades nature by faintness and diminution, by obscuring its appearances, and weakening its effects."[4] In *Chevy Chase* there is not much of either bombast or affectation; but there is chill and lifeless imbecillity. The story cannot possibly be told in a manner that shall make less impression on the mind.

Before the profound observers of the present race repose too securely on the consciousness of their superiority to Addison, let them consider his Remarks on Ovid, in which may be found specimens of criticism sufficiently subtle and refined; let them peruse likewise his Essays on *Wit*,[5] and on the *Pleasures of Imagination*,[6] in which he founds art on the base of nature, and draws the principles of invention from dispositions inherent in the mind of man, with skill and elegance, such as his contemners will not easily attain.

As a describer of life and manners, he must be allowed to stand perhaps the first of the first rank. His humour, which, as Steele observes, is peculiar to himself, is so happily diffused as to give the grace of novelty to domestick scenes and daily occurrences. He never *outsteps the modesty of nature* nor raises merriment or wonder by the violation of truth. His figures neither divert by

---

[3] *Spectator*, Nos. 70, 74.

[4] Cf. Dennis, "Of Simplicity in Poetical Compositions"; "Remarks on Cato." *Critical Works*, ed. Hooker, II, 29–42.

[5] *Spectator*, Nos. 58–63.

[6] *Ibid.*, Nos. 411–421.

distortion, nor amaze by aggravation. He copies life with so much fidelity, that he can be hardly said to invent; yet his exhibitions have an air so much original, that it is difficult to suppose them not merely the product of imagination.

As a teacher of wisdom, he may be confidently followed. His religion has nothing in it enthusiastick or superstitious: he appears neither weakly credulous nor wantonly sceptical; his morality is neither dangerously lax, nor impracticably rigid. All the enchantment of fancy, and all the cogency of argument, are employed to recommend to the reader his real interest, the care of pleasing the Author of his being. Truth is shewn sometimes as the phantom of a vision, sometimes appears half-veiled in an allegory; sometimes attracts regard in the robes of fancy, and sometimes steps forth in the confidence of reason. She wears a thousand dresses, and in all is pleasing.

Mille habet ornatus, mille decenter habet.[7]

His prose is the model of the middle style; on grave subjects not formal, on light occasions not groveling; pure without scrupulosity, and exact without apparent elaboration; always equable, and always easy, without glowing words or pointed sentences. Addison never deviates from his track to snatch a grace; he seeks no ambitious ornaments, and tries no hazardous innovations. His page is always luminous, but never blazes in unexpected splendour.

It was apparently his principal endeavour to avoid all harshness and severity of diction; he is therefore sometimes verbose in his transitions and connections, and sometimes descends too much to the language of conversation: yet if his language had been less idiomatical, it might have lost somewhat of its genuine Anglicism. What he attempted, he performed; he is never feeble, and he did not wish to be energetick; he is never rapid, and he never stagnates. His sentences have neither studied amplitude, nor affected brevity: his periods, though not diligently rounded, are voluble and easy. Whoever wishes to attain an English style, familiar but not coarse, and elegant but not ostentatious, must give his days and nights to the volumes of Addison.

[7] *Tibullus*, IV. ii. 14.

_1688 –_

The Life of Pope

Alexander Pope was born in London, May 22,[1] 1688, of parents whose rank or station was never ascertained: we are informed that they were of *gentle blood*; that his father was of a family of which the Earl of Downe was the head, and that his mother was the daughter of William Turner, Esquire, of York, who had likewise three sons, one of whom had the honour of being killed, and the other of dying, in the service of Charles the First; the third was made a general officer in Spain, from whom the sister inherited what sequestrations and forfeitures had left in the family.

This, and this only, is told by Pope; who is more willing, as I have heard observed, to shew what his father was not, than what he was. It is allowed that he grew rich by trade; but whether in a shop or on the Exchange was never discovered, till Mr. Tyers told, on the authority of Mrs. Racket,[2] that he was a linen-draper in the Strand. Both parents were papists.

[1] May 21 is correct.
[2] Pope's half-sister.

Pope was from his birth of a constitution tender and delicate; but is said to have shewn remarkable gentleness and sweetness of disposition. The weakness of his body continued through his life, but the mildness of his mind perhaps ended with his childhood. His voice, when he was young, was so pleasing, that he was called in fondness the *little Nightingale*.

Being not sent early to school, he was taught to read by an aunt; and when he was seven or eight years old, became a lover of books. He first learned to write by imitating printed books; a species of penmanship in which he retained great excellence through his whole life, though his ordinary hand was not elegant.

When he was about eight, he was placed in Hampshire under Taverner, a Romish priest, who, by a method very rarely practised, taught him the Greek and Latin rudiments together. He was now first regularly initiated in poetry by the perusal of Ogylby's *Homer,* and Sandys's *Ovid:* Ogylby's assistance he never repaid with any praise; but of Sandys's he declared, in his notes to the *Iliad,* that English poetry owed much of its present beauty to his translations. Sandys very rarely attempted original composition.

From the care of Taverner, under whom his proficiency was considerable, he was removed to a school at Twyford near Winchester, and again to another school about Hyde-park Corner; from which he used sometimes to stroll to the playhouse, and was so delighted with theatrical exhibitions, that he formed a kind of play from Ogylby's *Iliad,* with some verses of his own intermixed, which he persuaded his schoolfellows to act, with the addition of his master's gardener, who personated *Ajax.*

At the two last schools he used to represent himself as having lost part of what Taverner had taught him, and on his master at Twyford he had already exercised his poetry in a lampoon. Yet under those masters he translated more than a fourth part of the *Metamorphoses.* If he kept the same proportion in his other exercises, it cannot be thought that his loss was great.

He tells of himself, in his poems,[3] that *he lisp'd in numbers;* and used to say that he could not remember the time when he

---

[3] *Epistle to Dr. Arbuthnot,* l. 128.

began to make verses. In the style of fiction it might have been said of him as of Pindar, that when he lay in his cradle, *the bees swarmed about his mouth.*[4]

About the time of the Revolution his father, who was undoubtedly disappointed by the sudden blast of popish prosperity, quitted his trade, and retired to Binfield in Windsor Forest, with about twenty thousand pounds; for which, being conscientiously determined not to entrust it to the government, he found no better use than that of locking it up in a chest, and taking from it what his expences required; and his life was long enough to consume a great part of it, before his son came to the inheritance.

To Binfield Pope was called by his father when he was about twelve years old; and there he had for a few months the assistance of one Deane, another priest, of whom he learned only to construe a little of *Tully's Offices.* How Mr. Deane could spend, with a boy who had translated so much of *Ovid,* some months over a small part of *Tully's Offices,* it is now vain to enquire.

Of a youth so successfully employed, and so conspicuously improved, a minute account must be naturally desired; but curiosity must be contended with confused, imperfect, and sometimes improbable intelligence. Pope, finding little advantage from external help, resolved thenceforward to direct himself, and at twelve formed a plan of study which he completed with little other incitement than the desire of excellence.

His primary and principal purpose was to be a poet, with which his father accidentally concurred, by proposing subjects, and obliging him to correct his performances by many revisals; after which the old gentleman, when he was satisfied, would say, *these are good rhymes.*

In his perusal of the English poets he soon distinguished the versification of Dryden, which he considered as the model to be studied, and was impressed with such veneration for his instructer, that he persuaded some friends to take him to the coffee-house which Dryden frequented, and pleased himself with having seen him.

[4] *Pausanias,* IX. 23.

Dryden died May 1, 1701,[5] some days before Pope was twelve; so early must he therefore have felt the power of harmony, and the zeal of genius. Who does not wish that Dryden could have known the value of the homage that was paid him, and foreseen the greatness of his young admirer?

The earliest of Pope's productions is his *Ode on Solitude,* written before he was twelve, in which there is nothing more than other forward boys have attained, and which is not equal to Cowley's performances at the same age.

His time was now spent wholly in reading and writing. As he read the Classicks, he amused himself with translating them; and at fourteen made a version of the first book of the *Thebais,* which, with some revision, he afterwards published. He must have been at this time, if he had no help, a considerable proficient in the Latin tongue.

By Dryden's Fables, which had then been not long published, and were much in the hands of poetical readers, he was tempted to try his own skill in giving Chaucer a more fashionable appearance, and put *January and May,* and the *Prologue of the Wife of Bath,* into modern English. He translated likewise the Epistle of *Sappho to Phaon* from Ovid, to complete the version, which was before imperfect; and wrote some other small pieces, which he afterwards printed.

He sometimes imitated the English poets, and professed to have written at fourteen his poem upon *Silence,* after Rochester's *Nothing.* He had now formed his versification, and in the smoothness of his numbers surpassed his original: but this is a small part of his praise; he discovers such acquaintance both with human life and public affairs, as is not easily conceived to have been attainable by a boy of fourteen in *Windsor Forest.*

Next year he was desirous of opening to himself new sources of knowledge, by making himself acquainted with modern languages; and removed for a time to London, that he might study French and Italian, which, as he desired nothing more than to read them, were by diligent application soon dispatched. Of

[5] 1700.

Italian learning he does not appear to have ever made much use in his subsequent studies.

He then returned to Binfield, and delighted himself with his own poetry. He tried all styles, and many subjects. He wrote a comedy, a tragedy, an epick poem, with panegyricks on all the princes of Europe; and, as he confesses, *thought himself the greatest genius that ever was.* Self-confidence is the first requisite to great undertakings; he, indeed, who forms his opinion of himself in solitude, without knowing the powers of other men, is very liable to errour; but it was the felicity of Pope to rate himself at his real value.

Most of his puerile productions were, by his maturer judgement, afterwards destroyed; *Alcander,* the epick poem, was burnt by the persuasion of Atterbury.[6] The tragedy was founded on the legend of *St. Genevieve.* Of the comedy there is no account.

Concerning his studies it is related, that he translated Tully *on old Age;* and that, besides his books of poetry and criticism, he read *Temple's Essays* and *Locke On human Understanding.* His reading, though his favourite authors are not known, appears to have been sufficiently extensive and multifarious; for his early pieces shew, with sufficient evidence, his knowledge of books.

He that is pleased with himself, easily imagines that he shall please others. Sir William Trumbal, who had been ambassador at Constantinople, and secretary of state, when he retired from business, fixed his residence in the neighbourhood of Binfield. Pope, not yet sixteen, was introduced to the statesman of sixty, and so distinguished himself, that their interviews ended in friendship and correspondence. Pope was, through his whole life, ambitious of splendid acquaintance, and he seems to have wanted neither diligence nor success in attracting the notice of the great; for from his first entrance into the world, and his entrance was very early, he was admitted to familiarity with those whose rank or station made them most conspicuous.

[6] Francis Atterbury (1662–1732), Bishop of Rochester, later intrigued with the Jacobites, and was imprisoned in the Tower and thereafter banished for attempting to restore the Stuarts to the throne. His friendship (and correspondence) with Pope was longlasting and sincere.

From the age of sixteen the life of Pope, as an author, may be properly computed. He now wrote his pastorals, which were shewn to the Poets and Criticks of that time; as they well deserved, they were read with admiration, and many praises were bestowed upon them and upon the Preface, which is both elegant and learned in a high degree: they were, however, not published till five years afterwards.

Cowley, Milton, and Pope, are distinguished among the English Poets by the early exertion of their powers; but the works of Cowley alone were published in his childhood, and therefore of him only can it be certain that his puerile performances received no improvement from his maturer studies.

At this time began his acquaintance with Wycherley, a man who seems to have had among his contemporaries his full share of reputation, to have been esteemed without virtue, and caressed without good-humour. Pope was proud of his notice; Wycherley wrote verses in his praise, which he was charged by Dennis with writing to himself,[7] and they agreed for a while to flatter one another. It is pleasant to remark how soon Pope learned the cant of an author, and began to treat criticks with contempt, though he had yet suffered nothing from them.

But the fondness of Wycherley was too violent to last. His esteem of Pope was such, that he submitted some poems to his revision; and when Pope, perhaps proud of such confidence, was sufficiently bold in his criticisms, and liberal in his alterations, the old scribbler was angry to see his pages defaced, and felt more pain from the detection than content from the amendment of his faults. They parted; but Pope always considered him with kindness, and visited him a little time before he died.

Another of his early correspondents was Mr. Cromwell, of whom I have learned nothing particular but that he used to ride a-hunting in a tye-wig. He was fond, and perhaps vain, of amusing himself with poetry and criticism; and sometimes sent his

[7] *Reflections . . . upon An Essay upon Criticism,* 1711. Dennis, *Critical Works,* ed. Hooker, 1939, I, 417.

performances to Pope, who did not forbear such remarks as were now-and-then unwelcome. Pope, in his turn, put the juvenile version of *Statius* into his hands for correction.

Their correspondence afforded the publick its first knowledge of Pope's Epistolary Powers; for his Letters were given by Cromwell to one Mrs. Thomas, and she many years afterwards sold them to Curll, who inserted them in a volume of his Miscellanies.[8]

Walsh, a name yet preserved among the minor poets, was one of his first encouragers. His regard was gained by the Pastorals, and from him Pope received the counsel [9] by which he seems to have regulated his studies. Walsh advised him to correctness, which, as he told him, the English poets had hitherto neglected, and which therefore was left to him as a basis of fame; and, being delighted with rural poems, recommended to him to write a pastoral comedy, like those which are read so eagerly in Italy; a design which Pope probably did not approve, as he did not follow it.

Pope had now declared himself a poet; and, thinking himself entitled to poetical conversation, began at seventeen to frequent Will's, a coffee-house on the north side of Russel-street in Covent-garden, where the wits of that time used to assemble, and where Dryden had, when he lived, been accustomed to preside.

During this period of his life he was indefatigably diligent, and insatiably curious; wanting health for violent, and money for expensive pleasures, and having certainly excited in himself very strong desires of intellectual eminence, he spent much of his time over his books; but he read only to store his mind with facts and images, seizing all that his authors presented with undistinguishing voracity, and with an appetite for knowledge too eager to be nice. In a mind like his, however, all the faculties were at once involuntarily improving. Judgement is forced upon us by experience. He that reads many books must compare one opinion or one style with another; and when he compares, must necessarily

[8] *Familiar Letters to Mr. Cromwell, Esq. by Mr. Pope.* Curll, *Miscellanea,* 1727.

[9] 1783: council.

distinguish, reject, and prefer. But the account given by himself of his studies was, that from fourteen to twenty he read only for amusement, from twenty to twenty-seven for improvement and instruction; that in the first part of this time he desired only to know, and in the second he endeavoured to judge.

The Pastorals, which had been for some time handed about among poets and criticks, were at last printed (1709) in Tonson's Miscellany, in a volume which began with the Pastorals of Philips, and ended with those of Pope.

The same year was written the *Essay on Criticism*; a work which displays such extent of comprehension, such nicety of distinction, such acquaintance with mankind, and such knowledge both of ancient and modern learning, as are not often attained by the maturest age and longest experience. It was published about two years afterwards, and being praised by Addison in *The Spectator*[10] with sufficient liberality, met with so much favour as enraged Dennis, "who," he says, "found himself attacked, without any manner of provocation on his side, and attacked in his person, instead of his writings, by one who was wholly a stranger to him, at a time when all the world knew he was persecuted by fortune; and not only saw that this was attempted in a clandestine manner, with the utmost falsehood and calumny, but found that all this was done by a little affected hypocrite, who had nothing in his mouth at the same time but truth, candour, friendship, good-nature, humanity, and magnanimity." [11]

How the attack was clandestine is not easily perceived, nor how his person is depreciated; but he seems to have known something of Pope's character, in whom may be discovered an appetite to talk too frequently of his own virtues.

The pamphlet is such as rage might be expected to dictate. He supposes himself to be asked two questions: whether the Essay will succeed, and who or what is the author.

Its success he admits to be secured by the false opinions then prevalent; the author he concludes to be *young and raw*.

[10] No. 253.
[11] Dennis, ed. Hooker, 1939, I, 396.

First, because he discovers a sufficiency beyond his little ability, and hath rashly undertaken a task infinitely above his force. Secondly, while this little author struts, and affects the dictatorian air, he plainly shews that at the same time he is under the rod; and while he pretends to give law to others, is a pedantick slave to authority and opinion. Thirdly, he hath, like schoolboys, borrowed both from living and dead. Fourthly, he knows not his own mind, and frequently contradicts himself. Fifthly, he is almost perpetually in the wrong.[12]

All these positions he attempts to prove by quotations and remarks; but his desire to do mischief is greater than his power. He has, however, justly criticised some passages, in these lines,

> There are whom heaven has bless'd with store of wit,
> Yet want as much again to manage it;
> For wit and judgment ever are at strife———[13]

it is apparent that *wit* has two meanings, and that what is wanted, though called *wit,* is truly judgment. So far Dennis is undoubtedly right; but, not content with argument, he will have a little mirth, and triumphs over the first couplet in terms too elegant to be forgotten. "By the way, what rare numbers are here! Would not one swear that this youngster had espoused some antiquated Muse, who had sued out a divorce on account of impotence from some superannuated sinner; and, having been p-xed by her former spouse, has got the gout in her decrepit age, which makes her hobble so damnably." [14] This was the man who would reform a nation sinking into barbarity.

In another place Pope himself allowed that Dennis had detected one of those blunders which are called *bulls.* The first edition had this line:

> What is this wit———
> Where wanted, scorn'd; and envied where acquir'd?

[12] *Op. cit.,* abridged from I, 398–402.
[13] *An Essay on Criticism,* II. 80–82.
[14] *Op. cit.,* I, 404.

"How," says the critick, "can wit be *scorn'd* where it is not? Is not this a figure frequently employed in Hibernian land? The person that wants this wit may indeed be scorned, but the scorn shews the honour which the contemner has for wit." [15] Of this remark Pope made the proper use, by correcting the passage.[16]

I have preserved, I think, all that is reasonable in Dennis's criticism; it remains that justice be done to his delicacy.

> For his acquaintance (says Dennis) he names Mr. Walsh, who had by no means the qualification which this author reckons absolutely necessary to a critick, it being very certain that he was, like this Essayer, a very indifferent poet; he loved to be well-dressed; and I remember a little young gentleman whom Mr. Walsh used to take into his company, as a double foil to his person and capacity. —Enquire between *Sunninghill* and *Oakingham* for a young, short, squab gentleman, the very bow of the God of Love, and tell me whether he be a proper author to make personal reflections?—He may extol the antients, but he has reason to thank the gods that he was born a modern; for had he been born of Grecian parents, and his father consequently had by law had the absolute disposal of him, his life had been no longer than that of one of his poems, the life of half a day.—Let the person of a gentleman of his parts be never so contemptible, his inward man is ten times more ridiculous; it being impossible that his outward form, though it be that of downright monkey, should differ so much from human shape, as his unthinking immaterial part does from human understanding.[17]

Thus began the hostility between Pope and Dennis, which, though it was suspended for a short time, never was appeased. Pope seems, at first, to have attacked him wantonly; but though he always professed to despise him, he discovers, by mentioning him very often, that he felt his force or his venom.

[15] *Ibid.*, I, 411.
[16] *An Essay on Criticism*, ll. 500 ff.
[17] Inexactly abridged from Dennis (ed. Hooker, 1939, I, 416–417).

Of this Essay Pope declared that he did not expect the sale to be quick, because *not one gentleman in sixty, even of liberal education, could understand it.* The gentlemen, and the education of that time, seem to have been of a lower character than they are of this. He mentioned a thousand copies as a numerous impression.

Dennis was not his only censurer; the zealous papists thought the monks treated with too much contempt, and Erasmus too studiously praised; but to these objections he had not much regard.

The *Essay* has been translated into French by *Hamilton,* author of the *Comte de Grammont,* whose version was never printed, by *Robotham,* secretary to the King for Hanover, and by *Resnel;* and commented by Dr. Warburton, who has discovered in it such order and connection as was not perceived by Addison, nor, as is said, intended by the author.

Almost every poem, consisting of precepts, is so far arbitrary and immethodical, that many of the paragraphs may change places with no apparent inconvenience; for of two or more positions, depending upon some remote and general principle, there is seldom any cogent reason why one should precede the other. But for the order in which they stand, whatever it be, a little ingenuity may easily give a reason. *It is possible,* says Hooker, *that by long circumduction, from any one truth all truth may be inferred.*[18] Of all homogeneous truths at least, of all truths respecting the same general end, in whatever series they may be produced, a concatenation by intermediate ideas may be formed, such as, when it is once shewn, shall appear natural; but if this order be reversed, another mode of connection equally specious may be found or made. Aristotle is praised for naming Fortitude first of the cardinal virtues,[19] as that without which no other virtue can steadily be practised; but he might, with equal propriety, have placed Prudence and Justice before it, since without Prudence Fortitude is mad; without Justice, it is mischievous.

As the end of method is perspicuity, that series is sufficiently regular that avoids obscurity; and where there is no obscurity it will not be difficult to discover method.

[18] *Ecclesiastical Polity,* II, i. 2, quoted from memory.
[19] *Nicomachean Ethics,* III, 6–9.

In the *Spectator*[20] was published the *Messiah*, which he first submitted to the perusal of Steele, and corrected in compliance with his criticisms.

It is reasonable to infer, from his Letters, that the verses on the *Unfortunate Lady* were written about the time when his *Essay* was published. The Lady's name and adventures I have sought with fruitless enquiry.

I can therefore tell no more than I have learned from Mr. Ruffhead,[21] who writes with the confidence of one who could trust his information. She was a woman of eminent rank and large fortune, the ward of an unkle, who, having given her a proper education, expected like other guardians that she should make at least an equal match; and such he proposed to her, but found it rejected in favour of a young gentleman of inferior condition.

Having discovered the correspondence between the two lovers, and finding the young lady determined to abide by her own choice, he supposed that separation might do what can rarely be done by arguments, and sent her into a foreign country, where she was obliged to converse only with those from whom her unkle had nothing to fear.

Her lover took care to repeat his vows; but his letters were intercepted and carried to her guardian, who directed her to be watched with still greater vigilance; till of this restraint she grew so impatient, that she bribed a woman-servant to procure her a sword, which she directed to her heart.

From this account, given with evident intention to raise the Lady's character, it does not appear that she had any claim to praise, nor much to compassion. She seems to have been impatient, violent, and ungovernable. Her unkle's power could not have lasted long; the hour of liberty and choice would have come in time. But her desires were too hot for delay, and she liked self-murder better than suspence.

Nor is it discovered that the unkle, whoever he was, is with

---

[20] No. 378.
[21] Owen Ruffhead, *Life of Pope*, 1769.

much justice delivered to posterity as a *false Guardian;* he seems to have done only that for which a guardian is appointed; he endeavoured to direct his niece till she should be able to direct herself. Poetry has not often been worse employed than in dignifying the amorous fury of a raving girl.

Not long after, he wrote the *Rape of the Lock,* the most airy, the most ingenious, and the most delightful of all his compositions, occasioned by a frolick of gallantry, rather too familiar, in which Lord Petre cut off a lock of Mrs. Arabella Fermor's hair. This, whether stealth or violence, was so much resented, that the commerce of the two families, before very friendly, was interrupted. Mr. Caryl, a gentleman who, being secretary to King James's Queen, had followed his Mistress into France, and who being the author of *Sir Solomon Single,* a comedy, and some translations, was entitled to the notice of a Wit, solicited Pope to endeavour a reconciliation by a ludicrous poem, which might bring both the parties to a better temper. In compliance with Caryl's request, though his name was for a long time marked only by the first and last letter, C—l, a poem of two cantos was written (1711), as is said, in a fortnight, and sent to the offended Lady, who liked it well enough to shew it; and, with the usual process of literary transactions, the author, dreading a surreptitious edition, was forced to publish it.

The event is said to have been such as was desired; the pacification and diversion of all to whom it related, except Sir *George Brown,* who complained with some bitterness that, in the character of *Sir Plume,* he was made to talk nonsense. Whether all this be true, I have some doubt; for at Paris, a few years ago, a niece of Mrs. Fermor, who presided in an English Convent, mentioned Pope's work with very little gratitude, rather as an insult than an honour; and she may be supposed to have inherited the opinion of her family.

At its first appearance it was termed by Addison *merum sal.*[22] Pope, however, saw that it was capable of improvement; and, having luckily contrived to borrow his machinery from the *Rosicru-*

[22] I.e., the perfection of wit.

cians, imparted the scheme with which his head was teeming to Addison, who told him that his work, as it stood, was *a delicious little thing,* and gave him no encouragement to retouch it.

This has been too hastily considered as an instance of Addison's jealousy; for as he could not guess the conduct of the new design, or the possibilities of pleasure comprised in a fiction of which there had been no examples, he might very reasonably and kindly persuade the author to acquiesce in his own prosperity, and forbear an attempt which he considered as an unnecessary hazard.

Addison's counsel was happily rejected. Pope foresaw the future efflorescence of imagery then budding in his mind, and resolved to spare no art, or industry of cultivation. The soft luxuriance of his fancy was already shooting, and all the gay varieties of diction were ready at his hand to colour and embellish it.

His attempt was justified by its success. The *Rape of the Lock* stands forward, in the classes of literature, as the most exquisite example of ludicrous poetry. Berkeley congratulated him upon the display of powers more truly poetical than he had shewn before; with elegance of description and justness of precepts, he had now exhibited boundless fertility of invention.

He always considered the intermixture of the machinery with the action as his most successful exertion of poetical art. He indeed could never afterwards produce any thing of such unexampled excellence. Those performances, which strike with wonder, are combinations of skilful genius with happy casualty; and it is not likely that any felicity, like the discovery of a new race of preternatural agents, should happen twice to the same man.

Of this poem the author was, I think, allowed to enjoy the praise for a long time without disturbance. Many years afterwards Dennis published some remarks upon it,[23] with very little force, and with no effect; for the opinion of the publick was already settled, and it was no longer at the mercy of criticism.

About this time he published the *Temple of Fame,* which, as he tells Steele in their correspondence, he had written two years before; that is, when he was only twenty-two years old, an early

[23] Apparently commenced 1714, but published 1728.

time of life for so much learning and so much observation as that work exhibits.

On this poem Dennis afterwards published some remarks, of which the most reasonable is, that some of the lines represent *motion* as exhibited by *sculpture.*[24]

Of the Epistle from *Eloisa to Abelard*, I do not know the date. His first inclination to attempt a composition of that tender kind arose, as Mr. Savage told me, from his perusal of Prior's *Nut-brown Maid*. How much he has surpassed Prior's work it is not necessary to mention, when perhaps it may be said with justice, that he has excelled every composition of the same kind. The mixture of religious hope and resignation gives an elevation and dignity to disappointed love, which images merely natural cannot bestow. The gloom of a convent strikes the imagination with far greater force than the solitude of a grove.

This piece was, however, not much his favourite in his latter years, though I never heard upon what principle he slighted it.

In the next year (1713) he published *Windsor Forest;* of which part was, as he relates, written at sixteen, about the same time as his Pastorals, and the latter part was added afterwards: where the addition begins, we are not told. The lines relating to the Peace confess their own date. It is dedicated to Lord Lansdowne,[25] who was then high in reputation and influence among the Tories; and it is said, that the conclusion of the poem gave great pain to Addison, both as a poet and a politician. Reports like this are often spread with boldness very disproportionate to their evidence. Why should Addison receive any particular disturbance from the last lines of *Windsor Forest?* If contrariety of opinion could poison a politician, he would not live a day; and, as a poet, he must have felt Pope's force of genius much more from many other parts of his works.

The pain that Addison might feel it is not likely that he would confess; and it is certain that he so well suppressed his discontent, that Pope now thought himself his favourite; for having been

---

[24] Dennis, ed. Hooker, II, 142–143.

[25] George Granville, Baron Lansdowne (1667–1735), whose biography appears among Johnson's *Lives of the Poets.*

consulted in the revisal of *Cato,* he introduced it by a Prologue; and, when Dennis published his Remarks, undertook not indeed to vindicate but to revenge his friend, by a *Narrative of the Frenzy of John Dennis.*

There is reason to believe that Addison gave no encouragement to this disingenuous hostility; for, says Pope, in a Letter to him,[26] "indeed your opinion, that 'tis entirely to be neglected, would be my own in my own case; but I felt more warmth here than I did when I first saw his book against myself (though indeed in two minutes it made me heartily merry)." Addison was not a man on whom such cant of sensibility could make much impression. He left the pamphlet to itself, having disowned it to Dennis, and perhaps did not think Pope to have deserved much by his officiousness.

This year was printed in the *Guardian*[27] the ironical comparison between the Pastorals of Philips and Pope; a composition of artifice, criticism, and literature, to which nothing equal will easily be found. The superiority of Pope is so ingeniously dissembled, and the feeble lines of Philips so skilfully preferred, that Steele, being deceived, was unwilling to print the paper lest Pope should be offended. Addison immediately saw the writer's design; and, as it seems, had malice enough to conceal his discovery, and to permit a publication which, by making his friend Philips ridiculous, made him forever an enemy to Pope.

It appears that about this time Pope had a strong inclination to unite the art of Painting with that of Poetry, and put himself under the tuition of Jervas.[28] He was near-sighted and therefore not formed by nature for a painter: he tried, however, how far he could advance, and sometimes persuaded his friends to sit. A picture of Betterton, supposed to be drawn by him, was in the possession of Lord Mansfield: if this was taken from the life, he must have begun to paint earlier; for Betterton was now dead.

[26] Dated July 20, 1713.
[27] No. 40.
[28] Charles Jervas (1675?–1739), a pupil of Kneller; a successful portrait-painter, who painted, among others, portraits of Swift, Arbuthnot, Newton, and of Pope three times.

Pope's ambition of this new art produced some encomiastick verses to Jervas, which certainly shew his power as a poet, but I have been told that they betray his ignorance of painting.

He appears to have regarded Betterton with kindness and esteem; and after his death published, under his name, a version into modern English of Chaucer's Prologues, and one of his Tales, which, as was related by Mr. Harte, were believed to have been the performance of Pope himself by Fenton,[29] who made him a gay offer of five pounds, if he would shew them in the hand of Betterton.

The next year (1713) produced a bolder attempt, by which profit was sought as well as praise. The poems which he had hitherto written, however they might have diffused his name, had made very little addition to his fortune. The allowance which his father made him, though, proportioned to what he had, it might be liberal, could not be large; his religion hindered him from the occupation of any civil employment, and he complained that he wanted even money to buy books.

He therefore resolved to try how far the favour of the publick extended, by soliciting a subscription to a version of the *Iliad*, with large notes.

To print by subscription was, for some time, a practice peculiar to the English. The first considerable work for which this expedient was employed is said to have been Dryden's *Virgil*; and it had been tried again with great success when the *Tatlers* were collected into volumes.

There was reason to believe that Pope's attempt would be successful. He was in the full bloom of reputation, and was personally known to almost all whom dignity of employment or splendour of reputation had made eminent; he conversed indifferently with both parties, and never disturbed the publick with his political opinions; and it might be naturally expected, as each faction then boasted its literary zeal, that the great men, who on other occasions practised all the violence of opposition, would

[29] Elijah Fenton (1683–1730), who assisted Pope in translating the *Odyssey*. See later in the present *Life*.

emulate each other in their encouragement of a poet who had delighted all, and by whom none had been offended.

With those hopes, he offered an English *Iliad* to subscribers, in six volumes in quarto, for six guineas; a sum, according to the value of money at that time, by no means inconsiderable, and greater than I believe to have been ever asked before. His proposal, however, was very favourably received, and the patrons of literature were busy to recommend his undertaking, and promote his interest. Lord Oxford,[30] indeed, lamented that such a genius should be wasted upon a work not original; but proposed no means by which he might live without it: Addison recommended caution and moderation, and advised him not to be content with the praise of half the nation, when he might be universally favoured.

The greatness of the design, the popularity of the author, and the attention of the literary world, naturally raised such expectations of the future sale, that the booksellers made their offers with great eagerness; but the highest bidder was *Bernard Lintot,* who became proprietor on condition of supplying, at his own expence, all the copies which were to be delivered to subscribers, or presented to friends, and paying two hundred pounds for every volume.

Of the Quartos it was, I believe, stipulated that none should be printed but for the author, that the subscription might not be depreciated; but Lintot impressed the same pages upon a small Folio, and paper perhaps a little thinner; and sold exactly at half the price, for half a guinea each volume, books so little inferior to the Quartos, that, by a fraud of trade, those Folios, being afterwards shortened by cutting away the top and bottom, were sold as copies printed for the subscribers.

Lintot printed two hundred and fifty on royal paper in Folio for two guineas a volume; of the small Folio, having printed seven-

---

[30] Robert Harley, first Earl of Oxford (1661–1724), statesman and collector of the great Harleian library, upon the Catalogue of which Johnson was variously employed, assisting in its compilation, writing proposals and preface; and Introduction to selected tracts published from it in eight volumes.

teen hundred and fifty copies of the first volume, he reduced the number in the other volumes to a thousand.

It is unpleasant to relate that the bookseller, after all his hopes and all his liberality, was, by a very unjust and illegal action, defrauded of his profit. An edition of the English *Iliad* was printed in Holland in Duodecimo, and imported clandestinely for the gratification of those who were impatient to read what they could not yet afford to buy. This fraud could only be counteracted by an edition equally cheap and more commodious; and Lintot was compelled to contract his Folio at once into a Duodecimo, and lose the advantage of an intermediate gradation. The notes, which in the Dutch copies were placed at the end of each book, as they had been in the large volumes, were now subjoined to the text in the same page, and are therefore more easily consulted. Of this edition two thousand five hundred were first printed, and five thousand a few weeks afterwards; but indeed great numbers were necessary to produce considerable profit.

Pope, having now emitted his proposals, and engaged not only his own reputation, but in some degree that of his friends who patronised his subscription, began to be frighted at his own undertaking; and finding himself at first embarrassed with difficulties, which retarded and oppressed him, he was for a time timorous and uneasy; had his nights disturbed by dreams of long journeys through unknown ways, and wished, as he said, *that somebody would hang him.*

This misery, however, was not of long continuance; he grew by degrees more acquainted with Homer's images and expressions, and practice increased his facility of versification. In a short time he represents himself as dispatching regularly fifty verses a day, which would shew him by an easy computation the termination of his labour.

His own diffidence was not his only vexation. He that asks a subscription soon finds that he has enemies. All who do not encourage him defame him. He that wants money will rather be thought angry than poor, and he that wishes to save his money conceals his avarice by his malice. Addison had hinted his suspicion that Pope was too much a Tory; and some of the Tories suspected his principles because he had contributed to the *Guardian*, which was carried on by Steele.

To those who censured his politicks were added enemies yet more dangerous, who called in question his knowledge of Greek, and his qualifications for a translator of Homer. To these he made no publick opposition; but in one of his Letters[31] escapes from them as well as he can. At an age like his, for he was not more than twenty-five, with an irregular education, and a course of life of which much seems to have passed in conversation, it is not very likely that he overflowed with Greek. But when he felt himself deficient he sought assistance; and what man of learning would refuse to help him? Minute enquiries into the force of words are less necessary in translating Homer than other poets, because his positions are general, and his representations natural, with very little dependence on local or temporary customs, on those changeable scenes of artificial life, which, by mingling original with accidental notions, and crowding the mind with images which time effaces, produce ambiguity in diction, and obscurity in books. To this open display of unadulterated nature it must be ascribed, that Homer has fewer passages of doubtful meaning than any other poet either in the learned or in modern languages. I have read of a man, who being, by his ignorance of Greek, compelled to gratify his curiosity with the Latin printed on the opposite page, declared that from the rude simplicity of the lines literally rendered, he formed nobler ideas of the Homeric majesty than from the laboured elegance of polished versions.

Those literal translations were always at hand, and from them he could easily obtain his author's sense with sufficient certainty; and among the readers of Homer the number is very small of those who find much in the Greek more than in the Latin, except the musick of the numbers.

If more help was wanting, he had the poetical translation[32] of *Eobanus Hessus*, an unwearied writer of Latin verses; he had the

[31] To Addison, January 30, 1713/14.
[32] Published 1540.

French Homers of *La Valterie*[33] and *Dacier*,[34] and the English of *Chapman*,[35] *Hobbes*,[36] and *Ogylby*.[37] With Chapman, whose work, though now totally neglected, seems to have been popular almost to the end of the last century, he had very frequent consultations, and perhaps never translated any passage till he had read his version, which indeed he has been sometimes suspected of using instead of the original.

Notes were likewise to be provided; for the six volumes would have been very little more than six pamphlets without them. What the mere perusal of the text could suggest, Pope wanted no assistance to collect or methodize; but more was necessary; many pages were to be filled, and learning must supply materials to wit and judgment. Something might be gathered from Dacier; but no man loves to be indebted to his contemporaries, and Dacier was accessible to common readers. Eustathius[38] was therefore necessarily consulted. To read Eustathius, of whose work there was then no Latin version, I suspect Pope, if he had been willing, not to have been able; some other was therefore to be found, who had leisure as well as abilities, and he was doubtless most readily employed who would do much work for little money.

The history of the notes has never been traced. Broome,[39] in his preface to his poems, declares himself the commentator *in part upon the Iliad*; and it appears from Fenton's Letter, preserved in the Museum, that Broome was at first engaged in consulting Eustathius; but that after a time, whatever was the reason, he desisted: another man of Cambridge was the[n] employed, who soon grew weary of the work; and a third, that was recommended by *Thirlby*, is now discovered to have been *Jortin*, a man since

[33] Dated 1682.
[34] *Iliad*, 1699; *Odyssey*, 1708.
[35] Between 1598 and 1615.
[36] 1674–1675.
[37] 1660 and 1665.
[38] A late twelfth-century Byzantine scholar, commentator on Homer and Pindar, and Archbishop of Thessalonica.
[39] William Broome was later to translate for Pope eight books of the *Odyssey*.

well known to the learned world,[40] who complained that Pope, having accepted and approved his performance, never testified any curiosity to see him, and who professed to have forgotten the terms on which he worked. The terms which Fenton uses are very mercantile: *I think at first sight that his performance is very commendable, and have sent word for him to finish the 17th book, and to send it with his demands for his trouble. I have here enclosed the specimen; if the rest come before the return, I will keep them till I receive your order.*

Broome then offered his service a second time, which was probably accepted, as they had afterwards a closer correspondence. Parnell contributed the Life of Homer, which Pope found so harsh, that he took great pains in correcting it; and by his own diligence, with such help as kindness or money could procure him, in somewhat more than five years he completed his version of the *Iliad*, with the notes. He began it in 1712, his twenty-fifth year, and concluded it in 1718, his thirtieth year.

When we find him translating fifty lines a day, it is natural to suppose that he would have brought his work to a more speedy conclusion. The *Iliad*, containing less than sixteen thousand verses, might have been despatched in less than three hundred and twenty days by fifty verses in a day. The notes, compiled with the assistance of his mercenaries, could not be supposed to require more time than the text. According to this calculation, the progress of Pope may seem to have been slow; but the distance is commonly very great between actual performances and speculative possibility. It is natural to suppose, that as much as has been done to-day may be done to-morrow; but on the morrow some difficulty emerges, or some external impediment obstructs. Indolence, interruption, business, and pleasure, all take their turns of retardation; and every long work is lengthened by a thousand causes that can, and ten thousand that cannot, be recounted. Perhaps no extensive and multifarious performance was ever effected within the term originally fixed in the undertaker's mind. He that runs against Time, has an antagonist not subject to casualties.

[40] Boyle lecturer in Cambridge, and archdeacon of London, 1764. Author of a life of Erasmus, 1758. Thirlby was his Cambridge tutor.

The encouragement given to this translation, though report seems to have over-rated it, was such as the world has not often seen. The subscribers were five hundred and seventy-five. The copies for which subscriptions were given were six hundred and fifty-four; and only six hundred and sixty were printed. For those copies Pope had nothing to pay; he therefore received, including the two hundred pounds a volume, five thousand three hundred and twenty pounds four shillings, without deduction, as the books were supplied by Lintot.

By the success of his subscription Pope was relieved from those pecuniary distresses with which, notwithstanding his popularity, he had hitherto struggled. Lord Oxford had often lamented his disqualification for publick employment, but never proposed a pension. While the translation of *Homer* was in its progress, Mr. Craggs, then secretary of state, offered to procure him a pension, which, at least during his ministry, might be enjoyed with secrecy. This was not accepted by Pope, who told him, however, that, if he should be pressed with want of money, he would send to him for occasional supplies. Craggs was not long in power, and was never solicited for money by Pope, who disdained to beg what he did not want.

With the product of this subscription, which he had too much discretion to squander, he secured his future life from want, by considerable annuities. The estate of the Duke of Buckingham was found to have been charged with five hundred pounds a year, payable to Pope, which doubtless his translation enabled him to purchase.

It cannot be unwelcome to literary curiosity, that I deduce thus minutely the history of the English *Iliad*. It is certainly the noblest version of poetry which the world has ever seen; and its publication must therefore be considered as one of the great events in the annals of Learning.

To those who have skill to estimate the excellence and difficulty of this great work, it must be very desirable to know how it was performed, and by what gradations it advanced to correctness. Of such an intellectual process the knowledge has very rarely been attainable; but happily there remains the original copy of the *Iliad*, which, being obtained by Bolingbroke as a curiosity, descended from him to Mallet, and is now by the solicitation of the late Dr. Maty reposited in the Museum.[41]

Between this manuscript, which is written upon accidental fragments of paper, and the printed edition, there must have been an intermediate copy, that was perhaps destroyed as it returned from the press. . . .[42]

The *Iliad* was published volume by volume, as the translation proceeded; the four first books appeared in 1715. The expectation of this work was undoubtedly high, and every man who had connected his name with criticism, or poetry, was desirous of such intelligence as might enable him to talk upon the popular topick. Halifax, who, by having been first a poet,[43] and then a patron of poetry, had acquired the right of being a judge, was willing to hear some books while they were yet unpublished. Of this rehearsal Pope afterwards gave the following account.

> The famous Lord Halifax was rather a pretender to taste than really possessed of it.——When I had finished the two or three first books of my translation of the *Iliad,* that Lord desired to have the pleasure of hearing them read at his house.——Addison, Congreve, and Garth, were there at the reading. In four or five places, Lord Halifax stopt me very civilly, and with a speech each time, much of the same kind, "I beg your pardon, Mr. Pope; but there is something in that passage that does not quite please me.—— Be so good as to mark the place, and consider it a little at your leisure.——I am sure you can give it a little turn." I returned from Lord Halifax's with Dr. Garth, in his chariot; and, as we were going along, was saying to the

[41] The British Museum, of which Maty was a librarian.

[42] Here Johnson introduces specimens of Pope's revisions in manuscript and print.

[43] In his *Life,* Johnson gives short shrift to the poetry, "of which a short time has withered the beauties. It would now be esteemed no honour, by a contributor to the monthly bundles of verses, to be told, that, in strains either familiar or solemn, he sings like Montague" [Charles Montagu, first Earl of Halifax, 1661–1715].

Doctor, that my Lord had laid me under a good deal of difficulty by such loose and general observations; that I had been thinking over the passages almost ever since, and could not guess at what it was that offended his Lordship in either of them. Garth laughed heartily at my embarrassment; said, I had not been long enough acquainted with Lord Halifax to know his way yet; that I need not puzzle myself about looking those places over and over, when I got home. "All you need do (says he) is to leave them just as they are; call on Lord Halifax two or three months hence, thank him for his kind observations on those passages, and then read them to him as altered. I have known him much longer than you have, and will be answerable for the event." I followed his advice; waited on Lord Halifax some time after; said, I hoped he would find his objections to those passages removed; read them to him exactly as they were at first: and his Lordship was extremely pleased with them, and cried out, *Ay, now they are perfectly right: nothing can be better.*

It is seldom that the great or the wise expect that they are despised or cheated. Halifax, thinking this a lucky opportunity of securing immortality, made some advances of favour and some overtures of advantage to Pope, which he seems to have received with sullen coldness. All our knowledge of this transaction is derived from a single Letter (Dec. 1, 1714), in which Pope says,

I am obliged to you, both for the favours you have done me, and those you intend me. I distrust neither your will nor your memory, when it is to do good; and if I ever become troublesome or solicitous, it must not be out of expectation, but out of gratitude. Your Lordship may cause me to live agreeably in the town, or contentedly in the country, which is really all the difference I set between an easy fortune and a small one. It is indeed a high strain of generosity in you to think of making me easy all my life, only because I have been so happy as to divert you some few hours; but, if I may have leave to

> add it is because you think me no enemy to my native
> country, there will appear a better reason; for I must of
> consequence be very much (as I sincerely am) yours,
> &c.

These voluntary offers, and this faint acceptance, ended without effect. The patron was not accustomed to such frigid gratitude, and the poet fed his own pride with the dignity of independence. They probably were suspicious of each other. Pope would not dedicate till he saw at what rate his praise was valued; he would be *troublesome out of gratitude, not expectation*. Halifax thought himself entitled to confidence; and would give nothing, unless he knew what he should receive. Their commerce had its beginning in hope of praise on one side, and of money on the other, and ended because Pope was less eager of money than Halifax of praise. It is not likely that Halifax had any personal benevolence to Pope; it is evident that Pope looked on Halifax with scorn and hatred.[44]

The reputation of this great work failed of gaining him a patron; but it deprived him of a friend. Addison and he were now at the head of poetry and criticism; and both in such a state of elevation, that, like the two rivals in the Roman state, one could no longer bear an equal, nor the other a superior. Of the gradual abatement of kindness between friends, the beginning is often scarcely discernible by themselves, and the process is continued by petty provocations, and incivilities sometimes peevishly returned, and sometimes contemptuously neglected, which would escape all attention but that of pride, and drop from any memory but that of resentment. That the quarrel of these two wits should be minutely deduced, is not to be expected from a writer to whom, as Homer says, *nothing but rumour has reached, and who has no personal knowledge*.[45]

Pope doubtless approached Addison, when the reputation of

---

[44] Pope had him in mind in the Epistle to *Dr. Arbuthnot*:
     Proud, as *Apollo* on his forked hill,
       Sate full-blown *Bufo*, puff'd by ev'ry quill. (ll. 231–2).
[45] *Iliad*, II. 485–486.

their wit first brought them together, with the respect due to a man whose abilities were acknowledged, and who, having attained that eminence to which he was himself aspiring, had in his hands the distribution of literary fame. He paid court with sufficient diligence by his Prologue to *Cato,* by his abuse of Dennis, and, with praise yet more direct, by his poem on the *Dialogues on Medals,* of which the immediate publication was then intended. In all this there was no hypocrisy; for he confessed that he found in Addison something more pleasing than in any other man.

It may be supposed, that as Pope saw himself favoured by the world, and more frequently compared his own powers with those of others, his confidence increased, and his submission lessened; and that Addison felt no delight from the advances of a young wit, who might soon contend with him for the highest place. Every great man, of whatever kind be his greatness, has among his friends those who officiously, or insidiously, quicken his attention to offences, heighten his disgust, and stimulate his resentment. Of such adherents Addison doubtless had many, and Pope was now too high to be without them.

From the emission and reception of the Proposals for the *Iliad,* the kindness of Addison seems to have abated. Jervas the painter once pleased himself (Aug. 20, 1714) with imagining that he had re-established their friendship; and wrote to Pope that Addison once suspected him of too close a confederacy with Swift, but was now satisfied with his conduct. To this Pope answered, a week after, that his engagements to Swift were such as his services in regard to the subscription demanded, and that the Tories never put him under the necessity of asking leave to be grateful. *But,* says he, *as Mr. Addison must be* the judge *in what regards himself, and seems to have no very just one in regard to me, so I must own to you I expect nothing but civility from him.*[46] In the same Letter he mentions Philips, as having been busy to kindle animosity between them; but, in a Letter to Addison, he expresses some consciousness of behaviour, inattentively deficient in respect.

Of Swift's industry in promoting the subscription there remains the testimony of Kennet, no friend to either him or Pope.

[46] To Jervas, August 27, 1714.

> Nov. 2, 1713, Dr. Swift came into the coffee-house, and
> had a bow from every body but me, who, I confess, could
> not but despise him. When I came to the ante-chamber
> to wait, before prayers, Dr. Swift was the principal man
> of talk and business, and acted as master of requests.——
> Then he instructed a young nobleman that the *best Poet
> in England* was *Mr. Pope* (a papist), who had begun a
> translation of *Homer* into English verse, for which *he
> must have them all subscribe;* for, says he, the author
> *shall not* begin to print till *I have* a thousand guineas for
> him.[47]

About this time it is likely that Steele, who was, with all his po-
litical fury, good-natured and officious, procured an interview
between these angry rivals, which ended in aggravated malevo-
lence. On this occasion, if the reports be true, Pope made his com-
plaint with frankness and spirit, as a man undeservedly neglected
or opposed; and Addison affected a contemptuous unconcern,
and, in a calm even voice, reproached Pope with his vanity, and,
telling him of the improvements which his early works had re-
ceived from his own remarks and those of Steele, said, that he,
being now engaged in publick business, had no longer any care
for his poetical reputation; nor had any other desire, with regard
to Pope, than that his should not, by too much arrogance, alienate
the publick.

To this Pope is said to have replied with great keenness and
severity, upbraiding Addison with perpetual dependance, and with
the abuse of those qualifications which he had obtained at the
publick cost, and charging him with mean endeavours to obstruct
the progress of rising merit. The contest rose so high, that they
parted at last without any interchange of civility.

The first volume of *Homer* was (1715) in time published;
and a rival version of the first *Iliad*, for rivals the time of their
appearance inevitably made them, was immediately printed, with
the name of Tickell. It was soon perceived that, among the fol-

[47] Bishop Kennet's Diary, Swift's *Works*, 1883, XVI, 75.

lowers of Addison, Tickell had the preference, and the criticks and poets divided into factions. *I*, says Pope, *have the town, that is, the mob, on my side; but it is not uncommon for the smaller party to supply by industry what it wants in numbers.—I appeal to the people as my rightful judges, and, while they are not inclined to condemn me, shall not fear the high-flyers at Button's.*[48] This opposition he immediately imputed to Addison, and complained of it in terms sufficiently resentful to Craggs, their common friend.

When Addison's opinion was asked, he declared the versions to be both good, but Tickell's the best that had ever been written; and sometimes said that they were both good, but that Tickell had more of *Homer*.

Pope was now sufficiently irritated; his reputation and his interest were at hazard. He once intended to print together the four versions of Dryden, Maynwaring,[49] Pope, and Tickell, that they might be readily compared, and fairly estimated. This design seems to have been defeated by the refusal of Tonson, who was the proprietor of the other three versions.

Pope intended at another time a rigorous criticism of Tickell's translation, and had marked a copy, which I have seen, in all places that appeared defective. But while he was thus meditating defence or revenge, his adversary sunk before him without a blow; the voice of the publick were [*sic*] not long divided, and the preference was universally given to Pope's performance.

He was convinced, by adding one circumstance to another, that the other translation was the work of Addison himself; but if he knew it in Addison's life-time, it does not appear that he told it. He left his illustrious antagonist to be punished by what has been considered as the most painful of all reflections, the remembrance of a crime perpetrated in vain.

The other circumstances of their quarrel were thus related by Pope:

[48] To Craggs, July 15, 1715.
[49] His translation of the bulk of *Iliad*, Bk. I, was published in Tonson's *Miscellany*, Vol. V, 1703.

Philips seemed to have been encouraged to abuse me in coffee-houses, and conversations: and Gildon wrote a thing about Wycherley,[50] in which he had abused both me and my relations very grossly. Lord Warwick himself told me one day, that it was in vain for me to endeavour to be well with Mr. Addison; that his jealous temper would never admit of a settled friendship between us: and, to convince me of what he had said, assured me, that Addison had encouraged Gildon to publish those scandals, and had given him ten guineas after they were published. The next day, while I was heated with what I had heard, I wrote a Letter to Mr. Addison, to let him know that I was not unacquainted with this behaviour of his; that if I was to speak severely of him, in return for it, it should [not?] be in such a dirty way, that I should rather tell him, himself, fairly of his faults, and allow his good qualities; and that it should be something in the following manner: I then adjoined the first sketch of what has since been called my satire on Addison. Mr. Addison used me very civilly ever after.[51]

The verses on Addison, when they were sent to Atterbury, were considered by him as the most excellent of Pope's performances; and the writer was advised,[52] since he knew where his strength lay, not to suffer it to remain unemployed.

This year (1715) being, by the subscription, enabled to live more by choice, having persuaded his father to sell their estate at Binfield, he purchased, I think only for his life, that house at Twickenham to which his residence afterwards procured so much celebration, and removed thither with his father and mother.

Here he planted the vines and the quincunx which his verses mention; and being under the necessity of making a subterraneous passage to a garden on the other side of the road, he adorned it with fossile bodies, and dignified it with the title of a grotto; a place of silence and retreat, from which he endeavoured to per-

---

[50] Memoirs of Wycherley, 1718.
[51] Spence, Anecdotes, ed. Singer, 1802, p. 148.
[52] Atterbury to Pope, February 26, 1721/22.

suade his friends and himself that cares and passions could be excluded.

A grotto is not often the wish or pleasure of an Englishman, who has more frequent need to solicit than exclude the sun; but Pope's excavation was requisite as an entrance to his garden, and, as some men try to be proud of their defects, he extracted an ornament from an inconvenience, and vanity produced a grotto where necessity enforced a passage. It may be frequently remarked of the studious and speculative, that they are proud of trifles, and that their amusements seem frivolous and childish; whether it be that men conscious of great reputation think themselves above the reach of censure, and safe in the admission of negligent indulgences, or that mankind expect from elevated genius an uniformity of greatness, and watch its degradation with malicious wonder; like him who having followed with his eye an eagle into the clouds, should lament that she ever descended to a perch.

While the volumes of his *Homer* were annually published he collected his former works (1717) into one quarto volume, to which he prefixed a Preface, written with great spriteliness and elegance, which was afterwards reprinted, with some passages subjoined that he at first omitted; other marginal additions of the same kind he made in the later editions of his poems. Waller remarks[53] that poets lose half their praise, because the reader knows not what they have blotted. Pope's voracity of fame taught him the art of obtaining the accumulated honour both of what he had published, and of what he had suppressed.

In this year his father died suddenly, in his seventy-fifth year, having passed twenty-nine years in privacy. He is not known but by the character which his son has given him. If the money with which he retired was all gotten by himself, he had traded very successfully in times when sudden riches were rarely attainable.

The publication of the *Iliad* was at last completed in 1720. The splendour and success of this work raised Pope many enemies, that endeavoured to depreciate his abilities; Burnet, who was afterwards a Judge of no mean reputation, censured him in a piece

---

[53] On Roscommon's *Horace*, l. 41.

called *Homerides* before it was published; Ducket likewise endeavoured to make him ridiculous.[54] Dennis was the perpetual persecutor of all his studies. But, whoever his criticks were, their writings are lost, and the names which are preserved, are preserved in the *Dunciad*.

In this disastrous year (1720) of national infatuation, when more riches than Peru can boast were expected from the South Sea, when the contagion of avarice tainted every mind, and even poets panted after wealth, Pope was seized with the universal passion, and ventured some of his money. The stock rose in its price, and he for a while thought himself *the Lord of thousands*. But this dream of happiness did not last long, and he seems to have waked soon enough to get clear with the loss only of what he once thought himself to have won, and perhaps not wholly of that.

Next year he published some select poems of his friend Dr. Parnell, with a very elegant Dedication to the Earl of Oxford; who, after all his struggles and dangers, then lived in retirement, still under the frown of a victorious faction, who could take no pleasure in hearing his praise.

He gave the same year (1721)[55] an edition of *Shakspeare*. His name was now of so much authority, that Tonson thought himself entitled, by annexing it, to demand a subscription of six guineas for Shakspeare's plays in six quarto volumes; nor did his expectation much deceive him; for of seven hundred and fifty which he printed, he dispersed a great number at the price proposed. The reputation of that edition indeed sunk afterwards so low, that one hundred and forty copies were sold at sixteen shillings each.

On this undertaking, to which Pope was induced by a reward of two hundred and seventeen pounds twelve shillings, he seems never to have reflected afterwards without vexation; for Theobald, a man of heavy diligence, with very slender powers, first, in a

[54] The work (1715, 1716) was a collaborative effort of Sir Thomas Burnet and George Duckett.

[55] The agreement with Tonson was made in this year, but the work was published four years later.

book called *Shakespeare Restored*,[56] and then in a formal edition, detected his deficiencies with all the insolence of victory; and, as he was now high enough to be feared and hated, Theobald had from others all the help that could be supplied, by the desire of humbling a haughty character.

From this time Pope became an enemy to editors, collaters, commentators, and verbal criticks; and hoped to persuade the world, that he miscarried in this undertaking only by having a mind too great for such minute employment.

Pope in his edition undoubtedly did many things wrong, and left many things undone; but let him not be defrauded of his due praise. He was the first that knew, at least the first that told, by what helps the text might be improved. If he inspected the early editions negligently, he taught others to be more accurate. In his Preface he expanded with great skill and elegance the character which had been given of Shakspeare by Dryden; and he drew the publick attention upon his works, which, though often mentioned, had been little read.

Soon after the appearance of the *Iliad,* resolving not to let the general kindness cool, he published proposals for a translation of the *Odyssey,* in five volumes, for five guineas. He was willing, however, now to have associates in his labour, being either weary with toiling upon another's thoughts, or having heard, as Ruffhead relates, that Fenton and Broome had already begun the work, and liking better to have them confederates than rivals.

In the patent, instead of saying that he had *translated* the *Odyssey,* as he had said of the *Iliad,* he says that he had *undertaken* a translation; and in the proposals the subscription is said to be not solely for his own use, but for that of *two of his friends who have assisted him in this work.*

In 1723, while he was engaged in this new version, he appeared before the Lords at the memorable trial of Bishop Atterbury, with whom he had lived in great familiarity, and frequent correspondence. Atterbury had honestly recommended to him the study of the popish controversy, in hope of his conversion; to

---

[56] 1726, and then 1734.

which Pope answered in a manner that cannot much recommend his principles, or his judgement. In questions and projects of learning, they agreed better. He was called at the trial to give an account of Atterbury's domestick life, and private employment, that it might appear how little time he had left for plots. Pope had but few words to utter, and in those few he made several blunders.

His letters to Atterbury express the utmost esteem, tenderness, and gratitude: *perhaps,* says he, *it is not only in this world that I may have cause to remember the Bishop of Rochester.*[57] At their last interview in the Tower, Atterbury presented him with a Bible.

Of the *Odyssey* Pope translated only twelve books; the rest were the work of Broome and Fenton: the notes were written wholly by Broome, who was not over-liberally rewarded. The Public was carefully kept ignorant of the several shares; and an account was subjoined at the conclusion, which is now known not to be true.

The first copy of Pope's books, with those of Fenton, are to be seen in the Museum. The parts of Pope are less interlined than the *Iliad,* and the latter books of the *Iliad* less than the former. He grew dexterous by practice, and every sheet enabled him to write the next with more facility. The books of Fenton have very few alterations by the hand of Pope. Those of Broome have not been found; but Pope complained, as it is reported, that he had much trouble in correcting them.

His contract with Lintot was the same as for the *Iliad,* except that only one hundred pounds were to be paid him for each volume. The number of subscribers was five hundred and seventy-four, and of copies eight hundred and nineteen; so that his profit, when he had paid his assistants, was still very considerable. The work was finished in 1725, and from that time he resolved to make no more translations.

The sale did not answer Lintot's expectation, and he then pretended to discover something of fraud in Pope, and commenced, or threatened, a suit in Chancery.

On the English *Odyssey* a criticism was published by Spence,[58]

[57] To Atterbury, April 20, 1723.
[58] *An Essay on Pope's Odyssey,* 1726–1727.

at that time Prelector of Poetry at Oxford; a man whose learning was not very great, and whose mind was not very powerful. His criticism, however, was commonly just; what he thought, he thought rightly; and his remarks were recommended by his coolness and candour. In him Pope had the first experience of a critick without malevolence, who thought it as much his duty to display beauties as expose faults; who censured with respect, and praised with alacrity.

With this criticism Pope was so little offended, that he sought the acquaintance of the writer, who lived with him from that time in great familiarity, attended him in his last hours, and compiled memorials of his conversation. The regard of Pope recommended him to the great and powerful, and he obtained very valuable preferments in the Church.

Not long after Pope was returning home from a visit in a friend's coach, which, in passing a bridge, was overturned into the water; the windows were closed, and being unable to force them open, he was in danger of immediate death, when the postilion snatched him out by breaking the glass, of which the fragments cut two of his fingers in such a manner, that he lost their use.

Voltaire, who was then in England, sent him a Letter of Consolation. He had been entertained by Pope at his table, where he talked with so much grossness that Mrs. Pope was driven from the room. Pope discovered, by a trick, that he was a spy for the Court, and never considered him as a man worthy of confidence.

He soon afterwards (1727) joined with Swift, who was then in England, to publish three volumes of Miscellanies, in which amongst other things he inserted the *Memoirs of a Parish Clerk*, in ridicule of Burnet's importance in his own History, and a *Debate upon Black and White Horses*, written in all the formalities of a legal process by the assistance, as is said, of Mr. Fortescue, afterwards Master of the Rolls. Before these Miscellanies is a preface signed by Swift and Pope, but apparently written by Pope; in which he makes a ridiculous and romantick complaint of the robberies committed upon authors by the clandestine seizure and sale of their papers. He tells, in tragick strains, how *the cabinets*

*of the Sick and the closets of the Dead have been broke open and
ransacked;* as if those violences were often committed for papers
of uncertain and accidental value, which are rarely provoked by
real treasures; as if epigrams and essays were in danger where
gold and diamonds are safe. A cat, hunted for his musk, is, ac-
cording to Pope's account, but the emblem of a wit winded by
booksellers.

His complaint, however, received some attestation; for the same
year the Letters written by him to Mr. Cromwell, in his youth,
were sold by Mrs. Thomas to Curll, who printed them.

In these Miscellanies was first published the *Art of Sinking in
Poetry,* which, by such a train of consequences as usually passes
in literary quarrels, gave in a short time, according to Pope's
account, occasion to the *Dunciad.*

In the following year (1728) he began to put Atterbury's ad-
vice in practice, and shewed his satirical powers by publishing the
Dunciad, one of his greatest and most elaborate performances, in
which he endeavoured to sink into contempt all the writers by
whom he had been attacked, and some others whom he thought
unable to defend themselves.

At the head of the Dunces he placed poor Theobald, whom he
accused of ingratitude; but whose real crime was supposed to be
that of having revised Shakspeare more happily than himself.
This satire had the effect which he intended, by blasting the
characters which it touched. Ralph, who, unnecessarily interpos-
ing in the quarrel,[59] got a place in a subsequent edition, com-
plained that for a time he was in danger of starving, as the book-
sellers had no longer any confidence in his capacity.

The prevalence of this poem was gradual and slow: the plan,
if not wholly new, was little understood by common readers.
Many of the allusions required illustration; the names were
often expressed only by the initial and final letters, and, if they
had been printed at length, were such as few had known or recol-
lected. The subject itself had nothing generally interesting, for
whom did it concern to know that one or another scribbler was a

[59] James Ralph, Pennsylvanian by birth, came to England with Frank-
lin in 1724, and satirized Pope gratuitously in 1728. He died in 1762.

dunce? If therefore it had been possible for those who were attacked to conceal their pain and their resentment, the *Dunciad* might have made its way very slowly in the world.

This, however, was not to be expected: every man is of importance to himself, and therefore, in his own opinion, to others; and, supposing the world already acquainted with all his pleasures and his pains, is perhaps the first to publish injuries or misfortunes, which had never been known unless related by himself, and at which those that hear them will only laugh; for no man sympathises with the sorrows of vanity.

The history of the *Dunciad* is very minutely related by Pope himself, in a Dedication which he wrote to Lord Middlesex[60] in the name of Savage.

> I will relate the war of the *Dunces* (for so it has been commonly called), which began in the year 1727, and ended in 1730.
>
> When Dr. Swift and Mr. Pope thought it proper, for reasons specified in the Preface to their Miscellanies, to publish such little pieces of theirs as had casually got abroad, there was added to them the *Treatise of the Bathos*, or the *Art of Sinking in Poetry*. It happened that in one chapter of this piece the several species of bad poets were ranged in classes, to which were prefixed almost all the letters of the alphabet (the greatest part of them at random); but such was the number of poets eminent in that art, that some one or other took every letter to himself: all fell into so violent a fury, that, for half a year or more, the common newspapers (in most of which they had some property, as being hired writers) were filled with the most abusive falshoods and scurrilities they could possibly devise. A liberty no way to be wondered at in those people, and in those papers, that for many years, during the uncontrouled license of the press, had aspersed almost all the great characters of the age; and this with impunity, their own persons and names being utterly secret and obscure.

[60] Charles Sackville, second Duke of Dorset (1711–69).

This gave Mr. Pope the thought, that he had now some opportunity of doing good, by detecting and dragging into light these common enemies of mankind; since to invalidate this universal slander, it sufficed to shew what contemptible men were the authors of it. He was not without hopes, that, by manifesting the dulness of those who had only malice to recommend them, either the booksellers would not find their account in employing them, or the men themselves, when discovered, want courage to proceed in so unlawful an occupation. This it was that gave birth to the *Dunciad;* and he thought it an happiness, that, by the late flood of slander on himself, he had acquired such a peculiar right over their names as was necessary to this design.

On the 12th of March, 1729, at St. James's, that poem was presented to the King and Queen (who had before been pleased to read it) by the right honourable Sir Robert Walpole; and some days after the whole impression was taken and dispersed by several noblemen and persons of the first distinction.

It is certainly a true observation, that no people are so impatient of censure as those who are the greatest slanderers, which was wonderfully exemplified on this occasion. On the day the book was first vended, a crowd of authors besieged the shop; intreaties, advices, threats of law and battery, nay cries of treason, were all employed to hinder the coming-out of the *Dunciad:* on the other side, the booksellers and hawkers made as great efforts to procure it. What could a few poor authors do against so great a majority as the publick? There was no stopping a torrent with a finger, so out it came.

Many ludicrous circumstances attended it. The *Dunces* (for by this name they were called) held weekly clubs, to consult of hostilities against the author: one wrote a Letter to a great minister, assuring him Mr. Pope was the greatest enemy the government had; and another bought his image in clay, to execute him in effigy, with which sad sort of satisfaction the gentlemen were a little comforted.

Some false editions of the book having an owl in their frontispiece, the true one, to distinguish it, fixed in its stead an ass laden with authors. Then another surreptitious one being printed with the same ass, the new edition in octavo returned for distinction to the owl again. Hence arose a great contest of booksellers against booksellers, and advertisements against advertisements; some recommending the edition of the owl, and others the edition of the ass; by which names they came to be distinguished, to the great honour also of the gentlemen of the *Dunciad*.[61]

Pope appears by this narrative to have contemplated his victory over the *Dunces* with great exultation; and such was his delight in the tumult which he had raised, that for a while his natural sensibility was suspended, and he read reproaches and invectives without emotion, considering them only as the necessary effects of that pain which he rejoiced in having given.

It cannot however be concealed that, by his own confession, he was the aggressor; for nobody believes that the letters in the *Bathos* were placed at random; and it may be discovered that, when he thinks himself concealed, he indulges the common vanity of common men, and triumphs in those distinctions which he had affected to despise. He is proud that his book was presented to the King and Queen by the right honourable Sir Robert Walpole; he is proud that they had read it before; he is proud that the edition was taken off by the nobility and persons of the first distinction.

The edition of which he speaks was, I believe, that, which by telling in the text the names and in the notes the characters of those whom he had satirised, was made intelligible and diverting. The criticks had now declared their approbation of the plan, and the common reader began to like it without fear; those who were strangers to petty literature, and therefore unable to decypher initials and blanks, had now names and persons brought within

[61] *A Collection of Pieces* . . . *on occasion of the Dunciad*, 1732.

their view; and delighted in the visible effect of those shafts of malice, which they had hitherto contemplated, as shot into the air.

Dennis, upon the fresh provocation now given him, renewed the enmity which had for a time been appeased by mutual civilities; and published remarks, which he had till then suppressed, upon the *Rape of the Lock*. Many more grumbled in secret, or vented their resentment in the newspapers by epigrams or invectives.

Ducket, indeed, being mentioned as loving Burnet with *pious passion,* pretended that his moral character was injured, and for some time declared his resolution to take vengeance with a cudgel. But Pope appeased him, by changing *pious passion* to *cordial friendship,* and by a note, in which he vehemently disclaims the malignity of meaning imputed to the first expression.

Aaron Hill, who was represented as diving for the prize, expostulated with Pope in a manner so much superior to all mean solicitation, that Pope was reduced to sneak and shuffle, sometimes to deny, and sometimes to apologize: he first endeavours to wound, and is then afraid to own that he meant a blow.

The *Dunciad,* in the complete edition, is addressed to Dr. Swift: of the notes, part was written by Dr. Arbuthnot, and an apologetical Letter was prefixed, signed by Cleland,[62] but supposed to have been written by Pope.

After this general war upon dulness, he seems to have indulged himself awhile in tranquillity; but his subsequent productions prove that he was not idle. He published (1731) a poem on *Taste,* in which he very particularly and severely criticises the house, the furniture, the gardens, and the entertainments of *Timon,* a man of great wealth and little taste. By *Timon* he was universally supposed, and by the Earl of Burlington, to whom the poem is addressed, was privately said, to mean the Duke of Chandos; a man perhaps too much delighted with pomp and show, but of a temper kind and beneficent, and who had consequently the voice of the publick in his favour.

[62] William Cleland (1674?–1741), commissioner of taxes (not the novelist).

A violent outcry was therefore raised against the ingratitude and treachery of Pope, who was said to have been indebted to the patronage of Chandos for a present of a thousand pounds, and who gained the opportunity of insulting him by the kindness of his invitation.

The receipt of the thousand pounds Pope publickly denied;[63] but from the reproach which the attack on a character so amiable brought upon him, he tried all means of escaping. The name of Cleland was again employed in an apology, by which no man was satisfied; and he was at last reduced to shelter his temerity behind dissimulation, and endeavour to make that disbelieved which he never had confidence openly to deny. He wrote an exculpatory letter to the Duke, which was answered with great magnanimity, as by a man who accepted his excuse without believing his professions. He said, that to have ridiculed his taste, or his buildings, had been an indifferent action in another man; but that in Pope, after the reciprocal kindness that had been exchanged between them, it had been less easily excused.

Pope, in one of his Letters, complaining of the treatment which his poem had found, *owns that such criticks can intimidate him, nay almost persuade him to write no more, which is a compliment this age deserves.*[64] The man who threatens the world is always ridiculous; for the world can easily go on without him, and in a short time will cease to miss him. I have heard of an idiot, who used to revenge his vexations by lying all night upon the bridge. *There is nothing,* says Juvenal,[65] *that a man will not believe in his own favour.* Pope had been flattered till he thought himself one of the moving powers in the system of life. When he talked of laying down his pen, those who sat round him intreated and implored, and self-love did not suffer him to suspect that they went away and laughed.

The following year deprived him of Gay, a man whom he had known early, and whom he seemed to love with more tenderness than any other of his literary friends. Pope was now forty-four

---

[63] *Epistle to Dr. Arbuthnot,* l. 375n.

[64] To Burlington, March 7, 1731.

[65] *Satires,* IV. 70.

years old; an age at which the mind begins less easily to admit new confidence, and the will to grow less flexible, and when therefore the departure of an old friend is very acutely felt.

In the next year he lost his mother, not by an unexpected death, for she had lasted to the age of ninety-three; but she did not die unlamented. The filial piety of Pope was in the highest degree amiable and exemplary; his parents had the happiness of living till he was at the summit of poetical reputation, till he was at ease in his fortune, and without a rival in his fame, and found no diminution of his respect or tenderness. Whatever was his pride, to them he was obedient; and whatever was his irritability, to them he was gentle. Life has, among its soothing and quiet comforts, few things better to give than such a son.

One of the passages of Pope's life, which seems to deserve some enquiry, was a publication of Letters between him and many of his friends, which falling into the hands of Curll, a rapacious bookseller of no good fame, were by him printed and sold. This volume containing some Letters from noblemen, Pope incited a prosecution against him in the House of Lords for breach of privilege, and attended himself to stimulate the resentment of his friends. *Curll* appeared at the bar, and, knowing himself in no great danger, spoke of Pope with very little reverence. *He has,* said Curll, *a knack at versifying, but in prose I think myself a match for him.* When the orders of the House were examined, none of them appeared to have been infringed; Curll went away triumphant, and Pope was left to seek some other remedy.

Curll's account was, that one evening a man in a clergyman's gown, but with a lawyer's band, brought and offered to sale a number of printed volumes, which he found to be Pope's epistolary correspondence; that he asked no name, and was told none, but gave the price demanded, and thought himself authorised to use his purchase to his own advantage.

That Curll gave a true account of the transaction, it is reasonable to believe, because no falshood was ever detected; and when some years afterwards I mentioned it to Lintot, the son of Bernard, he declared his opinion to be that Pope knew better than any body else how Curll obtained the copies, because another parcel was at the same time sent to himself, for which no price had ever been demanded, as he made known his resolution not to pay a porter, and consequently not to deal with a nameless agent.

Such care had been taken to make them publick, that they were sent at once to two booksellers; to Curll, who was likely to seize them as a prey, and to Lintot, who might be expected to give Pope information of the seeming injury. Lintot, I believe, did nothing; and Curll did what was expected. That to make them publick was the only purpose may be reasonably supposed, because the numbers offered to sale by the private messengers shewed that hope of gain could not have been the motive of the impression.

It seems that Pope, being desirous of printing his Letters, and not knowing how to do, without imputation of vanity, what has in this country been done very rarely, contrived an appearance of compulsion; that when he could complain that his letters were surreptitiously published, he might decently and defensively publish them himself.

Pope's private correspondence, thus promulgated, filled the nation with praises of his candour, tenderness, and benevolence, the purity of his purposes, and the fidelity of his friendship. There were some Letters which a very good or a very wise man would wish suppressed; but, as they had been already exposed, it was impracticable now to retract them.

From the perusal of those Letters, Mr. Allen[66] first conceived the desire of knowing him; and with so much zeal did he cultivate the friendship which he had newly formed, that when Pope told his purpose of vindicating his own property by a genuine edition, he offered to pay the cost.

This however Pope did not accept; but in time solicited a subscription for a Quarto volume, which appeared (1737) I believe, with sufficient profit. In the Preface he tells that his Letters were reposited in a friend's library, said to be the Earl of

[66] Ralph Allen of Bath, eulogized by Pope in Epilogue to *Satires*, I. 135; and by Fielding in *Tom Jones*, Bk. VIII, ch. 1. Fielding dedicated *Amelia* to him.

Oxford's, and that the copy thence stolen was sent to the press. The story was doubtless received with different degrees of credit. It may be suspected that the Preface to the Miscellanies was written to prepare the publick for such an incident; and to strengthen this opinion, James Worsdale, a painter, who was employed in clandestine negotiations, but whose veracity was very doubtful, declared that he was the messenger who carried, by Pope's direction, the books to Curll.

When they were thus published and avowed, as they had relation to recent facts, and persons either then living or not yet forgotten, they may be supposed to have found readers; but as the facts were minute, and the characters being either private or literary, were little known, or little regarded, they awakened no popular kindness or resentment: the book never became much the subject of conversation; some read it as contemporary history, and some perhaps as a model of epistolary language; but those who read it did not talk of it. Not much therefore was added by it to fame or envy; nor do I remember that it produced either publick praise or publick censure.

It had however, in some degree the recommendation of novelty. Our language has few Letters, except those of statesmen. Howel indeed, about a century ago, published his Letters, which are commended by *Morhoff,* and which alone of his hundred volumes continue his memory.[67] Loveday's Letters were printed only once;[68] those of Herbert and Suckling are hardly known. Mrs. Phillip's [*Orinda*'s] are equally neglected; and those of Walsh seem written as exercises, and were never sent to any living mistress or friend. Pope's epistolary excellence had an open field; he had no English rival, living or dead.

Pope is seen in this collection as connected with the other contemporary wits, and certainly suffers no disgrace in the comparison; but it must be remembered, that he had the power of favouring himself: he might have originally had publication in his mind, and have writ[t]en with care, or have afterwards selected those which he had most happily conceived, or most diligently laboured; and I know not whether there does not

[67] James Howell, *Epistolae Ho-Elianae,* 1645.
[68] Robert Loveday, *Letters Domestick and Forrein,* 1659 and later (!).

appear something more studied and artificial in his productions than the rest, except one long Letter by Bolingbroke, composed with all the skill and industry of a professed author. It is indeed not easy to distinguish affectation from habit; he that has once studiously formed a style, rarely writes afterwards with complete ease. Pope may be said to write always with his reputation in his head; Swift perhaps like a man who remembered that he was writing to Pope; but Arbuthnot like one who lets thoughts drop from his pen as they rise into his mind.

Before these Letters appeared, he published the first part of what he persuaded himself to think a system of Ethicks, under the title of an *Essay on Man;* which, if his Letter to Swift (of Sept. 14, 1725) be rightly explained by the commentator, had been eight years under his consideration, and of which he seems to have desired the success with great solicitude. He had now many open and doubtless many secret enemies. The *Dunces* were yet smarting with the war; and the superiority which he publickly arrogated, disposed the world to wish his humiliation.

All this he knew, and against all this he provided. His own name, and that of his friend to whom the work is inscribed, were in the first editions carefully suppressed; and the poem, being of a new kind, was ascribed to one or another, as favour determined, or conjecture wandered; it was given, says Warburton, to every man, except him only who could write it. Those who like only when they like the author, and who are under the dominion of a name, condemned it; and those admired it who are willing to scatter praise at random, which while it is unappropriated excites no envy. Those friends of Pope, that were trusted with the secret, went about lavishing honours on the new-born poet, and hinting that Pope was never so much in danger from any former rival.

To those authors whom he had personally offended, and to those whose opinion the world considered as decisive, and whom he suspected of envy or malevolence, he sent his essay as a present before publication, that they might defeat their own enmity by praises, which they could not afterwards decently retract.

With these precautions, in 1733 was published the first part of the *Essay on Man*. There had been for some time a report that Pope was busy upon a System of Morality, but this design was not discovered in the new poem, which had a form and a title with which its readers were unacquainted. Its reception was not uniform; some thought it a very imperfect piece, though not without good lines. While the author was unknown, some, as will always happen, favoured him as an adventurer, and some censured him as an intruder; but all thought him above neglect; the sale increased, and editions were multiplied.

The subsequent editions of the first Epistle exhibited two memorable corrections. At first, the poet and his friend

> Expatiate freely o'er this scene of man,
> A mighty maze *of walks without a plan*.[69]

For which he wrote afterwards,

> A mighty maze, *but not without a plan*:

for, if there were no plan, it was in vain to describe or to trace the maze.

The other alteration was of these lines:

> And spite of pride, *and in thy reason's spite*,
> One truth is clear, whatever is, right,[70]

but having afterwards discovered, or been shewn, that the *truth* which subsisted *in spite of reason* could not be very *clear*, he substituted

> And spite of pride, *in erring reason's spite*.

To such oversights will the most vigorous mind be liable, when it is employed at once upon argument and poetry.

The second and third Epistles were published; and Pope was, I believe, more and more suspected of writing them; at last, in

[69] I. 5–6.
[70] I. 293–294.

1734, he avowed the fourth, and claimed the honour of a moral poet.

In the conclusion it is sufficiently acknowledged, that the doctrine of the *Essay on Man* was received from Bolingbroke, who is said to have ridiculed Pope, among those who enjoyed his confidence, as having adopted and advanced principles of which he did not perceive the consequence, and as blindly propagating opinions contrary to his own. That those communications had been consolidated into a scheme regularly drawn, and delivered to Pope, from whom it returned only transformed from prose to verse, has been reported, but hardly can be true. The Essay plainly appears the fabrick of a poet: what Bolingbroke supplied could be only the first principles; the order, illustration, and embellishments must all be Pope's.

These principles it is not my business to clear from obscurity, dogmatism, or falsehood; but they were not immediately examined; philosophy and poetry have not often the same readers; and the Essay abounded in splendid amplifications and sparkling sentences, which were read and admired, with no great attention to their ultimate purpose; its flowers caught the eye, which did not see what the gay foliage concealed, and for a time flourished in the sunshine of universal approbation. So little was any evil tendency discovered, that, as innocence as unsuspicious, many read it for a manual of piety.

Its reputation soon invited a translator. It was first turned into French prose, and afterwards by Resnel into verse. Both translations fell into the hands of Crousaz, who first, when he had the version in prose, wrote a general censure,[71] and afterwards reprinted Resnel's version, with particular remarks upon every paragraph.[72]

Crousaz was a professor of Switzerland, eminent for his treatise of Logick, and his *Examen de Pyrrhonisme*, and, however little known or regarded here, was no mean antagonist. His mind was one of those in which philosophy and piety are happily united.

[71] *Examen de l'essai de Monsieur Pope*, 1737.
[72] *Commentaire sur la traduction en vers de M. L'Abbé du Resnel*, etc., 1738.

He was accustomed to argument and disquisition, and perhaps was grown too desirous of detecting faults; but his intentions were always right, his opinions were solid, and his religion pure.

His incessant vigilance for the promotion of piety disposed him to look with distrust upon all metaphysical systems of Theology, and all schemes of virtue and happiness purely rational; and therefore it was not long before he was persuaded that the positions of Pope, as they terminated for the most part in natural religion, were intended to draw mankind away from revelation, and to represent the whole course of things as a necessary concatenation of indissoluble fatality; and it is undeniable, that in many passages a religious eye may easily discover expressions not very favourable to morals, or to liberty.

About this time Warburton began to make his appearance in the first ranks of learning. He was a man of vigorous faculties, a mind fervid and vehement, supplied by incessant and unlimited enquiry, with wonderful extent and variety of knowledge, which yet had not oppressed his imagination, nor clouded his perspicacity. To every work he brought a memory full fraught, together with a fancy fertile of original combinations, and at once exerted the powers of the scholar, the reasoner, and the wit. But his knowledge was too multifarious to be always exact, and his pursuits were too eager to be always cautious. His abilities gave him an haughty confidence, which he disdained to conceal or mollify; and his impatience of opposition disposed him to treat his adversaries with such contemptuous superiority as made his readers commonly his enemies, and excited against the advocate the wishes of some who favoured the cause. He seems to have adopted the Roman Emperor's determination, *oderint dum metuant;*[73] he used no allurements of gentle language, but wished to compel rather than persuade.

His style is copious without selection, and forcible without neatness; he took the words that presented themselves: his diction is coarse and impure, and his sentences are unmeasured.

He had, in the early part of his life, pleased himself with the notice of inferior wits, and corresponded with the enemies of

[73] "So they but fear, let them hate."—Suetonius, *Caligula,* xxx.

Pope. A Letter was produced, when he had perhaps himself forgotten it, in which he tells *Concanen,* "Dryden *I observe borrows for want of leasure, and* Pope *for want of genius:* Milton *out of pride, and* Addison *out of modesty."* [74] And when Theobald published *Shakespeare,* in opposition to Pope, the best notes were supplied by Warburton.

But the time was now come when Warburton was to change his opinion, and Pope was to find a defender in him who had contributed so much to the exaltation of his rival.

The arrogance of Warburton excited against him every artifice of offence, and therefore it may be supposed that his union with Pope was censured as hypocritical inconstancy; but surely to think differently, at different times, of poetical merit, may be easily allowed. Such opinions are often admitted, and dismissed, without nice examination. Who is there that has not found reason for changing his mind about questions of greater importance?

Warburton, whatever was his motive, undertook, without solicitation, to rescue Pope from the talons of Crousaz, by freeing him from the imputation of favouring fatality, or rejecting revelation; and from month to month continued a vindication of the *Essay on Man,* in the literary journal of that time called *The Republick of Letters.*

Pope, who probably began to doubt the tendency of his own work, was glad that the positions, of which he perceived himself not to know the full meaning, could by any mode of interpretation be made to mean well. How much he was pleased with his gratuitous defender, the following Letter evidently shews:

March 24 [, 1739.[75]]

Sir,

    I have just received from Mr. R. two more of your Letters. It is in the greatest hurry imaginable that I write this; but I cannot help thanking you in particular for

---

[74] Cf. Nichols, *Illustrations of the Literary History of the Eighteenth Century,* II, 195.

[75] The edition of 1783 gives the wrong date, 1743.

your third Letter, which is so extremely clear, short, and full, that I think Mr. Crousaz ought never to have another answer, and deserved not so good an one. I can only say, you do him too much honour, and me too much right, so odd as the expression seems; for you have made my system as clear as I ought to have done, and could not. It is indeed the same system as mine, but illustrated with a ray of your own, as they say our natural body is the same still when it is glorified. I am sure I like it better than I did before, and so will every man else. I know I meant just what you explain; but I did not explain my own meaning so well as you. You understand me as well as I do myself, but you express me better than I could express myself. Pray accept the sincerest acknowledgements. I cannot but wish these Letters were put together in one Book, and intend (with your leave) to procure a translation of part, at least, of all of them into French; but I shall not proceed a step without your consent and opinion, &c.

By this fond and eager acceptance of an exculpatory comment, Pope testified that, whatever might be the seeming or real import of the principles which he had received from Bolingbroke, he had not intentionally attacked religion; and Bolingbroke, if he meant to make him without his own consent an instrument of mischief, found him now engaged with his eyes open on the side of truth.

It is known that Bolingbroke concealed from Pope his real opinions. He once discovered them to Mr. Hooke, who related them again to Pope, and was told by him that he must have mistaken the meaning of what he heard; and Bolingbroke, when Pope's uneasiness incited him to desire an explanation, declared that Hooke had misunderstood him.

Bolingbroke hated Warburton, who had drawn his pupil from him; and a little before Pope's death they had a dispute, from which they parted with mutual aversion.

From this time Pope lived in the closest intimacy with his commentator, and amply rewarded his kindness and his zeal; for he

introduced him to Mr. Murray,[76] by whose interest he became
preacher at Lincoln's Inn, and to Mr. Allen, who gave him his
niece and his estate, and by consequence a bishoprick. When he
died, he left him the property of his works; a legacy which may
be reasonably estimated at four thousand pounds.

Pope's fondness for the *Essay on Man* appeared by his desire
of its propagation. Dobson, who had gained reputation by his
version of Prior's *Solomon,* was employed by him to translate it
into Latin verse, and was for that purpose some time at Twicken-
ham; but he left his work, whatever was the reason, unfinished;
and, by Benson's invitation, undertook the longer task of *Paradise
Lost.* Pope then desired his friend to find a scholar who should
turn his Essay into Latin prose; but no such performance has ever
appeared.

Pope lived at this time among the great,[77] with that reception
and respect to which his works entitled him, and which he had
not impaired by any private misconduct or factious partiality.
Though Bolingbroke was his friend, Walpole was not his enemy;
but treated him with so much consideration as, at his request, to
solicit and obtain from the French Minister an abbey for Mr.
Southcot, whom he considered himself as obliged to reward, by
this exertion of his interest, for the benefit which he had received
from his attendance in a long illness.

It was said, that, when the Court was at Richmond, Queen
Caroline had declared her intention to visit him. This may have
been only a careless effusion, thought on no more: the report of
such notice, however, was soon in many mouths; and, if I do not
forget or misapprehend Savage's account, Pope, pretending to
decline what was not yet offered, left his house for a time, not,
I suppose, for any other reason than lest he should be thought
to stay at home in expectation of an honour which would not be
conferred. He was therefore angry at Swift, who represents him
as *refusing the visits of a Queen,*[78] because he knew that what
had never been offered, had never been refused.

[76] Afterward Lord Mansfield.
[77] Pope, *Imitations of Horace, Satires,* II. i. 133.
[78] Pope to Swift, March 4, 1729/30.

Beside the general system of morality supposed to be contained in the *Essay on Man,* it was his intention to write distinct poems upon the different duties or conditions of life; one of which is the Epistle to Lord Bathurst (1733) on the *Use of Riches,* a piece on which he declared great labour to have been bestowed.

Into this poem some incidents are historically thrown, and some known characters are introduced, with others of which it is difficult to say how far they are real or fictitious; but the praise of *Kyrl,* the *Man of Ross,* deserves particular examination, who, after a long and pompous enumeration of his publick works and private charities, is said to have diffused all those blessings from *five hundred a year.* Wonders are willingly told, and willingly heard. The truth is, that *Kyrl* was a man of known integrity, and active benevolence, by whose solicitation the wealthy were persuaded to pay contributions to his charitable schemes; this influence he obtained by an example of liberality exerted to the utmost extent of his power, and was thus enabled to give more than he had. This account Mr. *Victor* received from the minister of the place, and I have preserved it, that the praise of a good man being made more credible, may be more solid. Narrations of romantick and impracticable virtue will be read with wonder, but that which is unattainable is recommended in vain; that good may be endeavoured, it must be shewn to be possible.

> This is the only piece in which the author has given a hint of his religion, by ridiculing the ceremony of burning the pope, and by mentioning with some indignation the inscription on the Monument.[79]

When this poem was first published, the dialogue, having no letters of direction, was perplexed and obscure. Pope seems to have written with no very distinct idea; for he calls that an *Epistle to Bathurst,* in which Bathurst is introduced as speaking.

He afterwards (1734) inscribed to Lord Cobham his *Characters of Men,* written with close attention to the operations of the mind and modifications of life. In this poem he has endeavoured to establish and exemplify his favourite theory of the

[79] See Pope, *Moral Essays,* III, ll. 339–40 (*Epistle to Bathurst*).

Ruling Passion, by which he means an original direction of desire to some particular object, an innate affection which gives all action a determinate and invariable tendency, and operates upon the whole system of life, either openly, or more secretly by the intervention of some accidental or subordinate propension.

Of any passion, thus innate and irresistible, the existence may reasonably be doubted. Human characters are by no means constant; men change by change of place, of fortune, of acquaintance; he who is at one time a lover of pleasure, is at another a lover of money. Those indeed who attain any excellence, commonly spend life in one pursuit, for excellence is not often gained upon easier terms. But to the particular species of excellence men are directed, not by an ascendant planet or predominating humour, but by the first book which they read, some early conversation which they heard, or some accident which excited ardour and emulation.

It must be at least allowed that this *ruling Passion,* antecedent to reason and observation, must have an object independent on human contrivance; for there can be no natural desire of artificial good. No man therefore can be born, in the strict acceptation, a lover of money; for he may be born where money does not exist; nor can he be born, in a moral sense, a lover of his country; for society, politically regulated, is a state contradistinguished from a state of nature; and any attention to that coalition of interests which makes the happiness of a country, is possible only to those whom enquiry and reflection have enabled to comprehend it.

This doctrine is in itself pernicious as well as false: its tendency is to produce the belief of a kind of moral predestination, or overruling principle which cannot be resisted; he that admits it, is prepared to comply with every desire that caprice or opportunity shall excite, and to flatter himself that he submits only to the lawful dominion of Nature, in obeying the resistless authority of his *ruling Passion.*

Pope has formed his theory with so little skill, that, in the examples by which he illustrates and confirms it, he has confounded passions, appetites, and habits.

To the *Characters of Men* he added soon after, in an Epistle supposed to have been addressed to Martha Blount, but which the last edition has taken from her, the *Characters of Women*. This poem, which was laboured with great diligence, and, in the author's opinion with great success, was neglected at its first publication, as the commentator supposes, because the publick was informed by an advertisement, that it contained *no Character drawn from the Life;* an assertion which Pope probably did not expect or wish to have been believed, and which he soon gave his readers sufficient reason to distrust, by telling them in a note, that the work was imperfect, because part of his subject was *Vice too high* to be yet exposed.

The time however soon came, in which it was safe to display the Dutchess of Malborough under the name of *Atossa;* and her character was inserted with no great honour to the writer's gratitude.

He published from time to time (between 1730 and 1740) Imitations of different poems of Horace, generally with his name, and once as was suspected without it. What he was upon moral principles ashamed to own, he ought to have suppressed. Of these pieces it is useless to settle the dates, as they had seldom much relation to the times, and perhaps had been long in his hands.

This mode of imitation, in which the ancients are familiarised, by adapting their sentiments to modern topicks, by making Horace say of Shakespeare what he originally said of Ennius, and accommodating his satires on Pantolabus and Nomentanus to the flatterers and prodigals of our own time, was first practised in the reign of Charles the Second by Oldham and Rochester, at least I remember no instances more ancient. It is a kind of middle composition between translation and original design, which pleases when the thoughts are unexpectedly applicable, and the parallels lucky. It seems to have been Pope's favourite amusement; for he has carried it further than any former poet.

He published likewise a revival, in smoother numbers, of Dr. Donne's Satires, which was recommended to him by the Duke of Shrewsbury and the Earl of Oxford. They made no great impression on the publick. Pope seems to have known their imbecillity, and therefore suppressed them while he was yet contending to rise in reputation, but ventured them when he thought their deficiencies more likely to be imputed to Donne than to himself.

The Epistle to Dr. Arbuthnot, which seems to be derived in its first design from Boileau's Address *à son Esprit*,[80] was published in January 1735, about a month before the death of him to whom it is inscribed. It is to be regretted that either honour or pleasure should have been missed by Arbuthnot; a man estimable for his learning, amiable for his life, and venerable for his piety.

Arbuthnot was a man of great comprehension, skilful in his profession, versed in the sciences, acquainted with ancient literature, and able to animate his mass of knowledge by a bright and active imagination; a scholar with great brilliancy of wit; a wit, who, in the crowd of life, retained and discovered a noble ardour of religious zeal.

In this poem Pope seems to reckon with the publick. He vindicates himself from censures; and with dignity, rather than arrogance, enforces his own claims to kindness and respect.

Into this poem are interwoven several paragraphs which had been before printed as a fragment, and among them the satirical lines upon Addison, of which the last couplet has been twice corrected. It was at first,

> Who would not smile if such a man there be?
> Who would not laugh if Addison were he?

Then,

> Who would not grieve if such a man there be?
> Who would not laugh if Addison were he?

At last it is,

> Who but must laugh if such a man there be?
> Who would not weep if Atticus were he? [81]

[80] Hill takes this to be a reference to the *Épître à mes vers*.
[81] Lines 213–214.

He was at this time at open war with Lord Hervey, who had distinguished himself as a steady adherent to the Ministry; and, being offended with a contemptuous answer to one of his pamphlets, had summoned Pulteney to a duel. Whether he or Pope made the first attack, perhaps cannot now be easily known: he had written an invective against Pope, whom he calls, *Hard as thy heart, and as thy birth obscure;* and hints that his father was a *hatter.* To this Pope wrote a reply in verse and prose: the verses are in this poem;[82] and the prose, though it was never sent, is printed among his Letters, but to a cool reader of the present time exhibits nothing but tedious malignity.

His last Satires, of the general kind, were two Dialogues, named from the year in which they were published *Seventeen Hundred and Thirty-eight.* In these poems many are praised and many are reproached. Pope was then entangled in the opposition; a follower of the Prince of Wales, who dined at his house, and the friend of many who obstructed and censured the conduct of the Ministers. His political partiality was too plainly shewn; he forgot the prudence with which he passed, in his earlier years, uninjured and unoffending through much more violent conflicts of faction.

In the first Dialogue, having an opportunity of praising Allen of Bath, he asked his leave to mention him as a man not illustrious by any merit of ancestors, and called him in his verses *low-born Allen.* Men are seldom satisfied with praise introduced or followed by any mention of defect. Allen seems not to have taken any pleasure in his epithet, which was afterwards softened into *humble Allen.*[83]

In the second Dialogue he took some liberty with one of the *Foxes,* among others;[84] which *Fox,* in a reply to Lyttelton, took an opportunity of repaying, by reproaching him with the friendship of a lampooner, who scattered his ink without fear or decency, and against whom he hoped the resentment of the Legislature would quickly be discharged.

[82] Lines 305–333.
[83] *Epilogue to the Satires:* Dialogue I, 135.
[84] *Epilogue, Dialogue* I, 71–2; II, 166.

About this time Paul Whitehead, a small poet, was summoned before the Lords for a poem called *Manners,* together with Dodsley his publisher. Whitehead, who hung loose upon society, sculked and escaped; but Dodsley's shop and family made his appearance necessary. He was, however, soon dismissed; and the whole process was probably intended rather to intimidate Pope than to punish Whitehead.

Pope never afterwards attempted to join the patriot with the poet, nor drew his pen upon statesmen. That he desisted from his attempts of reformation is imputed, by his commentator,[85] to his despair of prevailing over the corruption of the time. He was not likely to have been ever of opinion that the dread of his satire would countervail the love of power or of money; he pleased himself with being important and formidable, and gratified sometimes his pride, and sometimes his resentment; till at last he began to think he should be more safe, if he were less busy.

The *Memoirs of Scriblerus,* published about this time, extend only to the first book of a work, projected in concert by Pope, Swift, and Arbuthnot, who used to meet in the time of Queen Anne, and denominated themselves the *Scriblerus Club.* Their purpose was to censure the abuses of learning by a fictitious Life of an infatuated Scholar. They were dispersed; the design was never completed; and Warburton laments its miscarriage, as an event very disastrous to polite letters.

If the whole may be estimated by this specimen, which seems to be the production of Arbuthnot, with a few touches perhaps by Pope, the want of more will not be much lamented, for the follies which the writer ridicules are so little practised, that they are not known; nor can the satire be understood but by the learned: he raises phantoms of absurdity, and then drives them away. He cures diseases that were never felt.

For this reason this joint production of three great writers has never obtained any notice from mankind; it has been little read, or when read has been forgotten, as no man could be wiser, better, or merrier, by remembering it.

[85] Here, and elsewhere, Warburton is to be understood by this term.

The design cannot boast of much originality; for, besides its
general resemblance to *Don Quixote,* there will be found in it
particular imitations of the History of Mr. *Ouffle.*[86]

Swift carried so much of it into Ireland as supplied him with
hints for his *Travels;* and with those the world might have been
contented, though the rest had been suppressed.

Pope had sought for images and sentiments in a region not
known to have been explored by many other of the English
writers; he had consulted the modern writers of Latin poetry, a
class of authors whom Boileau endeavoured to bring into con-
tempt, and who are too generally neglected. Pope, however, was
not ashamed of their acquaintance, nor ungrateful for the ad-
vantages which he might have derived from it. A small selection
from the Italians who wrote in Latin had been published at
London, about the latter end of the last century, by a man who
concealed his name, but whom his Preface shews to have been
well qualified for his undertaking.[87] This collection Pope ampli-
fied by more than half, and (1740) published it in two volumes,
but injuriously omitted his predecessor's preface. To these books,
which had nothing but the mere text, no regard was paid, the
authors were still neglected, and the editor was neither praised
nor censured.

He did not sink into idleness; he had planned a work, which
he considered as subsequent to his *Essay on Man,* of which he
has given this account to Dr. Swift.

March 25, 1736.

If ever I write any more Epistles in verse, one of them
shall be addressed to you. I have long concerted it, and
begun it; but I would make what bears your name as
finished as my last work ought to be, that is to say, more
finished than any of the rest. The subject is large, and
will divide into four Epistles, which naturally follow the
Essay on Man, viz. 1. Of the Extent and Limits of Human

---

[86] L. Bordelot, *Histoire des imaginations extravagantes de M. Oufle,*
1710; English translation, 1711.

[87] *Anthologia,* 1684 (attributed to Thomas Power).

Reason and Science. 2. A View of the useful and there-
fore attainable, and of the unuseful and therefore unattain-
able Arts. 3. Of the Nature, Ends, Application, and Use
of different Capacities. 4. Of the Use of *Learning*, of the
Science, of the *World*, and of *Wit*. It will conclude with
a satire against the Misapplication of all these, exempli-
fied by Pictures, Characters, and Examples.

This work in its full extent, being now afflicted with an asthma,
and finding the powers of life gradually declining, he had no
longer courage to undertake; but, from the materials which he
had provided, he added, at Warburton's request, another book to
the *Dunciad*, of which the design is to ridicule such studies as
are either hopeless or useless, as either pursue what is unattain-
able, or what, if it be attained, is of no use.

When this book was printed (1742) the laurel had been for
some time upon the head of Cibber; a man whom it cannot be
supposed that Pope could regard with much kindness or esteem,
though in one of the Imitations of *Horace*[88] he has liberally
enough praised the *Careless Husband*. In the *Dunciad*, among
other worthless scribblers, he had mentioned Cibber, who, in
his *Apology*, complains of the great poet's unkindness as more
injurious, *because*, says he, *I never have offended him*.

It might have been expected that Pope should have been, in
some degree, mollified by this submissive gentleness; but no such
consequence appeared. Though he condescended to commend
Cibber once, he mentioned him afterwards contemptuously in
one of his Satires, and again in his Epistle to Arbuthnot,[89] and
in the fourth book of the *Dunciad* attacked him with acrimony,
to which the provocation is not easily discoverable. Perhaps he
imagined that, in ridiculing the Laureat, he satirised those by
whom the laurel had been given, and gratified that ambitious
petulance with which he affected to insult the great.

The severity of this satire left Cibber no longer any patience.
He had confidence enough in his own powers to believe that he

[88] *Epistles*, II. i. 91.
[89] *Satires*, II. i. 34 and *Epistle to Dr. Arbuthnot*, l. 373.

could disturb the quiet of his adversary, and doubtless did not want instigators, who, without any care about the victory, desired to amuse themselves by looking on the contest. He therefore gave the town a pamphlet,[90] in which he declares his resolution from that time never to bear another blow without returning it, and to tire out his adversary by perseverance, if he cannot conquer him by strength.

The incessant and unappeasable malignity of Pope he imputes to a very distant cause. After the *Three Hours after Marriage*[91] had been driven off the stage, by the offence which the mummy and crocodile gave the audience, while the exploded scene was yet fresh in memory, it happened that Cibber played *Bayes* in the *Rehearsal*; and, as it had been usual to enliven the part by the mention of any recent theatrical transactions, he said that he once thought to have introduced his lovers disguised in a Mummy and a Crocodile. "This," says he, "was received with loud claps, which indicated contempt of the play." Pope, who was behind the scenes, meeting him as he left the stage, attacked him, as he says, with all the virulence of a *Wit out of his senses*; to which he replied, "that he would take no other notice of what was said by so particular a man than to declare, that, as often as he played that part, he would repeat the same provocation."

He shews his opinion to be, that Pope was one of the authors of the play which he so zealously defended; and adds an idle story of Pope's behaviour at a tavern.

The pamphlet was written with little power of thought or language, and, if suffered to remain without notice, would have been very soon forgotten. Pope had now been enough acquainted with human life to know, if his passion had not been too powerful for his understanding, that, from a contention like his with Cibber, the world seeks nothing but diversion, which is given at the expence of the higher character. When Cibber lampooned Pope, curiosity was excited; what Pope would say of Cibber nobody enquired, but in hope that Pope's asperity might betray his pain and lessen his dignity.

[90] *A Letter to Mr. Pope,* 1742.
[91] By Gay, Arbuthnot, and Pope, 1717.

He should, therefore, have suffered the pamphlet to flutter and die, without confessing that it stung him. The dishonour of being shewn as Cibber's antagonist could never be compensated by the victory. Cibber had nothing to lose; when Pope had exhausted all his malignity upon him, he would rise in the esteem both of his friends and his enemies. Silence only could have made him despicable: the blow which did not appear to be felt, would have been struck in vain.

But Pope's irascibility prevailed, and he resolved to tell the whole English world that he was at war with Cibber; and to shew that he thought him no common adversary, he prepared no common vengeance: he published a new edition of the *Dunciad,* in which he degraded *Theobald* from his painful pre-eminence, and enthroned *Cibber* in his stead. Unhappily the two heroes were of opposite characters, and Pope was unwilling to lose what he had already written; he has therefore depraved his poem by giving to Cibber the old books, the cold pedantry and sluggish pertinacity of Theobald.

Pope was ignorant enough of his own interest, to make another change, and introduced Osborne contending for the prize among the booksellers. Osborne was a man intirely destitute of shame, without sense of any disgrace but that of poverty.[92] He told me, when he was doing that which raised Pope's resentment, that he should be put into the *Dunciad;* but he had the fate of Cassandra; I gave no credit to his prediction, till in time I saw it accomplished. The shafts of satire were directed equally in vain against Cibber and Osborne; being repelled by the impenetrable impudence of one, and deadened by the impassive dulness of the other, Pope confessed his own pain by his anger; but he gave no pain to those who had provoked him. He was able to hurt none but himself; by transferring the same ridicule from one to another, he destroyed its efficacy; for, by shewing that what he had said of one he was ready to say of another, he reduced himself to the insignificance of his own magpye, who from his cage calls cuckold at a venture.[93]

[92] His impertinence provoked a beating from Johnson.—Boswell, *Life,* I, 154.

[93] *Moral Essays,* I. 5.

Cibber, according to his engagement, repaid the *Dunciad* with another pamphlet,[94] which, Pope said, *would be as good as a dose of hartshorn to him;* but his tongue and his heart were at variance. I have heard Mr. Richardson[95] relate, that he attended his father the painter on a visit, when one of Cibber's pamphlets came into the hands of Pope, who said, *These things are my diversion.* They sat by him while he perused it, and saw his features writhen with anguish; and young Richardson said to his father, when they returned, that he hoped to be preserved from such diversion as had been that day the lot of Pope.

From this time, finding his diseases more oppressive, and his vital powers gradually declining, he no longer strained his faculties with any original composition, nor proposed any other employment for his remaining life than the revisal and correction of his former works; in which he received advice and assistance from Warburton, whom he appears to have trusted and honoured in the highest degree.

He laid aside his Epick Poem, perhaps without much loss to mankind; for his hero was *Brutus* the Trojan, who, according to a ridiculous fiction, established a colony in Britain. The subject therefore was of the fabulous age; the actors were a race upon whom imagination has been exhausted, and attention wearied, and to whom the mind will not easily be recalled, when it is invited in blank verse, which Pope had adopted with great imprudence, and, I think, without due consideration of the nature of our language. The sketch is, at least in part, preserved by Ruffhead; by which it appears, that Pope was thoughtless enough to model the names of his heroes with terminations not consistent with the time or country in which he places them.

He lingered through the next year; but perceived himself, as he expresses it, *going down the hill.*[96] He had for at least five years been afflicted with an asthma, and other disorders, which his physicians were unable to relieve. Towards the end of his life he consulted Dr. Thomson, a man who had, by large promises,

[94] *Another Occasional Letter from Mr. Cibber to Mr. Pope,* 1744.
[95] Jonathan Richardson.
[96] To Warburton, February 21, 1743/44.

and free censures of the common practice of physick, forced himself up into sudden reputation. Thomson declared his distemper to be a dropsy, and evacuated part of the water by tincture of jalap; but confessed that his belly did not subside. Thomson had many enemies, and Pope was persuaded to dismiss him.

While he was yet capable of amusement and conversation, as he was one day sitting in the air with Lord Bolingbroke and Lord Marchmont, he saw his favourite Martha Blount at the bottom of the terrace, and asked Lord Bolingbroke to go and hand her up. Bolingbroke, not liking his errand, crossed his legs, and sat still; but Lord Marchmont, who was younger and less captious, waited on the Lady; who, when he came to her, asked, *What, is he not dead yet?* She is said to have neglected him with shameful unkindness, in the latter time of his decay; yet, of the little which he had to leave, she had a very great part. Their acquaintance began early; the life of each was pictured on the other's mind; their conversation therefore was endearing, for when they met, there was an immediate coalition of congenial notions. Perhaps he considered her unwillingness to approach the chamber of sickness as female weakness, or human frailty; perhaps he was conscious to himself of peevishness and impatience, or, though he was offended by her inattention, might yet consider her merit as overbalancing her fault; and, if he had suffered his heart to be alienated from her, he could have found nothing that might fill her place; he could have only shrunk within himself; it was too late to transfer his confidence or fondness.

In May 1744, his death was approaching; on the sixth, he was all day delirious, which he mentioned four days afterwards as a sufficient humiliation of the vanity of man; he afterwards complained of seeing things as through a curtain, and in false colours; and one day, in the presence of Dodsley, asked what arm it was that came out from the wall. He said that his greatest inconvenience was inability to think.

Bolingbroke sometimes wept over him in this state of helpless decay; and being told by Spence, that Pope, at the intermission of his deliriousness, was always saying something kind either of his present or absent friends, and that his humanity seemed to have survived his understanding, answered, *It has so.* And added, *I never in my life knew a man that had so tender a heart for his particular friends, or a more general friendship for mankind.* At another time he said, *I have known Pope these thirty years, and value myself more in his friendship than*—[97] his grief then suppressed his voice.

Pope expressed undoubting confidence of a future state. Being asked by his friend Mr. Hooke, a papist, whether he would not die like his father and mother, and whether a priest should not be called, he answered, *I do not think it essential, but it will be very right; and I thank you for putting me in mind of it.*

In the morning, after the priest had given him the last sacraments, he said, "There is nothing that is meritorious but virtue and friendship, and indeed friendship itself is only a part of virtue."

He died in the evening of the thirtieth day of May, 1744, so placidly, that the attendants did not discern the exact time of his expiration. He was buried at Twickenham, near his father and mother, where a monument has been erected to him by his commentator, the Bishop of Gloucester.

He left the care of his papers to his executors, first to Lord Bolingbroke, and if he should not be living to the Earl of Marchmont, undoubtedly expecting them to be proud of the trust, and eager to extend his fame. But let no man dream of influence beyond his life. After a decent time Dodsley the bookseller went to solicit preference as the publisher, and was told that the parcel had not been yet inspected; and whatever was the reason, the world has been disappointed of what was *reserved for the next age.*

He lost, indeed, the favour of Bolingbroke by a kind of posthumous offence. The political pamphlet called *The Patriot King* had been put into his hands that he might procure the impression of a very few copies, to be distributed according to the author's direction among his friends, and Pope assured him that no more had been printed than were allowed; but, soon after his death, the printer brought and resigned a complete edition of fifteen hundred copies, which Pope had ordered him to print, and to retain in

[97] Spence, *Anecdotes*, p. 321.

secret. He kept, as was observed, his engagement to Pope better than Pope had kept it to his friend; and nothing was known of the transaction, till, upon the death of his employer, he thought himself obliged to deliver the books to the right owner, who, with great indignation, made a fire in his yard, and delivered the whole impression to the flames.

Hitherto nothing had been done which was not naturally dictated by resentment of violated faith; resentment more acrimonious, as the violator had been more loved or more trusted. But here the anger might have stopped; the injury was private, and there was little danger from the example.

Bolingbroke, however, was not yet satisfied; his thirst of vengeance excited him to blast the memory of the man over whom he had wept in his last struggles; and he employed Mallet, another friend of Pope, to tell the tale to the publick, with all its aggravations. Warburton, whose heart was warm with his legacy, and tender by the recent separation, thought it proper for him to interpose; and undertook, not indeed to vindicate the action, for breach of trust has always something criminal, but to extenuate it by an apology. Having advanced, what cannot be denied, that moral obliquity is made more or less excusable by the motives that produce it, he enquires what evil purpose could have induced Pope to break his promise. He could not delight his vanity by usurping the work, which, though not sold in shops, had been shewn to a number more than sufficient to preserve the author's claim; he could not gratify his avarice; for he could not sell his plunder till Bolingbroke was dead; and even then, if the copy was left to another, his fraud would be defeated, and if left to himself, would be useless.

Warburton therefore supposes, with great appearance of reason, that the irregularity of his conduct proceeded wholly from his zeal for Bolingbroke, who might perhaps have destroyed the pamphlet, which Pope thought it his duty to preserve, even without its author's approbation. To this apology an answer was written in a *Letter to the most impudent man living*.[98]

[98] By Bolingbroke: *A Familiar Epistle to the Most Impudent Man Living*, 1749.

He brought some reproach upon his own memory by the petulant and contemptuous mention made in his will of Mr. Allen, and an affected repayment of his benefactions. Mrs. Blount, as the known friend and favourite of Pope, had been invited to the house of Allen, where she comported herself with such indecent arrogance, that she parted from Mrs. Allen in a state of irreconcileable dislike, and the door was for ever barred against her. This exclusion she resented with so much bitterness as to refuse any legacy from Pope, unless he left the world with a disavowal of obligation to Allen. Having been long under her dominion, now tottering in the decline of life, and unable to resist the violence of her temper, or, perhaps with the prejudice of a lover, persuaded that she had suffered improper treatment, he complied with her demand, and polluted his will with female resentment. Allen accepted the legacy, which he gave to the Hospital at Bath; observing that Pope was always a bad accomptant, and that if to 150£ he had put a cypher more, he had come nearer to the truth.

THE person of Pope is well known not to have been formed by the nicest model. He has, in his account of the *Little Club*,[99] compared himself to a spider, and by another is described as protuberant behind and before. He is said to have been beautiful in his infancy; but he was of a constitution originally feeble and weak; and as bodies of a tender frame are easily distorted, his deformity was probably in part the effect of his application. His stature was so low, that, to bring him to a level with common tables, it was necessary to raise his seat. But his face was not displeasing, and his eyes were animated and vivid.

By natural deformity, or accidental distortion, his vital functions were so much disordered, that his life was a *long disease*.[100] His most frequent assailant was the headach, which he used to relieve by inhaling the steam of coffee, which he very frequently required.

[99] *The Guardian*, No. 92.
[100] *Epistle to Dr. Arbuthnot*, l. 131.

Most of what can be told concerning his petty peculiarities was communicated by a female domestick of the Earl of Oxford, who knew him perhaps after the middle of life. He was then so weak as to stand in perpetual need of female attendance; extremely sensible of cold, so that he wore a kind of fur doublet, under a shirt of very coarse warm linen with fine sleeves. When he rose, he was invested in boddice made of stiff canvass, being scarce able to hold himself erect till they were laced, and he then put on a flannel waistcoat. One side was contracted. His legs were so slender, that he enlarged their bulk with three pair of stockings, which were drawn on and off by the maid; for he was not able to dress or undress himself, and neither went to bed nor rose without help. His weakness made it very difficult for him to be clean.

His hair had fallen almost all away; and he used to dine sometimes with Lord Oxford, privately, in a velvet cap. His dress of ceremony was black with a tye-wig, and a little sword.

The indulgence and accommodation which his sickness required, had taught him all the unpleasing and unsocial qualities of a valetudinary man. He expected that every thing should give way to his ease or humour, as a child, whose parents will not hear her cry, has an unresisted dominion in the nursery.

> C'est que l'enfant toûjours est homme,
> C'est que l'homme est toûjours enfant.

When he wanted to sleep he *nodded in company;*[101] and once slumbered at his own table while the Prince of Wales was talking of poetry.

The reputation which his friendship gave, procured him many invitations; but he was a very troublesome inmate. He brought no servant, and had so many wants, that a numerous attendance was scarcely able to supply them. Wherever he was, he left no room for another, because he exacted the attention, and employed the activity of the whole family. His errands were so frequent and

[101] *Imitations of Horace, Satires,* II. i. 13.

frivolous, that the footmen in time avoided and neglected him; and the Earl of Oxford discharged some of the servants for their resolute refusal of his messages. The maids, when they had neglected their business, alleged that they had been employed by Mr. Pope. One of his constant demands was of coffee in the night, and to the woman that waited on him in his chamber he was very burthensome; but he was careful to recompense her want of sleep; and Lord Oxford's servant declared, that in a house where her business was to answer his call, she would not ask for wages.

He had another fault, easily incident to those who, suffering much pain, think themselves entitled to whatever pleasures they can snatch. He was too indulgent to his appetite; he loved meat highly seasoned and of strong taste; and, at the intervals of the table, amused himself with biscuits and dry conserves. If he sat down to a variety of dishes, he would oppress his stomach with repletion, and though he seemed angry when a dram was offered him, did not forbear to drink it. His friends, who knew the avenues to his heart, pampered him with presents of luxury, which he did not suffer to stand neglected. The death of great men is not always proportioned to the lustre of their lives. Hannibal, says Juvenal,[102] did not perish by a javelin or a sword; the slaughters of Cannæ were revenged by a ring. The death of Pope was inputed by some of his friends to a silver saucepan, in which it was his delight to heat potted lampreys.

That he loved too well to eat, is certain; but that his sensuality shortened his life will not be hastily concluded, when it is remembered that a conformation so irregular lasted six and fifty years, notwithstanding such pertinacious diligence of study and meditation.

In all his intercourse with mankind, he had great delight in artifice, and endeavoured to attain all his purposes by indirect and unsuspected methods. *He hardly drank tea without a stratagem.*[103] If, at the house of his friends, he wanted any accommodation, he was not willing to ask for it in plain terms, but would mention it remotely as something convenient; though, when it was pro-

---

[102] *Satires*, X. 163–166.
[103] Edward Young, *Satires*, VI, 188.

cured, he soon made it appear for whose sake it had been recommended. Thus he teized Lord Orrery till he obtained a screen. He practised his arts on such small occasions, that Lady Bolingbroke used to say, in a French phrase, that *he plaid the politician about cabbages and turnips.* His unjustifiable impression of the *Patriot King,* as it can be imputed to no particular motive, must have proceeded from his general habit of secrecy and cunning; he caught an opportunity of a sly trick, and pleased himself with the thought of outwitting Bolingbroke.

In familiar or convivial conversation, it does not appear that he excelled. He may be said to have resembled Dryden, as being not one that was distinguished by vivacity in company. It is remarkable, that, so near his time, so much should be known of what he has written, and so little of what he has said: traditional memory retains no sallies of raillery, nor sentences of observation; nothing either pointed or solid, either wise or merry. One apophthegm only stands upon record. When an objection raised against his inscription for Shakspeare was defended by the authority of *Patrick,* he replied—*horresco referens*—that *he would allow the publisher*[104] *of a Dictionary to know the meaning of a single word, but not of two words put together.*

He was fretful, and easily displeased, and allowed himself to be capriciously resentful. He would sometimes leave Lord Oxford silently, no one could tell why, and was to be courted back by more letters and messages than the footmen were willing to carry. The table was indeed infested by Lady Mary Wortley, who was the friend of Lady Oxford, and who, knowing his peevishness, could by no intreaties be restrained from contradicting him, till their disputes were sharpened to such asperity that one or the other quitted the house.

He sometimes condescended to be jocular with servants or inferiors; but by no merriment, either of others or his own, was he even seen excited to laughter.

[104] Johnson means *compiler,* and of course "shudders" because he was, like Patrick, one himself. Pope's inscription contained the questionable Latin phrase, "Amor Publicus Posuit," i.e. the monument was erected to Shakespeare by his countrymen's love.

Of his domestick character, frugality was a part eminently re-markable. Having determined not to be dependent, he deter-mined not to be in want, and therefore wisely and magnanimously rejected all temptations to expence unsuitable to his fortune. This general care must be universally approved; but it sometimes appeared in petty artifices of parsimony, such as the practice of writing his compositions on the back of letters, as may be seen in the remaining copy of the *Iliad,* by which perhaps in five years five shillings were saved; or in a niggardly reception of his friends, and scantiness of entertainment, as, when he had two guests in his house, he would set at supper a single pint upon the table; and having himself taken two small glasses would retire, and say, *Gentlemen, I leave you to your wine.* Yet he tells his friends, that *he has a heart for all, a house for all, and, whatever they may think, a fortune for all.*[105]

He sometimes, however, made a splendid dinner, and is said to have wanted no part of the skill or elegance which such per-formances require. That this magnificence should be often dis-played, that obstinate prudence with which he conducted his affairs would not permit; for his revenue, certain and casual, amounted only to about eight hundred pounds a year, of which however he declares himself able to assign one hundred to charity.

Of this fortune, which as it arose from publick approbation was very honourably obtained, his imagination seems to have been too full: it would be hard to find a man, so well entitled to notice by his wit, that ever delighted so much in talking of his money. In his Letters, and in his Poems, his garden and his grotto, his quincunx and his vines, or some hints of his opulence, are always to be found. The great topick of his ridicule is poverty; the crimes with which he reproaches his antagonists are their debts, their habitation in the Mint, and their want of a dinner. He seems to be of an opinion not very uncommon in the world, that to want money is to want every thing.

Next to the pleasure of contemplating his possessions, seems

[105] Pope, *Works,* ed. Elwin and Courthope, VII, 357. Letter to Swift, March 23, 1736/37.

to be that of enumerating the men of high rank with whom he was acquainted, and whose notice he loudly proclaims not to have been obtained by any practices of meanness or servility; a boast which was never denied to be true, and to which very few poets have ever aspired. Pope never set genius to sale; he never flattered those whom he did not love, or praised those whom he did not esteem. Savage however remarked, that he began a little to relax his dignity when he wrote a distich for *his Highness's dog*.[106]

His admiration of the Great seems to have increased in the advance of life. He passed over peers and statemen to inscribe his *Iliad* to Congreve, with a magnanimity of which the praise had been compleat, had his friend's virtue been equal to his wit. Why he was chosen for so great an honour, it is not now possible to know; there is no trace in literary history of any particular intimacy between them. The name of Congreve appears in the Letters among those of his other friends, but without any observable distinction or consequence.

To his latter works, however, he took care to annex names dignified with titles, but was not very happy in his choice; for, except Lord Bathurst, none of his noble friends were such as that a good man would wish to have his intimacy with them known to posterity: he can derive little honour from the notice of Cobham, Burlington, or Bolingbroke.

Of his social qualities, if an estimate be made from his Letters, an opinion too favourable cannot easily be formed; they exhibit a perpetual and unclouded effulgence of general benevolence, and particular fondness. There is nothing but liberality, gratitude, constancy, and tenderness. It has been so long said as to be commonly believed, that the true characters of men may be found in their Letters, and that he who writes to his friend lays his heart open before him. But the truth is, that such were the simple friendships of the *Golden Age,* and are now the friendships only of children.)Very few can boast of hearts which they dare lay open to themselves, and of which, by whatever accident exposed, they do not shun a distinct and continued view; and, certainly, what

---

[106] *Works, ed. cit.,* IV, 449.

﹥we hide from ourselves we do not shew to our friends. There is, indeed, no transaction which offers stronger temptations to fallacy and sophistication than epistolary intercourse.[107] In the eagerness of conversation the first emotions of the mind often burst out, before they are considered; in the tumult of business, interest and passion have their genuine effect; but a friendly Letter is a calm and deliberate performance, in the cool of leisure, in the stillness of solitude, and surely no man sits down to depreciate by design his own character.

Friendship has no tendency to secure veracity; for by whom can a man so much wish to be thought better than he is, as by him whose kindness he desires to gain or keep? Even in writing to the world there is less constraint; the author is not confronted with his reader, and takes his chance of approbation among the different dispositions of mankind; but a Letter is addressed to a single mind, of which the prejudices and partialities are known; and must therefore please, if not by favouring them, by forbearing to oppose them.

To charge those favorable representations, which men give of their own minds, with the guilt of hypocritical falshood, would shew more severity than knowledge. The writer commonly believes himself. Almost every man's thoughts, while they are general, are right; and most hearts are pure while temptation is away. It is easy to awaken generous sentiments in privacy; to despise death when there is no danger; to glow with benevolence when there is nothing to be given. While such ideas are formed they are felt, and﹥self-love does not suspect the gleam of virtue to be the meteor of fancy.﹤

If the Letters of Pope are considered merely as compositions, they seem to be premeditated and artificial. It is one thing to write because there is something which the mind wishes to discharge, and another, to solicit the imagination because ceremony or vanity requires something to be written. Pope confesses his early Letters to be vitiated with *affectation and ambition*:[108] to know whether he

---

[107] For the inverse of these sentiments, see the letter to Mrs. Thrale, 27 October, 1777 (*ante*, p. 25).

[108] Pope's Preface to *Letters*, 1737.

disentangled himself from these perverters of epistolary integrity, his book and his life must be set in comparison.

One of his favorite topicks is contempt of his own poetry. For this, if it had been real, he would deserve no commendation, and in this he was certainly not sincere; for his high value of himself was sufficiently observed, and of what could he be proud but of his poetry? He writes, he says, when *he has just nothing else to do;*[109] yet Swift complains that he was never at leisure for conversation, because he *had always some poetical scheme in his head.*[110] It was punctually required that his writing-box should be set upon his bed before he rose; and Lord Oxford's domestick related, that, in the dreadful winter of Forty, she was called from her bed by him four times in one night, to supply him with paper, lest he should lose a thought.

He pretends insensibility to censure and criticism, though it was observed by all who knew him that every pamphlet disturbed his quiet, and that his extreme irritability laid him open to perpetual vexation; but he wished to despise his criticks, and therefore hoped that he did despise them.

As he happened to live in two reigns when the Court paid little attention to poetry, he nursed in his mind a foolish disesteem of Kings, and proclaims that *he never sees Courts.*[111] Yet a little regard shewn him by the Prince of Wales melted his obduracy; and he had not much to say when he was asked by his Royal Highness, *how he could love a Prince while he disliked Kings?* [112]

He very frequently professes contempt of the world, and represents himself as looking on mankind, sometimes with gay indifference, as on emmets of a hillock, below his serious attention; and sometimes with gloomy indignation, as on monsters more worthy of hatred than of pity. These were dispositions apparently counterfeited. How could he despise those whom he lived by pleasing, and on whose approbation his esteem of himself was

[109] Preface to *Works,* 1717.
[110] Swift, *Works,* XVIII, 138.
[111] Swift, *Works,* VII. 111.
[112] Ruffhead, *Pope,* p. 535.

superstructed? Why should he hate those to whose favour he owed his honour and his ease? Of things that terminate in human life, the world is the proper judge; to despise its sentence, if it were possible, is not just; and if it were just, is not possible. Pope was far enough from this unreasonable temper; he was sufficiently *a fool to Fame*,[113] and his fault was that he pretended to neglect it. His levity and his sullenness were only in his Letters; he passed through common life, sometimes vexed, and sometimes pleased, with the natural emotions of common men.

His scorn of the Great is repeated too often to be real; no man thinks much of that which he despises; and as falsehood is always in danger of inconsistency, he makes it his boast at an-other time that he lives among them.

It is evident that his own importance swells often in his mind. He is afraid of writing, lest the clerks of the Post-office should know his secrets; he has many enemies; he considers himself as sur-rounded by universal jealousy; *after many deaths, and many dis-persions, two or three of us,* says he, *may still be brought together, not to plot, but to divert ourselves, and the world too, if it pleases;* and they can live together, and *shew what friends wits may be, in spite of all the fools in the world.*[114] All this while it was likely that the clerks did not know his hand; he certainly had no more enemies than a publick character like his inevitably excites, and with what degree of friendship the wits might live, very few were so much fools as ever to enquire.

Some part of this pretended discontent he learned from Swift, and expresses it, I think, most frequently in his correspondence with him. Swift's resentment was unreasonable, but it was sin-cere; Pope's was the mere mimickry of his friend, a fictitious part which he began to play before it became him. When he was only twenty-five years old, he related that *a glut of study and retirement had thrown him on the world,* and that there was danger lest *a glut of the world should throw him back upon study and retire-ment.*[115] To this Swift answered with great propriety, that Pope had

[113] *Epistle to Dr. Arbuthnot,* l. 127.
[114] To Swift, September 14, 1725, and March 23, 1736/37.
[115] *Works, ed. cit.,* VII, 37.

not yet either acted or suffered enough in the world to have become weary of it. And, indeed, it must be some very powerful reason that can drive back to solitude him who has once enjoyed the pleasures of society.

In the Letters both of Swift and Pope there appears such narrowness of mind, as makes them insensible of any excellence that has not some affinity with their own, and confines their esteem and approbation to so small a number, that whoever should form his opinion of the age from their representation, would suppose them to have lived amidst ignorance and barbarity, unable to find among their contemporaries either virtue or intelligence, and persecuted by those that could not understand them.

When Pope murmurs at the world, when he professes contempt of fame, when he speaks of riches and poverty, of success and disappointment, with negligent indifference, he certainly does not express his habitual and settled sentiments, but either wilfully disguises his own character, or, what is more likely, invests himself with temporary qualities, and sallies out in the colours of the present moment. His hopes and fears, his joys and sorrows, acted strongly upon his mind; and if he differed from others, it was not by carelessness; he was irritable and resentful; his malignity to Philips, whom he had first made ridiculous, and then hated for being angry, continued too long. Of his vain desire to make Bentley contemptible, I never heard any adequate reason. He was sometimes wanton in his attacks; and, before Chandos, Lady Wortley, and Hill, was mean in his retreat.

The virtues which seem to have had most of his affection were liberality and fidelity of friendship, in which it does not appear that he was other than he describes himself. His fortune did not suffer his charity to be splendid and conspicuous; but he assisted Dodsley with a hundred pounds, that he might open a shop; and of the subscription of forty pounds a year that he raised for Savage, twenty were paid by himself. He was accused of loving money, but his love was eagerness to gain, not solicitude to keep it.

In the duties of friendship he was zealous and constant: his early maturity of mind commonly united him with men older than

himself, and therefore, without attaining any considerable length
of life, he saw many companions of his youth sink into the grave;
but it does not appear that he lost a single friend by coldness or
by injury; those who loved him once, continued their kindness.
His ungrateful mention of Allen in his will, was the effect of his
adherence to one whom he had known much longer, and whom
he naturally loved with greater fondness. His violation of the
trust reposed in him by Bolingbroke could have no motive in-
consistent with the warmest affection; he either thought the
action so near to indifferent that he forgot it, or so laudable that
he expected his friend to approve it.

It was reported, with such confidence as almost to enforce
belief, that in the papers intrusted to his executors was found a
defamatory Life of Swift, which he had prepared as an instrument
of vengeance to be used, if any provocation should be ever given.
About this I enquired of the Earl of Marchmont, who assured me
that no such piece was among his remains.

The religion in which he lived and died was that of the Church
of Rome, to which in his correspondence with Racine he professes
himself a sincere adherent.[116] That he was not scrupulously pious
in some part of his life, is known by many idle and indecent appli-
cations of sentences taken from the Scriptures; a mode of merri-
ment which a good man dreads for its profaneness, and a witty
man disdains for its easiness and vulgarity. But to whatever levities
he has been betrayed, it does not appear that his principles were
ever corrupted, or that he ever lost his belief of Revelation. The
positions which he transmitted from Bolingbroke he seems not
to have understood, and was pleased with an interpretation that
made them orthodox.

A man of such exalted superiority, and so little moderation,
would naturally have all his delinquences observed and aggra-
vated: those who could not deny that he was excellent, would
rejoice to find that he was not perfect.

Perhaps it may be imputed to the unwillingness with which

[116] Cf. Pope's *Correspondence*, ed. George Sherburn, 1956, IV, 415–
16. Louis Racine, in his poem, *La Religion* (1742), had impugned Pope's
Essay on Man on grounds that Pope repudiated.

the same man is allowed to possess many advantages, that his learning has been depreciated. He certainly was in his early life a man of great literary curiosity; and when he wrote his *Essay on Criticism* had, for his age, a very wide acquaintance with books. When he entered into the living world, it seems to have happened to him as to many others, that he was less attentive to dead masters; he studied in the academy of Paracelsus, and made the universe his favourite volume. He gathered his notions fresh from reality, not from the copies of authors, but the originals of Nature. Yet there is no reason to believe that literature ever lost his esteem; he always professed to love reading; and Dobson, who spent some time at his house translating his *Essay on Man,* when I asked him what learning he found him to possess, answered, *More than I expected.* His frequent references to history, his allusions to various kinds of knowledge, and his images selected from art and nature, with his observations on the operations of the mind and the modes of life, shew an intelligence perpetually on the wing, excursive, vigorous, and diligent, eager to pursue knowledge, and attentive to retain it.

From this curiosity arose the desire of travelling, to which he alludes in his verses to Jervas, and which, though he never found an opportunity to gratify it, did not leave him till his life declined.

Of his intellectual character, the constituent and fundamental principle was Good Sense, a prompt and intuitive perception of consonance and propriety. He saw immediately, of his own conceptions, what was to be chosen, and what to be rejected; and, in the works of others, what was to be shunned, and what was to be copied.

But good sense alone is a sedate and quiescent quality, which manages its possessions well, but does not increase them; it collects few materials for its own operations, and preserves safety, but never gains supremacy. Pope had likewise genius; a mind active, ambitious, and adventurous, always investigating, always aspiring; in its widest searches still longing to go forward, in its highest flights still wishing to be higher; always imagining something greater than it knows, always endeavouring more than it can do.

To assist these powers, he is said to have had great strength and exactness of memory. That which he had heard or read was not easily lost; and he had before him not only what his own meditation suggested, but what he had found in other writers, that might be accommodated to his present purpose.

These benefits of nature he improved by incessant and unwearied diligence; he had recourse to every source of intelligence, and lost no opportunity of information; he consulted the living as well as the dead; he read his compositions to his friends, and was never content with mediocrity when excellence could be attained. He considered poetry as the business of his life, and however he might seem to lament his occupation, he followed it with constancy; to make verses was his first labour, and to mend them was his last.

From his attention to poetry he was never diverted. If conversation offered any thing that could be improved, he committed it to paper; if a thought, or perhaps an expression more happy than was common, rose to his mind, he was careful to write it; an independent distich was preserved for an opportunity of insertion, and some little fragments have been found containing lines, or parts of lines, to be wrought upon at some other time.

He was one of those few whose labour is their pleasure: he was never elevated to negligence, nor wearied to impatience; he never passed a fault unamended by indifference, nor quitted it by despair. He laboured his works first to gain reputation, and afterwards to keep it.

Of composition there are different methods. Some employ at once memory and invention, and, with little intermediate use of the pen, form and polish large masses by continued meditation, and write their productions only when, in their own opinion, they have completed them. It is related of Virgil that his custom was to pour out a great number of verses in the morning, and pass the day in retrenching exuberances and correcting inaccuracies. The method of Pope, as may be collected from his translation, was to write his first thoughts in his first words, and gradually to amplify, decorate, rectify, and refine them.

With such faculties, and such dispositions, he excelled every other writer in *poetical prudence*; he wrote in such a manner as

heroic couplet

might expose him to few hazards. He used almost always the same fabrick of verse; and, indeed, by those few essays which he made of any other, he did not enlarge his reputation. Of this uniformity the certain consequence was readiness and dexterity. By perpetual practice, language had in his mind a systematical arrangement; having always the same use for words, he had words so selected and combined as to be ready at his call. This increase of facility he confessed himself to have perceived in the progress of his translation.

But what was yet of more importance, his effusions were always voluntary, and his subjects chosen by himself. His independence secured him from drudging at a task, and labouring upon a barren topick: he never exchanged praise for money, nor opened a shop of condolence or congratulation. His poems, therefore, were scarce ever temporary. He suffered coronations and royal marriages to pass without a song, and derived no opportunities from recent events, nor any popularity from the accidental disposition of his readers. He was never reduced to the necessity of soliciting the sun to shine upon a birth-day, of calling the Graces and Virtues to a wedding, or of saying what multitudes have said before him. When he could produce nothing new, he was at liberty to be silent.

His publications were for the same reason never hasty. He is said to have sent nothing to the press till it had lain two years under his inspection: it is at least certain, that he ventured nothing without nice examination. He suffered the tumult of imagination to subside, and the novelties of invention to grow familiar. He knew that the mind is always enamoured of its own productions, and did not trust his first fondness. He consulted his friends, and listened with great willingness to criticism; and, what was of more importance, he consulted himself, and let nothing pass against his own judgement.

He professed to have learned his poetry from Dryden, whom, whenever an opportunity was presented, he praised through his whole life with unvaried liberality; and perhaps his character may receive some illustration if he be compared with his master.

Integrity of understanding and nicety of discernment were not

allotted in a less proportion to Dryden than to Pope. The rectitude
of Dryden's mind was sufficiently shewn by the dismission of his
poetical prejudices, and the rejection of unnatural thoughts and
rugged numbers. But Dryden never desired to apply all the judge-
ment that he had. He wrote, and professed to write, merely for
the people; and when he pleased others, he contented himself. He
spent no time in struggles to rouse latent powers; he never at-
tempted to make that better which was already good, nor often
to mend what he must have known to be faulty. He wrote, as he
tells us, with very little consideration; when occasion or necessity
called upon him, he poured out what the present moment hap-
pened to supply, and, when once it had passed the press, ejected
it from his mind; for when he had no pecuniary interest, he had
no further solicitude.

Pope was not content to satisfy; he desired to excel, and there-
fore always endeavoured to do his best: he did not court the can-
dour, but dared the judgement of his reader, and, expecting no in-
dulgence from others, he shewed none to himself. He examined
lines and words with minute and punctilious observation, and
retouched every part with indefatigable diligence, till he had left
nothing to be forgiven.

For this reason he kept his pieces very long in his hands, while
he considered and reconsidered them. The only poems which can
be supposed to have been written with such regard to the times
as might hasten their publication, were the two satires of *Thirty-
eight*; of which Dodsley told me, that they were brought to him
by the author, that they might be fairly copied. "Almost every
line," he said, "was then written twice over; I gave him a clean
transcript, which he sent some time afterwards to me for the press,
with almost every line written twice over a second time."

His declaration that his care for his works ceased at their publi-
cation, was not strictly true. His parental attention never aban-
doned them; what he found amiss in the first edition, he silently
corrected in those that followed. He appears to have revised the
Iliad, and freed it from some of its imperfections; and the *Essay on
Criticism* received many improvements after its first appearance.
It will seldom be found that he altered without adding clearness,

elegance, or vigour. Pope had perhaps the judgement of Dryden; but Dryden certainly wanted the diligence of Pope.

In acquired knowledge, the superiority must be allowed to Dryden, whose education was more scholastick, and who before he became an author had been allowed more time for study, with better means of information. His mind has a larger range, and he collects his images and illustrations from a more extensive circumference of science. Dryden knew more of man in his general nature, and Pope in his local manners. The notions of Dryden were formed by comprehensive speculation, and those of Pope by minute attention. There is more dignity in the knowledge of Dryden, and more certainty in that of Pope.

Poetry was not the sole praise of either; for both excelled likewise in prose; but Pope did not borrow his prose from his predecessor. The style of Dryden is capricious and varied, that of Pope is cautious and uniform; Dryden obeys the motions of his own mind, Pope constrains his mind to his own rules of composition. Dryden is sometimes vehement and rapid; Pope is always smooth, uniform, and gentle. Dryden's page is a natural field, rising into inequalities, and diversified by the varied exuberance of abundant vegetation; Pope's is a velvet lawn, shaven by the scythe, and levelled by the roller.

Of genius, that power which constitutes a poet; that quality without which judgement is cold and knowledge is inert; that energy which collects, combines, amplifies, and animates; the superiority must, with some hesitation, be allowed to Dryden. It is not to be inferred that of this poetical vigour Pope had only a little, because Dryden had more; for every other writer since Milton must give place to Pope; and even of Dryden it must be said, that if he has brighter paragraphs, he has not better poems. Dryden's performances were always hasty, either excited by some external occasion, or extorted by domestick necessity; he composed without consideration, and published without correction. What his mind could supply at call, or gather in one excursion, was all that he sought, and all that he gave. The dilatory caution of Pope enabled him to condense his sentiments, to multiply his images, and to accumulate all that study might produce, or chance might supply. If the flights of Dryden therefore are higher, Pope continues longer on the wing. If of Dryden's fire the blaze is brighter, of Pope's the heat is more regular and constant. Dryden often surpasses expectation, and Pope never falls below it. Dryden is read with frequent astonishment, and Pope with perpetual delight.

This parallel will, I hope, when it is well considered, be found just; and if the reader should suspect me, as I suspect myself, of some partial fondness for the memory of Dryden, let him not too hastily condemn me; for meditation and enquiry may, perhaps, shew him the reasonableness of my determination.

THE Works of Pope are now to be distinctly examined, not so much with attention to slight faults or petty beauties, as to the general character and effect of each performance.

It seems natural for a young poet to initiate himself by Pastorals, which, not professing to imitate real life, require no experience, and, exhibiting only the simple operation of unmingled passions, admit no subtle reasoning or deep enquiry. Pope's Pastorals are not however composed but with close thought; they have reference to the times of the day, the seasons of the year, and the periods of human life. The last, that which turns the attention upon age and death, was the author's favourite. To tell of disappointment and misery, to thicken the darkness of futurity, and perplex the labyrinth of uncertainty, has been always a delicious employment of the poets. His preference was probably just. I wish, however, that his fondness had not overlooked a line in which the *Zephyrs* are made *to lament in silence.*[117]

To charge these Pastorals with want of invention, is to require what never was intended. The imitations are so ambitiously frequent, that the writer evidently means rather to shew his literature than his wit. It is surely sufficient for an author of sixteen not only to be able to copy the poems of antiquity with judicious selection, but to have obtained sufficient power of language, and skill in metre, to exhibit a series of versification, which had in English poetry no precedent, nor has since had an imitation.

[117] *Pastorals,* IV, 49.

The design of *Windsor Forest* is evidently derived from *Cooper's Hill*, with some attention to Waller's poem on *The Park*; but Pope cannot be denied to excel his masters in variety and elegance, and the art of interchanging description, narrative, and morality. The objection made by Dennis is the want of plan, of a regular subordination of parts terminating in the principal and original design.[118] There is this want in most descriptive poems, because as the scenes, which they must exhibit successively, are all subsisting at the same time, the order in which they are shewn must by necessity be arbitrary, and more is not to be expected from the last part than from the first. The attention, therefore, which cannot be detained by suspense, must be excited by diversity, such as his poem offers to its reader.

But the desire of diversity may be too much indulged; the parts of *Windsor Forest* which deserve least praise, are those which were added to enliven the stillness of the scene, the appearance of Father Thames, and the transformation of *Lodona*. Addison had in his *Campaign* derided the *Rivers* that *rise from their oozy beds* to tell stories of heroes,[119] and it is therefore strange that Pope should adopt a fiction not only unnatural but lately censured. The story of *Lodona*[120] is told with sweetness; but a new metamorphosis is a ready and puerile expedient; nothing is easier than to tell how a flower was once a blooming virgin, or a rock an obdurate tyrant.

The *Temple of Fame* has, as Steele warmly declared, *a thousand beauties*. Every part is splendid; there is great luxuriance of ornaments; the original vision of Chaucer was never denied to be much improved; the allegory is very skilfully continued, the imagery is properly selected, and learnedly displayed: yet, with all this comprehension of excellence, as its scene is laid in remote ages, and its sentiments, if the concluding paragraph be excepted, have little relation to general manners or common life, it never obtained much notice, but is turned silently over, and seldom quoted or mentioned with either praise or blame.

[118] Remarks on Pope's Homer. *Critical Works*, ed. Hooker, II, 136.
[119] *The Campaign*, l. 470.
[120] *Windsor Forest*, l. 171.

That the *Messiah* excels the *Pollio*[121] is no great praise, if it be considered from what original [122] the improvements are derived.

The *Verses on the unfortunate Lady* have drawn much attention by the illaudable singularity of treating suicide with respect; and they must be allowed to be written in some parts with vigorous animation, and in others with gentle tenderness; nor has Pope produced any poem in which the sense predominates more over the diction. But the tale is not skilfully told: it is not easy to discover the character of either the Lady or her Guardian. History relates that she was about to disparage herself by a marriage with an inferior; Pope praises her for the dignity of ambition, and yet condemns the unkle to detestation for his pride; the ambitious love of a niece may be opposed by the interest, malice, or envy of an unkle, but never by his pride. On such an occasion a poet may be allowed to be obscure, but inconsistency never can be right.

The *Ode for St. Cecilia's Day* was undertaken at the desire of Steele: in this the author is generally confessed to have miscarried, yet he has miscarried only as compared with Dryden; for he has far outgone other competitors. Dryden's plan is better chosen; history will always take stronger hold of the attention than fable: the passions excited by Dryden are the pleasures and pains of real life, the scene of Pope is laid in imaginary existence; Pope is read with calm acquiescence, Dryden with turbulent delight; Pope hangs upon the ear, and Dryden finds the passes of the mind.

Both the odes want the essential constituent of metrical compositions, the stated recurrence of settled numbers. It may be alleged, that Pindar is said by Horace to have written *numeris lege solutis:* [123] but as no such lax performances have been transmitted to us, the meaning of that expression cannot be fixed; and perhaps the like return might properly be made to a modern Pindarist, as Mr. Cobb received from Bentley, who, when he found his criticisms upon a Greek Exercise, which Cobb had presented, refuted one after another by Pindar's authority, cried

[121] Virgil's *Eclogue* IV.
[122] *Isaiah.*
[123] *Odes,* IV. ii. 11: "in free verse."

out at last, *Pindar was a bold fellow, but thou art an impudent one.*

If Pope's Ode be particularly inspected, it will be found that the first stanza consists of sounds well chosen indeed, but only sounds.

The second consists of hyperbolical common-places, easily to be found, and perhaps without much difficulty to be as well expressed.

In the third, however, there are numbers, images, harmony, and vigour, not unworthy the antagonist of Dryden. Had all been like this—but every part cannot be the best.

The next stanzas place and detain us in the dark and dismal regions of mythology, where neither hope nor fear, neither joy nor sorrow can be found: the poet however faithfully attends us; we have all that can be performed by elegance of diction, or sweetness of versification; but what can form avail without better matter?

The last stanza recurs again to common-places. The conclusion is too evidently modelled by that of Dryden; and it may be remarked that both end with the same fault, the comparison of each is literal on one side, and metaphorical on the other.

Poets do not always express their own thoughts; Pope, with all this labour in the praise of Musick, was ignorant of its principles, and insensible of its effects.

One of his greatest though of his earliest works is the *Essay on Criticism,* which, if he had written nothing else would have placed him among the first criticks and the first poets, as it exhibits every mode of excellence that can embellish or dignify didactick composition, selection of matter, novelty of arrangement, justness of precept, splendour of illustration, and propriety of digression. I know not whether it be pleasing to consider that he produced this piece at twenty, and never afterwards excelled it: he that delights himself with observing that such powers may be soon attained, cannot but grieve to think that life was ever after at a stand.

To mention the particular beauties of the Essay would be unprofitably tedious; but I cannot forbear to observe, that the com-

parison of a student's progress in the sciences with the journey of
a traveller in the Alps,[124] is perhaps the best that English poetry
can shew. A simile, to be perfect, must both illustrate and ennoble
the subject; must shew it to the understanding in a clearer view,
and display it to the fancy with greater dignity: but either of
these qualities may be sufficient to recommend it. In didactick
poetry, of which the great purpose is instruction, a simile may be
praised which illustrates, though it does not ennoble; in heroicks,
that may be admitted which ennobles, though it does not illustrate.
That it may be complete, it is required to exhibit, independently
of its references, a pleasing image; for a simile is said to be a short
episode. To this antiquity was so attentive, that circumstances
were sometimes added, which, having no parallels, served only to
fill the imagination, and produced what Perrault ludicrously called
comparisons with a long tail. In their similes the greatest writers
have sometimes failed; the ship-race, compared with the chariot-
race, is neither illustrated nor aggrandised;[125] land and water make
all the difference: when Apollo, running after Daphne, is likened
to a greyhound chasing a hare,[126] there is nothing gained; the
ideas of pursuit and flight are too plain to be made plainer, and
a god and the daughter of a god are not represented much to their
advantage, by a hare and dog. The simile of the Alps has no use-
less parts, yet affords a striking picture by itself; it makes the
foregoing position better understood, and enables it to take faster
hold on the attention; it assists the apprehension, and elevates the
fancy.

Let me likewise dwell a little on the celebrated paragraph,[127]
in which it is directed that *the sound should seem an echo to the
sense*; a precept which Pope is allowed to have observed beyond
any other English poet.

This notion of representative metre, and the desire of dis-
covering frequent adaptations of the sound to the sense, have
produced, in my opinion, many wild conceits and imaginary beau-

[124] *An Essay on Criticism*, ll. 219 ff.
[125] *Æneid*, V. 144–147.
[126] Ovid, *Metamorphoses*, I. 533–538.
[127] *Essay*, ll. 337–383.

ties. All that can furnish this representation are the sounds of
the words considered singly, and the time in which they are pro-
nounced. Every language has some words framed to exhibit the
noises which they express, as *thump, rattle, growl, hiss*. These
however are but few, and the poet cannot make them more, nor
can they be of any use but when sound is to be mentioned. The
time of pronunciation was in the dactylick measures of the learned
languages capable of considerable variety; but that variety could
be accommodated only to motion or duration, and different degrees
of motion were perhaps expressed by verses rapid or slow, without
much attention of the writer, when the image had full posses-
sion of his fancy; but our language having little flexibility, our
verses can differ very little in their cadence. The fancied re-
semblances, I fear, arise sometimes merely from the ambiguity of
words; there is supposed to be some relation between a *soft* line
and a *soft* couch, or between *hard* syllables and *hard* fortune.

Motion, however, may be in some sort exemplified; and yet it
may be suspected that even in such resemblances the mind often
governs the ear, and the sounds are estimated by their meaning.
One of the most successful attempts has been to describe the
labour of Sisyphus:

> With many a weary step, and many a groan,
> Up a high hill he heaves a huge round stone;
> The huge round stone, resulting with a bound,
> Thunders impetuous down, and smoaks along the ground.[128]

Who does not perceive the stone to move slowly upward, and roll
violently back? But set the same numbers to another sense;

> While many a merry tale, and many a song,
> Chear'd the rough road, we wish'd the rough road long.
> The rough road then, returning in a round,
> Mock'd our impatient steps, for all was fairy ground.

We have now surely lost much of the delay, and much of the
rapidity.

[128] Pope's *Odyssey*, XI. 735–738.

But to shew how little the greatest master of numbers can fix
the principles of representative harmony, it will be sufficient to
remark that the poet, who tells us that

> When Ajax strives [some rock's vast weight to throw,
> The line too labours and] the words move slow:
> Not so when swift Camilla scours the plain,
> Flies o'er th' unbending corn, and skims along the main;[129]

when he had enjoyed for about thirty years the praise of Camilla's
lightness of foot, tried another experiment upon *sound* and *time*,
and produced this memorable triplet:

> Waller was smooth; but Dryden taught to join
> The varying verse, the full resounding line,
> The long majestick march, and energy divine.[130]

Here are the swiftness of the rapid race, and the march of
slow-paced majesty, exhibited by the same poet in the same se-
quence of syllables, except that the exact prosodist will find the
line of *swiftness* by one time[131] longer than that of *tardiness*.

Beauties of this kind are commonly fancied; and when real,
are technical and nugatory, not to be rejected, and not to be
solicited.

To the praises which have been accumulated on *The Rape of
the Lock* by readers of every class, from the critick to the waiting-
maid, it is difficult to make any addition. Of that which is uni-
versally allowed to be the most attractive of all ludicrous compo-
sitions, let it rather be now enquired from what sources the power
of pleasing is derived.

Dr. Warburton, who excelled in critical perspicacity, has re-
marked that the preternatural agents are very happily adapted
to the purposes of the poem. The heathen deities can no longer
gain attention: we should have turned away from a contest

---

[129] *Essay*, ll. 370–373.
[130] *Imitations of Horace, Epistles*, II. i. 267–269.
[131] Unit of prosodic measurement equal to a short syllable.

between Venus and Diana. The employment of allegorical persons always excites conviction of its own absurdity; they may produce effects, but cannot conduct actions; when the phantom is put in motion, it dissolves; thus *Discord* may raise a mutiny, but *Discord* cannot conduct a march, nor besiege a town. Pope brought into view a new race of Beings, with powers and passions proportionate to their operation. The sylphs and gnomes act at the toilet and the tea-table, what more terrifick and more powerful phantoms perform on the stormy ocean, or the field of battle, they give their proper help, and do their proper mischief.

Pope is said, by an objector, not to have been the inventer of this petty nation; a charge which might with more justice have been brought against the author of the *Iliad,* who doubtless adopted the religious system of his country; for what is there but the names of his agents which Pope has not invented? Has he not assigned them characters and operations never heard of before? Has he not, at least, given them their first poetical existence? If this is not sufficient to denominate his work original, nothing original ever can be written.

In this work are exhibited, in a very high degree, the two most engaging powers of an author. New things are made familiar, and familiar things are made new. A race of aerial people, never heard of before, is presented to us in a manner so clear and easy, that the reader seeks for no further information, but immediately mingles with his new acquaintance, adopts their interests, and attends their pursuits, loves a sylph, and detests a gnome.

That familiar things are made new, every paragraph will prove. The subject of the poem is an event below the common incidents of common life; nothing real is introduced that is not seen so often as to be no longer regarded, yet the whole detail of a female-day is here brought before us invested with so much art of decoration, that, though nothing is disguised, every thing is striking, and we feel all the appetite of curiosity for that from which we have a thousand times turned fastidiously away.

The purpose of the Poet is, as he tells us, to laugh at *the little unguarded follies of the female sex*. It is therefore without justice that Dennis charges the *Rape of the Lock* with the want of a moral,[132] and for that reason sets it below the *Lutrin,* which exposes the pride and discord of the clergy. Perhaps neither Pope nor Boileau has made the world much better than he found it; but if they had both succeeded, it were easy to tell who would have deserved most from publick gratitude. The freaks, and humours, and spleen, and vanity of women, as they embroil families in discord, and fill houses with disquiet, do more to obstruct the happiness of life in a year than the ambition of the clergy in many centuries. It has been well observed, that the misery of man proceeds not from any single crush of overwhelming evil, but from small vexations continually repeated.

It is remarked by Dennis likewise, that the machinery is superfluous;[133] that, by all the bustle of preternatural operation, the main event is neither hastened nor retarded. To this charge an efficacious answer is not easily made. The sylphs cannot be said to help or to oppose, and it must be allowed to imply some want of art, that their power has not been sufficiently intermingled with the action. Other parts may likewise be charged with want of connection; the game at *ombre* might be spared, but if the Lady had lost her hair while she was intent upon her cards, it might have been inferred that those who are too fond of play will be in danger of neglecting more important interests. Those perhaps are faults; but what are such faults to so much excellence!

The Epistle of *Eloise to Abelard* is one of the most happy productions of human wit: the subject is so judiciously chosen, that it would be difficult, in turning over the annals of the world, to find another which so many circumstances concur to recommend. We regularly interest ourselves most in the fortune of those who most deserve our notice. Abelard and Eloise were conspicuous in their days for eminence of merit. The heart naturally loves truth. The adventures and misfortunes of this illustrious pair are known from undisputed history. Their fate does not leave the mind in hopeless dejection; for they both found quiet and consolation in retirement and piety. So new and so affecting is their story, that

[132] Dennis, *Critical Works,* ed. Hooker, II, 330–331.
[133] *Ibid.,* p. 328.

it supersedes invention, and imagination ranges at full liberty without straggling into scenes of fable.

The story, thus skilfully adopted, has been diligently improved. Pope has left nothing behind him, which seems more the effect of studious perseverance and laborious revisal. Here is particularly observable the *curiosa felicitas,* a fruitful soil, and careful cultivation. Here is no crudeness of sense, nor asperity of language.

The sources from which sentiments, which have so much vigour and efficacy, have been drawn, are shewn to be the mystick writers by the learned author of the *Essay on the Life and Writings of Pope;*[134] a book which teaches how the brow of Criticism may be smoothed, and how she may be enabled, with all her severity, to attract and to delight.

The train of my disquisition has now conducted me to that poetical wonder, the translation of the *Iliad;* a performance which no age or nation can pretend to equal. To the Greeks translation was almost unknown; it was totally unknown to the inhabitants of Greece. They had no recourse to the Barbarians for poetical beauties, but sought for every thing in Homer, where, indeed, there is but little which they might not find.

The Italians have been very diligent translators; but I can hear of no version, unless perhaps Anguillara's Ovid[135] may be excepted, which is read with eagerness. The *Iliad*[136] of Salvini every reader may discover to be punctiliously exact; but it seems to be the work of a linguist skilfully pedantick, and his countrymen, the proper judges of its power to please, reject it with disgust.

Their predecessors the Romans have left some specimens of translation behind them, and that employment must have had some credit in which Tully and Germanicus engaged; but unless we suppose, what is perhaps true, that the plays of Terence were versions of Menander, nothing translated seems ever to have risen to high reputation. The French, in the meridian hour of their learning, were very laudably industrious to enrich their own lan-

[134] Joseph Warton, *An Essay on the Genius and Writings of Pope,* Vol. I, 1756.

[135] *Metamorfosi,* 1584, in ottava rima.

[136] 1723.

guage with the wisdom of the ancients; but found themselves reduced, by whatever necessity, to turn the Greek and Roman poetry into prose. Whoever could read an author, could translate him. From such rivals little can be feared.

The chief help of Pope in this arduous undertaking was drawn from the versions of Dryden. Virgil had borrowed much of his imagery from Homer, and part of the debt was now paid by his translator. Pope searched the pages of Dryden for happy combinations of heroic diction, but it will not be denied that he added much to what he found. He cultivated our language with so much diligence and art, that he has left in his *Homer* a treasure of poetical elegances to posterity. His version may be said to have tuned the English tongue; for since its appearance no writer, however deficient in other powers, has wanted melody. Such a series of lines so elaborately corrected, and so sweetly modulated, took possession of the publick ear; the vulgar was enamoured of the poem, and the learned wondered at the translation.

But in the most general applause discordant voices will always be heard. It has been objected by some, who wish to be numbered among the sons of learning, that Pope's version of Homer is not Homerical; that it exhibits no resemblance of the original and characteristick manner of the Father of Poetry, as it wants his awful simplicity, his artless grandeur, his unaffected majesty. This cannot be totally denied; but it must be remembered that *necessitas quod cogit defendit;* that may be lawfully done which cannot be forborn. Time and place will always enforce regard. In estimating this translation, consideration must be had of the nature of our language, the form of our metre, and, above all, of the change which two thousand years have made in the modes of life and the habits of thought. Virgil wrote in a language of the same general fabrick with that of Homer, in verses of the same measure, and in an age nearer to Homer's time by eighteen hundred years; yet he found, even then, the state of the world so much altered, and the demand for elegance so much increased, that mere nature would be endured no longer; and perhaps, in the multitude of borrowed passages, very few can be shewn which he has not embellished.

There is a time when nations emerging from barbarity, and falling into regular subordination, gain leisure to grow wise, and feel the shame of ignorance and the craving pain of unsatisfied curiosity. To this hunger of the mind plain sense is grateful; that which fills the void removes uneasiness, and to be free from pain for a while is pleasure; but repletion generates fastidiousness; a saturated intellect soon becomes luxurious, and knowledge finds no willing reception till it is recommended by artificial diction. Thus it will be found, in the progress of learning, that in all nations the first writers are simple, and that every age improves in elegance. One refinement always makes way for another, and what was expedient to Virgil was necessary to Pope.

I suppose many readers of the English *Iliad*, when they have been touched with some unexpected beauty of the lighter kind, have tried to enjoy it in the original, where, alas! it was not to be found. Homer doubtless owes to his translator many *Ovidian* graces not exactly suitable to his character; but to have added can be no great crime, if nothing be taken away. Elegance is surely to be desired, if it be not gained at the expence of dignity. A hero would wish to be loved, as well as to be reverenced.

To a thousand cavils one answer is sufficient; the purpose of a writer is to be read, and the criticism which would destroy the power of pleasing must be blown aside. Pope wrote for his own age and his own nation: he knew that it was necessary to colour the images and point the sentiments of his author; he therefore made him graceful, but lost him some of his sublimity.

The copious notes with which the version is accompanied, and by which it is recommended to many readers, though they were undoubtedly written to swell the volumes, ought not to pass without praise: commentaries which attract the reader by the pleasure of perusal have not often appeared; the notes of others are read to clear difficulties, those of Pope to vary entertainment.

It has however been objected, with sufficient reason, that there is in the commentary too much of unseasonable levity and affected gaiety; that too many appeals are made to the Ladies, and the ease which is so carefully preserved is sometimes the ease of a trifler. Every art has its terms, and every kind of instruction its proper style; the gravity of common criticks may be tedious, but is less despicable than childish merriment.

Of the *Odyssey* nothing remains to be observed: the same general praise may be given to both translations, and a particular examination of either would require a large volume. The notes were written by Broome, who endeavoured not unsuccessfully to imitate his master.

Of the *Dunciad* the hint is confessedly taken from Dryden's *Mac Flecknoe*; but the plan is so enlarged and diversified as justly to claim the praise of an original, and affords perhaps the best specimen that has yet appeared of personal satire ludicrously pompous.

That the design was moral, whatever the author might tell either his readers or himself, I am not convinced. The first motive was the desire of revenging the contempt with which Theobald had treated his *Shakspeare*, and regaining the honour which he had lost, by crushing his opponent. Theobald was not of bulk enough to fill a poem, and therefore it was necessary to find other enemies with other names, at whose expence he might divert the publick.

In this design there was petulance and malignity enough; but I cannot think it very criminal. An author places himself uncalled before the tribunal of Criticism, and solicits fame at the hazard of disgrace. Dulness or deformity are not culpable in themselves, but may be very justly reproached when they pretend to the honour of wit or the influence of beauty. If bad writers were to pass without reprehension, what should restrain them? *impune diem consumpserit ingens Telephus;*[137] and upon bad writers only will censure have much effect. The satire which brought Theobald and Moore[138] into contempt, dropped impotent from Bentley, like the javelin of Priam.[139]

All truth is valuable, and satirical criticism may be considered

---

[137] Juvenal, *Satires*, I. 5: "Shall a vast *Telephus* take up the whole day without penalty?"

[138] Cf. *Dunciad*, II. 35–50, 109–120.

[139] *Æneid*, II. 544.

as useful when it rectifies error and improves judgement; he that refines the publick taste is a publick benefactor.

The beauties of this poem are well known; its chief fault is the grossness of its images. Pope and Swift had an unnatural delight in ideas physically impure, such as every other tongue utters with unwillingness, and of which every ear shrinks from the mention.

But even this fault, offensive as it is, may be forgiven for the excellence of other passages; such as the formation and dissolution of Moore, the account of the Traveller,[140] the misfortune of the Florist,[141] and the crouded thoughts and stately numbers which dignify the concluding paragraph.

The alterations which have been made in the *Dunciad,* not always for the better, require that it should be published, as in the last collection, with all its variations.

The *Essay on Man* was a work of great labour and long consideration, but certainly not the happiest of Pope's performances. The subject is perhaps not very proper for poetry, and the poet was not sufficiently master of his subject; metaphysical morality was to him a new study, he was proud of his acquisitions, and, supposing himself master of great secrets, was in haste to teach what he had not learned. Thus he tells us, in the first Epistle, that from the nature of the Supreme Being may be deduced an order of beings such as mankind, because Infinite Excellence can do only what is best. He finds out that these beings must be *somewhere,* and that *all the question is whether man be in a wrong place.* Surely if, according to the poet's Leibnitian reasoning, we may infer that man ought to be, only because he is, we may allow that his place is the right place, because he has it. Supreme Wisdom is not less infallible in disposing than in creating. But what is meant by *somewhere* and *place,* and *wrong place,* it had been vain to ask Pope, who probably had never asked himself.

Having exalted himself into the chair of wisdom, he tells us much that every man knows, and much that he does not know himself; that we see but little, and that the order of the universe

[140] *Dunciad,* IV. 293–336.
[141] *Ibid.,* ll. 403–436.

is beyond our comprehension; an opinion not very uncommon; and that there is a chain of subordinate beings *from infinite to nothing,* of which himself and his readers are equally ignorant. But he gives us one comfort, which, without his help, he supposes unattainable, in the position *that though we are fools, yet God is wise.*

This Essay affords an egregious instance of the predominance of genius, the dazzling splendour of imagery, and the seductive powers of eloquence. Never were penury of knowledge and vulgarity of sentiment so happily disguised. The reader feels his mind full, though he learns nothing; and when he meets it in its new array, no longer knows the talk of his mother and his nurse. When these wonder-working sounds sink into sense, and the doctrine of the Essay, disrobed of its ornaments, is left to the powers of its naked excellence, what shall we discover? That we are, in comparison with our Creator, very weak and ignorant; that we do not uphold the chain of existence, and that we could not make one another with more skill than we are made. We may learn yet more; that the arts of human life were copied from the instinctive operations of other animals; that if the world be made for man, it may be said that man was made for geese. To these profound principles of natural knowledge are added some moral instructions equally new: that self-interest, well understood, will produce social concord; that men are mutual gainers by mutual benefits; that evil is sometimes balanced by good; that human advantages are unstable and fallacious, of uncertain duration and doubtful effect; that our true honour is, not to have a great part, but to act it well: that virtue only is our own; and that happiness is always in our power.

Surely a man of no very comprehensive search may venture to say that he has heard all this before; but it was never till now recommended by such a blaze of embellishment, or such sweetness of melody. The vigorous contraction of some thoughts, the luxuriant amplification of others, the incidental illustrations, and sometimes the dignity, sometimes the softness of the verses, enchain philosophy, suspend criticism, and oppress judgement by overpowering pleasure.

This is true of many paragraphs; yet if I had undertaken to exemplify Pope's felicity of composition before a rigid critick, I should not select the *Essay on Man,* for it contains more lines unsuccessfully laboured, more harshness of diction, more thoughts imperfectly expressed, more levity without elegance, and more heaviness without strength, than will easily be found in all his other works.

The *Characters of Men and Women* are the product of diligent speculation upon human life; much labour has been bestowed upon them, and Pope very seldom laboured in vain. That his excellence may be properly estimated, I recommend a comparison of his *Characters of Women* with Boileau's Satire; it will then be seen with how much more perspicacity female nature is investigated, and female excellence selected; and he surely is no mean writer to whom Boileau shall be found inferior. The *Characters of Men,* however, are written with more, if not with deeper, thought, and exhibit many passages exquisitely beautiful. The *Gem and the Flower* will not easily be equalled.[142] In the women's part are some defects; the character of *Atossa* is not so neatly finished as that of *Clodio;*[143] and some of the female characters may be found perhaps more frequently among men; what is said of *Philomede*[144] was true of *Prior.*

In the Epistles to Lord Bathurst and Lord Burlington, Dr. Warburton has endeavoured to find a train of thought which was never in the writer's head, and, to support his hypothesis, has printed that first which was published last. In one, the most valuable passage is perhaps the Elogy on *Good Sense,*[145] and the other the *End of the Duke of Buckingham.*[146]

The Epistle to Arbuthnot, now arbitrarily called the *Prologue to the Satires,* is a performance consisting, as it seems, of many fragments wrought into one design, which by this union of scattered beauties contains more striking paragraphs than could prob-

---

[142] *Moral Essays,* I. 141–148.

[143] *Ibid.,* II. 115; I. 179.

[144] *Ibid.,* II. 83.

[145] *Ibid.,* IV. 39.

[146] *Ibid.,* III. 299.

ably have been brought together into an occasional work. As there
is no stronger motive to exertion than self-defence, no part has
more elegance, spirit, or dignity, than the poet's vindication of his
own character. The meanest passage is the satire upon *Sporus.*[147]

Of the two poems which derived their names from the year, and
which are called the *Epilogue to the Satires,* it was very justly
remarked by Savage, that the second was in the whole more
strongly conceived, and more equally supported, but that it had
no single passages equal to the contention in the first for the dig-
nity of Vice, and the celebration of the triumph of Corruption.[148]

The Imitations of Horace seem to have been written as relaxa-
tions of his genius. This employment became his favourite by
its facility; the plan was ready to his hand, and nothing was re-
quired but to accommodate as he could the sentiments of an old
author to recent facts or familiar images; but what is easy is seldom
excellent; such imitations cannot give pleasure to common readers;
the man of learning may be sometimes surprised and delighted by
an unexpected parallel; but the comparison requires knowledge of
the original, which will likewise often detect strained applications.
Between Roman images and English manners there will be an
irreconcileable dissimilitude, and the work will be generally un-
couth and party-coloured; neither original nor translated, neither
ancient nor modern.

Pope had, in proportions very nicely adjusted to each other, all
the qualities that constitute genius. He had *Invention,* by which
new trains of events are formed, and new scenes of imagery
displayed, as in the *Rape of the Lock*; and by which extrinsick
and adventitious embellishments and illustrations are connected
with a known subject, as in the *Essay on Criticism.* He had *Imag-
ination,* which strongly impresses on the writer's mind, and en-
ables him to convey to the reader, the various forms of nature,
incidents of life, and energies of passion, as in his *Eloisa, Windsor
Forest,* and the *Ethick Epistles.* He had *Judgement* which selects
from life or nature what the present purpose requires, and, by

---

[147] Lines 305–333.
[148] *Epilogue,* I. 114, 142.

THE LIFE OF POPE

separating the essence of things from its concomitants, often makes the representation more powerful than the reality: and he had colours of language always before him, ready to decorate his matter with every grace of elegant expression, as when he accommodates his diction to the wonderful multiplicity of Homer's sentiments and descriptions.

Poetical expression includes sound as well as meaning; *Musick,* says Dryden, *is inarticulate poetry;*[149] among the excellences of Pope, therefore, must be mentioned the melody of his metre. By perusing the works of Dryden, he discovered the most perfect fabrick of English verse, and habituated himself to that only which he found the best; in consequence of which restraint, his poetry has been censured as too uniformly musical, and as glutting the ear with unvaried sweetness. I suspect this objection to be the cant of those who judge by principles rather than perception: and who would even themselves have less pleasure in his works, if he had tried to relieve attention by studied discords, or affected to break his lines and vary his pauses.

But though he was thus careful of his versification, he did not oppress his powers with superfluous rigour. He seems to have thought with Boileau, that the practice of writing might be refined till the difficulty should overbalance the advantage. The construction of his language is not always strictly grammatical; with those rhymes which prescription had conjoined he contented himself, without regard to Swift's remonstrances,[150] though there was no striking consonance; nor was he very careful to vary his terminations, or to refuse admission at a small distance to the same rhymes.

To Swift's edict for the exclusion of Alexandrines and Triplets he paid little regard; he admitted them, but, in the opinion of Fenton, too rarely; he uses them more liberally in his translation than his poems.

He has a few double rhymes; and always, I think, unsuccessfully, except once in the *Rape of the Lock.*

[149] Preface to *Tyrannic Love. Works,* 1821, III, 350.
[150] Swift to Pope, June 28, 1715.

Expletives he very early ejected from his verses; but he now and then admits an epithet rather commodious than important. Each of the six first lines of the *Iliad* might lose two syllables with very little diminution of the meaning; and sometimes, after all his art and labour, one verse seems to be made for the sake of another. In his latter productions the diction is sometimes vitiated by French idioms, with which Bolingbroke had perhaps infected him.

I have been told that the couplet by which he declared his own ear to be most gratified was this:

> Lo, where Mæotis sleeps, and hardly flows
> The freezing Tanais thro' a waste of snows.[151]

But the reason of this preference I cannot discover.

It is remarked by Watts,[152] that there is scarcely a happy combination of words, or a phrase poetically elegant in the English language, which Pope has not inserted into his version of Homer. How he obtained possession of so many beauties of speech, it were desirable to know. That he gleaned from authors, obscure as well as eminent, what he thought brilliant or useful, and preserved it all in a regular collection, is not unlikely. When, in his last years, Hall's Satires[153] were shewn him, he wish'd that he had seen them sooner.

New sentiments and new images others may produce; but to attempt any further improvement of versification will be dangerous. Art and diligence have now done their best, and what shall be added will be the effort of tedious toil and needless curiosity.

After all this, it is surely superfluous to answer the question that has once been asked, Whether Pope was a poet? otherwise than by asking in return, If Pope be not a poet, where is poetry to be found? To circumscribe poetry by a definition will only shew the narrowness of the definer, though a definition which shall exclude Pope will not easily be made. Let us look round upon the present time, and back upon the past; let us enquire to whom

---

[151] *Dunciad*, III. 87–88.
[152] *The Improvement of the Mind*, 1741, ch. 20, sec. 36.
[153] *Virgidemiarum*, 1597–1598.

the voice of mankind has decreed the wreath of poetry; let their productions be examined, and their claims stated, and the pretensions of Pope will be no more disputed. Had he given the world only his version, the name of poet must have been allowed him: if the writer of the *Iliad* were to class his successors, he would assign a very high place to his translator, without requiring any other evidence of Genius.

The Life of Savage

It has been observed in all ages, that the advantages of nature or of fortune have contributed very little to the promotion of happiness; and that those whom the splendour of their rank, or the extent of their capacity, have placed upon the summits of human life, have not often given any just occasion to envy in those who look up to them from a lower station: whether it be that apparent superiority incites great designs, and great designs are naturally liable to fatal miscarriages; or that the general lot of mankind is misery, and the misfortunes of those whose eminence drew upon them an universal attention, have been more carefully recorded, because they were more generally observed, and have in reality been only more conspicuous than those of others, not more frequent, or more severe.

That affluence and power, advantages extrinsic and adventitious, and therefore easily separable from those by whom they are possessed, should very often flatter the mind with expectations of felicity which they cannot give, raises no astonishment; but it seems rational to hope, that intellectual greatness should produce better effects: that minds qualified for great attainments should first endeavour their own benefit; and that they who are most able to teach others the way to happiness, should with most certainty follow it themselves.

But this expectation, however plausible, has been very frequently disappointed. The heroes of literary as well as civil history have been very often no less remarkable for what they have atchieved; and volumes have been written only to enumerate the miseries of the learned, and relate their unhappy lives, and untimely deaths.

To these mournful narratives, I am about to add the Life of Richard Savage, a man whose writings entitle him to an eminent rank in the classes of learning, and whose misfortunes claim a degree of compassion, not always due to the unhappy, as they were often the consequences of the crimes of others, rather than his own.

In the year 1697, Anne Countess of Macclesfield, having lived for some time upon very uneasy terms with her husband, thought a public confession of adultery the most obvious and expeditious method of obtaining her liberty; and therefore declared, that the child, with which she was then great, was begotten by the Earl Rivers. This, as may be imagined, made her husband no less desirous of a separation than herself, and he prosecuted his design in the most effectual manner; for he applied not to the ecclesiastical courts for a divorce, but to the parliament for an act, by which his marriage might be dissolved, the nuptial contract totally annulled, and the children of his wife illegitimated. This act, after the usual deliberation, he obtained, though without the approbation of some, who considered marriage as an affair only cognizable by ecclesiastical judges; and on March 3d was separated from his wife, whose fortune, which was very great, was repaid her, and who having, as well as her husband, the liberty of making another choice, was in a short time married to Colonel Brett.

While the Earl of Macclesfield was prosecuting this affair, his wife was, on the 10th of January 1697–8, delivered of a son, and the Earl Rivers, by appearing to consider him as his own, left none any reason to doubt of the sincerity of her declaration; for he was his godfather, and gave him his own name, which was by his direction inserted in the register of St. Andrew's parish in Holborn, but unfortunately left him to the care of his mother, whom, as she was now set free from her husband, he probably imagined likely to treat with great tenderness the child that had contributed to so pleasing an event. It is not indeed easy to discover what motives could be found to over-balance that natural affection of a parent, or what interest could be promoted by neglect or cruelty. The dread of shame or of poverty, by which some wretches have been incited to abandon or to murder their children, cannot be supposed to have affected a woman who had proclaimed her crimes and solicited reproach, and on whom the clemency of the legislature had undeservedly bestowed a fortune, which would have been very little diminished by the expences which the care of her child could have brought upon her. It was therefore not likely that she would be wicked without temptation, that she would look upon her son from his birth with a kind of resentment and abhorrence; and, instead of supporting, assisting, and defending him, delight to see him struggling with misery, or that she would take every opportunity of aggravating his misfortunes, and obstructing his resources, and with an implacable and restless cruelty continue her persecution from the first hour of his life to the last.

But whatever were her motives, no sooner was her son born, than she discovered a resolution of disowning him; and in a very short time removed him from her sight, by committing him to the care of a poor woman, whom she directed to educate him as her own, and injoined never to inform him of his true parents.

Such was the beginning of the life of Richard Savage. Born with a legal claim to honour and to affluence, he was in two months illegitimated by the parliament, and disowned by his mother, doomed to poverty and obscurity, and launched upon the ocean of life, only that he might be swallowed by its quicksands or dashed upon its rocks.

His mother could not indeed infect others with the same cruelty. As it was impossible to avoid the inquiries which the curiosity or tenderness of her relations made after her child, she was obliged to give some account of the measures that she had taken; and her mother, the Lady Mason, whether in approbation of her design, or to prevent more criminal contrivances, engaged to transact with the nurse, to pay her for her care, and to superintend the education of the child.

In this charitable office she was assisted by his godmother, Mrs. Lloyd, who, while she lived, always looked upon him with that tenderness, which the barbarity of his mother made peculiarly necessary; but her death, which happened in his tenth year, was another of the misfortunes of his childhood; for though she kindly endeavoured to alleviate his loss by a legacy of three hundred pounds; yet, as he had none to prosecute his claim, to shelter him from oppression, or call-in law to the assistance of justice, her will was eluded by the executors, and no part of the money was ever paid.

He was, however, not yet wholly abandoned. The Lady Mason still continued her care, and directed him to be placed at a small grammar-school near St. Alban's, where he was called by the name of his nurse, without the least intimation that he had a claim to any other.

Here he was initiated in literature, and passed through several of the classes, with what rapidity or what applause cannot now be known. As he always spoke with respect of his master, it is probable that the mean rank, in which he then appeared, did not hinder his genius from being distinguished, or his industry from being rewarded; and if in so low a state he obtained distinction and rewards, it is not likely that they were gained but by genius and industry.

It is very reasonable to conjecture, that his application was equal to his abilities, because his improvement was more than proportioned to the opportunities which he enjoyed; nor can it be doubted, that if his earliest productions had been preserved, like those of happier students, we might in some have found vigorous sallies of that sprightly humour which distinguishes *The Author to be let,* and in others strong touches of that ardent imagination which painted the solemn scenes of *The Wanderer.*

While he was thus cultivating his genius, his father the Earl Rivers was seized with a distemper, which in a short time put an end to his life. He had frequently inquired after his son, and had always been amused [1] with fallacious and evasive answers; but, being now in his own opinion on his death-bed, he thought it his duty to provide for him among his other natural children, and therefore demanded a positive account of him, with an importunity not to be diverted or denied. His mother, who could no longer refuse an answer, determined at least to give such as should cut him off for ever from that happiness which competence affords, and therefore declared that he was dead; which is perhaps the first instance of a lye invented by a mother to deprive her son of a provision which was designed him by another, and which she could not expect herself, though he should lose it.

This was therefore an act of wickedness which could not be defeated, because it could not be suspected; the Earl did not imagine there could exist in a human form a mother that would ruin her son without enriching herself, and therefore bestowed upon some other person six thousand pounds, which he had in his will bequeathed to Savage.

The same cruelty which incited his mother to intercept this provision which had been intended him, prompted her in a short time to another project, a project worthy of such a disposition. She endeavoured to rid herself from the danger of being at any time made known to him, by sending him secretly to the American plantations.

By whose kindness this scheme was counteracted, or by what interposition she was induced to lay aside her design, I know not; it is not improbable that the Lady Mason might persuade or compel her to desist, or perhaps she could not easily find accomplices wicked enough to concur in so cruel an action; for it may be conceived, that those who had by a long gradation of guilt hardened their hearts against the sense of common wickedness, would yet be shocked at the design of a mother to expose her son to slavery and want, to expose him without interest, and without provocation; and Savage might on this occasion find protectors and advocates among those who had long traded in crimes, and whom compassion had never touched before.

[1] i.e., beguiled.

Being hindered, by whatever means, from banishing him into another countr.., she formed soon after a scheme for burying him in poverty and obscurity in his own; and, that his station of life, if not the place of his residence, might keep him for ever at a distance from her, she ordered him to be placed with a shoemaker in Holborn, that, after the usual time of trial, he might become his apprentice.

It is generally reported, that this project was for some time successful, and that Savage was employed at the awl longer than he was willing to confess; nor was it perhaps any great advantage to him, that an unexpected discovery determined him to quit his occupation.

About this time his nurse, who had always treated him as her own son, died; and it was natural for him to take care of those effects, which by her death were, as he imagined, become his own; he therefore went to her house, opened her boxes, and examined her papers, among which he found some letters written to her by the Lady Mason, which informed him of his birth, and the reasons for which it was concealed.

He was no longer satisfied with the employment which had been allotted him, but thought he had a right to share the affluence of his mother; and therefore without scruple applied to her as her son, and made use of every art to awaken her tenderness, and attract her regard. But neither his letters, nor the interposition of those friends which his merit or his distress procured him, made any impression upon her mind. She still resolved to neglect, though she could no longer disown him.

It was to no purpose that he frequently solicited her to admit him to see her; she avoided him with the most vigilant precaution, and ordered him to be excluded from her house, by whomsoever he might be introduced, and what reason soever he might give for entering it.

Savage was at the same time so touched with the discovery of his real mother, that it was his frequent practice to walk in the dark evenings for several hours before her door, in hopes of seeing her as she might come by accident to the window, or cross her apartment with a candle in her hand.

But all his assiduity and tenderness were without effect, for he could neither soften her heart, nor open her hand, and was reduced to the utmost miseries of want, while he was endeavouring to awaken the affection of a mother: He was therefore obliged to seek some other means of support; and, having no profession, became by necessity an author.

At this time the attention of all the literary world was engrossed by the Bangorian controversy, which filled the press with pamphlets, and the coffee-houses with disputants. Of this subject, as most popular, he made choice for his first attempt, and without any other knowledge of the question than he had casually collected from conversation, published a poem against the Bishop.[2]

What was the success or merit of this performance, I know not; it was probably lost among the innumerable pamphlets to which that dispute gave occasion. Mr. Savage was himself in a little time ashamed of it, and endeavoured to suppress it, by destroying all the copies that he could collect.

He then attempted a more gainful kind of writing, and in his eighteenth year offered to the stage a comedy borrowed from a Spanish plot, which was refused by the players, and was therefore given by him to Mr. Bullock, who, having more interest, made some slight alterations, and brought it upon the stage,[3] under the title of WOMAN's A RIDDLE, but allowed the unhappy author no part of the profit.

Not discouraged, however, at his repulse, he wrote two years afterwards LOVE IN A VEIL, another comedy, borrowed likewise from the Spanish, but with little better success than before; for though it was received and acted,[4] yet it appeared so late in the

[2] Benjamin Hoadley, at that time (1717–20) Bishop of Bangor. His discourses denying absolute authority to institutions divine as well as secular gave rise to the so-called Bangorian Controversy, "one of the most intricate tangles of fruitless logomachy in the language" (Leslie Stephen, History of English Thought in the Eighteenth Century, ch. X, par. 31). Savage's poem was "The Convocation," 1717.

[3] Christopher Bullock was joint manager of Lincoln's Inn Fields theatre. The play appeared 1716.

[4] At Drury Lane Theatre, 1718, according to Jacob, Poetical Register, I, 298.

year, that the author obtained no other advantage from it, than the acquaintance of Sir Richard Steele, and Mr. Wilks, by whom he was pitied, caressed, and relieved.

Sir Richard Steele, having declared in his favour with all the ardour of benevolence which constituted his character, promoted his interest with the utmost zeal, related his misfortunes, applauded his merit, took all the opportunities of recommending him, and asserted, that "the inhumanity of his mother had given him a right to find every good man his father."

Nor was Mr. Savage admitted to his acquaintance only, but to his confidence, of which he sometimes related an instance too extraordinary to be omitted, as it affords a very just idea of his patron's character.

He was once desired by Sir Richard, with an air of the utmost importance, to come very early to his house the next morning. Mr. Savage came as he had promised, found the chariot at the door, and Sir Richard waiting for him, and ready to go out. What was intended, and whither they were to go, Savage could not conjecture, and was not willing to enquire; but immediately seated himself with Sir Richard; the coachman was ordered to drive, and they hurried with the utmost expedition to Hyde-Park Corner, where they stopped at a petty tavern, and retired to a private room. Sir Richard than informed him, that he intended to publish a pamphlet, and that he had desired him to come thither that he might write for him. They soon sat down to the work. Sir Richard dictated, and Savage wrote, till the dinner that had been ordered was put upon the table. Savage was surprized at the meanness of the entertainment, and after some hesitation ventured to ask for wine, which Sir Richard, not without reluctance, ordered to be brought. They then finished their dinner, and proceeded in their pamphlet, which they concluded in the afternoon.

Mr. Savage then imagined his task over, and expected that Sir Richard would call for the reckoning, and return home; but his expectations deceived him, for Sir Richard told him, that he was without money, and that the pamphlet must be sold before the dinner could be paid for; and Savage was therefore obliged to go and offer their new production to sale for two guineas, which with some difficulty he obtained. Sir Richard then returned home, having retired that day only to avoid his creditors, and composed the pamphlet only to discharge his reckoning.

Mr. Savage related another fact equally uncommon, which, though it has no relation to his life, ought to be preserved. Sir Richard Steele having one day invited to his house a great number of persons of the first quality, they were surprized at the number of liveries which surrounded the table; and after dinner, when wine and mirth had set them free from the observation of rigid ceremony, one of them enquired of Sir Richard, how such an expensive train of domestics could be consistent with his fortune. Sir Richard very frankly confessed, that they were fellows of whom he would very willingly be rid. And being then asked, why he did not discharge them, declared that they were bailiffs who had introduced themselves with an execution, and whom, since he could not send them away, he had thought it convenient to embellish with liveries, that they might do him credit while they staid.

His friends were diverted with the expedient, and, by paying the debt, discharged their attendance, having obliged Sir Richard to promise that they should never again find him graced with a retinue of the same kind.

Under such a tutor, Mr. Savage was not likely to learn prudence or frugality; and perhaps many of the misfortunes, which the want of those virtues brought upon him in the following parts of his life, might be justly imputed to so unimproving an example.

Nor did the kindness of Sir Richard end in common favours. He proposed to have established him in some settled scheme of life, and to have contracted a kind of alliance with him, by marrying him to a natural daughter, on whom he intended to bestow a thousand pounds. But though he was always lavish of future bounties, he conducted his affairs in such a manner, that he was very seldom able to keep his promises, or execute his own intentions; and, as he was never able to raise the sum which he had offered, the marriage was delayed. In the mean time he was officiously informed, that Mr. Savage had ridiculed him; by which he was so much exasperated, that he withdrew the allowance which he had paid him, and never afterwards admitted him to his house.

It is not indeed unlikely that Savage might by his imprudence, expose himself to the malice of a tale-bearer; for his patron had many follies, which, as his discernment easily discovered, his imagination might sometimes incite him to mention too ludicrously. A little knowledge of the world is sufficient to discover that such weakness is very common, and that there are few who do not sometimes, in the wantonness of thoughtless mirth, or the heat of transient resentment, speak of their friends and benefactors with levity and contempt, though in their cooler moments they want neither sense of their kindness, nor reverence for their virtue. The fault therefore of Mr. Savage was rather negligence than ingratitude; but Sir Richard must likewise be acquitted of severity, for who is there that can patiently bear contempt from one whom he has relieved and supported, whose establishment he has laboured, and whose interest he has promoted?

He was now again abandoned to fortune, without any other friend than Mr. Wilks; a man, who, whatever were his abilities or skill as an actor, deserves at least to be remembered for his virtues, which are not often to be found in the world, and perhaps less often in his profession than in others. To be humane, generous, and candid, is a very high degree of merit in any case; but those qualities deserve still greater praise, when they are found in that condition, which makes almost every other man, for whatever reason, contemptuous, insolent, petulant, selfish, and brutal.[5]

As Mr. Wilks was one of those to whom calamity seldom complained without relief, he naturally took an unfortunate wit into his protection, and not only assisted him in any casual distresses, but continued an equal and steady kindness to the time of his death.

[5] Robert Wilks (1665?–1732), one of the leading actors of his day, long popular in London (Drury Lane and Haymarket theatres) and in Dublin.

By his interposition Mr. Savage once obtained from his mother fifty pounds,[6] and a promise of one hundred and fifty more; but it was the fate of this unhappy man, that few promises of any advantage to him were performed. His mother was infected among others with the general madness of the South Sea traffic; and, having been disappointed in her expectations, refused to pay what perhaps nothing but the prospect of sudden affluence prompted her to promise.

Being thus obliged to depend upon the friendship of Mr. Wilks, he was consequently an assiduous frequenter of the theatres; and in a short time the amusements of the stage took such possession of his mind, that he never was absent from a play in several years.

This constant attendance naturally procured for him the acquaintance of the players, and, among others, of Mrs. Oldfield,[7] who was so much pleased with his conversation, and touched with his misfortunes, that she allowed him a settled pension of fifty pounds a year, which was during her life regularly paid.

That this act of generosity may receive its due praise, and that the good actions of Mrs. Oldfield may not be sullied by her general character, it is proper to mention what Mr. Savage often declared in the strongest terms, that he never saw her alone, or in any other place than behind the scenes.

At her death he endeavoured to show his gratitude in the most decent manner, by wearing mourning as for a mother; but did not celebrate her in elegies, because he knew that too great profusion of praise would only have revived those faults which his natural equity did not allow him to think less, because they were committed by one who favoured him; but of which, though his virtue would not endeavour to palliate them, his gratitude would not suffer him to prolong the memory, or diffuse the censure.

In his *Wanderer*, he has indeed taken an opportunity of mentioning her, but celebrates her not for her virtue, but her beauty, an excellence which none ever denied her: this is the only en-

[6] This I write upon the credit of the author of his life, which was published 1727. JOHNSON.

[7] Anne Oldfield (1683–1730), a great actress, celebrated in both tragic and comic rôles.

comium with which he has rewarded her liberality, and perhaps
he has even in this been too lavish of his praise. He seems to have
thought, that never to mention his benefactress would have an
appearance of ingratitude, though to have dedicated any particu-
lar performance to her memory would have only betrayed an
officious partiality, that, without exalting her character, would
have depressed his own.

He had sometimes, by the kindness of Mr. Wilks, the advan-
tage of a benefit,[8] on which occasions he often received uncom-
mon marks of regard and compassion; and was once told by the
Duke of Dorset, that it was just to consider him as an injured
nobleman, and that in his opinion the nobility ought to think
themselves obliged, without solicitation, to take every opportunity
of supporting him by their countenance and patronage. But he
had generally the mortification to hear that the whole interest of
his mother was employed to frustrate his applications, and that
she never left any expedient untried, by which he might be cut
off from the possibility of supporting life. The same disposition
she endeavoured to diffuse among all those over whom nature or
fortune gave her any influence, and indeed succeeded too well in
her design; but could not always propagate her effrontery with
her cruelty, for some of those, whom she incited against him,
were ashamed of their own conduct, and boasted of that relief
which they never gave him.

In this censure I do not indiscriminately involve all his rela-
tions; for he has mentioned with gratitude the humanity of one
Lady, whose name I am now unable to recollect, and to whom
therefore I cannot pay the praises which she deserves for having
acted well in opposition to influence, precept, and example.

The punishment which our laws inflict upon those parents who
murder their infants is well known, nor has its justice ever been
contested; but if they deserve death who destroy a child in its
birth, what pains can be severe enough for her who forbears to
destroy him only to inflict sharper miseries upon him; who pro-
longs his life only to make him miserable; and who exposes him,

[8] i.e., the house profits of an evening's theatrical performance.

without care and without pity, to the malice of oppression, the
caprices of chance, and the temptations of poverty; who rejoices
to see him overwhelmed with calamities; and, when his own in-
dustry, or the charity of others, has enabled him to rise for a short
time above his miseries, plunges him again into his former dis-
tress?

The kindness of his friends not affording him any constant
supply, and the prospect of improving his fortune by enlarging
his acquaintance necessarily leading him to places of expence, he
found it necessary to endeavour once more at dramatic poetry,[9]
for which he was now better qualified by a more extensive knowl-
edge, and longer observation. But having been unsuccessful in
comedy, though rather for want of opportunities than genius, he
resolved now to try whether he should not be more fortunate in
exhibiting a tragedy.

The story which he chose for the subject, was that of Sir
Thomas Overbury, a story well adapted to the stage, though per-
haps not far enough removed from the present age, to admit
properly the fictions necessary to complete the plan: for the mind,
which naturally loves truth, is always most offended with the
violation of those truths of which we are most certain; and we of
course conceive those facts most certain, which approach nearest
to our own time.

Out of this story he formed a tragedy, which, if the circum-
stances in which he wrote it be considered, will afford at once
an uncommon proof of strength of genius, and evenness of mind,
of a serenity not to be ruffled, and an imagination not to be sup-
pressed.

During a considerable part of the time in which he was em-
ployed upon this performance, he was without lodging, and often
without meat; nor had he any other conveniences for study than
the fields or the street allowed him; there he used to walk and
form his speeches, and afterwards step into a shop, beg for a few
moments the use of the pen and ink, and write down what he had
composed, upon paper which he had picked up by accident.

If the performance of a writer thus distressed is not perfect, its

[9] In 1724. JOHNSON.

faults ought surely to be imputed to a cause very different from want of genius, and must rather excite pity than provoke censure.

But when under these discouragements the tragedy was finished, there yet remained the labour of introducing it on the stage, an undertaking, which, to an ingenuous mind, was in a very high degree vexatious and disgusting; for, having little interest or reputation, he was obliged to submit himself wholly to the players, and admit, with whatever reluctance, the emendations of Mr. Cibber, which he always considered as the disgrace of his performance.

He had indeed in Mr. Hill [10] another critic of a very different class, from whose friendship he received great assistance on many occasions, and whom he never mentioned but with the utmost tenderness and regard. He had been for some time distinguished by him with very particular kindness, and on this occasion it was natural to apply to him as an author of an established character. He therefore sent this tragedy to him, with a short copy of verses, in which he desired his correction. Mr. Hill, whose humanity and politeness are generally known, readily complied with his request; but as he is remarkable for singularity of sentiment, and bold experiments in language, Mr. Savage did not think his play much improved by his innovation, and had even at that time the courage to reject several passages which he could not approve; and, what is still more laudable, Mr. Hill had the generosity not to resent the neglect of his alterations, but wrote the prologue and epilogue, in which he touches on the circumstances of the author with great tenderness.

After all these obstructions and compliances, he was only able to bring his play upon the stage in the summer, when the chief actors had retired, and the rest were in possession of the house for their own advantage. Among these, Mr. Savage was admitted to play the part of Sir Thomas Overbury, by which he gained no great reputation, the theatre being a province for which nature seemed not to have designed him; for neither his voice, look, nor

[10] Aaron Hill (1685–1750), poet, dramatist, and critical journalist, conducted *The Plain Dealer* (1724), wrote the libretto for Handel's *Rinaldo* (1711), was ridiculed by Pope, whom he attacked.

gesture, were such as were expected on the stage; and he was so much ashamed of having been reduced to appear as a player, that he always blotted out his name from the list, when a copy of his tragedy was to be shown to his friends.

In the publication of his performance he was more successful, for the rays of genius that glimmered in it, that glimmered through all the mists which poverty and Cibber had been able to spread over it, procured him the notice and esteem of many persons eminent for their rank, their virtue, and their wit.

Of this play, acted, printed, and dedicated, the accumulated profits arose to an hundred pounds, which he thought at that time a very large sum, having been never master of so much before.

In the Dedication, for which he received ten guineas, there is nothing remarkable. The Preface contains a very liberal encomium on the blooming excellences of Mr. Theophilus Cibber, which Mr. Savage could not in the latter part of his life see his friends about to read without snatching the play out of their hands. The generosity of Mr. Hill did not end on this occasion; for afterwards, when Mr. Savage's necessities returned, he en-encouraged a subscription to a Miscellany of Poems in a very extraordinary manner, by publishing his story in the *Plain Dealer*,[11] with some affecting lines, which he asserts to have been written by Mr. Savage upon the treatment received by him from his mother, but of which he was himself the author, as Mr. Savage afterwards declared. These lines, and the paper in which they were inserted, had a very powerful effect upon all but his mother, whom, by making her cruelty more public, they only hardened in her aversion.

Mr. Hill not only promoted the subscription to the Miscellany, but furnished likewise the greatest part of the Poems of which it is composed, and particularly *The Happy Man*, which he published as a specimen.

[11] The *Plain Dealer* was a periodical paper, written by Mr. Hill and Mr. Bond, whom Mr. Savage called the two contending powers of light and darkness. They wrote by turns each six Essays; and the character of the work was observed regularly to rise in Mr. Hill's weeks, and fall in Mr. Bond's. JOHNSON.

The subscriptions of those whom these papers should influence to patronize merit in distress, without any other solicitation, were directed to be left at Button's coffee-house; and Mr. Savage going thither a few days afterwards, without expectation of any effect from his proposal, found to his surprise seventy guineas, which had been sent him in consequence of the compassion excited by Mr. Hill's pathetic representation.

To this Miscellany he wrote a Preface, in which he gives an account of his mother's cruelty in a very uncommon strain of humour, and with a gaiety of imagination, which the success of his subscription probably produced.

The Dedication is addressed to the Lady Mary Wortley Montagu, whom he flatters without reserve, and, to confess the truth, with very little art. The same observation may be extended to all his Dedications: his compliments are constrained and violent, heaped together without the grace of order, or the decency of introduction; he seems to have written his panegyrics for the perusal only of his patrons, and to have imagined that he had no other task than to pamper them with praises however gross, and that flattery would make its way to the heart, without the assistance of elegance or invention.

Soon afterwards, the death of the king furnished a general subject for a poetical contest, in which Mr. Savage engaged, and is allowed to have carried the prize of honour from his competitors; but I know not whether he gained by his performance any other advantage than the increase of his reputation; though it must certainly have been with farther views that he prevailed upon himself to attempt a species of writing, of which all the topics had been long before exhausted, and which was made at once difficult by the multitudes that failed in it, and those that had succeeded.

He was now advancing in reputation, and though frequently involved in very distressful perplexities, appeared however to be gaining upon mankind, when both his fame and his life were endangered by an event, of which it is not yet determined, whether it ought to be mentioned as a crime or a calamity.

On the 20th of November 1727, Mr. Savage came from Rich-

mond, where he then lodged, that he might pursue his studies
with less interruption, with an intent to discharge another lodg-
ing which he had in Westminster; and accidentally meeting two
gentlemen his acquaintances, whose names were Merchant and
Gregory, he went in with them to a neighbouring coffee-house,
and sat drinking till it was late, it being in no time of Mr. Savage's
life any part of his character to be the first of the company that
desired to separate. He would willingly have gone to bed in the
same house; but there was not room for the whole company, and
therefore they agreed to ramble about the streets, and divert them-
selves with such amusements as should offer themselves till morn-
ing.

In this walk they happened unluckily to discover a light in
Robinson's coffee-house, near Charing–cross, and therefore went
in. Merchant, with some rudeness, demanded a room, and was
told that there was a good fire in the next parlour, which the com-
pany were about to leave, being then paying their reckoning.
Merchant, not satisfied with this answer, rushed into the room,
and was followed by his companions. He then petulantly placed
himself between the company and the fire, and soon after kicked
down the table. This produced a quarrel, swords were drawn on
both sides, and one Mr. James Sinclair was killed. Savage, hav-
ing wounded likewise a maid that held him, forced his way with
Merchant out of the house; but being intimidated and confused,
without resolution either to fly or stay, they were taken in a
back-court by one of the company and some soldiers, whom he
had called to his assistance.

Being secured and guarded that night, they were in the morn-
ing carried before three justices, who committed them to the
Gatehouse, from whence, upon the death of Mr. Sinclair, which
happened the same day, they were removed in the night to New-
gate, where they were however treated with some distinction, ex-
empted from the ignominy of chains, and confined, not among
the common criminals, but in the Press-yard.

When the day of trial came, the court was crowded in a very
unusual manner, and the public appeared to interest itself as in
a cause of general concern. The witnesses against Mr. Savage
and his friends were, the woman who kept the house, which was

a house of ill-fame, and her maid, the men who were in the room with Mr. Sinclair, and a woman of the town, who had been drinking with them, and with whom one of them had been seen in bed. They swore in general, that Merchant gave the provocation, which Savage and Gregory drew their swords to justify; that Savage drew first, and that he stabbed Sinclair when he was not in a posture of defence, or while Gregory commanded his sword; that after he had given the thrust he turned pale, and would have retired, but that the maid clung round him, and one of the company endeavoured to detain him, from whom he broke, by cutting the maid on the head, but was afterwards taken in a court.

There was some difference in their depositions; one did not see Savage give the wound, another saw it given when Sinclair held his point towards the ground; and the woman of the town asserted, that she did not see Sinclair's sword at all: this difference however was very far from amounting to inconsistency; but it was sufficient to shew, that the hurry of the dispute was such, that it was not easy to discover the truth with relation to particular circumstances, and that therefore some deductions were to be made from the credibility of the testimonies.

Sinclair had declared several times before his death, that he received his wound from Savage, nor did Savage at his trial deny the fact, but endeavoured partly to extenuate it, by urging the suddenness of the whole action, and the impossibility of any ill design, or premeditated malice, and partly to justify it by the necessity of self-defence, and the hazard of his own life, if he had lost that opportunity of giving the thrust: he observed, that neither reason nor law obliged a man to wait for the blow which was threatened, and which, if he should suffer it, he might never be able to return; that it was always allowable to prevent an assault, and to preserve life, by taking away that of the adversary, by whom it was endangered.

With regard to the violence with which he endeavoured to escape, he declared, that it was not his design to fly from justice, or decline a trial, but to avoid the expences and severities of a prison; and that he intended to have appeared at the bar without compulsion.

This defence, which took up more than an hour, was heard by

the multitude that thronged the court with the most attentive and respectful silence: those who thought he ought not to be acquitted, owned that applause could not be refused him; and those who before pitied his misfortunes, now reverenced his abilities.

The witnesses which appeared against him were proved to be persons of characters which did not entitle them to much credit; a common strumpet, a woman by whom strumpets were entertained, and a man by whom they were supported; and the character of Savage was by several persons of distinction asserted to be that of a modest inoffensive man, not inclined to broils, or to insolence, and who had, to that time, been only known for his misfortunes and his wit.

Had his audience been his judges, he had undoubtedly been acquitted; but Mr. Page, who was then upon the bench, treated him with his usual insolence and severity, and when he had summed up the evidence, endeavoured to exasperate the jury, as Mr. Savage used to relate it, with this eloquent harangue:

'Gentlemen of the jury, you are to consider that Mr. Savage is a very great man, a much greater man than you or I, gentlemen of the jury; that he wears very fine clothes, much finer clothes than you or I, gentlemen of the jury; that he has abundance of money in his pocket, much more money than you or I, gentlemen of the jury; but, gentlemen of the jury, is it not a very hard case, gentlemen of the jury, that Mr. Savage should therefore kill you or me, gentlemen of the jury?'

Mr. Savage, hearing his defence thus misrepresented, and the men who were to decide his fate incited against him by invidious comparisons, resolutely asserted, that his cause was not candidly explained, and began to recapitulate what he had before said with regard to his condition, and the necessity of endeavouring to escape the expences of imprisonment; but the judge having ordered him to be silent, and repeated his orders without effect, commanded that he should be taken from the bar by force.

The jury then heard the opinion of the judge, that good characters were of no weight against positive evidence, though they might turn the scale where it was doubtful; and that though, when two men attack each other, the death of either is only manslaughter; but where one is the aggressor, as in the case before them, and, in pursuance of his first attack, kills the other, the law supposes action, however sudden, to be malicious. They then deliberated upon their verdict, and determined that Mr. Savage and Mr. Gregory were guilty of murder, and Mr. Merchant, who had no sword, only of manslaughter.

Thus ended this memorable trial, which lasted eight hours. Mr. Savage and Mr. Gregory were conducted back to prison, where they were more closely confined, and loaded with irons of fifty pounds weight: four days afterwards they were sent back to the court to receive sentence; on which occasion Mr. Savage made, as far as it could be retained in memory, the following speech.

'It is now, my Lord, too late to offer any thing by way of defence or vindication; nor can we expect from your Lordships, in this court, but the sentence which the law requires you, as judges, to pronounce against men of our calamitous condition.—But we are also persuaded, that as mere men, and out of this seat of rigorous justice, you are susceptive of the tender passions, and too humane, not to commiserate the unhappy situation of those, whom the law sometimes perhaps—exacts—from you to pronounce upon. No doubt you distinguish between offences, which arise out of premeditation, and a disposition habituated to vice or immorality, and transgressions, which are the unhappy and unforeseen effects of casual absence of reason, and sudden impulse of passion: we therefore hope you will contribute all you can to an extension of that mercy, which the gentlemen of the jury have been pleased to shew Mr. Merchant, who (allowing facts as sworn against us by the evidence) has led us into this our calamity. I hope this will not be construed, as if we meant to reflect upon that gentleman, or remove any thing from us upon him, or that we repine the more at our fate, because he has no participation of it: No, my Lord! For my part, I declare nothing could more soften my grief, than to be without any companion in so great a misfortune.[12]

Mr. Savage had now no hopes of life, but from the mercy of

[12] Quoted from the Life of Savage, 1727 [p. 23], on which see the note further on.

the crown, which was very earnestly solicited by his friends, and which, with whatever difficulty the story may obtain belief, was obstructed only by his mother.

To prejudice the Queen against him, she made use of an incident, which was omitted in the order of time, that it might be mentioned together with the purpose which it was made to serve. Mr. Savage, when he had discovered his birth, had an incessant desire to speak to his mother, who always avoided him in publick, and refused him admission into her house. One evening walking, as it was his custom, in the street that she inhabited, he saw the door of her house by accident open; he entered it, and finding no person in the passage to hinder him, went up stairs to salute her. She discovered him before he could enter her chamber, alarmed the family with the most distressful outcries, and when she had by her screams gathered them about her, ordered them to drive out of the house that villain, who had forced himself in upon her, and endeavoured to murder her. Savage, who had attempted with the most submissive tenderness to soften her rage, hearing her utter so detestable an accusation, thought it prudent to retire; and, I believe, never attempted afterwards to speak to her.

But, shocked as he was with her falsehood and her cruelty, he imagined that she intended no other use of her lye, than to set herself free from his embraces and solicitations, and was very far from suspecting that she would treasure it in her memory, as an instrument of future wickedness, or that she would endeavour for this fictitious assault to deprive him of his life.

But when the Queen was solicited for his pardon, and informed of the severe treatment which he had suffered from his judge, she answered, that, however unjustifiable might be the manner of his trial, or whatever extenuation the action for which he was condemned might admit, she could not think that man a proper object of the King's mercy, who had been capable of entering his mother's house in the night, with an intent to murder her.

By whom this atrocious calumny had been transmitted to the Queen; whether she that invented had the front to relate it; whether she found any one weak enough to credit it, or corrupt enough to concur with her in her hateful design, I know not: but methods had been taken to persuade the Queen so strongly of the truth of it, that she for a long time refused to hear any of those who petitioned for his life.

Thus had Savage perished by the evidence of a bawd, a strumpet, and his mother, had not justice and compassion procured him an advocate of rank too great to be rejected unheard, and of virtue too eminent to be heard without being believed. His merit and his calamities happened to reach the ear of the Countess of Hertford, who engaged in his support with all the tenderness that is excited by pity, and all the zeal which is kindled by generosity; and, demanding an audience of the Queen, laid before her the whole series of his mother's cruelty, exposed the improbability of an accusation by which he was charged with an intent to commit a murder that could produce no advantage, and soon convinced her how little his former conduct could deserve to be mentioned as a reason for extraordinary severity.

The interposition of this lady was so successful, that he was soon after admitted to bail, and, on the 9th of March 1728, pleaded the King's pardon.

It is natural to enquire upon what motives his mother could prosecute him in a manner so outrageous and implacable; for what reason she could employ all the arts of malice, and all the snares of calumny, to take away the life of her own son, of a son who never injured her, who was never supported by her expence, nor obstructed any prospect of pleasure or advantage; why she should endeavour to destroy him by a lye—a lye which could not gain credit, but must vanish of itself at the first moment of examination, and of which only this can be said to make it probable, that it may be observed from her conduct, that the most execrable crimes are sometimes committed without apparent temptation.

This mother is still alive, and may perhaps even yet, though her malice was so often defeated, enjoy the pleasure of reflecting, that the life, which she often endeavoured to destroy, was at least shortened by her maternal offices; that though she could not transport her son to the plantations, bury him in the shop of a mechanic, or hasten the hand of the public executioner, she has yet had the satisfaction of imbittering all his hours, and forcing him into exigences that hurried on his death.

It is by no means necessary to aggravate the enormity of this woman's conduct, by placing it in opposition to that of the Countess of Hertford; no one can fail to observe how much more amiable it is to relieve, than to oppress, and to rescue innocence from destruction, than to destroy without an injury.

Mr. Savage, during his imprisonment, his trial, and the time in which he lay under sentence of death, behaved with great firmness and equality of mind, and confirmed by his fortitude the esteem of those who before admired him for his abilities. The peculiar circumstances of his life were made more generally known by a short account,[13] which was then published, and of which several thousands were in a few weeks dispersed over the nation: and the compassion of mankind operated so powerfully in his favour, that he was enabled, by frequent presents, not only to support himself, but to assist Mr. Gregory in prison; and, when he was pardoned and released, he found the number of his friends not lessened.

The nature of the act for which he had been tried was in itself doubtful; of the evidences which appeared against him, the character of the man was not unexceptionable, that of the woman notoriously infamous: she, whose testimony chiefly influenced the jury to condemn him, afterwards retracted her assertions. He always himself denied that he was drunk, as had been generally reported. Mr. Gregory, who is now Collector of Antigua, is said to declare him far less criminal than he was imagined, even by some who favoured him: and Page himself afterwards confessed, that he had treated him with uncommon rigour. When all these particulars are rated together, perhaps the memory of Savage may not be much sullied by his trial.

Some time after he had obtained his liberty, he met in the street the woman that had sworn with so much malignity against him. She informed him, that she was in distress, and, with a

[13] Written by Mr. Beckingham and another gentleman. JOHNSON. Charles Beckingham (1699–1731), poet and dramatist, had two plays performed (by the age of twenty) at Lincoln's Inn Fields theatre.

degree of confidence not easily attainable, desired him to relieve her. He, instead of insulting her misery, and taking pleasure in the calamities of one who had brought his life into danger, reproved her gently for her perjury; and changing the only guinea that he had, divided it equally between her and himself.

This is an action which in some ages would have made a saint, and perhaps in others a hero, and which, without any hyperbolical encomiums, must be allowed to be an instance of uncommon generosity, an act of complicated virtue; by which he at once relieved the poor, corrected the vicious, and forgave an enemy; by which he at once remitted the strongest provocations, and exercised the most ardent charity.

Compassion was indeed the distinguishing quality of Savage; he never appeared inclined to take advantage of weakness, to attack the defenceless, or to press upon the falling: whoever was distressed was certain at least of his good wishes; and when he could give no assistance to extricate them from misfortunes, he endeavoured to sooth them by sympathy and tenderness.

But when his heart was not softened by the sight of misery, he was sometimes obstinate in his resentment, and did not quickly lose the remembrance of an injury. He always continued to speak with anger of the insolence and partiality of Page, and a short time before his death revenged it by a satire.[14]

It is natural to enquire in what terms Mr. Savage spoke of this fatal action, when the danger was over, and he was under no necessity of using any art to set his conduct in the fairest light. He was not willing to dwell upon it; and, if he transiently mentioned it, appeared neither to consider himself as a murderer, nor as a man wholly free from the guilt of blood. How much and how long he regretted it, appeared in a poem which he published many years afterwards. On occasion of a copy of verses, in which the failings of good men were recounted, and in which the author had endeavoured to illustrate his position, that "the best may sometimes deviate from virtue," by an instance of murder committed by Savage in the heat of wine, Savage re-

[14] Reprinted as "A Character," in *The Poetical Works of Richard Savage,* ed. Clarence Tracy, 1962, p. 243.

marked, that it was no very just representation of a good man, to suppose him liable to drunkenness, and disposed in his riots to cut throats.

He was now indeed at liberty, but was, as before, without any other support than accidental favours and uncertain patronage afforded him; sources by which he was sometimes very liberally supplied, and which at other times were suddenly stopped; so that he spent his life between want and plenty; or, what was yet worse, between beggary and extravagance; for as whatever he received was the gift of chance, which might as well favour him at one time as another, he was tempted to squander what he had, because he always hoped to be immediately supplied.

Another cause of his profusion was the absurd kindness of his friends, who at once rewarded and enjoyed his abilities, by treating him at taverns, and habituating him to pleasures which he could not afford to enjoy, and which he was not able to deny himself, though he purchased the luxury of a single night by the anguish of cold and hunger for a week.

The experience of these inconveniences determined him to endeavour after some settled income, which, having long found submission and intreaties fruitless, he attempted to extort from his mother by rougher methods. He had now, as he acknowledged, lost that tenderness for her, which the whole series of her cruelty had not been able wholly to repress, till he found, by the efforts which she made for his destruction, that she was not content with refusing to assist him, and being neutral in his struggles with poverty, but was as ready to snatch every opportunity of adding to his misfortunes, and that she was to be considered as an enemy implacably malicious, whom nothing but his blood could satisfy. He therefore threatened to harass her with lampoons, and to publish a copious narrative of her conduct, unless she consented to purchase an exemption from infamy, by allowing him a pension.

This expedient proved successful. Whether shame still survived, though virtue was extinct, or whether her relations had more delicacy than herself, and imagined that some of the darts which satire might point at her would glance upon them; Lord Tyrconnel, whatever were his motives, upon his promise to lay aside his design of exposing the cruelty of his mother, received him into his family, treated him as his equal, and engaged to allow him a pension of two hundred pounds a year.[15]

This was the golden part of Mr. Savage's life; and for some time he had no reason to complain of fortune; his appearance was splendid, his expences large, and his acquaintance extensive. He was courted by all who endeavoured to be thought men of genius, and caressed by all who valued themselves upon a refined taste. To admire Mr. Savage, was a proof of discernment; and to be acquainted with him, was a title to poetical reputation. His presence was sufficient to make any place of publick entertainment popular; and his approbation and example constituted the fashion. So powerful is genius, when it is invested with the glitter of affluence! Men willingly pay to fortune that regard which they owe to merit, and are pleased when they have an opportunity at once of gratifying their vanity, and practising their duty.

This interval of prosperity furnished him with opportunities of enlarging his knowledge of human nature, by contemplating life from its highest gradations to its lowest; and, had he afterwards applied to dramatic poetry, he would perhaps not have had many superiors; for as he never suffered any scene to pass before his eyes without notice, he had treasured in his mind all the different combinations of passions, and the innumerable mixtures of vice and virtue, which distinguish one character from another; and, as his conception was strong, his expressions were clear, he easily received impressions from objects, and very forcibly transmitted them to others.

Of his exact observations on human life he has left a proof, which would do honour to the greatest names, in a small pamphlet, caled *The Author to be let,* where he introduces Iscariot Hackney, a prostitute scribbler, giving an account of his birth, his education, his disposition and morals, habits of life, and

---

[15] Tyrconnel's mother and Savage's putative mother were sisters.

maxims of conduct. In the introduction are related many secret
histories of the petty writers of that time, but sometimes mixed
with ungenerous reflections on their birth, their circumstances, or
those of their relations; nor can it be denied, that some passages
are such as Iscariot Hackney might himself have produced.

He was accused likewise of living in an appearance of friend-
ship with some whom he satirised, and of making use of the con-
fidence which he gained by a seeming kindness to discover
failings and expose them: it must be confessed, that Mr. Savage's
esteem was no very certain possession, and that he would
lampoon at one time those whom he had praised at another.

It may be alleged, that the same man may change his princi-
ples, and that he, who was once deservedly commended, may be
afterwards satirised with equal justice, or that the poet was
dazzled with the appearance of virtue, and found the man whom
he had celebrated, when he had an opportunity of examining
him more narrowly, unworthy of the panegyrick which he had
too hastily bestowed; and that, as a false satire ought to be re-
canted, for the sake of him whose reputation may be injured,
false praise ought likewise to be obviated, lest the distinction
between vice and virtue should be lost, lest a bad man should be
trusted upon the credit of his encomiast, or lest others should
endeavour to obtain the like praises by the same means.

But though these excuses may be often plausible, and some-
times just, they are very seldom satisfactory to mankind; and the
writer, who is not constant to his subject, quickly sinks into
contempt, his satire loses its force, and his panegyrick its value,
and he is only considered at one time as a flatterer, and as a
calumniator at another.

To avoid these imputations, it is only necessary to follow the
rules of virtue, and to preserve an unvaried regard to truth. For
though it is undoubtedly possible that a man, however cautious,
may be sometimes deceived by an artful appearance of virtue, or
by false evidences of guilt, such errors will not be frequent; and
it will be allowed, that the name of an author would never have
been made contemptible, had no man ever said what he did not
think, or misled others but when he was himself deceived.

If[16] *The Author to be let* was first published in a single pamphlet, and afterwards inserted in a collection of pieces relating to the *Dunciad*, which were addressed by Mr. Savage to the Earl of Middlesex, in a dedication which he was prevailed upon to sign, though he did not write it, and in which there are some positions, that the true author would perhaps not have published under his own name, and on which Mr. Savage afterwards reflected with no great satisfaction; the enumeration of the bad effects of the uncontroled freedom of the press, and the assertion that the "liberties taken by the writers of Journals with their superiors were exorbitant and unjustifiable," very ill became men, who have themselves not always shewn the exactest regard to the laws of subordination in their writings, and who have often satirised those that at least thought themselves their superiors, as they were eminent for their hereditary rank, and employed in the highest offices of the kingdom. But this is only an instance of that partiality which almost every man indulges with regard to himself; the liberty of the press is a blessing when we are inclined to write against others, and a calamity when we find ourselves overborne by the multitude of our assailants; as the power of the crown is always thought too great by those who suffer by its influence and too little by those in whose favour it is exerted; and a standing army is generally accounted necessary by those who command, and dangerous and oppressive by those who support it.

Mr. Savage was likewise very far from believing, that the letters[17] annexed to each species of bad poets in the *Bathos*, were, as he was directed to assert, "set down at random;" for when he was charged by one of his friends with putting his name to such an improbability, he had no answer to make, than that "he did not think of it;" and his friends had too much tenderness to reply, that next to the crime of writing contrary to what he thought, was that of writing without thinking.

After having remarked what is false in this dedication, it is

[16] "If," here, is equivalent to "Considering that." Hill (*Lives*, II, 360, par. 107) omits it, and begins a new sentence at "The enumeration."

[17] I.e., initials of proper names affixed to quotations.

proper that I observe the impartiality which I recommend, by declaring what Savage asserted, that the account of the circumstances which attended the publication of the Dunciad, however strange and improbable, was exactly true.

The publication of this piece at this time raised Mr. Savage a great number of enemies among those that were attacked by Mr. Pope, with whom he was considered as a kind of confederate, and whom he was suspected of supplying with private intelligence and secret incidents: so that the ignominy of an informer was added to the terror of a satirist.

That he was not altogether free from literary hypocrisy, and that he sometimes spoke one thing, and wrote another, cannot be denied; because he himself confessed, that, when he lived in great familiarity with Dennis, he wrote an epigram against him.[18]

Mr. Savage however set all the malice of all the pigmy writers at defiance, and thought the friendship of Mr. Pope cheaply purchased by being exposed to their censure and their hatred; nor had he any reason to repent of the preference, for he found Mr. Pope a steady and unalienable friend almost to the end of his life.

About this time, notwithstanding his avowed neutrality with regard to party, he published a panegyrick on Sir Robert Walpole, for which he was rewarded by him with twenty guineas, a sum not very large, if either the excellence of the performance, or the affluence of the patron be considered; but greater than he afterwards obtained from a person of yet higher rank, and more desirous in appearance of being distinguished as a patron of literature.

As he was very far from approving the conduct of Sir Robert Walpole, and in conversation mentioned him sometimes with acrimony, and generally with contempt; as he was one of those who were always zealous in their assertions of the justice of the

[18] Johnson prints in a footnote Savage's cruel epigram, believing it yet unpublished. Hill reprints it (II, 362), noting that it had appeared in *Gent. Mag.*, 1731, p. 306, slightly varied, and again in Washington's edition of Pope. Tracy does not include it in his edition of Savage's Poetry, though he gives another, on p. 182.

late opposition, jealous of the rights of the people, and alarmed by the long-continued triumph of the court; it was natural to ask him what could induce him to employ his poetry in praise of that man who was, in his opinion, an enemy to liberty, and an oppressor of his country? He alleged, that he was then dependent upon the Lord Tyrconnel, who was an implicit follower of the ministry; and that being enjoined by him, not without menaces, to write in praise of his leader, he had not resolution sufficient to sacrifice the pleasure of affluence to that of integrity.

On this, and on many other occasions, he was ready to lament the misery of living at the tables of other men, which was his fate from the beginning to the end of his life; for I know not whether he ever had, for three months together, a settled habitation, in which he could claim a right of residence.

To this unhappy state it is just to impute much of the inconsistancy of his conduct; for though a readiness to comply with the inclination of others was no part of his natural character, yet he was sometimes obliged to relax his obstinacy, and submit his own judgement, and even his virtue, to the government of those by whom he was supported: so that, if his miseries were sometimes the consequences of his faults, he ought not yet to be wholly excluded from compassion, because his faults were very often the effects of his misfortunes.

In this gay period of his life, while he was surrounded by affluence and pleasure, he published *The Wanderer*, a moral poem, of which the design is comprised in these lines:

> I fly all public care, all venal strife,
> To try the still compar'd with active life;
> To prove, by these the sons of men may owe
> The fruits of bliss to bursting clouds of woe;
> That ev'n calamity, by thought refin'd,
> Inspirits and adorns the thinking mind.

And more distinctly in the following passage:

> By woe, the soul to daring action swells;
> By woe, in plaintless patience it excels;

> From patience, prudent clear experience springs,
> And traces knowledge thro' the course of things!
> Thence hope is form'd, thence fortitude, success,
> Renown:——whate'er men covet and caress.

This performance was always considered by himself as his master-piece; and Mr. Pope, when he asked his opinion of it, told him, that he read it once over, and was not displeased with it, that it gave him more pleasure at the second perusal, and delighted him still more at the third.

It has been generally objected to *The Wanderer,* that the disposition of the parts is irregular; that the design is obscure, and the plan perplexed; that the images, however beautiful, succeed each other without order; and that the whole performance is not so much a regular fabrick, as a heap of shining materials thrown together by accident, which strikes rather with the solemn magnificence of a stupendous ruin, than the elegant grandeur of a finished pile.

This criticism is universal, and therefore it is reasonable to believe it at least in a great degree just; but Mr. Savage was always of a contrary opinion, and thought his drift could only be missed by negligence or stupidity, and that the whole plan was regular, and the parts distinct.

It was never denied to abound with strong representations of nature, and just observations upon life; and it may easily be observed, that most of his pictures have an evident tendency to illustrate his first great position, "that good is the consequence of evil." The sun that burns up the mountains, fructifies the vales; the deluge that rushes down the broken rocks with dreadful impetuosity, is separated into purling brooks; and the rage of the hurricane purifies the air.

Even in this poem he has not been able to forbear one touch upon the cruelty of his mother, which, though remarkably delicate and tender, is a proof how deep an impression it had upon his mind.

This must be at least acknowledged, which ought to be thought equivalent to many other excellences, that this poem can promote no other purposes than those of virtue, and that it is written with a very strong sense of the efficacy of religion.

But my province is rather to give the history of Mr. Savage's performances, than to display their beauties, or to obviate the criticisms which they have occasioned; and therefore I shall not dwell upon the particular passages which deserve applause: I shall neither shew the excellence of his descriptions, nor expatiate on the terrifick portrait of suicide, nor point out the artful touches, by which he has distinguished the intellectual features of the rebels, who suffered death in his last canto. It is, however, proper to observe, that Mr. Savage always declared the characters wholly fictitious, and without the least allusion to any real persons or actions.

From a poem so diligently laboured, and so successfully finished, it might be reasonably expected that he should have gained considerable advantage; nor can it, without some degree of indignation and concern, be told, that he sold the copy for ten guineas, of which he afterwards returned two, that the two last sheets of the work might be reprinted, of which he had in his absence intrusted the correction to a friend, who was too indolent to perform it with accuracy.

A superstitious regard to the correction of his sheets was one of Mr. Savage's peculiarities: he often altered, revised, recurred to his first reading or punctuation, and again adopted the alteration; he was dubious and irresolute without end, as on a question of the last importance, and at last was seldom satisfied: the intrusion or omission of a comma was sufficient to discompose him, and he would lament an error of a single letter as a heavy calamity. In one of his letters relating to an impression of some verses, he remarks, that he had, with regard to the correction of the proof, "a spell upon him;" and indeed the anxiety with which he dwelt upon the minutest and most trifling niceties, deserved no other name than that of fascination.

That he sold so valuable a performance for so small a price, was not to be imputed either to necessity, by which the learned and ingenious are often obliged to submit to very hard conditions; or to avarice, by which the book-sellers are frequently incited to oppress that genius by which they are supported; but to that intemperate desire of pleasure, and habitual slavery to his passions, which involved him in many perplexities. He happened at that time to be engaged in the pursuit of some trifling gratification, and, being without money for the present occasion, sold his poem to the first bidder, and perhaps for the first price that was proposed, and would probably have been content with less, if less had been offered him.

This poem was addressed to the Lord Tyrconnel, not only in the first lines, but in a formal dedication filled with the highest strains of panegyrick, and the warmest professions of gratitude, but by no means remarkable for delicacy of connection or elegance of style.

These praises in a short time he found himself inclined to retract, being discarded by the man on whom he had bestowed them, and whom he then immediately discovered not to have deserved them. Of this quarrel, which every day made more bitter, Lord Tyrconnel and Mr. Savage assigned very different reasons, which might perhaps all in reality concur, though they were not all convenient to be alleged by either party. Lord Tyrconnel affirmed, that it was the constant practice of Mr. Savage to enter a tavern with any company that proposed it, drink the most expensive wines with great profusion, and when the reckoning was demanded, to be without money: If, as it often happened, his company were willing to defray his part, the affair ended, without any ill consequences; but, if they were refractory, and expected that the wine should be paid for by him that drank it, his method of composition was, to take them with him to his own apartment, assume the government of the house, and order the butler in an imperious manner to set the best wine in the cellar before his company, who often drank till they forgot the respect due to the house in which they were entertained, indulged themselves in the utmost extravagance of merriment, practised the most licentious frolicks, and committed all the outrages of drunkenness.

Nor was this the only charge which Lord Tyrconnel brought against him: Having given him a collection of valuable books, stamped with his own arms, he had the mortification to see them in a short time exposed to sale upon the stalls, it being usual with

Mr. Savage, when he wanted a small sum, to take his books to the pawnbroker.

Whoever was acquainted with Mr. Savage easily credited both these accusations: for, having been obliged, from his first entrance into the world, to subsist upon expedients, affluence was not able to exalt him above them; and so much was he delighted with wine and conversation, and so long had he been accustomed to live by chance, that he would at any time to go to the tavern without scruple, and trust for the reckoning to the liberality of his company, and frequently of company to whom he was very little known. This conduct indeed very seldom drew upon him those inconveniences that might be feared by any other person; for his conversation was so entertaining, and his address so pleasing, that few thought the pleasure which they received from him dearly purchased, by paying for his wine. It was his peculiar happiness, that he scarcely ever found a stranger, whom he did not leave a friend; but it must likewise be added, that he had not often a friend long, without obliging him to become a stranger.

Mr. Savage, on the other hand, declared, that Lord Tyrconnel quarrelled with him, because he would subtract from his own luxury and extravagance what he had promised to allow him, and that his resentment was only a plea for the violation of his promise: He asserted, that he had done nothing that ought to exclude him from that subsistence which he thought not so much a favour, as a debt, since it was offered him upon conditions, which he had never broken; and that his only fault was, that he could not be supported with nothing.

He acknowledged, that Lord Tyrconnel often exhorted him to regulate his method of life, and not to spend all his nights in taverns, and that he appeared very desirous, that he would pass those hours with him, which he so freely bestowed upon others. This demand Mr. Savage considered as a censure of his conduct, which he could never patiently bear; and which, in the latter and cooler part of his life, was so offensive to him, that he declared it as his resolution, "to spurn that friend who should presume to dictate to him;" and it is not likely, that in his earlier years he received admonitions with more calmness.

He was likewise inclined to resent such expectations, as tending to infringe his liberty, of which he was very jealous, when it was necessary to the gratification of his passions; and declared, that the request was still more unreasonable, as the company to which he was to have been confined was insupportably disagreeable. This assertion affords another instance of that inconsistency of his writings with his conversation, which was so often to be observed. He forgot how lavishly he had, in his Dedication to *The Wanderer,* extolled the delicacy and penetration, the humanity and generosity, the candour and politeness, of the man, whom, when he no longer loved him, he declared to be a wretch without understanding, without good-nature, and without justice; of whose name he thought himself obliged to leave no trace in any future edition of his writings; and accordingly blotted it out of that copy of *The Wanderer* which was in his hands.

During his continuance with the Lord Tyrconnel, he wrote *The Triumph of Health and Mirth,* on the recovery of Lady Tyrconnel from a languishing illness. This performance is remarkable, not only for the gaiety of the ideas, and the melody of the numbers, but for the agreeable fiction upon which it is formed. Mirth, overwhelmed with sorrow for the sickness of her favourite, takes a flight in quest of her sister Health, whom she finds reclined upon the brow of a lofty mountain, amidst the fragrance of perpetual spring, with the breezes of the morning sporting about her. Being solicited by her sister Mirth, she readily promises her assistance, flies away in a cloud, and impregnates the waters of Bath with new virtues, by which the sickness of Belinda is relieved.

As the reputation of his abilities, the particular circumstances of his birth and life, the splendour of his appearance, and the distinction which was for some time paid him by Lord Tyrconnel, intitled him to familiarity with persons of higher rank than those to whose conversation he had been before admitted, he did not fail to gratify that curiosity, which induced him to take a nearer view of those whom their birth, thier employments, or their fortunes, necessarily place at a distance from the greatest part of mankind, and to examine whether their merit was magnified or diminished by the medium through which it was contemplated; whether the splendour with which they dazzled their admirers was inherent in themselves, or only reflected on them by the objects that surrounded them; and whether great men were selected for high stations, or high stations made great men.

For this purpose he took all opportunities of conversing familiarly with those who were most conspicuous at that time for their power or their influence; he watched their looser moments, and examined their domestick behaviour, with that acuteness which nature had given him, and which the uncommon variety of his life had contributed to increase, and that inquisitiveness which must always be produced in a vigorous mind, by an absolute freedom from all pressing or domestick engagements. His discernment was quick, and therefore he soon found in every person, and in every affair, something that deserved attention; he was supported by others, without any care for himself, and was therefore at leisure to pursue his observations.

More circumstances to constitute a critick on human life could not easily concur; nor indeed could any man, who assumed from accidental advantages more praise than he could justly claim from his real merit, admit an acquaintance more dangerous than that of Savage; of whom likewise it must be confessed, that abilities really exalted above the common level, or virtue refined from passion, or proof against corruption, could not easily find an abler judge, or a warmer advocate.

What was the result of Mr. Savage's enquiry, though he was not much accustomed to conceal his discoveries, it may not be entirely safe to relate, because the persons whose characters he criticised are powerful; and power and resentment are seldom strangers; nor would it perhaps be wholly just, because what he asserted in conversation might, though true in general, be heightened by some momentary ardour of imagination, and, as it can be delivered only from memory, may be imperfectly represented; so that the picture at first aggravated, and then unskilfully copied, may be justly suspected to retain no great resemblance of the original.

It may however be observed, that he did not appear to have

formed very elevated ideas of those to whom the administration of
affairs, or the conduct of parties, has been intrusted; who have
been considered as the advocates of the crown, or the guardians
of the people; and who have obtained the most implicit confi-
dence, and the loudest applauses. Of one particular person, who
has been at one time so popular as to be generally esteemed, and
at another so formidable as to be universally detested, he observed,
that his acquisitions had been small, or that his capacity was
narrow, and that the whole range of his mind was from obscenity
to politicks, and from politicks to obscenity.[19]

But the opportunity of indulging his speculations on great
characters was now at an end. He was banished from the table of
Lord Tyrconnel, and turned again adrift upon the world, without
prospect of finding quickly any other harbour. As prudence was
not one of the virtues by which he was distinguished, he had
made no provision against a misfortune like this. And though it
is not to be imagined but that the separation must for some time
have been preceded by coldness, peevishness, or neglect, though
it was undoubtedly the consequence of accumulated provocations
on both sides; yet every one that knew Savage will readily believe,
that to him it was sudden as a stroke of thunder; that, though
he might have transiently suspected it, he had never suffered any
thought so unpleasing to sink into his mind, but that he had
driven it away by amusements, or dreams of future felicity and
affluence, and had never taken any measures by which he might
prevent a precipitation from plenty to indigence.

This quarrel and separation, and the difficulties to which Mr.
Savage was exposed by them, were soon known both to his friends
and enemies; nor was it long before he perceived, from the be-
haviour of both, how much is added to the lustre of genius by the
ornaments of wealth.

His condition did not appear to excite much compassion; for he
had not always been careful to use the advantages he enjoyed
with that moderation which ought to have been with more than
usual caution preserved by him, who knew, if he had reflected,

[19] Sir Robert Walpole.

that he was only a dependant on the bounty of another, whom he could expect to support him no longer than he endeavoured to preserve his favour by complying with his inclinations, and whom he nevertheless set at defiance, and was continually irritating by negligence or encroachments.

Examples need not be sought at any great distance to prove, that superiority of fortune has a natural tendency to kindle pride, and that pride seldom fails to exert itself in contempt and insult; and if this is often the effect of hereditary wealth, and of honours enjoyed only by the merit of others, it is some extenuation of any indecent triumphs to which this unhappy man may have been betrayed, that his prosperity was heightened by the force of novelty, and made more intoxicating by a sense of the misery in which he had so long languished, and perhaps of the insults which he had formerly borne, and which he might now think himself entitled to revenge. It is too common for those who have unjustly suffered pain, to inflict it likewise in their turn with the same injustice, and to imagine that they have a right to treat others as they have themselves been treated.

That Mr. Savage was too much elevated by any good fortune, is generally known; and some passages of his Introduction to *The Author to be let* sufficiently shew, that he did not wholly refrain from such satire as he afterwards thought very unjust, when he was exposed to it himself; for when he was afterwards ridiculed in the character of a distressed poet, he very easily discovered that distress was not a proper subject for merriment, or topick of invective. He was then able to discern, that, if misery be the effect of virtue, it ought to be reverenced; if of ill-fortune, to be pitied; and if of vice, not to be insulted, because it is perhaps itself a punishment adequate to the crime by which it was produced. And the humanity of that man can deserve no panegyrick, who is capable of reproaching a criminal in the hands of the executioner.

But these reflections, though they readily occurred to him in the first and last parts of his life, were, I am afraid, for a long time forgotten; at least they were, like many other maxims, treasured up in his mind, rather for shew than use, and operated

very little upon his conduct, however elegantly he might some-
times explain, or however forcibly he might inculcate, them.

His degradation therefore from the condition which he had
enjoyed with such wanton thoughtlessness, was considered by
many as an occasion of triumph. Those who had before paid their
court to him without success, soon returned the contempt which
they had suffered; and they who had received favours from him,
for of such favours as he could bestow he was very liberal, did
not always remember them. So much more certain are the effects
of resentment than of gratitude; it is not only to many more
pleasing to recollect those faults which place others below them,
than those virtues by which they are themselves comparatively
depressed; but it is likewise more easy to neglect, than to re-
compense; and though there are few who will practise a laborious
virtue, there will never be wanting multitudes that will indulge
an easy vice.

Savage, however, was very little disturbed at the marks of
contempt which his ill-fortune brought upon him, from those
whom he never esteemed, and with whom he never considered
himself as levelled by any calamities: and though it was not
without some uneasiness that he saw some, whose friendship he
valued, change their behaviour; he yet observed their coldness
without much emotion, considered them as the slaves of fortune
and the worshippers of prosperity, and was more inclined to
despise them, than to lament himself.

It does not appear that, after this return of his wants, he found
mankind equally favourable to him, as at his first appearance in
the world. His story, though in reality not less melancholy, was
less affecting, because it was no longer new; it therefore procured
him no new friends; and those that had formerly relieved him,
thought they might now consign him to others. He was now like-
wise considered by many rather as criminal, than as unhappy; for
the friends of Lord Tyrconnel, and of his mother, were suffici-
ently industrious to publish his weaknesses, which were indeed
very numerous; and nothing was forgotten, that might make him
either hateful or ridiculous.

It cannot but be imagined, that such representations of his

faults must make great numbers less sensible of his distress; many, who had only an opportunity to hear one part, made no scruple to propagate the account which they received; many assisted their circulation from malice or revenge; and perhaps many pretended to credit them, that they might with a better grace withdraw their regard, or withhold their assistance.

Savage however was not one of those, who suffered himself to be injured without resistance, nor was less diligent in exposing the faults of Lord Tyrconnel, over whom he obtained at least this advantage, that he drove him first to the practice of outrage and violence; for he was so much provoked by the wit and virulence of Savage, that he came with a number of attendants, that did no honour to his courage, to beat him at a coffee-house. But it happened that he had left the place a few minutes, and his lordship had, without danger, the pleasure of boasting how he would have treated him. Mr. Savage went next day to repay his visit at his own house; but was prevailed on, by his domesticks, to retire without insisting upon seeing him.

Lord Tyrconnel was accused by Mr. Savage of some actions, which scarcely any provocations will be thought sufficient to justify; such as seizing what he had in his lodgings, and other instances of wanton cruelty, by which he increased the distress of Savage, without any advantage to himself.

These mutual accusations were retorted on both sides, for many years, with the utmost degree of virulence and rage; and time seemed rather to augment than diminish their resentment. That the anger of Mr. Savage should be kept alive, is not strange, because he felt every day the consequences of the quarrel; but it might reasonably have been hoped, that Lord Tyrconnel might have relented, and at length have forgot those provocations, which, however they might have once inflamed him, had not in reality much hurt him.

The spirit of Mr. Savage indeed never suffered him to solicit a reconciliation; he returned reproach for reproach, and insult for insult; his superiority of wit supplied the disadvantages of his fortune, and enabled him to form a party, and prejudice great numbers in his favour.

But though this might be some gratification of his vanity, it afforded very little relief to his necessities; and he was very frequently reduced to uncommon hardships, of which, however, he never made any mean or importunate complaints, being formed rather to bear misery with fortitude, than enjoy prosperity with moderation.

He now thought himself again at liberty to expose the cruelty of his mother, and therefore, I believe, about this time, published *The Bastard,* a poem remarkable for the vivacious sallies of thought in the beginning, where he makes a pompous enumeration of the imaginary advantages of base birth; and the pathetick sentiments at the end, where he recounts the real calamities which he suffered by the crime of his parents.

The vigour and spirit of the verses, the peculiar circumstances of the author, the novelty of the subject, and the notoriety of the story to which the allusions are made, procured this performance a very favourable reception; great numbers were immediately dispersed, and editions were multiplied with unusual rapidity.

One circumstance attended the publication, which Savage used to relate with great satisfaction. His mother, to whom the poem was with "due reverence" inscribed, happened then to be at Bath, where she could not conveniently retire from censure, or conceal herself from observation; and no sooner did the reputation of the poem begin to spread, than she heard it repeated in all places of concourse, nor could she enter the assembly-rooms, or cross the walks, without being saluted with some lines from *The Bastard.*

This was perhaps the first time that ever she discovered a sense of shame, and on this occasion the power of wit was very conspicuous; the wretch who had, without scruple, proclaimed herself an adulteress, and who had first endeavoured to starve her son, then to transport him, and afterwards to hang him, was not able to bear the representation of her own conduct; but fled from reproach, though she felt no pain from guilt, and left Bath with the utmost haste, to shelter herself among the crowds of London.

Thus Savage had the satisfaction of finding, that, though he could not reform his mother, he could punish her, and that he did not always suffer alone.

The pleasure which he received from this increase of his poetical reputation, was sufficient for some time to overbalance the miseries of want, which this performance did not much alleviate; for it was sold for a very trivial sum to a bookseller, who, though the success was so uncommon that five impressions were sold, of which many were undoubtedly very numerous, had not generosity sufficient to admit the unhappy writer to any part of the profit.

The sale of this poem was always mentioned by Savage with the utmost elevation of heart, and deferred to by him as an incontestable proof of a general acknowledgement of his abilities. It was indeed the only production of which he could justly boast a general reception.

But though he did not lose the opportunity which success gave him, of setting a high rate on his abilities, but paid due deference to the suffrages of mankind when they were given in his favour, he did not suffer his esteem of himself to depend upon others, nor found any thing sacred in the voice of the people when they were inclined to censure him; he then readily shewed the folly of expecting that the publick should judge right, observed how slowly poetical merit had often forced its way into the world; he contented himself with the applause of men of judgement, and was somewhat disposed to exclude all those from the character of men of judgement who did not applaud him.

But he was at other times more favourable to mankind than to think them blind to the beauties of his works, and imputed the slowness of their sale to other causes; either they were published at a time when the town was empty, or when the attention of the publick was engrossed by some struggle in the parliament, or some other object of general concern; or they were by the neglect of the publisher not diligently dispersed, or by his avarice not advertised with sufficient frequency. Address, or industry, or liberality, was always wanting; and the blame was laid rather on any person than the author.

By arts like these, arts which every man practises in some

degree, and to which too much of the little tranquillity of life is to be ascribed, Savage was always able to live at peace with himself. Had he indeed only made use of these expedients to alleviate the loss or want of fortune or reputation, or any other advantages, which it is not in man's power to bestow upon himself, they might have been justly mentioned as instances of a philosophical mind, and very properly proposed to the imitation of multitudes, who, for want of diverting their imaginations with the same dexterity, languish under afflictions which might be easily removed.

It were doubtless to be wished, that truth and reason were universally prevalent; that every thing were esteemed according to its real value; and that men would secure themselves from being disappointed in their endeavours after happiness, by placing it only in virtue, which is always to be obtained; but if adventitious and foreign pleasures must be pursued, it would be perhaps of some benefit, since that pursuit must frequently be fruitless, if the practice of Savage could be taught, that folly might be an antidote to folly, and one fallacy be obviated by another.

But the danger of this pleasing intoxication must not be concealed; nor indeed can any one, after having observed the life of Savage, need to be cautioned against it. By imputing none of his miseries to himself, he continued to act upon the same principles, and to follow the same path; was never made wiser by his sufferings, nor preserved by one misfortune from falling into another. He proceeded throughout his life to tread the same steps on the same circle; always applauding his past conduct, or at least forgetting it, to amuse himself with phantoms of happiness, which were dancing before him; and willingly turned his eyes from the light of reason, when it would have discovered the illusion, and shewn him, what he never wished to see, his real state.

He is even accused, after having lulled his imagination with those ideal opiates, of having tried the same experiment upon his conscience; and, having accustomed himself to impute all deviations from the right to foreign causes, it is certain that he was upon every occasion too easily reconciled to himself, and that he appeared very little to regret those practices which had impaired his reputation. The reigning error of his life was, that he mistook the love for the practice of virtue, and was indeed not so much a good man, as the friend of goodness.

This at least must be allowed him, that he always preserved a strong sense of the dignity, the beauty, and the necessity of virtue, and that he never contributed deliberately to spread corruption amongst mankind. His actions, which were generally precipitate, were often blameable; but his writings, being the productions of study, uniformly tended to the exaltation of the mind, and the propagation of morality and piety.

These writings may improve mankind, when his failings shall be forgotten; and therefore he must be considered, upon the whole, as a benefactor to the world; nor can his personal example do any hurt, since, whoever hears of his faults, will hear of the miseries which they brought upon him, and which would deserve less pity, had not his condition been such as made his faults pardonable. He may be considered as a child exposed to all the temptations of indigence, at an age when resolution was not yet strengthened by conviction, nor virtue confirmed by habit; a circumstance which in his *Bastard* he laments in a very affecting manner:

—No Mother's care
Shielded my infant innocence with prayer:
No Father's guardian–hand my youth maintain'd,
Call'd forth my virtues, or from vice restrain'd.

The Bastard, however it might provoke or mortify his mother, could not be expected to melt her to compassion, so that he was still under the same want of the necessities of life; and he therefore exerted all the interest which his wit, or his birth, or his misfortunes, could procure, to obtain, upon the death of Eusden,[20] the place of Poet Laureat, and prosecuted his application with so much diligence, that the King publickly declared it his intention to bestow it upon him; but such was the fate of Savage, that even the King, when he intended his advantage, was disappointed

[20] Lawrence Eusden died Sept. 27, 1730.

in his schemes; for the Lord Chamberlain, who has the disposal of the laurel, as one of the appendages of his office, either did not know the King's design, or did not approve it, or thought the nomination of the Laureat an encroachment upon his rights, and therefore bestowed the laurel upon Colley Cibber.

Mr. Savage, thus disappointed, took a resolution of applying to the queen, that, having once given him life, she would enable him to support it, and therefore published a short poem on her birth-day, to which he gave the odd title of *Volunteer Laureat*. The event of this essay he has himself related in the following letter, which he prefixed to the poem, when he afterwards re-printed it in *The Gentleman's Magazine,* from whence I have copied it intire, as this was one of the few attempts in which Mr. Savage succeeded.

"Mr. Urban, In your Magazine for February you published the last *Volunteer Laureat*, written on a very melancholy occasion, the death of the royal patroness of arts and literature in general, and of the author of that poem in particular; I now send you the first that Mr. Savage wrote under that title.—This gentleman, notwithstanding a very considerable interest, being, on the death of Mr. Eusden, disappointed of the Laureat's place, wrote the before-mentioned poem; which was no sooner published, but the late Queen sent to a bookseller for it: the author had not at that time a friend either to get him introduced, or his poem presented at court; yet such was the unspeakable goodness of that Princess, that notwithstanding this act of ceremony was wanting, in a few days after publication, Mr. Savage received a Bank-bill of fifty pounds, and a gracious message from her Majesty, by the Lord North and Guilford, to this effect; 'That her Majesty was highly pleased with the verses; that she took particularly kind his lines there relating to the King; that he had permission to write annu-ally on the same subject; and that he should yearly receive the like present, till something better (which was her Majesty's in-tention) could be done for him.' After this, he was permitted to present one of his annual poems to her Majesty, had the honour of kissing her hand, and met with the most gracious reception. Yours, &c."

Such was the performance, and such its reception; a reception which, though by no means unkind, was not yet in the highest degree generous: to chain down the genius of a writer to an annual panegyric, shewed in the Queen too much desire of hearing her own praises, and a greater regard to herself than to him on whom her bounty was conferred. It was a kind of avaricious generosity, by which flattery was rather purchased, than genius rewarded.

Mrs. Oldfield had formerly given him the same allowance with much more heroic intention; she had no other view than to enable him to prosecute his studies, and to set himself above the want of assistance, and was contented with doing good without stipulating for encomiums.

Mr. Savage however was not at liberty to make exceptions, but was ravished with the favours which he had received, and probably yet more with those which he was promised; he considered himself now as a favourite of the Queen, and did not doubt but a few annual poems would establish him in some profitable employment.

He therefore assumed the title of *Volunteer Laureat*, not without some reprehensions from Cibber, who informed him, that the title of *Laureat* was a mark of honour conferred by the King, from whom all honour is derived, and which therefore no man has a right to bestow upon himself; and added, that he might, with equal propriety, style himself a Volunteer Lord, or Volunteer Baronet. It cannot be denied that the remark was just; but Savage did not think any title, which was conferred upon Mr. Cibber, so honourable as that the usurpation of it could be imputed to him as an instance of very exorbitant vanity, and therefore continued to write under the same title, and received every year the same reward.

He did not appear to consider these encomiums as tests of his abilities, or as any thing more than annual hints to the Queen of her promise, or acts of ceremony, by the performance of which he was intitled to his pension, and therefore did not labour them with great diligence, or print more than fifty each year, except that for some of the last years he regularly inserted them in *The*

Gentleman's Magazine, by which they were dispersed over the kingdom.

Of some of them he had himself so low an opinion, that he intended to omit them in the collection of poems, for which he printed proposals, and solicited subscriptions; nor can it seem strange, that, being confined to the same subject, he should be at some times indolent, and at others unsuccessful; that he should sometimes delay a disagreeable task, till it was too late to perform it well; or that he should sometimes repeat the same sentiment on the same occasion, or at others be misled by an attempt after novelty to forced conceptions and far-fetched images.

He wrote indeed with a double intention, which supplied him with some variety; for his business was to praise the Queen for the favours which he had received, and to complain to her of the delay of those which she had promised: in some of his pieces, therefore, gratitude is predominant, and in some discontent; in some he represents himself as happy in her patronage, and in others as disconsolate to find himself neglected.

Her promise, like other promises made to this unfortunate man, was never performed, though he took sufficient care that it should not be forgotten. The publication of his *Volunteer Laureat* procured him no other reward than a regular remittance of fifty pounds.

He was not so depressed by his disappointments as to neglect any opportunity that was offered of advancing his interest. When the Princess Anne was married,[21] he wrote a poem upon her departure, only, as he declared, "because it was expected from him," and he was not willing to bar his own prospects by any appearance of neglect.

He never mentioned any advantage gained by this poem, or any regard that was paid to it; and therefore it is likely that it was considered at court as an act of duty to which he was obliged by his dependence, and which it was therefore not necessary to reward by any new favour: or perhaps the Queen really intended

[21] On March 14, 1734. The poem was entitled "The Genius of Liberty."

his advancement, and therefore thought it superfluous to lavish presents upon a man whom she intended to establish for life.

About this time not only his hopes were in danger of being frustrated, but his pension likewise of being obstructed, by an accidental calumny. The writer of *The Daily Courant,* a paper then published under the direction of the ministry, charged him with a crime, which, though not very great in itself, would have been remarkably invidious in him, and might very justly have incensed the Queen against him. He was accused by name of influencing elections against the court, by appearing at the head of a tory mob; nor did the accuser fail to aggravate his crime, by representing it as the effect of the most atrocious ingratitude, and a kind of rebellion against the Queen, who had first preserved him from an infamous death, and afterwards distinguished him by her favour, and supported him by her charity. The charge, as it was open and confident, was likewise by good fortune very particular. The place of the transaction was mentioned, and the whole series of the rioter's conduct related. This exactness made Mr. Savage's vindication easy; for he never had in his life seen the place which was declared to be the scene of his wickedness, nor ever had been present in any town when its representatives were chosen. This answer he therefore made haste to publish, with all the circumstances necessary to make it credible; and very reasonably demanded, that the accusation should be retracted in the same paper, that he might no longer suffer the imputation of sedition and ingratitude. This demand was likewise pressed by him in a private letter to the author of the paper, who, either trusting to the protection of those whose defence he had undertaken, or having entertained some personal malice against Mr. Savage, or fearing, lest, by retracting so confident an assertion, he should impair the credit of his paper, refused to give him that satisfaction.

Mr. Savage therefore thought it necessary, to his own vindication, to prosecute him in the King's Bench; but as he did not find any ill effects from the accusation, having sufficiently cleared his innocence, he thought any further procedure would have the appearance of revenge; and therefore willingly dropped it.

He saw soon afterwards a process commenced in the same court
against himself, on an information in which he was accused of
writing and publishing an obscene pamphlet.

It was always Mr. Savage's desire to be distinguished; and,
when any controversy became popular, he never wanted some
reason for engaging in it with great ardour, and appearing at the
head of the party which he had chosen. As he was never cele-
brated for his prudence, he had no sooner taken his side, and
informed himself of the chief topicks of the dispute, than he
took all opportunities of asserting and propagating his principles,
without much regard to his own interest, or any other visible de-
sign than that of drawing upon himself the attention of man-
kind.

The dispute between the bishop of London and the chancellor[22]
is well known to have been for some time the chief topick of
political conversation; and therefore Mr. Savage, in pursuance of
his character, endeavoured to become conspicuous among the
controvertists with which every coffee-house was filled on that
occasion. He was an indefatigable opposer of all the claims of
ecclesiastical power, though he did not know on what they were
founded; and was therefore no friend to the Bishop of London.
But he had another reason for appearing as a warm advocate for
Dr. Rundle; for he was the friend of Mr. Foster and Mr. Thom-
son,[23] who were the friends of Mr. Savage.

Thus remote was his interest in the question, which, however,
as he imagined, concerned him so nearly, that it was not sufficient
to harangue and dispute, but necessary likewise to write upon it.

He therefore engaged with great ardour in a new Poem, called
by him, *The Progress of a Divine;* in which he conducts a
profligate priest by all the gradations of wickedness from a poor

[22] The Bishop of London was Edmund Gibson (1669–1748); the
Chancellor, Charles Talbot (1685–1737): the quarrel was about appoint-
ing Thomas Rundle Bishop of Gloucester. Rundle was made Bishop of
Derry in the event.

[23] Thomson was the poet; James Foster a Nonconformist minister, "a
man of mean ability," said Johnson elsewhere, "and of no original think-
ing." (*Johnsonian Miscellanies,* ed. Hill, II, 41).

curacy in the country, to the highest preferments of the Church, and describes with that humour which was natural to him, and that knowledge which was extended to all the diversities of human life, his behaviour in every station; and insinuates that this priest, thus accomplished, found at last a patron in the Bishop of London.

When he was asked by one of his friends, on what pretence he could charge the bishop with such an action? he had no more to say than that he had only inverted the accusation, and that he thought it reasonable to believe, that he who obstructed the rise of a good man without reason, would for bad reasons promote the exaltation of a villain.

The clergy were universally provoked by this satire; and Savage, who, as was his constant practice, had set his name to his performance, was censured in *The Weekly Miscellany* with severity which he did not seem inclined to forget.

But a return of invective was not thought a sufficient punishment. The Court of King's Bench was therefore moved against him, and he was obliged to return an answer to a charge of obscenity. It was urged, in his defence, that obscenity was criminal when it was intended to promote the practice of vice; but that Mr. Savage had only introduced obscene ideas with the view of exposing them to detestation, and of amending the age by showing the deformity of wickedness. This plea was admitted; and Sir Philip Yorke, who then presided in that court, dismissed the information with encomiums upon the purity and excellence of Mr. Savage's writings.

The prosecution, however, answered in some measure the purpose of those by whom it was set on foot; for Mr. Savage was so far intimidated by it, that, when the edition of his poem was sold, he did not venture to reprint it; so that it was in a short time forgotten, or forgotten by all but those whom it offended.

It is said that some endeavours were used to incense the Queen against him: but he found advocates to obviate at least part of their effect; for though he was never advanced, he still continued to receive his pension.

This poem drew more infamy upon him than any incident of

his life; and, as his conduct cannot be vindicated, it is proper
to secure his memory from reproach, by informing those whom he
made his enemies, that he never intended to repeat the provoca-
tion; and that, though, whenever he thought he had any reason
to complain of the clergy, he used to threaten them with a new
edition of *The Progress of a Divine,* it was his calm and settled
resolution to suppress it for ever.

He once intended to have made a better reparation for the
folly or injustice with which he might be charged, by writing
another poem, called *The Progress of a Freethinker,* whom he in-
tended to lead through all the stages of vice and folly, to convert
him from virtue to wickedness, and from religion to infidelity, by
all the modish sophistry used for that purpose; and at last to
dismiss him by his own hand into the other world.

That he did not execute this design is a real loss to mankind,
for he was too well acquainted with all the scenes of debauchery
to have failed in his representations of them, and too zealous for
virtue not to have represented them in such a manner as should
expose them either to ridicule or detestation.

But this plan was, like others, formed and laid aside till the
vigour of his imagination was spent, and the effervescence of in-
vention had subsided; but soon gave way to some other design,
which pleased by its novelty for a while, and then was neglected
like the former.

He was still in his usual exigences, having no certain support
but the pension allowed him by the Queen, which, though it
might have kept an exact economist from want, was very far
from being sufficient for Mr. Savage, who had never been ac-
customed to dismiss any of his appetites without the gratification
which they solicited, and whom nothing but want of money with-
held from partaking of every pleasure that fell within his view.

His conduct with regard to his pension was very particular. No
sooner had he changed the bill, than he vanished from the sight
of all his acquaintances, and lay for some time out of the reach
of all the enquiries that friendship or curiosity could make after
him; at length he appeared again pennyless as before, but never

informed even those whom he seemed to regard most, where he had been, nor was his retreat ever discovered.

This was his constant practice during the whole time that he received the pension from the Queen: He regularly disappeared and returned. He indeed affirmed that he retired to study, and that the money supported him in solitude for many months; but his friends declared, that the short time in which it was spent sufficiently confuted his own account of his conduct.

His politeness and his wit still raised him friends, who were desirous of setting him at length free from that indigence by which he had been hitherto oppressed; and therefore solicited Sir Robert Walpole in his favour with so much earnestness, that they obtained a promise of the next place that should become vacant, not exceeding two hundred pounds a year. This promise was made with an uncommon declaration, "that it was not the promise of a minister to a petitioner, but of a friend to his friend."

Mr. Savage now concluded himself set at ease for ever, and, as he observes in a poem written on that incident of his life, trusted and was trusted; but soon found that his confidence was ill-grounded, and this friendly promise was not inviolable. He spent a long time in solicitations, and at last despaired and desisted.

He did not indeed deny that he had given the minister some reason to believe that he should not strengthen his own interest by advancing him, for he had taken care to distinguish himself in coffee-houses as an advocate for the ministry of the last years of Queen Anne, and was always ready to justify the conduct, and exalt the character of Lord Bolingbroke, whom he mentions with great regard in an epistle upon authors, which he wrote about that time, but was too wise to publish, and of which only some fragments have appeared, inserted by him in the *Magazine* after his retirement.[24]

To despair was not, however, the character of Savage; when one patronage failed, he had recourse to another. The prince was now

[24] "Satire on False Historians," in *The Gentleman's Magazine,* 1741, p. 491.

extremely popular, and had very liberally rewarded the merit of some writers whom Mr. Savage did not think superior to himself, and therefore he resolved to address a poem to him.

For this purpose he made choice of a subject, which could regard only persons of the highest rank and highest affluence, and which was therefore proper for a poem intended to procure the patronage of a prince; and having retired for some time to Richmond, that he might prosecute his design in full tranquillity, without the temptations of pleasure, or the solicitations of creditors, by which his meditations were in equal danger of being disconcerted, he produced a poem *On Public Spirit, with regard to Publick Works.*

The plan of this poem is very extensive, and comprises a multitude of topicks, each of which might furnish matter sufficient for a long performance, and of which some have already employed more eminent writers; but as he was perhaps not fully acquainted with the whole extent of his own design, and was writing to obtain a supply of wants too pressing to admit of long or accurate enquiries, he passes negligently over many publick works, which, even in his own opinion, deserved to be more elaborately treated.

But though he may sometimes disappoint his reader by transient touches upon these subjects, which have often been considered, and therefore naturally raise expectations, he must be allowed amply to compensate his omissions, by expatiating, in the conclusion of his work, upon a kind of beneficence not yet celebrated by any eminent poet, though it now appears more susceptible of embellishments, more capable to exalt the ideas, and affect the passions, than many of those which have hitherto been thought worthy of the ornaments of verse. The settlement of colonies in uninhabited countries, the establishment of those in security, whose misfortunes have made their own country no longer pleasing or safe, the acquisition of property without injury to any, the appropriation of the waste and luxuriant bounties of nature, and the enjoyment of those gifts which heaven has scattered upon regions uncultivated and unoccupied, cannot be considered without giving rise to a great number of pleasing ideas, and bewildering the imagination in delightful prospects; and, therefore, whatever speculations they may produce in those who have confined themselves to political studies, naturally fixed the attention, and excited the applause, of a poet. The politician, when he considers men driven into other countries for shelter, and obliged to retire to forest and deserts, and pass their lives and fix their posterity in the remotest corners of the world, to avoid those hardships which they suffer or fear in their native place, may very properly enquire, why the legislature does not provide a remedy for these miseries, rather than encourage an escape from them. He may conclude, that the flight of every honest man is a loss to the community; that those who are unhappy without guilt ought to be relieved; and the life, which is overburthened by accidental calamities, set at ease by the care of the publick; and that those, who have by misconduct forfeited their claim to favour, ought rather to be made useful to the society which they have injured than driven from it.[25] But the poet is employed in a more pleasing undertaking than that of proposing laws, which, however just or expedient, will never be made; or endeavouring to reduce to rational schemes of government societies which were formed by chance, and are conducted by the private passions of those who preside in them. He guides the unhappy fugitive from want and persecution, to plenty, quiet, and security, and seats him in scenes of peaceful solitude, and undisturbed repose.

Savage has not forgotten, amidst the pleasing sentiments which this prospect of retirement suggested to him, to censure those crimes which have been generally committed by the discoverers of new regions, and to expose the enormous wickedness of making war upon barbarous nations because they cannot resist, and of invading countries because they are fruitful; of extending navigation only to propagate vice, and of visiting distant lands only to lay them waste. He has asserted the natural equality of mankind, and endeavoured to suppress that pride which inclines men to imagine that right is the consequence of power.

His description of the various miseries which force men to seek

[25] Johnson himself discusses these topics in his *Journey to the Western Isles.*

for refuge in distant countries, affords another instance of his proficiency in the important and extensive study of human life; and the tenderness with which he recounts them, another proof of his humanity and benevolence.

It is observable, that the close of this poem discovers a change which experience had made in Mr. Savage's opinions. In a poem written by him in his youth, and published in his Miscellanies, he declares his contempt of the contracted views and narrow prospects of the middle state of life, and declares his resolution either to tower like the cedar, or be trampled like the shrub; but in this poem, though addressed to a prince, he mentions this state of life as comprising those who ought most to attract reward, those who merit most the confidence of power, and the familiarity of greatness; and, accidentally mentioning this passage to one of his friends, declared, that in his opinion all the virtue of mankind was comprehended in that state.

In describing villas and gardens, he did not omit to condemn that absurd custom which prevails among the English, of permitting servants to receive money from strangers for the entertainment that they receive, and therefore inserted in his poem these lines;

> But what the flowering pride of gardens rare,
> However royal, or however fair,
> If gates, which to access should still give way,
> Ope but, like Peter's paradise, for pay?
> If perquisited varlets frequent stand,
> And each new walk must a new tax demand?
> What foreign eye but with contempt surveys?
> What Muse shall from oblivion snatch their praise?

But before the publication of his performance he recollected that the Queen allowed her garden and cave at Richmond to be shewn for money, and that she so openly countenanced the practice, that she had bestowed the privilege of shewing them as a place of profit on a man, whose merit she valued herself upon rewarding, though she gave him only the liberty of disgracing his country.

He therefore thought, with more prudence than was often exerted by him, that the publication of these lines might be officiously represented as an insult upon the Queen, to whom he owed his life and his subsistence; and that the propriety of his observation would be no security against the censures which the unseasonableness of it might draw upon him; he therefore suppressed the passage in the first edition, but after the Queen's death thought the same caution no longer necessary, and restored it to the proper place.

The poem was therefore published without any political faults, and inscribed to the prince; but Mr. Savage, having no friend upon whom he could prevail to present it to him, had no other method of attracting his observation than the publication of frequent advertisements, and therefore received no reward from his patron, however generous on other occasions.

This disappointment he never mentioned without indignation, being by some means or other confident that the Prince was not ignorant of his address to him; and insinuated, that, if any advances in popularity could have been made by distinguishing him, he had not written without notice, or without reward.

He was once inclined to have presented his poem in person, and sent to the printer for a copy with that design; but either his opinion changed, or his resolution deserted him, and he continued to resent neglect without attempting to force himself into regard.

Nor was the publick much more favorable than his patron, for only seventy-two were sold, though the performance was much commended by some whose judgement in that kind of writing is generally allowed. But Savage easily reconciled himself to mankind without imputing any defect to his work, by observing that his poem was unluckily published two days after the prorogation of the parliament, and by consequence at a time when all those who could be expected to regard it were in the hurry of preparing for their departure, or engaged in taking leave of others upon their dismission from publick affairs.

It must be however allowed, in justification of the publick, that this performance is not the most excellent of Mr. Savage's works;

and that, though it cannot be denied to contain many striking sentiments, majestic lines, and just observations, it is in general not sufficiently polished in the language, or enlivened in the imagery, or digested in the plan.

Thus his poem contributed nothing to the alleviation of his poverty, which was such as very few could have supported with equal patience; but to which it must likewise be confessed, that few would have been exposed who received punctually fifty pounds a year; a salary which, though by no means equal to the demands of vanity and luxury, is yet found sufficient to support families above want, and was undoubtedly more than the necessities of life require.

But no sooner had he received his pension, than he withdrew to his darling privacy, from which he returned in a short time to his former distress, and for some part of the year generally lived by chance, eating only when he was invited to the tables of his acquaintances, from which the meanness of his dress often excluded him, when the politeness and variety of his conversation would have been thought a sufficient recompense for his entertainment.

He lodged as much by accident as he dined, and passed the night sometimes in mean houses, which are set open at night to any casual wanderers, sometimes in cellars, among the riot and filth of the meanest and most profligate of the rabble; and sometimes, when he had not money to support even the expences of these receptacles, walked about the streets till he was weary, and lay down in the summer upon a bulk, or in the winter, with his associates in poverty, among the ashes of a glass-house.

In this manner were passed those days and those nights which nature had enabled him to have employed in elevated speculations, useful studies, or pleasing conversation. On a bulk, in a cellar, or in a glass-house among thieves and beggars, was to be found the Author of *The Wanderer,* the man of exalted sentiments, extensive views, and curious observations; the man whose remarks on life might have assisted the statesman, whose ideas of virtue might have enlightened the moralist, whose eloquence might have influenced senates, and whose delicacy might have polished courts.

It cannot but be imagined that such necessities might sometimes force him upon disreputable practices: and it is probable that these lines in *The Wanderer* were occasioned by his reflections on his own conduct:

> Though misery leads to happiness and truth,
> Unequal to the load, this languid youth,
> (Oh, let none censure, if, untried by grief,
> If, amidst woe, untempted by relief,)
> He stoop'd reluctant to low arts of shame,
> Which then, ev'n then he scorn'd, and blush'd to name.

Whoever was acquainted with him was certain to be solicited for small sums, which the frequency of the request made in time considerable, and he was therefore quickly shunned by those who were become familiar enough to be trusted with his necessities; but his rambling manner of life, and constant appearance at houses of public resort, always procured him a new succession of friends, whose kindness had not been exhausted by repeated requests; so that he was seldom absolutely without resources, but had in his utmost exigences this comfort, that he always imagined himself sure of speedy relief.

It was observed, that he always asked favours of this kind without the least submission or apparent consciousness of dependence, and that he did not seem to look upon a compliance with his request as an obligation that deserved any extraordinary acknowledgements; but a refusal was resented by him as an affront, or complained of as an injury; nor did he readily reconcile himself to those who either denied to lend, or gave him afterwards any intimation that they expected to be repaid.

He was sometimes so far compassionated by those who knew both his merits and distresses, that they received him into their families, but they soon discovered him to be a very incommodious inmate; for, being always accustomed to an irregular manner of life, he could not confine himself to any stated hours, or pay any regard to the rules of a family, but would prolong his conversation till midnight, without considering that business might require his friend's application in the morning: and, when he had persuaded himself to retire to bed, was not, without equal difficulty, called up to dinner; it was therefore impossible to pay him any distinction without the entire subversion of all economy, a kind of establishment which, wherever he went, he always appeared ambitious to overthrow.

It must therefore be acknowledged, in justification of mankind, that it was not always by the negligence or coldness of his friends that Savage was distressed, but because it was in reality very difficult to preserve him long in a state of ease. To supply him with money was a hopeless attempt; for no sooner did he see himself master of a sum sufficient to set him free from care for a day, than he became profuse and luxurious. When once he had entered a tavern, or engaged in a scheme of pleasure, he never retired till want of money obliged him to some new expedient. If he was entertained in a family, nothing was any longer to be regarded there but amusements and jollity; wherever Savage entered, he immediately expected that order and business should fly before him, that all should thenceforward be left to hazard, and that no dull principle of domestic management should be opposed to his inclination, or intrude upon his gaiety.

His distresses, however afflictive, never dejected him; in his lowest state he wanted not spirit to assert the natural dignity of wit, and was always ready to repress that insolence which superiority of fortune incited, and to trample on that reputation which rose upon any other basis than that of merit: he never admitted any gross familiarities, or submitted to be treated otherwise than as an equal. Once, when he was without lodging, meat, or clothes, one of his friends, a man not indeed remarkable for moderation in his prosperity, left a message, that he desired to see him about nine in the morning. Savage knew that his intention was to assist him; but was very much disgusted that he should presume to prescribe the hour of his attendance, and, I believe, refused to visit him, and rejected his kindness.

The same invincible temper, whether firmness or obstinacy, appeared in his conduct to the Lord Tyrconnel, from whom he very frequently demanded that the allowance which was once paid him should be restored; but with whom he never appeared to entertain for a moment the thought of soliciting a reconciliation, and whom he treated at once with all the haughtiness of superiority, and all the bitterness of resentment. He wrote to him, not in a style of supplication or respect, but of reproach, menace, and contempt; and appeared determined, if he ever regained his allowance, to hold it only by the right of conquest.

As many more can discover, that a man is richer than that he is wiser than themselves, superiority of understanding is not so readily acknowledged as that of fortune; nor is that haughtiness, which the consciousness of great abilities incites, born with the same submission as the tyranny of affluence; and therefore Savage, by asserting his claim to deference and regard, and by treating those with contempt whom better fortune animated to rebel against him, did not fail to raise a great number of enemies in the different classes of mankind. Those who thought themselves raised above him by the advantages of riches, hated him because they found no protection from the petulance of his wit. Those who were esteemed for their writings feared him as a critic, and maligned him as a rival, and almost all the smaller wits were his professed enemies.

Among these Mr. Miller so far indulged his resentment as to introduce him in a farce,[26] and direct him to be personated on the stage, in a dress like that which he then wore; a mean insult, which only insinuated that Savage had but one coat, and which was therefore despised by him rather than resented; for though he wrote a lampoon against Miller, he never printed it: and as no other person ought to prosecute that revenge from which the person who was injured desisted, I shall not preserve what Mr. Savage suppressed: of which the publication would indeed have been a punishment too severe for so impotent an assault.

The great hardships of poverty were to Savage not the want of lodging or of food, but the neglect and contempt which it drew

[26] Hill surmises that James Miller, author of The Coffee House, 1737, is meant, but finds nothing in this or his other plays to substantiate the charge.

upon him. He complained, that as his affairs grew desperate, he found his reputation for capacity visibly decline; that his opinion in questions of criticism was no longer regarded, when his coat was out of fashion; and that those who, in the interval of his prosperity, were always encouraging him to great undertakings by encomiums on his genius and assurances of success, now received any mention of his designs with coldness, thought that the subjects on which he proposed to write were very difficult, and were ready to inform him, that the event of a poem was uncertain, that an author ought to employ much time in the consideration of his plan, and not presume to sit down to write in confidence of a few cursory ideas, and a superficial knowledge; difficulties were started on all sides, and he was no longer qualified for any performance but *The Volunteer Laureat*.

Yet even this kind of contempt never depressed him; for he always preserved a steady confidence in his own capacity, and believed nothing above his reach which he should at any time earnestly endeavour to attain. He formed schemes of the same kind with regard to knowledge and to fortune, and flattered himself with advances to be made in science, as with riches, to be enjoyed in some distant period of his life. For the acquisition of knowledge he was indeed far better qualified than for that of riches; for he was naturally inquisitive and desirous of the conversation of those from whom any information was to be obtained, but by no means solicitous to improve those opportunities that were sometimes offered of raising his fortune; and he was remarkably retentive of his ideas, which, when once he was in possession of them, rarely forsook him; a quality which could never be communicated to his money.

While he was thus wearing out his life in expectation that the Queen would some time recollect her promise, he had recourse to the usual practice of writers, and published proposals for printing his works by subscription, to which he was encouraged by the success of many who had not a better right to the favour of the publick; but, whatever was the reason, he did not find the world equally inclined to favour him; and he observed with some discontent, that, though he offered his works at half a guinea, he was able to procure but a small number in comparison with those who subscribed twice as much to Duck.

Nor was it without indignation that he saw his proposals neglected by the Queen, who patronised Mr. Duck's with uncommon ardour, and incited a competition among those who attended the court, who should most promote his interest, and who should first offer a subscription.[27] This was a distinction to which Mr. Savage made no scruple of asserting that his birth, his misfortunes, and his genius, gave him a fairer title, than could be pleaded by him on whom it was conferred.

Savage's applications were however not universally unsuccessful; for some of the nobility countenanced his design, encouraged his proposals, and subscribed with great liberality. He related of the Duke of Chandos particularly, that, upon receiving his proposals, he sent him ten guineas.

But the money which his subscriptions afforded him was not less volatile than that which he received from his other schemes; whenever a subscription was paid him, he went to a tavern; and, as money so collected is necessarily received in small sums, he never was able to send his poems to the press, but for many years continued his solicitation, and squandered whatever he obtained.

This project of printing his works was frequently revived; and, as his proposals grew obsolete, new ones were printed with fresher dates. To form schemes for the publication was one of his favourite amusements; nor was he ever more at ease than when, with any friend who readily fell in with his schemes, he was adjusting the print, forming the advertisements, and regulating the dispersion of his new edition, which he really intended some time to publish, and which, as long as experience had shewn him the impossibility of printing the volume together, he at last determined to divide into weekly or monthly numbers, that the profits of the first might supply the expences of the next.

Thus he spent his time in mean expedients and tormenting suspense, living for the greatest part in the fear of prosecutions from

[27] Queen Caroline made Stephen Duck (1705–1756), the "thresher poet," her librarian at Richmond. He later became Rector of Byfleet, but, in a fit of depression, drowned himself.

his creditors, and consequently skulking in obscure parts of the town, of which he was no stranger to the remotest corners. But wherever he came, his address secured him friends, whom his necessities soon alienated; so that he had perhaps a more numerous acquaintance than any man ever before attained, there being scarcely any person eminent on any account to whom he was not known, or whose character he was not in some degree able to delineate.

To the acquisition of this extensive acquaintance every circumstance of his life contributed. He excelled in the arts of conversation, and therefore willingly practised them. He had seldom any home, or even a lodging in which he could be private; and therefore was driven into public-houses for the common conveniences of life and supports of nature. He was always ready to comply with every invitation, having no employment to withhold him, and often no money to provide for himself; and by dining with one company, he never failed of obtaining an introduction into another.

Thus dissipated was his life, and thus casual his subsistence; yet did not the distraction of his views hinder him from reflection, nor the uncertainty of his condition depress his gaiety. When he had wandered about without any fortunate adventure by which he was led into a tavern, he sometimes retired into the fields, and was able to employ his mind in study, or amuse it with pleasing imaginations; and seldom appeared to be melancholy, but when some sudden misfortune had just fallen upon him, and even then in a few moments he would disentangle himself from his perplexity, adopt the subject of conversation, and apply his mind wholly to the objects that others presented to it.

This life, unhappy as it may be already imagined, was yet imbittered, in 1738, with new calamities. The death of the Queen deprived him of all the prospects of preferment with which he so long entertained his imagination; and, as Sir Robert Walpole had before given him reason to believe that he never intended the performance of his promise, he was now abandoned again to fortune.

He was however, at that time, supported by a friend; and as it was not his custom to look out for distant calamities, or to feel any other pain than that which forced itself upon his senses, he was not much afflicted at his loss, and perhaps comforted himself that his pension would be now continued without the annual tribute of a panegyric.

Another expectation contributed likewise to support him: he had taken a resolution to write a second tragedy upon the story of Sir Thomas Overbury, in which he preserved a few lines of his former play, but made a total alteration of the plan, added new incidents, and introduced new characters; so that it was a new tragedy, not a revival of the former.

Many of his friends blamed him for not making choice of another subject; but, in vindication of himself, he asserted, that it was not easy to find a better; and that he thought it his interest to extinguish the memory of the first tragedy, which he could only do by writing one less defective upon the same story; by which he should entirely defeat the artifice of the booksellers, who, after the death of any author of reputation, are always industrious to swell his works, by uniting his worst productions with his best.

In the execution of this scheme, however, he proceeded but slowly, and probably only employed himself upon it when he could find no other amusement; but he pleased himself with counting the profits, and perhaps imagined, that the theatrical reputation which he was about to acquire, would be equivalent to all that he had lost by the death of his patroness.

He did not, in confidence of his approaching riches, neglect the measures proper to secure the continuance of his pension, though some of his favourers thought him culpable for omitting to write on her death; but on her birth-day next year, he gave a proof of the solidity of his judgement, and the power of his genius. He knew that the track of elegy had been so long beaten, that it was impossible to travel in it without treading in the footsteps of those who had gone before him; and that therefore it was necessary, that he might distinguish himself from the herd of encomiasts, to find out some new walk of funeral panegyrick.

This difficult task he performed in such a manner, that his poem may be justly ranked among the best pieces that the death of princes has produced. By transferring the mention of her death to her birth-day, he has formed a happy combination of topicks, which any other man would have thought it very difficult to connect in one view, but which he has united in such a manner, that the relation between them appears natural; and it may be justly said, that what no other man would have thought on, it now appears scaraely possible for any man to miss.

The beauty of this peculiar combination of images is so masterly, that it is sufficient to set this poem above censure, and therefore it is not necessary to mention many other delicate touches which may be found in it, and which would deservedly be admired in any other performance.

To these proofs of his genius may be added, from the same poem, an instance of his prudence, an excellence for which he was not so often distinguished; he does not forget to remind the King, in the most delicate and artful manner, of continuing his pension.

With regard to the success of this address, he was for some time in suspence, but was in no great degree solicitous about it; and continued his labour upon his new tragedy with great tranquillity, till the friend who had for a considerable time supported him, removing his family to another place, took occasion to dismiss him. It then became necessary to enquire more diligently what was determined in his affair, having reason to suspect that no great favour was intended him, because he had not received his pension at the usual time.

It is said, that he did not take those methods of retrieving his interest, which were most likely to succeed; and some of those who were employed in the Exchequer, cautioned him against too much violence in his proceedings; but Mr. Savage, who seldom regulated his conduct by the advice of others, gave way to his passion, and demanded of Sir Robert Walpole, at his levee, the reason of the distinction that was made between him and the other pensioners of the Queen, with a degree of roughness which perhaps determined him to withdraw what had been only delayed.

Whatever was the crime of which he was accused or suspected, and whatever influence was employed against him, he received soon after an account that took from him all hopes of regaining his pension; and he had now no prospect of subsistence but from his

play, and he knew no way of living for the time required to finish
it.

So peculiar were the misfortunes of this man, deprived of an
estate and title by a particular law, exposed and abandoned by a
mother, defrauded by a mother of a fortune which his father had
allotted him, he entered the world without a friend; and though
his abilities forced themselves into esteem and reputation, he was
never able to obtain any real advantage, and whatever prospects
arose were always intercepted as he began to approach them. The
king's intentions in his favour were frustrated; his dedication to the
Prince, whose generosity on every other occasion was eminent, pro-
cured him no reward; Sir Robert Walpole, who valued himself
upon keeping his promise to others, broke it to him without regret;
and the bounty of the Queen was, after her death, withdrawn
from him, and from him only.

Such were his misfortunes, which yet he bore, not only with
decency, but with cheerfulness; nor was his gaiety clouded even
by his last disappointments, though he was in a short time reduced
to the lowest degree of distress, and often wanted both lodging and
food. At this time he gave another instance of the insurmountable
obstinacy of his spirit: his clothes were worn out; and he received
notice, that at a coffee-house some clothes and linen were left for
him: the person who sent them did not, I believe, inform him to
whom he was to be obliged, that he might spare the perplexity of
acknowledging the benefit; but though the offer was so far gener-
ous, it was made with some neglect of ceremonies, which Mr.
Savage so much resented, that he refused the present, and de-
clined to enter the house till the clothes that had been designed
for him were taken away.

His distress was now publickly known, and his friends, there-
fore, thought it proper to concert some measures for his relief; and
one of them wrote a letter to him, in which he expressed his con-
cern "for the miserable withdrawing of his pension;" and gave him
hopes, that in a short time he should find himself supplied with a
competence, "without any dependence on those little creatures
whom we are pleased to call the Great." [28]

The scheme proposed for this happy and independent subsist-

[28] The writer was Pope.

ence, was, that he should retire into Wales, and receive an allow-
ance of fifty pounds a year, to be raised by a subscription, on
which he was to live privately in a cheap place, without aspiring
any more to affluence, or having any farther care of reputation.

This offer Mr. Savage gladly accepted, though with intentions
very different from those of his friends; for they proposed that he
should continue an exile from London for ever, and spend all the
remaining part of his life at Swansea; but he designed only to take
the opportunity, which their scheme offered him, of retreating for
a short time, that he might prepare his play for the stage, and his
other works for the press, and then to return to London to exhibit
his tragedy, and live upon the profits of his own labour.

With regard to his works, he proposed very great improvements,
which would have required much time, or great application; and
when he had finished them, he designed to do justice to his sub-
scribers, by publishing them according to his proposals.

As he was ready to entertain himself with future pleasures, he
had planned out a scheme of life for the country, of which he had
no knowledge but from pastorals and songs. He imagined that he
should be transported to scenes of flowery felicity, like those
which one poet has reflected to another; and had projected a
perpetual round of innocent pleasures, of which he suspected no
interruption from pride, or ignorance, or brutality.

With these expectations he was so enchanted, that when he was
once gently reproached by a friend for submitting to live upon a
subscription, and advised rather by a resolute exertion of his
abilities to support himself, he could not bear to debar himself
from the happiness which was to be found in the calm of a cottage,
or lose the opportunity of listening, without intermission, to the
melody of the nightingale, which he believed was to be heard
from every bramble, and which he did not fail to mention as a
very important part of the happiness of a country life.

While this scheme was ripening, his friends directed him to take
a lodging in the liberties of the Fleet,[29] that he might be secure
from his creditors, and sent him every Monday a guinea, which
he commonly spent before the next morning, and trusted, after his

[29] An area surrounding Fleet Prison, made free to the debtors consigned
to it.

usual manner, the remaining part of the week to the bounty of fortune.

He now began very sensibly to feel the miseries of dependence. Those by whom he was to be supported, began to prescribe to him with an air of authority, which he knew not how decently to resent, nor patiently to bear; and he soon discovered, from the conduct of most of his subscribers, that he was yet in the hands of "little creatures."

Of the insolence that he was obliged to suffer, he gave many instances, of which none appeared to raise his indignation to a greater height, than the method which was taken of furnishing him with clothes. Instead of consulting him, and allowing him to send a taylor his orders for what they thought proper to allow him, they proposed to send for a taylor to take his measure, and then to consult how they should equip him.

This treatment was not very delicate, nor was it such as Savage's humanity would have suggested to him on a like occasion; but it had scarcely deserved mention, had it not, by affecting him in an uncommon degree, shewn the peculiarity of his character. Upon hearing the design that was formed, he came to the lodging of a friend with the most violent agonies of rage; and, being asked what it could be that gave him such disturbance, he replied with the utmost vehemence of indignation, "That they had sent for a taylor to measure him."

How the affair ended was never enquired, for fear of renewing his uneasiness. It is probable, that, upon recollection, he submitted with a good grace to what he could not avoid, and that he discovered no resentment where he had no power.

He was, however, not humbled to implicit and universal compliance; for when the gentleman, who had first informed him of the design to support him by a subscription, attempted to procure a reconciliation with the Lord Tyrconnel, he could by no means be prevailed upon to comply with the measures that were proposed.

A letter was written for him[30] to Sir William Lemon,[31] to pre-

[30] By Mr. Pope. JOHNSON
[31] Lemon, or Leman, was the son-in-law of Mrs. Brett (Savage's "mother's" name by a later marriage).

vail upon him to interpose his good offices with Lord Tyrconnel, in which he solicited Sir William's assistance, "for a man who really needed it as much as any man could well do;" and informed him, that he was retiring "for ever to a place where he should no more trouble his relations, friends, or enemies;" he confessed, that his passion had betrayed him to some conduct with regard to Lord Tyrconnel, for which he could not but heartily ask his pardon; and as he imagined Lord Tyrconnel's passion might be yet so high, that he would not "receive a letter from him," begged that Sir William would endeavour to soften him; and expressed his hopes that he would comply with his request, and that "so small a relation would not harden his heart against him."

That any man should presume to dictate a letter to him, was not very agreeable to Mr. Savage; and therefore he was, before he had opened it, not much inclined to approve it. But when he read it, he found it contained sentiments entirely opposite to his own, and, as he asserted, to the truth; and therefore, instead of copying it, wrote his friend a letter full of masculine resentment and warm expostulations. He very justly observed, that the style was too supplicatory, and the representation too abject, and that he ought at least to have made him complain with "the dignity of a gentleman in distress." He declared that he would not write the paragraph in which he was to ask Lord Tyrconnel's pardon; for, "he despised his pardon, and therefore could not heartily, and would not hypocritically, ask it." He remarked, that his friend made a very unreasonable distinction between himself and him; for, says he, when you mention men of high rank "in your own character," they are "those little creatures whom we are pleased to call the great"; but when you address them "in mine," no servility is sufficiently humble. He then with great propriety explained the ill consequences which might be expected from such a letter, which his relations would print in their own defence, and which would for ever be produced as a full answer to all that he should allege against them; for he always intended to publish a minute account of the treatment which he had received. It is to be remembered, to the honour of the gentleman by whom this letter was drawn up, that he yielded to Mr. Savage's reasons, and agreed that it ought to be suppressed.

After many alterations and delays, a subscription was at length raised, which did not amount to fifty pounds a year, though twenty were paid by one gentleman; such was the generosity of mankind, that what had been done by a player without solicitation, could not now be effected by application and interest; and Savage had a great number to court and to obey for a pension less than that which Mrs. Oldfield paid him without exacting any servilities.

Mr. Savage however was satisfied, and willing to retire, and was convinced that the allowance, though scanty, would be more than sufficient for him, being now determined to commence a rigid œconomist, and to live according to the exactest rules of frugality; for nothing was in his opinion more contemptible than a man, who, when he knew his income, exceeded it; and yet he confessed, that instances of such folly were too common, and lamented that some men were not to be trusted with their own money.

Full of these salutary resolutions, he left London in July 1739, having taken leave with great tenderness of his friends, and parted from the author of this narrative with tears in his eyes. He was furnished with fifteen guineas, and informed, that they would be sufficient, not only for the expence of his journey, but for his support in Wales for some time; and that there remained but little more of the first collection. He promised a strict adherence to his maxims of parsimony, and went away in the stage-coach; nor did his friends expect to hear from him, till he informed them of his arrival at Swansea.

But when they least expected, arrived a letter dated the four-teenth day after his departure, in which he sent them word, that he was yet upon the road, and without money; and that he there-fore could not proceed without a remittance. They then sent him the money that was in their hands, with which he was enabled to reach Bristol, from whence he was to go to Swansea by water.

At Bristol he found an embargo laid upon the shipping, so that he could not immediately obtain a passage; and being therefore obliged to stay there some time, he with his usual felicity, in-gratiated himself with many of the principal inhabitants, was invited to their houses, distinguished at their publick feasts, and treated with a regard that gratified his vanity, and therefore easily engaged his affection.

He began very early after his retirement to complain of the conduct of his friends in London, and irritated many of them so much by his letters, that they withdrew, however honourably, their contributions; and it is believed, that little more was paid than the twenty pounds a year, which were allowed him by the gentleman who proposed the subscription.

After some stay at Bristol he retired to Swansea, the place originally proposed for his residence, where he lived about a year, very much dissatisfied with the diminution of his salary; but contracted, as in other places, acquaintance with those who were most distinguished in that country, among whom he has celebrated Mr. Powel and Mrs. Jones, by some verses which he inserted in *The Gentleman's Magazine*.

Here he completed his tragedy, of which two acts were wanting when he left London, and was desirous of coming to town to bring it upon the stage. This design was very warmly opposed, and he was advised by his chief benefactor to put it into the hands of Mr. Thomson and Mr. Mallet, that it might be fitted for the stage, and to allow his friends to receive the profits, out of which an annual pension should be paid him.

This proposal he rejected with the utmost contempt.[32] He was by no means convinced that the judgement of those, to whom he was required to submit, was superior to his own. He was now determined, as he expressed it, to be "no longer kept in leading-strings," and had no elevated idea of "his bounty, who proposed to pension him out of the profits of his own labours."

He attempted in Wales to promote a subscription for his works, and had once hopes of success; but in a short time afterwards formed a resolution of leaving that part of the country, to which he thought it not reasonable to be confined for the gratification of those, who, having promised him a liberal income, had no sooner

[32] In a letter from Pope to Savage, 15 Sept., 1742, Pope writes defensively: "What mortal would take your play . . . out of your hands, if you could come, and attend it yourself? It was only in defect of that, these offices of the two gentlemen you are so angry at, were offered. What interest but trouble could they have had in it?" (Pope's *Correspondence*, ed. Sherburn, IV, 418.)

banished him to a remote corner, than they reduced his allowance to a salary scarcely equal to the necessities of life.

His resentment of this treatment, which, in his own opinion at least, he had not deserved, was such, that he broke off all correspondence with most of his contributors, and appeared to consider them as persecutors and oppressors; and in the latter part of his life declared, that their conduct toward him, since his departure from London, "had been perfidiousness improving on perfidiousness, and inhumanity on inhumanity."

It is not to be supposed, that the necessities of Mr. Savage did not sometimes incite him to satirical exaggerations of the behaviour of those by whom he thought himself reduced to them. But it must be granted, that the diminution of his allowance was a great hardship, and that those who withdrew their subscription from a man, who, upon the faith of their promise, had gone into a kind of banishment, and abandoned all those by whom he had been before relieved in his distress, will find it no easy task to vindicate their conduct.

It may be alleged, and perhaps justly, that he was petulant and contemptuous; that he more frequently reproached his subscribers for not giving him more, than thanked them for what he received; but it is to be remembered, that his conduct, and this is the worst charge that can be drawn up against him, did them no real injury; and that it therefore ought rather to have been pitied than resented; at least, the resentment it might provoke ought to have been generous and manly; epithets which his conduct will hardly deserve that starves the man whom he has persuaded to put himself into his power.

It might have been reasonably demanded by Savage, that they should, before they had taken away what they promised, have replaced him in his former state, that they should have taken no advantages from the situation to which the appearance of their kindness had reduced him, and that he should have been recalled to London before he was abandoned. He might justly represent, that he ought to have been considered as a lion in the toils, and demand to be released before the dogs should be loosed upon him.

He endeavoured, indeed, to release himself, and, with an intent to return to London, went to Bristol, where a repetition of the kindness which he had formerly found invited him to stay. He was not only caressed and treated, but had a collection made for him of about thirty pounds, with which it had been happy if he had immediately departed for London; but his negligence did not suffer him to consider, that such proofs of kindness were not often to be expected, and that this ardour of benevolence was in a great degree the effect of novelty, and might, probably, be every day less; and therefore he took no care to improve the happy time, but was encouraged by one favour to hope for another, till at length generosity was exhausted, and officiousness wearied.

Another part of his misconduct was the practice of prolonging his visits to unseasonable hours, and disconcerting all the families into which he was admitted. This was an error in a place of commerce which all the charms of his conversation could not compensate; for what trader would purchase such airy satisfaction by the loss of solid gain, which must be the consequence of midnight merriment, as those hours which were gained at night were generally lost in the morning?

Thus Mr. Savage, after the curiosity of the inhabitants was gratified, found the number of his friends daily decreasing, perhaps without suspecting for what reason their conduct was altered; for he still continued to harass, with his nocturnal intrusions, those that yet countenanced him, and admitted him to their houses.

But he did not spend all the time of his residence at Bristol in visits or at taverns, for he sometimes returned to his studies, and began several considerable designs. When he felt an inclination to write, he always retired from the knowledge of his friends, and lay hid in an obscure part of the suburbs, till he found himself again desirous of company, to which it is likely that intervals of absence made him more welcome.

He was always full of his design of returning to London, to bring his tragedy upon the stage; but, having neglected to depart with the money that was raised for him, he could not afterwards procure a sum sufficient to defray the expences of his journey; nor perhaps would a fresh supply have had any other effect, than, by putting immediate pleasures in his power, to have driven the thoughts of his journey out of his mind.

While he was thus spending the day in contriving a scheme for the morrow, distress stole upon him by imperceptible degrees. His conduct had already wearied some of those who were at first enamoured of his conversation; but he might, perhaps, still have devolved to others, whom he might have entertained with equal success, had not the decay of his clothes made it no longer consistent with their vanity to admit him to their tables, or to associate with him in publick places. He now began to find every man from home at whose house he called; and was therefore no longer able to procure the necessaries of life, but wandered about the town, slighted and neglected, in quest of a dinner, which he did not always obtain.

To complete his misery, he was pursued by the officers for small debts which he had contracted; and was therefore obliged to withdraw from the small number of friends from whom he had still reason to hope for favours. His custom was to lie in bed the greatest part of the day, and to go out in the dark with the utmost privacy, and after having paid his visit return again before morning to his lodging, which was in the garret of an obscure inn.

Being thus excluded on one hand, and confined on the other, he suffered the utmost extremities of poverty, and often fasted so long that he was seized with faintness, and had lost his appetite, not being able to bear the smell of meat, till the action of his stomach was restored by a cordial.

In this distress, he received a remittance of five pounds from London,[33] with which he provided himself a decent coat, and determined to go to London, but unhappily spent his money at a favourite tavern. Thus was he again confined to Bristol, where he was every day hunted by bailiffs. In this exigence he once more found a friend, who sheltered him in his house, though at the usual inconveniences with which his company was attended; for he neither could be persuaded to go to bed in the night, nor to rise in the day.

It is observable, that in these various scenes of misery, he was always disengaged and cheerful: he at some times pursued his studies, and at others continued or enlarged his epistolary corre-

[33] Again from Pope.

spondence; nor was he ever so far dejected as to endeavour to procure an increase of his allowance by any other methods than accusations and reproaches.

He had now no longer any hopes of assistance from his friends at Bristol, who as merchants, and by consequence sufficiently studious of profit, cannot be supposed to have looked with much compassion upon negligence and extravagance, or to think any excellence equivalent to a fault of such consequence as neglect of œconomy. It is natural to imagine, that many of those, who would have relieved his real wants, were discouraged from the exertion of their benevolence by observation of the use which was made of their favours, and conviction that relief would only be momentary, and that the same necessity would quickly return.

At last he quitted the house of his friend, and returned to his lodging at the inn, still intending to set out in a few days for London; but on the 10th of January 1742–3, having been at supper with two of his friends, he was at his return to his lodgings arrested for a debt of about eight pounds, which he owed at a coffee-house, and conducted to the house of a sheriff's officer. The account which he gives of this misfortune, in a letter to one of the gentlemen with whom he had supped, is too remarkable to be omitted.

"It was not a little unfortunate for me, that I spent yesterday's evening with you; because the hour hindered me from entering on my new lodging; however, I have now got one, but such a one as I believe nobody would choose.

"I was arrested at the suit of Mrs. Read, just as I was going up stairs to bed, at Mr. Bowyer's; but taken in so private a manner, that I believe nobody at the White Lion is apprised of it. Though I let the officers know the strength (or rather weakness) of my pocket, yet they treated me with the utmost civility; and even when they conducted me to confinement, it was in such a manner, that I verily believe I could have escaped, which I would rather be ruined than have done, notwithstanding the whole amount of my finances was but three pence halfpenny.

"In the first place I must insist, that you will industriously conceal this from Mrs. S——s, because I would not have her good-nature suffer that pain, which, I know, she would be apt to feel on this occasion.

"Next, I conjure you, dear Sir, by all the ties of friendship, by no means to have one uneasy thought on my account; but to have the same pleasantry of countenance, and unruffled serenity of mind, which (God be praised!) I have in this, and have had in a much severer calamity. Furthermore, I charge you, if you value my friendship as truly as I do yours, not to utter, or even harbour, the least resentment against Mrs. Read. I believe she has ruined me, but I freely forgive her; and (though I will never more have any intimacy with her) I would, at a due distance, rather do her an act of good, than ill will. Lastly (pardon the expression), I absolutely command you not to offer me any pecuniary assistance, nor to attempt getting me any from any one of your friends. At another time, or on any other occasion, you may, dear friend, be well assured, I would rather write to you in the submissive style of a request, than that of a peremptory command.

"However, that my truly valuable friend may not think I am too proud to ask a favour, let me entreat you to let me have your boy to attend me for this day, not only for the sake of saving me the expence of porters, but for the delivery of some letters to people whose names I would not have known to strangers.

"The civil treatment I have thus far met from those whose prisoner I am, makes me thankful to the Almighty, that, though he has thought fit to visit me (on my birth-night) with affliction, yet (such is his great goodness!) my affliction is not without alleviating circumstances. I murmur not; but am all resignation to the divine will. As to the world, I hope that I shall be endued by Heaven with that presence of mind, that serene dignity in misfortune, that constitutes the character of a true nobleman; a dignity far beyond that of coronets; a nobility arising from the just principles of philosophy, refined and exalted by those of Christianity."———

He continued five days at the officer's, in hopes that he should be able to procure bail, and avoid the necessity of going to prison. The state in which he passed his time, and the treatment which he received, are very justly expressed by him in a letter which he wrote to a friend: "The whole day," says he, "has been employed in various peoples' filling my head with their foolish chimerical systems, which has obliged me coolly (as far as nature will admit) to digest, and accommodate myself to, every different person's ways of thinking; hurried from one wild system to another, till it has quite made a chaos of my imagination, and nothing done——promised——disappointed——ordered to send, every hour, from one part of the town to the other."——

When his friends, who had hitherto caressed and applauded, found that to give bail and pay the debt was the same, they all refused to preserve him from a prison at the expence of eight pounds; and therefore, after having been some time at the officer's house, "at an immense expense," as he observes in his letter, he was at length removed to Newgate.

This expence he was enabled to support by the generosity of Mr. Nash,[34] at Bath, who, upon receiving from him an account of his condition, immediately sent him five guineas, and promised to promote his subscription at Bath with all his interest.

By his removal to Newgate, he obtained at least a freedom from suspense, and rest from the disturbing vicissitudes of hope and disappointment; he now found that his friends were only companions, who were willing to share his gaiety, but not to partake of his misfortunes; and therefore he no longer expected any assistance from them.

It must however be observed of one gentleman, that he offered to release him by paying the debt; but that Mr. Savage would not consent, I suppose because he thought he had before been too burthensome to him.

He was offered by some of his friends, that a collection should be made for his enlargement; but he "treated the proposal," and declared, "he should again treat it, with disdain. As to writing any mendicant letters, he had too high a spirit, and determined only to write to some ministers of state, to try to regain his pension."

He continued to complain of those that had sent him into the country, and objected to them, that he had "lost the profits of his play, which had been finished three years;" and in another letter declares his resolution to publish a pamphlet, that the world might know how "he had been used."

[34] i.e., "Beau" Nash, "King of Bath." For his charitable conduct, see Goldsmith's Life of him.

This pamphlet was never written; for he in a very short time recovered his usual tranquillity, and cheerfully applied himself to more inoffensive studies. He indeed steadily declared, that he was promised a yearly allowance of fifty pounds, and never received half the sum; but he seemed to resign himself to that as well as to other misfortunes, and lose the remembrance of it in his amusements and employments.

The cheerfulness with which he bore his confinement, appears from the following letter, which he wrote, January the 30th, to one of his friends in London:

"I now write to you from my confinement in Newgate, where I have been ever since Monday last was se'nnight, and where I enjoy myself with much more tranquillity than I have known for upwards of a twelvemonth past; having a room entirely to myself, and pursuing the amusement of my poetical studies, uninterrupted, and agreeable to my mind. I thank the Almighty, I am now all collected in myself; and, though my person is in confinement, my mind can expatiate on ample and useful subjects with all the freedom imaginable. I am now more conversant with the Nine than ever; and if, instead of a Newgate-bird, I may be allowed to be a bird of the Muses, I assure you Sir, I sing very freely in my cage; sometimes indeed in the plaintive notes of the nightingale; but, at others, in the cheerful strains of the lark."——

In another letter he observes, that he ranges from one subject to another, without confining himself to any particular task; and that he was employed one week upon one attempt, and the next upon another.

Surely the fortitude of this man deserves, at least, to be mentioned with applause; and, whatever faults may be imputed to him, the virtue of suffering well cannot be denied him. The two powers which, in the opinion of Epictetus, constituted a wise man, are those of bearing and forbearing, which cannot indeed be affirmed to have been equally possessed by Savage; and indeed the want of one obliged him very frequently to practise the other.

He was treated by Mr. Dagg, the keeper of the prison, with great humanity; was supported by him at his own table without any certainty of recompence; had a room to himself, to which he could at any time retire from all disturbance; was allowed to stand at the door of the prison, and sometimes taken out into the fields; so that he suffered fewer hardships in prison than he had been accustomed to undergo in the greatest part of his life.[35]

The keeper did not confine his benevolence to a gentle execution of his office, but made some overtures to the creditor for his release, though without effect; and continued, during the whole time of his imprisonment, to treat him with the utmost tenderness and civility.

Virtue is undoubtedly most laudable in that state which makes it most difficult; and therefore the humanity of a gaoler certainly deserves this public attestation; and the man, whose heart has not been hardened by such an employment, may be justly proposed as a pattern of benevolence. If an inscription was once engraved "to the honest toll-gatherer," less honours ought not to be paid "to the tender gaoler."

Mr. Savage very frequently received visits, and sometimes presents, from his acquaintances: but they did not amount to a subsistence, for the greater part of which he was indebted to the generosity of this keeper; but these favours, however they might endear to him the particular persons from whom he received them, were very far from impressing upon his mind any advantageous ideas of the people of Bristol, and therefore he thought he could not more properly employ himself in prison, than in writing a poem called "London and Bristol Delineated."[36]

When he had brought this poem to its present state, which, without considering the chasm, is not perfect, he wrote to London an account of his design, and informed his friend, that he was determined to print it with his name; but enjoined him not to communicate his intention to his Bristol acquaintance. The gentleman,[37] surprised at his resolution, endeavoured to dissuade him

---

[35] In the Spring of 1739, George Whitefield and John Wesley began the Methodist open-air preaching at Bristol, and Dagg, who permitted Whitefield to speak to the prisoners every day, appears to have been an early convert.

[36] In the first edition of the *Life,* 1744, Johnson printed the poem.

[37] Edward Cave, the Printer, originator of *The Gentleman's Magazine.*

from publishing it, at least from prefixing his name; and declared, that he could not reconcile the injunction of secrecy with his resolution to own it at its first appearance. To this Mr. Savage returned an answer agreeable to his character in the following terms:

"I received yours this morning; and not without a little surprise at the contents. To answer a question with a question, you ask me concerning London and Bristol, Why will I add delineated? Why did Mr. Woolaston add the same word to his *Religion of Nature*? I suppose that it was his will and pleasure to add it in his case; and it is mine to do so in my own. You are pleased to tell me, that you understand not why secrecy is enjoined, and yet I intend to set my name to it. My answer is—I have my private reasons, which I am not obliged to explain to any one. You doubt my friend Mr. S———[38] would not approve of it—And what is it to me whether he does or not? Do you imagine that Mr. S——— is to dictate to me? If any man who calls himself my friend should assume such an air, I would spurn at his friendship with contempt. You say, I seem to think so by not letting him know it—And suppose I do, what then? Perhaps I can give reasons for that disapprobation, very foreign from what you would imagine. You go on in saying, Suppose I should not put my name to it—My answer is, that I will not suppose any such thing, being determined to the contrary: neither, Sir, would I have you suppose, that I applied to you for want of another press: nor would I have you imagine, that I owe Mr. S——— obligations which I do not."

Such was his imprudence, and such his obstinate adherence to his own resolutions, however absurd. A prisoner! supported by charity! and whatever insults he might have received during the latter part of his stay in Bristol, once caressed, esteemed, and presented with a liberal collection, he could forget on a sudden his danger and his obligations, to gratify the petulance of his wit, or the eagerness of his resentment, and publish a satire, by which he might reasonably expect that he should alienate those who then supported him, and provoke those whom he could neither resist nor escape.

[38] Strong, Bristol Post-Master, from whom Cave obtained letters and other information about Savage which Johnson was able to use.

This resolution, from the execution of which it is probable that only his death could have hindered him, is sufficient to shew, how much he disregarded all considerations that opposed his present passions, and how readily he hazarded all future advantages for any immediate gratifications. Whatever was his predominant inclination, neither hope nor fear hindered him from complying with it; nor had opposition any other effect than to heighten his ardour, and irritate his vehemence.

This performance was however laid aside, while he was employed in soliciting assistance from several great persons; and one interruption succeeding another, hindered him from supplying the chasm, and perhaps from retouching the other parts, which he can hardly be imagined to have finished in his own opinion; for it is very unequal, and some of the lines are rather inserted to rhyme to others, than to support or improve the sense; but the first and last parts are worked up with great spirit and elegance.

His time was spent in the prison for the most part in study, or in receiving visits; but sometimes he descended to lower amusements, and diverted himself in the kitchen with the conversation of the criminals; for it was not pleasing to him to be much without company; and though he was very capable of a judicious choice, he was often contented with the first that offered: for this he was sometimes reproved by his friends, who found him surrounded with felons; but the reproof was on that, as on other occasions, thrown away; he continued to gratify himself, and to set very little value on the opinion of others.

But here, as in every other scene of his life, he made use of such opportunities as occurred of benefiting those who were more miserable than himself, and was always ready to perform any office of humanity to his fellow-prisoners.

He had now ceased from corresponding with any of his subscribers except one, who yet continued to remit him the twenty pounds a year which he had promised him, and by whom it was expected that he would have been in a very short time enlarged, because he had directed the keeper to enquire after the state of his debts.[39]

[39] Pope again.

However, he took care to enter his name according to the forms of the court, that the creditor might be obliged to make him some allowance, if he was continued a prisoner, and when on that occasion he appeared in the hall was treated with very unusual respect.

But the resentment of the city was afterwards raised by some accounts that had been spread of the satire, and he was informed that some of the merchants intended to pay the allowance which the law required, and to detain him a prisoner at their own expence. This he treated as an empty menace; and perhaps might have hastened the publication, only to shew how much he was superior to their insults, had not all his schemes been suddenly destroyed.

When he had been six months in prison, he received from one of his friends,[40] in whose kindness he had the greatest confidence, and on whose assistance he chiefly depended, a letter, that contained a charge of very atrocious ingratitude, drawn up in such terms as sudden resentment dictated.[41] Henley, in one of his advertisements, had mentioned *Pope's treatment of Savage*. This was supposed by Pope to be the consequence of a complaint made by Savage to Henley, and was therefore mentioned by him with much resentment. Mr. Savage returned a very solemn protestation of his innocence, but however appeared much disturbed at the accusation. Some days afterwards he was seized with a pain in his back and side, which, as it was not violent, was not suspected to be dangerous; but growing daily more languid and dejected, on the 25th of July he confined himself to his room, and a fever seized his spirits. The symptoms grew every day more formidable, but his condition did not enable him to procure any assistance. The last time that the keeper saw him was on July the 31st, 1743; when Savage, seeing him at his bed-side, said, with an uncommon earnestness, "I have something to say to you, Sir;" but, after a pause, moved his hand in a melancholy manner; and, finding him-

[40] Mr. Pope. JOHNSON
[41] The following two sentences were not in the earlier text. John Henley gave weekly public orations, advertised beforehand in a flamboyant manner; he was no friend of Pope's.

self unable to recollect what he was going to communicate, said, " 'Tis gone!" The keeper soon after left him; and the next morning he died. He was buried in the church-yard of St. Peter, at the expence of the keeper.

Such were the life and death of Richard Savage, a man equally distinguished by his virtues and vices; and at once remarkable for his weaknesses and abilities.

He was of a middle stature, of a thin habit of body, a long visage, coarse features, and melancholy aspect; of a grave and manly deportment, a solemn dignity of mien; but which, upon a nearer acquaintance, softened into an engaging easiness of manners. His walk was slow, and his voice tremulous and mournful. He was easily excited to smiles, but very seldom provoked to laughter.

His mind was in an uncommon degree vigorous and active. His judgment was accurate, his apprehension quick, and his memory so tenacious, that he was frequently observed to know what he had learned from others in a short time, better than those by whom he was informed; and could frequently recollect incidents, with all their combination of circumstances, which few would have regarded at the present time, but which the quickness of his apprehension impressed upon him. He had the peculiar felicity, that his attention never deserted him; he was present to every object, and regardful of the most trifling occurrences. He had the art of escaping from his own reflections, and accommodating himself to every new scene.

To this quality is to be imputed the extent of his knowledge, compared with the small time which he spent in visible endeavours to acquire it. He mingled in cursory conversation with the same steadiness of attention as others apply to a lecture; and, amidst the appearance of thoughtless gaiety, lost no new idea that was started, nor any hint that could be improved. He had therefore made in coffee-houses the same proficiency as others in their closets: and it is remarkable, that the writings of a man of little education and little reading have an air of learning scarcely to be found in any other performances, but which perhaps as often obscures as embellishes them.

His judgement was eminently exact both with regard to writings and to men. The knowledge of life was indeed his chief attainment; and it is not without some satisfaction, that I can produce the suffrage of Savage in favour of human nature, of which he never appeared to entertain such odious ideas as some, who perhaps had neither his judgement nor experience, have published, either in ostentation of their sagacity, vindication of their crimes, or gratification of their malice.

His method of life particularly qualified him for conversation, of which he knew how to practise all the graces. He was never vehement or loud, but at once modest and easy, open and respectful; his language was vivacious and elegant, and equally happy upon grave or humourous subjects. He was generally censured for not knowing when to retire; but that was not the defect of his judgement, but of his fortune: when he left his company, he was frequently to spend the remaining part of the night in the street, or at least was abandoned to gloomy reflections, which it is not strange that he delayed as long as he could; and sometimes forgot that he gave others pain to avoid it himself.

It cannot be said, that he made use of his abilities for the direction of his own conduct: an irregular and dissipated manner of life had made him the slave of every passion that happened to be excited by the presence of its object, and that slavery to his passions reciprocally produced a life irregular and dissipated. He was not master of his own motions, nor could promise any thing for the next day.

With regard to his œconomy, nothing can be added to the relation of his life. He appeared to think himself born to be supported by others, and dispensed from all necessity of providing for himself; he therefore never prosecuted any scheme of advantage, nor endeavoured even to secure the profits which his writings might have afforded him. His temper was, in consequence of the dominion of his passions, uncertain and capricious; he was easily engaged, and easily disgusted; but he is accused of retaining his hatred more tenaciously than his benevolence.

He was compassionate both by nature and principle, and always ready to perform offices of humanity; but when he was provoked (and small offences were sufficient to provoke him), he would prosecute his revenge with the utmost acrimony till his passion had subsided.

His friendship was therefore of little value; for though he was zealous in the support or vindication of those whom he loved, yet it was always dangerous to trust him, because he considered himself as discharged by the first quarrel from all ties of honour or gratitude; and would betray those secrets which, in the warmth of confidence, had been imparted to him. This practice drew upon him an universal accusation of ingratitude: nor can it be denied that he was very ready to set himself free from the load of an obligation; for he could not bear to conceive himself in a state of dependence, his pride being equally powerful with his other passions, and appearing in the form of insolence at one time, and of vanity at another. Vanity, the most innocent species of pride, was most frequently predominant: He could not easily leave off, when he had once begun to mention himself or his works; nor ever read his verses without stealing his eyes from the page, to discover, in the faces of his audience, how they were affected with any favourite passage.

A kinder name than that of vanity ought to be given to the delicacy with which he was always careful to separate his own merit from every other man's, and to reject that praise to which he had no claim. He did not forget, in mentioning his performances, to mark every line that had been suggested or amended; and was so accurate, as to relate that he owed three words in *The Wanderer* to the advice of his friends.

His veracity was questioned, but with little reason; his accounts, though not indeed always the same, were generally consistent. When he loved any man, he suppressed all his faults; and, when he had been offended by him, concealed all his virtues: but his characters were generally true, so far as he proceeded; though it cannot be denied, that his partiality might have sometimes the effect of falsehood.

In cases indifferent, he was zealous for virtue, truth, and justice: he knew very well the necessity of goodness to the present and future happiness of mankind; nor is there perhaps any writer, who has less endeavoured to please by flattering the appetites, or perverting the judgement.

As an author, therefore, and he now ceases to influence mankind in any other character, if one piece which he had resolved to suppress be excepted, he has very little to fear from the strictest moral or religious censure. And though he may not be altogether secure against the objections of the critic, it must however be acknowledged, that his works are the productions of a genius truly poetical; and, what many writers who have been more lavishly applauded cannot boast, that they have an original air, which has no resemblance of any foregoing work, that the versification and sentiments have a cast peculiar to themselves, which no man can imitate with success, because what was nature in Savage, would in another be affectation. It must be confessed, that his descriptions are striking, his images animated, his fictions justly imagined, and his allegories artfully pursued; that his diction is elevated, though sometimes forced, and his numbers sonorous and majestic, though frequently sluggish and encumbered. Of his style, the general fault is harshness, and its general excellence is dignity; of his sentiments, the prevailing beauty is sublimity, and uniformity the prevailing defect.

For his life, or for his writings, none, who candidly consider his fortune, will think an apology either necessary or difficult. If he was not always sufficiently instructed in his subject, his knowledge was at least greater than could have been attained by others in the same state. If his works were sometimes unfinished, accuracy cannot reasonably be exacted from a man oppressed with want, which he has no hope of relieving but by a speedy publication. The insolence and resentment of which he is accused were not easily to be avoided by a great mind, irritated by perpetual hardships, and constrained hourly to return the spurns of contempt, and repress the insolence of prosperity; and vanity may surely readily be pardoned in him, to whom life afforded no other comforts than barren praises, and the consciousness of deserving them.

Those are no proper judges of his conduct, who have slumbered away their time on the down of plenty; nor will any wise man presume to say, "Had I been in Savage's condition, I should have lived or written better than Savage."

This relation will not be wholly without its use, if those, who languish under any part of his sufferings, shall be enabled to fortify their patience, by reflecting that they feel only those afflictions from which the abilities of Savage did not exempt him; or those, who, in confidence of superior capacities or attainments, disregard the common maxims of life, shall be reminded, that nothing will supply the want of prudence; and that negligence and irregularity, long continued, will make knowledge useless, wit ridiculous, and genius contemptible.

FROM Thomson

As a writer, he is entitled to one praise of the highest kind: his mode of thinking, and of expressing his thoughts, is original. His blank verse is no more the blank verse of Milton, or of any other poet, than the rhymes of Prior are the rhymes of Cowley. His numbers, his pauses, his diction, are of his own growth, without transcription, without imitation. He thinks in a peculiar train, and he thinks always as a man of genius; he looks round on Nature and on Life, with the eye which Nature bestows only on a poet; the eye that distinguishes, in every thing presented to its view, whatever there is on which imagination can delight to be detained, and with a mind that at once comprehends the vast, and attends to the minute. The reader of the *Seasons* wonders that he never saw before what Thomson shews him, and that he never yet has felt what Thomson impresses.

His is one of the works in which blank verse seems properly used; Thomson's wide expansion of general views, and his enumeration of circumstantial varieties, would have been obstructed and embarrassed by the frequent intersection[s] of the sense, which are the necessary effects of rhyme.

His descriptions of extended scenes and general effects bring before us the whole magnificence of Nature, whether pleasing or dreadful. The gaiety of *Spring,* the splendour of *Summer,* the tranquillity of *Autumn,* and the horror of *Winter,* take in their turns possession of the mind. The poet leads us through the appearances of things as they are successively varied by the vicissitudes of the year, and imparts to us so much of his own enthusiasm, that our thoughts expand with his imagery, and kindle with his sentiments. Nor is the naturalist without his part in the entertainment; for he is assisted to recollect and to combine, to arrange his discoveries, and to amplify the sphere of his contemplation.

The great defect of the *Seasons* is want of method; but for this I know not that there was any remedy. Of many appearances subsisting all at once, no rule can be given why one should be mentioned before another; yet the memory wants the help of order, and the curiosity is not excited by suspense or expectation.

His diction is in the highest degree florid and luxuriant, such as may be said to be to his images and thoughts *both their lustre and their shade;* such as invest[s] them with splendour, through which perhaps they are not always easily discerned. It is too exuberant, and sometimes may be charged with filling the ear more than the mind.

These Poems, with which I was acquainted at their first appearance, I have since found altered and enlarged by subsequent revisals, as the author supposed his judgement to grow more exact, and as books or conversation extended his knowledge and opened his prospects. They are, I think, improved in general; yet I know not whether they have not lost part of what Temple calls their *race;* a word which, applied to wines, in its primitive sense, means the flavour of the soil.

Liberty, when it first appeared, I tried to read, and soon desisted. I have never tried again, and therefore will not hazard either praise or censure.

The highest praise which he has received ought not to be supprest; it is said by Lord Lyttelton in the Prologue to his posthumous play, that his works contained

No line which, dying, he could wish to blot.

The Life of Gray

Thomas Gray, the son of Mr. Philip Gray, a scrivener of London, was born in Cornhill, November 26, 1716. His grammatical education he received at Eton under the care of Mr. Antrobus, his mother's brother, then assistant to Dr. George; and when he left school, in 1734, entered a pensioner at Peterhouse in Cambridge.

The transition from the school to the college is, to most young scholars, the time from which they date their years of manhood, liberty, and happiness; but Gray seems to have been very little delighted with academical gratifications; he liked at Cambridge neither the mode of life nor the fashion of study, and lived sullenly on to the time when his attendance on lectures was no longer required. As he intended to profess the Common Law, he took no degree.

When he had been at Cambridge about five years, Mr. Horace Walpole, whose friendship he had gained at Eton, invited him to travel with him as his companion. They wandered through France into Italy; and Gray's Letters contain a very pleasing account of many parts of their journey. But unequal friendships are easily dissolved: at Florence they quarrelled, and parted; and Mr. Walpole is now content to have it told that it was by his fault. If we look however without prejudice on the world, we shall find that men, whose consciousness of their own merit sets them above the compliances of servility, are apt enough in their association with superiors to watch their own dignity with troublesome and punctilious jealousy, and in the fervour of independance to exact that attention which they refuse to pay. Part they did, whatever was the quarrel, and the rest of their travels was doubtless more unpleasant to them both. Gray continued his journey in a manner suitable to his own little fortune, with only an occasional servant.

He returned to England in September 1741, and in about two months afterwards buried his father; who had, by an injudicious waste of money upon a new house, so much lessened his fortune, that Gray thought himself too poor to study the law. He therefore retired to Cambridge, where he soon after became Bachelor of Civil Law; and where, without liking the place or its inhabitants, or professing to like them, he passed, except a short residence at London, the rest of his life.

About this time he was deprived of Mr. West, the son of a chancellor of Ireland, a friend on whom he appears to have set a high value, and who deserved his esteem by the powers which he shews in his Letters, and in the Ode to *May*, which Mr. Mason has preserved, as well as by the sincerity with which, when Gray sent him part of *Agrippina*, a tragedy that he had just begun, he gave an opinion which probably intercepted the progress of the work, and which the judgement of every reader will confirm. It was certainly no loss to the English stage that *Agrippina* was never finished.

In this year (1742) Gray seems first to have applied himself seriously to poetry; for in this year were produced the *Ode to Spring*, his *Prospect of Eton*, and his *Ode to Adversity*. He began likewise a Latin poem, *de Principiis cogitandi*.

It may be collected from the narrative of Mr. Mason, that his first ambition was to have excelled in Latin poetry: perhaps it were reasonable to wish that he had prosecuted his design; for though there is at present some embarrassment in his phrase, and some harshness in his Lyrick numbers, his copiousness of language is such as very few possess; and his lines, even when imperfect, discover a writer whom practice would quickly have made skilful.

He now lived on at Peterhouse, very little solicitous what others did or thought, and cultivated his mind and enlarged his views without any other purpose than of improving and amusing himself; when Mr. Mason, being elected fellow of Pembroke-hall, brought him a companion who was afterwards to be his editor, and whose fondness and fidelity has kindled in him a zeal of admiration, which cannot be reasonably expected from the neutrality of a stranger and the coldness of a critick.

In this his retirement he wrote (1747) an ode on the *Death of Mr. Walpole's Cat*; and the year afterwards attempted a poem of more importance, on *Government and Education,* of which the fragments which remain have many excellent lines.

His next production (1750) was his far-famed *Elegy in the Church-yard*, which, finding its way into a Magazine,[1] first, I believe, made him known to the publick.

An invitation from lady Cobham about this time gave occasion to an odd composition called a *Long Story,* which adds little to Gray's character.

Several of his pieces were published (1753), with designs, by Mr. Bentley; and, that they might in some form or other make a book, only one side of each leaf was printed. I believe the poems and the plates recommended each other so well, that the whole impression was soon bought. This year he lost his mother.

Some time afterwards (1756) some young men of the college, whose chambers were near his, diverted themselves with disturbing him by frequent and troublesome noises, and, as is said, by pranks yet more offensive and contemptuous. This insolence, having endured it a while, he represented to the governors of the society, among whom perhaps he had no friends; and, finding his complaint little regarded, removed himself to Pembroke-hall.

In 1757 he published *The Progress of Poetry* and *The Bard*,

[1] In *The Magazine of Magazines,* February, 1751; *The London Magazine,* March, 1751; *The Grand Magazine of Magazines,* April, 1751; and *The True Briton,* March and April, 1751.

two compositions at which the readers of poetry were at first content to gaze in mute amazement. Some that tried them confessed their inability to understand them, though Warburton said that that they were understood as well as the work of Milton and Shakspeare, which it is the fashion to admire. Garrick wrote a few lines in their praise. Some hardy champions undertook to rescue them from neglect, and in a short time many were content to be shewn beauties which they could not see.

Gray's reputation was now so high, that, after the death of Cibber, he had the honour of refusing the laurel, which was then bestowed on Mr. Whitehead.

His curiosity, not long after, drew him away from Cambridge to a lodging near the Museum,[2] where he resided near three years, reading and transcribing; and, so far as can be discovered, very little affected by two odes on *Oblivion* and *Obscurity*, in which his Lyrick performances were ridiculed with much contempt and much ingenuity.[3]

When the Professor of Modern History at Cambridge died, he was, as he says, *cockered and spirited up,* till he asked it of lord Bute, who sent him a civil refusal; and the place was given to Mr. Brocket, the tutor of Sir James Lowther.

His constitution was weak, and believing that his health was promoted by exercise and change of place, he undertook (1765) a journey into Scotland, of which his account, so far as it extends, is very curious and elegant; for as his comprehension was ample, his curiosity extended to all the works of art, all the appearances of nature, and all the monuments of past events. He naturally contracted a friendship with Dr. Beattie, whom he found a poet, a philosopher, and a good man. The Mareschal College at Aberdeen offered him the degree of Doctor of Laws, which, having omitted to take it at Cambridge, he thought it decent to refuse.

What he had formerly solicited in vain, was at last given him without solicitation. The Professorship of History became again vacant, and he received (1768) an offer of it from the duke of Grafton. He accepted, and retained it to his death; always design-

---

[2] i.e., the British Museum, founded in 1753.
[3] By G. Colman and Robert Lloyd.

ing lectures, but never reading them; uneasy at his neglect of duty, and appeasing his uneasiness with designs of reformation, and with a resolution which he believed himself to have made of resigning the office, if he found himself unable to discharge it.

Ill health made another journey necessary, and he visited (1769) Westmoreland and Cumberland. He that reads his epistolary narration wishes, that to travel, and to tell his travels, had been more of his employment; but it is by studying at home that we must obtain the ability of travelling with intelligence and improvement.

His travels and his studies were now near their end. The gout, of which he had sustained many weak attacks, fell upon his stomach, and, yielding to no medicines, produced strong convulsions, which (July 30, 1771) terminated in death.

His character I am willing to adopt, as Mr. Mason has done, from a Letter written to my friend Mr. Boswell, by the Rev. Mr. Temple, rector of St. Gluvias in Cornwall; and am as willing as his warmest well-wisher to believe it true.

> Perhaps he was the most learned man in Europe. He was equally acquainted with the elegant and profound parts of science, and that not superficially but thoroughly. He knew every branch of history, both natural and civil; had read all the original historians of England, France, and Italy; and was a great antiquarian. Criticism, metaphysics, morals, politics, made a principal part of his study; voyages and travels of all sorts were his favourite amusements; and he had a fine taste in painting, prints, architecture, and gardening. With such a fund of knowledge, his conversation must have been equally instructing and entertaining; but he was also a good man, a man of virtue and humanity. There is no character without some speck, some imperfection; and I think the greatest defect in his was an affectation in delicacy, or rather effeminacy, and a visible fastidiousness, or contempt and disdain of his inferiors in science. He also had, in some degree, that weakness which disgusted Voltaire so much in Mr. Congreve: though he seemed to value others chiefly according to the progress they had made in knowledge, yet he could

not bear to be considered himself merely as a man of
letters; and though without birth, or fortune, or station,
his desire was to be looked upon as a private independent
gentleman, who read for his amusement. Perhaps it may
be said, What signifies so much knowledge, when it
produced so little? Is it worth taking so much pains to
leave no memorial but a few poems? But let it be con-
sidered that Mr. Gray was, to others, at least innocently
employed; to himself, certainly beneficially. His time
passed agreeably; he was every day making some new
acquisition in science; his mind was enlarged, his heart
softened, his virtue strengthened; the world and man-
kind were shewn to him without a mask; and he was
taught to consider every thing as trifling, and unworthy
of the attention of a wise man, except the pursuit of
knowledge and practice of virtue, in that state wherein
God hath placed us.

To this character Mr. Mason has added a more particular ac-
count of Gray's skill in zoology. He has remarked, that Gray's
effeminacy was affected most *before those whom he did not wish
to please;*[4] and that he is unjustly charged with making knowledge
his sole reason of preference, as he paid his esteem to none whom
he did not likewise believe to be good.

What has occurred to me, from the slight inspection of his Let-
ters in which my undertaking has engaged me, is, that his mind
had a large grasp; that his curiosity was unlimited, and his judge-
ment cultivated; that he was a man likely to love much where he
loved at all, but that he was fastidious and hard to please. His
contempt however is often employed, where I hope it will be
approved, upon scepticism and infidelity. His short account of
Shaftesbury I will insert.

You say you cannot conceive how lord Shaftesbury
came to be a philosopher in vogue; I will tell you: first, he
was a lord; secondly, he was as vain as any of his readers;
thirdly, men are very prone to believe what they do not

W. Mason, *Memoirs of Gray,* 1775, II, 322.

understand; fourthly, they will believe any thing at all, provided they are under no obligation to believe it; fifthly, they love to take a new road, even when that road leads no where; sixthly, he was reckoned a fine writer, and seems always to mean more than he said. Would you have any more reasons? An interval of above forty years has pretty well destroyed the charm. A dead lord ranks with commoners: vanity is no longer interested in the matter; for a new road is become an old one.[5]

Mr. Mason has added, from his own knowledge, that though Gray was poor, he was not eager of money; and that, out of the little that he had, he was very willing to help the necessitous.[6]

As a writer he had this peculiarity, that he did not write his pieces first rudely, and then correct them, but laboured every line as it arose in the train of composition; and he had a notion not very peculiar, that he could not write but at certain times, or at happy moments; a fantastick foppery, to which my kindness for a man of learning and of virtue wishes him to have been superior.

GRAY's Poetry is now to be considered; and I hope not to be looked on as an enemy to his name, if I confess that I contemplate it with less pleasure than his life.

His ode on *Spring* has something poetical, both in the language and the thought; but the language is too luxuriant, and the thoughts have nothing new. There has of late arisen a practice of giving to adjectives, derived from substantives, the termination of participles; such as the *cultured* plain, the *daisied* bank; but I was sorry to see, in the lines of a scholar like Gray, the *honied* Spring. The morality is natural, but too stale; the conclusion is pretty.

The poem on the *Cat* was doubtless by its author considered as a trifle, but it is not a happy trifle. In the first stanza *the azure flowers* that *blow,* shew resolutely a rhyme is sometimes made when it cannot easily be found. *Selima,* the *Cat,* is called a nymph, with some violence both to language and sense; but there is good use made of it when it is done; for of the two lines,

[5] From a letter to Stonehewer, August 18, 1758.
[6] Mason, *Memoirs,* II, 235.

> What female heart can gold despise?
> What cat's averse to fish?

the first relates merely to the nymph, and the second only to the cat. The sixth stanza contains a melancholy truth, that *a favourite has no friend,* but the last ends in a pointed sentence of no relation to the purpose; if *what glistered* had been *gold,* the cat would not have gone into the water; and, if she had, would not less have been drowned.

> The *Prospect of Eton College* suggests nothing to Gray, which every beholder does not equally think and feel. His supplication to father *Thames,* to tell him who drives the hoop or tosses the ball, is useless and puerile. Father *Thames* has no better means of knowing than himself. His epithet *buxom health* is not elegant; he seems not to understand the word. Gray thought his language more poetical as it was more remote from common use: finding in Dryden *honey redolent of Spring,* an expression that reaches the utmost limits of our language, Gray drove it a little more beyond common apprehension, by making *gales* to be redolent of joy and youth.

Of the *Ode on Adversity,* the hint was at first taken from *O Diva, gratum quæ regis Antium;*[7] but Gray has excelled his original by the variety of his sentiments, and by their moral application. Of this piece, at once poetical and rational, I will not by slight objections violate the dignity.

My process has now brought me to the *wonderful Wonder of Wonders,* the two Sister Odes; by which, though either vulgar ignorance or common sense at first universally rejected them, many have been since persuaded to think themselves delighted. I am one of those that are willing to be pleased, and therefore would gladly find the meaning of the first stanza of the *Progress of Poetry.*

Gray seems in his rapture to confound the images of *spreading sound* and *running water.* A *stream of musick* may be allowed; but where does *Musick,* however *smooth and strong,* after having visited the *verdant vales, rowl down the steep amain,* so as that

[7] Horace, *Odes,* I. 35.

rocks and nodding groves rebellow to the roar? If this be said of *Musick,* it is nonsense; if it be said of *Water,* it is nothing to the purpose.

The second stanza, exhibiting Mars's car and Jove's eagle, is unworthy of further notice. Criticism disdains to chase a schoolboy to his common-places.

To the third it may likewise be objected, that it is drawn from Mythology, though such as may be more easily assimilated to real life. Idalia's *velvet-green* has something of cant. An epithet or metaphor drawn from Nature ennobles Art; an epithet or metaphor drawn from Art degrades Nature. Gray is too fond of words arbitrarily compounded. *Many-twinkling* was formerly censured as not analogical; we may say *many-spotted,* but scarcely *many-spotting.* This stanza, however, has something pleasing.

Of the second ternary of stanzas, the first endeavours to tell something, and would have told it, had it not been crossed by Hyperion: the second describes well enough the universal prevalence of Poetry; but I am afraid that the conclusion will not rise from the premises. The caverns of the North and the plains of Chili are not the residences of *Glory and generous Shame.* But that Poetry and Virtue go always together is an opinion so pleasing, that I can forgive him who resolves to think it true.

The third stanza sounds big with *Delphi,* and *Egean,* and *Ilissus,* and *Meander,* and *hallowed fountain* and *solemn sound;* but in all Gray's odes there is a kind of cumbrous splendor which we wish away. His position is at last false: in the time of Dante and Petrarch, from whom he derives our first school of Poetry, Italy was over-run by *tyrant power* and *coward vice;* nor was our state much better when we first borrowed the Italian arts.

Of the third ternary, the first gives a mythological birth of Shakspeare. What is said of that mighty genius is true; but it is not said happily: the real effects of this poetical power are put out of sight by the pomp of machinery. Where truth is sufficient to fill the mind, fiction is worse than useless; the counterfeit debases the genuine.

His account of Milton's blindness, if we suppose it caused by study in the formation of his poem, a supposition surely allowable, is poetically true, and happily imagined. But the *car* of Dryden, with his *two coursers,* has nothing in it peculiar; it is a car in which any other rider may be placed.

The Bard appears, at the first view, to be, as Algarotti and others have remarked, an imitation of the prophecy of Nereus.[8] Algarotti thinks it superior to its original; and, if preference depends only on the imagery and animation of the two poems, his judgement is right. There is in *The Bard* more force, more thought, and more variety. But to copy is less than to invent, and the copy has been unhappily produced at a wrong time. The fiction of Horace was to the Romans credible; but its revival disgusts us with apparent and unconquerable falsehood. *Incredulus odi.*[9]

To select a singular event, and swell it to a giant's bulk by fabulous appendages of spectres and predictions, has little difficulty, for he that forsakes the probable may always find the marvellous. And it has little use; we are affected only as we believe; we are improved only as we find something to be imitated or declined. I do not see that *The Bard* promotes any truth, moral or political.

His stanzas are too long, especially his epodes; the ode is finished before the ear has learned its measures, and consequently before it can receive pleasure from their consonance and recurrence.

Of the first stanza the abrupt beginning has been celebrated; but technical beauties can give praise only to the inventor. It is in the power of any man to rush abruptly upon his subject, that has read the ballad of *Johnny Armstrong,*

Is there ever a man in all Scotland—

The initial resemblances, or alliterations, *ruin, ruthless, helm or hauberk,* are below the grandeur of a poem that endeavours at sublimity.

In the second stanza the *Bard* is well described; but in the third we have the puerilities of obsolete mythology. When we are told that *Cadwallo hush'd the stormy main,* and that *Modred* made

[8] Horace, *Odes,* I. 15.
[9] Horace, *Ars Poetica,* I. 188. "Not believing, I hate it."

huge Plinlimmon bow his cloud-top'd head, attention recoils from the repetition of a tale that, even when it was first heard, was heard with scorn.

The *weaving* of the *winding sheet* he borrowed, as he owns, from the northern Bards; but their texture, however, was very properly the work of female powers, as the art of spinning the thread of life in another mythology. Theft is always dangerous; Gray has made weavers of his slaughtered bards, by a fiction outrageous and incongruous. They are then called upon to *Weave the warp, and weave the woof,* perhaps with no great propriety; for it is by crossing the *woof* with the *warp* that men *weave* the *web* or piece; and the first line was dearly bought by the admission of its wretched correspondent, *Give ample room and verge enough.* He has, however, no other line as bad.

The third stanza of the second ternary is commended, I think, beyond its merit. The personification is indistinct. *Thirst* and *Hunger* are not alike; and their features, to make the imagery perfect, should have been discriminated. We are told, in the same stanza, how *towers* are *fed.* But I will no longer look for particular faults; yet let it be observed that the ode might have been concluded with an action of better example; but suicide is always to be had, without expence of thought.

These odes are marked by glittering accumulations of ungraceful ornaments; they strike, rather than please; the images are magnified by affectation; the language is laboured into harshness. The mind of the writer seems to work with unnatural violence. *Double, double, toil and trouble.* He has a kind of strutting dignity, and is tall by walking on tiptoe. His art and his struggle are too visible, and there is too little appearance of ease and nature.

To say that he has no beauties, would be unjust: a man like him, of great learning and great industry, could not but produce something valuable. When he pleases least, it can only be said that a good design was ill directed.

His translations of Northern and Welsh poetry deserve praise; the imagery is preserved, perhaps often improved; but the language is unlike the language of other poets.

In the character of his Elegy I rejoice to concur with the common reader; for by the common sense of readers uncorrupted with literary prejudices, after all the refinements of subtilty and the dogmatism of learning, must be finally decided all claim to poetical honours. The *Church-yard* abounds with images which find a mirrour in every mind, and with sentiments to which every bosom returns an echo. The four stanzas beginning *Yet even these bones,* are to me original: I have never seen the notions in any other place; yet he that reads them here, persuades himself that he has always felt them. Had Gray written often thus, it had been vain to blame, and useless to praise him.

FROM Collins

Mr. Collins was a man of extensive literature, and of vigorous faculties. He was acquainted not only with the learned tongues, but with the Italian, French, and Spanish languages. He had employed his mind chiefly upon works of fiction, and subjects of fancy; and, by indulging some peculiar habits of thought, was eminently delighted with those flights of imagination which pass the bounds of nature, and to which the mind is reconciled only by a passive acquiescence in popular traditions. He loved fairies, genii, giants, and monsters; he delighted to rove through the meanders of inchantment, to gaze on the magnificence of golden palaces, to repose by the waterfalls of Elysian gardens.

This was however the character rather of his inclination than his genius; the grandeur of wildness, and the novelty of extravagance, were always desired by him, but were not always attained. Yet as diligence is never wholly lost, if his efforts sometimes caused harshness and obscurity, they likewise produced in happier moments sublimity and splendour. This idea which he had formed of excellence, led him to oriental fictions and allegorical imagery; and perhaps, while he was intent upon description, he did not sufficiently cultivate sentiment. His poems are the productions of a

inspiration

mind not deficient in fire, nor unfurnished with knowledge either of books or life, but somewhat obstructed in its progress by deviation in quest of mistaken beauties.

His morals were pure, and his opinions pious: in a long continuance of poverty, and long habits of dissipation, it cannot be expected that any character should be exactly uniform. There is a degree of want by which the freedom of agency is almost destroyed; and long association with fortuitous companions will at last relax the strictness of truth, and abate the fervour of sincerity. That this man, wise and virtuous as he was, passed always unentangled through the snares of life, it would be prejudice and temerity to affirm; but it may be said that at least he preserved the source of action unpolluted, that his principles were never shaken, that his distinctions of right and wrong were never confounded, and that his faults had nothing of malignity or design, but proceeded from some unexpected pressure, or casual temptation.

The latter part of his life cannot be remembered but with pity and sadness. He languished some years under that depression of mind which enchains the faculties without destroying them, and leaves reason the knowledge of right without the power of pursuing it. These clouds which he perceived gathering on his intellects, he endeavoured to disperse by travel, and passed into France; but found himself constrained to yield to his malady, and returned. He was for some time confined in a house of lunaticks, and afterwards retired to the care of his sister in Chichester, where death in 1756 came to his relief.

After his return from France, the writer of this character paid him a visit at Islington, where he was waiting for his sister, whom he had directed to meet him: there was then nothing of disorder discernible in his mind by any but himself; but he had withdrawn from study, and travelled with no other book than an English Testament, such as children carry to the school: when his friend took it into his hand, out of curiosity to see what companion a Man of Letters had chosen, *I have but one book,* said Collins, *but that is the best.*

Such was the fate of Collins, with whom I once delighted to converse, and whom I yet remember with tenderness.

He was visited at Chichester, in his last illness, by his learned friends Dr. Warton and his brother, to whom he spoke with disapprobation of his Oriental Eclogues, as not sufficiently expressive of Asiatick manners, and called them his Irish Eclogues. . . .

To what I have formerly said of his writings may be added, that his diction was often harsh, unskilfully laboured, and injudiciously selected. He affected the obsolete when it was not worthy of revival; and he puts his words out of the common order, seeming to think, with some later candidates for fame, that not to write prose is certainly to write poetry. His lines commonly are of slow motion, clogged and impeded with clusters of consonants. As men are often esteemed who cannot be loved, so the poetry of Collins may sometimes extort praise when it gives little pleasure.

FICTION

The History of Rasselas,

PRINCE OF ABISSINIA

I

DESCRIPTION OF A PALACE IN A VALLEY

Ye who listen with credulity to the whispers of fancy, and persue with eagerness the phantoms of hope; who expect that age will perform the promises of youth, and that the deficiencies of the present day will be supplied by the morrow; attend to the history of Rasselas prince of Abissinia.[1]

Rasselas was the fourth son of the mighty emperour, in whose dominions the Father of waters begins his course; whose bounty pours down the streams of plenty, and scatters over half the world the harvests of Egypt.

According to the custom which has descended from age to age among the monarchs of the torrid zone, Rasselas was confined in a private palace, with the other sons and daughters of Abissinian royalty, till the order of succession should call him to the throne.

[1] *Rasselas. Ras* means *chief* or *head,* according to Father Jerome Lobo, whose *Voyage to Abyssinia* Johnson translated in 1735.

The place, which the wisdom or policy of antiquity had destined for the residence of the Abissinian princes, was a spacious valley in the kingdom of Amhara, surrounded on every side by mountains, of which the summits overhang the middle part. The only passage, by which it could be entered, was a cavern that passed under a rock, of which it has long been disputed whether it was the work of nature or of human industry. The outlet of the cavern was concealed by a thick wood, and the mouth which opened into the valley was closed with gates of iron, forged by the artificers of ancient days, so massy that no man could, without the help of engines, open or shut them.

From the mountains on every side, rivulets descended that filled all the valley with verdure and fertility, and formed a lake in the middle inhabited by fish of every species, and frequented by every fowl whom nature has taught to dip the wing in water. This lake discharged its superfluities by a stream which entered a dark cleft of the mountain on the northern side, and fell with dreadful noise from precipice to precipice till it was heard no more.

The sides of the mountains were covered with trees, the banks of the brooks were diversified with flowers; every blast shook spices from the rocks, and every month dropped fruits upon the ground. All animals that bite the grass, or brouse the shrub, whether wild or tame, wandered in this extensive circuit, secured from beasts of prey by the mountains which confined them. On one part were flocks and herds feeding in the pastures, on another all the beasts of chase frisking in the lawns; the sprightly kid was bounding on the rocks, the subtle monkey frolicking in the trees, and the solemn elephant reposing in the shade. All the diversities of the world were brought together, the blessings of nature were collected, and its evils extracted and excluded.

The valley, wide and fruitful, supplied its inhabitants with the necessaries of life, and all delights and superfluities were added at the annual visit which the emperour paid his children, when the iron gate was opened to the sound of musick; and during eight days every one that resided in the valley was required to propose whatever might contribute to make seclusion pleasant, to fill up the vacancies of attention, and lessen the tediousness of time. Every desire was immediately granted. All the artificers of pleasure were called to gladden the festivity; the musicians exerted the power of harmony, and the dancers shewed their activity before the princes, in hope that they should pass their lives in this blissful captivity, to which th[o]se only were admitted whose performance was thought able to add novelty to luxury. Such was the appearance of security and delight which this retirement afforded, that they to whom it was new always desired that it might be perpetual; and as those, on whom the iron gate had once closed, were never suffered to return, the effect of longer experience could not be known. Thus every year produced new schemes of delight, and new competitors for imprisonment.

The palace stood on an eminence raised about thirty paces above the surface of the lake. It was divided into many squares or courts, built with greater or less magnificence according to the rank of those for whom they were designed. The roofs were turned into arches of massy stone joined with a cement that grew harder by time, and the building stood from century to century, deriding the solstitial rains and equinoctial hurricanes, without need of reparation.

This house, which was so large as to be fully known to none but some ancient officers who successively inherited the secrets of the place, was built as if suspicion herself had dictated the plan. To every room there was an open and secret passage, every square had a communication with the rest, either from the upper stories by private galleries, or by subterranean passages from the lower apartments. Many of the columns had unsuspected cavities, in which a long race of monarchs had reposited their treasures. They then closed up the opening with marble, which was never to be removed but in the utmost exigencies of the kingdom; and recorded their accumulations in a book which was itself concealed in a tower not entered but by the emperour, attended by the prince who stood next in succession.[2]

[2] The description here seems "planted" for future narrative development. Johnson never exploits it, however, having his mind on events of a different order.

II

THE DISCONTENT OF RASSELAS IN THE HAPPY VALLEY

Here the sons and daughters of Abissinia lived only to know the soft vicissitudes of pleasure and repose, attended by all that were skilful to delight, and gratified with whatever the senses can enjoy. They wandered in gardens of fragrance, and slept in the fortresses of security. Every art was practised to make them pleased with their own condition. The sages who instructed them, told them of nothing but the miseries of publick life, and described all beyond the mountains as regions of calamity, where discord was always raging, and where man preyed upon man.

To heighten their opinion of their own felicity, they were daily entertained with songs, the subject of which was the *happy valley*. Their appetites were excited by frequent enumerations of different enjoyments, and revelry and merriment was the business of every hour from the dawn of morning to the close of even.

These methods were generally successful; few of the Princes had ever wished to enlarge their bounds, but passed their lives in full conviction that they had all within their reach that art or nature could bestow, and pitied those whom fate had excluded from this seat of tranquility, as the sport of chance, and the slaves of misery.

Thus they rose in the morning, and lay down at night, pleased with each other and with themselves, all but Rasselas, who, in the twenty-sixth year of his age, began to withdraw himself from their pastimes and assemblies, and to delight in solitary walks and silent meditation. He often sat before tables covered with luxury, and forgot to taste the dainties that were placed before him: he rose abruptly in the midst of the song, and hastily retired beyond the sound of musick. His attendants observed the change and endeavoured to renew his love of pleasure: he neglected their officiousness, repulsed their invitations, and spent day after day on the banks of rivulets sheltered with trees, where he sometimes listened to the birds in the branches, sometimes observed the fish playing in the stream, and anon cast his eyes upon the pastures and mountains filled with animals, of which some were biting the herbage, and some sleeping among the bushes.

This singularity of his humour made him much observed. One of the Sages, in whose conversation he had formerly delighted, followed him secretly, in hope of discovering the cause of his disquiet. Rasselas, who knew not that any one was near him, having for some time fixed his eyes upon the goats that were brousing among the rocks, began to compare their condition with his own.

"What," said he, "makes the difference between man and all the rest of the animal creation? Every beast that strays beside me has the same corporal necessities with myself; he is hungry and crops the grass, he is thirsty and drinks the stream, his thirst and hunger are appeased, he is satisfied and sleeps; he rises again and is hungry, he is again fed and is at rest. I am hungry and thirsty like him, but when thirst and hunger cease I am not at rest; I am, like him, pained with want, but am not, like him, satisfied with fulness. The intermediate hours are tedious and gloomy; I long again to be hungry that I may again quicken my attention. The birds peck the berries or the corn, and fly away to the groves where they sit in seeming happiness on the branches, and waste their lives in tuning one unvaried series of sounds. I likewise can call the lutanist and the singer, but the sounds that pleased me yesterday weary me to day, and will grow yet more wearisome to morrow. I can discover within me no power of perception which is not glutted with its proper pleasure, yet I do not feel myself delighted. Man has surely some latent sense for which this place affords no gratification, or he has some desires distinct from sense which must be satisfied before he can be happy."

After this he lifted up his head, and seeing the moon rising, walked towards the palace. As he passed through the fields, and saw the animals around him, "Ye, said he, are happy, and need not envy me that walk thus among you, burthened with myself; nor do I, ye gentle beings, envy your felicity; for it is not the felicity of man. I have many distresses from which ye are free; I fear pain when I do not feel it; I sometimes shrink at evils recollected, and sometimes start at evils anticipated: surely the equity of providence has ballanced peculiar sufferings with peculiar enjoyments."

With observations like these the prince amused himself as he returned, uttering them with a plaintive voice, yet with a look that discovered him to feel some complacence in his own perspicacity, and to receive some solace of the miseries of life, from consciousness of the delicacy with which he felt, and the eloquence with which he bewailed them. He mingled cheerfully in the diversions of the evening, and all rejoiced to find that his heart was lightened.

III

THE WANTS OF HIM THAT WANTS NOTHING

On the next day his old instructor, imagining that he had now made himself acquainted with his disease of mind, was in hope of curing it by counsel, and officiously sought an opportunity of conference, which the prince, having long considered him as one whose intellects were exhausted, was not very willing to afford: "Why, said he, does this man thus intrude upon me; shall I be never suffered to forget those lectures which pleased only while they were new, and to become new again must be forgotten?" He then walked into the wood, and composed himself to his usual meditations; when, before his thoughts had taken any settled form, he perceived his persuer at his side, and was at first prompted by his impatience to go hastily away; but, being unwilling to offend a man whom he had once reverenced and still loved, he invited him to sit down with him on the bank.

The old man, thus encouraged, began to lament the change which had been lately observed in the prince, and to enquire why he so often retired from the pleasures of the palace, to loneliness and silence. "I fly from pleasure, said the prince, because pleasure has ceased to please; I am lonely because I am miserable, and am unwilling to cloud with my presence the happiness of others." "You, Sir, said the sage, are the first who has complained of misery in the *happy valley*. I hope to convince you that your complaints have no real cause. You are here in full possession of all that the emperour of Abissinia can bestow; here is neither labour to be endured nor danger to be dreaded, yet here is all that labour or danger can procure or purchase. Look round and tell me which of your wants is without supply: if you want nothing, how are you unhappy?"

"That I want nothing, said the prince, or that I know not what I want, is the cause of my complaint; if I had any known want, I should have a certain wish; that wish would excite endeavour, and I should not then repine to see the sun move so slowly towards the western mountain, or lament when the day breaks and sleep will no longer hide me from myself. When I see the kids and the lambs chasing one another, I fancy that I should be happy if I had something to persue. But, possessing all that I can want, I find one day and one hour exactly like another, except that the latter is still more tedious than the former. Let your experience inform me how the day may now seem as short as in my child-hood, while nature was yet fresh, and every moment shewed me what I never had observed before. I have already enjoyed too much; give me something to desire."

The old man was surprized at this new species of affliction, and knew not what to reply, yet was unwilling to be silent. "Sir, said he, if you had seen the miseries of the world, you would know how to value your present state." "Now, said the prince, you have given me something to desire; I shall long to see the miseries of the world, since the sight of them is necessary to happiness."

IV

THE PRINCE CONTINUES TO GRIEVE AND MUSE

At this time the sound of musick proclaimed the hour of repast, and the conversation was concluded. The old man went away sufficiently discontented to find that his reasonings had produced the only conclusion which they were intended to prevent. But in the decline of life shame and grief are of short duration; whether it be that we bear easily what we have born long, or that, finding ourselves in age less regarded, we less regard others; or, that we look with slight regard upon afflictions, to which we know that the hand of death is about to put an end.

The prince, whose views were extended to a wider space, could not speedily quiet his emotions. He had been before terrified at the length of life which nature promised him, because he considered that in a long time much must be endured; he now rejoiced in his youth, because in many years much might be done.

This first beam of hope, that had been ever darted into his mind, rekindled youth in his cheeks, and doubled the lustre of his eyes. He was fired with the desire of doing something, though he knew not yet with distinctness, either end or means.

He was now no longer gloomy and unsocial; but, considering himself as master of a secret stock of happiness, which he could enjoy only by concealing it, he affected to be busy in all schemes of diversion, and endeavoured to make others pleased with the state of which he himself was weary. But pleasures never can be so multiplied or continued, as not to leave much of life unemployed; there were many hours, both of the night and day, which he could spend without suspicion in solitary thought. The load of life was much lightened: he went eagerly into the assemblies, because he supposed the frequency of his presence necessary to the success of his purposes; he retired gladly to privacy, because he had now a subject of thought.

His chief amusement was to picture to himself that world which he had never seen; to place himself in various conditions; to be entangled in imaginary difficulties, and to be engaged in wild adventures: but his benevolence always terminated his projects in the relief of distress, the detection of fraud, the defeat of oppression, and the diffusion of happiness.

Thus passed twenty months of the life of Rasselas. He busied himself so intensely in visionary bustle, that he forgot his real solitude, and, amidst hourly preparations for the various incidents of human affairs, neglected to consider by what means he should mingle with mankind.

One day, as he was sitting on a bank, he feigned to himself an orphan virgin robbed of her little portion by a treacherous lover, and crying after him for restitution and redress.[3] So strongly was the image impressed upon his mind, that he started up in the maid's defence, and run forward to seize the plunder with all the eagerness of real persuit. Fear naturally quickens the flight of guilt. Rasselas could not catch the fugitive with his utmost efforts; but, resolving to weary, by perseverance, him whom he could not surpass in speed, he pressed on till the foot of the mountain stopped his course.

Here he recollected himself, and smiled at his own useless impetuosity. Then raising his eyes to the mountain, "This, said he, is the fatal obstacle that hinders at once the enjoyment of pleasure, and the exercise of virtue. How long is it that my hopes and wishes have flown beyond this boundary of my life, which yet I never have attempted to surmount!"

Struck with this reflection, he sat down to muse, and remembered, that since he first resolved to escape from his confinement, the sun had passed twice over him in his annual course. He now felt a degree of regret with which he had never been before acquainted. He considered how much might have been done in the time which had passed, and left nothing real behind it. He compared twenty months with the life of man. "In life, said he, is not to be counted the ignorance of infancy, or imbecility of age. We are long before we are able to think, and we soon cease from the power of acting. The true period of human existence may be reasonably estimated as forty years, of which I have mused away the four and twentieth part. What I have lost was certain, for I have certainly possessed it; but of twenty months to come who can assure me?"

The consciousness of his own folly pierced him deeply, and he was long before he could be reconciled to himself. "The rest of my time, said he, has been lost by the crime or folly of my ancestors, and the absurd institutions of my country; I remember it with disgust, yet without remorse: but the months that have

---

[3] In keeping with the romantic idealism of his sheltered upbringing, the prince's day-dreams may be said to exemplify "the dangerous prevalence of imagination" in its most naive condition ("*orphan* virgin!"). For discussion, consult chapter 44.

passed since new light darted into my soul, since I formed a
scheme of reasonable felicity, have been squandered by my own
fault. I have lost that which can never be restored: I have seen
the sun rise and set for twenty months, an idle gazer on the light
of heaven: In this time the birds have left the nest of their mother,
and committed themselves to the woods and to the skies: the kid
has forsaken the teat, and learned by degrees to climb the rocks
in quest of independant sustenance. I only have made no ad-
vances, but am still helpless and ignorant. The moon by more
than twenty changes, admonished me of the flux of life; the
stream that rolled before my feet upbraided my inactivity. I sat
feasting on intellectual luxury, regardless alike of the examples
of the earth, and the instructions of the planets. Twenty months
are passed, who shall restore them!"

These sorrowful meditations fastened upon his mind; he past
four months in resolving to lose no more time in idle resolves, and
was awakened to more vigorous exertion by hearing a maid, who
had broken a porcelain cup, remark, that what cannot be repaired
is not to be regretted.

This was obvious; and Rasselas reproached himself that he had
not discovered it, having not known, or not considered, how many
useful hints are obtained by chance, and how often the mind,
hurried by her own ardour to distant views, neglects the truths
that lie open before her. He, for a few hours, regretted his regret,
and from that time bent his whole mind upon the means of es-
caping from the valley of happiness.

V

THE PRINCE MEDITATES HIS ESCAPE

He now found that it would be very difficult to effect that which
it was very easy to suppose effected. When he looked round about
him, he saw himself confined by the bars of nature which had
never yet been broken, and by the gate, through which none that
once had passed it were ever able to return. He was now impatient
as an eagle in a grate. He passed week after week in clambering
the mountains, to see if there was any aperture which the bushes
might conceal, but found all the summits inaccessible by their

prominence. The iron gate he despaired to open; for it was not only secured with all the power of art, but was always watched by successive sentinels, and was by its position exposed to the perpetual observation of all the inhabitants.

He then examined the cavern through which the waters of the lake were discharged; and, looking down at a time when the sun shone strongly upon its mouth, he discovered it to be full of broken rocks, which, though they permitted the stream to flow through many narrow passages, would stop any body of solid bulk. He returned discouraged and dejected; but, having now known the blessing of hope, resolved never to despair.

In these fruitless searches he spent ten months. The time, however, passed chearfully away: in the morning he rose with new hope, in the evening applauded his own diligence, and in the night slept sound after his fatigue. He met a thousand amusements which beguiled his labour, and diversified his thoughts. He discerned the various instincts of animals, and properties of plants, and found the place replete with wonders, of which he purposed to solace himself with the contemplation, if he should never be able to accomplish his flight; rejoicing that his endeavours, though yet unsuccessful, had supplied him with a source of inexhaustible enquiry.

But his original curiosity was not yet abated; he resolved to obtain some knowledge of the ways of men. His wish still continued, but his hope grew less. He ceased to survey any longer the walls of his prison, and spared to search by new toils for interstices which he knew could not be found, yet determined to keep his design always in view, and lay hold on any expedient that time should offer.

VI

A DISSERTATION ON THE ART OF FLYING

Among the artists that had been allured into the happy valley, to labour for the accommodation and pleasure of its inhabitants, was a man eminent for his knowledge of the mechanick powers, who had contrived many engines both of use and recreation. By a wheel, which the stream turned, he forced the water into a tower, whence it was distributed to all the apartments of the palace. He erected a pavillion in the garden, around which he kept the air always cool by artificial showers. One of the groves, appropriated to the ladies, was ventilated by fans, to which the rivulet that run through it gave a constant motion; and instruments of soft musick were placed at proper distances, of which some played by the impulse of the wind, and some by the power of the stream.

This artist was sometimes visited by Rasselas, who was pleased with every kind of knowledge, imagining that the time would come when all his acquisitions should be of use to him in the open world. He came one day to amuse himself in his usual manner, and found the master busy in building a sailing chariot: he saw that the design was practicable upon a level surface, and with expressions of great esteem solicited its completion. The workman was pleased to find himself so much regarded by the prince, and resolved to gain yet higher honours. "Sir, said he, you have seen but a small part of what the mechanick sciences can perform. I have been long of opinion, that, instead of the tardy conveyance of ships and chariots, man might use the swifter migration of wings; that the fields of air are open to knowledge, and that only ignorance and idleness need crawl upon the ground."

This hint rekindled the prince's desire of passing the mountains; having seen what the mechanist had already performed, he was willing to fancy that he could do more; yet resolved to enquire further before he suffered hope to afflict him by disappointment. "I am afraid, said he to the artist, that your imagination prevails over your skill, and that you now tell me rather what you wish than what you know. Every animal has his element assigned him; the birds have the air, and man and beasts the earth." "So, replied the mechanist, fishes have the water, in which yet beasts can swim by nature, and men by art. He that can swim needs not despair to fly: to swim is to fly in a grosser fluid, and to fly is to swim in a subtler. We are only to proportion our power of resistance to the different density of the matter through which we are to pass. You will be necessarily upborn by the air, if you can renew any impulse upon it, faster than the air can recede from the pressure."

"But the exercise of swimming, said the prince, is very laborious; the strongest limbs are soon wearied; I am afraid the act of flying will be yet more violent, and wings will be of no great use, unless we can fly further than we can swim."

"The labour of rising from the ground, said the artist, will be great, as we see it in the heavier domestick fowls; but, as we mount higher, the earth's attraction, and the body's gravity, will be gradually diminished, till we shall arrive at a region where the man will float in the air without any tendency to fall: no care will then be necessary, but to move forwards, which the gentlest impulse will effect. You, Sir, whose curiosity is so extensive, will easily conceive with what pleasure a philosopher, furnished with wings, and hovering in the sky, would see the earth, and all it's inhabitants, rolling beneath him, and presenting to him successively, by it's diurnal motion, all the countries within the same parallel. How must it amuse the pendent spectator to see the moving scene of land and ocean, cities and desarts! To survey with equal security the marts of trade, and the fields of battle; mountains infested by barbarians, and fruitful regions gladdened by plenty, and lulled by peace! How easily shall we then trace the Nile through all his passage; pass over to distant regions, and examine the face of nature from one extremity of the earth to the other!"

"All this, said the prince, is much to be desired, but I am afraid that no man will be able to breathe in these regions of speculation and tranquility. I have been told, that respiration is difficult upon lofty mountains, yet from these precipices, though so high as to produce great tenuity of the air, it is very easy to fall: therefore I suspect, that from any height, where life can be supported, there may be danger of too quick descent."

"Nothing, replied the artist, will ever be attempted, if all possible objections must be first overcome. If you will favour my project I will try the first flight at my own hazard. I have considered the structure of all volant animals, and find the folding continuity of the bat's wings most easily accommodated to the human form. Upon this model I shall begin my task to morrow, and in a year expect to tower into the air beyond the malice or persuit of man. But I will work only on this condition, that the art shall not be divulged, and that you shall not require me to make wings for any but ourselves."

"Why, said Rasselas, should you envy others so great an advantage? All skill ought to be exerted for universal good; every man has owed much to others, and ought to repay the kindness that he has received."

"If men were all virtuous, returned the artist, I should with great alacrity teach them all to fly. But what would be the security of the good, if the bad could at pleasure invade them from the sky? Against an army sailing through the clouds neither walls, nor mountains, nor seas, could afford any security. A flight of northern savages might hover in the wind, and light at once with irresistible violence upon the capital of a fruitful region that was rolling under them. Even this valley, the retreat of princes, the abode of happiness, might be violated by the sudden descent of some of the naked nations that swarm on the coast of the southern sea."

The prince promised secrecy, and waited for the performance, not wholly hopeless of success. He visited the work from time to time, observed its progress, and remarked many ingenious contrivances to facilitate motion, and unite levity with strength. The artist was every day more certain that he should leave vultures and eagles behind him, and the contagion of his confidence seized upon the prince.

In a year the wings were finished, and, on a morning appointed, the maker appeared furnished for flight on a little promontory: he waved his pinions a while to gather air, then leaped from his stand, and in an instant dropped into the lake. His wings, which were of no use in the air, sustained him in the water, and the prince drew him to land, half dead with terrour and vexation.

VII

THE PRINCE FINDS A MAN OF LEARNING

The prince was not much afflicted by this disaster, having suffered himself to hope for a happier event, only because he had no other means of escape in view. He still persisted in his design to leave the happy valley by the first opportunity.

His imagination was now at a stand; he had no prospect of entering into the world; and, notwithstanding all his endeavours to support himself, discontent by degrees preyed upon him, and he began again to lose his thoughts in sadness, when the rainy season, which in these countries is periodical, made it inconvenient to wander in the woods.

The rain continued longer and with more violence than had been ever known: the clouds broke on the surrounding mountains, and the torrents streamed into the plain on every side, till the cavern was too narrow to discharge the water. The lake overflowed its banks, and all the level of the valley was covered with the inundation. The eminence, on which the palace was built, and some other spots of rising ground, were all that the eye could now discover. The herds and flocks left the pastures, and both the wild beasts and the tame retreated to the mountains.

This inundation confined all the princes to domestick amusements, and the attention of Rasselas was particularly seized by a poem, which Imlac rehearsed upon the various conditions of humanity. He commanded the poet to attend him in his apartment, and recite his verses a second time; then entering into familiar talk, he thought himself happy in having found a man who knew the world so well, and could so skilfully paint the scenes of life. He asked a thousand questions about things, to which, though common to all other mortals, his confinement from childhood had kept him a stranger. The poet pitied his ignorance, and loved his curiosity, and entertained him from day to day with novelty and instruction, so that the prince regretted the necessity of sleep, and longed till the morning should renew his pleasure.

As they were sitting together, the prince commanded Imlac to relate his history, and to tell by what accident he was forced, or by what motive induced, to close his life in the happy valley. As he was going to begin his narrative, Rasselas was called to a concert, and obliged to restrain his curiosity till the evening.

VIII

THE HISTORY OF IMLAC

The close of the day is, in the regions of the torrid zone, the only season of diversion and entertainment, and it was therefore midnight before the musick ceased, and the princesses retired. Rasselas then called for his companion and required him to begin the story of his life.

"Sir, said Imlac, my history will not be long: the life that is devoted to knowledge passes silently away, and is very little diversified by events. To talk in publick, to think in solitude, to read and to hear, to inquire, and answer inquiries, is the business of a scholar. He wanders about the world without pomp or terrour, and is neither known nor valued but by men like himself.

"I was born in the kingdom of Goiama, at no great distance from the fountain of the Nile. My father was a wealthy merchant, who traded between the inland countries of Africk and the ports of the red sea. He was honest, frugal and diligent, but of mean sentiments, and narrow comprehension: he desired only to be rich, and to conceal his riches, lest he should be spoiled by the governours of the province."

"Surely, said the prince, my father must be negligent of his charge, if any man in his dominions dares take that which belongs to another. Does he not know that kings are accountable for injustice permitted as well as done? If I were emperour, not the meanest of my subjects should be oppressed with impunity. My blood boils when I am told that a merchant durst not enjoy his honest gains for fear of losing them by the rapacity of power. Name the governour who robbed the people, that I may declare his crimes to the emperour."

"Sir, said Imlac, your ardour is the natural effect of vertue animated by youth: the time will come when you will acquit your father, and perhaps hear with less impatience of the governour. Oppression is, in the Abissinian dominions, neither frequent nor tolerated; but no form of government has been yet discovered, by which cruelty can be wholly prevented. Subordination supposes power on one part and subjection on the other; and if power be in the hands of men, it will sometimes be abused. The vigilance of the supreme magistrate may do much, but much will still remain undone. He can never know all the crimes that are committed, and can seldom punish all that he knows."

"This, said the prince, I do not understand, but I had rather hear thee than dispute. Continue thy narration."

"My father, proceeded Imlac, originally intended that I should have no other education, than such as might qualify me for commerce; and discovering in me great strength of memory, and quickness of apprehension, often declared his hope that I should be some time the richest man in Abissinia."

"Why, said the prince, did thy father desire the increase of his wealth, when it was already greater than he durst discover or enjoy? I am unwilling to doubt thy veracity, yet inconsistencies cannot both be true."

"Inconsistencies, answered Imlac, cannot be right, but, imputed to man, they may both be true. Yet diversity is not inconsistency. My father might expect a time of greater security. However, some desire is necessary to keep life in motion, and he, whose real wants are supplied, must admit those of fancy."

"This, said the prince, I can in some measure conceive. I repent that I interrupted thee."

"With this hope, proceeded Imlac, he sent me to school; but when I had once found the delight of knowledge, and felt the pleasure of intelligence and the pride of invention, I began silently to despise riches, and determined to disappoint the purpose of my father, whose grossness of conception raised my pity. I was twenty years old before his tenderness would expose me to the fatigue of travel, in which time I had been instructed, by successive masters, in all the literature of my native country. As every hour taught me something new, I lived in a continual course of gratifications; but, as I advanced towards manhood, I lost much of the reverence with which I had been used to look on my instructors; because, when the lesson was ended, I did not find them wiser or better than common men.

"At length my father resolved to initiate me in commerce, and, opening one of his subterranean treasuries, counted out ten thousand pieces of gold. This, young man, said he, is the stock with which you must negociate. I began with less than the fifth part, and you see how diligence and parsimony have increased it. This is your own to waste or to improve. If you squander it by negligence or caprice, you must wait for my death before you will be rich: if, in four years, you double your stock, we will thenceforward let subordination cease, and live together as friends and partners; for he shall always be equal with me, who is equally skilled in the art of growing rich.

"We laid our money upon camels, concealed in bales of cheap goods, and travelled to the shore of the red sea. When I cast my eye on the expanse of waters my heart bounded like that of a prisoner escaped. I felt an unextinguishable curiosity kindle in my mind, and resolved to snatch this opportunity of seeing the manners of other nations, and of learning sciences unknown in Abissinia.

"I remembered that my father had obliged me to the improvement of my stock, not by a promise which I ought not to violate, but by a penalty which I was at liberty to incur; and therefore determined to gratify my predominant desire, and by drinking at the fountains of knowledge, to quench the thirst of curiosity.

"As I was supposed to trade without connexion with my father, it was easy for me to become acquainted with the master of a ship, and procure a passage to some other country. I had no motives of choice to regulate my voyage; it was sufficient for me that, wherever I wandered, I should see a country which I had not seen before. I therefore entered a ship bound for Surat, having left a letter for my father declaring my intention.

IX

THE HISTORY OF IMLAC CONTINUED

"When I first entered upon the world of waters, and lost sight of land, I looked round about me with pleasing terrour, and thinking my soul enlarged by the boundless prospect, imagined that I could gaze round for ever without satiety; but, in a short time, I grew weary of looking on barren uniformity, where I could only see again what I had already seen. I then descended into the ship, and doubted for a while whether all my future pleasures would not end like this in disgust and disappointment. Yet surely, said I, the ocean and the land are very different; the only variety of water is rest and motion, but the earth has mountains and vallies, desarts and cities: it is inhabited by men of different customs and contrary opinions; and I may hope to find variety in life, though I should miss it in nature.

"With this thought I quieted my mind; and amused myself during the voyage, sometimes by learning from the sailors the art of navigation, which I have never practised, and sometimes by forming schemes for my conduct in different situations, in not one of which I have been ever placed.

"I was almost weary of my naval amusements when we landed safely at Surat. I secured my money, and purchasing some commodities for show, joined myself to a caravan that was passing into the inland country. My companions, for some reason or other, conjecturing that I was rich, and, by my inquiries and admiration, finding that I was ignorant, considered me as a novice whom they had a right to cheat, and who was to learn at the usual expence the art of fraud. They exposed me to the theft of servants, and the exaction of officers, and saw me plundered upon false pretences, without any advantage to themselves, but that of rejoicing in the superiority of their own knowledge."

"Stop a moment, said the prince. Is there such depravity in man, as that he should injure another without benefit to himself? I can easily conceive that all are pleased with superiority; but your ignorance was merely accidental, which, being neither your crime nor your folly, could afford them no reason to applaud themselves; and the knowledge which they had, and which you wanted, they might as effectually have shewn by warning, as betraying you."

"Pride, said Imlac, is seldom delicate, it will please itself with very mean advantages; and envy feels not its own happiness, but when it may be compared with the misery of others. They were my enemies because they grieved to think me rich, and my oppressors because they delighted to find me weak."

"Proceed, said the prince: I doubt not of the facts which you relate, but imagine that you impute them to mistaken motives."

"In this company, said Imlac, I arrived at Agra, the capital of Indostan, the city in which the great Mogul commonly resides. I applied myself to the language of the country, and in a few months was able to converse with the learned men; some of whom I found morose and reserved, and others easy and communicative; some were unwilling to teach another what they had with difficulty learned themselves; and some shewed that the end of their studies was to gain the dignity of instructing.

"To the tutor of the young princes I recommended myself so much, that I was presented to the emperour as a man of uncommon knowledge. The emperour asked me many questions concerning my country and my travels; and though I cannot now recollect any thing that he uttered above the power of a common man, he dismissed me astonished at his wisdom, and enamoured of his goodness.[4]

"My credit was now so high, that the merchants, with whom I had travelled, applied to me for recommendations to the ladies of the court. I was surprised at their confidence of solicitation, and gently reproached them with their practices on the road. They heard me with cold indifference, and shewed no tokens of shame or sorrow.

"They then urged their request with the offer of a bribe; but what I would not do for kindness I would not do for money; and refused them, not because they had injured me, but because I would not enable them to injure others; for I knew they would have made use of my credit to cheat those who should buy their wares.

"Having resided at Agra till there was no more to be learned, I travelled into Persia, where I saw many remains of ancient magnificence, and observed many new accommodations[5] of life.

[4] This quietly sardonic understatement is almost Chaucerian.
[5] *accommodations*: conveniences.

The Persians are a nation eminently social, and their assemblies afforded me daily opportunities of remarking characters and manners, and of tracing human nature through all its variations.

"From Persia I passed into Arabia, where I saw a nation at once pastoral and warlike; who live without any settled habitation; whose only wealth is their flocks and herds; and who have yet carried on, through all ages, an hereditary war with all mankind, though they neither covet nor envy their possessions.

 X

IMLAC'S HISTORY CONTINUED. A DISSERTATION UPON POETRY

"Wherever I went, I found that Poetry was considered as the highest learning, and regarded with a veneration somewhat approaching to that which man would pay to the Angelick Nature. And it yet fills me with wonder, that, in almost all countries, the most ancient poets are considered as the best: whether it be that every other kind of knowledge is an acquisition gradually attained, and poetry is a gift conferred at once; or that the first poetry of every nation surprised them as a novelty, and retained the credit by consent which it received by accident at first: or whether, as the province of poetry is to describe Nature and Passion, which are always the same, the first writers took possession of the most striking objects for description, and the most probable occurrences for fiction, and left nothing to those that followed them, but transcription of the same events, and new combinations of the same images. Whatever be the reason, it is commonly observed that the early writers are in possession of nature, and their followers of art: that the first excel in strength and invention, and the latter in elegance and refinement.

"I was desirous to add my name to this illustrious fraternity. I read all the poets of Persia and Arabia, and was able to repeat by memory the volumes that are suspended in the mosque of Mecca. But I soon found that no man was ever great by imitation. My desire of excellence impelled me to transfer my attention to nature and to life. Nature was to be my subject, and men to be my auditors: I could never describe what I had not seen: I could not hope to move those with delight or terrour, whose interests and opinions I did not understand.

"Being now resolved to be a poet, I saw every thing with a new purpose; my sphere of attention was suddenly magnified: no kind of knowledge was to be overlooked. I ranged mountains and deserts for images and resemblances, and pictured upon my mind every tree of the forest and flower of the valley. I observed with equal care the crags of the rock and the pinnacles of the palace. Sometimes I wandered along the mazes of the rivulet, and sometimes watched the changes of the summer clouds. To a poet nothing can be useless. Whatever is beautiful, and whatever is dreadful, must be familiar to his imagination: he must be conversant with all that is awfully vast or elegantly little.[6] The plants of the garden, the animals of the wood, the minerals of the earth, and meteors of the sky, must all concur to store his mind with inexhaustible variety: for every idea is useful for the inforcement or decoration of moral or religious truth; and he, who knows most, will have most power of diversifying his scenes, and of gratifying his reader with remote allusions and unexpected instruction.

"All the appearances of nature I was therefore careful to study, and every country which I have surveyed has contributed something to my poetical powers."

"In so wide a survey, said the prince, you must surely have left much unobserved. I have lived, till now, within the circuit of these mountains, and yet cannot walk abroad without the sight of something which I had never beheld before, or never heeded."

"The business of a poet, said Imlac, is to examine, not the individual, but the species; to remark general properties and large appearances: he does not number the streaks of the tulip, or describe the different shades in the verdure of the forest. He is to exhibit in his portraits of nature such prominent and striking features, as recal the original to every mind; and must neglect the minuter discriminations, which one may have remarked, and

[6] The passage reflects Johnson's awareness of Burke's recent *Enquiry into the Origin of our Ideas of the Sublime and Beautiful*, 1757.

another have neglected, for those characteristicks which are alike obvious to vigilance and carelessness.

"But the knowledge of nature is only half the task of a poet; he must be acquainted likewise with all the modes of life. His character requires that he estimate the happiness and misery of every condition; observe the power of all the passions in all their combinations, and trace the changes of the human mind as they are modified by various institutions and accidental influences of climate or custom, from the spriteliness of infancy to the despondence of decrepitude. He must divest himself of the prejudices of his age or country; he must consider right and wrong in their abstracted and invariable state; he must disregard present laws and opinions, and rise to general and transcendental truths, which will always be the same: he must therefore content himself with the slow progress of his name; contemn the applause of his own time, and commit his claims to the justice of posterity. He must write as the interpreter of nature, and the legislator of mankind, and consider himself as presiding over the thoughts and manners of future generations; as a being superiour to time and place.

"His labour is not yet at an end: he must know many languages and many sciences; and, that his stile may be worthy of his thoughts, must, by incessant practice, familiarize to himself every delicacy of speech and grace of harmony."

XI

IMLAC'S NARRATIVE CONTINUED. A HINT ON PILGRIMAGE

Imlac now felt the enthusiastic fit, and was proceeding to aggrandize his own profession, when the prince cried out, "Enough! Thou hast convinced me, that no human being can ever be a poet. Proceed with thy narration."

"To be a poet, said Imlac, is indeed very difficult." "So difficult, returned the prince, that I will at present hear no more of his labours. Tell me whither you went when you had seen Persia."

"From Persia, said the poet, I travelled through Syria, and for three years resided in Palestine, where I conversed with great

numbers of the northern and western nations of Europe; the
nations which are now in possession of all power and all knowl-
edge; whose armies are irresistible, and whose fleets command
the remotest parts of the globe. When I compared these men
with the natives of our own kingdom, and those that surround
us, they appeared almost another order of beings. In their
countries it is difficult to wish for any thing that may not be
obtained: a thousand arts, of which we never heard, are con-
tinually labouring for their convenience and pleasure; and what-
ever their own climate has denied them is supplied by their com-
merce."

"By what means, said the prince, are the Europeans thus power-
ful? or why, since they can so easily visit Asia and Africa for
trade or conquest, cannot the Asiaticks and Africans invade their
coasts, plant colonies in their ports, and give laws to their natural
princes? The same wind that carries them back would bring us
thither."

"They are more powerful, Sir, than we, answered Imlac, be-
cause they are wiser; knowledge will always predominate over
ignorance, as man governs the other animals. But why their
knowledge is more than ours, I know not what reason can be
given, but the unsearchable will of the Supreme Being."

"When, said the prince with a sigh, shall I be able to visit
Palestine, and mingle with this mighty confluence of nations?
Till that happy moment shall arrive, let me fill up the time with
such representations as thou canst give me. I am not ignorant
of the motive that assembles such numbers in that place, and
cannot but consider it as the center of wisdom and piety, to which
the best and wisest men of every land must be continually resort-
ing."

"There are some nations, said Imlac, that send few visitants to
Palestine; for many numerous and learned sects in Europe,
concur to censure pilgrimage as superstitious, or deride it as
ridiculous."

"You know, said the prince, how little my life has made me
acquainted with diversity of opinions: it will be too long to hear
the arguments on both sides; you, that have considered them,
tell me the result."

"Pilgrimage, said Imlac, like many other acts of piety, may be reasonable or superstitious, according to the principles upon which it is performed. Long journies in search of truth are not commanded. Truth, such as is necessary to the regulation of life, is always found where it is honestly sought. Change of place is no natural cause of the increase of piety, for it inevitably produces dissipation of mind. Yet, since men go every day to view the fields where great actions have been performed, and return with stronger impressions of the event, curiosity of the same kind may naturally dispose us to view that country whence our religion had its beginning; and I believe no man surveys those awful scenes without some confirmation of holy resolutions. That the Supreme Being may be more easily propitiated in one place than in another, is the dream of idle superstition; but that some places may operate upon our own minds in an uncommon manner, is an opinion which hourly experience will justify.[7] He who supposes that his vices may be more successfully combated in Palestine, will, perhaps, find himself mistaken, yet he may go thither without folly: he who thinks they will be more freely pardoned, dishonours at once his reason and religion."

"These, said the prince, are European distinctions. I will consider them another time. What have you found to be the effect of knowledge? Are those nations happier than we?"

"There is so much infelicity, said the poet, in the world, that scarce any man has leisure from his own distresses to estimate the comparative happiness of others. Knowledge is certainly one of the means of pleasure, as is confessed by the natural desire which every mind feels of increasing its ideas. Ignorance is mere privation, by which nothing can be produced: it is a vacuity in which the soul sits motionless and torpid for want of attraction; and, without knowing why, we always rejoice when we learn, and grieve when we forget. I am therefore inclined to conclude, that,

[7] Johnson reverts to this topic in a memorable passage in his *Journey to the Western Islands:* "Far from me and from my friends be such frigid philosophy as may conduct us indifferent and unmoved over any ground which has been dignified by wisdom, bravery, or virtue. That man is little to be envied whose patriotism would not gain force upon the plain of Marathon or whose piety would not grow warmer among the ruins of Iona."

if nothing counteracts the natural consequence of learning, we grow more happy as our minds take a wider range.

"In enumerating the particular comforts of life we shall find many advantages on the side of the Europeans. They cure wounds and diseases with which we languish and perish. We suffer inclemencies of weather which they can obviate. They have engines for the despatch of many laborious works, which we must perform by manual industry. There is such communication between distant places, that one friend can hardly be said to be absent from another. Their policy removes all publick inconveniencies: they have roads cut through their mountains, and bridges laid upon their rivers. And, if we descend to the privacies of life, their habitations are more commodious, and their possessions are more secure."

"They are surely happy, said the prince, who have all these conveniencies, of which I envy none so much as the facility with which separated friends interchange their thoughts."

"The Europeans, answered Imlac, are less unhappy than we, but they are not happy. Human life is every where a state in which much is to be endured, and little to be enjoyed."

XII

THE STORY OF IMLAC CONTINUED

"I am not yet willing, said the prince, to suppose that happiness is so parsimoniously distributed to mortals; nor can believe but that, if I had the choice of life, I should be able to fill every day with pleasure. I would injure no man, and should provoke no resentment: I would relieve every distress, and should enjoy the benedictions of gratitude. I would choose my friends among the wise, and my wife among the virtuous; and therefore should be in no danger from treachery, or unkindness. My children should, by my care, be learned and pious, and would repay to my age what their childhood had received. What would dare to molest him who might call on every side to thousands enriched by his bounty, or assisted by his power? And why should not life glide quietly away in the soft reciprocation of protection and reverence?

THE HISTORY OF RASSELAS

All this may be done without the help of European refinements, which appear by their effects to be rather specious than useful. Let us leave them and persue our journey."

"From Palestine, said Imlac, I passed through many regions of Asia; in the more civilized kingdoms as a trader, and among the Barbarians of the mountains as a pilgrim. At last I began to long for my native country, that I might repose after my travels, and fatigues, in the places where I had spent my earliest years, and gladden my old companions with the recital of my adventures. Often did I figure to myself those, with whom I had sported away the gay hours of dawning life, sitting round me in its evening, wondering at my tales, and listening to my counsels.

"When this thought had taken possession of my mind, I considered every moment as wasted which did not bring me nearer to Abissinia. I hastened into Egypt, and, notwithstanding my impatience, was detained ten months in the contemplation of its ancient magnificence, and in enquiries after the remains of its ancient learning. I found in Cairo a mixture of all nations; some brought thither by the love of knowledge, some by the hope of gain, and many by the desire of living after their own manner without observation, and of lying hid in the obscurity of multitudes: for, in a city, populous as Cairo, it is possible to obtain at the same time the gratifications of society, and the secrecy of solitude.

"From Cairo I travelled to Suez, and embarked on the Red sea, passing along the coast till I arrived at the port from which I had departed twenty years before. Here I joined myself to a caravan and re-entered my native country.

"I now expected the caresses of my kinsmen, and the congratulations of my friends, and was not without hope that my father, whatever value he had set upon riches, would own with gladness and pride a son who was able to add to the felicity and honour of the nation. But I was soon convinced that my thoughts were vain. My father had been dead fourteen years, having divided his wealth among my brothers, who were removed to some other provinces. Of my companions the greater part was in the grave, of the rest some could with difficulty remember me, and some considered me as one corrupted by foreign manners.

"A man used to vicissitudes is not easily dejected. I forgot, after a time, my disappointment, and endeavoured to recommend myself to the nobles of the kingdom: they admitted me to their tables, heard my story, and dismissed me. I opened a school, and was prohibited to teach. I then resolved to sit down in the quiet of domestick life, and addressed a lady that was fond of my conversation, but rejected my suit, because my father was a merchant.

"Wearied at last with solicitation and repulses, I resolved to hide myself for ever from the world, and depend no longer on the opinion or caprice of others. I waited for the time when the gate of the *happy valley* should open, that I might bid farewell to hope and fear: the day came; my performance was distinguished with favour, and I resigned myself with joy to perpetual confinement."

"Hast thou here found happiness at last? said Rasselas. Tell me without reserve; art thou content with thy condition? or, dost thou wish to be again wandering and inquiring? All the inhabitants of this valley celebrate their lot, and, at the annual visit of the emperour, invite others to partake of their felicity."

"Great prince, said Imlac, I shall speak the truth: I know not one of all your attendants who does not lament the hour when he entered this retreat. I am less unhappy than the rest, because I have a mind replete with images, which I can vary and combine at pleasure. I can amuse my solitude by the renovation of the knowledge which begins to fade from my memory, and by recollection of the accidents of my past life. Yet all this ends in the sorrowful consideration, that my acquirements are now useless, and that none of my pleasures can be again enjoyed. The rest, whose minds have no impression but of the present moment, are either corroded by malignant passions, or sit stupid in the gloom of perpetual vacancy."

"What passions can infest those, said the prince, who have no rivals? We are in a place where impotence precludes malice, and where all envy is repressed by community of enjoyments."

"There may be community, said Imlac, of material possessions, but there can never be community of love or of esteem. It must happen that one will please more than another; he that knows himself despised will always be envious; and still more envious and malevolent, if he is condemned to live in the presence of those who despise him. The invitations, by which they allure others to a state which they feel to be wretched, proceed from the natural malignity of hopeless misery. They are weary of themselves, and of each other, and expect to find relief in new companions. They envy the liberty which their folly has forfeited, and would gladly see all mankind imprisoned like themselves.

"From this crime, however, I am wholly free. No man can say that he is wretched by my persuasion. I look with pity on the crowds who are annually soliciting admission to captivity, and wish that it were lawful for me to warn them of their danger."

"My dear Imlac, said the prince, I will open to thee my whole heart. I have long meditated an escape from the happy valley. I have examined the mountains on every side, but find myself insuperably barred: teach me the way to break my prison; thou shalt be the companion of my flight, the guide of my rambles, the partner of my fortune, and my sole director in the *choice of life*."

"Sir, answered the poet, your escape will be difficult, and, perhaps, you may soon repent your curiosity. The world, which you figure to yourself smooth and quiet as the lake in the valley, you will find a sea foaming with tempests, and boiling with whirlpools: you will be sometimes overwhelmed by the waves of violence, and sometimes dashed against the rocks of treachery. Amidst wrongs and frauds, competitions and anxieties, you will wish a thousand times for these seats of quiet, and willingly quit hope to be free from fear."

"Do not seek to deter me from my purpose, said the prince: I am impatient to see what thou hast seen; and, since thou art thyself weary of the valley, it is evident, that thy former state was better than this. Whatever be the consequence of my experiment, I am resolved to judge with my own eyes of the various conditions of men, and then to make deliberately my *choice of life*."

"I am afraid, said Imlac, you are hindered by stronger restraints than my persuasions; yet, if your determination is fixed, I do not counsel you to despair. Few things are impossible to diligence and skill."

XIII

RASSELAS DISCOVERS THE MEANS OF ESCAPE

The prince now dismissed his favourite to rest, but the narrative of wonders and novelties filled his mind with perturbation. He revolved all that he had heard, and prepared innumerable questions for the morning.

Much of his uneasiness was now removed. He had a friend to whom he could impart his thoughts, and whose experience could assist him in his designs. His heart was no longer condemned to swell with silent vexation. He thought that even the *happy valley* might be endured with such a companion, and that, if they could range the world together, he should have nothing further to desire.

In a few days the water was discharged, and the ground dried. The prince and Imlac then walked out together to converse without the notice of the rest. The prince, whose thoughts were always on the wing, as he passed by the gate, said, with a countenance of sorrow, "Why art thou so strong, and why is man so weak?"

"Man is not weak, answered his companion; knowledge is more than equivalent to force. The master of mechanicks laughs at strength. I can burst the gate, but cannot do it secretly. Some other expedient must be tried."

As they were walking on the side of the mountain, they observed that the conies, which the rain had driven from their burrows, had taken shelter among the bushes, and formed holes behind them, tending upwards in an oblique line. "It has been the opinion of antiquity, said Imlac, that human reason borrowed many arts from the instinct of animals; let us, therefore, not think ourselves degraded by learning from the coney. We may escape by piercing the mountain in the same direction. We will begin where the summit hangs over the middle part, and labour upward till we shall issue out beyond the prominence."

The eyes of the prince, when he heard this proposal, sparkled with joy. The execution was easy, and the success certain.

No time was now lost. They hastened early in the morning to chuse a place proper for their mine. They clambered with great fatigue among crags and brambles, and returned without having discovered any part that favoured their design. The second and the third day were spent in the same manner, and with the same frustration. But, on the fourth, they found a small cavern, concealed by a thicket, where they resolved to make their experiment.

Imlac procured instruments proper to hew stone and remove earth, and they fell to their work on the next day with more eagerness than vigour. They were presently exhausted by their efforts, and sat down to pant upon the grass. The prince, for a moment, appeared to be discouraged. "Sir, said his companion, practice will enable us to continue our labour for a longer time; mark, however, how far we have advanced, and you will find that our toil will some time have an end. Great works are performed, not by strength, but perseverance: yonder palace was raised by single stones, yet you see its height and spaciousness. He that shall walk with vigour three hours a day will pass in seven years a space equal to the circumference of the globe."

They returned to their work day after day, and, in a short time, found a fissure in the rock, which enabled them to pass far with very little obstruction. This Rasselas considered as a good omen. "Do not disturb your mind, said Imlac, with other hopes or fears than reason may suggest: if you are pleased with prognosticks of good, you will be terrified likewise with tokens of evil, and your whole life will be a prey to superstition. Whatever facilitates our work is more than an omen, it is a cause of success. This is one of those pleasing surprises which often happen to active resolution. Many things difficult to design prove easy to performance."

XIV

RASSELAS AND IMLAC RECEIVE AN UNEXPECTED VISIT

They had now wrought their way to the middle, and solaced their toil with the approach of liberty, when the prince, coming down to refresh himself with air, found his sister Nekayah standing before the mouth of the cavity. He started and stood confused, afraid to tell his design, and yet hopeless to conceal it. A few moments determined him to repose on her fidelity, and secure her secrecy by a declaration without reserve.

"Do not imagine, said the princess, that I came hither as a spy: I had long observed from my window, that you and Imlac directed your walk every day towards the same point, but I did not suppose you had any better reason for the preference than a cooler shade, or more fragrant bank; nor followed you with any other design than to partake of your conversation. Since then not suspicion but fondness has detected you, let me not lose the advantage of my discovery. I am equally weary of confinement with yourself, and not less desirous of knowing what is done or suffered in the world. Permit me to fly with you from this tasteless tranquility, which will yet grow more loathsome when you have left me. You may deny me to accompany you, but cannot hinder me from following."

The prince, who loved Nekayah above his other sisters, had no inclination to refuse her request, and grieved that he had lost an opportunity of shewing his confidence by a voluntary communication. It was therefore agreed that she should leave the valley with them; and that, in the mean time, she should watch, lest any other straggler should, by chance or curiosity, follow them to the mountain.

At length their labour was at an end; they saw light beyond the prominence, and, issuing to the top of the mountain, beheld the Nile, yet a narrow current, wandering beneath them.

The prince looked round with rapture, anticipated all the pleasures of travel, and in thought was already transported beyond his father's dominions. Imlac, though very joyful at his escape, had less expectation of pleasure in the world, which he had before tried, and of which he had been weary.

Rasselas was so much delighted with a wider horizon, that he could not soon be persuaded to return into the valley. He informed his sister that the way was open, and that nothing now remained but to prepare for their departure.

XV

THE PRINCE AND PRINCESS LEAVE THE VALLEY, AND SEE
MANY WONDERS

The prince and princess had jewels sufficient to make them rich whenever they came into a place of commerce, which, by Imlac's direction, they hid in their cloaths, and, on the night of the next full moon, all left the valley. The princess was followed only by a single favourite, who did not know whither she was going.

They clambered through the cavity, and began to go down on the other side. The princess and her maid turned their eyes towards every part, and, seeing nothing to bound their prospect, considered themselves as in danger of being lost in a dreary vacuity. They stopped and trembled. "I am almost afraid, said the princess, to begin a journey of which I cannot perceive an end, and to venture into this immense plain where I may be approached on every side by men whom I never saw." The prince felt nearly the same emotions, though he thought it more manly to conceal them.

Imlac smiled at their terrours, and encouraged them to proceed; but the princess continued irresolute till she had been imperceptibly drawn forward too far to return.

In the morning they found some shepherds in the field, who set milk and fruits before them. The princess wondered that she did not see a palace ready for her reception, and a table spread with delicacies; but, being faint and hungry, she drank the milk and eat the fruits, and thought them of a higher flavour than the products of the valley.

They travelled forward by easy journeys, being all unaccustomed to toil or difficulty, and knowing, that though they might be missed, they could not be persued. In a few days they came into a more populous region, where Imlac was diverted with the admiration which his companions expressed at the diversity of manners, stations and employments.

Their dress was such as might not bring upon them the suspicion of having any thing to conceal, yet the prince, wherever he came, expected to be obeyed, and the princess was frighted, because those that came into her presence did not prostrate themselves before her. Imlac was forced to observe them with great vigilance, lest they should betray their rank by their unusual behaviour, and detained them several weeks in the first village to accustom them to the sight of common mortals.

By degree the royal wanderers were taught to understand that they had for a time laid aside their dignity, and were to expect only such regard as liberality and courtesy could procure. And Imlac, having, by many admonitions, prepared them to endure the tumults of a port, and the ruggedness of the commercial race, brought them down to the sea-coast.

The prince and his sister, to whom every thing was new, were gratified equally at all places, and therefore remained for some months at the port without any inclination to pass further. Imlac was content with their stay, because he did not think it safe to expose them, unpractised in the world, to the hazards of a foreign country.

At last he began to fear lest they should be discovered, and proposed to fix a day for their departure. They had no pretensions to judge for themselves, and referred the whole scheme to his direction. He therefore took passage in a ship to Suez; and, when the time came, with great difficulty prevailed on the princess to enter the vessel. They had a quick and prosperous voyage, and from Suez travelled by land to Cairo.

XVI

THEY ENTER CAIRO, AND FIND EVERY MAN HAPPY

As they approached the city, which filled the strangers with astonishment, "This, said Imlac to the prince, is the place where travellers and merchants assemble from all the corners of the earth. You will here find men of every character, and every occupation. Commerce is here honourable: I will act as a merchant, and you shall live as strangers, who have no other end of travel than curiosity; it will soon be observed that we are rich; our reputation will procure us access to all whom we shall desire to know; you will see all the conditions of humanity, and enable yourself at leisure to make your *choice of life.*"

They now entered the town, stunned by the noise, and offended by the crowds. Instruction had not yet so prevailed over habit, but that they wondered to see themselves pass undistinguished along the street, and met by the lowest of the people without reverence or notice. The princess could not at first bear the thought of being levelled with the vulgar, and, for some days, continued in her chamber, where she was served by her favourite Pekuah as in the palace of the valley.

Imlac, who understood traffick, sold part of the jewels the next day, and hired a house, which he adorned with such magnificence, that he was immediately considered as a merchant of great wealth. His politeness attracted many acquaintance, and his generosity made him courted by many dependants. His table was crowded by men of every nation, who all admired his knowledge, and solicited his favour. His companions, not being able to mix in the conversation, could make no discovery of their ignorance or surprise, and were gradually initiated in the world as they gained knowledge of the language.

The prince had, by frequent lectures, been taught the use and nature of money; but the ladies could not, for a long time, comprehend what the merchants did with small pieces of gold and silver, or why things of so little use should be received as equivalent to the necessaries of life.

They studied the language two years, while Imlac was preparing to set before them the various ranks and conditions of mankind. He grew acquainted with all who had any thing uncommon in their fortune or conduct. He frequented the voluptuous and the frugal, the idle and the busy, the merchants and the men of learning.

The prince, being now able to converse with fluency, and having learned the caution necessary to be observed in his intercourse with strangers, began to accompany Imlac to places of resort, and to enter into all assemblies, that he might make his *choice of life.*

For some time he thought choice needless, because all appeared to him equally happy. Wherever he went he met gayety and kindness, and heard the song of joy, or the laugh of carelessness. He began to believe that the world overflowed with universal plenty, and that nothing was withheld either from want or merit; that every hand showered liberality, and every heart melted with benevolence: "and who then, says he, will be suffered to be wretched?"

Imlac permitted the pleasing delusion, and was unwilling to crush the hope of inexperience; till one day, having sat a while silent, "I know not, said the prince, what can be the reason that I am more unhappy than any of our friends. I see them perpetually and unalterably chearful, but feel my own mind restless and uneasy. I am unsatisfied with those pleasures which I seem most to court; I live in the crowds of jollity, not so much to enjoy company as to shun myself, and am only loud and merry to conceal my sadness."

"Every man, said Imlac, may, by examining his own mind, guess what passes in the minds of others: when you feel that your own gaiety is counterfeit, it may justly lead you to suspect that of your companions not to be sincere. Envy is commonly reciprocal. We are long before we are convinced that happiness is never to be found, and each believes it possessed by others, to keep alive the hope of obtaining it for himself. In the assembly, where you passed the last night, there appeared such spriteliness of air, and volatility of fancy, as might have suited beings of an higher order, formed to inhabit serener regions inaccessible to care or sorrow: yet, believe me, prince, there was not one who did not dread the moment when solitude should deliver him to the tyranny of reflection."

"This, said the prince, may be true of others, since it is true of me; yet, whatever be the general infelicity of man, one condition is more happy than another, and wisdom surely directs us to take the least evil in the *choice of life*."

"The causes of good and evil, answered Imlac, are so various and uncertain, so often entangled with each other, so diversified by various relations, and so much subject to accidents which cannot be foreseen, that he who would fix his condition upon incontestable reasons of preference, must live and die inquiring and deliberating."

"But surely, said Rasselas, the wise men, to whom we listen with reverence and wonder, chose that mode of life for themselves which they thought most likely to make them happy."

"Very few, said the poet, live by choice. Every man is placed in his present condition by causes which acted without his foresight, and with which he did not always willingly cooperate; and therefore you will rarely meet one who does not think the lot of his neighbour better than his own."

"I am pleased to think, said the prince, that my birth has given me at least one advantage over others, by enabling me to determine for myself. I have here the world before me; I will review it at leisure: surely happiness is somewhere to be found."

XVII

THE PRINCE ASSOCIATES WITH YOUNG MEN OF SPIRIT AND GAIETY

Rasselas rose next day, and resolved to begin his experiments upon life. "Youth, cried he, is the time of gladness: I will join myself to the young men, whose only business is to gratify their desires, and whose time is all spent in a succession of enjoyments."

To such societies he was readily admitted, but a few days brought him back weary and disgusted. Their mirth was without images,[8] their laughter without motive; their pleasures were gross and sensual, in which the mind had no part; their conduct was at once wild and mean; they laughed at order and at law, but the frown of power dejected, and the eye of wisdom abashed them.

The prince soon concluded, that he should never be happy in a course of life of which he was ashamed. He thought it unsuitable to a reasonable being to act without a plan, and to be sad or chearful only by chance. "Happiness, said he, must be something solid and permanent, without fear and without uncertainty."

But his young companions had gained so much of his regard by their frankness and courtesy, that he could not leave them with-

[8] *without images:* Johnson, in his Dictionary, defines Image: "An idea; a representation of any thing to the mind; a picture drawn in the fancy."

out warning and remonstrance. "My friends, said he, I have seriously considered our manners and our prospects, and find that we have mistaken our own interest. The first years of man must make provision for the last. He that never thinks never can be wise. Perpetual levity must end in ignorance; and intemperance, though it may fire the spirits for an hour, will make life short or miserable. Let us consider that youth is of no long duration, and that in maturer age, when the enchantments of fancy shall cease, and phantoms of delight dance no more about us, we shall have no comforts but the esteem of wise men, and the means of doing good. Let us, therefore, stop, while to stop is in our power: let us live as men who are sometime to grow old, and to whom it will be the most dreadful of all evils not to count their past years but by follies, and to be reminded of their former luxuriance of health only by the maladies which riot has produced."

They stared a while in silence one upon another, and, at last, drove him away by a general chorus of continued laughter.

The consciousness that his sentiments were just, and his intentions kind, was scarcely sufficient to support him against the horrour of derision. But he recovered his tranquility, and persued his search.

XVIII

THE PRINCE FINDS A WISE AND HAPPY MAN

As he was one day walking in the street, he saw a spacious building which all were, by the open doors, invited to enter: he followed the stream of people, and found it a hall or school of declamation, in which professors read lectures to their auditory. He fixed his eye upon a sage raised above the rest, who discoursed with great energy on the government of the passions. His look was venerable, his action graceful, his pronunciation clear, and his diction elegant. He shewed, with great strength of sentiment, and variety of illustration, that human nature is degraded and debased, when the lower faculties predominate over the higher; that when fancy, the parent of passion, usurps the dominion of the mind, nothing ensues but the natural effect of unlawful government, perturbation and confusion; that she betrays the fortresses of the intellect to rebels, and excites her children to sedition against reason their lawful sovereign. He compared reason to the sun, of which the light is constant, uniform, and lasting; and fancy to a meteor, of bright but transitory lustre, irregular in its motion, and delusive in its direction.[9]

He then communicated the various precepts given from time to time for the conquest of passion, and displayed the happiness of those who had obtained the important victory, after which man is no longer the slave of fear, nor the fool of hope; is no more emaciated by envy, inflamed by anger, emasculated by tenderness, or depressed by grief; but walks on calmly through the tumults or the privacies of life, as the sun persues alike his course through the calm or the stormy sky.

He enumerated many examples of heroes immovable by pain or pleasure, who looked with indifference on those modes or accidents to which the vulgar give the names of good and evil. He exhorted his hearers to lay aside their prejudices, and arm themselves against the shafts of malice or misfortune, by invulnerable patience, concluding, that this state only was happiness, and that this happiness was in every one's power.

Rasselas listened to him with the veneration due to the instructions of a superiour being, and, waiting for him at the door, humbly implored the liberty of visiting so great a master of true wisdom. The lecturer hesitated a moment, when Rasselas put a purse of gold into his hand, which he received with a mixture of joy and wonder.

"I have found, said the prince at his return to Imlac, a man who can teach all that is necessary to be known, who, from the unshaken throne of rational fortitude, looks down on the scenes of life changing beneath him. He speaks, and attention watches his lips. He reasons, and conviction closes his periods. This man shall

---

[9] The dichotomy of reason and imagination (fancy), and the question of due proportions between them, occasioned endless discussion, both ethical and aesthetic; of which, in morals, *Rasselas,* as announced in its opening sentence, is itself an important part.

be my future guide: I will learn his doctrines, and imitate his life."

"Be not too hasty, said Imlac, to trust, or to admire, the teachers of morality: they discourse like angels, but they live like men."

Rasselas, who could not conceive how any man could reason so forcibly without feeling the cogency of his own arguments, paid his visit in a few days, and was denied admission. He had now learned the power of money, and made his way by a piece of gold to the inner apartment, where he found the philosopher in a room half darkened, with his eyes misty, and his face pale. "Sir, said he, you are come at a time when all human friendship is useless; what I suffer cannot be remedied, what I have lost cannot be supplied. My daughter, my only daughter, from whose tenderness I expected all the comforts of my age, died last night of a fever. My views, my purposes, my hopes are at an end: I am now a lonely being disunited from society."

"Sir, said the prince, mortality is an event by which a wise man can never be surprised: we know that death is always near, and it should therefore always be expected." "Young man, answered the philosopher, you speak like one that has never felt the pangs of separation." "Have you then forgot the precepts, said Rasselas, which you so powerfully enforced? Has wisdom no strength to arm the heart against calamity? Consider, that external things are naturally variable, but truth and reason are always the same." "What comfort, said the mourner, can truth and reason afford me? of what effect are they now, but to tell me, that my daughter will not be restored?"

The prince, whose humanity would not suffer him to insult misery with reproof, went away convinced of the emptiness of rhetorical sound, and the inefficacy of polished periods and studied sentences.

XIX

A GLIMPSE OF PASTORAL LIFE

He was still eager upon the same enquiry; and, having heard of a hermit, that lived near the lowest cataract of the Nile, and filled the whole country with the fame of his sanctity, resolved to visit his retreat, and enquire whether that felicity, which publick life could not afford, was to be found in solitude; and whether a man, whose age and virtue made him venerable, could teach any peculiar art of shunning evils, or enduring them.

Imlac and the princess agreed to accompany him, and, after the necessary preparations, they began their journey. Their way lay through fields, where shepherds tended their flocks, and the lambs were playing upon the pasture. "This, said the poet, is the life which has been often celebrated for its innocence and quiet: let us pass the heat of the day among the shepherds tents, and know whether all our searches are not to terminate in pastoral simplicity." [10]

The proposal pleased them, and they induced the shepherds, by small presents and familiar questions, to tell their opinion of their own state: they were so rude and ignorant, so little able to compare the good with the evil of the occupation, and so indistinct in their narratives and descriptions, that very little could be learned from them. But it was evident that their hearts were cankered with discontent; that they considered themselves as condemned to labour for the luxury of the rich, and looked up with stupid malevolence toward those that were placed above them.

The princess pronounced with vehemence, that she would never suffer these envious savages to be her companions, and that she should not soon be desirous of seeing any more specimens of rustick happiness; but could not believe that all the accounts of primeval pleasures were fabulous, and was yet in doubt whether life had any thing that could be justly preferred to the placid gratifications of fields and woods. She hoped that the time would come, when with a few virtuous and elegant companions, she should gather flowers planted by her own hand, fondle the lambs of her own ewe, and listen, without care, among brooks and breezes, to one of her maidens reading in the shade.

[10] Johnson's dislike of pastorals is notorious. Cf. *ante*, p. 335.

XX

THE DANGER OF PROSPERITY

On the next day they continued their journey, till the heat compelled them to look round for shelter. At a small distance they saw a thick wood, which they no sooner entered than they perceived that they were approaching the habitations of men. The shrubs were diligently cut away to open walks where the shades were darkest; the boughs of opposite trees were artificially interwoven; seats of flowery turf were raised in vacant spaces, and a rivulet, that wantoned along the side of a winding path, had its banks sometimes opened into small basons, and its stream sometimes obstructed by little mounds of stone heaped together to increase its murmurs.[11]

They passed slowly through the wood, delighted with such unexpected accommodations, and entertained each other with conjecturing what, or who, he could be, that, in those rude and unfrequented regions, had leisure and art for such harmless luxury.

As they advanced, they heard the sound of musick, and saw youths and virgins dancing in the grove; and, going still further, beheld a stately palace built upon a hill surrounded with woods. The laws of eastern hospitality allowed them to enter, and the master welcomed them like a man liberal and wealthy.

He was skilful enough in appearances soon to discern that they were no common guests, and spread his table with magnificence. The eloquence of Imlac caught his attention, and the lofty courtesy of the princess excited his respect. When they offered to depart he entreated their stay, and was the next day still more unwilling to dismiss them than before. They were easily persuaded to stop, and civility grew up in time to freedom and confidence.

The prince now saw all the domesticks chearful, and all the

[11] Johnson was inveterately cool toward the efforts of the landscape gardeners and great landowners of his day to transform the face of nature. His description here seems more appropriate to Vauxhall Gardens than to Egyptian scenery.

face of nature smiling round the place, and could not forbear to hope that he should find here what he was seeking; but when he was congratulating the master upon his possessions, he answered with a sigh, "My condition has indeed the appearance of happiness, but appearances are delusive. My prosperity puts my life in danger; the Bassa of Egypt is my enemy, incensed only by my wealth and popularity. I have been hitherto protected against him by the princes of the country; but, as the favour of the great is uncertain, I know not how soon my defenders may be persuaded to share the plunder with the Bassa. I have sent my treasures into a distant country, and, upon the first alarm, am prepared to follow them. Then will my enemies riot in my mansion, and enjoy the gardens which I have planted."

They all joined in lamenting his danger, and deprecating his exile; and the princess was so much disturbed with the tumult of grief and indignation, that she retired to her apartment. They continued with their kind inviter a few days longer, and then went forward to find the hermit.

XXI

THE HAPPINESS OF SOLITUDE. THE HERMIT'S HISTORY

They came on the third day, by the direction of the peasants, to the hermit's cell: it was a cavern in the side of a mountain, overshadowed with palm-trees; at such a distance from the cataract, that nothing more was heard than a gentle uniform murmur, such as composed the mind to pensive meditation, especially when it was assisted by the wind whistling among the branches. The first rude essay of nature had been so much improved by human labour, that the cave contained several apartments, appropriated to different uses, and often afforded lodging to travellers, whom darkness or tempests happened to overtake.

The hermit sat on a bench at the door, to enjoy the coolness of the evening. On one side lay a book with pens and papers, on the other mechanical instruments of various kinds. As they approached him unregarded, the princess observed that he had not the countenance of a man that had found, or could teach, the way to happiness.

They saluted him with great respect, which he repaid like a man not unaccustomed to the forms of courts. "My children, said he, if you have lost your way, you shall be willingly supplied with such conveniencies for the night as this cavern will afford. I have all that nature requires, and you will not expect delicacies in a hermit's cell."

They thanked him, and, entering, were pleased with the neatness and regularity of the place. The hermit set flesh and wine before them, though he fed only upon fruits and water. His discourse was chearful without levity, and pious without enthusiasm.[12] He soon gained the esteem of his guests, and the princess repented of her hasty censure.

At last Imlac began thus: "I do not now wonder that your reputation is so far extended; we have heard at Cairo of your wisdom, and came hither to implore your direction for this young man and maiden in the *choice of life*."

"To him that lives well, answered the hermit, every form of life is good; nor can I give any other rule for choice, than to remove from all apparent evil."

"He will remove most certainly from evil, said the prince, who shall devote himself to that solitude which you have recommended by your example."

"I have indeed lived fifteen years in solitude, said the hermit, but have no desire that my example should gain any imitators. In my youth I professed arms, and was raised by degrees to the highest military rank. I have traversed wide countries at the head of my troops, and seen many battles and sieges. At last, being disgusted by the preferment of a younger officer, and feeling that my vigour was beginning to decay, I resolved to close my life in peace, having found the world full of snares, discord, and misery. I had once escaped from the persuit of the enemy by the shelter of this cavern, and therefore chose it for my final residence. I employed artificers to form it into chambers, and stored it with all that I was likely to want.

"For some time after my retreat, I rejoiced like a tempest-beaten sailor at his entrance into the harbour, being delighted with

---

[12] *enthusiasm:* "A vain belief of private revelation." (Dictionary)

the sudden change of the noise and hurry of war, to stillness and repose. When the pleasure of novelty went away, I employed my hours in examining the plants which grow in the valley, and the minerals which I collected from the rocks. But that enquiry is now grown tasteless and irksome. I have been for some time unsettled and distracted: my mind is disturbed with a thousand perplexities of doubt, and vanities of imagination, which hourly prevail upon me, because I have no opportunities of relaxation or diversion. I am sometimes ashamed to think that I could not secure myself from vice, but by retiring from the exercise of virtue, and begin to suspect that I was rather impelled by resentment, than led by devotion, into solitude. My fancy riots in scenes of folly, and I lament that I have lost so much, and have gained so little. In solitude, if I escape the example of bad men, I want likewise the counsel and conversation of the good. I have been long comparing the evils with the advantages of society, and resolve to return into the world to morrow. The life of a solitary man will be certainly miserable, but not certainly devout."

They heard his resolution with surprise, but, after a short pause, offered to conduct him to Cairo. He dug up a considerable treasure which he had hid among the rocks, and accompanied them to the city, on which, as he approached it, he gazed with rapture.

XXII

THE HAPPINESS OF A LIFE LED ACCORDING TO NATURE

Rasselas went often to an assembly of learned men, who met at stated times to unbend their minds, and compare their opinions. Their manners were somewhat coarse, but their conversation was instructive, and their disputations acute, though sometimes too violent, and often continued till neither controvertist remembered upon what question they began. Some faults were almost general among them: every one was desirous to dictate to the rest, and every one was pleased to hear the genius or knowledge of another depreciated.

In this assembly Rasselas was relating his interview with the hermit, and the wonder with which he heard him censure a course of life which he had so deliberately chosen, and so laudably followed. The sentiments of the hearers were various. Some were of opinion, that the folly of his choice had been[13] justly punished by condemnation to perpetual perseverance. One of the youngest among them, with great vehemence, pronounced him an hypocrite. Some talked of the right of society to the labour of individuals, and considered retirement as a desertion of duty. Others readily allowed, that there was a time when the claims of the publick were satisfied, and when a man might properly sequester himself, to review his life, and purify his heart.

One, who appeared more affected with the narrative than the rest, thought it likely, that the hermit would, in a few years, go back to his retreat, and, perhaps, if shame did not restrain, or death intercept him, return once more from his retreat into the world: "For the hope of happiness, said he, is so strongly impressed, that the longest experience is not able to efface it. Of the present state, whatever it be, we feel, and are forced to confess, the misery, yet, when the same state is again at a distance, imagination paints it as desirable. But the time will surely come, when desire will be no longer our torment, and no man shall be wretched but by his own fault."

"This, said a philosopher, who had heard him with tokens of great impatience, is the present condition of a wise man. The time is already come, when none are wretched but by their own fault. Nothing is more idle, than to inquire after happiness, which nature has kindly placed within our reach. The way to be happy is to live according to nature, in obedience to that universal and unalterable law with which every heart is originally impressed; which is not written on it by precept, but engraven by destiny, not instilled by education, but infused at our nativity. He that lives according to nature will suffer nothing from the delusions of hope, or importunities of desire: he will receive and reject with equability of temper; and act or suffer as the reason of things shall alternately prescribe. Other men may amuse themselves

[13] i.e., would have been.

with subtle definitions, or intricate ra[t]iocination. Let them learn to be wise by easier means: let them observe the hind of the forest, and the linnet of the grove: let them consider the life of animals, whose motions are regulated by instinct; they obey their guide and are happy. Let us therefore, at length, cease to dispute, and learn to live; throw away the incumbrance of precepts, which they who utter them with so much pride and pomp do not understand, and carry with us this simple and intelligible maxim, That deviation from nature is deviation from happiness."

When he had spoken, he looked round him with a placid air, and enjoyed the consciousness of his own beneficence. "Sir, said the prince, with great modesty, as I, like all the rest of mankind, am desirous of felicity, my closest attention has been fixed upon your discourse: I doubt not the truth of a position which a man so learned has so confidently advanced. Let me only know what it is to live according to nature."

"When I find young men so humble and so docile, said the philosopher, I can deny them no information which my studies have enabled me to afford. To live according to nature, is to act always with due regard to the fitness arising from the relations and qualities of causes and effects; to concur with the great and unchangeable scheme of universal felicity; to co-operate with the general disposition and tendency of the present system of things."

The prince soon found that this was one of the sages whom he should understand less as he heard him longer. He therefore bowed and was silent, and the philosopher, supposing him satisfied, and the rest vanquished, rose up and departed with the air of a man that had co-operated with the present system.

XXIII

THE PRINCE AND HIS SISTER DIVIDE BETWEEN THEM THE WORK OF OBSERVATION

Rasselas returned home full of reflexions, doubtful how to direct his future steps. Of the way to happiness he found the learned and simple equally ignorant; but, as he was yet young, he flattered himself that he had time remaining for more experiments, and further enquiries. He communicated to Imlac his observations and his doubts, but was answered by him with new doubts, and remarks that gave him no comfort. He therefore discoursed more frequently and freely with his sister, who had yet the same hope with himself, and always assisted him to give some reason why, through he had been hitherto frustrated, he might succeed at last.

"We have hitherto, said she, known but little of the world: we have never yet been either great or mean. In our own country, though we had royalty, we had no power, and in this we have not yet seen the private recesses of domestick peace. Imlac favours not our search, lest we should in time find him mistaken. We will divide the task between us: you shall try what is to be found in the splendour of courts, and I will range the shades of humbler life. Perhaps command and authority may be the supreme blessings, as they afford most opportunities of doing good: or, perhaps, what this world can give may be found in the modest habitations of middle fortune; too low for great designs, and too high for penury and distress."

XXIV

THE PRINCE EXAMINES THE HAPPINESS OF HIGH STATIONS

Rasselas applauded the design, and appeared next day with a splendid retinue at the court of the Bassa. He was soon distinguished for his magnificence, and admitted, as a prince whose curiosity had brought him from distant countries, to an intimacy with the great officers, and frequent conversation with the Bassa himself.

He was at first inclined to believe, that the man must be pleased with his own condition, whom all approached with reverence, and heard with obedience, and who had the power to extend his edicts to a whole kingdom. "There can be no pleasure, said he, equal to that of feeling at once the joy of thousands all made happy by wise administration. Yet, since, by the law of subordination, this sublime delight can be in one nation but the lot

of one, it is surely reasonable to think that there is some satis-
faction more popular and accessible, and that millions can hardly
be subjected to the will of a single man, only to fill his particular
breast with incommunicable content."

These thoughts were often in his mind, and he found no solu-
tion of the difficulty. But as presents and civilities gained him more
familiarity, he found that almost every man who stood high in
employment hated all the rest, and was hated by them, and that
their lives were a continual succession of plots and detections,
stratagems and escapes, faction and treachery. Many of those, who
surrounded the Bassa, were sent only to watch and report his
conduct; every tongue was muttering censure and every eye was
searching for a fault.

At last the letters of revocation arrived, the Bassa was carried
in chains to Constantinople, and his name was mentioned no
more.

"What are we now to think of the prerogatives of power, said
Rasselas to his sister; is it without any efficacy to good? or, is the
subordinate degree only dangerous, and the supreme safe and
glorious? Is the Sultan the only happy man in his dominions?
or, is the Sultan himself subject to the torments of suspicion, and
the dread of enemies?"

In a short time the second Bassa was deposed. The Sultan, that
had advanced him, was murdered by the Janisaries, and his suc-
cessor had other views and different favourites.

XXV

THE PRINCESS PERSUES HER ENQUIRY WITH MORE DILIGENCE THAN SUCCESS

The princess, in the mean time, insinuated herself into many
families; for there are few doors, through which liberality, joined
with good humour, cannot find its way. The daughters of many
houses were airy[14] and chearful, but Nekayah had been too long

---

[14] *airy:* as equivalent terms, the Dictionary gives "sprightly: vivacious;
lively."

accustomed to the conversation of Imlac and her brother to be much pleased with childish levity and prattle which had no meaning. She found their thoughts narrow, their wishes low, and their merriment often artificial. Their pleasures, poor as they were, could not be preserved pure, but were embittered by petty competitions and worthless emulation. They were always jealous of the beauty of each other; of a quality to which solicitude can add nothing, and from which detraction can take nothing away. Many were in love with triflers like themselves, and many fancied that they were in love when in truth they were only idle. Their affection was seldom fixed on sense or virtue, and therefore seldom ended but in vexation. Their grief, however, like their joy, was transient; every thing floated in their mind unconnected with the past or future, so that one desire easily gave way to another, as a second stone cast into the water effaces and confounds the circles of the first.

With these girls she played as with inoffensive animals, and found them proud of her countenance, and weary of her company.

But her purpose was to examine more deeply, and her affability easily persuaded the hearts that were swelling with sorrow to discharge their secrets in her ear: and those whom hope flattered, or prosperity delighted, often courted her to partake their pleasures.

The princess and her brother commonly met in the evening in a private summer-house on the bank of the Nile, and related to each other the occurrences of the day. As they were sitting together, the princess cast her eyes upon the river that flowed before her. "Answer, said she, great father of waters, thou that rollest thy floods through eighty nations, to the invocations of the daughter of thy native king. Tell me if thou waterest, through all thy course, a single habitation from which thou dost not hear the murmurs of complaint?"

"You are then, said Rasselas, not more successful in private houses than I have been in courts." "I have, since the last partition of our provinces,[15] said the princess, enabled myself to enter

---

[15] *provinces:* "proper offices or business." (Dictionary)

familiarly into many families, where there was the fairest show of prosperity and peace, and know not one house that is not haunted by some fury that destroys its quiet.

"I did not seek ease among the poor, because I concluded that there it could not be found. But I saw many poor whom I had supposed to live in affluence. Poverty has, in large cities, very different appearances: it is often concealed in splendour, and often in extravagance. It is the care of a very great part of mankind to conceal their indigence from the rest: they support themselves by temporary expedients, and every day is lost in contriving for the morrow.

"This, however, was an evil, which, though frequent, I saw with less pain, because I could relieve it. Yet some have refused my bounties; more offended with my quickness to detect their wants, than pleased with my readiness to succour them: and others, whose exigencies compelled them to admit my kindness, have never been able to forgive their benefactress. Many, however, have been sincerely grateful without the ostentation of gratitude, or the hope of other favours."

XXVI

THE PRINCESS CONTINUES HER REMARKS UPON PRIVATE LIFE

Nekayah perceiving her brother's attention fixed, proceeded in her narrative.

"In families, where there is or is not poverty, there is commonly discord: if a kingdom be, as Imlac tells us, a great family, a family likewise is a little kingdom, torn with factions and exposed to revolutions. An unpractised observer expects the love of parents and children to be constant and equal; but this kindness seldom continues beyond the years of infancy: in a short time the children become rivals to their parents. Benefits are allayed[16] by reproaches, and gratitude debased by envy.

---

[16] *allayed*: Johnson admitted both *alloy* and *allay* in much the sense: mixed with baser material. "Gold is allayed with silver and copper."

"Parents and children seldom act in concert: each child endeavours to appropriate the esteem or fondness of the parents, and the parents, with yet less temptation, betray each other to their children; thus some place their confidence in the father, and some in the mother, and, by degrees, the house is filled with artifices and feuds.

"The opinions of children and parents, of the young and the old, are naturally opposite, by the contrary effects of hope and despondence, of expectation and experience, without crime or folly on either side. The colours of life in youth and age appear different, as the face of nature in spring and winter. And how can children credit the assertions of parents, which their own eyes show them to be false?

"Few parents act in such a manner as much to enforce their maxims by the credit of their lives. The old man trusts wholly to slow contrivance and gradual progression: the youth expects to force his way by genius, vigour, and precipitance. The old man pays regard to riches, and the youth reverences virtue. The old man deifies prudence: the youth commits himself to magnanimity and chance. The young man, who intends no ill, believes that none is intended, and therefore acts with openness and candour: but his father, having suffered the injuries of fraud, is impelled to suspect, and too often allured to practice it. Age looks with anger on the temerity of youth, and youth with contempt on the scrupulosity of age. Thus parents and children, for the greatest part, live on to love less and less: and, if those whom nature has thus closely united are the torments of each other, where shall we look for tenderness and consolation?"

"Surely, said the prince, you must have been unfortunate in your choice of acquaintance: I am unwilling to believe, that the most tender of all relations is thus impeded in its effects by natural necessity."

"Domestick discord, answered she, is not inevitably and fatally necessary; but yet is not easily avoided. We seldom see that a whole family is virtuous: the good and evil cannot well agree; and the evil can yet less agree with one another: even the virtuous fall sometimes to variance, when their virtues are of different kinds, and tending to extremes.[17] In general, those parents have most reverence who most deserve it: for he that lives well cannot be despised.

"Many other evils infest private life. Some are the slaves of servants whom they have trusted with their affairs. Some are kept in continual anxiety to the caprice of rich relations, whom they cannot please, and dare not offend. Some husbands are imperious, and some wives perverse: and, as it is always more easy to do evil than good, though the wisdom or virtue of one can very rarely make many happy, the folly or vice of one may often make many miserable."

"If such be the general effect of marriage, said the prince, I shall, for the future, think it dangerous to connect my interest with that of another, lest I should be unhappy by my partner's fault."

"I have met, said the princess, with many who live single for that reason; but I never found that their prudence ought to raise envy. They dream away their time without friendship, without fondness, and are driven to rid themselves of the day, for which they have no use, by childish amusements, or vicious delights. They act as beings under the constant sense of some known inferiority, that fills their minds with rancour, and their tongues with censure. They are peevish at home, and malevolent abroad; and, as the out-laws of human nature, make it their business and their pleasure to disturb that society which debars them from its privileges. To live without feeling or exciting sympathy, to be fortunate without adding to the felicity of others, or afflicted without tasting the balm of pity, is a state more gloomy than solitude: it is not retreat but exclusion from mankind. Marriage has many pains, but celibacy has no pleasures."

"What then is to be done? said Rasselas; the more we enquire, the less we can resolve. Surely he is most likely to please himself that has no other inclination to regard."

[17] Johnson once remarked to Boswell that altercation was more likely to arise between those who were "good different ways," who differed in the color of their virtue, than between good men and bad.

XXVII

DISQUISITION UPON GREATNESS

The conversation had a short pause. The prince, having considered his sister's observations, told her, that she had surveyed life with prejudice, and supposed misery where she did not find it. "Your narrative, says he, throws yet a darker gloom upon the prospects of futurity: the predictions of Imlac were but faint sketches of the evils painted by Nekayah. I have been lately convinced that quiet is not the daughter of grandeur, or of power: that her presence is not to be bought by wealth, nor enforced by conquest. It is evident, that as any man acts in a wider compass, he must be more exposed to opposition from enmity or miscarriage from chance; whoever has many to please or to govern, must use the ministry of many agents, some of whom will be wicked, and some ignorant; by some he will be misled, and by others betrayed. If he gratifies one he will offend another: those that are not favoured will think themselves injured; and, since favours can be conferred but upon few, the greater number will be always discontented."

"The discontent, said the princess, which is thus unreasonable, I hope that I shall always have spirit to despise, and you, power to repress."

"Discontent, answered Rasselas, will not always be without reason under the most just or vigilant administration of publick affairs. None, however attentive, can always discover that merit which indigence or faction may happen to obscure; and none, however powerful, can always reward it. Yet, he that sees inferiour desert advanced above him, will naturally impute that preference to partiality or caprice; and, indeed, it can scarcely be hoped that any man, however magnanimous by nature, or exalted by condition, will be able to persist for ever in fixed and inexorable justice of distribution: he will sometimes indulge his own affections, and sometimes those of his favourites; he will permit some to please him who can never serve him; he will discover in those whom he loves qualities which in reality they do not possess; and to those, from whom he receives pleasure, he will in his turn endeavour to give it. Thus will recommendations sometimes prevail which were purchased by money, or by the more destructive bribery of flattery and servility.

"He that has much to do will do something wrong, and of that wrong must suffer the consequences; and, if it were possible that he should always act rightly, yet when such numbers are to judge of his conduct, the bad will censure and obstruct him by malevolence, and the good sometimes by mistake.

"The highest stations cannot therefore hope to be the abodes of happiness, which I would willingly believe to have fled from thrones and palaces to seats of humble privacy and placid obscurity. For what can hinder the satisfaction, or intercept the expectations, of him whose abilities are adequate to his employments, who sees with his own eyes the whole circuit of his influence, who chooses by his own knowledge all whom he trusts, and whom none are tempted to deceive by hope or fear? Surely he has nothing to do but to love and to be loved, to be virtuous and to be happy."

"Whether perfect happiness would be procured by perfect goodness, said Nekayah, this world will never afford an opportunity of deciding. But this, at least, may be maintained, that we do not always find visible happiness in proportion to visible virtue. All natural and almost all political evils, are incident alike to the bad and good: they are confounded in the misery of a famine, and not much distinguished in the fury of a faction; they sink together in a tempest, and are driven together from their country by invaders. All that virtue can afford is quietness of conscience, a steady prospect of a happier state; this may enable us to endure calamity with patience; but remember that patience must suppose pain."

XXVIII

RASSELAS AND NEKAYAH CONTINUE THEIR CONVERSATION

"Dear princess, said Rasselas, you fall into the common errours of exaggeratory declamation, by producing, in a familiar disquisition, examples of national calamities, and scenes of extensive misery, which are found in books rather than in the world, and which, as they are horrid, are ordained to be rare. Let us not imagine evils which we do not feel, nor injure life by misrepresentations. I cannot bear that quer[u]lous eloquence which threatens every city with a siege like that of Jerusalem, that makes famine attend on every flight of locusts, and suspends pestilence on the wing of every blast that issues from the south.

"On necessary and inevitable evils, which overwhelm kingdoms at once, all disputation is vain: when they happen they must be endured. But it is evident, that these bursts of universal distress are more dreaded than felt: thousands and ten thousands flourish in youth, and wither in age, without the knowledge of any other than domestick evils, and share the same pleasures and vexations whether their kings are mild or cruel, whether the armies of their country persue their enemies, or retreat before them. While courts are disturbed with intestine competitions, and ambassadours are negotiating in foreign countries, the smith still plies his anvil, and the husbandman drives his plow forward; the necessaries of life are required and obtained, and the successive business of the seasons continues to make its wonted revolutions.

"Let us cease to consider what, perhaps, may never happen, and what, when it shall happen, will laugh at human speculation. We will not endeavour to modify the motions of the elements, or to fix the destiny of kingdoms. It is our business to consider what beings like us may perform; each labouring for his own happiness, by promoting within his circle, however narrow, the happiness of others.

"Marriage is evidently the dictate of nature; men and women were made to be companions of each other, and therefore I cannot be persuaded but that marriage is one of the means of happiness."

"I know not, said the princess, whether marriage be more than one of the innumerable modes of human misery. When I see and reckon the various forms of connubial infelicity, the unexpected causes of lasting discord, the diversities of temper, the oppositions of opinion, the rude collisions of contrary desire where both are urged by violent impulses, the obstinate contests of disagreeing virtues, where both are supported by consciousness of good intention, I am sometimes disposed to think with the severer casuists[18] of most nations, that marriage is rather permitted than approved, and that none, but by the instigation of a passion too much indulged, entangle themselves with indissoluble compacts."

"You seem to forget, replied Rasselas, that you have, even now, represented celibacy as less happy than marriage. Both conditions may be bad, but they cannot both be worst. Thus it happens when wrong opinions are entertained, that they mutually destroy each other, and leave the mind open to truth."

"I did not expect, answered the princess, to hear that imputed to falsehood which is the consequence only of frailty. To the mind, as to the eye, it is difficult to compare with exactness objects vast in their extent, and various in their parts. Where we see or conceive the whole at once we readily note the discriminations and decide the preference: but of two systems, of which neither can be surveyed by any human being in its full compass of magnitude and multiplicity of complication, where is the wonder, that judging of the whole by parts, I am alternately affected by one and the other as either presses on my memory or fancy? We differ from ourselves just as we differ from each other, when we see only part of the question, as in the multifarious relations of politicks and morality: but when we perceive the whole at once, as in numerical computations, all agree in one judgment, and none ever varies his opinion."

"Let us not add, said the prince, to the other evils of life, the bitterness of controversy, nor endeavour to vie with each other in subtilties of argument. We are employed in a search, of which both are equally to enjoy the success, or suffer by the miscarriage. It is therefore fit that we assist each other. You surely conclude too hastily from the infelicity of marriage against its institution; will not the misery of life prove equally that life cannot be the gift of heaven? The world must be peopled by marriage, or peopled without it."

"How the world is to be peopled, returned Nekayah, is not my

[18] *casuists;* a casuist is "one that studies and settles cases of conscience." (Dictionary)

care, and needs not be yours. I see no danger that the present generation should omit to leave successors behind them: we are not now enquiring for the world, but for ourselves."

XXIX

THE DEBATE ON MARRIAGE CONTINUED

"The good of the whole, says Rasselas, is the same with the good of all its parts. If marriage be best for mankind it must be evidently best for individuals, or a permanent and necessary duty must be the cause of evil, and some must be inevitably sacrificed to the convenience of others. In the estimate which you have made of the two states, it appears that the incommodities of a single life are, in a great measure, necessary and certain, but those of the conjugal state accidental and avoidable.

"I cannot forbear to flatter myself that prudence and benevolence will make marriage happy. The general folly of mankind is the cause of general complaint. What can be expected but disappointment and repentance from a choice made in the immaturity of youth, in the ardour of desire, without judgment, without foresight, without enquiry after conformity of opinions, similarity of manners, rectitude of judgment, or purity of sentiment.

"Such is the common process of marriage. A youth and maiden meeting by chance, or brought together by artifice, exchange glances, reciprocate civilities, go home, and dream of one another. Having little to divert attention, or diversify thought, they find themselves uneasy when they are apart, and therefore conclude that they shall be happy together. They marry, and discover what nothing but voluntary blindness had before concealed; they wear out life in altercations, and charge nature with cruelty.

"From those early marriages proceeds likewise the rivalry of parents and children: the son is eager to enjoy the world before the father is willing to forsake it, and there is hardly room at once for two generations. The daughter begins to bloom before the mother can be content to fade, and neither can forbear to wish for the absence of the other.

"Surely all these evils may be avoided by that deliberation and delay which prudence prescribes to irrevocable choice. In the variety and jollity of youthful pleasures life may be well enough supported without the help of a partner. Longer time will increase experience, and wider views will allow better opportunities of enquiry and selection: one advantage, at least, will be certain; the parents will be visibly older than their children."

"What reason cannot collect, said Nekayah, and what experiment has not yet taught, can be known only from the report of others. I have been told that late marriages are not eminently happy. This is a question too important to be neglected, and I have often proposed it to those, whose accuracy of remark, and comprehensiveness of knowledge, made their suffrages worthy of regard. They have generally determined, that it is dangerous for a man and woman to suspend their fate upon each other, at a time when opinions are fixed, and habits are established; when friendships have been contracted on both sides, when life has been planned into method, and the mind has long enjoyed the contemplation of its own prospects.

"It is scarcely possible that two travelling through the world under the conduct of chance, should have been both directed to the same path, and it will not often happen that either will quit the track which custom has made pleasing. When the desultory levity of youth has settled into regularity, it is soon succeeded by pride ashamed to yield, or obstinacy delighting to contend. And even though mutual esteem produces mutual desire to please, time itself, as it modifies unchangeably the external mien, determines likewise the direction of the passions, and gives an inflexible rigidity to the manners. Long customs are not easily broken: he that attempts to change the course of his own life, very often labours in vain; and how shall we do that for others which we are seldom able to do for ourselves?"

"But surely, interposed the prince, you suppose the chief motive of choice forgotten or neglected. Whenever I shall seek a wife, it shall be my first question, whether she be willing to be led by reason?"

"Thus it is, said Nekayah, that philosophers are deceived. There

are a thousand familiar disputes which reason never can decide;
questions that elude investigation, and make logick ridiculous;
cases where something must be done, and where little can be said.
Consider the state of mankind, and enquire how few can be sup-
posed to act upon any occasions, whether small or great, with all
the reasons of action present to their minds. Wretched would be
the pair above all names of wretchedness, who should be doomed
to adjust by reason every morning all the minute detail of a do-
mestick day.

"Those who marry at an advanced age, will probably escape the
encroachments of their children; but, in diminution of this ad-
vantage, they will be likely to leave them, ignorant and helpless,
to a guardian's mercy: or, if that should not happen, they must at
least go out of the world before they see those whom they love
best either wise or great.

"From their children, if they have less to fear, they have less
also to hope, and they lose, without equivalent, the joys of early
love, and the convenience of uniting with manners pliant, and
minds susceptible of new impressions, which might wear away
their dissimilitudes by long cohabitation, as soft bodies, by con-
tinual attrition, conform their surfaces to each other.

"I believe it will be found that those who marry late are best
pleased with their children, and those who marry early with their
partners."

"The union of these two affections, said Rasselas, would pro-
duce all that could be wished. Perhaps there is a time when mar-
riage might unite them, a time neither too early for the father,
nor too late for the husband."

"Every hour, answered the princess, confirms my prejudice in
favour of the position so often uttered by the mouth of Imlac,
'That nature sets her gifts on the right hand and on the left.'
Those conditions, which flatter hope and attract desire, are so
constituted, that, as we approach one, we recede from another.
There are goods so opposed that we cannot seize both, but, by too
much prudence, may pass between them at too great a distance to
reach either. This is often the fate of long consideration; he does
nothing who endeavours to do more than is allowed to humanity.

Flatter not yourself with contrarieties of pleasure. Of the blessings set before you make your choice, and be content. No man can taste the fruits of autumn while he is delighting his scent with the flowers of the spring: no man can, at the same time, fill his cup from the source and from the mouth of the Nile."

XXX

IMLAC ENTERS, AND CHANGES THE CONVERSATION

Here Imlac entered, and interrupted them. "Imlac, said Rasselas, I have been taking from the princess the dismal history of private life, and am almost discouraged from further search."

"It seems to me, said Imlac, that while you are making the choice of life, you neglect to live. You wander about a single city, which, however large and diversified, can now afford few novelties, and forget that you are in a country, famous among the earliest monarchies for the power and wisdom of its inhabitants; a country where the sciences first dawned that illuminate the world, and beyond which the arts cannot be traced of civil society or domestick life.

"The old Egyptians have left behind them monuments of industry and power before which all European magnificence is confessed to fade away. The ruins of their architecture are the schools of modern builders, and from the wonders which time has spared we may conjecture, though uncertainly, what it has destroyed."

"My curiosity, said Rasselas, does not very strongly lead me to survey piles of stone, or mounds of earth; my business is with man. I came hither not to measure fragments of temples, or trace choaked aqueducts, but to look upon the various scenes of the present world."

"The things that are now before us, said the princess, require attention, and deserve it. What have I to do with the heroes or the monuments of ancient times? with times which never can return, and heroes, whose form of life was different from all that the present condition of mankind requires or allows."

"To know any thing, returned the poet, we must know its

effects; to see men we must see their works, that we may learn what reason has dictated, or passion has incited, and find what are the most powerful motives of action. To judge rightly of the present we must oppose it to the past; for all judgment is comparative, and of the future nothing can be known. The truth is, that no mind is much employed upon the present: recollection and anticipation fill up almost all our moments. Our passions are joy and grief, love and hatred, hope and fear. Of joy and grief the past is the object, and the future of hope and fear; even love and hatred respect the past, for the cause must have been before the effect.

"The present state of things is the consequence of the former, and it is natural to inquire what were the sources of the good that we enjoy, or of the evil that we suffer. If we act only for ourselves, to neglect the study of history is not prudent: if we are entrusted with the care of others, it is not just. Ignorance, when it is voluntary, is criminal; and he may properly be charged with evil who refused to learn how he might prevent it.

"There is no part of history so generally useful as that which relates the progress of the human mind, the gradual improvement of reason, the successive advances of science, the vicissitudes of learning and ignorance, which are the light and darkness of thinking beings, the extinction and resuscitation of arts, and all the revolutions of the intellectual world. If accounts of battles and invasions are peculiarly the business of princes, the useful or elegant arts are not to be neglected; those who have kingdoms to govern, have understandings to cultivate.

"Example is always more efficacious than precept. A soldier is formed in war, and a painter must copy pictures. In this, contemplative life has the advantage: great actions are seldom seen, but the labours of art are always at hand for those who desire to know what art has been able to perform.

"When the eye or the imagination is struck with any uncommon work the next transition of an active mind is to the means by which it was performed. Here begins the true use of such contemplation; we enlarge our comprehension by new ideas, and perhaps recover some art lost to mankind, or learn what is less perfectly known in our own country. At least we compare our own with former times, and either rejoice at our improvements, or, what is the first motion towards good, discover our defects."

"I am willing, said the prince, to see all that can deserve my search." "And I, said the princess, shall rejoice to learn something of the manners of antiquity."

"The most pompous monument of Egyptian greatness, and one of the most bulky works of manual industry, said Imlac, are the pyramids; fabricks raised before the time of history, and of which the earliest narratives afford us only uncertain traditions. Of these the greatest is still standing, very little injured by time."

"Let us visit them to morrow, said Nekayah. I have often heard of the Pyramids, and shall not rest, till I have seen them within and without with my own eyes."

XXXI

THEY VISIT THE PYRAMIDS

The resolution being thus taken, they set out the next day. They laid tents upon their camels, being resolved to stay among the pyramids till their curiosity was fully satisfied. They travelled gently, turned aside to every thing remarkable, stopped from time to time and conversed with the inhabitants, and observed the various appearances of towns, ruined and inhabited, of wild and cultivated nature.

When they came to the great pyramid they were astonished at the extent of the base, and the height of the top. Imlac explained to them the principles upon which the pyramidal form was chosen for a fabrick intended to co-extend its duration with that of the world: he showed that its gradual diminution gave it such stability, as defeated all the common attacks of the elements, and could scarcely be overthrown by earthquakes themselves, the least resistible of natural violence. A concussion that should shatter the pyramid would threaten the dissolution of the continent.

They measured all its dimensions, and pitched their tents at its foot. Next day they prepared to enter its interiour apartments, and having hired the common guides climbed up to the first passage, when the favourite of the princess, looking into the cavity, stepped back and trembled. "Pekuah, said the princess, of what art thou afraid?" "Of the narrow entrance, answered the lady, and of the dreadful gloom. I dare not enter a place which must surely be inhabited by unquiet souls. The original possessors of these dreadful vaults will start up before us, and, perhaps, shut us in for ever." She spoke, and threw her arms round the neck of her mistress.

"If all your fear be of apparitions, said the prince, I will promise you safety: there is no danger from the dead; he that is once buried will be seen no more."

"That the dead are seen no more, said Imlac, I will not undertake to maintain against the concurrent and unvaried testimony of all ages, and of all nations. There is no people, rude or learned, among whom apparitions of the dead are not related and believed. This opinion, which, perhaps, prevails as far as human nature is diffused, could become universal only by its truth: those, that never heard of one another, would not have agreed in a tale which nothing but experience can make credible. That it is doubted by single cavillers can very little weaken the general evidence, and some who deny it with their tongues confess it by their fears.

"Yet I do not mean to add new terrours to those which have already seized upon Pekuah. There can be no reason why spectres should haunt the pyramid more than other places, or why they should have power or will to hurt innocence and purity. Our entrance is no violation of their priviledges; we can take nothing from them, how then can we offend them?"

"My dear Pekuah, said the princess, I will always go before you, and Imlac shall follow you. Remember that you are the companion of the princess of Abissinia."

"If the princess is pleased that her servant should die, returned the lady, let her command some death less dreadful than enclosure in this horrid cavern. You know I dare not disobey you: I must go if you command me; but, if I once enter, I never shall come back."

The princess saw that her fear was too strong for expostulation or reproof, and embracing her, told her that she should stay in the tent till their return. Pekuah was yet not satisfied, but entreated the princess not to persue so dreadful a purpose as that of entering the recesses of the pyramid. "Though I cannot teach courage, said Nekayah, I must not learn cowardise; nor leave at last undone what I came hither only to do."

XXXII

THEY ENTER THE PYRAMID

Pekuah descended to the tents, and the rest entered the pyramid: they passed through the galleries, surveyed the vaults of marble, and examined the chest in which the body of the founder is supposed to have been reposited. They then sat down in one of the most spacious chambers to rest a while before they attempted to return.

"We have now, said Imlac, gratified our minds with an exact view of the greatest work of man, except the wall of China.

"Of the wall it is very easy to assign the motives. It secured a wealthy and timorous nation from the incursions of Barbarians, whose unskilfulness in arts made it easier for them to supply their wants by rapine than by industry, and who from time to time poured in upon the habitations of peaceful commerce, as vultures descend upon domestick fowl. Their celerity and fierceness made the wall necessary, and their ignorance made it efficacious.

"But for the pyramids no reason has ever been given adequate to the cost and labour of the work. The narrowness of the chambers proves that it could afford no retreat from enemies, and treasures might have been reposited at far less expence with equal security. It seems to have been erected only in compliance with that hunger of imagination which preys incessantly upon life, and must be always appeased by some employment. Those who have already all that they can enjoy, must enlarge their desires. He that has built for use, till use is supplied, must begin to build for vanity, and extend his plan to the utmost power of human performance, that he may not be soon reduced to form another wish.

"I consider this mighty structure as a monument of the insufficiency of human enjoyments. A king, whose power is unlimited, and whose treasures surmount all real and imaginary wants, is compelled to solace, by the erection of a pyramid, the satiety of dominion and tasteles[s]ness of pleasures, and to amuse the tediousness of declining life, by seeing thousands labouring without end, and one stone, for no purpose, laid upon another. Whoever thou art, that, not content with a moderate condition, imaginest happiness in royal magnificence, and dreamest that command or riches can feed the appetite of novelty with perpetual gratifications, survey the pyramids, and confess thy folly!"

XXXIII

THE PRINCESS MEETS WITH AN UNEXPECTED MISFORTUNE

They rose up, and returned through the cavity at which they had entered, and the princess prepared for her favourite a long narrative of dark labyrinths, and costly rooms, and of the different impressions which the varieties of the way had made upon her. But, when they came to their train, they found every one silent and dejected: the men discovered shame and fear in their countenances, and the women were weeping in the tents.

What had happened they did not try to conjecture, but immediately enquired. "You had scarcely entered into the pyramid, said one of the attendants, when a troop of Arabs rushed upon us: we were too few to resist them, and too slow to escape. They were about to search the tents, set us on our camels, and drive us along before them, when the approach of some Turkish horsemen put them to flight; but they seized the lady Pekuah with her two maids, and carried them away: the Turks are now persuing them by our instigation, but I fear they will not be able to overtake them."

The princess was overpowered with surprise and grief. Rasselas, in the first heat of his resentment, ordered his servants to follow him, and prepared to persue the robbers with his sabre in his hand. "Sir, said Imlac, what can you hope from violence or valour?

the Arabs are mounted on horses trained to battle and retreat; we have only beasts of burden. By leaving our present station we may lose the princess, but cannot hope to regain Pekuah."

In a short time the Turks returned, having not been able to reach the enemy. The princess burst out into new lamentations, and Rasselas could scarcely forbear to reproach them with cowardice; but Imlac was of opinion, that the escape of the Arabs was no addition to their misfortune, for, perhaps, they would have killed their captives rather than have resigned them.

XXXIV

THEY RETURN TO CAIRO WITHOUT PEKUAH

There was nothing to be hoped from longer stay. They returned to Cairo repenting of their curiosity, censuring the negligence of the government, lamenting their own rashness which had neglected to procure a guard, imagining many expedients by which the loss of Pekuah might have been prevented, and resolving to do something for her recovery, though none could find any thing proper to be done.

Nekayah retired to her chamber, where her women attempted to comfort her, by telling her that all had their troubles, and that lady Pekuah had enjoyed much happiness in the world for a long time, and might reasonably expect a change of fortune. They hoped that some good would befal her wheresoever she was, and that their mistress would find another friend who might supply her place.

The princess made them no answer, and they continued the form of condolence, not much grieved in their hearts that the favourite was lost.

Next day the prince presented to the Bassa a memorial of the wrong which he had suffered, and a petition for redress. The Bassa threatened to punish the robbers, but did not attempt to catch them, nor, indeed, could any account or description be given by which he might direct the persuit.

It soon appeared that nothing would be done by authority.

Governors, being accustomed to hear of more crimes than they can punish, and more wrongs than they can redress, set themselves at ease by indiscriminate negligence, and presently forget the request when they lose sight of the petitioner.

Imlac then endeavoured to gain some intelligence by private agents. He found many who pretended to an exact knowledge of all the haunts of the Arabs, and to regular correspondence with their chiefs, and who readily undertook the recovery of Pekuah. Of these, some were furnished with money for their journey, and came back no more; some were liberally paid for accounts which a few days discovered to be false. But the princess would not suffer any means, however improbable, to be left untried. While she was doing something she kept her hope alive. As one expedient failed, another was suggested; when one messenger returned unsuccessful, another was despatched to a different quarter.

Two months had now passed, and of Pekuah nothing had been heard; the hopes which they had endeavoured to raise in each other grew more languid, and the princess, when she saw nothing more to be tried, sunk down inconsolable in hopeless dejection. A thousand times she reproached herself with the easy compliance by which she permitted her favourite to stay behind her. "Had not my fondness, said she, lessened my authority, Pekuah had not dared to talk of her terrours. She ought to have feared me more than spectres. A severe look would have overpowered her; a peremptory command would have compelled obedience. Why did foolish indulgence prevail upon me? Why did I not speak and refuse to hear?"

"Great princess, said Imlac, do not reproach yourself for your virtue, or consider that as blameable by which evil has accidentally been caused. Your tenderness for the timidity of Pekuah was generous and kind. When we act according to our duty, we commit the event to him by whose laws our actions are governed, and who will suffer none to be finally punished for obedience. When, in prospect of some good, whether natural or moral, we break the rules prescribed us, we withdraw from the direction of superiour wisdom, and take all consequences upon ourselves. Man cannot so far know the connexion of causes and events, as that he may venture to do wrong in order to do right. When we persue our end by lawful means, we may always console our miscarriage by the hope of future recompense. When we consult only our own policy, and attempt to find a nearer way to good, by overleaping the settled boundaries of right and wrong, we cannot be happy even by success, because we cannot escape the consciousness of our fault; but, if we miscarry, the disappointment is irremediably embittered. How comfortless is the sorrow of him, who feels at once the pangs of guilt, and the vexation of calamity which guilt has brought upon him?

"Consider, princess, what would have been your condition, if the lady Pekuah had entreated to accompany you, and, being compelled to stay in the tents, had been carried away; or how would you have born the thought, if you had forced her into the pyramid, and she had died before you in agonies of terrour."

"Had either happened, said Nekayah, I could not have endured life till now: I should have been tortured to madness by the remembrance of such cruelty, or must have pined away in abhorrence of myself."

"This at least, said Imlac, is the present reward of virtuous conduct, that no unlucky consequence can oblige us to repent it."

XXXV

THE PRINCESS LANGUISHES FOR WANT OF PEKUAH

Nekayah, being thus reconciled to herself, found that no evil is insupportable but that which is accompanied with consciousness of wrong. She was, from that time, delivered from the violence of tempestuous sorrow, and sunk into silent pensiveness and gloomy tranquillity. She sat from morning to evening recollecting all that had been done or said by her Pekuah, treasured up with care every trifle on which Pekuah had set an accidental value, and which might recal to mind any little incident or careless conversation. The sentiments of her, whom she now expected to see no more, were treasured in her memory as rules of life, and she deliberated to no other end than to conjecture on any occasion what would have been the opinion and counsel of Pekuah.

The women, by whom she was attended, knew nothing of her real condition, and therefore she could not talk to them but with caution and reserve. She began to remit her curiosity, having no great care to collect notions which she had no convenience of uttering. Rasselas endeavoured first to comfort and afterwards to divert her; he hired musicians, to whom she seemed to listen, but did not hear them, and procured masters to instruct her in various arts, whose lectures, when they visited her again, were again to be repeated. She had lost her taste of pleasure and her ambition of excellence. And her mind, though forced into short excursions, always recurred to the image of her friend.

Imlac was every morning earnestly enjoined to renew his enquiries, and was asked every night whether he had yet heard of Pekuah, till not being able to return the princess the answer that she desired, he was less and less willing to come into her presence. She observed his backwardness, and commanded him to attend her. "You are not, said she, to confound impatience with resentment, or to suppose that I charge you with negligence, because I repine at your unsuccessfulness. I do not much wonder at your absence; I know that the unhappy are never pleasing, and that all naturally avoid the contagion of misery. To hear complaints is wearisome alike to the wretched and the happy; for who would cloud by adventitious grief the short gleams of gaiety which life allows us? or who, that is struggling under his own evils, will add to them the miseries of another?

"The time is at hand, when none shall be disturbed any longer by the sighs of Nekayah: my search after happiness is now at an end. I am resolved to retire from the world with all its flatteries and deceits, and will hide myself in solitude, without any other care than to compose my thoughts, and regulate my hours by a constant succession of innocent occupations, till, with a mind purified from all earthly desires, I shall enter into that state, to which all are hastening, and in which I hope again to enjoy the friendship of Pekuah."

"Do not entangle your mind, said Imlac, by irrevocable determinations, nor increase the burthen of life by a voluntary accumulation of misery: the weariness of retirement will continue or increase when the loss of Pekuah is forgotten. That you have been deprived of one pleasure is no very good reason for rejection of the rest."

"Since Pekuah was taken from me, said the princess, I have no pleasure to reject or to retain. She that has no one to love or trust has little to hope. She wants the radical principle of happiness. We may, perhaps, allow that what satisfaction this world can afford, must arise from the conjunction of wealth, knowledge and goodness: wealth is nothing but as it is bestowed, and knowledge nothing but as it is communicated: they must therefore be imparted to others, and to whom could I now delight to impart them? Goodness affords the only comfort which can be enjoyed without a partner, and goodness may be practised in retirement."

"How far solitude may admit goodness, or advance it, I shall not, replied Imlac, dispute at present. Remember the confession of the pious hermit. You will wish to return into the world, when the image of your companion has left your thoughts." "That time, said Nekayah, will never come. The generous frankness, the modest obsequiousness, and the faithful secrecy of my dear Pekuah, will always be more missed, as I shall live longer to see vice and folly."

"The state of a mind oppressed with a sudden calamity, said Imlac, is like that of the fabulous inhabitants of the new created earth, who, when the first night came upon them, supposed that day never would return. When the clouds of sorrow gather over us, we see nothing beyond them, nor can imagine how they will be dispelled: yet a new day succeeded to the night, and sorrow is never long without a dawn of ease. But they who restrain themselves from receiving comfort, do as the savages would have done, had they put out their eyes when it was dark. Our minds, like our bodies, are in continual flux; something is hourly lost, and something acquired. To lose much at once is inconvenient to either, but while the vital powers remain uninjured, nature will find the means of reparation. Distance has the same effect on the mind as on the eye, and while we glide along the stream of time, whatever we leave behind us is always lessening, and that which we approach increasing in magnitude. Do not suffer life to stagnate; it will grow muddy for want of motion: commit yourself again to the current of the world; Pekuah will vanish by degrees; you will meet in your way some other favourite, or learn to diffuse yourself in general conversation."

"At least, said the prince, do not despair before all remedies have been tried: the enquiry after the unfortunate lady is still continued, and shall be carried on with yet greater diligence, on condition that you will promise to wait a year for the event, without any unalterable resolution."

Nekayah thought this a reasonable demand, and made the promise to her brother, who had been advised by Imlac to require it. Imlac had, indeed, no great hope of regaining Pekuah, but he supposed, that if he could secure the interval of a year, the princess would be then in no danger of a cloister.

XXXVI

PEKUAH IS STILL REMEMBERED. THE PROGRESS OF SORROW

Nekayah, seeing that nothing was omitted for the recovery of her favourite, and having, by her promise, set her intention of retirement at a distance, began imperceptibly to return to common cares and common pleasures. She rejoiced without her own consent at the suspension of her sorrows, and sometimes caught herself with indignation in the act of turning away her mind from the remembrance of her, whom yet she resolved never to forget.

She then appointed a certain hour of the day for meditation on the merits and fondness of Pekuah, and for some weeks retired constantly at the time fixed, and returned with her eyes swollen and her countenance clouded. By degrees she grew less scrupulous, and suffered any important and pressing avocation to delay the tribute of daily tears. She then yielded to less occasions; sometimes forgot what she was indeed afraid to remember, and, at last, wholly released herself from the duty of periodical affliction.

Her real love of Pekuah was yet not diminished. A thousand

occurrences brought her back to memory, and a thousand wants, which nothing but the confidence of friendship can supply, made her frequently regretted. She, therefore, solicited Imlac never to desist from enquiry, and to leave no art of intelligence untried, that, at least, she might have the comfort of knowing that she did not suffer by negligence or sluggishness. "Yet what, said she, is to be expected from our persuit of happiness, when we find the state of life to be such, that happiness itself is the cause of misery? Why should we endeavour to attain that, of which the possession cannot be secured? I shall henceforward fear to yield my heart to excellence, however bright, or to fondness, however tender, lest I should lose again what I have lost in Pekuah."

XXXVII

THE PRINCESS HEARS NEWS OF PEKUAH

In seven months, one of the messengers, who had been sent away upon the day when the promise was drawn from the princess, returned, after many unsuccessful rambles, from the borders of Nubia, with an account that Pekuah was in the hands of an Arab chief, who possessed a castle or fortress on the extremity of Egypt. The Arab, whose revenue was plunder, was willing to restore her, with her two attendants, for two hundred ounces of gold.

The price was no subject of debate. The princess was in extasies when she heard that her favourite was alive, and might so cheaply be ransomed. She could not think of delaying for a moment Pekuah's happiness or her own, but entreated her brother to send back the messenger with the sum required. Imlac, being consulted, was not very confident of the veracity of the relator, and was still more doubtful of the Arab's faith, who might, if he were too liberally trusted, detain at once the money and the captives. He thought it dangerous to put themselves in the power of the Arab, by going into his district, and could not expect that the Rover would so much expose himself as to come into the lower country, where he might be seized by the forces of the Bassa.

It is difficult to negotiate where neither will trust. But Imlac, after some deliberation, directed the messenger to propose that Pekuah should be conducted by ten horsemen to the monastry of St. Anthony, which is situated in the deserts of Upper-Egypt, where she should be met by the same number, and her ransome should be paid.

That no time might be lost, as they expected that the proposal would not be refused, they immediately began their journey to the monastry; and, when they arrived, Imlac went forward with the former messenger to the Arab's fortress. Rasselas was desirous to go with them, but neither his sister nor Imlac would consent. The Arab, according to the custom of his nation, observed the laws of hospitality with great exactness to those who put themselves into his power, and, in a few days, brought Pekuah with her maids, by easy journeys, to their place appointed, where receiving the stipulated price, he restored her with great respect to liberty and her friends, and undertook to conduct them back towards Cairo beyond all danger of robbery or violence.

The princess and her favourite embraced each other with transport too violent to be expressed, and went out together to pour the tears of tenderness in secret, and exchange professions of kindness and gratitude. After a few hours they returned into the refectory of the convent, where, in the presence of the prior and his brethren, the prince required of Pekuah the history of her adventures.

XXXVIII

THE ADVENTURES OF THE LADY PEKUAH

"At what time, and in what manner, I was forced away, said Pekuah, your servants have told you. The suddenness of the event struck me with surprise, and I was at first rather stupified than agitated with any passion of either fear or sorrow. My confusion was encreased by the speed and tumult of our flight while we were followed by the Turks, who, as it seemed, soon despaired to overtake us, or were afraid of those whom they made a shew of menacing.

"When the Arabs saw themselves out of danger they slackened their course, and, as I was less harassed by external violence, I began to feel more uneasiness in my mind. After some time we stopped near a spring shaded with trees in a pleasant meadow, where we were set upon the ground, and offered such refreshments as our masters were partaking. I was suffered to sit with my maids apart from the rest, and none attempted to comfort or insult us. Here I first began to feel the full weight of my misery. The girls sat weeping in silence, and from time to time looked on me for succour. I knew not to what condition we were doomed, nor could conjecture where would be the place of our captivity, or whence to draw any hope of deliverance. I was in the hands of robbers and savages, and had no reason to suppose that their pity was more than their justice, or that they would forbear the gratification of any ardour of desire, or caprice of cruelty. I, however, kissed my maids, and endeavoured to pacify them by remarking, that we were yet treated with decency, and that, since we were now carried beyond persuit, there was no danger of violence to our lives.

"When we were to be set again on horseback, my maids clung round me, and refused to be parted, but I commanded them not to irritate those who had us in their power. We travelled the remaining part of the day through an unfrequented and pathless country, and came by moonlight to the side of a hill, where the rest of the troop was stationed. Their tents were pitched, and their fires kindled, and our chief was welcomed as a man much beloved by his dependants.

"We were received into a large tent, where we found women who had attended their husbands in the expedition. They set before us the supper which they had provided, and I eat it rather to encourage my maids than to comply with any appetite of my own. When the meat was taken away they spread the carpets for repose. I was weary, and hoped to find in sleep that remission of distress which nature seldom denies. Ordering myself therefore to be undrest, I observed that the women looked very earnestly upon me, not expecting, I suppose, to see me so submissively attended. When my upper vest was taken off, they were apparently struck with the splendour of my cloaths, and one of them timorously laid her hand upon the embroidery. She then went out, and, in a short time, came back with another woman, who seemed to be of higher rank, and greater authority. She did, at her entrance, the usual act of reverence, and, taking me by the hand, placed me in a smaller tent, spread with finer carpets, where I spent the night quietly with my maids.

"In the morning, as I was sitting on the grass, the chief of the troop came towards me. I rose up to receive him, and he bowed with great respect. "Illustrious lady, said he, my fortune is better than I had presumed to hope; I am told by my women, that I have a princess in my camp." Sir, answered I, your women have deceived themselves and you; I am not a princess, but an unhappy stranger who intended soon to have left this country, in which I am now to be imprisoned for ever. "Whoever, or whencesoever, you are, returned the Arab, your dress, and that of your servants, show your rank to be high, and your wealth to be great. Why should you, who can so easily procure your ransome, think yourself in danger of perpetual captivity? The purpose of my incursions is to encrease my riches, or more properly to gather tribute. The sons of Ishmael are the natural and hereditary lords of this part of the continent, which is usurped by late invaders, and low-born tyrants, from whom we are compelled to take by the sword what is denied to justice. The violence of war admits no distinction; the lance that is lifted at guilt and power will sometimes fall on innocence and gentleness."

"How little, said I, did I expect that yesterday it should have fallen upon me."

"Misfortunes, answered the Arab, should always be expected. If the eye of hostility could learn reverence or pity, excellence like yours had been exempt from injury. But the angels of affliction spread their toils alike for the virtuous and the wicked, for the mighty and the mean. Do not be disconsolate; I am not one of the lawless and cruel rovers of the desert; I know the rules of civil life: I will fix your ransome, give a pasport to your messenger, and perform my stipulation with nice punctuality."

"You will easily believe that I was pleased with his courtesy; and finding that his predominant passion was desire of money, I began now to think my danger less, for I knew that no sum would be thought too great for the release of Pekuah. I told him that he should have no reason to charge me with ingratitude, if I was used with kindness, and that any ransome, which could be expected for a maid of comon rank, would be paid, but that he must not persist to rate me as a princess. He said, he would consider what he should demand, and then, smiling, bowed and retired.

"Soon after the women came about me, each contending to be more officious[19] than the other, and my maids themselves were served with reverence. We travelled onward by short journeys. On the fourth day the chief told me, that my ransome must be two hundred ounces of gold, which I not only promised him, but told him, that I would add fifty more, if I and my maids were honourably treated.

"I never knew the power of gold before. From that time I was the leader of the troop. The march of every day was longer or shorter as I commanded, and the tents were pitched where I chose to rest. We now had camels and other conveniencies for travel, my own women were always at my side, and I amused myself with observing the manners of the vagrant nations, and with viewing remains of ancient edifices with which these deserted countries appear to have been, in some distant age, lavishly embellished.

"The chief of the band was a man far from illiterate: he was able to travel by the stars or the compass, and had marked in his erratick expeditions such places as are most worthy the notice of a passenger. He observed to me, that buildings are always best preserved in places little frequented, and difficult of access: for, when once a country declines from its primitive splendour, the more inhabitants are left, the quicker ruin will be made. Walls supply stones more easily than quarries, and palaces and temples will be demolished to make stables of granate, and cottages of porphyry.

[19] *officious:* either "kind, doing good offices," or "importunately forward." (Dictionary)

XXXIX

THE ADVENTURES OF PEKUAH CONTINUED

"We wandered about in this manner for some weeks, whether, as
our chief pretended, for my gratification, or, as I rather suspected,
for some convenience of his own. I endeavoured to appear con-
tented where sullenness and resentment would have been of no
use, and that endeavour conduced much to the calmness of my
mind; but my heart was always with Nekayah, and the troubles of
the night much overbalanced the amusements of the day. My
women, who threw all their cares upon their mistress, set their
minds at ease from the time when they saw me treated with re-
spect, and gave themselves up to the incidental alleviations of our
fatigue without solicitude or sorrow. I was pleased with their
pleasure, and animated with their confidence. My condition had
lost much of its terrour, since I found that the Arab ranged the
country merely to get riches. Avarice is an uniform and tractable
vice: other intellectual distempers are different in different con-
stitutions of mind; that which sooths the pride of one will offend
the pride of another; but to the favour of the covetous there is a
ready way, bring money and nothing is denied.

"At last we came to the dwelling of our chief, a strong and
spacious house built with stone in an island of the Nile, which lies,
as I was told, under the tropick. "Lady, said the Arab, you shall
rest after your journey a few weeks in this place, where you are
to consider yourself as sovereign. My occupation is war: I have
therefore chosen this obscure residence, from which I can issue
unexpected, and to which I can retire unpersued. You may now
repose in security: here are few pleasures, but here is no danger."
He then led me into the inner apartments, and seating me on the
richest couch, bowed to the ground. His women, who considered
me as a rival, looked on me with malignity; but being soon in-
formed that I was a great lady detained only for my ransome, they
began to vie with each other in obsequiousness and reverence.

"Being again comforted with new assurances of speedy liberty,
I was for some days diverted from impatience by the novelty of the

place. The turrets overlooked the country to a great distance, and afforded a view of many windings of the stream. In the day I wandered from one place to another as the course of the sun varied the splendour of the prospect, and saw many things which I had never seen before. The crocodiles and river-horses[20] are common in this unpeopled region, and I often looked upon them with terrour, though I knew that they could not hurt me. For some time I expected to see mermaids and tritons, which, as Imlac has told me, the European travellers have stationed in the Nile, but no such beings ever appeared, and the Arab, when I enquired after them, laughed at my credulity.

"At night the Arab always attended me to a tower set apart for celestial observations, where he endeavoured to teach me the names and courses of the stars. I had no great inclination to this study, but an appearance of attention was necessary to please my instructor, who valued himself for his skill, and, in a little while, I found some employment requisite to beguile the tediousness of time, which was to be passed always amidst the same objects. I was weary of looking in the morning on things from which I had turned away weary in the evening: I therefore was at last willing to observe the stars rather than do nothing, but could not always compose my thoughts, and was very often thinking on Nekayah when others imagined me contemplating the sky. Soon after the Arab went upon another expedition, and then my only pleasure was to talk with my maids about the accident by which we were carried away, and the happiness that we should all enjoy at the end of our captivity."

"There were women in your Arab's fortress, said the princess, why did you not make them your companions, enjoy their conversation, and partake their diversions? In a place where they found business or amusement, why should you alone sit corroded with idle melancholy? or why could not you bear for a few months that condition to which they were condemned for life?"

"The diversions of the women, answered Pekuah, were only childish play, by which the mind accustomed to stronger operations could not be kept busy. I could do all which they delighted

[20] *river-horses:* English for hippopotami.

in doing by powers merely sensitive,[21] while my intellectual faculties were flown to Cairo. They ran from room to room as a bird hops from wire to wire in his cage. They danced for the sake of motion, as lambs frisk in a meadow. One sometimes pretended to be hurt that the rest might be alarmed, or hid herself that another might seek her. Part of their time passed in watching the progress of light bodies that floated on the river, and part in marking the various forms into which clouds broke in the sky.

"Their business was only needlework, in which I and my maids sometimes helped them; but you know that the mind will easily straggle from the fingers, nor will you suspect that captivity and absence from Nekayah could receive solace from silken flowers.

"Nor was much satisfaction to be hoped from their conversation: for of what could they be expected to talk? They had seen nothing; for they had lived from early youth in that narrow spot: of what they had not seen they could have no knowledge, for they could not read. They had no ideas but of the few things that were within their view, and had hardly names for any thing but their cloaths and their food. As I bore a superiour character, I was often called to terminate their quarrels, which I decided as equitably as I could. If it could have amused me to hear the complaints of each against the rest, I might have been often detained by long stories, but the motives of their animosity were so small that I could not listen without intercepting the tale."

"How, said Rasselas, can the Arab, whom you represented as a man of more than common accomplishments, take any pleasure in his seraglio, when it is filled only with women like these? Are they exquisitely beautiful?"

"They do not, said Pekuah, want that unaffecting and ignoble beauty which may subsist without spriteliness or sublimity, without energy of thought or dignity of virtue. But to a man like the Arab such beauty was only a flower casually plucked and carelessly thrown away. Whatever pleasures he might find among them, they were not those of friendship or society. When they were playing about him he looked on them with inattentive superiority: when they vied for his regard he sometimes turned away disgusted.

[21] *sensitive:* "having sense or perception but not reason."

As they had no knowledge, their talk could take nothing from the tediousness of life: as they had no choice, their fondness, or appearance of fondness, excited in him neither pride nor gratitude; he was not exalted in his own esteem by the smiles of a woman who saw no other man, nor was much obliged by that regard, of which he could never know the sincerity, and which he might often perceive to be exerted not so much to delight him as to pain a rival. That which he gave, and they received, as love, was only a careless distribution of superfluous time, such love as man can bestow upon that which he despises, such as has neither hope nor fear, neither joy nor sorrow."

"You have reason, lady, to think yourself happy, said Imlac, that you have been thus easily dismissed. How could a mind, hungry for knowledge, be willing, in an intellectual famine, to lose such a banquet as Pekuah's conversation?"

"I am inclined to believe, answered Pekuah, that he was for some time in suspense; for, notwithstanding his promise, whenever I proposed to dispatch a messenger to Cairo, he found some excuse for delay. While I was detained in his house he made many incursions into the neighbouring countries, and, perhaps, he would have refused to discharge me, had his plunder been equal to his wishes. He returned always courteous, related his adventures, delighted to hear my observations, and endeavoured to advance my acquaintance with the stars. When I importuned him to send away my letters, he soothed me with professions of honour and sincerity; and, when I could be no longer decently denied, put his troop again in motion, and left me to govern in his absence. I was much afflicted by this studied procrastination, and was sometimes afraid that I should be forgotten; that you would leave Cairo, and I must end my days in an island of the Nile.

"I grew at last hopeless and dejected, and cared so little to entertain him, that he for a while more frequently talked with my maids. That he should fall in love with them, or with me, might have been equally fatal, and I was not much pleased with the growing friendship. My anxiety was not long; for, as I recovered some degree of chearfulness, he returned to me, and I could not forbear to despise my former uneasiness.

"He still delayed to send for my ransome, and would, perhaps, never have determined, had not your agent found his way to him. The gold, which he would not fetch, he could not reject when it was offered. He hastened to prepare for our journey hither, like a man delivered from the pain of an intestine conflict. I took leave of my companions in the house, who dismissed me with cold indifference."

Nekayah, having heard her favourite's relation, rose and embraced her, and Rasselas gave her an hundred ounces of gold, which she presented to the Arab for the fifty that were promised.

XL

THE HISTORY OF A MAN OF LEARNING

They returned to Cairo, and were so well pleased at finding themselves together, that none of them went much abroad. The prince began to love learning, and one day declared to Imlac, that he intended to devote himself to science, and pass the rest of his days in literary solitude.

"Before you make your final choice, answered Imlac, you ought to examine its hazards, and converse with some of those who are grown old in the company of themselves. I have just left the observatory of one of the most learned astronomers in the world, who has spent forty years in unwearied attention to the motions and appearances of the celestial bodies, and has drawn out his soul in endless calculations. He admits a few friends once a month to hear his deductions and enjoy his discoveries. I was introduced as a man of knowledge worthy of his notice. Men of various ideas and fluent conversation are commonly welcome to those whose thoughts have been long fixed upon a single point, and who find the images of other things stealing away. I delighted him with my remarks, he smiled at the narrative of my travels, and was glad to forget the constellations, and descend for a moment into the lower world.

"On the next day of vacation I renewed my visit, and was so

fortunate as to please him again. He relaxed from that time the severity of his rule, and permitted me to enter at my own choice. I found him always busy, and always glad to be relieved. As each knew much which the other was desirous of learning, we exchanged our notions with great delight. I perceived that I had every day more of his confidence, and always found new cause of admiration in the profundity of his mind. His comprehension is vast, his memory capacious and retentive, his discourse is methodical, and his expression clear.

"His integrity and benevolence are equal to his learning. His deepest researches and most favourite studies are willingly interrupted for any opportunity of doing good by his counsel or his riches. To his closest retreat, at his most busy moments, all are admitted that want his assistance: "For though I exclude idleness and pleasure, I will never, says he, bar my doors against charity. To man is permitted the contemplation of the skies, but the practice of virtue is commanded."

"Surely, said the princess, this man is happy."

"I visited him, said Imlac, with more and more frequency, and was every time more enamoured of his conversation: he was sublime without haughtiness, courteous without formality, and communicative without ostentation. I was at first, great princess, of your opinion, thought him the happiest of mankind, and often congratulated him on the blessing that he enjoyed. He seemed to hear nothing with indifference but the praises of his condition, to which he always returned a general answer, and diverted the conversation to some other topick.

"Amidst this willingness to be pleased, and labour to please, I had quickly reason to imagine that some painful sentiment pressed upon his mind. He often looked up earnestly towards the sun, and let his voice fall in the midst of his discourse. He would sometimes, when we were alone, gaze upon me in silence with the air of a man who longed to speak what he was yet resolved to suppress. He would often send for me with vehement injunctions of haste, though, when I came to him, he had nothing extraordinary to say. And sometimes, when I was leaving him, would call me back, pause a few moments and then dismiss me.

XLI

THE ASTRONOMER DISCOVERS THE CAUSE OF HIS UNEASINESS

"At last the time came when the secret burst his reserve. We were sitting together last night in the turret of his house, watching the emersion[22] of a satellite of Jupiter. A sudden tempest clouded the sky, and disappointed our observation. We sat a while silent in the dark, and then he addressed himself to me in these words: "Imlac, I have long considered thy friendship as the greatest blessing of my life. Integrity without knowledge is weak and useless, and knowledge without integrity is dangerous and dreadful. I have found in thee all the qualities requisite for trust, benevolence, experience, and fortitude. I have long discharged an office which I must soon quit at the call of nature, and shall rejoice in the hour of imbecility and pain to devolve it upon thee."

"I thought myself honoured by this testimony, and protested that whatever could conduce to his happiness would add likewise to mine."

"Hear, Imlac, what thou wilt not without difficulty credit. I have possessed for five years the regulation of weather, and the distribution of the seasons: the sun has listened to my dictates, and passed from tropick to tropick by my direction; the clouds, at my call, have poured their waters, and the Nile has overflowed at my command; I have restrained the rage of the dog-star, and mitigated the fervours of the crab. The winds alone, of all the elemental powers, have hitherto refused my authority, and multitudes have perished by equinoctial tempests which I found myself unable to prohibit or restrain. I have administered this great office with exact justice, and made to the different nations of the earth an impartial dividend of rain and sunshine. What must have been the misery of half the globe, if I had limited the clouds to particular regions, or confined the sun to either side of the equator?"

[22] *emersion:* reappearance after being obscured by proximity to the sun or a brighter body.

XLII

THE OPINION OF THE ASTRONOMER IS EXPLAINED AND JUSTIFIED

"I suppose he discovered in me, through the obscurity of the room, some tokens of amazement and doubt, for, after a short pause, he proceeded thus:"

"Not to be easily credited will neither surprise nor offend me; for I am, probably, the first of human beings to whom this trust has been imparted. Nor do I know whether to deem this distinction a reward or punishment; since I have possessed it I have been far less happy than before, and nothing but the consciousness of good intention could have enabled me to support the weariness of unremitted vigilance."

"How long, Sir, said I, has this great office been in your hands?"

"About ten years ago, said he, my daily observations of the changes of the sky led me to consider, whether, if I had the power of the seasons, I could confer greater plenty upon the inhabitants of the earth. This contemplation fastened on my mind, and I sat days and nights in imaginary dominion, pouring upon this country and that the showers of fertility, and seconding every fall of rain with a due proportion of sunshine. I had yet only the will to do good, and did not imagine that I should ever have the power.

"One day as I was looking on the fields withering with heat, I felt in my mind a sudden wish that I could send rain on the southern mountains, and raise the Nile to an inundation. In the hurry of my imagination I commanded rain to fall, and, by comparing the time of my command, with that of the inundation, I found that the clouds had listned to my lips."

"Might not some other cause, said I, produce this concurrence? the Nile does not always rise on the same day."

"Do not believe, said he with impatience, that such objections could escape me: I reasoned long against my own conviction, and laboured against truth with the utmost obstinacy. I sometimes suspected myself of madness, and should not have dared to impart this secret but to a man like you, capable of distinguishing the wonderful from the impossible, and the incredible from the false."

"Why, Sir, said I, do you call that incredible, which you know, or think you know, to be true?"

"Because, said he, I cannot prove it by any external evidence; and I know too well the laws of demonstration to think that my conviction ought to influence another, who cannot, like me, be conscious of its force. I, therefore, shall not attempt to gain credit by disputation. It is sufficient that I feel this power, that I have long possessed, and every day exerted it. But the life of man is short, the infirmities of age increase upon me, and the time will soon come when the regulator of the year must mingle with the dust. The care of appointing a successor has long disturbed me; the night and the day have been spent in comparisons of all the characters which have come to my knowledge, and I have yet found none so worthy as thyself.

XLIII

THE ASTRONOMER LEAVES IMLAC HIS DIRECTIONS

"Hear therefore, what I shall impart, with attention, such as the welfare of a world requires. If the task of a king be considered as difficult, who has the care only of a few millions, to whom he cannot do much good or harm, what must be the anxiety of him, on whom depend the action of the elements, and the great gifts of light and heat!——Hear me therefore with attention.

"I have diligently considered the position of the earth and sun, and formed innumerable schemes in which I changed their situation. I have sometimes turned aside the axis of the earth, and sometimes varied the ecliptick of the sun: but I have found it impossible to make a disposition by which the world may be advantaged; what one region gains, another loses by any imaginable alteration, even without considering the distant parts of the solar system with which we are unacquainted. Do not, therefore, in thy administration of the year, indulge thy pride by innovation; do not please thyself with thinking that thou canst make thyself renowned to all future ages, by disordering the seasons. The memory of mischief is no desirable fame. Much less will it become thee to let kindness or interest prevail. Never rob other countries of rain to pour it on thine own. For us the Nile is sufficient."

"I promised that when I possessed the power, I would use it with inflexible integrity, and he dismissed me, pressing my hand." "My heart, said he, will be now at rest, and my benevolence will no more destroy my quiet: I have found a man of wisdom and virtue, to whom I can chearfully bequeath the inheritance of the sun."

The prince heard this narration with very serious regard, but the princess smiled, and Pekuah convulsed herself with laughter. "Ladies, said Imlac, to mock the heaviest of human afflictions is neither charitable nor wise. Few can attain this man's knowledge, and few practise his virtues; but all may suffer his calamity. Of the uncertainties of our present state, the most dreadful and alarming is the uncertain continuance of reason."

The princess was recollected, and the favourite was abashed. Rasselas, more deeply affected, enquired of Imlac, whether he thought such maladies of the mind frequent, and how they were contracted.

XLIV

THE DANGEROUS PREVALENCE OF IMAGINATION

"Disorders of intellect, answered Imlac, happen much more often than superficial observers will easily believe. Perhaps, if we speak with rigorous exactness, no human mind is in its right state. There is no man whose imagination does not sometimes predominate over his reason, who can regulate his attention wholly by his will, and whose ideas will come and go at his command. No man will be found in whose mind airy[23] notions do not sometimes tyrannise, and force him to hope or fear beyond the limits of sober probability. All power of fancy over reason is a degree of insanity; but while this power is such as we can controul and repress, it is not visible to others, nor considered as any depravation of the mental

[23] *airy*: imaginary.

faculties: it is not pronounced madness but when it comes ungovernable, and apparently[24] influences speech or action.

"To indulge the power of fiction, and send imagination out upon the wing, is often the sport of those who delight too much in silent speculation. When we are alone we are not always busy; the labour of excogitation is too violent to last long; the ardour of enquiry will sometimes give way to idleness or satiety. He who has nothing external that can divert him, must find pleasure in his own thoughts, and must conceive himself what he is not; for who is pleased with what he is? He then expatiates in boundless futurity, and culls from all imaginable conditions that which for the present moment he should most desire, amuses his desires with impossible enjoyments, and confers upon his pride unattainable dominion. The mind dances from scene to scene, unites all pleasures in all combinations, and riots in delights which nature and fortune, with all their bounty, cannot bestow.

"In time some particular train of ideas fixes the attention, all other intellectual gratifications are rejected, the mind, in weariness or leisure, recurs constantly to the favourite conception, and feasts on the luscious falsehood whenever she is offended with the bitterness of truth. By degrees the reign of fancy is confirmed; she grows first imperious, and in time despotick. Then fictions begin to operate as realities, false opinions fasten upon the mind, and life passes in dreams of rapture or of anguish.

"This, Sir, is one of the dangers of solitude, which the hermit has confessed not always to promote goodness, and the astronomer's misery has proved to be not always propitious to wisdom."

"I will no more, said the favourite, imagine myself the queen of Abissinia. I have often spent the hours, which the princess gave to my own disposal, in adjusting ceremonies and regulating the court; I have repressed the pride of the powerful, and granted the petitions of the poor; I have built new palaces in more happy situations, planted groves upon the tops of mountains, and have exulted in the beneficence of royalty, till, when the princess entered, I had almost forgotten to bow down before her."

---

[24] *apparently:* manifestly.

"And I, said the princess, will not allow myself any more to play the shepherdess in my waking dreams. I have often soothed my thoughts with the quiet and innocence of pastoral employments, till I have in my chamber heard the winds whistle, and the sheep bleat; sometimes freed the lamb entangled in the thicket, and sometimes with my crook encountered the wolf. I have a dress like that of the village maids, which I put on to help my imagination, and a pipe on which I play softly, and suppose myself followed by my flocks."

"I will confess, said the prince, an indulgence of fantastick delight more dangerous than yours. I have frequently endeavoured to image the possibility of a perfect government, by which all wrong should be restrained, all vice reformed, and all the subjects preserved in tranquility and innocence. This thought produced innumerable schemes of reformation, and dictated many useful regulations and salutary edicts. This has been the sport and some-times the labour of my solitude; and I start, when I think with how little anguish I once supposed the death of my father and my brothers."

"Such, says Imlac, are the effects of visionary schemes: when we first form them we know them to be absurd, but familiarise them by degrees, and in time lose sight of their folly."

XLV

THEY DISCOURSE WITH AN OLD MAN

The evening was now far past, and they rose to return home. As they walked along the bank of the Nile, delighted with the beams of the moon quivering on the water, they saw at a small distance an old man, whom the prince had often heard in the assembly of the sages. "Yonder, said he, is one whose years have calmed his passions, but not clouded his reason: let us close the disquisitions of the night, by enquiring what are his sentiments of his own state, that we may know whether youth alone is to struggle with vexation, and whether any better hope remains for the latter part of life."

Here the sage approached and saluted them. They invited him
to join their walk, and prattled a while as acquaintance that had
unexpectedly met one another. The old man was chearful and
talkative, and the way seemed short in his company. He was
pleased to find himself not disregarded, accompanied them to their
house, and, at the prince's request, entered with them. They placed
him in the seat of honour, and set wine and conserves before him.

"Sir, said the princess, an evening walk must give to a man of
learning, like you, pleasures which ignorance and youth can
hardly conceive. You know the qualities and the causes of all that
you behold, the laws by which the river flows, the periods in
which the planets perform their revolutions. Every thing must
supply you with contemplation, and renew the consciousness of
your own dignity."

"Lady, answered he, let the gay and the vigorous expect pleasure
in their excursions, it is enough that age can obtain ease. To me
the world has lost its novelty: I look round, and see what I remem-
ber to have seen in happier days. I rest against a tree, and consider,
that in the same shade I once disputed upon the annual overflow
of the Nile with a friend who is now silent in the grave. I cast my
eyes upwards, fix them on the changing moon, and think with pain
on the vicissitudes of life. I have ceased to take much delight in
physical truth; for what have I to do with those things which I
am soon to leave?"

"You may at least recreate yourself, said Imlac, with the recollec-
tion of an honourable and useful life, and enjoy the praise which
all agree to give you."

"Praise, said the sage, with a sigh, is to an old man an empty
sound. I have neither mother to be delighted with the reputation
of her son, nor wife to partake the honours of her husband. I have
outlived my friends and my rivals. Nothing is now of much impor-
tance; for I cannot extend my interest beyond myself. Youth is
delighted with applause, because it is considered as the earnest of
some future good, and because the prospect of life is far extended:
but to me, who am now declining to decrepitude, there is little to
be feared from the malevolence of men, and yet less to be hoped

from their affection or esteem. Something they may yet take away, but they can give me nothing. Riches would now be useless, and high employment would be pain. My retrospect of life recalls to my view many opportunities of good neglected, much time squandered upon trifles, and more lost in idleness and vacancy. I leave many great designs unattempted, and many great attempts unfinished. My mind is burthened with no heavy crime, and therefore I compose myself to tranquility; endeavour to abstract my thoughts from hopes and cares, which, though reason knows them to be vain, still try to keep their old possession of the heart; expect, with serene humility, that hour which nature cannot long delay; and hope to possess in a better state that happiness which here I could not find, and that virtue which here I have not attained."

He rose and went away, leaving his audience not much elated with the hope of long life. The prince consoled himself with remarking, that it was not reasonable to be disappointed by this account; for age had never been considered as the season of felicity, and, if it was possible to be easy in decline and weakness, it was likely that the days of vigour and alacrity might be happy: that the noon of life might be bright, if the evening could be calm.

The princess suspected that age was querulous and malignant, and delighted to repress the expectations of those who had newly entered the world. She had seen the possessors of estates look with envy on their heirs, and known many who enjoy pleasure no longer than they can confine it to themselves.

Pekuah conjectured, that the man was older than he appeared, and was willing to impute his complaints to delirious dejection; or else supposed that he had been unfortunate, and was therefore discontented: "For nothing, said she, is more common than to call our own condition, the condition of life."

Imlac, who had no desire to see them depressed, smiled at the comforts which they could so readily procure to themselves, and remembered, that at the same age, he was equally confident of unmingled prosperity, and equally fertile of consolatory expedients. He forbore to force upon them unwelcome knowledge, which time itself would too soon impress. The princess and her lady retired;

the madness of the astronomer hung upon their minds, and they desired Imlac to enter upon his office, and delay next morning the rising of the sun.

XLVI

THE PRINCESS AND PEKUAH VISIT THE ASTRONOMER

The princess and Pekuah having talked in private of Imlac's astronomer, thought his character at once so amiable and so strange, that they could not be satisfied without a nearer knowledge, and Imlac was requested to find the means of bringing them together.

This was somewhat difficult; the philosopher had never received any visits from women, though he lived in a city that had in it many Europeans who followed the manners of their own countries, and many from other parts of the world that lived there with European liberty. The ladies would not be refused, and several schemes were proposed for the accomplishment of their design. It was proposed to introduce them as strangers in distress, to whom the sage was always accessible; but, after some deliberation, it appeared, that by this artifice, no acquaintance could be formed, for their conversation would be short, and they could not decently importune him often. "This, said Rasselas, is true; but I have yet a stronger objection against the misrepresentation of your state. I have always considered it as treason against the great republick of human nature, to make any man's virtues the means of deceiving him, whether on great or little occasions. All imposture weakens confidence and chills benevolence. When the sage finds that you are not what you seemed, he will feel the resentment natural to a man who, conscious of great abilities, discovers that he has been tricked by understandings meaner than his own, and, perhaps, the distrust, which he can never afterwards wholly lay aside, may stop the voice of counsel, and close the hand of charity; and where will you find the power of restoring his benefactions to mankind, or his peace to himself?"

To this no reply was attempted, and Imlac began to hope that their curiosity would subside; but, next day, Pekuah told him, she had now found an honest pretence for a visit to the astronomer, for she would solicit permission to continue under him the studies in which she had been initiated by the Arab, and the princess might go with her either as a fellow-student, or because a woman could not decently come alone. "I am afraid, said Imlac, that he will be soon weary of your company: men advanced far in knowledge do not love to repeat the elements of their art, and I am not certain that even of the elements, as he will deliver them connected with inferences, and mingled with reflections, you are a very capable auditress." "That, said Pekuah, must be my care: I ask of you only to take me thither. My knowledge is, perhaps, more than you imagine it, and by concurring always with his opinions I shall make him think it greater than it is."

The astronomer, in pursuance of this resolution, was told, that a foreign lady, travelling in search of knowledge, had heard of his reputation, and was desirous to become his scholar. The uncommonness of the proposal raised at once his surprize and curiosity, and when, after a short deliberation, he consented to admit her, he could not stay without impatience till the next day.

The ladies dressed themselves magnificently, and were attended by Imlac to the astronomer, who was pleased to see himself approached with respect by persons of so splendid an appearance. In the exchange of the first civilities he was timorous and bashful; but when the talk became regular, he recollected his powers, and justified the character which Imlac had given. Enquiring of Pekuah what could have turned her inclination towards astronomy, he received from her a history of her adventure at the pyramid, and of the time passed in the Arab's island. She told her tale with ease and elegance, and her conversation took possession of his heart. The discourse was then turned to astronomy: Pekuah displayed what she knew: he looked upon her as a prodigy of genius, and intreated her not to desist from a study which she had so happily begun.

They came again and again, and were every time more welcome than before. The sage endeavoured to amuse them, that they might prolong their visits, for he found his thoughts grow brighter in their company; the clouds of solicitude vanished by degrees, as he forced himself to entertain them, and he grieved when he was left at their departure to his old employment of regulating the seasons.

The princess and her favourite had now watched his lips for several months, and could not catch a single word from which they could judge whether he continued, or not, in the opinion of his preternatural commission. They often contrived to bring him to an open declaration, but he easily eluded all their attacks, and on which side soever they pressed him escaped from them to some other topick.

As their familiarity increased they invited him often to the house of Imlac, where they distinguished him by extraordinary respect. He began gradually to delight in sublunary pleasures. He came early and departed late; laboured to recommend himself by assiduity and compliance; excited their curiosity after new arts, that they might still want his assistance; and when they made any excursion of pleasure or enquiry, entreated to attend them.

By long experience of his integrity and wisdom, the prince and his sister were convinced that he might be trusted without danger; and lest he should draw any false hopes from the civilities which he received, discovered to him their condition, with the motives of their journey, and required his opinion on the choice of life.

"Of the various conditions which the world spreads before you, which you shall prefer, said the sage, I am not able to instruct you. I can only tell that I have chosen wrong. I have passed my time in study without experience; in the attainment of sciences which can, for the most part, be but remotely useful to mankind. I have purchased knowledge at the expence of all the common comforts of life: I have missed the endearing elegance of female friendship, and the happy commerce of domestick tenderness. If I have obtained any prerogatives above other students, they have been accompanied with fear, disquiet, and scrupulosity; but even of these prerogatives, whatever they were, I have, since my thoughts have been diversified by more intercourse with the world, begun to question the reality. When I have been for a few days lost in pleasing dissipation, I am always tempted to think that my enquiries have ended in errour, and that I have suffered much, and suffered it in vain."

Imlac was delighted to find that the sage's understanding was breaking through its mists, and resolved to detain him from the planets till he should forget his task of ruling them, and reason should recover its original influence.

From this time the astronomer was received into familiar friendship, and partook of all their projects and pleasures: his respect kept him attentive, and the activity of Rasselas did not leave much time unengaged. Something was always to be done; the day was spent in making observations which furnished talk for the evening, and the evening was closed with a scheme for the morrow.

The sage confessed to Imlac, that since he had mingled in the gay tumults of life, and divided his hours by a succession of amusements, he found the conviction of his authority over the skies fade gradually from his mind, and began to trust less to an opinion which he never could prove to others, and which he now found subject to variation from causes in which reason had no part. "If I am accidentally left alone for a few hours, said he, my inveterate persuasion rushes upon my soul, and my thoughts are chained down by some irresistible violence, but they are soon disentangled by the prince's conversation, and instantaneously released at the entrance of Pekuah. I am like a man habitually afraid of spectres, who is set at ease by a lamp, and wonders at the dread which harrassed him in the dark, yet, if his lamp be extinguished, feels again the terrours which he knows that when it is light he shall feel no more. But I am sometimes afraid lest I indulge my quiet by criminal negligence, and voluntarily forget the great charge with which I am intrusted. If I favour myself in a known errour, or am determined by my own ease in a doubtful question of this importance, how dreadful is my crime!"

"No disease of the imagination, answered Imlac, is so difficult of cure, as that which is complicated with the dread of guilt: fancy and conscience then act interchangeably upon us, and so often shift their places, that the illusions of one are not distinguished from the dictates of the other. If fancy presents images not moral or religious, the mind drives them away when they give it pain, but when melancholick notions take the form of duty, they lay hold on the faculties without opposition, because we are afraid to exclude or banish them. For this reason the superstitious are often melancholy, and the melancholy almost always superstitious.

"But do not let the suggestions of timidity overpower your better reason: the danger of neglect can be but as the probability of the obligation, which when you consider it with freedom, you find very little, and that little growing every day less. Open your heart to the influence of the light, which, from time to time, breaks in upon you: when scruples importune you, which you in your lucid moments know to be vain, do not stand to parley, but fly to business or to Pekuah, and keep this thought always prevalent, that you are only one atom of the mass of humanity, and have neither such virtue nor vice, as that you should be singled out for supernatural favours or afflictions."

XLVII

THE PRINCE ENTERS AND BRINGS A NEW TOPICK

"All this, said the astronomer, I have often thought, but my reason has been so long subjugated by an uncontrolable and overwhelming idea, that it durst not confide in its own decisions. I now see how fatally I betrayed my quiet, by suffering chimeras to prey upon me in secret; but melancholy shrinks from communication, and I never found a man before, to whom I could impart my troubles, though I had been certain of relief. I rejoice to find my own sentiments confirmed by yours, who are not easily deceived, and can have no motive or purpose to deceive. I hope that time and variety will dissipate the gloom that has so long surrounded me, and the latter part of my days will be spent in peace."

"Your learning and virtue, said Imlac, may justly give you hopes."

Rasselas then entered with the princess and Pekuah, and enquired whether they had contrived any new diversion for the next day. "Such, said Nekayah, is the state of life, that none are happy but by the anticipation of change: the change itself is nothing; when we have made it, the next wish is to change again. The world is not yet exhausted; let me see something to morrow which I never saw before."

"Variety, said Rasselas, is so necessary to content, that even the happy valley disgusted me by the recurrence of its luxuries; yet I could not forbear to reproach myself with impatience, when I saw the monks of St. Anthony support without complaint, a life, not of uniform delight, but uniform hardship."

"Those men, answered Imlac, are less wretched in their silent convent than the Abissinian princes in their prison of pleasure. Whatever is done by the monks is incited by an adequate and reasonable motive. Their labour supplies them with necessaries; it therefore cannot be omitted, and is certainly rewarded. Their devotion prepares them for another state, and reminds them of its approach, while it fits them for it. Their time is regularly distributed; one duty succeeds another, so that they are not left open to the distraction of unguided choice, nor lost in the shades of listless inactivity. There is a certain task to be performed at an appropriated hour; and their toils are cheerful, because they consider them as acts of piety, by which they are always advancing towards endless felicity."

"Do you think, said Nekayah, that the monastick rule is a more holy and less imperfect state than any other? May not he equally hope for future happiness who converses openly with mankind, who succours the distressed by his charity, instructs the ignorant by his learning, and contributes by his industry to the general system of life; even though he should omit some of the mortifications which are practised in the cloister, and allow himself such harmless delights as his condition may place within his reach?"

"This, said Imlac, is a question which has long divided the wise, and perplexed the good. I am afraid to decide on either part. He that lives well in the world is better than he that lives well in a monastery. But, perhaps, every one is not able to stem the temptations of publick life; and, if he cannot conquer, he may properly retreat. Some have little power to do good, and have likewise little strength to resist evil. Many are weary of their conflicts with adversity, and are willing to eject those passions which have long busied them in vain. And many are dismissed by age and diseases from the more laborious duties of society. In monasteries the weak and timorous may be happily sheltered, the weary may repose, and the penitent may meditate. Those retreats of prayer and contemplation have something so congenial to the mind of man, that, perhaps, there is scarcely one that does not purpose to close his life in pious abstraction with a few associates serious as himself."

"Such, said Pekuah, has often been my wish, and I have heard the princess declare, that she should not willingly die in a croud."

"The liberty of using harmless pleasures, proceeded Imlac, will not be disputed; but it is still to be examined what pleasures are harmless. The evil of any pleasure that Nekayah can image is not in the act itself, but in its consequences. Pleasure, in itself harmless, may become mischievous, by endearing to us a state which we know to be transient and probatory, and withdrawing our thoughts from that, of which every hour brings us nearer to the beginning, and of which no length of time will bring us to the end. Mortification is not virtuous in itself, nor has any other use, but that it disengages us from the allurements of sense. In the state of future perfection, to which we all aspire, there will be pleasure without danger, and security without restraint."

The princess was silent, and Rasselas, turning to the astronomer, asked him, whether he could not delay her retreat, by shewing her something which she had not seen before.

"Your curiosity, said the sage, has been so general, and your pursuit of knowledge so vigorous, that novelties are not now very easily to be found: but what you can no longer procure from the living may be given by the dead. Among the wonders of this country are the catacombs, or the ancient repositories, in which the bodies of the earliest generations were lodged, and where, by the virtue of the gums which embalmed them, they yet remain without corruption."

"I know not, said Rasselas, what pleasure the sight of the catacombs can afford; but, since nothing else is offered, I am resolved to view them, and shall place this with many other things which I have done, because I would do something."

They hired a guard of horsemen, and the next day visited the catacombs. When they were about to descend into the sepulchral caves, "Pekuah, said the princess, we are now again invading the habitations of the dead; I know that you will stay behind; let me find you safe when I return." "No, I will not be left, answered Pekuah; I will go down between you and the prince."

They then all descended, and roved with wonder through the labyrinth of subterraneous passages, where the bodies were laid in rows on either side.

XLVIII

IMLAC DISCOURSES ON THE NATURE OF THE SOUL

"What reason, said the prince, can be given, why the Egyptians should thus expensively preserve those carcasses which some nations consume with fire, others lay to mingle with the earth, and all agree to remove from their sight, as soon as decent rites can be performed?"

· "The original of ancient customs, said Imlac, is commonly unknown; for the practice often continues when the cause has ceased; and concerning superstitious ceremonies it is vain to conjecture; for what reason did not dictate reason cannot explain. I have long believed that the practice of embalming arose only from tenderness to the remains of relations or friends, and to this opinion I am more inclined, because it seems impossible that this care should have been general: had all the dead been embalmed, their repositories must in time have been more spacious than the dwellings of the living. I suppose only the rich or honourable were secured from corruption, and the rest left to the course of nature.

"But it is commonly supposed that the Egyptians believed the soul to live as long as the body continued undissolved, and therefore tried this method of eluding death."

"Could the wise Egyptians, said Nekayah, think so grosly of the soul? If the soul could once survive its separation, what could it afterwards receive or suffer from the body?"

"The Egyptians would doubtless think erroneously, said the

astronomer, in the darkness of heathenism, and the first dawn of philosophy. The nature of the soul is still disputed amidst all our opportunities of clearer knowledge: some yet say, that it may be material, who, nevertheless, believe it to be immortal."

"Some, answered Imlac, have indeed said that the soul is material, but I can scarcely believe that any man has thought it, who knew how to think; for all the conclusions of reason enforce the immateriality of mind, and all the notices of sense and investigations of science concur to prove the unconsciousness of matter.

"It was never supposed that cogitation is inherent in matter, or that every particle is a thinking being. Yet, if any part of matter be devoid of thought, what part can we suppose to think? Matter can differ from matter only in form, density, bulk, motion, and direction of motion: to which of these, however varied or combined, can consciousness be annexed? To be round or square, to be solid or fluid, to be great or little, to be moved slowly or swiftly one way or another, are modes of material existence, all equally alien from the nature of cogitation. If matter be once without thought, it can only be made to think by some new modification, but all the modifications which it can admit are equally unconnected with cogitative powers."

"But the materialists, said the astronomer, urge that matter may have qualities with which we are unacquainted."

"He who will determine, returned Imlac, against that which he knows, because there may be something which he knows not; he that can set hypothetical possibility against acknowledged certainty, is not to be admitted among reasonable beings. All that we know of matter is, that matter is inert, senseless and lifeless; and if this conviction cannot be opposed but by referring us to something that we know not, we have all the evidence that human intellect can admit. If that which is known may be over-ruled by that which is unknown, no being, not omniscient, can arrive at certainty."

"Yet let us not, said the astronomer, too arrogantly limit the Creator's power."

"It is no limitation of omnipotence, replied the poet, to suppose that one thing is not consistent with another, that the same proposition cannot be at once true and false, that the same number cannot be even and odd, that cogitation cannot be conferred on that which is created incapable of cogitation."

"I know not, said Nekayah, any great use of this question. Does that immateriality, which, in my opinion, you have sufficiently proved, necessarily include eternal duration?"

"Of immateriality, said Imlac, our ideas are negative, and therefore obscure. Immateriality seems to imply a natural power of perpetual duration as a consequence of exemption from all causes of decay: whatever perishes, is destroyed by the solution of its contexture, and separation of its parts; nor can we conceive how that which has no parts, and therefore admits no solution, can be naturally corrupted or impaired."

"I know not, said Rasselas, how to conceive any thing without extension: what is extended must have parts, and you allow, that whatever has parts may be destroyed."

"Consider your own conceptions, replied Imlac, and the difficulty will be less. You will find substance without extension. An ideal form is no less real than material bulk: yet an ideal form has no extension. It is no less certain, when you think on a pyramid, that your mind possesses the idea of a pyramid, than that the pyramid itself is standing. What space does the idea of a pyramid occupy more than the idea of a grain of corn? or how can either idea suffer laceration? As is the effect such is the cause; as thought is, such is the power that thinks; a power impassive and indiscerptible."

"But the Being, said Nekayah, whom I fear to name, the Being which made the soul, can destroy it."

"He, surely, can destroy it, answered Imlac, since, however unperishable, it receives from a superiour nature its power of duration. That it will not perish by any inherent cause of decay, or principle of corruption, may be shown by philosophy; but philosophy can tell no more. That it will not be annihilated by him that made it, we must humbly learn from higher authority."

The whole assembly stood a while silent and collected. "Let us return, said Rasselas, from this scene of mortality. How gloomy would be these mansions of the dead to him who did not know

that he shall never die; that what now acts shall continue its
agency, and what now thinks shall think on for ever. Those that
lie here stretched before us, the wise and the powerful of antient
times, warn us to remember the shortness of our present state: they
were, perhaps, snatched away while they were busy, like us, in the
choice of life."

"To me, said the princess, the choice of life is become less im-
portant; I hope hereafter to think only on the choice of eternity."

They then hastened out of the caverns, and, under the protec-
tion of their guard, returned to Cairo.

XLIX

THE CONCLUSION, IN WHICH NOTHING IS CONCLUDED

It was now the time of the inundation of the Nile: a few days after
their visit to the catacombs, the river began to rise.

They were confined to their house. The whole region being
under water gave them no invitation to any excursions, and, being
well supplied with materials for talk, they diverted themselves with
comparisons of the different forms of life which they had observed,
and with various schemes of happiness which each of them had
formed.

Pekuah was never so much charmed with any place as the con-
vent of St. Anthony, where the Arab restored her to the princess,
and wished only to fill it with pious maidens, and to be made
prioress of the order: she was weary of expectation and disgust,
and would gladly be fixed in some unvariable state.

The princess thought, that of all sublunary things, knowledge
was the best: She desired first to learn all sciences, and then pur-
posed to found a college of learned women, in which she would
preside, that, by conversing with the old, and educating the young,
she might divide her time between the acquisition and communica-
tion of wisdom, and raise up for the next age models of prudence,
and patterns of piety.

The prince desired a little kingdom, in which he might admin-
ister justice in his own person, and see all the parts of government

with his own eyes; but he could never fix the limits of his domin-
ion, and was always adding to the number of his subjects.

Imlac and the astronomer were contented to be driven along the
stream of life without directing their course to any particular port.

Of these wishes that they had formed they well knew that none
could be obtained. They deliberated a while what was to be done,
and resolved, when the inundation should cease, to return to
Abissinia.

FINIS

Rinehart Editions